# MORNNOVIN

## ALYSSA MARIE BETHANCOURT

### THE WAY OF THE FALLING STAR BOOK 1

Dogwood House LLC

Mornnovin
The Way of the Falling Star Book 1


This is a work of fiction.
All characters and events in this book are fictitious. Any resemblance to real persons alive or dead is coincidental.

When I started writing *Mornnovin*, eleven years ago, I was living in my own personal Hell and surrounded by people who kept telling me not to waste my time on writing. If not for the small handful of friends who believed in me then, gently (and sometimes bullishly) nudging me onward when I faltered, this story would never have happened.

Now here we are, and if not for the great big wonderful army who've gathered around me now with their love, encouragement, support, and sweet crowdsource dollars, this story would never have become the book you're holding right now. From my heart to yours, thank you.

And a special thank you to Ron Gonzales, who was so excited about this book and was as proud of me as if I were his own daughter. He never got to read *Mornnovin*, but he already knew he loved it. Here's hoping it lives up to your faith in me, Gonzo.

    – Alyssa

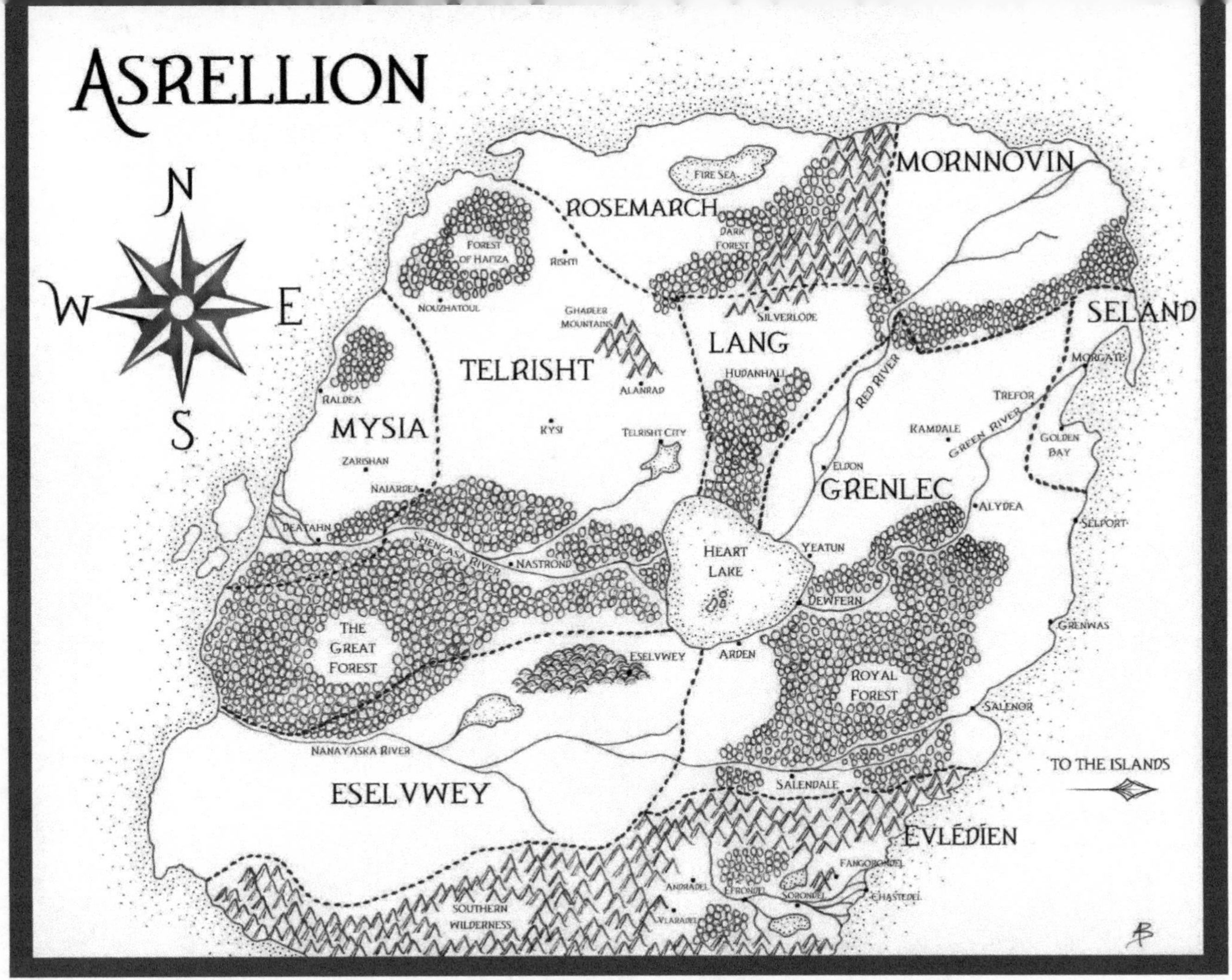
ASRELLION
N
W
E
S
MORNNOVIN
FIRE SEA
ROSEMARCH
DARK FOREST
FOREST OF HAFIZA
RISHTI
NOUZHATOUL
GHADLER MOUNTAINS
SILVERLODE
SELAND
LANG
TELRISHT
ALANRAD
HUDANHALL
MORGATE
RED RIVER
TREFOR
RALDEA
MYSIA
KYSI
TELRISHT CITY
RAMDALE
GREEN RIVER
GOLDEN BAY
ZARISHAN
ELDON
GRENLEC
NAIARDEA
ALYDEA
SELPORT
DEATAHN
SHENZASA RIVER
NASTROND
HEART LAKE
YEATUN
DEWFERN
GRENWAS
THE GREAT FOREST
ESELVWEY
ARDEN
ROYAL FOREST
SALENOR
NANAYASKA RIVER
TO THE ISLANDS
ESELVWEY
SALENDALE
EVLÉDIEN
FANGORONDEL
ANDRADEL
EFRONDEL
SORONDEL
CHASTEDEL
SOUTHERN WILDERNESS
VLARADEL

# a guide to Elven pronunciation

**a**  is always pronounced "ah"

**e**  makes a sound like in "bed" unless accented; then it sounds like "say"

**i**  always sounds like "kit" unless accented; then it sounds like "ee"

**o**  sounds like "for" unless accented; then it sounds like "box"

**u**  makes an "oo" sound, never "you"

**y**  behaves like "i" when between consonants; can function as a consonant when preceded or followed by a vowel

**ai**  sounds like "eye"

**oi**  sounds like "boy"

**c**  is always soft as in "citrus"

**ch**  always sounds like "sh"

**g**  always makes a hard sound, like in "go"

**j**  always soft like "zhe" (like the French *"je"*)

**q**  functions like "k"; there is no "qu"

**r**  is pronounced with a slight flip, not quite a roll

**s**  is always pronounced like "sail"; never like "as"

**th**  is not quite as hard as a straight "t" but harder than an English "th," with the tongue touching the back of the front teeth where they meet the gums

# Chapter One

By the time the sleeping village of Brannock became aware that anything was wrong, it was already the final breath past too late. The battle was over, and they had lost.

It was full night as troops disposed of the bodies and took possession of the town's resources. While not large or especially prosperous, Brannock was situated in a prime location for the staging of further incursions over the border. It would prove strategically useful for that reason alone.

In fact, the village's unimportance and remote location were perfectly suited to the plan. It would be weeks, maybe months, before the capital became aware of the situation.

The general gave precise orders, directing his men in the setup of their secret base inside hostile territory. This invasion, this war, had been a long time coming, and emotions were running high. Not a one of them pretended that it wasn't exciting to finally be underway and committed. They needed to be careful lest their zeal compromise the mission.

This was the first step – they were the front line. The success or failure of the entire war depended upon what they did here. It was a profound burden, but one they were all prepared to shoulder. A heavy death toll would soon be their legacy.

Or so they could only hope.

Loralíenasa Níelor Raia was not supposed to be where she was, but that was only part of the allure.

There were reasons aplenty political and historical why she'd chosen to break the law to be here. She prioritized those above personal reasons, though she had those as well.

But maybe more compelling than any other motive driving her into human lands – where she would be caught and likely killed on sight – the ancient forests of Grenlec were beautiful. Perhaps the most incredible place in all the world.

These trees, she mused, were nearly as old as the Exile. There were patches of forest floor that had not seen the sun since the days when her people had moved freely through Asrellion. The shadows here were deeper than mere darkness; they were tangible things, implacable, guarding their secrets from the light of reality. Even the woodland creatures seemed to *know* things.

As much as humans tried to deny it, there was magic here too. Raw, untamed. It was terrifying and exhilarating both at once. Like the world here was not fully formed, still malleable to the one audacious enough to claim mastery of such a powerful corner of Being.

She couldn't even say what kind of tree that was, the massive one owning the sky with branches spread wide enough to cover a tourney field. It had great flat leaves larger than the palm of her hand. A score of smaller trees cowered in its shade, acknowledging their lord. Whatever it was, it did not grow in the Valley.

The urge to climb to the top was strong, but she could see it wouldn't be easy: the branches of the enormous forest chieftain did not begin until well above her reach.

Loralíenasa tied and unsaddled her horse, spread the blanket upon the carpet of pine needles, and sat while allowing herself a share of her road rations. Even past midday, the air was cool and pleasantly damp. It was late summer, but this deep in the wood it was forever some *un*-season that did not and could not exist elsewhere.

That branch, she finally decided. Insane, maybe, but she would climb the smaller tree closest to the giant and leap from that branch to the curved one *there*. From that point it would be relatively easy, she hoped. She would find her way to the top once she had a better view of what she faced up higher.

Thoughts of her frustrating, wrong-headed guardian and the responsibilities waiting for her at home only entered her mind fleetingly, and were soon pushed away.

Packing up the remnants of her luncheon, shaking the pine needles out of the blanket, she gritted her teeth and set about her mission.

The bark was rough beneath her hands. As sheltered as she was, she found the sensation enjoyable. It felt good to do something so natural, so coarse. Not even sword practice had toughened her palms enough to prevent them from tearing as she hauled her weight up the trunk of the evergreen.

Finally high enough, she took a moment to gauge the distance she was about to cross in such a reckless manner. Part of her wanted to fall, to experience something so real. Her logical side told her how stupid that was. Besides which, it was no good to attempt a thing without intending to succeed.

The distance was not so far. In her younger days, before the Captain had let her hold a real sword, he'd made her complete a course of acrobatic training – tumbling and learning to control her body with absolute precision. This was reasonable, just needlessly risky. She reveled briefly in the fact that there was no one here to tell her not to do it.

Then she jumped.

There was a terrifying, exhilarating moment of weightlessness as she floated free between the branches. Then the palms of her hands hit hard, and she had to make herself concentrate on wrapping her fingers around the rough wood in the split second available. The lower half of her body continued to swing forward, but she braced the pointed toes of her boots against the trunk and bent her knees, absorbing the momentum, as her feet made contact. Her grip held firm. Pleased and breathless, she hoisted herself up onto the branch.

It was relatively easy from there – just a matter of plotting a course and following it through. She got well above the tops of the other trees before the branches were too thin to hold her weight any further up.

There was a strong wind up here, with a hint of distant rain in it. Now that the sky was no longer hidden, she could see that it was late in the afternoon. A sea of tree-tops in a breathtaking array of greens spread beneath her in every direction to the horizon, moving gently like a pebble-rippled pond. Her own massive tree was no more than a single point in the eternal sea of forest, she herself no more significant than a bug clinging to its spotted surface.

And even though she felt tiny, and unimportant, and almost lost in the vastness of existence, it was not a frightening sense of smallness. It was reassuring, actually, to realize that despite the constant pressure to uphold her family's legacy, she was not the most important thing alive. To see that time could and would continue on without her, that the universe would not notice if she fell short of the perfection expected of her.

Loralíenasa closed her eyes and drew in a deep, contented breath.

Moments like these, when she could feel the joy of simply being alive without having to be any-thing else, anything more – this was *it*. She could appreciate, in this moment, that there were things worth sacrificing for. She was even content to accept that, because of who she was, she might just have to be the one doing the sacrificing.

Right now, though, she was just here. And alive. And it was good.

She wanted to stay up on her high bough to watch the sunset, but she knew that would be foolish. Once the sun went down, night would fall quickly in the ancient forest and she would be left trying to make camp in the dark. But she could afford to wait just a little longer before climbing down.

Shifting amid the branches and the leaves, Loralíenasa moved so that she could take in the view on all sides. It was astounding how far the green sea stretched. To the west, her view did not extend as far because the terrain rose up in a series of hills. And to the east...

Her heart leaped up into her throat and also dropped into the pit of her stomach at the same time.

So deep in the forest, Loralíenasa had assumed she would be far from human settlements and any real danger. Even with her people's shamefully outdated knowledge of the kingdom of Grenlec, she knew she was nowhere near the major city in the area. But there, in plain view to the east of her vantage point, a dark castle loomed up out of the surrounding trees, too close.

*"Qijí,"* she swore quietly to herself.

Getting down was equal parts easier and more dangerous than getting up had been. Breaking her legs out here, alone in the middle of nowhere, would be a stupid thing to do. She managed not to fall, but she did have to jump the final five or so meters. She rolled into the landing, distributing the force of the impact through her body. As she climbed to her feet, she felt herself grinning.

A startled intake of breath behind her drew her instant attention.

A tall black-haired man was standing with her horse – had been stroking the animal's side, but his hand was currently frozen mid-motion. At his heels stood an enormous floppy-eared dog with a predominantly black shaggy coat, with distinctive white and golden brown markings. The man's expression, as he took in her sudden appearance from nowhere, was one of arrested shock.

In the handful of times Loralíenasa had ventured from the Valley, she'd always been careful to avoid being seen. At least, when she looked like herself. She had tried wearing an illusion once, in order to walk through a city marketplace, but she suspected from the strange glances that it had not been entirely convincing.

Still, this was her first time alone with a human, face-to-face; she was as startled and intrigued by him as he seemed to be by her.

He wasn't so much a *man*, she registered as she stood studying him. He seemed more like her age, or whatever the human equivalent would be. Not yet a man in his own right, exactly, but no longer a boy either.

Despite his height, he was not as big or bulky as she had expected a human to be. In fact, he was on the slender side. Wiry, she decided. His jaw was maybe a little more square than she was accustomed to seeing among her own people. His eyes were slightly rounder, his ears also lacking points. But, really, she wasn't seeing any grand difference. It was only little things. She found herself wondering what all the fuss was about. He had longish hair, and his eyes were noticeably bright and sharp in his pale, handsome face.

As much as she wanted to keep staring at him, Loralíenasa knew she was in real danger and needed to find out just how much. She closed her mouth and made an effort to look like she *wasn't* making an effort to look dignified – as dignified as a girl who had just jumped out of a tree and rolled through forest mulch could look. Still, not speaking the language of Grenlec, she wasn't sure where to go from there.

"You – you're not human," he declared unexpectedly. Even more of a surprise, he said it in her language. He didn't move any closer, but he did turn away from her horse to face her fully.

"You speak *Evlé'í*? How?" she blurted, then kicked herself mentally. *Years of the finest diplomatic training, and* this *is how you re-open communications with Grenlec. Top-notch, Loralíenasa.*

He didn't seem to notice the stupidity of the question, because he answered in earnest. "My mother taught me." His accent was flawless, that of a well-bred elven aristocrat. She could see him struggling to process the fact that she was real, and that his wild guess had been proven correct when she answered him in the same language.

His response, though, raised more questions than it answered. His mother had taught him, but who was *she*, and where had she learned? From whom? Why learn the dead language of a people who may never have existed? And if her understanding was wrong, if humans *did* in fact know that her people were alive somewhere, that changed everything about the world she'd been raised in and the reality she had been groomed to protect. Tomanasíl would need to know. Precautions would have to be taken.

Loralíenasa asked none of those questions.

Instead, she swallowed her nerves and stepped closer for a better look at him. This was insanity, but it was happening and she was already determined to see it through, wherever it led. The dog watched her warily as she approached but made no sign of aggression, which was a relief. It was far too large for her to want to tangle with.

It was clear from the expensive cut and fabric of the stranger's clothing, and the assured ease with which he held himself, that she was dealing with nobility. He carried no weapon that she could see, although he had the look of a man who knew how to use one. She guessed he was close to home, likely from that castle. Strangely, even though he was facing someone he would have reason to believe might mean him harm, he showed no sign of fear. Interest, caution, intelligence, watchfulness, even a little excitement – but not fear. She might have been inclined to question his sanity, but he had a sharp and lucid look.

A long time had passed since either of them had spoken when he said, "If I may ask, what are you doing here?"

Even though the question was a blunt one, he posed it with such formal courtesy that Loralíenasa found herself wanting to smile just a little and she realized she was actually trying to think of the most truthful way to answer him. This complete stranger, this *human* stranger to whom she owed absolutely nothing, in the middle of the forest. He was so serious, so earnest, that she wanted to trust him.

Loralíenasa raised an eyebrow, reaching for a nonchalant tone. "What are *you* doing here?"

One corner of his thin lips hitched up toward a smile. "I've already told you something about myself. It's your turn."

It pleased her that he had responded with so much spirit, which she promptly told herself was irrelevant. "Exploring," she finally decided to say. "This seems like an especially good place to go about it. Your turn."

"Exploring," he answered, then smiled suddenly. It did delightful things to his already captivating eyes. "You see? Not much of an answer, is it?"

Amused, feeling a strong surge of liking for the stranger, Loralíenasa nevertheless chose to ignore the jab. Instead she glanced at her horse, who had begun nuzzling the human in the shoulder. "He seems fond of you."

The man briefly shifted his attention back to the stallion's sleek white neck and gave it an admiring pat. As he moved, Loralíenasa observed idly that he had none of the oafish clumsiness she had been led to expect from a human.

"I confess, it was a bit of a shock to come across such a fine mount tethered to a tree out in the middle of nothing." He let his hand drop to rest upon the dog at his side, and his smile made a quick reappearance. "But not as much of a shock as it was when a woman fell out of the sky."

Loralíenasa had begun to decide that the man posed no threat to her, but she stepped closer just to be certain. His body language changed subtly as the distance between them shrank; his expression was guarded but still unafraid. She could see his heartbeat thrumming rapidly in his neck when she came close enough to catch his scent of living warmth and some manufactured perfume of a woodland flavor, but he made no move. Neither to escape nor attack. The dog inched forward and pushed a large wet nose into her hand.

"There's more you want to say, isn't there?" she tested quietly. "About my people? About what I'm doing here?"

He cleared his throat and swallowed, watching her carefully. "I could say the same to you. We're being terribly polite, aren't we?"

Somehow, another smile did not seem like the right response. A breeze gusted through the leaves and a bird sounded a shrill arpeggio as Loralíenasa tried to decide where this was going.

"Your mother – where did she learn to speak *Evlé'í*?" she asked, testing again.

Mild grief flickered in the man's bright eyes. "A tutor," he answered gamely. "An elf, she said, but people always assumed that was no more than a romantic tale."

Loralíenasa noted the grief and the use of past tense in speaking of his mother, and felt a predictable twinge of sympathy, but put that aside. "An elf for a tutor? I have to assume that is uncommon." Tomanasíl had declared it unlawful to leave the Valley, except under orders, almost as his first act as Regent, but that had been a formality. Her people were justly afraid of being discovered.

As she had just been discovered.

"It is unheard of," the man said.

They watched each other, wary and intrigued at the same time.

"Where…" The solemn young man trailed off, as though uncertain he should ask what he had been about to. He took a breath and forged ahead anyway. "Where do you–"

"Don't ask me that," she interrupted, more sharply than she had intended.

She knew it was only curiosity, like her own, but she still felt she couldn't bear for him to pursue a line of questioning that might have sinister undertones. She wanted to like him.

The man stopped speaking so abruptly it must have been difficult. He drew his fingers slowly through his unruly black hair, an obviously habitual gesture to help him collect his thoughts. Again, silence stretched long between them. Loralíenasa gave in and rubbed the dog's soft head.

Every question she wanted to ask felt completely inappropriate for whatever this surprised, stolen moment was.

*What is it like to be born knowing you're going to die – how does that affect the way the whole world looks and the way you have to live your life? Is it true that humans are less intelligent than elves? Are you as clumsy and destructive as the stories say? Do you even see colors the same way, hear the same subtleties in music and the wind and rain that we do, feel the same emotions?*

Most of all, she wanted to know why humans had hated elves enough to initiate the Purification, and if they still hated her people that much.

He was the first one to speak again, eventually. "Are you going to kill me?"

Loralíenasa was taken aback by the question, but even more shocked by the calm, sober way in which he asked it. As though, even if her answer was yes, he was prepared to accept what the moment had to bring. She fought for an equally calm response.

"Should I?"

He blinked. "I suppose that would depend entirely upon what you would hope to gain by it."

Again, he had taken her by surprise. "And what might I gain by it?"

This time his answer was more relaxed. "Only you would know that."

Loralíenasa smiled wryly, acknowledging another surge of liking. "You're a strange one, aren't you? Are you a philosopher, or just a quarrelsome pedant?"

"Both. Neither." He grinned, assailing her with the full effect of a disarming smile. "I'm too young to know yet what I am, but I do like to ask questions of the world."

Just like that, the tension was gone and she felt almost like they had known one another for ages and had bantered like this a hundred times before. "Why would you ask me that?" she wondered aloud. "Do I look like a killer?"

He lifted both shoulders and let them fall again in a strange hunching gesture that Loralíenasa was unfamiliar with. It looked equally evasive and apologetic. "Yes? I'm afraid I can't say *no*. I mean no offense. You are a charming young woman." He said it with no discernible irony, as if he had been four times his age and speaking to a girl at her first coming out. "But you are – well, we'll say intense. And armed."

She quirked her lips. "So should you be, out in the middle of nowhere. The world is a dangerous place."

"More so for you than for me, I should think," he replied lightly enough to take the sting out of the words. "Besides, I am almost certainly closer to home than you are, and I have company." He scratched his enormous dog behind its floppy ears; it lolled its pink tongue in a most unintimidating manner. "Why should you want me armed, anyway? Aren't you concerned that *I* might intend *you* harm?"

Although Loralíenasa fully intended to reply with another lighthearted dismissal, she found herself saying in all seriousness, "No. Not particularly."

The black-haired stranger considered that for a moment. "Why not?"

She didn't know the answer to that; she only knew that she honestly did not believe this man would willingly cause harm to another living being. Something about him made the very idea seem almost insulting. She twisted her fingers in a gesture meant to convey ambiguity. "I might look dangerous, but you do not."

"I wouldn't hurt you," he assured her, almost urgently, his voice pitched low. "I'm not like… I'm not one of *those*."

"A Purist?" she finished for him, stating what he had tried not to.

He winced, and she wished she hadn't said it so bluntly. "A Purist," he agreed quietly. "I am not one of those."

In the silence that fell on the heels of those sad words, Loralíenasa realized three things: that she already knew she was in no danger from him, that she needed to be gone from this place before that changed, and that what she really wanted was to stay and talk with this intriguing young man until they both ran out of questions.

She drew a deep breath and turned away from him, watching her feet as she took several steps over the crackling forest carpet.

"I believe it is time for me to be on my way," she informed him carefully, looking at her boots and the pine needles and browning leaves she was crushing beneath her soles.

The young man let out a sigh. "I was surprised when you didn't bolt right at the off." There was a crunching under his boots as he shifted his stance. "Though I'm glad you stayed. I'm glad to have met you."

Her throat clenched as the possible implication of those words struck her. "You mustn't tell anyone," she admonished. "Please. We are not meant to have survived."

When he made no immediate response she turned to look at him, and was struck again by how much he was not what she would have expected.

Eyes intent upon hers, he nodded slowly once he had her full attention. "You have my word, upon my honor. I told you, I am not the type to wish you ill."

Loralíenasa did not doubt for a moment that he meant it. "Thank you."

Moving with practiced care, the man began without discussion to saddle her horse for her. It felt odd to let him do it, but instead of being annoyed by the presumption, she chose to be amused and even a little charmed.

He worked quickly, his hands deft and clever, the movements familiar. It didn't take him long at all. And then it was time for her to go.

Loralíenasa sighed.

"Look," he said, coming toward her carefully. "This, meeting you – an elf... I want you to know, it changes things. I am–"

He went on to say something she didn't register, because she was rather more focused on the small, furry brown animal that had just fumbled its way out of the brush to investigate the two of them. The dog was making low warning sounds in its direction. A moment after she saw the thing, her mind started screaming alarmed curses at her.

"Dammit. Get on the horse," she told the man through stiff lips, interrupting. "Smoothly, no sudden movements. Just do it." Even as she spoke, she started inching forward too.

He stopped talking to look at the thing that had drawn her attention. "What? That? It's just a–"

"A young bear," she finished, pushing past him to swing up into the saddle. "Which means we are about to meet a protective mother bear who will not be at all happy to see us near her cub." She reached down to offer him a hand up.

At that moment, something large crashed through the trees nearby. It did not seem like a good time to continue discussing the matter. The man took her hand.

Loralíenasa had been lucky – or unfortunate – enough to experience a number of strange things in her life. None of them remotely compared to this particular moment. Just as she felt the warm skin of his hand making contact with hers, her entire body froze in a horrible paralysis as though she had been struck dead-on by a bolt of lightning. She seemed to come out of herself, to be inside his head instead of her own, to be looking at herself through his eyes and feeling what he was feeling. Besides being disorienting, it was *wrong*.

When the weird sensation passed, she found she was facedown, limbs akimbo, sputtering through a mouthful of blue wool doublet. A large dog loomed over her, alternating between licking her face and that of his master with a distinct sense of urgency. She pushed herself upright and looked down at the man she had flattened in falling from her horse's saddle.

Far from making amused, suggestive faces at her over their position, he was staring up at her with stunned, utter blankness – a fully accurate reflection of the expression on her own face. The small bear cub waddled up to them and snuffled inquisitively at the man's shoulder. His lips worked as though he was trying to say something, but no sound came out.

The mother bear said everything for them, emerging from the brush, in the form of a surprised and angry roar.

"Shit," her new acquaintance observed succinctly, finally finding his voice.

The dog dropped into a defensive stance between his master and the attacking monster, hackles raised and teeth bared. Loralíenasa knew with certainty that he would die protecting him, if she let him.

There was no making sense of any of this, and no time to try.

She scrambled to her feet ungracefully. She felt drunk. The bear was coming right at them, enormous and bristling with parental rage.

"Run!" the stranger advised from his position in the dirt and dead leaves.

There wasn't time for that. Frightened beyond speech, beyond thought, Loralíenasa drew her sword from its sheath at her back and slashed the bear's massive claw just as it came in for a swing at her face.

Obviously the creature did not love her for that.

The trees seemed to literally bend backward as the creature roared in pain. The bear was nearly twice her height and much more than twice as broad, with claws longer than her fingers and wickedly sharp, its teeth like horrible yellow knives in a maw large enough to tear her face off. It stank of urine and fish and rot, and she knew that she was about to be quite dead.

Of course, she was not inclined to accept that, even if it was inevitable. And she had no intention of seeing her handsome new acquaintance torn asunder. With that vague thought in mind and not thinking of much else, Loralíenasa danced out of the angry creature's reach while calling taunts in its direction – drawing it away from the man still immobile on the ground and the dog crouched over him protectively.

He yelled something at her, but she was past hearing.

The bear, with blood dripping from the matted fur of its paw, was ignoring the man now too. All of its attention was instead focused on Loralíenasa. She gripped her sword and tried to brace herself for another attack. There was no way she could have readied herself for the entire weight of the thing coming down on her with murderous intent.

Loralíenasa could do nothing but allow her instincts to take over, because she was by now completely incapable of forming anything like a rational plan. She was aware of hacking with her blade, of dodging and rolling. She was aware of an almost constant roar, and the heat of being too close to the giant animal; of hot blood on her skin. It was a nightmare of teeth and coarse fur and heavy strength overpowering her and a sense of being crushed. Something tore her shoulder apart, and she screamed.

Then, in one sudden moment of clarity, she saw an opening and was able to take it, thrusting her blade point-first into the monster's throat up into its skull. She was flat on her back, and had to make herself roll out of the way as the massive animal collapsed to the ground with a *thud* that she could feel in her joints.

And then there was silence.

# Chapter Two

The first time she surfaced from her delirium, and the second and third, Loralíenasa could not make any sense of her surroundings. She was supposed to be in the forest, alone, exploring the world outside the Valley against her guardian's wishes and without his knowledge. In fact, he would *kill* her if he knew where she was and what she was doing. The lengths to which she had gone in order to arrange the whole thing so he wouldn't even suspect her absence. The blatantly premeditated nature of her crime.

She was not supposed to be wherever this was, surrounded by concerned-looking humans murmuring things in a language she could not understand.

It felt like she was sleeping a minute at a time, waking and drifting off again at weirdly brief intervals and far too often, but never long enough to get any meaningful handle on reality. Sometimes when she opened her eyes *he* was there, and she would feel an inexplicable relief.

Eventually she woke from one of her not-sleeps lucid enough to process her situation in a mostly rational manner. She was in a bed, in a stone-walled room, in the company of a young serving-girl who was so intent upon the needlework in her lap that she had not yet noticed her charge's conscious state.

Loralíenasa's entire left side was numb, until she twitched her fingers experimentally. Then it stabbed and burned.

She must have made a noise, because the maidservant looked up at her suddenly and said something in an incomprehensible language. The girl had the archetypal dark hair, brown eyes, and pale white complexion of a Grenlecian – leaving little doubt that they were still in the human kingdom.

Loralíenasa restrained a groan.

The girl who was apparently her designated caretaker spoke again, no more intelligibly than the first time, but she accompanied her words with a clear enough gesture: offering water.

Loralíenasa tried to nod. The small movement caused a nauseating, tearing pain in the left side of her neck.

The girl said something stern-sounding, again gesturing clearly enough to convey that she ought not to move. The warning came a bit late, no matter how kindly it might have been intended.

Reaching over slowly with her right hand, Loralíenasa touched her neck, feeling her way down. It was all bandaged and tender, but to her relief everything still seemed to be attached. Somehow. She saw in her mind those last nightmarish seconds, the hair and the heat and the teeth and claws. The cold fear, and the desperation. That horrible moment when she had thought she would have to see her forest man mauled to death, all of it followed by chaos and calm. None of her training had prepared her for *this*.

Her examination was cut short by the Grenlecian girl, again offering water. This time she had cleverly devised a way, using a clean square of linen, to drip the liquid carefully into Loralíenasa's mouth so she would not have to try sitting up. It took a while to quench her thirst in this way, but they got there eventually.

Fatigued from the small effort, Loralíenasa closed her eyes. When she opened them again, hours seemed to have passed but the dark-haired serving girl was still there with her embroidery.

She noticed Loralíenasa more quickly this time, and again helped her to drink with the napkin technique. She was just spreading the cloth out to dry when the door opened and closed, and footsteps could be heard approaching the bed.

The elf could not turn her head to look, but she knew who it was. She could feel his presence.

A moment later he came into view over the bed, concern written across his pale, sharp features. He seemed to relax a little when he saw that she was awake and aware. He even smiled.

The maidservant said something to him in their language, to which he responded briefly. His voice was pleasant to listen to. They had a short exchange, then she rose from her seat and departed after what looked like an obligatory curtsey.

The man took up the chair at the side of the bed. He was alone this time; she hoped the dog had come out of the fray unharmed.

They watched each other in silence for a long time. Loralíenasa wondered if she had only imagined their whole conversation, him speaking her language. How could he have? And whatever that was, there at the end – that strange moment of connectedness and utter disorientation – that *had* to have been her imagination.

"You are not hurt?" she finally said, testing. She was dismayed at how weak and unsteady she sounded. "Your dog–"

His smile returned, a fleeting thing and solemn, but sincere. "We are both quite well, thanks to you," he answered in Elven.

A warmth of satisfaction washed over her.

He continued to study her with a mixture of curiosity and apprehension, as if expecting to find at any moment that she was made of smoke and would disappear. "You saved my life. And dog's."

The conspicuous lapse in his otherwise flawless Elven seemed odd. "That should be *'my dog's,'*" she corrected, watching his reaction with interest.

He chuckled sheepishly. "No, his name is Aiqa." The use of the word for *dog* as a name was understandably confusing. "It was meant to annoy my brother, but that tale is a long one. What you did for me…" he added, possibly trying to change the subject. "You are incredibly brave."

She wanted to bask in the praise, but her stronger desire was to appear calm and smooth in front of this unknown human. "Would you rather I had let her eat you?"

Another flash of his solemn smile. "You wouldn't have."

No. No she would not. "Maybe."

He watched her a moment longer, eyes bright and too perceptive. As close as he was – she could feel the heat of his body, smell the scent of him – she wished he would move closer.

"Where are we?" she asked, more because she wanted to hear him speak again than because she had any real interest in the answer. She was where she was, and that wasn't likely to change any time soon.

He flicked his eyes briefly around the room as if noticing it for the first time. "Castle Grenwold. These are my lands, this part of the forest. This castle is my holding, my home outside of the capital at Dewfern." He offered another small smile. "It is also where I grew up."

So her guess had been correct: nobility. She nearly nodded, but managed to stop herself in time.

There were so many things she wanted to ask him now that she apparently had the time for it, some of them too important to rush, some not important enough to pose at all. She wanted to know everything about Grenlec, about *him*. Whether or not he was having the same kind of reaction to her that she was to him.

She settled for something more pragmatic. "How bad is it?" she asked, gesturing vaguely at her bandaged neck and shoulder with her good hand.

The young man sobered again instantly, drawing his fingers back through his long black forelocks as though to put off having to answer. "There's some tearing, inside, and you lost a lot of blood," he told her reluctantly. "You made it through the night, though, which made the doctor happy. He says, barring infection, you should be whole again in a few weeks. Ten, perhaps twelve."

"Twelve weeks?" she echoed weakly. There was no way in the Dark One's Abyss she could stay here recovering for anything like that long. If she was not home before the season changed, Tomanasíl would come looking for her. And if he did that, he would find out that she was not where she was supposed to be.

And if that happened, she would wish the bear had been more thorough.

"The doctor says you're lucky to be alive," the human told her. His eyes were a dark shade of purple as he said it.

Hadn't they been brighter before, and more blue? Disoriented and unhappy, she remained silent for want of anything to say that would not come across as childishly surly. The last thing she wanted was for him to think of her as a child.

"Surely it won't be so bad, staying here with me for a while?" he tried, this time the smile endearingly shy.

So he *was* feeling something. Loralíenasa experienced a small and completely irrational rush of excitement, and watched as his eyes undeniably shifted in color back to a bright blue – lighter than they had been at their first meeting. It was both unnerving and delightful.

She allowed herself to return his smile. "We shall see."

"What am I to call you?" He seemed to have relaxed a little, seeing that she was not going to panic over the severity of her injuries.

She caught herself short of blurting her full name automatically. There were many reasons why that would be a bad idea. It was likely that her family name would mean nothing to him, so many years after the Exile, but it would be foolish to take the risk.

"Lorien," she finally offered instead. "You may call me Lorien."

He savored the name visibly for a moment, then he offered fair coin. "I am Naoise Raynesley, Duke of Lakeside, second son of Lorn King of Grenlec."

Son of the king. An involuntary shudder took her. Son of the *Grenlecian* king.

Though it was now many centuries in the past and so was the man, the things Grenlec's then-king had ordered done to her people in the time of the War were so unspeakable that Tomanasíl had not allowed her tutors to include any of the details in her curriculum. She'd had to weasel the stories out of her older friends, and then wished she hadn't. Even though she knew better now why her people would build a culture that glorified melancholy and loss, that knowledge came at a high price.

She tried to tell herself it didn't matter about this man – she had *known* he was Grenlecian; what difference did it make what family he came of? The War was so long ago as his people measured things, the blood of the ancestor who had initiated the atrocities had probably thinned entirely out of the line several generations ago. If indeed that particular line had even survived.

It didn't matter.

She had been silent for some time, and he was watching her struggle with the weight of his lineage. At length he leaned closer, all earnest sincerity. "I told you that you have nothing to fear from me. I meant it."

*That* was untrue. There were plenty of reasons she could think of to fear him, especially when he smiled and she could feel her pulse fluttering stupidly. But at least she believed he would not harm her.

"The doctor and Issa do not know what you are, and I will not betray you," he went on. "I'm simply happy to know your kind yet live."

"Not many of us," she said, then wished she had not. Tomanasíl would *kill* her.

His answering look was sympathetic and full of unspoken apology. His eyes had gone dark again, to that strange shade somewhere between blue and purple. It was mesmerizing.

Whatever he was about to say, however, was interrupted by the return of the maidservant Issa. She came in with a tray bearing a chunk of crusty bread and a steaming bowl of soup. Loralíenasa's stomach lurched at the thought of ingesting food.

"No," she told Naoise preemptively, in a low voice the girl could not overhear. "I cannot."

The prince looked at her, appraising, before turning his head to address the diligent serving girl in their language. He had a strong profile – hawkish nose balancing the lines of chin and brow and the prominence of his cheekbones. Issa replied with borderline insolent heat, but Naoise's response left no room for argument.

He did, however, resume his attention to Loralíenasa with evident regret. "I am being ordered out," he informed her quietly. "She tells me the doctor says if you are not able to eat, then you must rest. I am not to overtax you."

As a matter of fact, Loralíenasa was feeling tired. Not that she had any intention of admitting it, or wanted him to leave. She sighed. "When will you be back?"

The question sparked a pleased light in his eyes. "After you've slept," he promised. He said something else to the maidservant, then pushed himself smoothly to his feet. "Rest," he said gently. "I will return. And have no fear; you are safe here."

Though the truth of that remained debatable, Loralíenasa was not in the mood for pessimism. Instead, she found herself thinking of the brightness of Naoise's eyes and trying to recall where she had seen such eyes before as she drifted off to sleep.

History had never been Loralíenasa's favorite area of study, but from what she could see, Grenlec did not seem to have advanced much since the days of the War. It didn't take much in the way of observation to see that the place was *primitive*.

Some part of her was spitefully glad that humans had obviously experienced a dark age of intellectual and technological decline since expelling their elven mentors. They deserved it. More of her, though, was simply horrified. Especially when it occurred to her that she was going to have to live in these conditions until she was well enough to be on her way.

This was brought home to her most awfully when she managed to convey to the girl Issa through a complicated and tiring one-armed pantomime that she had a pressing need to relieve her bladder, and the girl responded by showing her the chamber pot.

Surely, even without elves to teach them and help them aspire to greater heights of education, humans could have figured out the basic concepts of plumbing and bodily waste disposal by now? By Vaian's great godly fingers, how could they choose to live this way? How weary their servants must be, always hauling water back and forth, up and down flights of stairs. And how much money they must spend in a year, keeping themselves in candles and lamp oil.

Had it never occurred to them that there had to be a more efficient way to get on? But of course, she'd been taught that humans had an irrational fear of any knowledge or technological advancement they considered to fall into the vague and foolish category of "magic."

When Issa stepped out in order to dispose of the chamber pot, scarcely a moment had passed before it struck Loralíenasa that she was finally alone.

Moving carefully, she eased herself into the dressing gown draped over the end of her bed and slipped out into the hall for a little exploration. She was probably in no shape to be doing this, but she had already come too far into this strange and ill-advised adventure to let a thing like common sense stop her now.

It was night – which night, she realized she did not know – and the corridors of the castle were quiet and mostly unlit. The stone of the walls was rough-hewn, a mottled grey darkened by wear and time. Clearly, as far as human dwellings went, this was not a recent construction. Not as old as the War, certainly. She doubted they had the knowledge or skill to make their buildings last that many thousands of years, but the place had obviously been lived in by many generations. She could feel them, the residual layers of the memories of so many years, almost like the nuanced bouquet of a complex perfume.

Loralíenasa moved down the hallway in darkness like one of the ghosts she could hear whispering in the quietest corners of her mind.

Not only was the stone rough, she soon noticed, but the finished woods too were only crudely worked. If this was the best they could do in one of their high houses, she was not impressed. Most of the windows were simply shuttered or barred – no glass to filter the light or keep the elements at bay. There were some admittedly nice tapestries lining the walls, but nothing she would call fine. Some of the wrought-iron-work in the candelabras and hinges and in the banisters was quite pretty, even expertly done. If there was a little too much of it and she was not seeing the gleam of gold or silver, of crystal or marble, or richly polished woods like she was accustomed to in the Valley, that was no more than a mean-spirited quibble.

Actually, she realized after a solid half hour of wandering that she was being ungraciously, unfairly judgmental. Holding people she had never met to a standard they had never even been exposed to. Instead of condemning them based on what she was seeing here, she decided to do her best to use it to understand them.

It soon emerged that the present master of this castle seemed to have a real appreciation for art and an eye for detail. Even though the sheer volume of paintings, wall hangings, sculptures, decorative wood carvings, and other pieces of ornamentation indicated vast wealth, there was an obvious preference for small masterpieces over ostentatious display. One hallway was lined on both sides by miniature portraits, hundreds of tiny human moments captured in time to stare out at their descendants through the years to come.

There was a music room as well, as much a museum as a functional studio, from her perspective. She was somewhat deflated to see that there seemed to be no human approximation of the *sònoreth*, her instrument, but there were many others to catch her interest. Lutes, viols, harps big and small, drums of many varieties, several flute-like pipes, some enormous upright wooden thing that made a rich, sonorous tone when she plucked at the strings. It was instructive, as complete a view into Grenlec's current level of cultural advancement as she could have wanted. The quality of the woodworking and the resin on the sound boxes, the fineness of the strings, the precision of the tuning – all of these told her things about the skill of human craftsmanship that she would have misjudged otherwise.

In fact, the refinement of their instruments had her impressed. She'd been estimating human knowledge and ability far below what this showed her. She had to remind herself again to be fair, and she felt a surge of irritation toward every teacher or elder who had taken pains to explain to her how coarse and boorish their human cousins were. It was starting to ring of hateful propaganda, standing in this room looking at these works of art.

Loralíenasa found her way down to ground level, but was so dizzy by the time she reached the bottom of the stairs that she had to sit for a moment to gather her strength. She'd been hoping the doctor's assessment of her condition had been inaccurately bleak because he thought his patient human, but she was forced now to admit that maybe she was hurt as badly as he said.

While she huddled on the bottom step, recovering, she heard footsteps and had to find a quick hiding spot in what turned out to be some kind of supply room. She waited until the way was clear before peeking out again and continuing on with her exploration.

It wasn't until after she emerged from the tiny room that she saw it was really an extra corner of sorts that had resulted from the confluence of two separate structures. She soon came to the conclusion that the castle had started as a far humbler residence and had only evolved into something more complicated over time, piece by piece. It became an intriguing game, trying to determine which parts were the oldest.

Soon she came to the dining hall. It was fairly small. During mealtimes, the room would be lit by a pair of intricate wrought-iron chandeliers suspended from the high ceiling; at the moment, it was dark and she was seeing by the light of the moon coming in at the window casements. The cold stone of the walls was warmed and softened by several large tapestries, among the largest she had ever seen, some of which had been worked in gleaming metal-wire thread.

The most impressive of these showed what she deduced to be the royal crest – the heraldry was dominated by a massive crown sewn with gold thread and several substantial emeralds – over an elaborately detailed forest scene that must have taken literally years or an army of needleworkers to embroider.

She fingered a corner of the extraordinary tapestry and considered all she had seen so far.

Admittedly, humans had not advanced as far after sending elves into exile as they might have otherwise. It was not a matter for debate that they still lived more roughly than they had to – almost immeasurably more roughly than her people did. What was impressive, she realized, was that despite their innate disadvantages, they were still trying. It still mattered to them to reach for something better even if they could never get it in their grasp.

There was something so tragic in that, and so admirable, that Loralíenasa found herself feeling sad as she drifted down the hallway with one hand absently rubbing rough against the old stone wall.

What must it be like, she wondered, to live knowing that you would probably never reach the goals you set for yourself? No matter how earnestly you pursued them, no matter how devoutly you applied yourself to their accomplishment? With infinite years ahead of her and a mind that was always seeking the *why* of everything, Loralíenasa could not imagine accepting that there were things she would die short of achieving. The advantages of her family and position only made it harder for her to envision; if there was something she wanted to learn, or make, or do, it was simply a fact that she would eventually have the time and the resources to see it happen. And that was just the way the world worked.

But to be born with death already sitting by the roadside, waiting for you to catch up – what would that do to your perception of the world? She tried to get her head around the idea and couldn't manage it.

Loralíenasa was wrestling with these philosophical issues when she heard voices, echoing from somewhere close by. Two male voices, she decided after a moment of listening. One was Prince Naoise. It struck her as both fascinating and alarming to realize that she would already know his voice – the rich resonance of it – anywhere. The other speaker was new to her, but brash and young-sounding.

As she was in a curious mood, and already fully invested in her exploration, she didn't even stop to think about whether she ought to turn back. Following the echoes, she crept close, carefully quiet.

No one who knew him would ever have accused Naoise Raynesley of being a country rustic, but frankly he could only take so much city-living before he had to get away. Not that he disliked people, because he really didn't, but by nature he had a need for far more personal time than a prince of the realm was able to come by in the capital. That was why he retreated to Grenwold as often as his father would let him. His family knew this about him.

And that was why he was justly irritated when his brother turned up.

Dairinn Raynesley was more than a handful – he was a force of nature. One of the Immutable Laws, all unto himself. When he came into a room, there was no ignoring him to carry on with one's business. No matter how unwilling one was to oblige, he took as much attention as he wanted, by some occult means that could neither be contested nor denied. He was a classically handsome man, and physically intimidating as well, and was rarely denied anything – or anyone – he set his eyes on.

Most people considered it a privilege to be singled out by the Crown Prince as a suitable audience for the ongoing performance that was his life, but as much as Naoise loved his brother, he found it tiring to so often be the one Dairinn wanted around.

Naoise could almost tangibly feel the energy draining out of him, as if he were donning several heavy cloaks one after another, the moment his steward informed him that the Crown Prince had been sighted riding up to the castle gates. By the time Dairinn swept into the library – that incandescent smile of his filling the whole place with a forceful cheer – Naoise was exhausted already and wondering how early he could possibly be allowed to call the evening.

"Brother!" Dairinn cried happily. Curled up on the rug under the table, Aiqa raised his head with an expectant whine upon seeing him. Dairinn crossed the entirety of the room in four great strides and had Naoise up out of his chair in a rib-cracking hug before the younger prince could say anything. "By the god, have I got news, and you'll not believe a word of it!"

When he had wrestled his way free and found his breath again, Naoise managed a smile. "That's to standard, then. I never believe a word of what you say, Dair."

The elder prince laughed and clapped him hard on the back, sending him forward a step. "All this time by yourself has you feeling saucy, I see. We've got to get you back to the real world straightaway, before you start fancying yourself a wit." He was looking well, and very much like he had lately been getting himself into exactly the kinds of trouble he most enjoyed in the two months since they'd seen one another.

"What are you doing here?" Naoise asked, attempting to recover his lost place in the book Dairinn had made him drop. He set the marker and put the tome aside, safely out of range. He simply had to resign himself to belonging to Dairinn now for as long as his brother wanted the attention. "I thought you were summering in Yeatun. Surely that has to be infinitely more exciting than my small corner of nowhere."

Dairinn grinned wolfishly as he bent to give Aiqa a good petting. "I was," he replied, "and it is. But this news I mentioned cannot wait. I am on my way to tell Father at once, and I know he will want you there with him when it all comes down."

Intrigued, Naoise opened his mouth to invite his brother to share these astonishing tidings of his, but Dairinn stood up suddenly and pounded his gloved fist on the table Naoise had been seated at.

"I'll be damned if I'm delivering news of this character in a room this full of books and so dry of good alcohol," the Crown Prince asserted. "Where do you keep the spirits around here, little brother?"

A quarter of an hour later, they were comfortably installed in the small formal receiving room downstairs with a snifter each of something strong – although Naoise had only poured for himself in order to be sociable. It wasn't so long ago that he'd still been too young for drink by their father's reckoning, and he had not acquired anything like Dairinn's taste for it.

Dairinn drained his first glass in one long, impressive gulp, then poured another before peeling off his riding gloves and tossing them somewhere out of sight.

"I say. *Much* better," the road-weary prince declared. He glanced at the bottle sitting on the low table between them. "This is Father's, is it not? I think I remember sneaking a fair glug of it when I was nine." He laughed heartily at the memory. "Couldn't see straight for hours. Good job it was Mum who found me in the herb garden half-passed-out and bibbling about fairy frogs, else I'd have been beaten to a blister."

Even though five years had passed since her death, it still gave Naoise a twinge to hear Dairinn invoke their mother so casually. It took him a moment to recall the incident in question, and when he did he found it dim and fuzzed-over with the confusion of youth. "You were *drunk*? Mum said you were sick."

That only made Dairinn laugh harder. "And sick I was, my brother."

Naoise shook his head fondly and invited Aiqa to snuggle against his legs. The large dog settled there warmly and put his head down on his white paws.

As pressing as the elder prince seemed to think his reason for being here, however, he insisted on sharing several trivial anecdotes and stories of questionable nature from his summer in Yeatun before Naoise could bring him back on point.

"By the good god," Dairinn swore when he finally remembered his purpose. "I set out at once when word came to Yeatun: Telrisht has invaded Lang, and they're pushing all the way through. They'll be on our doorstep by the end of the month. It's war, Naoise."

It took a moment for the news to be real to Naoise. "Telrisht... in Lang? But *why?* The Ayiz only just came to the throne... what? Half a year ago? And did he not just conclude peaceful trade negotiations with the King of Lang?"

"You're asking me?" Dairinn shifted restlessly in his seat. "Sod that. I don't care *why* the plague-cursed Ayiz wants to bring an army onto our soil, and it isn't my job to puzzle it out. More importantly, we get to send him and his damn *Rahd* screaming back to their heathen god and he asked us to do it."

Of course that would be Dairinn's outlook on the matter. He was excited. Naoise was unsettled, to say the least.

War; he could not deny that the word evoked a certain youthful rush of his blood. But was he ready for it, for all it would mean? As a prince of the realm, he would be expected to show leadership and courage on the field of battle – did he have that in him?

And what if they lost? The Telrishti were notoriously bloodthirsty in war, which they had honed into a science over the centuries. The Rahd, their elite corps of knights, were like a nightmare out of legend, trained not only in the art of taking lives in battle but in the absolute pacification of the countryside through which they moved. What would the final cost be for Grenlec, in lives lost and property destroyed? What of Lang, too, their unfortunate ally caught in the middle? Even if Grenlec beat the enemy back, when if ever would Lang recover?

More questions kept coming, questions he could not answer and that he knew were not on his brother's mind. Which raised another point: what of Dairinn? Would their father let the Crown Prince take the field? If he did, would Dairinn have the common sense not to get himself killed?

That he was a strong young man and well-trained were facts no one would deny, but he was also reckless. He had no idea – would never have an idea – how often Naoise or their father had quietly saved him from his own indiscretions greater or lesser, and Naoise expected that to be his role for as long as he and his brother both lived. The love the people had for their boisterous Crown Prince would serve him well when his time came to rule. Unfortunately, he also had a rather breezy view of his own capabilities.

If they were not posted together, Naoise could do nothing to make sure his brother came out of the war alive.

Naoise realized he was shaking.

"So," Dairinn went on, completely disregarding Naoise's long silence, "get yourself packed up, little brother, because in the morning it's off to Dewfern for musters and war councils and some long-overdue bloodshed by-and-by."

Oh, *damn*. The realization hit Naoise like a bucket of cold water to the face: he wouldn't be going anywhere in the morning. He couldn't. He had this small matter of harboring an injured, couldn't't-possibly-be-real elf in secret. He had promised her that she would be taken care of, that she would be safe, and he couldn't guarantee that if he went gallivanting off to war.

"Dair." Naoise drew a deep breath. "It will be a few days before I can be on my way. I have some things to settle here first. You must go on without me. Father needs to hear this news as soon as possible."

In fact, he had to get Dairinn out of here with a quickness, before his brother spotted her. Because she was extraordinarily pretty. And Dairinn and pretty women were–

"Hullo," Dairinn said suddenly, sitting upright in his deeply-cushioned arm chair, his eyes bright and fixed upon something that had caught more of his interest than Naoise was used to seeing him give out. "I say. Who are *you*?"

# CHAPTER THREE

Already knowing perfectly well what he was about to see, Naoise sighed and followed his brother's gaze to the edge of the arched doorframe. Sure as he breathed, a certain white-faced young woman stood there and had apparently been watching the two of them for some time.

She seemed momentarily startled to have been noticed, but she recovered her poise quickly. Sometimes he thought perhaps she was younger than him, but mostly he assumed she was far older simply because of her composure and bearing. At moments like this, it was hard to tell.

Straightening, pushing off from the doorframe, the elf came two deliberate steps into the room as if to say, *"Yes. I was spying on you. So what? Are you going to do something about it?"*

Naoise liked her attitude, and she had a lot of it.

Dairinn stood slowly, his drink forgotten on the low table. "Hullo," he said again, this time in an entirely different tone.

One could hardly blame Dairinn for noticing the young woman, because she was eye-catching. Slender figure, uncommonly white skin, striking features. If there was something decidedly not-human about the high, wide structure of her cheekbones or the unusual tilt of her vivid green eyes, it did nothing at all to detract from her appeal. Actually it only made her more intriguing.

Naoise would have been lying to himself if he tried to pretend that he had not noticed how beautiful she was, but in the interest of proper gentlemanly chivalry, he was making an effort not to dwell on it. That was proving difficult for him just now, with her standing before him wearing only nightclothes, her long black curls tumbling unbound down her back and over her shoulders.

"Naoise," Dairinn said, a slow grin spreading across his face, "you are a bad man. A very bad man indeed, letting us all believe you come out here for the quiet contemplation. 'Some things to settle here' my rather well-formed ass."

"Oh." Naoise reconsidered the dressing gown and the loose hair and took his meaning. "Oh dear me, no. It isn't what you think."

Dairinn was ignoring him. With his best courtly grace, smiling his most handsome smile, he approached Loríen and reached for her hand to kiss it elegantly. "I am Dairinn, this rascal's responsible older brother. What is your name, my dove?"

It was at least amusing to see the flirtatious prince's most charming advances met with boredom, even if Naoise experienced a moment of panic as he wondered if his brother would believe the lie he had to tell. Naoise knew he was not much of a liar.

He cleared his throat and tried for an offhand tone. "She's Mysian, you moron. She can't understand a word."

"Really?" Dairinn replied, stretching the word lasciviously long, winking over his shoulder at his brother.

"I swear you have the basest imagination," Naoise said. "Do you not see that she's hurt?" The bandages were visible on her neck above the line of her dressing gown though the alarming state of her shoulder was hidden, and her color was still not what it ought to be after so much blood loss. "I found her in the forest, injured – mauled by a bear. She's here recovering."

"I'm sure she will wish to express her gratitude before she leaves," Dairinn said happily. He had not, Naoise noticed, let go of the girl's hand. A fact that made him somewhat cross.

"Shall I tell her you said that?" he suggested tersely.

Dairinn laughed in delight, half-turning his body to look back at him. "Oh my. How adorable. I don't believe I've ever seen you so bunched up over a woman before."

"I will kill you."

Loríen carefully took her hand away from Dairinn's and looked past him to meet Naoise's eyes from across the room. It was alarming and exhilarating at the same time to have her intense concentration focused on him. "What, exactly, does this great oaf think he is doing?" she asked in her fluid language.

Naoise laughed against his better judgment. "This is my older brother," he told her, somewhere halfway between an apology and an explanation. "Be careful with him – he has a reputation with women and he thinks he's irresistible."

She laughed in turn, and it was a delightful sound. "I see. And did I correctly hear you saying that I am Mysian? A well-conceived falsehood, if so."

"You did. I thought it would be the most believable."

"Come now," Dairinn interrupted. "Don't leave me out." He made a deliberate show of working his memory and said, brow furrowed in concentration, *"Vashallo, jeya. Dairinn va quae insae."* He grinned. "There. That's all the Mysian I know."

Naoise watched Loríen with some trepidation, uncertain how well she would be able to parse what had just been said to her if she did not speak Mysian. While it did have its roots in Elven, the modern language had evolved along its own distinct path. She raised a single eyebrow at the elder prince, the merest hint of a smile tweaking the corner of her mouth.

"My name is Loríen," she replied in prim, formal Mysian, "and I am most certainly not your darling."


Between the two brothers, the elder was much closer to what Loralíenasa had expected in a man of Grenlec. Big, loud, broad-shouldered, with thick arms and a square jaw and an inflated opinion of his own worth. And, despite the paradox of it, innocently harmless while conveying a sense that he would be capable of casual brutality at the slightest provocation. If not for the chestnut-red sheen to his short-cropped dark hair and the almost alarming blue of his eyes, he would be the perfect Grenlecian archetype.

It was curious how much Naoise obviously loved the raucous fellow.

But before things could get interesting – as she felt certain they were about to – they were interrupted by a flurry of indignant anger in the form of the maidservant, Issa. The girl burst into the receiving room practically quivering with rage, and launched into a forceful tirade when she saw the two princes and Loralíenasa in the midst of their strange meeting.

Not even knowing what was being said, she could see that Issa was accusing both men of gross misconduct and that they were striving vainly to defend themselves. Loralíenasa supposed getting dressed down would look the same in any language and she felt sorry for them, but could not help also being amused. In particular, Issa seemed most strongly to disapprove of the elder prince, Dairinn.

Eventually, the maidservant concluded her lecture and all but seized Loríen in order to drag her back to her room. Cooperating seemed like the thing to do in her current condition. Loríen met Naoise's eyes across the room and offered him a wry half-smile on her way out. He shook his head ruefully.

Something had been going on between the brothers before they'd noticed her spying on them. Even though she couldn't understand the words, she could easily see it.

At first, she'd only been watching because she found Naoise so pleasant to look at and listen to, and could hardly hope to find a better opportunity to get away with staring. But it would have been a lie to pretend that her curiosity had not been piqued by the fire in Dairinn's eyes and the grave contemplation with which Naoise had responded. And whatever they had been talking about, she felt certain that it was going to mean a change in her situation.

Hence, she was not at all surprised when Naoise came for a visit in the late watches of the night, after Issa had gone to sleep in the adjoining bedroom.

Feeling her independence after the evening's small adventure, Loralíenasa refused to receive her guest helpless in bed and moved instead to the wide seat in the window. Naoise joined her there, pleasantly close. He waded slowly through all of the expected trivialities, as though he was in no hurry to get to what lay on the other side of them. He inquired after her health and comfort and apologized for the earlier situation, and Issa's over-protectiveness, and his brother's rascally behavior.

"He's not as bad as he wants everyone to think." Naoise spoke with some care not to wake Issa next door, despite the sudden intensity of his manner as he said it. "I think it's just easier for him when people don't expect him to be… better. More."

Loralíenasa studied him, wondering why he should be so intent upon defending his brother when she had said nothing at all. She wanted to ask what was wrong, but they didn't know each other well enough for that.

"I find it hard to believe the two of you are related," she said instead, lightly. "You are nothing alike." That wasn't entirely true; she thought she could see the family resemblance, physically at least, but she didn't know how much of that was just the fact that they were both human and therefore strange to her in the same ways.

Naoise did not smile. "So I've been told."

She could make nothing of his meaning, whether he was offended or agreeing with her. He would practically blend in back home in the Valley, she thought a little sourly.

He looked out the window even though it was too dark outside to see anything. His profile was austere in a way she found appealing, but he seemed unhappy. "To speak truth," he said, "I have no idea how he would react if he knew what you are. None at all."

Loríen couldn't think of a way to respond to that without showing far too much anxiety or childish fear, so she remained silent. After a moment of observing the tension in his posture, she came to understand that this was an important issue to him and it distressed him that he could not predict his brother on it.

This would be entirely different if their roles were reversed. She could say, without asking, *exactly* how anyone at home would feel about discovering a human in their midst.

Finally his attention seemed to refocus and he sighed before turning sober eyes upon her. "I apologize for my distraction. I have had grave news this evening. I fear I must leave Grenwold, and it will not be safe here for you after I've gone."

She swallowed. Even her little jaunt around the castle had left her too exhausted to think about trying to make it any farther than her bed tonight; the long journey home, south and over the mountains, would be a ridiculous impossibility in her condition.

"I've been trying to think of a solution for you," he went on quietly, "but I confess that my attention is stretched in too many directions at the moment. I wish I–" He stopped, visibly reconsidering whatever he had been about to say, and made that strange hunching gesture with his shoulders again. "I'm sorry I seem to be so useless," he concluded after an awkward silence.

"What has happened?" she heard herself asking before she could tell herself it was none of her business. She berated herself inwardly for the slip, but there was no going back. "What is this news that has you so troubled?"

After considering her question for a moment during which she thought he was looking for a way to defer it, the human prince smiled grimly. "Timing is a funny thing, isn't it?" He shook his head. "I have here recovering in my home an elf out of myth, who was injured saving my life. And she is not only fascinating and witty, but also beautiful and mysterious enough to be a fever dream, and I cannot say just how dearly I would like the chance to become better acquainted. Of course this would be the precise moment when Telrisht would choose to start a war."

"Telrisht…" She swallowed, wrestling with at least a dozen conflicting emotions. Understandably, given the news that the two nations her people hated more than anything else in the world were shortly to be killing each other, in addition to the particular way the Grenlecian prince had chosen to share the information. And, with a war on, there was no way at all that she could manage to stay here any longer.

She didn't even know how she felt about the outcome of the war, either way. Telrisht and Grenlec both had done such terrible things to her people and as far as she was concerned they could send each other to the black Abyss and she wouldn't even blink.

But she didn't like the idea that Naoise might have to fight. And die. She didn't even like to imagine him with a sword in his hand.

Oh, Vaian. So irrelevant. What mattered here, she reminded herself, was that she was in a bad place at a worse time and she needed to think of a way out of it.

"Oh dear," she said when she realized she had no idea what to do.

Naoise sighed in agreement. Neither of them spoke for a long time.

During the long silence, while trying to think productively about the fact that she was all but trapped in enemy territory with more enemies coming on and no way to get home, Loralíenasa eventually realized that she wasn't thinking at all. That she was, instead, admiring Naoise's hands. He had the fingers of a musician, long and lean and restless.

As soon as she realized what she was doing, she was of course angry with herself. This was important, damn it. She made herself look elsewhere.

"This," she deadpanned, amusement tempered by disgust at her own folly and her bad luck, "is not the best situation I have ever been in."

He let out a short, quiet laugh before relapsing into a thoughtful stillness.

It did not fail to register that she was only in this mess because she was a stupid child who had blatantly and with defiant forethought *explicitly* disobeyed her elders. Damn them. Damn them for knowing better and being right.

Eventually Naoise asked, cautiously, "Is it far, your home? I don't mean to pry, of course–"

She allowed herself to look at him and found that he was searching her face for any sign that he was wading into unfriendly waters. She chose not to answer sharply, even though she had already warned him not to ask about this. "It is. Quite far."

He cleared his throat, clearly unhappy to be pressing what he knew was not a good subject. "Is there… perhaps… some way we could send a message? If someone could come for you–"

"No," she cut in.

The thought of sending one of the human prince's messengers to the Valley, revealing the secret location of her people's place of exile in order to deliver the news to Lord Tomanasíl Maiantar that she was wounded in Grenlec and in need of an escort…

Vaian, no. She shuddered.

She could of course use her tracking glass to contact the friend she was supposed to be staying with, but that didn't help either. It would be too long before any rescue Víara might send could reach her.

"I'm sorry." Naoise's voice was quiet. Full of true regret. She knew he had only been doing his best to offer solutions.

Loralíenasa reached out to give his arm a reassuring squeeze even though she couldn't manage to tell him the line of questioning had been welcome. He looked down at her hand, but said nothing more.

Something odd happened in the back of Loríen's mind as she sat with her hand resting on Naoise's lean forearm, and she had to concentrate to figure out what it was. She could feel him in a way that had nothing to do with contact or proximity, and it sent her back to the strange, panicked, lightning-struck moment just before the bear's attack when she had felt herself to be inside Naoise's head. For the last few days, she'd been trying to tell herself that the stress of the incident had made her memory unreliable, but…

Naoise looked up at her, and something about the inquisitive light in his eyes confirmed everything. He was recalling the same incident, wondering if it had been his imagination, and trying to decide whether or not to ask.

If it had really happened and they really had shared that moment of connection, Loríen was at a loss to understand it. She knew of only one possible explanation, and it made no sense; and if it really was the *Galvanos*, that would mean she had far worse problems than being trapped and wounded in Grenlec on the brink of war.

She had to get out. Now.

It occurred to her in that moment that there *was* no solution to her current conundrum. All she could do was make a bad choice and hope it wouldn't turn out to be the *worst* choice, and that she could survive it.

She put on a small smile for the human prince. "Don't worry about me. I'm sure we'll think of something," she lied breezily.

He was not even remotely fooled. It was a long time before he was able to answer with anything like the same kind of blithe nonchalance. "Perhaps we should both sleep on it. No doubt things will look less bleak in the morning." He didn't manage it as well as she had.

They both knew she was going to steal away in the night and hope she had the strength to make it home on her own. And that the only thing he could do to help was to let her.

Loralíenasa drew a deep breath and nodded. "No doubt." She did not want those to be her last words to him, and struggled to add something more. "But whatever the case, you have been so kind already to trouble yourself on my account. Thank you, for everything." Blurting that she wanted to kiss him didn't seem like the right thing to do, so she shut her mouth and mentally ordered herself not to be such a girlish idiot.

"I should leave you to your rest. Sleep well." Naoise pushed himself to his feet reluctantly, and her hand was somehow now in his, actually tingling where their skin touched. He brought it to his lips but merely held it there a moment without kissing it. She didn't know what to make of that.

A moment later he was gone, and they were both alone.

Prince Naoise could blame timing if he wanted, but Loralíenasa knew better. This had the stink of Fate all over it, from top to bottom. She had to get herself out of Grenlec before things got even worse than bad luck and her stupidity had already made them.

It was not yet anything like morning.

Naoise was not an especially late riser, but he could not help but consider this an indecent hour at which to have people in his room, yelling. Something about bad seeds and knavish behavior, not that he was able to take it in. The sun had not yet shown his face over the treeline, even. The unhappily woken prince responded with considerably less charm than he would have been able to manage in an hour or three. There was profanity involved, and if he had been more awake, he would have been sorry about that. There was only one person in the world he ever spoke to that way on purpose, and that was because Dairinn liked it.

In point of fact, it was only one individual in his room making loud and free with the imprecations, but Issa had enough attitude to seem like more than one woman when she wanted to. This, unfortunately, was one of those times.

Naoise had not yet figured out how such a young maidservant had managed to come by so much insolence. She treated him like a wayward younger brother whenever he was at home, even though he was fairly certain she was no older than he.

He sat up in bed, struggling out from beneath Aiqa's insistently heavy head and shrugging at least halfway into a dressing gown, and tried to make Issa's shrill accusations mean something despite the unseemly hour.

"Aren't you listening to me at all? My lord, I said she's gone. *Gone.* I'd lay money to it your no-good whore of a brother has her tupped in some broom closet right this breathing minute. You say she saved your idle hide out there. Don't you care half a copper ronan?"

Naoise blinked, fighting to get his brain to do anything besides wish the loud young woman would go away. "When you say 'she,' are you–" he had to pause for a yawn– "are you referring to Loríen?"

"Of *course* I am," Issa snapped.

"And... did I hear you calling the Crown Prince a *whore*?"

The girl grumbled something incoherent and gripped her skirt in two bloodless fists. "My lord prince, please, I'm worried about the lady. When I went in to check on her, she was gone. Bed not even slept in. Maybe your brother had naught to do with it, but it's no less worrisome for that."

Naoise listened to the frantic maidservant and sighed. He wished he had been wrong to expect this. "She's gone."

"That's what I've been trying to say, my lord." Her face was practically purple now with agitation, eyes so wide they almost looked like they might fall out. "How much drink did that foul-mouthed lout force down you last night anyway?"

Naoise sat up straighter and pushed a hand through his hair, taking on a more authoritative mien. "That is enough about my brother," he said quietly. He was rewarded with mild contrition. "The lady has left Grenwold, and is no longer our concern."

Issa's only response was an indignant sputter.

"I will see to it you are rewarded for the devoted care you have shown these last few days," he added. "Thank you, Issa." It was a dismissal.

There was obviously much more the maidservant wanted to say, but he had allowed no room for that in his tone. She had no choice but to drop a sullen curtsey and leave his presence.

The prince couldn't help sighing again. As true as it might have been that Loríen was gone from Grenwold, the part about her not being his concern anymore was a lie. He suspected he was going to keep thinking about her, worrying and wondering if she'd been able to make it home safely, until the day he died.

But that didn't matter now. Or at least, he couldn't let it. *Now*, what mattered was pulling himself together and getting back to his father's side. There was no time for elves or myths or magic.

Grenlec was at war.

A day. That was how much distance Loralíenasa estimated she'd put between herself and Grenwold before the fatigue hit her.

It wasn't even the normal tiredness of traveling stupidly while recovering from a fairly severe injury. This was a different sort of awful, and there were two reasons why she could only estimate when it had started. Not only did it come over her so gradually she couldn't say how long she had felt this way, but once it did, she found her brain doing unreliable things with time and her memory.

With an ache in her joints and a sick, poisoned feeling in her muscles, Loríen found a spot to collapse for a while out of sight. She wondered if her shoulder was infected after all, as the doctor had worried. That would be just her luck. She wasn't able to wonder anything more than that, because she either passed out or fell asleep immediately afterward.

When she came to, it was so dark she thought for a moment that she had gone blind. Then she saw the faint heat glow rising off her horse's back and was relieved to discover it was only night.

Her relief was short-lived. The further she came awake, the more she realized just how *not right* she felt. She would have been alarmed by it if her brain wasn't already so fuzzy, but it was, and that was part of the problem. It took her more time than she was able to calculate just to remember where she was and how she had gotten there, and even more to wonder why she felt this way.

A single word jumped into the forefront of her mind and would not leave: *Galvanos*. She told her imagination to be more useful or mind its own business, and climbed unsteadily to her feet.

The change in altitude made her feel queasy. Her stomach flopped and twitched, but eventually it stopped torturing her and she was able to move on again.

When she awoke after another brief nap, she felt so ill she wished she could die. Her face was damp with a sick sweat and every muscle in her body felt as sore and sensitive as if she'd been running for several days straight. The light burned her eyes. Her throat was dry and raw. Her brain seemed to be on fire.

Efrondel would be nearly three weeks off at her usual pace.

*I'm not going to make it. I'm going to die out here.*

It took several moments for her to convince her body to stand up and even longer to get into the saddle. Her arms were as weak as dry grass. When she managed it, at last, she wondered what the point was. There was no way in the name of Vaian or the Dark One's Abyss that she would be able to reach the Valley, and she knew it.

*Don't think; just ride. If you can't ride, then crawl. Forward. Just don't think about it.*

Trying to follow her own advice, she told her horse to move forward and hoped it would continue even after she next passed out. Every step she took away from *him* sapped a little more of her strength, required more of her will-power. And despite her best efforts not to think, she could not stop herself from remembering those impossibly bright eyes, the fall of his black hair, the austere lines of his profile. The dark velvet of his voice.

*Keep moving. Don't think about it. You* can't *think about it. Keep going.*

She rode for what might have been hours, her mind a fog and her body and heart a single ache. The pain became numbing. Mercifully, it soon grew almost impossible for her to form a coherent thought. Her only task was to cling to the saddle as her horse moved onward, and that was on the verge of too much. After riding longer than she thought she could, she collapsed for a brief rest. She slid out of consciousness for a while without knowing it. She tried to eat some of her trail rations, but they came back up almost at once.

When she eventually convinced herself that she would have to move on if she ever wanted to get home, she climbed weakly onto her horse's back and forced herself to continue.

Her strength was failing. The forest seemed to push down upon her, and she was having difficulty holding up beneath its solidity. Still, she made herself move forward. Her clothes were wet with perspiration and she felt bitterly cold – an entirely new feeling she had no experience with and that made no sense.

Loralíenasa collapsed into the underbrush without bothering to search for a campsite. She brought her arm up to lift the water to her lips, but she was out again before she could complete the gesture. For hours, until morning, she lay unmoving where she had fallen.

The sun in her eyes forced her to awaken, but it was not to any sense of healing or refreshment. She felt even worse than before, which she would not have thought possible. She groaned without knowing she did so, and rolled to her knees.

Her stomach churned and she found herself dry heaving. Her breath was coming in short, difficult gasps. A droplet of sweat rolled down her nose and plunked down painfully loud onto a dead leaf below her. She took a swallow of water, and then another, the effort leaving her breathless.

For several moments, she had trouble remembering which direction was which. Then, memory coming slowly, she used a nearby tree trunk to claw her way to her feet. She swayed dizzily, holding the tree for support. Her vision swam. It did not matter. She had to try to move on, no matter how difficult it was to do so. With a tired, feeble gait, she started off again heading south.

Her patient horse, forgotten in her delirium, followed behind.

It felt like she was walking against a gale. Every step was an ordeal. A part of her strongly wished, for reasons she could no longer make sense of, to turn back; the rest of her was equally determined to make it home because it seemed like an impossible feat. She did not know which to side with. The struggle was agonizing. Somehow, though, she just kept going.

Then she was sitting down and had been for some time. She could not remember having stopped. There seemed to be a fog surrounding her, through which she could neither see nor think, penetrated only by a constant dull ringing which was equally confounding.

She tilted her swollen head back and looked up at the sky. The sun was directly overhead, but no matter how hard she tried, she could not make that observation have a meaning. In truth, she could make no sense of the fact that she was sitting on the grass in the open. She forced herself to her feet again and kept going in what seemed to be the right direction.

Time passed, and distance with it, but she had already stopped being able to measure either. For hours or days or years she walked. Then she was on her knees, pushing herself onward with trembling arms.

After a while, she became aware that she was not moving any longer and that the light was gone. She tried to keep going, but her body did not obey her. She couldn't even *feel* her body anymore. It was a relief, after so much pain. But there was still pain, a different sort, and it went deeper than should have been possible.

It didn't matter, though. The burden of making the hard decision to continue had been lifted from her; she simply *could not* move any farther. She could not do anything but lie there and hope she would soon slide into blackness again, and stay there this time.

For a long time, she was not aware of herself. But then, she felt something rough and hard touching her with an insistence she would have found annoying if she was capable of feeling so strong an emotion as annoyance. Someone seemed to be saying something to her, but she could not understand the words. What language was the person speaking? What language did *she* speak? She opened her eyes slowly.

A face hovered above hers. A familiar face. Light blue eyes stared down at her, grave with concern. The lips formed a word. "Loralíenasa."

She tried to wet her lips, but found her tongue too dry to perform the task. Then water was sliding down her throat and she had to concentrate on not choking. The flow of liquid ceased after a moment. She tried again to speak.

"Lanas?" Her voice was little more than a husk of a whisper.

The face above hers broke into a tight, relieved smile. "Damn it, Loríen. Don't ever scare me like that again. Here, have some more water."

Loralíenasa obeyed and drank again from the proffered waterskin. Then she tried to make her eyes focus enough to have a look around. She was still in the forest, and she still felt awful, and it was night. But Lanoralas was there with her. It would be all right. It was his job to make sure she safe.

She swallowed, and swallowed again. "Lanas. How...?"

"Víara had one of her dreams and sent me out to bring you home. Vaian be praised I listened to her, and that you haven't lost your tracking glass," Lanas explained in a tone rough with worry.

Her memory was still fuzzy, but it seemed to her that she was not used to hearing him sound like this.

"I can't *believe* the two of you are stupid enough to play these kinds of games," he went on. "Flouting the law for larks and lying about it. Neither of you are *nearly* young enough to get away with being so irresponsible. Lord Maiantar will be furious." He stopped mid-rant when he seemed to realize that she wasn't processing anything he said. "What happened to you, Loríen?"

Loralíenasa tried to organize her thoughts, to remember. Lanas' reassuring familiarity was helping a little. The sequence of events and their meaning was proving elusive, though. "I... met a man. A human."

Lanas' mild blue eyes turned stormy with the suddenness of an angry seasky. "What did that savage do to you? Your shoulder–"

Loralíenasa shook her head. It hurt and was a mistake. "No." She fought to remember what had happened. "I was in the forest," she began again. "There was a tree, and we talked, then there was a bear. He was…"

She shivered as a chill caught her.

"You're delirious," Lanas observed, frowning. "I have to get you home. You need help. Oh, Vaian. Lord Maiantar is going to kill us *both*."

# Chapter Four

Lyn clambered soundlessly down the tree-trunk and onto the great boulder. Peering over the edge, she could see the top of Bryant's dark-haired head below. It looked like he was fletching arrows.

She grinned to herself and crawled over to the other side of the boulder, to the tree that grew right up against it. It was possible to reach the hollow in the trunk from here; she'd stashed a bucket of slimy pond-water there yesterday. Hauling it back across the boulder without making a noise was a challenge, but she'd been practicing. This was going to be perfect. She settled into place and prepared to unleash the bucket's contents upon her unsuspecting victim.

When she looked down to gauge the placement, Bryant was no longer there.

She darted her gaze across the clearing, but he was nowhere to be seen. An amused laugh floated up to her. Her eyebrows contracted in confusion, but the truth of the situation dawned on her a moment too late.

"Oh, great galloping goats, *no!*" she swore, and tried to move out of the way, but not fast enough. A bucket of mud came glopping down onto her from the branches above, thoroughly covering her head and most of her torso.

All of her planning, set at naught.

"No!" she cried indignantly. "That's not fair!"

Bryant laughed again and stepped out of hiding. He appeared even more pleased with himself than usual.

"Not fair?" he echoed. "And it's fair for you to try to douse a poor innocent fellow, without provocation, as he's trying to do something useful?"

Lyn sputtered, trying to put her frustration into words. "Innocent? No provocation? What do you call leaving that dead rat in my bed?"

Bryant grinned, assuming his typical look of not-quite-convincing virtue.

"That was an accident," he said austerely. "I had just misplaced it."

Snorting, Lyn pushed her golden braid over her shoulder and looked down at her begrimed condition. There was, she decided, only one way to fix the situation. She jumped off the rock onto Bryant with a playful growl.

He managed to catch some of her weight, but was still knocked to the ground by the force of her attack. She made certain to spread as much of the muck onto him as possible. They went rolling, her long braid tangling itself around them, until Bryant finally managed to pin her. Lyn's muddy assault had left his appearance less than immaculate, which he noted with a muffled oath.

That was all Lyn had hoped for. She laughed triumphantly.

"Do you yield?" he asked, smirking.

She smiled back and said, "For now. Get off me or I'll kick you."

Bryant laughed again and jumped to his feet.

"How did you know?" she demanded, trying to sound angry but not succeeding. She was laughing too hard. "I was *very* quiet."

"Not quiet enough," Bryant replied, grinning, "and you're so predictable." He offered her a hand up.

Lyn climbed to her feet without his help. "What are you talking about?" she demanded. She made an ineffectual attempt to brush some of the twigs, leaves, and mud from her clothes, then shrugged and awaited his explanation with her hands on her hips.

Bryant leaned smugly against the stone. "I've been doing my work in that spot all week. I *knew* you would decide to make use of it before too long. Like I said, you're predictable."

She thumbed her nose at him. At least he had a great smudge of mud across his pale cheek.

He ignored her and went on to explain the entirety of his cleverness, unable to resist. "I had the whole thing figured out – where you would sit, where you would hide the water, where to position the bucket above you. You're not that quiet. I heard you, and I smelled the water. So I pulled the rope I'd rigged. If you're going to play these games with a master, you can't complain when you get beaten. Or doused," he added with a smirk.

"A master," Lyn snorted. "A master idiot, you mean."

Bryant threw a handful of mud at her, and she ducked.

"That was an unkind thing to say, Lyn," a light voice said behind her.

Lyn turned quickly to face the speaker, a lady with gleaming platinum tresses nearly the same color as her skin, and fascinating sky blue eyes with deeper grey shadows. Though she had the appearance of an elf, like Lyn and Bryant, she was something else entirely. Despite the rebuke, her expression at the moment was mildly amused.

"Come on, Sun," Lyn objected. "Did you see what *he* did to *me*?"

"Don't try pleading innocence," the fairy said, a smile showing in her eyes. "I saw the whole thing."

Lyn's bottom lip curled downward into an exaggerated pout.

Both Bryant and Sun burst out laughing.

"Sorry, Lyn," Bryant chuckled. "Not going to work. We both know you too well."

"He's right, you know," Sun said. "If these are the kinds of games you want to play, you can't whine when he plays back."

"But he started it!" Lyn complained. Sometimes Sun was like this – siding with Bryant unaccountably – and it was vexing.

Bryant put both his hands up in a gesture of blamelessness. "Before I put the rat in your bed, you tried to put itching powder in my boots, remember?"

Lyn leaned toward him, hands still on hips. "And before that there was the time you froze the hot springs right before my bath." She felt her blood boiling as she thought of it. It wasn't fair when he used the magic for which it seemed he had a natural gift though she did not. There was no way for her to predict what he could do, using his powers. How was she supposed to play the game by those rules?

Sun laughed. "Look, you two, if you're going to argue over who started it, I'm afraid you're going to have to go back almost to the day I found you. You've been at it this whole time. My only point was that you shouldn't call Bryant an idiot, Lyn. Nothing more."

Lyn relaxed a bit. "Well, all right." She flashed Bryant a smile and held out an extremely muddy hand for him to shake. "Sorry about calling you an idiot."

Bryant stared at her filthy hand with one eyebrow raised, then shrugged and shook it anyway. "All right. Come on, I'll show you how to move more quietly."

Grinning, Lyn said, "Thanks, Bryant. Next time you won't hear me, I promise."

Bryant kindly allowed Lyn first go at the hot springs when they were done with their stealth lessons. He sat against a tree-trunk, idly shifting a fallen twig through the color spectrum, as he waited his turn. It had been an exceptionally good day and he was happy.

Most of his days were good. They could hardly be otherwise, living in this idyllic part of the forest with no responsibilities, no purpose except to enjoy himself, his only company a beautiful girl with an active sense of humor and a fairy who had been like his mother for as far back as his memory stretched.

Of course, his memory did not in fact reach back to the beginning of his life, and that gave him a twinge when he let himself think about it.

The fact was, he had already been a grown elf when he'd awakened one day to find the fairy bent over him, nursing him back to health from what had obviously been grievous injuries. He'd had no idea what his name was or where he came from, and the fairy had not been able to enlighten him. According to her, she had found him collapsed in a burning bush with Lyn in his arms. For her part, Lyn had been little more than an infant then, with few words at her command beyond her own name; he could hardly look to her for the answers he lacked.

That had been more than a hundred years ago, and no one had ever come looking for him; whatever he'd left behind was obviously not important. He could think of no life more pleasant than the one he now lived, and tried not to bother himself about a past he couldn't remember.

Lately, though, it had started to weigh on him now and then; he knew it had to do with Lyn. With the way he had started to feel about her as she left childhood behind and became a young woman. Sun had found them together, but that could mean anything. Was she his daughter, his sister, a stranger, his charge – what? Would it be appropriate for him to act on his feelings when she was older, or would he be doing something unwittingly awful?

Lyn looked nothing like him, so he was disinclined to believe they were related. Her skin was much darker than his, for a start. He was stark white, nearly as white as Sun, where Lyn was a beautiful burnished bronze. And his hair was black, nothing like her honey-gold tresses. His eyes were bright green to her blue. Some of their features were similar, but he didn't know what that meant – maybe it was just what elves looked like. With no basis for comparison, he couldn't say.

Sometimes, he thought he simply *had* to find out. Leave on a quest, or something. But he never knew where he would go, whom he would ask, what he could accomplish. The world beyond the forest was almost a complete enigma to him, what little he did know either teased from Sun or discovered on covert excursions that angered her when she learned of them. He always talked himself out of it.

*I'll ask Cole,* he thought.

It was about time he hunted his human friend down again, anyway. He chuckled as he imagined how surprised Cole would be when he found him this time. It was sort of a game for Bryant – much like the ones he played with Lyn. He didn't know how Cole thought of it, but it was hard to know how Cole felt about anything.

Instead of waiting for his turn in the hot spring, Bryant took a quick dip in the stream and then returned to the cottage to grab his bow and quiver of arrows, and a small bag containing only a waterskin, a loaf of bread, and his sketchbook and charcoal nibs. His knife was already in his belt. Having everything he needed and nearly everything he owned in the world, he called out a cheerful, "Bye, Sun. Back in a few days!" Wherever the fairy was, she would hear him eventually.

He set out into the forest humming a bright tune.

Bryant struck west, toward the small village at the edge of the Dark Forest. It was a journey of several days, but the time passed quickly because he was enjoying himself. The trip seemed to have only just begun when he saw chimney smoke on the horizon and had to go more carefully to avoid being seen. Something about his being an elf had seemed to make people uncomfortable in past forays, when he chanced to run into them.

As he went, he recalled bungling into the mercenary camp that first time. His lost memory often left him childlike when he discovered new things. He hadn't known who or what they were, and had gotten much closer than common sense would have dictated if he had any. That was when he'd met Cole on sentry duty. The recollection was a fond one.

He found Cole in his small workshop on the outskirts of town, against the verge of the forest where decent folk feared to dwell. His friend was assembling the various pieces of a chair he seemed to have just finished cutting. He was still new at his job, but seemed to be adapting to it well enough. If Bryant hadn't known Cole, he probably wouldn't have been able to tell that the compact, sandy-haired human had been a hardened professional killer only a few months earlier.

Bryant crept silently into the workshop and got directly behind his friend without him noticing. "Hello, Cole."

Cole reached instinctively for the nearest weapon, which happened to be a hammer, before turning to face his intruder. The tense readiness lingered on his stubbled face just long enough for Bryant to catch the expression. "Ah, you." He set the hammer down. "I was wondering when you'd turn up again. What've you been up to lately?"

"Not much," Bryant replied. "As usual. How's work going?" He made himself comfortable on top of a table, legs folded over each other in front of him, and cocked his head to await his friend's answer.

Cole shrugged, glancing down at the chair he was assembling. "Boring. But there are worse things than boring, I guess, and it's better than being run out of town. That's happened often enough." As he said it, a hint of the old anger came into his mild blue eyes, but was gone almost as soon as it appeared.

"Well, sorry to hear it's not as exciting as *killing* people," Bryant said. He'd had too many arguments with Cole over giving up his profession to allow him any quarter on the issue, now that he had finally convinced Cole to take a place among good people. When Cole didn't say anything in response to that, he said, "I've come to ask a question."

"You?" Cole said in a perfect deadpan. "A question? How unlike you."

"Ha, ha," Bryant said dryly. This was old, familiar ground for them. "What do you know about elves?" he asked, trying to sound as earnest as he really was. His suspicious human friend was always quick to assume he was kidding around, even when he was completely serious. Possibly because Bryant frequently pretended to be serious when he was just waiting for the opportune moment to break the jest.

Cole snorted. "I know *you*. Not that anyone would believe me if I told them about you. But that's it."

Brow furrowing, Bryant said, "They wouldn't believe you? Why's that?"

"Don't you know anything?" Despite the rough question, there was no malice in it. "Haven't we talked about this before?" He continued to fit the pieces of the chair together.

Bryant shook his head. "Well, you said something about humans trying to kill all the elves in Asrellion a while ago, but obviously that didn't work." *And I wasn't listening,* he thought but tactfully did not say. "I mean, here I am. And there's Lyn. We must have come from *somewhere*. You said that war was a long time ago. Thousands of years." He paused, examining his hands thoughtfully. "I don't *think* I'm that old. I know Lyn isn't. There must be more of us."

"Shouldn't you be asking your fairy about this?" Cole said. He finished with the chair and pushed it aside, then sat with his capable hands resting on his knees. They twitched as if impatient to be active again. "Sometimes I can't believe the things I have to say when I'm talking to you," he added in an undertone.

Bryant shrugged, a mannerism he had picked up from Cole. "She says she doesn't know where I came from. And when I asked her about that war, she sort of got angry and said she didn't think we should talk about it."

"I'm no teacher," Cole said, scowling again. "Get your schooling somewhere else, boy."

Bryant laughed. Even though he didn't know his actual age, they both knew he was far older than Cole. Had to be; he'd never aged, as far as he remembered. His friend had called him *boy* from the beginning, because of his innocent way of asking questions that everyone ought to know the answers to. "Well if your memory's going already, old man…"

Cole snorted. "Ass. If it matters, I've been hearing rumors lately about elves in the east."

"In the east?" Bryant echoed, thinking. "What kind of rumors? Like, rubbishy fairy-tale rumors, or possibly true rumors?"

"How in the seven hells should *I* know what's true and what's not?"

Bryant looked at him in fascination, his head cocked. "Why do you swear?" he asked. "By 'you' I mean 'humans,' not just *you*. Well, I guess I mean 'people,' since I don't know whether elves do it or not too. Probably they do. But you swear a lot, I think."

Glaring at Bryant until he shut up, Cole said, "Dunno. Everyone swears. Why *don't* you?" It was obvious that he was asking in the hope of getting Bryant to stop interrogating him for a moment at least.

Bryant shrugged again. "I don't know. Sun doesn't, I guess. East? On the coast, you mean? Seland? Or east Grenlec?"

Cole sighed. "I don't know. Just east. But it probably is just a 'rubbishy fairy-tale rumor' since no one's seen an elf since the War. Well. Almost no one," he added with a grimace. He sometimes said he must be half-insane for being able to claim to have met what should have been a fictional being. He knew anyone he told would certainly think him out of his mind.

It would hardly have mattered, Bryant reflected. Most people didn't think much of Cole anyway. Social stigmas, he supposed, were almost impossible to escape no matter how hard one tried. "So, you don't know *anything*?" he said without mentioning that.

"Isn't that what I've been saying?" Cole said with an entirely manufac-tured growl. They both knew it was his job to try to take Bryant down a few pegs and that it was Bryant's job to laugh at him for it. They had settled into their patterns long ago and it made them both comfortable.

Bryant was silent for a moment, thinking. Then he shrugged again. "Well all right then. See you later." He jumped down from the table.

A puzzled look crossed the young human's face. "That's it? You came all this way for a five minute conversation?"

"I'll be back soon," Bryant replied reproachfully. He waved once, then slipped out of the workshop and out of town, uncharacteristically pensive.


As Bryant neared the cottage in the woods that he shared with Sun and Lyn, a fierce cry sounded and something came plummeting out of the sky onto him. He was knocked to the ground and all the wind was forced from his body. For a moment he could only lay in the leaves, dazed and bewildered.

He heard laughter, and he struggled to regain his wits.

"You didn't hear me *that* time, did you?" Lyn crowed, climbing off of him. She was beaming. "I was up there," she added, and pointed to the high tree branches overhead.

He sat up. "Good gummed galipots, Lyn. You nearly killed me." He shook his swimming head. "Next time use the axe. It'll be less painful."

She laughed again and held out a hand to help him up. His dignity injured enough already by her clear victory, he ignored it and stood on his own.

"Where did you go?" she demanded, trying without much success to sound stern.

"To see my friend," he replied. He swayed a bit on his feet, but started walking again toward the cottage. She'd gotten him good.

She followed close behind him. "Who, that Cole fellow?"

"Yes, him," he replied.

"How is he?" Lyn pestered, poking him in the ribs. "When are you going to let me meet him, anyway?"

"Quit it," Bryant growled with pretended ferocity. "My head is still swimming. Can't you let me recover for a minute?"

Lyn pouted, relenting. "Sorry," she said. "I didn't mean to *hurt* you." She sulked a moment longer, then rushed ahead to open the door for him. "Here, Bryant." He went in past her and she said, "Let me get you some water."

Without waiting for an answer, she poured out a glass from the pitcher on the small kitchen table and brought it to him.

"Where's Sun?" Bryant asked after he had pushed a few gulps over his road-dry throat.

Lyn shrugged. "Wherever she goes. Why?"

"I need to talk to her."

The air in the cottage moved and the fairy appeared before them. "Welcome home, Bryant," she said lightly. "You had a pleasant journey?"

He nodded, then opened his mouth to tell her that he wanted to talk to her alone when she got the chance, but Sun spoke before he could say anything.

"Lyn, could you please fetch some more water from the spring?" she asked, favoring her foster daughter with a smile.

Lyn smiled back. "Sure." Without complaint, she picked up the large bucket in the kitchen and went out the door. He must have really made her feel bad about the aerial tackle.

"You wanted to talk?" Sun invited without hesitation.

Bryant blinked. She did that often – knew what he was going to say before he said it – but it was still disconcerting every time. "Yes," he said slowly. He still hadn't decided how to approach this without meeting with the stone wall he always got when he tried to ask her about his past. It occurred to him that maybe she knew that, and it was why she'd chosen to rush him into the conversation, but it was impossible to know how Sun thought.

All traces of the smile she'd offered Lyn a moment ago had vanished. "You've been having questions lately," the fairy murmured. "Questions about you and Lyn. Yes?"

He nodded. His throat was dry again. The atmosphere in the small cottage was quickly taking on a strange quality he could not account for. Almost a darkening like the sky clouding over before a storm. A warning, perhaps, but he chose to ignore it. "Yes. I've been–"

"I know," Sun cut in, and it was clear that she actually did. "So you feel you need to know who you both are." She drew a deep breath and let it out slowly – an odd affectation, Bryant thought, given that she didn't need to breathe. "Are you sure you want to hear this?"

Bryant nodded, eyes wide. If she was truly going to tell him this time, he found the change frightening. His voice was no more than a whisper. "I am."

"I wasn't telling the truth when I said I did not know who you are," Sun said, voicing the words he had been expecting her to. "Everything else was true. I did find you in that burning bush with Lyn. You were badly hurt, and you were unwell for many days." She paused, meeting his eyes intently. "But I do know who you are, and I also know how you came to be there."

He shook his head. He had started to shake. "Then why—"

"When you woke, you remembered nothing. You couldn't even remember how to talk. By the time I had taught you to speak, I'd grown fond of you, and of Lyn. I never told you who you are because I thought you'd be better off here, with this life. I was right, too," she added stubbornly. "Elves have been *useless* ever since the Exile. Sad all the time and glorifying the sadness, worshiping their loss. You don't want to know who you are and you *don't* want to go back. Please believe me."

Anger rose within him — anger like he had never felt before. It was a hot and unpleasant feeling that made his stomach hurt. "How dare you pass judgment on my people and decide for me what life I'm to lead?"

*How dare you lie to me all this time?* he thought. *How dare you take my identity from me?*

"I know nothing about my people or my home simply because you decided I'd like it better playing in the forest with you. Because *you* thought it would be *fun* to pretend to have children. You've *robbed* me. Who are you to have done this to me?" He had never felt such rage before in his life, and it was boiling in him almost out of control. The words didn't even feel like his own.

Sun's eyes hardened. "I have been your mother, and Lyn's. I have taken care of you. I have given you a better life, a happier life, than you would have had."

"You're not my mother," he cried, springing to his feet.

"No. *Your* mother is *dead*. Your father too. Your family is all *dead*."

That silenced him. He clenched his fists, his breath sawing in and out painfully. He felt like he was going to lose consciousness from the unfamiliar lightheaded feeling of so much fury.

"Trust me," Sun said, her voice gentle again. "You're better off here than you would have been in Evlédíen."

"Evlédíen..." he echoed. The name was stirring vague memories in his mind — feelings of coldness, of ice. Of belonging to something large and old, to a burden that was his birthright. "Who am I?" he demanded, his fists still clenched. "Tell me. Now."

The fairy sighed. "Your name is Gallanas."

Bryant was deafened by a roaring in his ears as memory came flooding in upon him. *Gallanas... Gallanas Vísairajenré Raía. Son of Andras and Melíara. The Harunomíya.*

He clutched at his head, gasping with the disorienting pain of so much knowledge all at once. He remembered a journey, and fire… The chaos in the road as people died and some few tried to flee. The sound of steel on steel ringing out above the roar of the flames – but more than that, the screaming. His father. Tomanasíl gripping his arms, a desperate plea in his eyes not to be sent from his side, as Gallanas asked him to find the girls, the little ones, and keep them safe. Heat, and then darkness.

"Lyn is my sister," he said flatly after a moment. "Or Lyllíen, I should say. Lyn was what we all called her, what she called herself." He looked up at the fairy. "I am the heir to the throne of Evlédíen, and my parents are dead; my people need me. I am not the only one you've robbed with your selfishness."

"I just wanted you to be happy," Sun objected. "I… thought *we* could be happy. A family. And we were. *No one* in Evlédíen is happy, Bryant."

"My name is Gallanas," he shouted, drawing himself up to his full height, his name bursting from him as though the truth was too large for one man to contain. His anger felt cold now, an icy river churning through his veins. He glared at the fairy one last time and bit back every furious thing he wanted to say, then strode past her and threw open the door of the cottage, escaping out into the sunlight.

Lyn was standing there, holding the forgotten water bucket in slack hands, surprise plain on her lovely face.

*She is my sister.*

Gallanas brushed past her without a word. He needed to be alone. He remembered so much, more with every minute, and the weight of those last memories was threatening to drive him to his knees. Mother, Father, so many friends, dead on that road. Had any of them survived? What of Tomanasíl, of Loralíenasa? What had the loss of the king done to his people? What had become of Evlédíen?

He heard Lyn call what she thought was his name behind him, but he could not reply. He was quickly remembering what it was to be an elf – a prince of elves. His people were not supposed to be so emotional, to allow their rage to control them the way his was at the moment. He knew he had to get a handle on himself before he would be able to tell her anything.

# CHAPTER FIVE

For a while, Lyn sat in the cottage trembling with a nameless fear. *Something* had just happened, something important, and she had no idea what it was.

She had never heard either Bryant or Sun yell before, had never seen such anger in anyone, and it frightened her. The fairy had not been in their home when Lyn went in to ask what had happened, nor had she returned since. That was nothing unusual in itself – Sun frequently vanished to do whatever it was fairies did. But she had always before appeared when Lyn or Bryant called for her, and something about her absence this time felt final, like the *memory* of her presence had been removed from the cottage.

When neither Bryant nor the fairy had returned with night drawing on, Lyn decided she had to go looking. Her nerves were twisted up to an unbearable pitch.

It turned out that Bryant hadn't gone far. He was sitting atop the stand of boulders by the hot springs, staring off into the distance in a way that had nothing to do with seeing what was in front of him. Though he must have been aware of her approach, he said nothing as she drew near and did not move in the slightest.

"Mind if I join you?" she asked tentatively.

He broke out of his reverie long enough to cast her an enigmatic look, then gestured at the stone.

She climbed up onto the boulder beside him but said nothing else. Something had happened, something had changed, and she was almost afraid to find out what.

After a few moments, Bryant drew a deep breath. "I need to leave again for a while. There are... things I must think on." He sounded strange. "And then we need to talk. There is much I must tell you."

She bit her lip and studied him, but could make nothing of his odd expression in the dusk light. "You just came back. You need to leave again?" *Not without telling me what's going on.* "Bryant, Sun's gone and I don't think she's coming back."

He raised his head, obviously surprised. Then he sighed. "I am sorry for that. It was not my intention to… But still I must go. I need to sort some things out."

"Without me?" Lyn dared to ask, feeling small and uncertain.

"I promise I'll soon return." It wasn't an answer to her question, but it also was, and it made her unhappy. Bryant gave a strained smile. "Wait here for me, please?"

There was something different about him, about the way he was talking and the way he held himself, that she could not identify. "I will," she whispered, more frightened than she wanted to be. She hesitated for a moment, then leaned close to embrace him, in desperate need of comfort.

To her horror, he recoiled with a look of distaste.

He reached out and took her hand hastily when her face showed how he'd wounded her. "I'm sorry, Lyn. It's just… Just wait here, please. I will come back to you soon." He gave her hand a faint pressure, then jumped down from the rock and disappeared into the night.

*Gallanas. Harunomíya Gallanas.*

The name was like an arrowhead burrowing deeper into a wound and drawing more blood where it passed, because every new old memory it dislodged in Gallanas' mind was a fresh source of pain. He stumbled through the forest bleeding memories all over the fabric of the only identity he had known before yesterday, until the familiar pattern began to blur and he had no idea anymore who he was supposed to be.

That day on the road…

He shrank away from those memories. There was nothing in them he wanted to revisit.

But Evlédíen. Home. Tomanasíl. Everything he loved, except Lyn, denied him by one of the inscrutable *Farín* – the enemies of his people more certainly, more implacably than humans ever had been. She hadn't even allowed him the ability to mourn his parents. It was not made better by the knowledge that everything she'd said about elves was true. Nor was it better that what should have been vibrant images of his own life felt distant and hard to reach on the far side of Bryant – whoever that was.

*Gallanas.* His own name didn't even feel like it belonged to him anymore. Or he no longer belonged to it. He had become something else out here in the forest and now he was no one, fit for nowhere.

No. He realized something eventually: *Cole* knew who he was. That was where he needed to go right now. It would be good to share his anger with someone who would understand. Cole *always* understood. Once he'd turned his steps in the direction of Cole's village, he realized that if nothing else, his friend deserved some explanation. A goodbye, if necessary.

When he reached the town, he was even more cautious than before about going unseen. He remembered too much now about the hatred of men for elves. He knew what humans had done to his kind.

It occurred to him to wonder why Cole had always been so good to him.

He slipped into Cole's workshop, but his friend was not there. Peering into the window of the human's small home, he saw Cole inside, hunched over a bowl of what looked like stew. Gallanas jumped in through the window almost without a sound, but Cole was well-trained. He looked up sharply.

"Don't you believe in doors?" the human growled. Then he saw the look on his friend's face and his own expression changed. "Something's wrong."

Gallanas paced the short length of the floor a few times before sinking into the one other chair at the table with a heavy sigh. "Not at all," he replied. "Only I've just discovered that half of my life has been a lie."

Cole set down his spoon and the heel of crusty bread in his other hand. "You found out who you are."

Gallanas had forgotten how quick Cole could be sometimes, but the former mercenary went out of his way to see that most people never noticed in the first place. The elf nodded. "I have. And that Sun knew all along, and had simply decided it would be better for me not to know." He brought his fist down onto the table-top.

"Shit," Cole said quietly. "I'm guessing you had some words?"

Gallanas gave a short laugh at Cole's deliberate understatement. "I think I ran her off, actually. I can't say I'm all that sorry. I've never been so furious in my life." He paused for a moment, still unused to the idea that he could in fact remember *all* of his life. "No, never," he added. He looked into his friend's eyes and saw that Cole was waiting for an explanation.

He sighed again. "This is what I remember: my name is Gallanas, and I am the son of a king. I came here from our kingdom in the south, which we call Evlédíen." He stopped to let his listener absorb the new names, as he looked momentarily lost. "Lyn, as it happens, is my little sister."

Sympathy flickered in Cole's eyes, but he said nothing.

The elf drew another deep breath and continued. "I suppose it was a bit more than a hundred years ago, if I've got my timeline right. That progressive fellow here in Rosemarch announced he was hosting a peace council, because he was tired of the constant warring between the human kingdoms and the way it ravages the common man."

Cole nodded. This much was common knowledge. "Adan," he confirmed, quietly. "Of Ravenwood."

Gallanas touched his nose to indicate that Cole was correct. "Well, my father is... was... a progressive man as well. When he heard about that council – he had his sources, I see that look – he decided it presented the perfect opportunity for elves to reveal themselves to the world once more. He never *was* happy about living in hiding," he added, remembering as he said it.

Andras the Golden. Andras the Wise. Andras the Reformer. Never satisfied with the status quo, always pushing for more, for better.

His father was dead.

Gallanas' hands began to shake, so he pressed them flat against the top of the table. Smooth surface; Cole did good work.

"It's *quite* a long journey from Evlédíen to Rosemarch, and a dangerous one," he went on. "We'd been traveling for weeks and had just crossed into Rosemarch when the attack came." His voice started to shake like his hands. He knew he was supposed to be better at controlling that. "It was a well-planned ambush. We were surrounded, fire-bombs exploding in our midst. Instant chaos. There were so many of them. My father..."

He broke off for fear that his tears would escape from the dark place where he had been hiding them ever since remembering the truth.

In an attempt to help in some way, Cole fetched another cup and poured dark ale for his friend. Gallanas drank it all in one long swig, grateful for the distraction. After a moment, he had himself under control again.

He drew another deep breath before continuing. "My father was cut down in the first wave of the assault. I believe he was the target. But my mother, I could not find. I could hear the screams... Smoke and fire everywhere, members of our party dying in all directions. We were fighting for our lives though we knew it was a losing battle; we were horribly outnumbered. Some broke into the woods and tried to flee, but I couldn't, not without my family. My mother, my sisters–"

"Sisters?" Cole echoed. "More than one?"

Gallanas nodded carefully. He had said the worst part already, but it still took an effort to keep his voice under control. "Lyn has a twin. Or had. I don't know if she, if she survived. I sent the man I loved to look for her while I searched as well, but…" He clutched the empty cup in both his hands. "I found Lyn," he went on, "but not Loríen. I looked as long as I could, but the fires were out of control, and the fighting so intense." He shuddered convulsively. Talking about it put him back there amid the smoke, and the smell, and the screaming. The ale wasn't sitting well. "I took Lyn and ran, but I was wounded. I suppose that's when I collapsed. And then Sun found me."

His head was pounding. He dropped the cup and put both hands to his temples. If he placed them just right, he could hold it all in, hold it back, stop remembering. For several moments he was hardly aware of his surroundings. Then, gradually, he realized that Cole was beside him and had put an arm about his shoulders. He took several deep breaths, forcing himself to regain his calm.

When Cole could see that Gallanas had calmed somewhat, he returned to his seat. "That's the worst story I've ever heard."

Gallanas gave a short, dry laugh.

"And the fairy didn't tell you because she hoped to spare you the grief?" Cole wondered, clearly trying to sort out what his friend needed from him.

He laughed again, and this time the sound was bitter. "Not exactly. She didn't tell me because she had decided, in her infallible fairy wisdom, that I wouldn't *want* to go home. What were her words?" he asked himself caustically. "That we had been useless and sad ever since the Exile. I wonder why *that* might be. And I have doubtless deepened their grief, as they must think me dead." *Tomsíl, I am so sorry.*

Cole studied him. "What are you going to do?"

The question was unexpected, though it shouldn't have been. Gallanas made his decision in that moment. "My people need me, and our sister may still be alive. I'm going back."

The other man nodded.

Leaning across the table in sudden earnest, Gallanas seized Cole by the wrist. "I must beg a favor of you, my friend."

The human's eyebrows went up. "Anything."

This idea had begun shortly after he'd remembered the truth, and had been growing in his mind ever since. He met Cole's eyes intently. "I believe that whoever attacked us on our way to that meeting wanted my family dead," he said. "Lyn and I have been safe, living in the forest under Sun's protection. But I believe our enemy may find us again when we leave."

Cole nodded slowly.

Gallanas' eyes did not leave his friend's. "This is what I want from you, Cole: I want you to come with us. And if anything should happen to me, I want you to swear to protect Lyn with your life."

A flicker of unease began in Cole's eyes as he spoke, blossoming into genuine agitation by the time he finished. Several moments passed before he said flatly, "I'm not in the habit of making promises, Bryant. Gallanas."

"That's because people have never believed you before," the elf pointed out matter-of-factly. "But you know *I* trust you. I don't care who or what your parents were. I know who *you* are."

A hard wall slammed down behind Cole's eyes. "I'm not talking about my parents."

"Neither am I," Gallanas countered. "I'm saying I trust you and no one else to take care of my sister if I'm killed."

Cole looked away, staring at the wall of his small cottage. "I'm *not* trustworthy, Bryant. Ask anyone."

Gallanas got out of his chair and walked around to kneel in the line of Cole's sight. He stared into his friend's eyes. "Please, Cole. This is important. I *need* to know Lyn will be safe. Who else can I trust?"

Cole made no reply, simply shook his head.

Grimacing, Gallanas said, "Stop being so ridiculous. Why would I have wasted my time on you if you're as horrible as you say?" He stood and grabbed his friend by both shoulders. "Deny it all you like, but *I* know what you really are. And I need you to make this promise to me. Please."

The human made no answer for a long time. Gallanas let go of him and left him alone with his thoughts; the time for pressing him had passed.

At last Cole drew a deep breath and said quietly, looking down at the table, "It'll take me a few days to settle things here."

Gallanas brightened. "So you'll do it? You promise?"

The look in Cole's eyes was as grim as if he had just offered his soul to the Dark One. "Listen to me say this once, Bryant. I've never made a promise before, to anyone. There isn't anyone in the world besides you that'd call my word good anyway. I don't know how loyal I'll end up being. I don't even know if it's *in* me to be loyal. If you want an oath from a man like that, I'll give it. But I think you're making a mistake."

Gallanas beamed. "You're wrong about yourself, Cole," he said. "Trust me. One day you'll know it as surely as I do."

Cole sighed. "Very well. I swear to you by whatever you like that if anything ever happens to you, I'll take care of Lyn and see her home." As soon as the words were out of his mouth, he stood abruptly and crossed to the sideboard, where there sat a bottle of some dark hard liquor and a single small ceramic drinking vessel. He poured himself a glass with shaking hands and drained it off in one swallow.

Laughing, Gallanas said, "Thank you. You've set my mind at rest. Finish what you have to and meet us at our cottage as soon as you can."

Even though the sun had been down for hours, the air was still as hot and close as a closet on fire. Naoise hated Telrisht.

The scout came back sooner than the prince expected, huffing and sweating in the oppressive heat. He poured half the contents of his waterskin over the rag he wore about his head and the other half down his throat before delivering his news.

"Everything is in place," the scout reported, "and the barracks are all settled for the night. We're good whenever you give the signal."

Naoise nodded, peering through the rocks at the walls of the quiet outpost. "Final count?"

"One hundred and twenty." The scout took one last pull from the skin before replacing it at his belt, nearly empty. "Twenty awake and on watch. Two at each tower, two on each wall, two at the gate, and two more at the storehouse."

The prince grunted, wishing Telrisht's mercenaries could employ a more minimalistic approach to their work. "Thank you, Doran. Take your position now."

The scout saluted and disappeared again into the darkness.

Everything had been planned meticulously and there was no more reason to put off the assault. Naoise glanced up at the westering moon. Three hours and a bit past midnight. He had hoped to wait for some wind, but the air had been oppressively still since noon and there was no indication that the weather would be changing. If there was ever a time to catch the enemy ill-prepared, it was now.

Naoise drew a deep breath with the same silent prayer he offered before every battle, and withdrew to the rocky defile where the rest of his unit lay in hiding.

*Father of us all, let me lead my men to see another dawn.*

Reid, his second-in-command, was mounted at the head of the formation, watching his approach with grim concentration. Naoise pulled out his tinderbox when he reached the horses and struck the flint until he had a decent flame going, then lit a torch and passed it back through the troops until every second rider was carrying his own fire. Reid held Naoise's while the prince swung into the saddle.

They all knew the plan already, and now was not the time for idle chatter. Naoise's men were the best, hand-picked for this unit, and they had already struck several outposts just like this one in the last two months.

Naoise raised his torch so that it could easily be seen all the way down the column. He waited only a moment to be certain all thirty of the men at his back were ready, then spurred his stallion into a brisk trot. This was followed by the sound of dozens of hoofs scrambling to action in his wake. A moment later, they were galloping full-tilt toward the walls of the silent outpost.

The two guards on the front-facing wall were dead almost before they knew an attack was underway, tumbling from their high position with flaming arrows buried in their chests. Naoise's men wasted no time casting their ropes.

By the time the enemy was able to respond to the siege, he and more than half of his men had mounted the wall. Those unlucky enough to have drawn sentry duty engaged the invaders on the walls, but the contest was a short one.

A moment later, when the barracks roared into flames, Naoise knew the ten men he had stationed to the rear of the compound had been able to make their way in. One hundred mercenaries came streaming out of the barracks in a confused panic, right into the line of Naoise's archers. The night erupted into the chaos of flames and the screams of the dying.

Someone had the presence of mind to figure out that they outnumbered the attacking force and ordered the survivors into two detachments – one to fight the fires, the other to deal with the hail of arrows coming from their own walls. They used the bodies of the fallen as shields. Naoise could hear a voice shouting furiously in Telrishti, cursing and demanding to know why no one was doing anything about the fire spreading to the storehouse.

The prince slung his bow over his shoulder and called for his lieutenant.

He didn't have to look to know that it was Reid at his side a moment later when he leaped down from the wall and rolled up into a sprint across the sandy courtyard toward the barracks. They dodged their way through the madness, striking down those who offered resistance, until they came to the far side of the inferno. It was so hot now that it literally stole Naoise's breath. He could feel the dry heat of the flames in his throat. He ignored that, ignored the roaring flames and the way the heat seemed to physically push back against him, and focused on the one mercenary with a level enough head to be giving orders.

The Telrishti leader was a giant of a man, tall and craggy, bristling with rage, black hair a sleep-disordered riot down his back. At the moment he stood behind the barracks directing the firefighting effort and screaming for someone to rescue the black powder from the storehouse.

He gave a cry when he spotted them and strode forward with sword in hand. Soot blackened his face and murder gleamed in his eyes. Reid rushed to engage him while Naoise paused a moment to assess the situation.

The mercenary was good, but Reid was better. Unfortunately, Naoise needed the man alive and he clearly didn't mean to be taken that way.

Between the brightness of the towering flame and the choking opacity of the smoke, it was nearly impossible to see what was happening, as intended. Bodies were rushing everywhere – fleeing the flames or fighting them, trying to clear the explosives, dodging the hail of arrows. Half of the men Naoise had sent in from the rear guarded the storehouse, forming a kill pocket in the doorway to keep the mercenaries from gaining access. The other half, he knew, would be securing the main gate. A tangible panic was building, as the Telrishti mercenaries began to grasp that they could not find their enemies to face them, and were not being allowed to escape. Soon, the panic would make them deadly.

Naoise had only a handful of moments left to force events onto the right course tonight, before the fires reached the storehouse and ended them all.

The mercenary dueling with Reid had neat footwork. Very methodical. Carefully, forcing himself to take steady breaths despite the pounding of his heart and the swirling ash, Naoise drew his bow and took aim. He waited for the smoke to clear, then waited for it to clear again to be sure he had the shot. Naoise released the string; the man moved forward again with a thrust at Reid's arm.

A second later, the Telrishti was nailed to the sand by the arrow through his foot.

Naoise lowered the bow and hastened to his lieutenant's side. Reid had his sword trained on the mercenary's throat. For his part, the paid fighter was breathing heavily, trying not to scream, his face mottled with rage and pain.

"Surrender?" Naoise shouted over the chaos.

The man gave a terse nod.

Naoise walked over, yanked the arrow out of the ground, set it alight, and shot it into the air.

The assault from the walls ceased. Naoise moved to help his men secure the black powder while Reid disarmed and bound the leader.

# CHAPTER SIX

Dawn was a weak, watery thing in an ash-choked sky by the time Naoise was able to see to the prisoners. Nearby, the outpost smoldered to its final rest. What had remained of the night after the surrender, the Grenlecian unit had spent trussing their captives and salvaging whatever they could that was of use from the storehouse. Everything else had been left to burn.

As Naoise examined their take, a persistent and disturbing idea nagged at the back of his mind, too oblique yet to make sense of. Something was wrong here, and he couldn't put a name to it.

There was no time to dwell on that yet. There was no time even to get a moment of rest before calling this business done. After seeing to the supplies, the prince gave his men a pass-through. No serious injuries, he was relieved to discover – just a few minor burns and some sore lungs, despite their precautions. Nothing that any of them would allow to slow their ride, when they set out.

Then, of course, there were the prisoners to be dealt with.

"I must say again that you are wasting your time with this, my lord," Reid complained, half a step behind Naoise as they walked through the camp. Reid was not as young as Naoise, but he was still young enough to have ambition and for that ambition to be resented by his more resigned elders. All the more so because he was a handsome man with classical Grenlecian features, he was competent, and he had a way of speaking his mind no matter how grossly he was outranked.

"Not only that," he went on, "but you risked all our lives needlessly by demanding live prisoners. It's luck alone saw us through that siege."

Naoise didn't bother looking back at his lieutenant. They had already had this argument, and his own opinion was not going to change. Reid knew that.

In the last month, they had hit three outposts just like this one and had destroyed them all, but there was something else going on. Something about the goods they seized that just didn't fit. They weren't going to get any answers unless they bothered to ask questions, and Naoise felt it was far past time for something to change. Too long had both sides held one another in check, sapping the resources of both kingdoms – losing men, losing wealth, losing land to the depredations of war.

He kept walking. "Your opinions have been noted."

Reid muttered, but knew a futile argument when he saw one. Naoise chose to be grateful that he had a second who made him reconsider his decisions.

More than half of the mercenary company had died in the attack. Many of the survivors were badly hurt or suffering the effects of smoke inhalation. Naoise judged it unlikely that the company would be fighting for Telrisht any time in the immediate future. The observation gave him some amount of professional satisfaction.

The surviving leaders of the company were lined up on their knees in the defile where Naoise's unit had made their camp, bound at wrist and ankle, awaiting the Grenlecians' pleasure. The captain was no more charming than expected when the prince came around to ask his questions. He rattled off a string of Telrishti curses and spat into the dirt at Naoise's feet. His eyes gleamed with resentment in his tawny brown face.

Naoise nodded once, looking down at the man. His wounded foot was certainly not contributing favorably to his view of Naoise's character. "I assume you do not approve of my tactics."

The captain grunted. "Yours is the conduct of a cheat and a coward."

Naoise felt something sink within him at that accusation, but he had no right to argue it. He made his command decisions knowing how others would see them and he just had to accept that. "Mine is the conduct of a man who has been at war for seven years," he replied calmly, "who would see it end before all the world is consumed by its relentless engines."

The mercenary's glower did not convey much in the way of sympathy, nor did his stolid silence.

"You have my apologies that I have come to favor expediency over courtesy on the field," Naoise said. "I am a man of the times in which we live. I do regret it. But you must forgive me – I've not presented myself. Naoise, Duke of Lakeside, Prince of Grenlec." He inclined his head briefly.

"And so they bring up their princes to be brigands in Grenlec. This is not surprising." As with most Telrishti with a better than passing knowledge of

Common, there was an archaic formality to his speech.

Ignoring the obvious goad, Naoise went on with the same grave civility. "I understand I have had the honor of facing Rammad Company, which means you must be Captain Adar. Your courage on the field is well-known; I saw confirmation of it myself last night."

Clearly, the Telrishti believed he had already said everything he needed to about Naoise's character, for he responded with silence.

The prince drew a deep breath. "Our objective was the outpost itself, and the disruption of the supply line. That goal having been met, I am prepared to release you and your men alive, Captain Adar. I only require the answers to certain questions before that can happen."

At Naoise's side, Reid grunted what might have been disagreement, but he said nothing.

The captain frowned, waiting. Naoise had no doubt he would prefer to put on a show of offended Telrishti honor, but as a paid sword was pragmatic enough to know when to cut his losses.

Into Captain Adar's line of sight, Naoise raised the sword he had carried to this parlay, still sheathed, salvaged from the storehouse. "Where did these come from?"

"That I could not tell you even did I desire it," the captain replied, grinning suddenly with ferocious satisfaction. "We take delivery, and we send on what we are delivered, but where the supply comes from is a matter of no mind to us. Call it intelligence beyond our pay, if you so please."

The heat of the day was already setting in, building on the heat of the oppressive night just past. Experience told Naoise that by noon it would be like the inside of a kiln. He was somehow both damp and dry with it, swaying on his feet from the combination of sun and sleeplessness, but his captives had to be suffering more, baking on the hard hot stones of the defile. The sooner he could be done with this, the sooner they could all find some relief.

Naoise lowered the sword. "Then tell me what you can," he invited, "about the delivery itself."

"What would you know, my lord?" the captain asked, still wearing that fierce, defiant grin.

Naoise gave it a moment of thought. "Who made the delivery? Describe them."

The smile faded from Adar's face as he considered his answer. "In truth, there is not much I can say to that." He shook his head. "Strange as it may be, we have never seen the agents who bring the goods."

A moment passed while Naoise tried to make sense of that. He frowned. "How does that work, exactly?"

"Twice a month," the captain explained, "a message arrives warning us that a shipment is imminent. On the day following, the goods are delivered by men clothed in black, their faces shrouded. They do not speak. They unload the wagons, take their payment, and depart again in silence."

"This has never been a cause for alarm?" Naoise asked.

The Telrishti lifted both shoulders and let them fall again, the gesture awkward with his hands bound behind his back. "We follow our orders, and we are paid well to do so without question."

Naoise again raised the salvaged sword, freeing several inches of the blade from the scabbard. Curved in the Telrishti fashion, the metal masterfully honed to an edge so lethal it could draw blood nearly on sight. It was a fine weapon.

Over the last seven years at war, he had become all too familiar with the works of every one of the major Telrishti swordmakers. Farid used an alloy of his own invention, devised for its flexibility, that gave off a distinctive rainbow sheen when tempered. Husam forged blades that were uglier than a hyena's smile, but they retained an edge like no other. Swords from the foundry of Zahir were beautiful, works of art each one. Those made by Raza had a tendency to break when met with a direct parry at the ricasso. It mattered, knowing which weapons he was up against in any given battle, and Naoise knew them all.

This blade came from none of them.

"When these black-garbed unknowns arrive," he tried again, frustrated and uneasy, "from what direction do they approach?"

Captain Adar blinked. "Why, they never make the same approach twice."

"So…" Naoise paced a handful of steps and then back again, trying to make sense of what he was hearing. Men shrouded so their identity and origin could not be traced? Weapons from an unknown source? Not just weapons, either. A great deal of grain had gone up in flames last night, which was a blow to Telrisht more severe than the loss of the weapons and black powder. They had little arable land left at this stage in the war and were now relying almost entirely on imports. But where in Asrellion *did* have the resources anymore to be parting with so much produce?

Only one answer presented itself, and Naoise had no liking for it.

Mysia, long ostracized by both Grenlec and Telrisht for their ancient ties to the elves that once were. Punished for that allegiance so heavily and so comprehensively for years by both kingdoms, after the War of Purification, that even so many generations later they had never reclaimed their former glory. Mysia's hatred for Grenlec ran deep, but no less was their mistrust of Telrisht. Would they possibly help one in order to prolong the war that taxed them both? What if their aid tipped the scales too far in Telrisht's favor?

Unless...

Naoise did not like any of the ideas this information provoked. He pushed a hand through his hair and turned back to face the mercenary captain.

"If there is nothing further you can tell me about the agents you dealt with, Captain Adar," he said wearily, "then I suppose all that remains is to have the full tally of your last several deliveries."

"And then, upon your word, you will release me and my men?"

"My word," Naoise agreed.

Reid grunted.

Bryant had been away for more than a week and Lyn was worried.

Sun still had not returned either. It became clearer every day that she wasn't going to. Lyn tried to carry on as if everything was normal, as if she knew that Bryant would be back at any moment; in truth, she had never been so frightened or confused in her uneventful life, and she didn't know what else to do.

She was sitting in the glade outside their cottage with her back to the large stone, weaving a circlet of flowers, when she heard footsteps approaching in the distance. A wave of relief left her dizzied and unable to stop herself from grinning.

*Bryant!*

Leaping to her feet, she cast the flowers aside and crept forward as silently as she could in her excitement. He deserved a good scare after making her worry for so long. She climbed the trunk of a tall tree, seeking a glimpse of him without being seen herself.

Lyn was well-hidden before Bryant came into sight. He wore an expression of calm happiness – of peace, even. Whatever had been wrong with him when he'd left, he appeared to have sorted it out. Maybe things would be all right after all, even if Sun wasn't coming back.

She watched him and gauged the speed of his approach, gathering herself to jump. Then she heard a twig snap in the woods behind her.

Bryant heard it too; he lifted his head and drew the knife from his belt in the same motion, alert as a hunting cat. Twenty menacing figures dressed all in black, their faces covered, leaped out of the surrounding undergrowth. Each was armed with a long, bare blade. Bryant's face drained of all color, but he held his ground and did not flinch.

Lyn gripped the tree branch with fingers that quickly went bloodless, silently offering the universe anything it wanted in exchange for the bow and arrows sitting back in the cottage. The universe was unable to oblige. She summoned Sun with all her will, but the fairy did not appear either. Lyn had to watch, unable to do anything, as the scene unfolded.

To her surprise, Bryant opened his mouth calmly to speak to the frightening circle of black-clad figures. To her even greater surprise, what he said with such assurance and a hint of wry humor was utter gibberish: *"Losí? Valo daiquro'í íta-qaior-qo sovora? Téo orían hana val jía? Aia, sur'lí jéha téo qaian chubíra."*

The mysterious attackers did not respond; they simply closed around Bryant in a unified circle.

Lyn held her breath.

Bryant raised his unarmed hand in a sudden sharp gesture. Lightning sparked from his fingertips, slamming into the chest of the nearest black-clad assassin and arcing from him to the two on either side. All three fell with choked off cries that revealed them as flesh-and-blood villains and not the terrifying wraiths they appeared to Lyn. As he collected himself for another blast, the remaining mass of assassins moved in all at once. He disappeared into their midst. Another flash of lightning, but this time it was deflected, shooting up toward the tree tops past Lyn and hitting none of the men who wanted to hurt him.

A sharp cry echoed through the trees.

She watched, powerless, as the black-clad figures receded to leave Bryant visible once more. He was lying on his back in the leaves, his green doublet quickly darkening. She felt a scream welling up inside her and had to clap a hand over her own mouth to prevent herself from making a sound.

There was a sudden roaring in her ears as Lyn realized that Bryant was looking up, directly at her. That he had known she was there all along. His eyes told her – begged her – to be quiet, to hide. To live.

As if the moment had not already reached a fever pitch of awful, it proceeded to get worse.

Two of the black-clad murderers knelt at Bryant's side. One of them produced a giant, dreadful knife with a horrible barb protruding back toward the handle from the tip. The other held a strangely-carved silver casket. Lyn tried to close her eyes but was unable to as they deftly carved into Bryant's chest with that terrible knife right through his doublet and laid open the vulnerable flesh. From her high perch, her view of what lay inside was all too clear. When he twitched and made a faint wheezing noise, she realized to her already dizzying horror that he was not yet dead.

They worked with cruel efficiency, Lyn their mesmerized unseen audience. They were sealing the lid on the silver casket, Bryant's heart within, almost before he had taken his final breath.

The assassins remained on the scene a moment longer, searching for something – *her*, she assumed. She kept her hands pressed over her mouth. When they did not find her readily, they went into the cottage and gave it a quick inspection. They came out again only a moment later, collected the bodies of their three fallen comrades, and vanished silently into the trees.

Several moments passed during which Lyn could not make herself think clearly. She had no idea what to do, and she knew she was not safe. Meanwhile, Bryant was lying below her with a big hole in his chest where his heart belonged, and there was nothing she could do to change that. Her eyes and then her cheeks were suddenly awash in hot tears.

Finally she decided she didn't care if the killers came back. Moving as silently as she ever had in her life, she slid down the tree-trunk and clambered to Bryant's side. She could hardly see for the tears flooding her eyes, but she could tell there was far too much blood. Bryant was gone. A moment ago he had been alive, smiling on his way home to her. Now he just... no longer existed, and in his place was this piece of ruined meat.

That made so little sense, was so upsetting, that she could feel another scream trying to push its way past her throat and it felt like the only possible response. She resisted the urge, knowing the sound would bring the murderers back. Instead, she crammed her fist into her mouth and bit hard on her knuckles. She couldn't even feel it.

*This can't be real. This is a nightmare. I'll wake up in a minute and everything'll be all right. Sun will be back and Bryant will be alive. Wake up, Lyn. Wake up!*

But it wasn't a nightmare, she realized eventually. She held Bryant's head in her lap and wept for a long time.

After she had cried herself into a kind of hollowed-out stillness, Lyn came to herself enough to recognize that she couldn't just leave him like this. She climbed to her feet slowly, her muscles cramped and sore, and went into their cottage to fetch the blanket from Bryant's bed. When she came back out, she noticed that night had fallen. She drew an unsteady breath, went to the path where Bryant's body still lay, and placed the blanket over him.

"I'm sorry," she murmured to his still form, "but you're going to have to wait until morning. It's too dark for me to dig right now." The idea of making his grave seemed inconceivable for more reasons than just the lack of light.

She stumbled into the cottage, collapsed into her bed, and fell at once into a troubled sleep fraught with violent nightmares.


In the morning, Lyn rolled out of bed with a groan. *Yesterday* struck her full-force as the sun hit her face through the open window. She burst into a fresh round of tears.

After a long, exhausting cry, she splashed her face with water and made herself go outside to do what she'd been unable to do the night before. But when she reached the spot where Bryant had fallen, she saw with alarm that the body was gone, only the blood-soaked patch of dirt and leaves attesting to the fact that he had ever lain there.

A quick perusal of the immediate area revealed that the body was nowhere to be found and indeed there were no drag marks or new footprints. It was just gone. Her eyes stung with new tears.

The only step into whatever new direction her life had taken that she had been able to contemplate was taking care of Bryant's body. If she couldn't do that, then she had no idea what to do with herself. What to do next. She dragged herself miserably back to the clearing to lean against the boulder for a while and cry again.

As she drew near, she noticed that a rectangular section of earth at the base of the rock was loose. On the face of the boulder, words had been inscribed since yesterday in a beautiful, flowing script.

*Here lies Gallanas Vísairajenré Raia*
*known also as Bryant*
*Lived from 3276 to 3553 of the Age of Exile*

Even in her disoriented state, Lyn was able to deduce that Sun had to be responsible for this, but she couldn't make anything of it. That strange name, his exact age...? She had again the excluded feeling she'd experienced after the argument. Obviously the fairy had been lying, about a lot of things, for a long time. Lyn couldn't decide how she was supposed to feel about that, but it was difficult to feel anything but the void left by Bryant's sudden *gone*-ness from her life.

At any rate, for better or worse the task had been taken care of and there was nothing left for Lyn to do. She was not grateful.

She sat by the grave for the rest of the day because she didn't know what else to do and every time she tried to think about it, it meant having to accept that she now lived in a world where she would never see Bryant again. She wasn't ready for that.

*Wait for me,* he had said – almost the last thing.

He had been so strange, that day. Angry, distant, distracted. Telling her nothing. Leaving again just after coming home. She was unable to account for such behavior; but then, everything had been wrong since that day, and she understood none of it. She had waited, but not for this.

What was she to do?

She kept waiting. She moved about in a sort of daze for the next few days, eating and sleeping and not much else. Most of the time, she sat by the boulder, thinking, wishing she had someone to talk to about any of this. Wishing she had Bryant. A few times, she thought she heard the men in black returning and she hid for a while. She had never been so quiet for so long in all her life.

Five days after Bryant's murder, something finally happened to break the horrible tension.

Lyn watched from the now-familiar safety of high tree branches as a man strolled into her clearing with a calm confidence that implied a lack of urgency. His clothing was simple – faded brown rough-woven trousers, battered doublet and knee-high boots of the same slightly darker shade of brown leather – but he wore a weapon at his hip that was like the long blades that had killed Bryant. He stopped when he saw the cottage and stared at it for a long time. Lyn stared at him.

She imagined that the forest was holding its breath.

Eventually he sighed, adjusted the strap of his knapsack on his shoulder, and approached the cottage door. He gave it three solid raps. Lyn mentally told the forest it could breathe again; she doubted that an assassin would have bothered to knock.

She dropped out of her tree not ten feet from the stranger and watched as he turned toward her, startled.

The only notable thing about the man was how much he did not look like Bryant. In fact, he was in every way that she could conceive of *not Bryant*. Apart from that, nothing about him seemed out of the ordinary.

Of course, he was only the second man Lyn had seen in her entire life.

The stranger dropped his hand from the hilt of his sword, where it had darted, when he took in Lyn's appearance. He blinked his pale blue eyes once, muscles easing as suddenly as they had tensed. "You must be Lyn." His voice was quieter and milder than she had expected it to be, and lower than Bryant's. He was darker than Bryant, too, but not by a lot. Beige seemed like a good word to describe him in a number of ways.

This was a situation Lyn had no idea how to handle, but that had been true for weeks now. She swallowed and made herself forge ahead, since there was no path backward. "That's me. You must be Cole."

A single brisk nod of the sandy-haired head confirmed as much. He studied her again, more carefully. "Where's your... Where's Bryant?"

More than anything else, Lyn wanted not to answer that question. She wanted this Cole not to be here, asking that question, the only living being besides Sun who could call her by name. The fact that he was standing here at all was proof that Bryant had known something was wrong and had tried to prepare for it.

Lyn tried to say the words. When they wouldn't come, she pointed toward the great boulder on the other side of the clearing. "Sun put him over there."

The lines of the man Cole's face did strange, angular things as he turned to see what she was talking about. An unnatural kind of stillness settled over him in stages, and even though he hadn't taken a single step toward the boulder, Lyn could actually *watch* him start to comprehend her meaning.

"He's dead." If he hadn't said them so respectfully, she probably would have punched him in the mouth for those words.

Lyn clenched her fists and didn't say anything.

"What happened?" he asked, still quiet, after several silent moments had passed.

Lyn drew a deep breath and then it all just poured out. "He had a fight with Sun and then they both left and I didn't know if either of them were coming back, then a bunch of fellows in black stabbed him and took his heart when he was coming home. I have no idea what's going on. And now that you're standing here, I feel like he knew it was going to happen, but I don't know why. I don't know anything. They just left me and now he's *gone*. I'm hoping *you* can tell *me* something."

"Shit," Cole murmured. "This isn't what I agreed to." He sighed and shifted his shoulder strap again with a broad, scarred hand. "Can I sit down and get a drink of something before we get into this?"

That answer confused her more than ever, but she nodded. "Come with me." He followed silently as she led him into the cottage.

She showed him a seat, got him a glass of water, and stood waiting with her arms folded across her chest. He made a disappointed face she didn't understand when he looked into the cup, but drank it anyway. The minutes plodded on, and he sat there still saying nothing, staring into the now-empty cup.

"Well?" Lyn eventually demanded. Her nerves were just about to snap.

Cole looked up at her wearily. "Dammit."

"What are you doing here?" she barked when he failed to offer the explanation she needed. "Who were those men? Where did Bryant go and why did he tell me to wait? What am I waiting *for*? I have no idea what's going on. I've been alone for days now, hiding, and no one wants to tell me why."

The man's thin lips twitched in the barest hint of a smile. It didn't make him appear any friendlier. "Just like Bryant." He shook his head and lowered his bag to the ground. It landed with a heavy thud. "I guess this is my job now. Bryant told me a lot of things you don't seem to know."

Lyn pulled up a chair and sat close, watching him expectantly.

"Right." He began to drum one of his rough sun-darkened hands on the table top. "Listen – I'm no good at this. Bryant came to me a few days ago. He was pretty upset. Said your fairy had been lying to him all these years. Knew who he was and where he came from. According to her, he's... he *was* a prince of the elves and his right name was Gallanas, and you're his sister."

Lyn felt the breath rushing out of her body as though she had been punched in the gut. "What's a prince?" It was the least important thing she could think to ask, and also the only thing she could manage to actually say.

*His sister.*

But Cole went on. "He asked me to go with the two of you back to where you come from, and he made me swear to protect you if anything happened to him. He *knew*," he added in apparent disbelief.

"Knew what?"

"Knew he was going to be attacked," the human explained. "He knew this would happen. He was so set on me swearing to protect you, like he just *knew* he'd– He could have told me there was someone after him." He said something unhappy under his breath and stopped drumming the table.

Eyes stinging, Lyn struggled to deal with all of this new information. "So you're staying?"

The blond human nodded solemnly. "I promised Bryant."

"How do I know you're telling the truth?" she asked, hating everything about everything.

Cole looked exhausted in a way that had nothing to do with being tired as he reached down to his pack and rummaged through it for a moment. He produced some battered papers which he slapped down onto the table and pushed across to Lyn without a word of explanation.

She took the papers. Two of them were maps, peppered with Bryant's familiar hand, one of them directing Cole to the cottage in which they both now sat. The other was more detailed, a map of the continent with more writing in his hand at the bottom. It said, "The password is *'Chanar thasa vaia.'*" In the Southern Mountains, instead of a solid mass of peaks, Bryant had drawn a valley and a pass leading to it. She blinked.

The third paper contained a brief note. Too brief.

*Lyn:*

*If you're looking at this, it means I was right and I didn't make it back to you. I'm sorry.*

*Trust Cole as you would trust me, listen to what he tells you, and go wherever he leads. You will find no truer companion in all of Asrellion, on that you have my word as one who loves you.*

*There is a life waiting for you at home in Evlédíen, my sister. Claim it and be happy.*

*All my love,*
*Bryant*

The human continued, oblivious to the sudden constriction in her throat. "He said your parents are dead, so he was needed on the throne. And... that you have a sister, a twin, who might still be alive."

"A twin sister?" she echoed, disbelieving. "That's impossible."

But as she said it, a vague memory stirred, an impression from her infant days of a *presence* that was like her own but different, always with her, *part* of her. She could not picture a face, but she found herself remembering the presence. The feeling of connection. She shook her head slowly, her thoughts a mad rush.

"A twin sister. I... wow. I guess I have to find her?" Looking up at the human, who was watching her without expression, she mused aloud, "I don't much like the idea of leaving the forest."

He sighed. "That's why Bryant made me promise to protect you, I expect."

She shook her head, scowling. Something about his weary acceptance of this duty, as if she were some onerous burden, was deeply galling. She wasn't sure if she wanted to walk out and find her way across the world by herself just to show him she could, punch him in the eye, or bury her face against his shoulder and cry like a child until he made Bryant come back.

What she did was square her shoulders and set her jaw. "No, I don't mean I'm scared. I mean I *like* it here. I don't understand the things you're talking about, but it sounds like a lot of responsibility and people telling me what to do. I'd prefer to stay here. But I guess if I have a sister somewhere, I do need to meet her, don't I?"

Cole looked at her skeptically, but he merely replied, "Yes, you do."

She cast her glance around the cottage, at all the familiar objects of the only life she knew. Most of them would have to stay behind. With Bryant. She drew a deep breath. "Right. Let me just get my things and we'll be on our way." She stood and started toward the peg on the wall that held her knapsack, but turned back to face the human when a belated thought struck her.

"By the way, Bryant talked about you a lot and it's nice to meet you."

He nodded once, almost politely. "Likewise."

# Chapter Seven

Sometimes, Loralíenasa had to wonder if Tomanasíl hated her. Sometimes, it seemed the only logical explanation for the indignities he subjected her to.

It made sense that the Eleven Noble Houses would begin to put forward candidates for her hand; she would soon be of age. Not that they expected her to make a choice right away, but they did want to familiarize her with her options. Tomanasíl had even made an official register of the names, just to keep it all transparent and above board, hoping to avoid the worst effects of any foolish rivalries. Loríen could hardly fault any of the Houses for hoping she would honor them with her choice.

She could, however, fault her individual suitors for being so unimpressive. For, in some cases, being quite odious.

Tomanasíl was forcing her to spend time with each and every one of them. He said it was *fair*. Said she had to cultivate the goodwill of her nobles, because much of her power as queen would come from them.

She wanted to tell him to go cultivate something else.

Loralíenasa looked across the dinner table at Qroíllenas Qaí and tried not to sigh. He was bad enough when she entertained him at the palace; at home in his own fine riverside villa, he was the insufferable, domineering Lord of the Manor.

"I assume the fare is to your liking," the dark-haired lord informed rather than asked her, one thin eyebrow arched.

Damn. Clearly Loralíenasa had allowed him to see her boredom, or he would not be bothering with the solicitude. He had seemed perfectly content, a moment ago, to go on indefinitely about his exceptional skill at the sònoreth.

"It is excellent," she replied, summoning a small polite smile. "Thank you, Qroíllen."

He had gone to great obvious expense to produce a meal that would impress the Míyahídéna. Obvious because he had not shrunk from calling her attention to several choice aspects of the spread and the quality of the preparation, throughout the evening, and had made sure she knew the name of the prestigious chef he'd procured for the occasion. She didn't especially want to see what would happen if she made him try harder for her attention.

He studied her a moment longer with cold blue eyes that were startlingly bright in his stark white face. Searching for any more cracks in the perfectly controlled mask she was supposed to wear in polite company. After a moment, apparently finding none, he drew a breath and continued his self-congratulations.

"But of course, no one entered in this year's tournament was any real competition for me. Quite a disappointing showing. I always enjoy the opportunity to distinguish myself—"

Loralíenasa made herself appear attentive while imagining Qroíllen with the entire crock of molten cheese dripping down his smug, handsome face.

That was one of Qroíllenas Qaí's chief faults: he was attractive and he knew it. He had his father's striking eyes and his features were cut with the chiseled perfection passed to him by his Chalaqar mother. He could be exceptionally graceful when he wanted to, he did genuinely possess laudable skills in music and in the Art, and his courtly etiquette was impeccable. He was wealthy and important and seemed to feel no need, given his natural gifts, for any effort at being at all personable.

A little arrogance wouldn't be so bad on its own, Loralíenasa mused, if only he was not constantly treating others as if they were so small, and generally making himself so impossible to like.

"Tell me," he demanded after moving the cheese course off to the impressive marble sideboard to make room for dessert. "I have heard a troubling rumor, and I hope you can set my mind at rest."

Loralíenasa stopped herself just on the verge of observing how *delightful* it was that he was going to allow her to have an opinion on something tonight. He would not appreciate the sarcasm, and Tomanasíl would make her suffer for it. He had instructed her to be polite to her suitors, all of them, until the time came to choose from among them. It was harder to get away with things when he had explicitly told her not to do them.

"If we're going to be gossiping," she answered instead, "then do make it good. I don't often indulge."

He blinked slowly and watched her for a moment, clearly trying to decide whether or not she was making a jab at him. She kept her expression carefully neutral.

It took him some time to arrange both of their plates and serve out the decadent chocolate creation he had paid to impress her with. He spoke while he worked. "I have heard it said that you are to be dueling Lanoralas Galvan. This week, in fact."

Loralíenasa nearly groaned, but stopped herself in time.

"Naturally, I was disturbed by this rumor," Qroíllen went on. "If the Captain has offended you in some way, certainly there are other avenues of redress open to a woman with your resources – of your status. Violence, Loralíenasa?" He made a disapproving sound with his tongue against his teeth. "Certainly you need not risk your safety and reputation in such a reckless and frankly barbaric fashion."

She didn't bother to hide her scowl.

"I would of course be happy to take your part, if your honor demands a duel be fought," he concluded, setting down the final plate and smoothing the wrinkles out of his silk sleeves one at a time. His tone was as prim as his posture.

It was a near thing, but Loralíenasa managed *not* to laugh at her conceited dinner companion. The thought of proper, urbane Qroíllen picking up a sword and facing off against the deadliest man in the Valley – just to prove a point to her about suitable behavior for a Raia – was almost too much. She almost could have thanked Qroíllen for the diversion of being thrown from annoyance to amusement so quickly. Almost. If he was not such an ass, and had not done it entirely without meaning to.

"It is possible someone was having you on," Loralíenasa replied diplomatically.

She did not tell him that Lanas would take him apart and leave him on his silk-clad backside, dazed and trying to recall his own name, in less than a minute. She did not tell him that she didn't welcome being told how to spend her few free hours, or that she suspected he was trying to win approval from her guardian by objecting to her aggressive and dangerous – and to his mind low-class – hobby. She did not tell him to mind his own damn affairs and to keep his priggish nose out of hers.

Instead, she tried a bite of the extravagant dessert. It was delicious.

The thin black eyebrow made another skyward journey. "Oh? You two have not in fact arranged to meet one another upon the East Green on Falaríyu next?"

For being apparently so well-informed, Qroíllen was amazingly thick.

"We are in fact dueling," Loralíenasa explained. "But you misunderstand our intent, and I am in no disquiet over my reputation." She felt herself growing cross with him and struggled to keep the smooth finish to her voice that was expected of her. "You know well that the Captain is my teacher and that I am more than able to acquit myself with a sword. The purpose of this duel, as I thought everyone knew, is to settle a friendly debate between us."

She had more of the chocolate confection. It was good enough that she supposed she would allow him to live despite being so frustrating.

Qroíllen watched her instead of enjoying his own dessert. "And the substance of this debate is–?"

This was common knowledge. Was he hoping to embarrass her by making her say it aloud? He didn't know her all that well. Perhaps he was trying to force her to make a dig at Lanas, one of his rivals for her hand. Maybe he enjoyed the thought of both possibilities at once. Maybe he was just deeply committed to feigning innocence as his only defense for this moronic conversational gambit.

"It began as a joke, really." Loralíenasa decided she didn't mind if her smile was a little too tight, the edge to her humor a little too sharp. "His men were harassing him one day during my lesson. Because I was doing so well against him." She ate more and hoped it wasn't obvious that she was trying to end the meal quickly. "They told him he ought to be careful, or I might have to take his place as Captain of the Guard. It was all in fun, of course. Later, we were teasing one another–" she was gratified to see Qroíllen lose some of his complexion at the reminder that Lanoralas had her favor and friendship– "bantering over who was better, and we decided to fight it out, for the general entertainment of the populace."

More to aggravate Tomanasíl, in point of fact, but that part did not need to be common knowledge. They had both laughed as they'd imagined his reaction to the news. They even had a side bet going: whether he would try to stop it from happening.

It suddenly occurred to Loralíenasa to wonder if this right now was Tomanasíl working clumsily through Qroíllenas to that end. That would explain his having been left ignorant on the finer points.

"...a joke?"

"This is amazing," Loralíenasa said instead of allowing the conversation to tread any further down this path, stabbing her fork into the dessert. "What is it called?"

He seemed put out, but she doubted he had the temerity to ignore her outright. A moment later she was proven correct. "I shall have to ask the chef for you. It is quite good."

Turning her sigh of relief into a sound of enjoyment as she took another bite, Loralíenasa decided there was nothing to do but push through the pain and hope the evening would be over quickly. "Lord Qroíllen, I've heard you are an expert on the works of Séochoría Ílím. And you have such lovely diction. I don't suppose I could convince you to recite a few verses?" She threw in a charming smile.

The lord's annoyance melted into smug satisfaction. "Of course, Míyahídéna. Anything to please you." He leaned back in his chair, eyes closed in concentration, and began the first stanza of a long poem.

Loralíenasa drank the rest of her wine and pretended to listen.


Even as she sat by the water's edge enjoying the breathtaking natural beauty of the scene, Loralíenasa knew that she was dreaming.

Not that the scene was too fantastical to be real – in fact, this was one of her favorite places to sit and meditate when time allowed, beneath the willow as it wept into this small, reed-fringed pond on the grounds behind the Crystal Palace. There were always flowers in bloom along the margin of the water, except in winter when the shadows were complex and beautiful upon the ice.

She knew she had to be asleep because there was a certain feel to these dreams, a particular too-lucid clarity, and she had them often enough to recognize it now. It had been a while since her last one, but it made sense tonight. Her unsatisfactory evening with Qroíllenas Qaí had left her feeling even more alone than usual, and she had no one to talk to about the things that weighed most on her mind. The price of being above peers.

Because this was a dream she'd had many times in various forms, she already knew what was going to happen next. It was no surprise when she heard a booted footfall behind her, determinedly approaching her place beside the water.

The footsteps stopped beside her. Glancing sidelong at the spot, she saw a pair of fine black leather boots, worn but well-cared-for, the toes squared and the wide folded tops extending above the knee. Grenlecian-style. She closed her eyes and took a deep breath as the wearer of the boots sank to the ground at her side. He smelled pleasantly of pine and cedar.

*Naoise.* Or, her dream of him.

Loralíenasa turned her head and drank in a good long view of the man who had been haunting her dreams for the last seven years despite the fact that she had only known the real version of him for four days.

Vaian, he was beautiful, but he looked older. Probably too much older for only seven years on. She tried to make her mind correct the image, but the exhaustion and the almost haunted look did not leave him. His face was still as pale, the skin as smooth and fine as she remembered. He just looked like he had seen too much. His eyes were weary. She wondered what she was trying to tell herself. Bad things had been happening in the wider world, so her scouts reported; it would be a lie to claim she didn't worry about him, and she had no need to lie to herself here.

His smile was a solemn thing as he studied her right back, but even so grim, she had missed the sight of it.

Above them, the sky was awash with the brilliance of the sun's last light, the willow sighing the song of a gentle autumn breeze as Loralíenasa moved closer to the man beside her and greeted him in the way she only could here, in dreams.

Full night had claimed their patch of earth beside the water by the time the headlong rush had passed and either one of them felt ready for words. Loríen was lying back on the grass gazing up at the stars, nestled comfortably between Naoise's arm and his chest, her head on his shoulder.

"I wish I could ever remember the best parts in the morning," dream Naoise sighed, expressing her own regret. His voice was just as she remembered it: strong and low and pleasant on the ear, the accent richly cultured. It was another curious feature of these dreams that she knew he was not speaking Elven, yet she understood him anyway.

In the beginning, after her return from that disastrous visit to Grenlec, she had seen him in her sleep almost nightly. Their conversations were even more enlivening and, soon, more intimate than those she'd had with his real life counterpart. It had been both a comfort and a sorrow during her long convalescence, being able to share her burdens but knowing she would never see him again in life. Knowing it was all just an illusion she had conjured for herself because in reality she was so alone.

The man, the real one, was exceptionally attractive. It hadn't taken long for the dreams to assume a different character, one of which she was not proud.

But even more embarrassing than that, it was a sad truth that her made-up dream version of a man she had known for all of four days had become her closest friend and only confidant. Sometimes, when she was awake, she wondered if she was losing her mind. Less frequently, she had the terrible, insidious idea that these dreams were not dreams – or at least not only her imagination. She desperately needed that not to be true.

Loralíenasa smiled up at the stars. She felt too good at the moment to want to engage in that kind of metaphysical speculation. "Of course you can't remember: you're just a dream." In the morning, she knew, the particulars of this strange too-real interlude would be cloudy. The feelings stayed with her, but the details never did.

He chuckled, and she could feel it resonating in his chest. "Maybe you're the dream."

She didn't want to think about what it meant that her subconscious was so contrary.

"I missed you tonight," she said instead.

"Oh?"

She nodded against his shoulder, enjoying the solidity of him. Would the real Naoise be this warm, his arm so tightly muscled? It was a shame she'd not had the time to find out. "Tomsíl is making me entertain suitors," she explained. "Most of them are decent enough, in their ways. Lanas is my oldest friend. I like Víqarío but we would never be... Well, shall we say I'm not his type. The others are mostly forgettable. Then there's Qroíllen. Vaian, but I do hate that man. *Such* a weed."

In the dream, Naoise answered in a teasing tone she'd never heard him use in real life. "Why bother with him? Beautiful as you are, surely you need not waste your time with dregs." He reached up and tweaked her cheek lightly.

Loríen blushed but didn't tell him to stop. No need for that, here. "He's not a dreg." She smiled at the thought that she was arguing against Qroíllen's worthlessness with herself. "He is unfortunately quite handsome and of impeccable breeding, and I cannot afford to slight his house." She raised herself up on one elbow to study her illusory Naoise again – the chiseled jaw and strong, hawkish nose, the noble brow, the features all sculpted like a master's work in marble. A lock of his black hair had fallen forward to obscure one eyebrow and the bright eye beneath.

As she looked at him, she remembered the incredible things he did to her in this dream place, and she felt her cheeks warming again. No real man could ever measure up to this fantasy she had concocted. "He's not you, though."

He regarded her with bright eyes that sparkled in the darkness, but he did not smile.

She sighed and lowered herself back to a more comfortable position.

"If the worst you have to worry about is odious suitors," dream Naoise said quietly after a long silence, "then I am happy you're still safe where you are. Out in the world, I'm afraid things are somewhat more grim of late."

That much was true. Even though her people kept themselves isolated from the world, Loríen had convinced Tomanasíl some time ago that they could not afford to be uninformed. It was the revelation of war between Grenlec and Telrisht, learned from the real Prince Naoise, that had led her to push her guardian on the subject. Their network of spies was still growing, but they were already able to tell her much about what was happening in wider Asrellion. She knew the war had not ended, and that the conflict was no longer between only Grenlec and Telrisht. She knew the human kingdoms were suffering, that countless thousands had died, that resources were steadily dwindling but neither side would relent.

"I don't mean to seem frivolous," she explained aloud. "I know other people have worse problems. I know–" she drew a deep breath and made herself be reasonable– "that there are people who would give much to have my life, such as it is. And I know you have been dealing with things I can only imagine, since… since we parted."

Naoise drew his hand slowly up her arm and down again. "I wasn't judging you. I truly am just relieved you're not dealing with what I am."

She nuzzled closer against him and felt less terrible about herself.

"To tell you the truth," Naoise said, "I don't even *know* what I'm dealing with lately."

Loralíenasa watched the clouds move across the stars and waited for an explanation.

"I've been fighting this war for so long that…" He trailed off, shook his head. His hair tickled her cheek. "At first, everything was so clear. We were the heroes, saving a beleaguered neighbor. My brother and I, we were proving our valor against an old enemy. But then, I don't know, something changed. The feel of it. Wars have a trajectory, they end, have a victor. This one just keeps on. It's like someone, somewhere, won't *let* us stop. We gather intelligence that turns the tide, then Telrisht receives vital supplies from an anonymous source that allow them to rally. Then the pendulum swings the other way. And back again. I feel like we're being controlled, manipulated."

Her dream construct was always so accommodating when she vented, so she played along. "Who? Who would want to keep you fighting?"

Naoise didn't answer right away. "The easy answer is Mysia." He sounded unhappy about it. "They've hated Grenlec and Telrisht both, with cause, ever since the days of–" he turned his head to offer an apologetic grimace– "the War of Purification."

She frowned back at him. "The War of Exile," she corrected.

Naoise sighed. "It would certainly serve them to see us both hobbled," he went on. "But, I don't know. That answer is almost too easy, and the timing makes no sense. King Eselakoto has sat the throne in Mysia for damn near fifty years. Why would he set something like this in motion after such a long and peaceful reign? At his advanced age?" He sounded genuinely agitated now, as though he had been thinking about these things a great deal and was upset by his inability to understand them.

"Fifty years," she repeated. "That is quite a long time for a human to rule, is it not?"

Naoise nodded, his hair again brushing her cheek.

"Advancing age…" she mused. "Perhaps his health is not what it was? And someone else has quietly seized control of the kingdom?"

Suddenly he was sitting up. "By the Father."

She sat up beside him and watched suspicion chase comprehension across his face. "I don't want that to be true," she thought aloud.

It was bad enough for Asrellion that the two mightiest kingdoms in the world were killing one another, with Lang helplessly ravaged in the middle, Rosemarch cut off to the north and concerned with its own internal problems, and Seland abandoned and vulnerable on the coast, the islands left to fend for themselves. She did not want to think of poor Mysia crushed in all the chaos, not after all they had already suffered for their loyalty to her people. And they would be, without question, if they were responsible for this present trouble and Grenlec or Telrisht ever caught on. In all the years that their conquerors called the Forbearance, they had never been allowed to grow again the military strength they would require to face either kingdom head-on.

Loralíenasa reached out and took the dream prince's hands in hers. His fingers were strong and lean – the hands of a musician, not a warrior – a thin white scar standing out against the second knuckle of his left hand. With everything in her, she silently willed his real-life counterpart not to harm Mysia.

"I don't want any of this," he answered tiredly. "And I hope I'm wrong to see a pattern here. Reid thought I was being paranoid. Said I was chasing shadows, risking all our lives on a manufactured crusade to give myself an inflated sense of my own importance."

Loríen raised her eyebrows at him.

He responded with a small smile that went away quickly. "Well, he didn't say it in those exact words." His voice sounded far away.

He was withdrawing from her, she could see. She was hit by the sudden knowledge that she was waking up. It came as a disappointment.

"Take care of yourself," she said while she still had the ability to do so.

The last thing the dream allowed her was a view of Naoise's intense eyes over a half-smile. By lunch, she would forget everything about the dream except that she'd had it.

Except, for some reason, she thought she had the memory of Naoise's voice saying, to her, "I miss you."

Before the day was over, Lyn had determined that Cole would be an all right sort if only he wasn't so terribly *dull*. She understood from Bryant that Cole had not had the most pleasant of lives, but she still thought he could stand to be less solemn. She spent the entire day trying to break through, only to be met by an increasingly blank wall of stoicism. The man was an enigma.

When they settled down to their campfire at dusk, she thought it would be amusing to slip a wet cloak under him as he sat down, and that it might finally elicit a reaction of some kind. Without comment, he calmly removed the offending item *before* sitting on it and deposited it close to the fire to dry, then took out a handful of dried meat from his bag and began to chew with mechanical efficiency.

"Aw, come on," she prodded. "Nothing?"

He frowned. "It doesn't upset you that your brother was just murdered?"

Heat rushed into her face. "Of course I'm upset. You have no idea what... what I saw." She felt her lips quivering with some combination of grief and rage and bit them until they stopped. "How else do you expect me to take my mind off it?"

The pair of furrows between his eyebrows deepened, but he made no reply.

She tried for several moments to let him have the silence he seemed to want, but it started to feel too thick and heavy and like it was pushing her down into the ground. Leaning forward, she angled for a better view of his eyes. "What are you thinking about?"

He did not look up. "How strange you are."

Lyn snorted. That was not at all what she had expected him to say. "I'm strange? How?"

"Dunno. Maybe Bryant's influence," he replied with a grunt.

She stared at him in disbelief. *Was that supposed to be a joke? He doesn't even* have *a sense of humor, does he?* "Hey, that was funny. Sort of. I mean you tried. You're not so bad, you know?"

His expression remained bland. "I'm sure I'm just as bad as you think I am."

"Mmm, not possible," Lyn replied. "I thought you were *boring* on top of everything else."

"Everything else?" he echoed. "Just what did he say about me?"

*Not as much as I'd have liked,* she thought, annoyed. "He said you used to do fighting for money," she answered, wrinkling her nose. "Have you killed a lot of people?"

Cole drew a slow breath but showed no other change to his stony demeanor. "A few." Finally looking directly into her eyes for the first time in the conversation, he added, "Don't you think we should get some rest?"

"I'm not tired," Lyn answered with a shrug.

"I'm not like you," he said, his tone finally terse. "Humans tire out after a day of marching."

"No need to be so surly," she pouted, but she didn't know what else to say. She realized after a moment that she'd never had to get to know anyone before – she had simply grown up with Bryant, and with Sun. They'd spent so much time together, she had always been able to say how one of them would react to anything. It was exhausting and fascinating, looking at this other person and having no idea what he might be thinking or feeling. She could see why Bryant had treated him almost like a toy – his own novel amusement.

Cole got up and moved around their campsite, preparing for sleep. She watched him, trying to decide whether or not he hated her. After a moment, he came back and rolled himself up into his blanket, facing away from her.

"You don't have to try so hard," he said eventually, surprising her. She wasn't sure she knew what he meant.

"Huh?"

"We don't have to like each other," he explained. "Let's just worry about getting you home safe."

Lyn felt her stomach sinking even lower. He definitely hated her. It wasn't enough that her entire world had collapsed out from under her, but now she was stuck tramping across the world with this dull man who hated her and was not Bryant.

It took them another day to come to the forest's edge, and when they did, Lyn slowed her pace until she'd stopped without realizing it. She stared at the last tree, having the strangest sensation like there was a gate in front of her that she couldn't pass through. Like she didn't have the keys. Sun had told her often enough not to leave the boundaries of the forest, but Lyn didn't think she was *forbidden* to do so. Still, she felt odd.

Cole turned toward her when he realized she'd stopped. "What's wrong?"

Lyn didn't know how to answer. Even more complex feelings were pushing their way forward, now that she'd paused to give them some attention. Bryant was behind her in the forest, along with the entire life she had known with him and Sun, and she was proposing to blithely walk out and leave it all behind, probably never to return.

*And what if they've forgotten about me in what's-it-called – that Elf Valley? Or what if they don't want me back? What if I don't like it there? They probably won't let me leave if things don't work out. And what if my sister didn't make it? Cole says she's in charge, but if she's dead they'll make me do it and I'll just die.*

Cole was still looking at her, waiting for a reply.

"I… I've decided not to go, after all," she said. "I think I'll just stay here, in the forest." She produced a watery smile.

The former mercenary frowned. "No. Bryant wanted you to go back to Evlédíen, and he made me promise to take you. It's not safe here," he added when he saw her features harden into a scowl. "Whoever killed Bryant's going to come back for you, and you won't be able to hide forever."

"Well, that's not your problem." Lyn didn't like the quaver she could hear in her own voice. "Go back home. I'll be fine."

He took several steps closer to her, and something about the movement seemed to carry a threat. She clenched her fists and held her ground. He stopped when he saw how she had tensed, hurt briefly flickering in his eyes, and he raised both hands in a placatory gesture. "Look, I won't force you to go anywhere, but it is my problem. I made a promise to Bryant. If you stay here, I have to stay with you." He paused, studying her as if trying to decide what would be the best thing to say.

She felt her resolve wavering.

"Don't you want to see your sister?" Cole asked quietly. "I'd give anything to find out I have family somewhere. It's a hard thing to be all alone in the world. Don't throw this away just because you're scared."

She bit her lip. "I'm not scared," she objected, even though she knew she was. She decided that she did not want this tough mercenary person thinking she was weak or so easily frightened. Her expression hardened into one of determination. "Let's go, then."

Cole said nothing; he merely waited for her.

"There's just something I have to do first," she said.

Her companion watched silently as she threw her head back and yelled, as loud as she could, *"Where are you?"* The leaves swallowed the echoes of her cry almost aggressively. Lyn waited, but Sun did not show herself.

She took a deep breath and deliberately walked past the tree, past the boundaries of the forest. All at once, the air seemed different; heavier, less pure, and she could taste something like sorrow in the wind. Everything seemed... *older*. More worn, not as clean. Like the world was contaminated by a grief that had settled into the rocks and the soil and lived in the running water.

It was stifling.

A desire to turn back came on almost irresistibly. She gritted her teeth and forced herself to continue forward.

Watching her without a word, Cole waited until she had come up beside him before he started off again.

# CHAPTER EIGHT

The weather was wild on the dark afternoon Naoise welcomed the King of Grenlec to his encampment in the mountains north of Alanrad. Telrisht did not often see rain, but there was wind and lightning enough to spare.

King Lorn traveled with a small escort of twenty, only fifteen of them soldiers – dangerous so deep into enemy territory, but he had opted for speed and stealth in response to his son's enigmatic message. Naoise could admire that, even if it shook him badly to see his father riding through peril and storm with so little protection.

They clasped arms, and exchanged all of the formal pleasantries at a shout to be heard over the squall while the party dismounted, Naoise's men moving to assist. Then the prince led his father to his own tent pitched amid the sharp crags of the Ghadeer Mountains, where they were sheltered somewhat from the gale force winds. The king sank gratefully into the camp chair offered him and accepted a skin of fresh water to wash the dust of the road from his throat.

Naoise studied his father while he drank. The ten months since they had seen each other last had not been kind to the king. There was more silver than black now in the neat beard, more lines worn into his pale face than ever. He looked tired, not that Naoise could blame him.

"I have assumed," Lorn, King of Grenlec said when he had caught his breath, "that you have *very* good cause for calling me out here to meet with you, son."

The prince bent his head, acknowledging the point his father wished to make. "My lord, I would not have asked for this audience if I did not think it vitally important," he assured the king.

"Well then, let's get right to it." Lorn returned Naoise's scrutiny with grey eyes that had lost none of their sharpness, despite the steep toll demanded of him by the last few years. "My scouts tell me you've had a busy season. Six outposts seized since the beginning of summer, reducing Telrishti supply lines in the east to the merest trickle. Excellent work, that. Your brother, meanwhile, has been occupying Alanrad with the Primary Wing since Redleaf last and is like to burst from the boredom. The Ayiz's main force remains pinned down and well-fortified in Nastrond. What is this intelligence you've acquired that you say will change things so greatly?"

Naoise lowered himself into the tent's only other chair and scrubbed at his brow with one hand while he composed his thoughts. He'd had some time to consider this, while waiting for his father to respond to his message. He had come to several conclusions, and he still wasn't sure how many of them he ought to share. It was a comfort to hear confirmation that his brother was alive and well, at least.

"I've a question for you first," he said, dreading the answer.

Lorn nodded. "If I can answer it, I will."

Outside, Naoise heard the howling of the winds, the rumbling of thunder that was not far enough distant. The clamor of scores of men and horses. The aural backdrop was appropriately apocalyptic for his present train of thought. "Where is Grenlec obtaining the bulk of its supplies?"

Lorn blinked. "That's not what I was expecting."

Naoise waited for an answer.

"Perhaps what you wanted was an audience with the quartermaster," the king replied. Somewhat cagily, Naoise could not help but feel.

Naoise pushed his hands through his hair and told himself this was necessary. "I mean it, Da. Where are we getting our arms, our provisions? We can hardly provide for our own people after the March of Fire; who is feeding the army?"

It was a long time before Lorn said anything. "Understand, Naoise." Not an encouraging start. "In war, you sometimes have to make decisions that don't feel right. Sometimes you just have to choose which evil you can best live with."

The hard decisions of war. Naoise did not need a lecture about *that*. He kept waiting.

"To be perfectly frank, I'm not sure who our supplier is," Lorn confessed when Naoise provided neither argument nor word of reproach. The chair creaked as he shifted. "We were facing a crisis, three years back. We'd had a bad harvest season and our farms were tapped, our armorers working at capacity and still unable to meet demand, the Ayiz burning everything from the

Lake to the Green River. The quartermaster told me it was time to seek either terms or a miracle."

"And then you got your miracle?" Naoise filled in grimly. He had been afraid of hearing just this. It was obvious what he had to do now, if his father would let him.

His father nodded. "Just so. The quartermaster came to me and said that he had been made an offer and could make the problem disappear, if I was willing to defer my questions. I didn't see how else to proceed."

"You don't have to justify yourself to me, sir," Naoise said, trying to keep the disappointment out of his voice. "I just needed to hear you say that, because I think I might begin now to see what's really happening."

The camp chair squealed again as Lorn leaned forward abruptly. "Oh?"

A particularly close growl of thunder forced Naoise to pause a moment before saying, "Yes. I have to go to Mysia."

Dairinn Raynesley had been occupying the same boring city in boring Telrisht for more than a year now, and he hated it. And was bored.

The locals never even tried to insurrect anymore, and any peacekeeping that *was* required was seen to by his captains. In fact, most everything was seen to by his captains. There was nothing for Dairinn to do but lose money dicing with his troops and disporting himself at the local brothels.

When his father appeared unexpectedly in Alanrad, Dairinn hoped it was to tell him to pick up and move out against a new military target. No open battles had been fought since the taking of the city. The war itself had all but come to a standstill. What action still went on lately had all come to him as news of the daring exploits of small stealth units like his brother's: dodging in and out of danger with reckless disregard for their own lives in order to achieve limited, focused objectives. This, what he was doing – camped in one spot with no one to fight while others chipped away at the enemy – was not his idea of a proper war.

Dairinn had the king shown to the decadent parlor that had once been the room where the Ayiz received his most honored guests. He made a habit of never coming here when he could help it.

In the state he had originally found it, the room had lacked chairs of any kind. Dairinn honestly could not understand why a desert-dwelling people would want to spend so much of their time on the ground, closer to the dust and sand that seemed to get *everywhere*. But the parlor was decorated to the height of Telrishti elegance, overfull of ornate censers and chandeliers, carved wooden screens, elaborate rugs, garish silk pillows, and exotic plants forced to survive indoors.

Of course, the rest of the palace was no better. People liked to talk about Telrishti opulence, but as far as Dairinn was concerned it was all just a too-bright muddle, and something about the art made him uncomfortable. He had tried to introduce an element of the familiar into the palace by filling it with his officers, but that only exacerbated another failing of Telrishti design: the openness and lack of privacy. It seemed like all he ever did since coming to Alanrad was find ways to compromise in order to minimize the misery of the place.

Maybe the king wasn't just here to issue new orders, Dairinn thought as he passed through the palace. Maybe he was here to report that the war was over, that they had won. It would be an anti-climactic end to such a bloody conflict, but they *had* been at it rather a long time.

He tried to decide which situation he would prefer as he made his way through the Ayiz's uncomfortable palace.

Another idea struck him hard then, and he slowed to a halt. What if his father bore tidings more grim? What if something had happened to Naoise? His younger brother was up at the front, such as it was these days, carrying out all manner of dangerous lunacy, and Dairinn knew Naoise hadn't the disposition for war. He wondered whose damn fool idea it had been to assign Naoise such a role. This was a man who had rescued a litter of abandoned kittens, nursing them all by hand until they were old enough to make their own way, mere months before he'd had to take up arms and march to war for his kingdom. It seemed near miraculous that no disaster had yet befallen him.

"My lord prince!" a familiar voice called out behind Dairinn.

He turned to regard the short but solid figure of Captain Edelmar hurrying up the arched hallway with no eye for the ornate screenwork all around them, hand on his sword to prevent it slapping against his boots. Dairinn was hardly surprised; any time something important was about to happen around here, he was never left to handle it on his own. He knew they didn't trust him to do more than swing his blade, nominal command of the Primary Wing notwithstanding. Sometimes it bothered him more than others. It would bother him less now if they were actually doing anything.

"Someone chasing you, Ed?" Dairinn asked with a grin as the captain drew up to him.

His subordinate offered a routine smile that moved almost none of the lines of his limestone-white face. "I'm told the king is here. Did we have no warning of this?"

Dairinn shook his head and started off again through the mazelike ways of the Ayiz's palace. At least he wasn't the only one caught unawares this time. "If this is a scheduled visit, I was never told of it."

Edelmar fell into step beside him. "That can't be good."

The prince shrugged. Cast the captain another grin, this one full of mischief. "Perhaps he just missed me."

Captain Edelmar snorted. The two men walked together in an almost-companionable silence.

Lorn was waiting in the parlor with a lacquered, brightly painted tray of refreshments at his elbow when they came in. Because Dairinn flatly refused to lounge on floor pillows in the Telrishti manner and had ordered real chairs brought into the palace, the king did not have to lever himself up from the ground when he stood to greet his son.

"Dairinn," Lorn said, clasping the prince about the shoulders. "It is grace itself to see you alive and well after so long a parting."

"Alive perhaps, but *well* may be something of an overstatement, sir," Dairinn replied. When his father displayed concern, Dairinn sighed with an extra infusion of drama. "Do you have any idea how long I've been trapped in this sand-choked pit of a city? I am like to lose my mind."

"I have some idea," Lorn said dryly. He nodded to the captain, who offered a soldier's salute in return.

"Your Majesty," Edelmar said when acknowledged. "This visit is unexpected." He stopped short of demanding to know what it meant; Dairinn was mildly impressed. Edelmar had long since stopped displaying such respectful restraint toward his prince. Then again, he was a seasoned veteran and nearly two decades Dairinn's senior, and viewed his role in the occupation of royal Alanrad with immeasurably more gravity than Dairinn did his.

Lorn eyed the soldier shrewdly. "And what might I have found different, had my presence been anticipated, Captain?"

Edelmar was not to be intimidated. Dairinn knew because he had already tried it every way he could think of without any observable effect. "Of course I meant to suggest no such thing, Your Majesty," he replied stoutly.

The king spared both Dairinn and the captain a rare smile. "Of course not. In answer to the question you did not ask, I am not here to issue new orders, merely to see my son."

"Ha!" Dairinn crowed, grinning. He hadn't expected to be right.

The captain offered another salute despite his obvious skepticism. "That being the case, I humbly withdraw with your permission until I am needed, my lord, Your Majesty." The hint was definitely there in his steely voice, that he strongly hoped he *would* be needed before the king returned to Grenlec.

Lorn dismissed the man, and Dairinn was alone with his father for the first time in… by the god, almost exactly a year. It was then that he noticed the strain in the king's bearing, the tightness around his grey eyes. King Lorn had always worn his years with a quiet dignity, but something had sucked all the blood from his now painfully white cheeks.

Not here with new orders; could it be Naoise after all?

Dairinn poured himself a glass of wine from the king's tray without invitation and helped himself to a handful of sugared dates. He would have preferred strawberries with cream, but this was Alanrad. "Well, Da," he declared. "Came all this way for me, did you? I'm flattered."

Lorn seated himself again and studied Dairinn before answering. "In truth, son, I did not."

The elder prince of Grenlec stopped with several dates in his mouth and stood blinking at his father. Hadn't he just said–? He swallowed too quickly and felt the dates sticking in his throat. "What, now?"

The king sighed. "I am here because of your brother, I'm afraid."

Dairinn's fears came roaring back tenfold. He'd spent seven years dreading this conversation, but now that it was here, he stood indecisive between wanting to yell something or to sit down abruptly. He drank all of his wine at a gulp and set the goblet down with a great effort to appear calmer than he felt. "What trouble has Naoise gotten himself into this time?"

Watching him for a moment as if considering whether to order him to sit, the king shook his head finally. "I've just been to his camp in the mountains. We had… an enlightening conversation."

"Then he's still alive?"

Lorn grunted, staring into his lap. "He has an uncanny way of cheating death, does your brother, or so his men say." He looked up at Dairinn and the worry lines around his eyes were quickly smoothed by compassion. "I'm sorry, Dair. I didn't mean to make you think– Yes, Naoise is alive and unharmed for the moment. Frustrated, as you are. Thinking too hard about everything, as always. He has had some interesting ideas of late."

In his relief, Dairinn sank into the nearest chair at the precise moment that his legs gave out beneath him. His father nodded with something like satisfaction. "Don't do that again, Da," he said, embarrassingly shaky.

Lorn reached out and squeezed his shoulder, but did not repeat his apology. "I stopped here after our talk in order to inform you that Naoise has departed for Mysia."

"Mysia?" Dairinn echoed stupidly. He'd gone from relieved to confused too fast to figure out what lay between. "What business have we in Mysia?"

"Your brother thinks it might be possible that someone is attempting to manipulate the outcome of this war," Lorn explained. He sounded like he might believe it; Dairinn wondered what Naoise had said to sell him on such a paranoid delusion. "He thinks there are answers to be found in Mysia, and he has gone to look for them."

Dairinn shook his head, trying to understand what Naoise was thinking. "Don't we stand in danger of sparking a diplomatic incident by running a strike force onto Mysian soil? They've stayed out of the war so far, but—"

"He has gone alone," Lorn explained tiredly.

"What?"

It was the king's turn to be on his feet. He paced the room, stopping to admire a painted vase he wasn't really looking at. "He believes—" he chuckled ruefully as if he could not believe what he had been talked into— "that it makes sense for him to go with only a diplomat's escort. He is a king's son and will be received with all appropriate honor as such at the Mysian court. Even if they *are* a pack of scheming weasels," he added in a mutter.

"And so…" Dairinn thought it through, but couldn't force Naoise's behavior to make any sense. "He's just abandoning his unit, running off across enemy soil to chase fantasies at the Mysian court? And what if he's right? The Father knows Mysia has always been full of backstabbing sneaks. Isn't he just jumping into danger with both feet?" His brother was too far up into his head and his complicated ideas to recognize the risk to himself. He was going to get himself killed and never see it coming.

"He made the point – and I am afraid he is right in this – that the fewer people share his suspicions at the present time, the better." Lorn stopped pretending to examine the room and turned back to Dairinn. His shoulders were bowed under an invisible burden. "Like it or not, if there is any truth to this mad idea, he *is* the best choice to investigate it. He speaks the language, is protected by the diplomatic immunity of his rank, is cautious by nature, and is far too young and unassuming to alarm our enemies should he encounter them. We can trust him to be discreet, and we know his mind is sharp. And," he bared his teeth in a grimace, "you know he has always been tolerant of Mysia's fascination with… old legends. He may even get on with those people. If there is a conspiracy, he will uncover it."

"And take a knife to the kidney for his trouble after they're done swapping fairy stories," Dairinn grunted. Another thought came to him. "What of his unit? Who will assume command?"

The shrewd gleam in Lorn's eyes showed that he guessed all too well what Dairinn wanted him to say. "His highly capable lieutenant has been promoted and will continue to strike at the Telrishti supply line. Never fear; that much is in hand."

Leaving only the small detail of Naoise heading into what might well be a trap with no one to guard his back. Dairinn didn't like the sound of that at all. "Let's go back to the beginning. I'd like to hear more about this conspiracy." And then decide whether or not the war had finally driven his bookish brother insane.

When Cole said they were being followed, Lyn didn't realize at first what he meant by it.

He woke her in the dead hours of the night, one calloused hand covering her startled exclamation, and led her with a gesture over brush and under branch like a man accustomed to creeping silently through darkness. They came at length to a place where she found herself looking down from a modest height at the smoldering remains of a small fire. Around the smoking fire-ring lay – she took a moment to count them – twelve sleeping figures dressed all in black.

Lyn clenched her fists so hard her fingers went numb.

The blond man continued to say nothing. He touched her shoulder and indicated with a jerk of his head that they should go back to their camp. She stared at him, and back down at the men she knew were Bryant's murderers. She wished she had not left her bow beside her bedroll, that she had magic arrows capable of killing them all before a single one of them could think another evil thought, and that Cole would let her do anything to them.

He touched her shoulder again; something in the way the moonlight hit his sad eyes told her he knew exactly what she was thinking, explosive arrowheads and all.

Lyn bit her lip and followed him back to their camp.

They didn't go back to sleep, of course. He let her speak now, but only quietly, and in low tones he explained that they needed to be as far away from here by dawn as they were physically capable of being. He said they might want to get their hands on some horses. He revealed that he had known they were being hunted since the day they left the Dark Forest.

Lyn wanted to hit someone. She decided it might as well be Cole, a solid jab to the gut that he didn't expect. He muffled a surprised expletive.

"Next time, *tell* me things," she hissed. "Don't just lead me around like a dumb cow on a rope. I want to see it coming. If I'm getting my heart cut out, I want those bastards to have to look me in the eye while they do it."

Cole grunted and packed the rest of his things in silence.

It wasn't really Cole she wanted to hit.


Lyn stared at the map and tried to make a decision.

It had been much easier when they'd been marching mostly due south. She had been able to tell herself it didn't matter which way they went because they'd get somewhere eventually, and everything she saw until then was a new experience worth having. Now Cole wanted her to make choices and be *responsible*. Being followed definitely took the shine off of things.

She was irritated that, on top of everything else those creeps were guilty of, they were ruining this too.

"I was going to take us to the Lake," Cole explained grimly. He didn't look at her as he said it, instead scanning the landscape behind them in the noon sun. "Catch a boat across to Arden, head south to the mountains from there. But with our tail so close behind..." He shook his head, as if the rest was obvious.

"With them so close behind, what?" Lyn pressed.

He cast a quick glance in her direction, frowning, before returning to his watch over their surroundings. "We don't want to get caught out on the water. No cover, no retreat."

"Well, obviously." Lyn scowled, feeling stupid. She had never had to think along these lines before. It was hard for her. She felt bad for Cole, that this was the way his mind just seemed to work naturally. Always seeing threats, calculating danger, assuming the worst, planning escape routes. For just a moment, she thought she understood why he never smiled. How could he, when his world was so forbidding and full of danger? Then she decided that was just a stupid way to live.

"So we need to come down on either side of the Lake?" she asked, even though he had already told her as much and had said he would do whatever she chose. She half hoped he would make the decision himself if she kept stalling. "And it doesn't matter which?"

"Both ways have advantages," he answered. She saw the muscles twitching in his square jaw beneath the blond stubble. "The terrain in Grenlec is better for getting lost in, and the two of us stand a better chance of blending in there. On the other hand, I've done more work in Telrisht. I know people."

"I'm betting by *people* you mean the less-than-savory kind." Bryant had told her stories. The kind of work Cole had done, the people he'd worked with. She wondered, briefly excited, if she might get to meet real criminals.

He shrugged. "The kind who'd be some help if we're in trouble."

"That's not a no."

Cole turned and frowned at her, maybe trying to decide whether or not she would seriously object to taking help from his contacts. Maybe wondering whether she *had* objections, or if she was just talking to talk. Either way, he wasn't amused. His hand clenched and unclenched on the hilt of his sword. "We've stayed in one place too long. Tell me where we're going and let's get moving."

Lyn folded the map up and tucked it away. She opened her mouth and let herself say whatever came out. "Telrisht."

"Fine." There was no way to tell from his tone whether he approved of the choice or not. He started walking, long strides right past her without looking back to be sure she was following. "I know a place not far off. We can get horses there."

Lyn had never been on a horse before. She wasn't sure she wanted to, or that she'd know what to do once she was up there, but she wasn't in any hurry to say that to this obnoxiously competent, dangerous man. She scrambled to catch up to him. "By 'get' you don't by any chance mean 'steal,' do you?"

His head came up stiffly, but he didn't look back at her. "There's a man owes me a favor," he answered, more curtly than usual.

She decided she had hurt his feelings. She waited until she was walking beside him, then peered up into his face. His expression was, as usual, bland and unreadable. "I mean, it'd be okay if you did plan to steal them," she extended as a generous peace offering. "I know you're just trying to keep me safe." Which she guessed she appreciated, considering that she'd be dead right now with a hole in her chest if not for him.

A look out of the corner of his eye told her what he thought of her peace offering, but he didn't say anything.

It was the season of sudden wind storms in Telrisht, the kind that sent walls of sand crashing across the arid landscape, leaving behind a path of devastation. Naoise and his token retinue – a valet and a single guard, minimal escort for a prince of the realm on official diplomatic business – had to batten down more than once on their journey. Despite the fact that it was now technically autumn, the heat had not yet broken. The people hated them and the land itself was no more hospitable. They were glad to put the place behind them.

The climate changed quickly over the border as the road climbed to a higher elevation and water became more plentiful, but that was not the comfort it should have been.

Coming to Mysia after the long trek through Telrisht was like entering another world. Specifically, it was like leaving the real world behind for a dream of the Lesser Demon's realm of eternal misery.

The Dread Abysm itself could not have been a more desolate place.

It was nearing dusk when they came to what should have been the border village of Eyso. After almost a score of days in the hostile Telrishti countryside, Naoise was eager for a bath and a deep sleep in neutral territory. He imagined his companions felt the same way.

But there was no rest to be had in Eyso.

The bleak scenery was the first clue. The fields through which they passed had been burned, the blackened skeletons of trees a forlorn silhouette against the sullen sky. The local fauna had fled to more hospitable pastures. The resulting silence was nothing short of unnerving. Not a single vole, finch, or fellow traveler did they see as they approached what should have been civilization.

An abandoned farmhouse with its roof collapsed stared at them in mute accusation from gaping, empty windows. The fields themselves had been raided before destruction, bare stalks lying haphazard and reduced to char on the dead soil. A faint stench lingered from the burning, clinging to the landscape with the persistence of death.

Naturally, this raised questions.

The soldier, Nicol, cleared his throat several times as they rode toward the eerie quiet of Eyso, but he never said anything. Lonan was a palpable source of anxiety, riding behind them both. Naoise had no words of reassurance to offer either of them. He himself was still trying to determine what it all meant. Their horses felt the strangeness and had to be coaxed onward, ears twitching and eyes rounding.

The three of them edged past the first outlying buildings and were not surprised when they saw no motion within. The village had been burned, just like the farmhouse. Everything was black and hollow, insubstantial as a dream after several rains. An ash-laced mist crawled through the streets to meet them, the only movement beside their own. A cheerless impression rose to Naoise's mind, unbidden, that they might be the only three people in the world left alive. There was no night noise to ease the sense of the unreal.

Naoise tried to suppress a shudder, knowing his men were watching him. They were apprehensive enough already.

"What do you suppose happened here, my lord?" Lonan blurted. His too-loud words were swallowed by the dead quiet as if it hungered for the sounds of life.

The prince shook his head and motioned for the valet to lower his voice. "Let us see what there is to be found out."

Something crashed in the distance, a sudden dim explosion of sound – wood falling on wood. His startled horse shied back a pace. Naoise steadied the beast with both hands and a soothing word before it could drive the other animals to panic.

He loosened his sword in its scabbard, and they rode deeper into the ghostly village.

Telrisht? Could they be responsible for this? This *was* their wartime practice: burning all farmholds through which they passed, and putting to death any enemy civilian in their path. But what would it mean if they had taken the war to Mysian soil? Did it prove Mysia was involved after all, or that they weren't? And if not Telrisht, who else could Mysia be at war with? How far in did the devastation go?

"Could this have been the Rahd?" Nicol whispered beside him.

Naoise eyed the black remains of the half-timbered village tavern. Something about the Telrishti assumption felt off, but he couldn't say why. He brought his horse's nervous steps to a halt and eased out of the saddle. A cloud of fine black ash swirled beneath his boots. His companions stared at him apprehensively for a moment, then Nicol joined him. So, after a moment, did Lonan. No doubt he had no wish to be left alone in the settling gloom.

Approaching the building with caution, looking for the safest way in, Naoise tried to figure out what it was that felt wrong.

"My lord, I don't think we should – it's not safe," Nicol advised. "The whole thing could come down any moment."

Naoise glanced at the soldier to show he acknowledged the concern, but went back to studying the ruin. After a moment of calculation, he traced a course over board and under beam into the heart of the devastation. When the others moved to follow, he motioned them back.

"I will be safer on my own," he explained as softly as he could and still be heard. The last thing he needed was to bring the upper floor down with his voice. "Stay with the horses and keep them calm."

His companions didn't like it, but they obeyed, and Naoise went on alone. He came out again only a moment later, soot-smeared and troubled. He couldn't make any sense of what he was seeing.

"There's nothing," he murmured to himself.

"My lord?" Nicol watched him intently for an answer.

Naoise raised his eyes to the view down the street, and across it, all about them, turning in a slow circle. Everywhere, it was the same thing. The truth slid into place.

"It's all destroyed," he said, "but not ravaged. The Telrishti... they raid. Everything here was burned as it was, nothing taken." Except for the crops, he realized. The fields had been stripped while the town burned intact. "And where are the bodies?" Not a one in sight nor a single carrion bird in the sky to show them where to look.

Nicol and Lonan both were watching him with wide, dark eyes, hoping he was about to supply them with the answers to these mysteries.

But there were no answers here – only more questions. Disquieting ones.

Another crash sounded, echoes swallowed by the creeping mist. Nicol's sword was out of its sheath faster than Naoise could have told him to be on his guard. The sound was followed by a low moan.

The prince and his men shared an uneasy glance. Something was alive out there after all.

"We should ride on," Lonan pleaded in a whisper pitched high by fear.

"All will be well," Naoise assured him though he felt no such confidence. "Wait here with the horses. Nicol, come with me."

"My lord, please," the valet squeaked.

Naoise briefly gripped Lonan's shoulder, but could not release him from the charge. He nodded to Nicol and together the two of them moved off in search of whatever still lived in this place of ash and shadows.

As they passed through the remains of Eyso, Naoise observed more of the same truth: there was no evidence of looting, and no sign that those living here had made any attempt to flee with their belongings. No sign either that any effort had been made to quench the flames. It was as if the entire town had simply vanished one night.

There wasn't much to the village – just one main thoroughfare with houses and a few trade shops fanning out in either direction. Before the burning, it had probably been home to fewer than a thousand souls. It did not take long to find the origin of the disturbance. Nor would it have taken an expert tracker to read the trail left through the ubiquitous soot.

"Your Highness, let me," Nicol said as they stared at the cellar hatch the small tracks had led them to. The house that had once stood on this plot was utterly destroyed, only charred floorboards now covering whatever lay beneath.

Or whomever.

"Go first if you like," Naoise allowed, "but I'm coming down as well."

Nicol nodded as though he had expected that answer, then waited a moment while the prince went back for a lantern from the saddlebags.

The hatch moaned when they eased it open. This was the sound they'd heard from the street outside the tavern, Naoise recognized. He followed Nicol and the light down a much-used ladder into the damp, cold cellar. The weak beam cast by their lantern against the darkness allowed him to see that this had once been the storeroom of a modestly wealthy household. The cell was roughly seven meters square and mazed with shelves. Many of them still held canned goods, though more than a few of the ceramic jars had shattered from the intense heat overhead during the burning.

But the shelves were not the only thing down here. Naoise could hear the desperately muffled breathing in the far corner.

"Show yourself, please," he said quietly. "We will not harm you."

The frightened breathing hitched, but there was no movement from the figure he knew to be huddled in the corner.

"Nicol, sheathe your sword," Naoise instructed. The soldier obeyed after a moment of hesitation. "You see?" he said into the darkness. "We are not your enemy. They have gone." When there was still no movement in the shadows, Naoise gestured Nicol forward with their small light.

The foot that first came into view within the dim yellow halo was so black that Naoise did not at first recognize it for what it was. When their beam had illuminated more – a knobby, scraped knee, a pair of soot-black hands raised in defense, a mop of filthy hair – he finally understood that they were looking at a frightened girl. She stared back at them with wide eyes that were more than half mad.

Naoise crouched before her and spoke gently in Mysian. "Are you all alone down here, little one?"

A whimper escaped the girl.

She was huddled upon a dirty blanket and a pile of rags that must have been her bed, Naoise noticed. She'd been living down here since the disaster that had claimed her village, all alone and left to shift for herself in the burnt-out carcass of her former life. Naoise was moved to pity.

"Come up into the light with us, child," he offered. "It's safe now, and we'll see that you get a hot meal." He extended a hand, but the girl shrank away.

"Shall I carry her out, my lord?" Nicol asked, squaring his shoulders in anticipation of the task.

Naoise shook his head. "She's frightened enough as it is." He reached out slowly, watching her track his movement with wild eyes, until he was just a finger's breadth from her hand. When she made no indication of flinching or biting, he reached the rest of the way and took her hand.

She screamed and jerked back, but he kept hold.

"Y-you," she croaked. Her voice had not been used in some time, but the sound of it told Naoise that she was older than he had originally estimated. This girl was thirteen, maybe fourteen. "You're... *real*."

He forced himself to smile despite the fact that his heart was racing. There had been a primal terror in her scream. "Yes, we're real, and we're going to help you."

"You're real," she repeated, voice cracking. "You're real."

"That's right," he confirmed. The bleak dread in her voice was making him feel nauseated.

"Come now," Nicol put in. The slight quaver in his words betrayed that he was feeling the same thing. "Let us help you out of this pit, girl."

She blinked up at the soldier. "Shades and shadows," she whispered.

Nicol swallowed. "She's mad, my lord."

Naoise searched her eyes for the spark of reason and couldn't find it. "Not surprising," he said grimly, "but she may yet be able to give us some clue as to what happened here." He carefully firmed his grip on her hand and moved to cup her elbow. "Come, my dear. Let us take a walk beneath the stars."

"Nothing but shades and shadows," she repeated breathlessly, but she did not object when he stood and brought her to her feet with him.

Nicol needed no prompting to lead them back out under the sky.

Even after a meal and three hours safe in Naoise's care, the girl wasn't speaking. Over his companions' objections, they made camp on what in better days had been the village green. Naoise didn't want to stray too far from Eyso until he had a clearer idea of what had happened here, what had happened to the lone survivor.

He needed answers. Unfortunately, she seemed unable or unwilling to provide them. He could not fault her.

Their campfire did little to hold back the gloom and crawling mist of the place, and Lonan was jumping at every crackle of the firewood. Naoise's bodyguard was only marginally less edgy, and neither of them were helping to put the traumatized child at ease.

Naoise studied her, first while she ate and then as she crouched as far away from the fire as she could while still remaining secure within its circle of light. Her entire body was covered in so many layers of soot that it was impossible to tell what she looked like or even what color her hair was, but she had the slack, desperate look of one who had not eaten well in weeks. It was clear that she had been living on scraps – for how long, Naoise hated to imagine.

Beyond that, she had obviously been damaged by whatever she'd witnessed in Eyso. To every offer or inquiry he made, she had so far returned nothing more than some whispered madness about shadows. There had to be some truth in it somewhere, but it was impossible to judge.

"Are you ready to tell us your name?" he tried again, as soothingly as he could.

The girl jumped at the sound of his voice and stared at him as though she had forgotten her earlier decision to believe he was real. She opened her mouth and closed it again, but no words were forthcoming.

"This is useless," Nicol declared from the other side of the fire. "She's cracked. Most like the Telrishti made her watch while they did her family – that'd be enough to make me want to forget everything I ever knew."

She darted a glance at Nicol then ducked her head as if trying to hide in plain sight. "Not people, shadows. You can't run from shadows. Can't run when it's already over."

Naoise listened distractedly, trying to come up with an explanation for Eyso that made sense. He shook his head at the soldier. "I don't think it was Telrisht." Someone just wanted it to look that way. "It doesn't make any sense. They're stretched thin enough on the eastern front and barely holding; why would they rouse an enemy to flank them, one that had stayed aloof from the war all these years?"

"All dead," the girl added, then repeated herself as if once simply did not express just how dead her entire village was.

"But if not Telrisht, then who?" Nicol argued.

"NOT PEOPLE!" the girl screamed suddenly, her voice a shrill accusation against the darkness.

Dead silence hung over the camp following that cry.

A log snapped in the fire and Lonan squeaked embarrassingly. Nicol let out a nervous sigh and Naoise unclenched his fists. Despite the chill night air, he found that his palms were damp.

"What are we going to do with her?" Lonan whispered, looking into the fire and not at the prince as he asked.

"We can't leave her here," Naoise temporized. In truth, he wasn't sure *what* to do with the girl. "I suppose we ought to take her with us until we find civilization, someone who can care for her."

Nicol grunted but didn't object. The valet seemed like he wanted to.

"The shadows made them disappear," the girl breathed, eyes wide and staring at Naoise as if she was looking through him into the blackness beyond. "But not me. I made myself disappear. When I was real again, it was over. They were never here."

"She's got to stop that," Lonan whined, terror at the edge of his voice.

"Get a hold of yourself, man," Nicol exhorted nervously.

Naoise drew a deep breath and fixed first one of them and then the other with a steady eye. "Both of you, hear me say this. The girl stays with us, and you will treat her with the courtesy due a lady. She has survived a horror we cannot comprehend because someone out there doesn't want us to. Someone is playing with all of our lives like game pieces on a blood-soaked board, setting us to destroy one another, laughing at our blind obedience to the pattern, *his* pattern. Killing us with impunity while we chase shadows we think we've cast ourselves." Both men were watching him, and even the girl had stopped muttering to listen, though he suspected she had no idea what he was saying.

"Whoever, whatever this someone is, I *will* find him out," he went on quietly, "if I have to search to the farthest corner of Asrellion to do so. And when I do, with my own hands I will make him choke on that laughter for the lives he has taken here and in Telrisht and at home in Grenlec. For the suffering he has caused, and the ruin. The kind of evil that would plunge all the world into death and darkness to slake some unknown thirst must not be allowed a place in Asrellion. It will not. By the Father, I swear he will be stopped."

# CHAPTER NINE

The bright leaves of autumn had begun their spectacular farewell to the year, and the air was crisp with the promise of cooler weather soon to come. The silver-leaved mitallía trees were burnished golden. Hints of distant song, and the lush scents of the harvest, drifted to the crowd gathered about the practice green in the shade of the Crystal Palace. It would be Festival soon.

Something of the carnival atmosphere seemed to have descended already upon the people of Efrondel. Loralíenasa saw smiles and high spirits in the audience that had come to watch her fight the Captain of the Guard, and smiles were a rare sight indeed in Evlédíen. It was true that she and Lanoralas had concocted a public and deliberately absurd rivalry in the weeks leading up to this duel in the hope of amusing *someone*. Their people needed it, they both agreed.

The performance seemed to have been a success. Most of the court had turned out, and the Guard, as well as much of the city. But, conspicuously, not the Lord Regent.

Loríen could imagine Tomanasíl looking down in judgment from his office window in the palace, frowning at the sight of her with a sword in her hand in front of so many spectators, determined not to dignify her behavior with acknowledgment. The image brightened her already excellent mood.

Lanoralas Galvan – her instructor in the sword, oldest friend, Captain of the Royal Guard, and least odious formal suitor – grinned at her from his corner of the roped-off fighting field. Despite his family's lofty status in the Valley and his own position of power, there was a frankness about the young captain that she found refreshing. Never more so than now, as he flipped his tail of ash blond hair back over his shoulder and informed her in a ringing voice for their audience's benefit that she was about to be humiliated before her subjects if she thought to prove herself his better.

Their spectators liked that a great deal, the Captain's supporters laughing and cheering him on. Riding the wave of the jocund mood, Loríen called back that he ought not to try too hard or he might break an aging hip on their first pass.

She could see him laughing at that as he gave his curved practice sword several test swings for the sake of those looking on. Lanoralas was, of course, not much older than Loríen – scarcely an adult himself, as she was often fond of pointing out when she was irritated with him. Usually when he was correcting her form or assigning particularly tedious drills.

"Impertinent little girl!" Lanoralas said to his Míyahídéna.

"Slow old man!" she replied breezily.

Scarcely had the words left her mouth but the Captain had crossed the green and was inside her guard, taking a precisely-judged swipe at her shoulder. Loríen spun out of the way, into a return cut aimed at the back of his neck that she knew he would dodge. He was gone before her sword could reach him, smiling at her from outside her range.

The crowd cheered the first pass, the Guard calling words of advice.

"Better not lose, sir, or we'll have to make *her* Captain of the Guard!" one guardsman taunted.

Their audience chuckled. Lanoralas spared a stage glare for his soldier.

Loríen took the initiative, throwing a flashy off-time series of thrusts for the entertainment of those watching. Lanas easily caught her intent and the sequence, meeting each attack but offering none of his own. The real contest had not yet begun; this was all for show.

She could see the change in his eyes, the moment he decided to be serious. Lanoralas was playful by nature, but swordwork was his life and his entire body was a natural weapon. He was also the finest fighter the Valley had ever seen, and though she was his best student, she had never beaten him in practice unless he wanted her to. She didn't consider it impossible that today might be the day, but only if she gave her all. She took a deep, centering breath to slow her suddenly leaping heartbeat.

He snaked his blade toward her with redoubled concentration, investigating. She parried easily and followed it up with an attack of her own, which he in turn easily blocked. Another beat passed as they sized up each other's defense. He was not dismissing her as a threat, which she accepted as a compliment and a helpful boost to her ego. She had a chance here, and he was admitting it.

All at once they began to trade blows so blindingly fast that the onlookers had difficulty following their progress.

A new intensity descended over the practice field, the only movement that of the two combatants. The series ended when Lanas' practice edge scored a thin red line of glowing energy across Loralíenasa's bicep, marking the wound he should have inflicted. She felt an accompanying sting that told her the cut would be a deep one. Her right arm would not have much fight left in it, she knew.

She made a decision that she hoped would not cost her the duel, tossing her sword over to her off-hand before Lanas could react. He smiled at her again, a more calculated expression than she saw from him anywhere but in combat, but he spared no more speech before bringing his sword back in line for another attack.

The crowd devoured the action, roaring when the Captain made his cut and cheering when the Míyahídéna kept fighting.

They fell to again, once more moving their blades so quickly their audience could not follow, eating up the field with their footwork. Lanoralas' supporters were sure now that he would win, but Lanoralas himself had taught her to be just as deadly with either hand. Wild speculations were flying as to which of them would prove to be the best fighter in the Valley.

They never had a chance to settle the question.

A young elf in the palace messengers' silver and blue livery came sprinting onto the field, horror twisting his face. "Míyahídéna!" he cried in a tone she had never heard before. Desperation, fear, something else dark and forceful, just on the verge of erupting into chaos.

Loralíenasa flung up a hand to call a halt, but Lanoralas was already lowering his weapon, his eyes on the frightened messenger.

"Míyahídéna," the boy repeated when he was closer, "the Lord Regent requires your presence. *Urgently!*"

Prompted by some sense, Loralíenasa looked beyond him and saw Tomanasíl approaching from the palace in haste, flanked by a member of the Guard. Oh, spite. Had he really felt he needed to come out himself to put a stop to their duel? After putting abject fear of the Abyss into this poor lad? And he was always calling *her* a child.

"He requires my presence?" she echoed dryly. "It seems that he could not bring himself to miss the sport after all."

The messenger whirled in surprise at her words to see the Regent making his way toward them. So he hadn't known Tomanasíl was following.

"You seem to be in some trouble," Lanas observed mildly.

The gathered audience murmured, some with amusement and others with concern, as they took in the changing situation.

But Loríen was noticing something in her guardian's steps. Tension rather than anger. Haste born not of righteous exasperation but of fear. When he was close enough for her to read his face, she saw his precise umber features contorted in a mask of grief. She had never before seen him show so much emotion of any kind, and he was doing so now *in public*.

What looked like a bit of folded parchment flapped in his hand as he walked. Loríen couldn't believe, a moment later, that she had spotted that detail before noticing the blood on the guardsman's blues.

She was suddenly acutely aware of their sizable audience, and in that same heartbeat she also knew that Tomanasíl was not. Fear washed over her, cold and paralyzing.

"Loríen," he began at far too great a distance, his voice pitched so that it could be heard by far too many, "something has happened." There was a terrible weight in each of those three innocent words.

Her eyes went to the guardsman's bloodied uniform, and again to the paper in her guardian's hands. "Perhaps this is something we should discuss in private, my lord."

Tomanasíl kept coming as though she had said nothing. "Something has happened," he repeated, "and a message has come for you." He sounded like a man who had struck his head and was uncertain of his own name.

"For me?" Loríen could not stop herself from echoing. "From whom?" Her eyes went back to the blood, drawn against her will. Nothing was right, here.

"I don't know," Tomanasíl answered, too loud, too flat. "I can't open the message."

She looked into his eyes and saw them numb with shock. "You *can't* open the message?"

He held it out to her. She saw that the message in question was a neatly-folded square of parchment sealed with blood red wax. The crest pressed into it appeared to be some vicious hunting bird poised to attack. She also saw that the hand presenting the message to her was scorched raw. When she took it from him, she felt a distinct thrill of power against her skin. Her full name was written in careful letters on the other side of the folded square.

Even though she knew, rationally, that she needed to disperse the crowd and get Tomanasíl somewhere quiet, Loríen was too intrigued and horrified to stop herself from asking, "How did this message come into your possession?"

It was the guard to his left who answered that, and she wished he hadn't. "My lady, I am Sergeant Callas, of the Border Guard. My unit was set upon in the mountains and slaughtered to a man. I escaped with my life only because they wanted it so, that I might deliver this message."

Lanoralas made an angry sound behind her, but she was too stunned to look back at him. "Who did this?" she demanded. More importantly, who knew of the Valley's secret location? Knew not only their whereabouts and the disposition of the Border Guard, but also her name? And the attack itself—

It was Lanas who asked the question for her. "Your unit – which side of the mountains were you patrolling?"

The guard frowned, grief and exhaustion etching deep lines in his face, but he saluted his captain before answering. "Were we attacked within the protective field, you mean? Aye, I'm afraid so. As for the who, I cannot say much." He shook his head tiredly. "They came on us out of the rocks like shadows, covered in black from hair to heel, and slew my men with never a word spoken. I took a hit that knocked me out, and when I came around that message was in my hand."

Loralíenasa looked again at the ominous letter she now held. The one Tomanasíl could not open. She broke the seal. Nothing happened. Her guardian let out a slow breath. She unfolded the creases and stared down at the neat writing in an ancient hand no longer used by her people, aware of the Captain's breath on the back of her neck. Tomanasíl came up on her other side and followed along as she read.

*"To the Míyahídéna Loralíenasa Níelor Raia of Evlédien, from Lord Katakí Kuromé of the freeholding of Mornnovin.*

*"I am as yet unknown to you, but that will soon change. These past centuries since the humans attempted our extermination, I have been building toward a remedy for that offense. Long have I stood as the sole guardian of the evlé'í legacy, as the people and the leaders of your Evlédien have cowered shamefully in their hole. I am our one hope of reclaiming a place in Asrellion. Before another year has passed, humans will be no more, and the rebuilding of our power shall finally begin.*

*"This message will be your one warning: do not hinder me in my work. You have by now seen evidence that the paltry magicians' shield about your borders, that you believe impregnable, poses no impediment to me. If you choose to raise your swords in defiance, I will break them.*

*"If, instead, you sit as still as you have through all the impotent years of*

*your exile and wait for me to destroy our enemies, I will be forgiving in the hour of victory. It is possible the two of us can come to an arrangement, Miyahídéna, for the continued existence of Evlédíen and the safety of her people.*

*"I require no answer, merely your forbearance as I complete my task. To ensure the proper decision, I offer a final reminder of the futility of pitting yourself as my enemy."*

Loríen looked up from the parchment, hardly seeing. In that moment, from the dazzling blue of a clear sky, a bolt of lightning slammed into the ground in the dead center of the practice green. Screams erupted from the audience, instant chaos descending upon the scene. Loríen could feel the shock reverberating inside her body, smell the stench of charred earth.

The Captain began calling for calm and order, but they were not to be had.

In the dream, Loríen was cold.

Snow and sky mirrored one another, stark whites and shadow blacks meeting and melding like the finger-paints of a sullen god. The only line separating their reality was the mist-shrouded darkness of majestic pine robed in ice – two rows of their solemn silence divided by a pristine strip of diamond-white snow. A narrow path between absolutes.

At the end of that path, the frozen air obscured the form of a man standing alone.

Even though he was too far away and the mist was close to opaque, Loríen knew the man. She began to walk in his direction and with dream-suddenness found herself before him.

Naoise wore a battered breastplate and greaves figured with the image of a many-branched tree, and a green cloak flowed from his shoulders. His eyes were a complexity of grief and need. He looked up at her only for a moment before returning his attention to the small object cradled gingerly in his gloved hands.

Loríen looked down and saw that it was a heart, and she knew that it was his. Live, red, veined and bloody and beating. Only, in the dream, there was no sound. Not to the biting wind that should have been whistling through pine boughs or to her footsteps crunching over snow, or to the living thing pulsing in Naoise's hands.

The silence seemed to roar inside her ears.

He stared at her in mute appeal. Even as his sad eyes bored into hers, the heart erupted into purple flames within his grasp. The firelight danced against the snow. Loríen knew she was shouting, but the silence reigned unbroken. Something drew her eye past the flames, and she saw standing behind Naoise a figure whose face she could not describe though she was staring into it.

It was all impression – a feeling of coldness, of control, of old anger.

She still had the image in her mind, of the look on Naoise's face as his heart burned silently, when she awoke.


An emergency council had not convened in Evlédíen since the deaths of King Andras and Queen Melíara, more than a century past. With the Harunomíya dead or gone in the same attack that claimed them both, and the sole surviving member of the family far too young to assume any responsibility herself, the power vacuum was an immediate problem. The lords and ladies of the Eleven Noble Houses had met in haste to remedy that.

Their decision at that time had provoked a great deal of controversy since.

Tomanasíl Maiantar was young, green, of a relatively unimportant house, and had no desire for a position of any authority. What he did have was a promise he refused to relinquish. To Gallanas, who had charged him in those last moments of blood and chaos on that distant road to find and take care of his young sister no matter what. When he informed the council of this promise and would not step aside in favor of a more experienced appointed guardian, the esteemed lords and ladies decided that giving him the Regency was the only way he could learn what he needed to teach her.

Dark days, those. The Valley in chaos, their royal family as old as Time itself all but gone. Everyone looking to someone else to have an answer, to bring the spinning to a halt.

This was just like those days.

Loralíenasa, of course, had only Tomanasíl's word for the comparison, and he was hardly in a mood for idle chatter just now. It was Lanoralas who told her in a whisper during the strained civility of the council that Lord Síthí hadn't been this upset since Tomanasíl was made Regent. She believed it. She had never seen Lord Síthí have an emotion before today.

When the assembled lords and ladies left the chill beauty of the council chamber after several hours of verbal hand-wringing, all any of them had managed to decide was that they did not want to die. An admirable resolution to be sure, Loralíenasa thought with some annoyance, but it hardly addressed the real issues. In fact, not much change from the default attitude of Evlédíen as a whole.

Tomanasíl sat slumped at the head of the black marble table, staring sightlessly at the swirling silver inlay, long after the last noble had gone. The silence reminded her of her nightmare. She had been trying not to think about it. Every time she did, she felt a heaviness that seemed to radiate from her gut until it was pulling even her fingertips toward the ground. It was obvious enough what she was afraid of, without having to dwell on the pointed imagery.

She watched her guardian, wishing she knew what to say. Wishing he would listen to her if she *did* know what to say.

The Captain had lingered behind. He exchanged a long look with her, and she knew he was having the same thought.

"Lord Maiantar," he said finally, "I await your command. Tell me what I am to do, and I will do it."

"I never asked for this," the Regent murmured. "I never wanted the responsibility. Damn you, Gallanas."

Lanoralas looked at her again, eyebrows raised. She gestured with fingers entwined, palms up, to indicate her uncertainty. She didn't know what tangent had her guardian tripped up at the moment, but there was no time to follow him into whatever territory this was.

"What do you intend to do?" she prompted. "The Houses were less than helpful, but at least that means you have license. They can hardly complain that you're acting against their consensus if they never came to one."

Beside her, Lanas snorted his amusement at that.

Tomanasíl regarded her with some surprise, misery etched into his dark brow. "What *can* I do?"

"Stop him!" Loríen blurted. How was he not as outraged as she over this?

He shook his head at the table. "*Stop* him? Child, even if we could stop this Katakí Kuromé, why would we? Why risk everything we've managed to preserve to save the very humans who want us dead?"

Loríen couldn't believe she was hearing Tomanasíl say this, even though a part of her had known this would be his reaction. "These are not the very humans who *anything*," she objected with a real effort to keep the heat out of her voice. The last thing she needed was for her guardian to dismiss her arguments on the grounds that she was failing to control her emotions. "There probably isn't even a human alive today who could trace his lineage back to the days of the War. Do you not understand how long ago that was for them? We are myths to them now."

Tomanasíl opened his mouth to deliver a cutting retort, but Lanoralas spoke over him.

"What about Mysia? You would abandon them to their fate as well?"

Loralíenasa added her silent agreement with all her heart, relieved that she had an ally in the Captain.

"I regret we cannot help Mysia, but what would you have me do, Lanoralas?" the Regent demanded.

"At least do some reconnaissance," the Captain proposed. "We know nothing about this Katakí Kuromé. You cannot trust his word to leave us in peace, even if he promised such a thing. He murdered our men unprovoked just to send a message. For all you know, this hint at forbearance might just hinge on a forced marriage with the Míyahídéna."

Oh, Vaian. Loríen hadn't even thought of that. Her innards twisted.

"And if he detects our agents, he will have them killed as well and any future discussion of peace will be out of the question." Tomanasíl shook his head. "We cannot risk angering an enemy so powerful that our barriers mean nothing to him."

"We can't afford to ignore him, either," Loralíenasa argued. Lanas glanced at her and nodded.

The Lord Regent of Evlédíen looked back and forth between her and the Captain of the Royal Guard, as twitchy as cornered prey. "I truly know not what you would have me do. It appears we are doomed no matter what we choose. I'd rather take the course that leads us to it less quickly, and perhaps circumstances will change."

Loríen shook her head. "You want a miracle."

"The world is only full of absolutes when you're young," her guardian told her in a tone she did not care for. "But there are more shades than black and white. Sometimes there are no good choices, only ones that are less bad."

"But you're choosing the worst," Loríen argued flatly, "if you plan to do nothing."

Lanoralas leaned across the table toward Tomanasíl. "Please, my lord, allow me to send out scouts. We'll determine the situation outside the Valley and *then* decide what to do. Or not do. You have my word that stealth will be key."

Tomanasíl was silent for a long time. Loralíenasa realized she was holding her breath, and forced herself to let it out slowly. At last he flattened both palms carefully against the marble table-top and said, "No."

"Lord Maiantar," Lanoralas began.

"No," Tomanasíl repeated. There was frost in his pale blue eyes as he fixed them first on the Captain and then on her. "I've seen this kingdom through many troubles in the last century, since your parents died." He sounded more tired and young and frightened than she could ever have imagined him capable of. "But nothing has prepared me for this. *I don't know what to do.*"

The Míyahídéna stared at her guardian, unsure of everything she had thought she'd known an hour ago.

All her life, Tomanasíl had been the rock that weathered every storm. He had always been so strong, so competent. For her, until now, the definition of Authority. She had no memories of her own parents aside from the confused images of infancy, and he had always been so much like a father to her that she often forgot how young he was. Most elves his age would be just marrying or graduating to journeyman at their crafts, if not still exploring the blithe freedom of their youth. He had borne the burden of acting as Regent for the kingdom as well as the responsibility of raising the heir to the throne, and he had done so with a quiet grace she could not help but admit even when she thought him too cold. As he'd said, he had seen Evlédíen through many difficult times.

And now he sat helpless as a babe while an invader threatened their home – threatened the known world in the name of vengeance. Loríen felt her heart contract with pained love for this man, the only parent she'd known, as she acknowledged to herself that he was not the infallible authority figure she had always needed him to be.

It was a hard truth to swallow, but he was just a man. A scared, young man with more power than he knew how to use.

And right now, he was wrong.

Loralíenasa and the Captain shared a glance, and she knew that the two of them were going to handle this on their own, whether Tomanasíl wanted them to or not.


As Naoise and his escort rode through the Mysian countryside, they encountered only more obliterated villages like Eyso and other towns living in terror of meeting their neighbors' fate.

No one was willing to take in the orphaned girl who traveled with them.

She was unsettling and said things no one wanted to hear about death and shadows, and they viewed her as an ill omen. One kindhearted matron at least bathed the girl, scrubbing the soot from her skin and brushing out her tangled hair. Now that she was clean and dressed in something other than rags, it was finally possible to see that the girl was in early adolescence, that her skin was the soft golden brown of a desert thrush, and that she was as fine-boned and fragile as that same bird.

She was still out of her mind, though.

The mysterious attacks did not seem to have advanced into the heart of the kingdom, but the fear was everywhere. The more he saw, the more Naoise felt in his heart that this was not a kingdom masterminding the destruction of mighty foes. He also came to be certain that Telrisht did not have a hand in what was happening here.

Zarishan was near the center of Mysia. By the time Naoise reached the capital, he knew what he would find there: the city was operating in a heightened state of panicked near-chaos.

Citizens went about their errands constantly watching for danger, the brightness of Mysian clothing and the broad, un-Grenlecian diversity of the people's coloring only adding to the jarring sense of too much energy under the circumstances. Conscripts were pouring in from the surrounding farmland, assembling in the city's wide courtyards with fear brittle in their every movement. Churchyards were bustling with crowds of the newly-devout come to pray for their lives. Doomsayers littered the busy market square, decrying Telrisht and the end of the long Forbearance.

All of the frenetic activity had Nicol on edge. He growled his response when Naoise told him to take his hand off his sword hilt as they rode through the market district. The soldier's obviously Grenlecian appearance wasn't winning the trust of the people as it was. Naoise didn't feel it would exactly help their cause to antagonize a crowd that was already pulsing with a fear of outsiders.

They made their way up the high street, past the exotic Mysian structures with their carved posts and lintels supporting gently curved rooflines with extended decorative eaves. Roof shingles were bright, walls primarily wood. Naoise noticed, taking it all in with some amount of fascination, that the Mysians used almost no stone in their construction. Gardens were part of homes, not accents to them. Buildings were made to blend into their natural environment rather than stand apart from it. The overall feel was completely unlike Dewfern, alien in a way that was also different from Telrisht's strangeness.

The Royal Palace, located at the highest point of the city, was a fine example of Zarishan's diversity. It stood on its hill as a glittering example of several hundred years of evolving architectural styles. At its sprawling foundation it was grey stone, but each level had the gleam of a different variety of Mysian wood. The gabled roofs, bright with jade green shingles, were smaller at each successive floor of the palace, terminating in a fluted golden spire flying the blue and white sun flag of Mysia.

Nicol shook his head the entire way to the palace, muttering something about foreigners and their damn unsettling ways. Naoise wondered how true the stories were – how much the Mysian aesthetic drew from the ancient elves who had been their allies.

As they approached the massive wooden gates barring their way into the palace courtyard, they were intercepted by a handful of armored soldiers.

"Halt, strangers, and state your business," the ranking soldier demanded. There was no welcome in his face as he took in their Grenlecian clothing and armor. This was not the protocol of a Mysia at peace, Naoise felt certain. Or perhaps he would find his reception here the same, as a Grenlecian, but he didn't like to imagine there was so much distrust in the world.

A smile would have been inappropriate, given the situation, but Naoise was careful to assume a palliative mien as he answered. "Good day to you, friend. I am Naoise, Duke of Lakeside, son of Lorn the King of Grenlec, come for an audience with your king." He showed his signet, to forestall any unnecessary debate.

The Mysian officer grunted and swept him with an appraising eye. "You will forgive me, my lord. These are not times in which we expect friendly visitors." He gestured for the gates to be opened. They swung apart slowly, groaning as they moved.

Naoise nodded. "Your caution is prudent, sir. I assure you we find no offense in it."

It was Nicol's turn to grunt, but Naoise held out a warning hand and the soldier subsided. The three of them and their oblivious passenger rode through the gates into the lush garden of the palace courtyard.

## Chapter Ten

The austere elegance inside the palace was at odds with the panic in the city, throwing into sharp relief just how unlike itself Mysia was at the moment. It was a serene world of polished woods and fine silks, graceful pillars and soaring ceilings, of air and light without the ostentation Naoise had left behind in Telrisht.

The serenity of the space was somewhat spoiled by the nervous clusters of palace officials rushing through the halls.

Even though the palace steward obligingly led Naoise to a sumptuous sitting room appointed with every comfort he could wish for, and showed his companions where they might rest until he needed them, more than an hour passed before anyone came to speak with him.

The man who entered the parlor at last was neither the King of Mysia nor another servant. His skin was the rich, mild color of ashwood and he had sharp features in the manner the Mysians called the Old Blood look, crowned by long golden hair that had to be a source of pride to him. His clothing was bright and beautifully embellished, of the style Naoise had seen on his way through Zarishan: loose, flowing trousers tucked into calf-hugging boots that came up just to the knee; and a shirt that hung down to the middle of the thigh under an even longer coat, both of them girdled by a wide, intricately-tooled leather belt.

Naoise rose to greet the newcomer, who did not bow as the steward had.

"My apologies that you have been kept waiting," the solemn-faced man said at once in Common. His Mysian accent was nearly undetectable, the mark of a well-educated noble. "I am Enyokoto." Eldest son of the king, Naoise knew. "And you, I am told, are one of my Grenlecian brothers. This is unexpected, but you are welcome to Zarishan."

It was not unreasonable for the prince to be the one to greet him, but Naoise sensed that all was not right here. He gave the Mysian a closer look.

Prince Enyokoto was a handsome man not much older than Naoise's brother Dairinn, but there were worry lines etched deep around his eyes and mouth. He gave the impression of being an open man by nature, one who hated secrets and lately had been made to keep many. The strain of it showed in him, in the tightness of those lines in his face.

Naoise might have been moved to greater sympathy if he was not so concerned for the welfare of his own people. If Enyokoto – if Mysia – was hiding anything that could help him untangle the whole mess, he could not afford to tiptoe around it until someone felt like sharing the truth.

"Enyokoto," Naoise echoed, pleasantly enough. "I am Naoise Raynesley. I could wish the circumstances prompting this visit were better, but it is a pleasure to meet you in any event. I look forward to being likewise honored by a meeting with your royal father."

The Mysian prince made a hasty effort to conceal his grimace in response to that, but wasn't fast enough. "Yes, well. My father the king is terribly busy. As you no doubt saw for yourself in your journey across the countryside, these are dark days for Mysia."

"They are dark days for all of Asrellion," Naoise pointed out mildly. "It is this fact I have come to discuss."

Enyokoto shifted. "Of course, cousin. We are well aware of Grenlec's long conflict with Telrisht. It is most unfortunate, to be sure." There was not the irony in his tone that Naoise would have expected. "But if you came here hoping to extract a promise of aid against your enemies… Well, you can see we have our own problems."

He was fishing, Naoise could tell. And not happy about being so cagey.

"I can indeed see that," Naoise replied. "And it is true that I came here seeking help, but not the kind you imagine. I think we might be in a position to help each other, if the talk in the street is to be believed. I believe we face a problem larger than Telrisht, and that we stand a chance of survival only if we put aside our old resentments and work in concert."

The Mysian appeared justifiably skeptical.

"Please," Naoise went on. "It is vital that I speak to the king immediately."

Enyokoto watched Naoise for a long time without answering. Weighing, considering. Without warning he moved to the lacquered wood tray on which the palace servants had brought refreshments for Naoise, and poured himself a glass of the honey wine. He drank it off slowly but all at once, his guest watching in some surprise. Then he sighed. A palpable tension went out of him, but a great deal remained.

"Prince Naoise," he said quietly, again studying his guest, "there is a sober earnestness about you that I find reassuring. Either you are a damn fine actor or an honorable man – both rare enough. My advisors would call for my head if they heard me saying this, but I want to trust you. I could sorely use an ally just now."

His instinct had been correct: something was terribly wrong here.

"You have my word," Naoise vowed, "upon my honor and the lives of my family and anything else you might like me to swear by, that I am not here to bring harm to Mysia. But by the Father, man, we cannot get down to it if you refuse to be straight with me. Either take me to the king or tell me why you will not do so."

The Prince of Mysia poured himself another glass, and one for Naoise this time, and gestured at the austere dark sofas facing one another. Naoise took the drink and the suggestion and sat facing the Mysian with some apprehension.

"The king," Enyokoto began sadly, "is indisposed." He drank, then shook his head. "Again, I ought not to be saying this. In these grim times, Mysia cannot afford to lack a strong king. For obvious reasons, we have kept quiet my poor father's condition. He is old and ailing, and in the last year has begun to forget himself."

Naoise tried to imagine his own father old and feebly losing possession of his faculties, but his mind flinched away from the thought.

"You have my sympathies," he said. "But Mysia *has* a strong leader, has it not? Are you not in command here?"

The Mysian nodded but accompanied it with a gesture of vague denial. "I am, but I am at my limit simply trying to keep the situation in the palace from bleeding out into the city, and keeping control of Zarishan. Not all of my father's advisors are willing to accept my orders over his while he yet lives, and he has lucid moments often enough to keep them protesting my misuse of what they see as his power. The state of the city itself is just on the edge of spinning into madness. Refugees from the countryside have been pouring in, spreading panic and tales of the End Times."

"What tales do they tell?" Naoise prompted. They might yet get somewhere, after all.

"They report the devastation of the borderlands," Enyokoto replied. "I cannot leave Zarishan myself as matters stand, but my agents confirm it: the farmlands have been ravaged. Entire villages gone, burned to ash. They tell me it is Telrisht, that the Forbearance is over as we always knew it would be, that now is the time to strike back while Telrisht's focus is split and the opportunity may never come again."

"The refugees say this?" Naoise had a hard time crediting that, given what he had seen and heard.

"No." Enyokoto shook his head again. "It is my father's generals who tell me that I must defend Mysia's ways against those who have always despised us." He drank the rest of the wine and put his glass aside with a firm gesture.

Naoise nodded. As grim as the situation was, he was encouraged by Enyokoto. The man was reasonable. In truth, he had not been entirely sure of his ability to convince an old king, set in his ways, of his suspicions of a conspiracy. The prince was dealing with conspiracies of his own and might be more likely to believe.

"So you're not certain it is Telrisht behind the attacks against your people?" Naoise asked.

The Prince of Mysia furrowed his brow in genuine puzzlement. "But who else would it be? Unless you're suggesting your own armies–"

"No." Naoise decided to try the wine. It wasn't as sweet as it smelled and was soothing on his road-dry throat. "Would it surprise you to learn that we too have been dealing with an enemy we do not know? And more, that Telrisht has as well?"

"Now that," Enyokoto protested, "you must explain." He frowned. "I must say I find the timing of your visit most curious. Mysia has watched your war with Telrisht these years from a safe distance. It is only now when we are attacked without provocation that Grenlec makes a diplomatic visit?"

"It is not *my* timing you should question," Naoise said grimly. "And it is most assuredly not a coincidence."

Enyokoto's look was grave as he paced between the sofas.

"I wish I could call these the fabrications of an overtaxed mind, Prince Naoise, but your words make a terrible kind of sense."

Naoise breathed a sigh of relief and finally allowed himself another glass of wine. His theories had taken him the better part of two hours to present in full, even though the Mysian prince had stopped him only occasionally to ask clarifying questions. Thirsty work, but it seemed to have borne fruit.

Then Enyokoto had insisted on sending for the girl, the child from Eyso. Her responses were as they had been all the way across Mysia. Even though it was as unsettling as ever to see the madness in her young eyes and listen to the gibberish she spouted, Naoise believed it was probably good for Enyokoto. The unusual circumstances at Eyso went a long way toward arguing against a conventional enemy.

"I wish I *were* only imagining this," Naoise replied wearily. Now that he knew he would not have to do any more convincing, he felt just how long he had been on the road and how desperate he was for a long sleep somewhere quiet. He missed home, he missed his family, and he missed his dog. Most of all, he wanted not to be fighting anymore. "Wars can be won. This is something else and the implications chill me to my marrow."

The Mysian scowled in thought. He now looked as exhausted as Naoise felt. "Even though you make sense, my friend, still you speak in riddles. Because who if not Telrisht seeks to destroy us both?"

Naoise shook his head. "I had hoped we might find the answer to that together."

Enyokoto subsided into an agitated silence.

A thought that Naoise disliked intensely had been pushing at the back of his mind for some weeks now. If there was ever the audience to give it the proper consideration, he had it now.

He leaned forward and stared down at his hands. "I am about to tell you something I have never said aloud to another living soul."

The Mysian prince waited.

Naoise went on carefully. "Seven years ago, on the eve of this war, I met a living elf – saw her with my own eyes. I never spoke of it because she was brave and good and I wanted her to be safe, but what it means is that… Well." He drew a deep breath. "They survived. Somewhere out in the world is a secret elven kingdom. How many of them yet remain, there is no way of knowing, but they're out there somewhere. What if–"

"No." He looked up and saw that Enyokoto was shaking his head.

Naoise fell silent.

"You cannot think that," Enyokoto argued. "You cannot *say* it. The elves would not attack us. Grenlec, Telrisht, that I could believe. You know you've earned their enmity. But elves would never betray Mysia. I don't expect you to understand, but do believe me. Our bonds run deeper than you know."

To that, Naoise had not the heart to make the reply that came to mind. He simply studied his new ally. "You don't seem terribly surprised by my revelation, in any event."

Enyokoto blinked. "That the elves survived? No. We know how strong they are, how determined. We paid a high enough cost in blood, and in sorrow in the years that followed, to see them safe. You should know that, Prince Naoise."

Naoise flinched.

The Mysian frowned apologetically. "It is not my intent to antagonize you. These are simply the facts. Yes, we suffered for our loyalty. Yes, we had reason to believe that suffering was not in vain, and the belief has been a balm to us through the years. I will confess I am jealous that if anyone was to see proof the elves survived, it had to be a Grenlecian."

Well, the man was honest. Naoise appreciated that. He also knew Enyokoto spoke sense. He just wished he could entirely dismiss his suspicions.

An image came into Naoise's mind, familiar and by now beloved in its familiarity, of his green-eyed forest woman. The elf whose existence had changed for him what the world meant. He had never believed his meeting her anything other than a blessing despite the long illness that had laid him flat after she left him. He knew – not thought, but *knew* – that she was good and at any rate would not be the cause of any harm to him. He still relived sometimes that moment when she had turned, blade in hand, to protect him from the beast that intended his death. He bore one of its claws with him always, on a leather band about his throat, to remind him of the time he had witnessed true bravery.

But she was not the only elf.

He could not deny that elves, if they lived, had cause to want his people dead. His people, Telrisht. Enyokoto had even said as much. Mysia made less sense, but...

"It isn't a pleasant thought, to be sure," he allowed, "but we must at least ask ourselves if it is possible. We have so many questions and none of them answered."

"Well." Enyokoto frowned, the worry lines tightening about his thin mouth. "Consider the question asked. My answer to it remains no."

Strangely, Naoise was relieved to hear him say it. As though footing that had seemed loose and treacherous had turned reassuringly solid. "In that case, we must ask ourselves a new question: how do we go about discovering the identity of our unknown enemy?"

The Mysian stopped pacing and returned to his seat. "You have assumed the answer to another question already, but I will do you the courtesy of con-firming it for you." He offered a quick, diplomatic smile. "Yes, I will work with you on this. The Creator knows Mysia and Grenlec have never been friends, Prince Naoise, but perhaps we can begin to change that. I've never met a Grenlecian quite like you."

Naoise returned the smile. "Have you ever met a Grenlecian?"

Enyokoto chuckled, but was not allowed the opportunity to answer.

A liveried messenger came into the parlor, his bright blue and silver uni-form at odds with the heavy mood choking the life out of Mysia. And there was terror in his eyes. "Your Highness," he said to Enyokoto. "A message has just come to the palace. It is… most urgent."

The two princes exchanged grave looks.

"Let me have it," Enyokoto commanded.

The messenger shifted diffidently. "It… the courier insists that he must de-liver it to you himself. And he…" The young man trailed off and glanced pointedly at Naoise.

"Be at ease, Seyam," Enyokoto said. "Prince Naoise is a trusted ally. You may speak freely in his presence."

Still the messenger hesitated. "But, my lord, he is Grenlecian. You need to know, the – the courier is – I mean we shouldn't–"

"Enough." There was steel in Enyokoto's voice. "You have been given an order by your prince."

The messenger tugged unhappily on his blue coat. "Yes, my lord. Well, then. The courier who insists on delivering his message in person is an elf."

Naoise realized after the fact that he and Enyokoto had both surged to their feet at the same time. The palace messenger looked back and forth between the two of them and swallowed.

Enyokoto drew a slow breath and said, carefully, "Bring him here. Mysia and Grenlec will both hear what he has to say."

After the messenger left to fetch this mysterious courier, Naoise spent the entire wait trying to figure out what to say to his counterpart. Enyokoto seemed to be doing the same thing.

"Thank you," Naoise said at last.

Then the door opened and an apparition out of legend stepped through.

Just like Loríen all those years ago, there was no mistaking this person for human. It was subtle, difficult to define, but there was an alien quality to the arrangement of his features that was intriguing and unsettling at the same time.

Clad in flowing, exotic garb, the elf moved with all the confidence and easy grace one would expect of a myth and was as sharp-featured and hand-some as the tales said he should be. He had, however, a fierce look about him. His skin was almost the color of burnished copper and reflected the light back as if it truly was wrought of metal. His almond-shaped eyes were dark and hard and inscrutable, his long yellow hair hanging down his back in martial braids that exposed the metal-clad tips of distinctly pointed ears. He was tall, corded with muscle, edgy with general anger, and had more than one weapon visible on his person.

The elf flicked his obsidian eyes between the princes but said nothing, waiting.

Enyokoto took a step forward. "On behalf of my father King Eselakoto, I welcome you to Zarishan, friend." He spoke Mysian now, his voice suddenly rich with a music it had lacked in his carefully flawless Common. "It has been too long since our people last met."

There was no change in the elf's hard expression as he answered in the same language. "It has been more than three thousand years since our people last met, prince."

Enyokoto sighed. "Indeed it has. And I'm glad those years have not meant extinction for your people." He offered the armed courier a polite smile. "Might I ask your name, sir?"

The elf grunted. "Sovoqatsu Zimají Farínaiqa." Though he addressed a prince, there was no deference in his manner. He was a warrior, not a soft pal-ace page. "I come with a message from the Míyahídéna of Evlédíen."

*Míyahídéna.* Naoise worked out the components of the word and realized it would approximate "Crown Princess." And *Evlédíen–* "elf valley." Plainly descriptive, if not terribly imaginative. Naoise had never heard the name be-fore today.

"I am told you will take the message in your father's place," the elf went on. "That is acceptable." From the folds of his long coat – not unlike Enyo-koto's in style – he produced a parchment square bearing a great blue wax seal. As he stepped forward to place the message in the prince's hands, he swept Naoise with a cold glance of appraisal but said nothing.

When Enyokoto took the parchment, Naoise saw that the crest pressed into the wax depicted a many-rayed star held within the circle of a crown.

The Mysian met Naoise's eyes briefly before he broke the seal.

It was a short message; Enyokoto was done only a moment later. All of the color had drained from his face.

Sovoqatsu drew himself up to his considerable full height, towering over both men. "I have been commanded to stay," he said to the Mysian prince, "and guide you back to Evlédíen. It is a long journey. We should begin at once."

Naoise sucked in a sharp breath. Enyokoto was still as pale as a cloudless dawn, but he turned his head at the sound and made an effort to rally himself. He passed Naoise the note without a word.

Short indeed. Cutting through the formal language of diplomacy, it said merely that the Crown Princess of Evlédíen was aware of the danger facing Mysia. That the enemy and his goal were known to her. Invited either Mysia's king or his surrogate to Evlédíen to discuss the matter at hand.

*The enemy and his goal were known.*

The Prince of Mysia collected himself admirably. "Thank you, Master Farínaiqa. I will... let you know of my chosen emissary as soon as I may."

Naoise stared down at the message penned in an elegant hand, and at the elven warrior bristling with weapons and hostility, and knew that whatever Enyokoto decided, he was going to Evlédíen.

He was going to find the answers. He was going to save Grenlec.

Lyn peered up at Cole from the dirt of the road. She couldn't tell which hurt more: her pride or her tailbone. "You said this was easy, you lying toad."

Cole looked down at her from his relaxed seat in his own saddle. "It *is* easy. When you don't upset the horse."

"I will end you."

It might have been her imagination, but she thought she saw a small smile quirking Cole's lips.

"Hey. Don't offer to help me up or anything," Lyn griped as she climbed to her feet.

"If you insist," Cole replied blandly.

Muttering imprecations under her breath, Lyn batted at the dirt on her formerly white breeches. The dappled grey she had acquired from Cole's associate in Telrisht City watched her placidly, giving no sign of the fit of pique that had landed Lyn in the middle of the road just a moment earlier.

"Listen, you great sweaty hairbag," she said to the horse. "All I want is a ride. There's no call to be so hostile just because I told you to go faster."

"Might have more to do with the way you keep digging in your heels," Cole pointed out. He easily weathered the glare she shot up at him.

"I mean it." Lyn tried unsuccessfully to catch hold of her horse's bridle. "Keep up with that smart mouth of yours and you'll be sorry you met me."

"What if I already am?"

Lyn picked up a chunk of dry Telrishti dirt and launched it in Cole's direction with an inarticulate squeal of irritation. He eased his horse aside and the clod went sailing harmlessly past his head.

"I had no idea you were going to turn out to be such a – such a – *oh*! I don't even know a word bad enough to call you!"

There was no mistaking it now: he was definitely smiling. Lyn had no intention of telling him she was glad to see it. Then he'd stop.

She made another grab at the bridle. The horse let her this time, chuffing its lips gently as though it had forgotten it was ever annoyed at her. Lyn gave it a stern glare before climbing back into the saddle, then leaned over to talk into its ear. "You're going to behave this time, right?"

Beside her, Cole snorted.

He made it look so simple, she thought wistfully. He was just *sitting* there. And then, when he wanted his horse to go somewhere, it *went*.

When *she* tried just sitting on her horse, she constantly felt like she was sliding off. Forget trying to make it go where she wanted it to. The more she told it to do something, the less it seemed to care what she wanted. And every time she tried to do any of the things she saw Cole doing, the awful beast bucked on her. The only bright point was that she was getting better at holding on when the thing was trying to unseat her.

"Maybe we should trade," she said to her stoic companion. "I think mine's broken."

Cole shook his head as if she made no sense, but she could still see traces of that stealth-smile trying to stay hidden. He clicked his tongue, and his superior horse started moving. "Come on. We don't know how far they are behind us and we have a long way to go."

Her stupid horse followed his with reluctance.

"I'm just saying you're the better horseman. We'd move faster if you took the broken one," she argued to Cole's back.

Was that – were his shoulders shaking?

"Hey! Are you *laughing* at me?" Lyn kicked her heels into the horse's sides to make it catch up.

She felt powerful muscles bunching beneath her as the horse bucked again.

Night came to Zarishan.

Prince Enyokoto asked Sovoqatsu for some time to decide what to do, and sent the dangerous elven courier with his people to find some dinner and rest. He considered Naoise for a moment before ordering food to be brought for the two of them.

"I have much to do yet today and my staff are certainly wondering why I've devoted so much of my time to a single visitor," he sighed tiredly, "but surely even I am allowed a moment to eat. I assume you could use a bit of something yourself."

Naoise was grateful – even more that his host was choosing not to cut him out of this important historic moment than for the offer of food. And he *was* hungry.

Servants came and lit the room's many beautiful lanterns and laid a meal for three at the black lacquered table. Naoise didn't recognize any of the dishes. Part of him was unreasonably pleased by this, as a curious traveler in a foreign place. The rest of him was tired and had been away from home for too long. He looked pointedly at the third setting and back up at Enyokoto.

"You have no idea how much I wish I could be the one to go," the Mysian said wistfully. "This invitation is…" He trailed off and shook his head, unable to express the enormity of what it meant.

Naoise didn't know about that. He knew how he felt about the thought of being the first human to set foot in the elven kingdom in more than three thousand years; he had *some* idea how much Enyokoto would give to be able to go himself.

"Alas that I cannot leave Mysia with matters such as they are," the prince went on. "But I know just the man for it."

"Who is he?"

"An old friend," Enyokoto answered. The light of fond memory had sparked in his eyes. "Sefaro Shinju. His family has always been close to mine; we were playmates as children and he remains like a brother to me. He's a good man, and he knows me well. I trust him absolutely to do what I would, were I there."

Naoise wished he knew anyone he could trust in that way. As much as he loved his brother, Dairinn wasn't exactly a responsible man. There was no predicting what he would do in any given situation, except probably overreact. And their younger sister, Alyra – as a woman in Grenlec, she moved in a different world from his. And then he had gone away to war. She was a bright young woman with a solid head on her shoulders, but to Naoise's regret, he simply couldn't say he knew her that well.

"He is also something of a gentleman expert on all things elven," Enyokoto added with what might have been a touch of amusement.

Naoise wondered just what that meant, in a country that itself prized its expertise where elves were concerned. The lord in question joined them a moment later, bowing just inside the doorway.

He was an unassuming man, Naoise observed. Neither slight nor brawny, of an average height, unremarkably handsome, hair and eyes both a pleasant shade of nut brown only marginally darker than his skin. Only when he smiled in greeting did Naoise see a hint of something extraordinary in him: the light of decency, of a life defined by love and loyalty.

"You sent for me, my prince?" he said to Enyokoto. His voice was as ordinary and mildly agreeable as the rest of him.

Enyokoto gestured at the empty seat and Sefaro moved to fill it. "I did. Thank you for being so prompt." He paused while his friend got settled. "Sefaro, I'd like you to meet Prince Naoise of Grenlec."

The lord betrayed his surprise only by the widening of his eyes. His tone was affable enough as he greeted Naoise.

Naoise did his host the kindness of letting the meal pass in light chat, setting aside for the moment the pressing issues that faced them all. Sefaro asked several polite questions about Grenlec, carrying the conversation forward on Naoise's responses with little apparent effort. It was easy to see why Enyokoto would choose this man to represent him at another court.

But despite his gracious manner, Sefaro clearly spent the meal wondering why he had been summoned in such company. As they were laying aside their utensils, the prince mercifully put an end to the suspense. "My friend, be at your ease. Naoise knows how bad things are in Mysia. They're worse in Grenlec. It's why he's come."

Naoise watched Sefaro and was interested to note that the polite openness did not leave him at this revelation. It wasn't an act.

"I need your help," Enyokoto went on.

"My lord, I am yours to command," Sefaro replied.

The Prince of Mysia sighed. The simple sound, to Naoise's ears, conveyed a complex weight of weariness, anxiety, and barely-restrained excitement. "I am about to ask much of you, Sef," he said quietly.

Lord Sefaro smiled crookedly back at his prince. "You should know I'm used to it by now. A lifetime in a prince's shadow prepares you for all kinds of things. What is it this time, Enyo? The moon and the stars? Or just that I entertain another dull country lord so you can spend time getting to know his daughter?"

Naoise chuckled at that while Prince Enyokoto tried unsuccessfully to look affronted.

But the flash of levity passed and Enyokoto leaned across the table, offering his friend the message from Evlédíen. He allowed a moment for the note to be read and then said, as Sefaro's face blanched at its contents, "I need you to serve as my ambassador, old friend."

To his credit, Sefaro did not hesitate. He simply blinked, set the message down, and said, "Are you certain I'm the right man for this?"

"I could not be more certain if I spent the year thinking it over," Enyokoto replied.

Before Sefaro could respond to that, Naoise said what he knew he had to. "And I know just the man to be your protection on the long road. A war veteran, even."

Both Mysians turned to him in some surprise.

He offered his most charming smile.

Enyokoto shook his head slowly. "I'm... not sure if that's... The message wasn't even for me, it was for my father. *I* trust you, Prince Naoise, but you're Grenlecian. I cannot make this decision on behalf of the elves."

Naoise had spent the evening preparing himself for this. "Can you decide for Grenlec, for Telrisht, for Lang and Seland and Rosemarch, and the Islands, that they shall all remain in the dark while they die? Can you make the decision that Mysia alone has the right to know what manner of destruction awaits us all?"

The Prince of Mysia frowned, looking more tired than ever. "I understand your concerns, truly. You have my word that whatever we learn, we will share with Grenlec. I'll put that in writing if you like."

"And can you assure me that your message will come in time to save Grenlec?" Naoise pressed. "That after Lord Sefaro here has returned to Zarishan and shared his findings with you, and you decide how much we're allowed to know, your messenger will not be riding to Dewfern merely to pray over our remains?"

"Guilt hardly endears your cause to me," Enyokoto snapped, but Naoise could see that his arguments were in fact having an effect.

"Forgive me," Naoise said. "It is not my intent to stir your guilt. I only wish to protect my people. If you plan to make a decision that puts us at risk, I think you should be certain you make that decision intentionally."

Enyokoto stared at his empty plate, brows drawn in thought. There was no sound but the hiss of the oil lamps for a long time.

Lord Sefaro cleared his throat. Both princes looked up at him, and he smiled disarmingly. "I've never been anything special with a blade. I could use a seasoned veteran watching my back on the road."

Enyokoto sighed.

"And let's face reality," Sefaro added in a more serious tone. "If Mysia and the elves are going to be on speaking terms again, the only way the rest of the world won't notice eventually is if the other kingdoms fall. I assume that's not what anyone here wants. I also assume the elves extended this invitation having calculated that risk."

Naoise looked at Sefaro and gave silent thanks to Enyokoto for choosing such a level-headed ambassador.

The Prince of Mysia muttered something under his breath and sighed again. "I *dearly* hope I'm not going to regret this, Prince Naoise."

Sefaro grinned. "Relax, Enyo. We're on the brink of total annihilation already. How much worse could things get?"

# Chapter Eleven

On a brisk, windblown afternoon, as the sun sank to its rest beyond the burnished gold horizon, the city of Efrondel prepared itself for another Autumn Festival.

Long ago, in the early days of the Homeland, Festival had been an event that came only once every six years – a special, rare occasion when elves gathered together to celebrate Vaian's Creation. After the War of Exile and the many years of suffering that followed, it had been Loralíenasa's father, King Andras, who decreed that Festival would become an annual affair. Their people sorely needed the diversion from their sorrow.

And because they needed it, because the rest of the year was devoted to mourning what had been lost, the elves took Festival and its rules seriously. People would do things on these three nights and the two days between them that would fly in the face of who they were. For some it would mean standing before a crowd at a tea or khala house and reciting poetry. For others it would mean entertainment of an altogether darker and more carnal character. What happened behind Festival masks was never spoken of again. Not even the Lord Regent was fool enough to touch Festival's traditions, though he loudly disapproved.

This year, as the people strove to forget what had happened on that practice green behind the palace, he was less inclined to interfere than ever.

Loralíenasa knew it.

Carefully disguised in sleek black fur and a black fox mask, she left the palace at dusk with the other revelers. She stopped at one of the food vendors' stalls that had been set up on the main thoroughfare for the occasion and purchased a skewer of honey-glazed fowl, a paper packet of one-bite cinnamon pastries, and a small glass of mitallía wine. She sat on the edge of the Starfont while she ate, listening to the musicians and watching the dancers already gathering in the Market Circle. When she was done eating, she joined the dance for a while beneath the emerging stars.

Then, when she saw Tomanasíl's spy melt into the crowd to enjoy his own Festival, satisfied that she was behaving herself, she bowed out of the dance and made her way north. Past red and gold swags and garlands of fall foliage, through surging crowds in bright and fantastical costumes, everywhere surrounded by music and laughter, all the way to the edge of the city.

On the lush plain below the mountains, where the River Efron flowed toward the sea, the elves who settled the Valley after fleeing the Homeland had paused and then halted on their long journey. They had found their new home, and it was beautiful.

The city they built there was like a diamond set upon green velvet, carefully engineered in the shape of an eight-pointed star and constructed out of crystal with all the skill of the Art and of science they had at their command. The rays of the star were encased all the way around by silver filigree walls. The cardinal points each terminated in an ornate gold gate – but for the southern point, which held the Crystal Palace and its grounds. At all eight points stood a guard tower. These had been manned every hour of every day since their construction, against the remote possibility of human invasion.

It was a lonely job, watching at the towers, and a mostly thankless one. The chances that humans might discover the one pass through the mountains and would then be able to overcome the magic defenses there were less than slim; in any case, the guards at the pass would alert Efrondel immediately if such a thing were to occur.

Nevertheless, the towers remained in operation, and it allowed Tomanasíl at least to sleep more easily. Even in these more complicated times, and in the wake of that one afternoon's disturbing events, the Regent liked to feel the Valley's defenses were more than adequate.

At the northernmost point of the city, in Nevethas Tower, a small crowd awaited Loralíenasa's arrival. She had a moment to muse, as she was let in by a man wearing a hawk mask, that this was her first time in any of the guard towers. There had never before been cause.

The vestibule was nicer than she had expected it to be – not merely utilitarian but beautiful – the walls silver covered with subtle tracework, the windows arched delicately and framed in pristine white marble. The stairs were the same white marble, winding all the way around the inner wall to the uppermost platform where the guards kept their watch. During the day, light would pour into the central well in glorious golden rays, setting the mosaicked floor aglow. By night it was lit by delicate silver globes that followed the curving line of the stairs all the way to the top of the tower.

Lanoralas removed his hawk mask once the door was closed behind Loríen. He nodded at the six other costumed elves and they unmasked as well.

Loralíenasa had not attended to her study of the Art in some years, but she was still able to see the power in the aurae of the tower's other inhabitants. Illusionists, able to bend other people's perceptions. The Valley's best scouts and only hope of gathering intelligence in the outer world without letting the humans know of their continued existence. Only a handful of them had been able to make it back to Efrondel in time, but the Regent had no idea they had still been in the field to begin with. This was the only way to meet without him knowing what she and Lanoralas had been up to.

She felt the lighthearted spirit of the Festival outside the walls of the tower sliding off like a discarded robe. The night ahead of them would be a long one, but Tomanasíl wasn't expecting her home until Festival ended. At least, she thought wryly, she was vindicating his mistrust by getting into just as much trouble as he expected her to. Just trouble of a different sort.

"All accounted for?"

The Captain shrugged off his feathered outer coat and tossed it onto the nearest bench. His clothing underneath was nearly normal. "Our man in Mornnovin didn't make it back. As far as the tracking glass can tell, he's somewhere in northern Grenlec."

"*Íyaqo*. We need him." Loralíenasa allowed herself to show her agitation as far as pacing the antechamber. Something about doing it in black fox fur felt satisfyingly predatory. "What have we learned?"

One of the scouts stepped forward. "Mysia is attacked, my lady."

Lanoralas growled.

The scout went on. "Mornnovin has been scrambling raids over the Mysian border meant to look like Telrisht. The people are confused and frightened. In Zarishan the army has begun to muster."

Loralíenasa responded with a stronger invective.

"In Lang the situation is even worse," a second scout reported. He had an especially low voice that made the news sound more dire than the previous report. "The war between Telrisht and Grenlec has been fought across their lands for so many years now that their fields lie fallow, their people starving. The cities are all but abandoned as the folk flee to the countryside to forage for food. The death toll from starvation is higher than anyone guesses. There is no army there to muster. They are ripe for Katakí's killing blow and it lies not within their power to stop it."

"And Seland?" Lanoralas asked angrily of the third scout.

"Destroyed," the smallest of the scouts replied. "No one even knew it was happening. If there were survivors, they have scattered into hiding and the great harbor at Seaport is a place of ghosts and silence. Their navy lies shattered down all the leagues of their shoreline."

Loralíenasa didn't want the answer, but she asked anyway, knowing she had to: "Rosemarch?"

"My lady, Rosemarch is engulfed in civil war," said the fourth scout predictably. "Three of the free city-provinces have risen up to claim control of the country. Those not fighting for preeminence are fighting to keep Rosemarch free of a central government as it has ever been."

"*Qotsu!*" Lanoralas exclaimed. Loralíenasa didn't often hear him use such strong language. He glanced at the remaining two scouts. "And we know Telrisht and Grenlec have one another decimated and pinned down. This Katakí Kuromé has done an amazing job of crushing any resistance he might have met with before it could be raised."

"It is said the Crown Prince of Grenlec has abandoned his post," added the tallest of the female scouts. "It was difficult to verify. Apparently he was no more than a figurehead for the Occupation, but there are whispers that he has vanished. It hasn't been good for morale. The news reportedly has driven the king to illness."

"And Telrisht is planning what they call a Final Push against Grenlec with the first of spring," said the final scout. "The Ayiz wants Grenlec out of his kingdom or to die fighting them."

"Perfect," Loralíenasa murmured. Was there any way the news could be worse? "Well there's nothing for it. We have to contact Iríjo." She looked to Lanoralas, who was frowning. "Do you have a tracking glass?"

The sounds of Festival rose and fell in an energetic wave outside the tower as the Captain sighed and reached into his sash.

"I'll do it," she told him, seeing his reluctance. It would be easier for her.

Farspeaking across this kind of distance was difficult enough even with the aid of empowered talismans like the tracking glass. For one with no gift for the Art, like Lanoralas, it was a definite strain. Loralíenasa hated to use the Art, and she had the gift. What she lacked was interest.

She took the small silver-rimmed looking glass from Lanoralas and settled on the floor with it in her lap.

Forming a mental picture of the missing scout, she called his name silently. She stared into the mirror, willing it to show sky instead of the inside of Nevethas Tower, a pair of blue eyes instead of her green, a man's face instead of her own. A headache started, like a band tightening about the crown of her skull, and she found her mind trying to drift to any task other than the one she wanted it to focus on. She wrestled her concentration back to the mirror and the face she needed to see there.

"Míyahídéna?"

There. Loralíenasa seized at the voice in her mind and the man it came from. An image formed in the mirror, dim but distinctly not her own reflection. There were leaves in the background, and a night sky with clouds glowing white. "Iríjo. We're all here – the Captain too. What can you tell us?"

The voice was projecting from the mirror now, the connection fully formed. They could all hear the brave scout who had infiltrated Mornnovin as he said, "Oh Vaian, I don't have long. They're after me and I can't stay still."

"Tell us what you can," Loralíenasa said as calmly as she could. She drew a carefully steady breath. "Who is chasing you?"

Lanoralas reached down and gripped her shoulder.

The answer did not put her at ease. "He has these... units of trained assassins. Elves. Our own kind. This Kataki has been building an army in the north: elves who followed him out of Eselvwey, more who joined him later rather than following the Retreat. Paid humans, even. An entire army."

"Followed him out of Eselvwey?" Lanoralas echoed quietly.

Loralíenasa repeated the question for the elf in the mirror and added, "Who is he, really? Where did he come from?"

"He fought in the War," the scout answered. "Different name in those days. Soríjuhí Volarín. Couldn't get anyone to talk about him beyond that, but it's known that he has a plan. A careful one. There's a terrible fear here, Míyahídéna. His own people fear him, but they're loyal too, blindly so. I was found out because I couldn't mimic that blind loyalty, was asking questions. Had to run for it."

"You were made?" A premonition of something awful slid down Loríen's spine. Tomanasíl had been afraid of what would happen if Kataki discovered them spying on him...

The face in the mirror nodded briskly. "Made me when I ran. They've been behind me ever since. Míyahídéna... if I can't outrun them I want you to know I'll see to it they get nothing from me. Please tell the Captain."

Loralíenasa swallowed hard. "He's here. He knows. What else can you tell me before you go? What about his defenses? His numbers?"

The scout raised his head suddenly and looked behind him at something Loralíenasa couldn't see. "No time. The defenses, they're insane. Traps, magic. He is *powerful*. His general is a legend. Don't try it. Vaian keep you, my lady; I must run."

The image in the mirror dissolved before she could offer a farewell.

Lanoralas squeezed her shoulder as she stared down at the circle of glass now reflecting only her own tightly-drawn face.

She let out a slow breath. Her head was pounding.

"We always knew we weren't going to be able to respond in numbers," the Captain said quietly. "This changes little. We just have to think it through and plan accordingly."

Magic. A name out of the past. Loralíenasa sighed. As much as she hated the fact, she knew what she had to do now: she had to speak to her former master. The question was whether or not Qíarna would speak to her.

But that would have to wait. It was Festival, and whether she liked it or not, real life would not resume in Efrondel until it was over.

And she had a life to celebrate.

She stood, mirror in hand, and met Lanoralas' eyes. "For Iríjo."

Seven voices echoed hers. "For Iríjo."

Naoise and Sefaro rode south from Zarishan with their elven guide, toward the Shenzasa River. Their course would take them east then to Heart Lake, where they would descend to the lowlands. Sovoqatsu would not say more about their way after that, but their path to the lake was calculated to take them in fairly straight lines while avoiding civilization. The last thing they needed was to cause a stir through Mysia by parading the elf past an awestruck populace.

Southern Mysia was a beautiful place replete with many stunning vistas of forest and dale, for the most part untouched by the destruction and despair of the north. There were wildflowers here Naoise had never seen in Grenlec, and the shape of the land itself had a stern grandeur that he found both daunting and oddly soothing. He felt he could enjoy vacationing here in better times.

In better company.

Sefaro was a delight to travel with, actually. Unfailingly cheerful without being overly talkative, supplied with an endless store of anecdotes, he was pleasant company and already becoming a friend.

Sovoqatsu Farínaiqa was another matter.

It was fascinating – the differences between the prickly, well-armed warrior and the bright-eyed, adventuresome young woman who had been Naoise's first experience with their kind. She had been suspicious and rightfully wary, but there had been so much more than that beneath the surface, curiosity not least. Sovoqatsu was hostility under a thin veneer of bad temper and showed no desire to accept either of his companions' invitations to conversation. That, of course, only piqued Naoise's interest.

They rode in haste and made good time, camping on the river bank seven days after leaving Zarishan. As usual, Sovoqatsu kept to himself, seeing to his horse with brisk efficiency and settling beside the fire with his own trail rations. Sefaro put a pot on the fire for stew. Naoise sat near Sovoqatsu and watched, intrigued, as the elf visibly withdrew.

"I should like to discuss Evlédíen."

Sovoqatsu stared at him over the fire.

"When was the kingdom founded?" Naoise asked, in Mysian so Sefaro could follow. "Who rules there?"

The elf grunted. "You're inquisitive for a bodyguard." He eyed Naoise. "Also small."

Naoise heard Sefaro choking back a laugh and looked over to see the Mysian smiling and shaking his head. He quirked his lips in amusement.

"Isn't it enough that you'll learn these things once you get there?" Sovoqatsu added irritably.

Naoise shrugged, determined to maintain his equanimity despite the other man's bad temper. "Is it so difficult to imagine that I might like to go in prepared with some knowledge of what to expect there?"

That drew an unexpected, fierce smile from the elf. "I could ask, in turn, if it would surprise you that I might not want you to know what to expect, Grenlecian."

"A touch," Sefaro laughed. "You must concede, Naoise."

The prince watched Sovoqatsu over the fire and listened to the sound of the wind in the trees, searching for the right words. There had to be a reason why this man had been chosen, why he alone had been sent to Mysia with this warning and this task.

"I want what you want," Naoise said finally. The elf stiffened. "You're here because your people owe Mysia a debt of gratitude and you want to see them survive. My people owe as well. Mysia, the elves. Telrisht. Grenlec has caused a great deal of suffering and we have much to repay. I'd like to start by seeing that we all make it through this – whatever this is."

Sovoqatsu leaned forward, so close to the flames that Naoise didn't know how he could stand it. "You have no idea why I'm here, human. You most certainly do not want what I want."

"I might surprise you," Naoise replied.

The elf smiled again, black eyes gleaming. "I would rather you didn't."

They heard the roar of the falls long before they could see the diamond mist billowing up from them, over the tops of the trees. It was a rumble so low and deep the earth itself seemed to shake. Naoise felt small, imagining how much water it would take to produce such a sound.

Of course they wouldn't actually be going over Scathan Falls – that would be death. But the stepped cliffs where the southern fork of the Shenzasa emptied into the lake were the best place to try a descent into the lowlands with horses.

Despite the dwindling length of the autumn days, they arrived at the falls with ample sunlight to make the climb down. It came as a surprise when Sovoqatsu stopped well before the cliff's edge was in sight and tied off his horse, then turned with dark eyes narrowed to face the path they had just followed.

"Is there a problem, my friend?" Sefaro asked, reining in.

The elf kept his eyes on the trees. "No problem. This is where we make our descent. But we must lose our tail before I will go any farther."

"Our tail?" Sefaro echoed. He turned in the saddle and looked behind them as though he expected to see a cohort of Rahd galloping through the trees.

Naoise kept his eyes on the elf. "How long have you known we were being followed?"

Sovoqatsu snorted. "How long have you?" Instead of waiting for an answer, he reached back and drew the narrow, elegantly curved sword he wore between his shoulder blades.

Their Mysian companion made a choking sound. "Don't you think we ought to find out who or what is behind us before we start skewering things?"

"What do you think the chances are that it's a clutch of children who forgot to throw their flowers at your feet as we left Zarishan?"

Naoise cleared his throat tactfully. The elf turned toward him and scowled.

"A little circumspection would be wise," Naoise advised. "If it *is* an enemy behind us, wouldn't it be helpful to be able to ask some questions?" He eyed Sovoqatsu's blade. "Hard to ask anything of the dead."

Sovoqatsu scowled harder and strode off into the trees. "Something else about the dead: they can't follow us into Evlédíen."

Naoise could feel Sefaro staring at him. He sighed. "I did try."

The elf made little sound as he disappeared into the brush, despite the carpet of pine needles and paper-dry fallen leaves. Sefaro and Naoise both strained to hear his progress, but he had effectively vanished. The prince shrugged philosophically and decided he might as well stretch his legs while they waited for their guide to return from his dark task.

"He doesn't like you much," Sefaro observed after taking a brief walk and refilling his skin at the river. He managed a perfectly straight delivery, which made Naoise chuckle.

"My friend," Naoise replied, "that fellow could find a way not to like *air*."

A short and rather high-pitched scream punctuated this claim from somewhere within the shrouded depths of the forest.

The two men turned toward the sound.

Sovoqatsu returned much more quickly than he had ventured forth, even though he now had a body draped over his shoulder.

"I don't know what this fool is," he said irritably as he strode into sight, "but this is not the enemy. Deal with him and let us be on our way." He dumped the body unceremoniously at the humans' feet with a clank of armor and moved to see to his horse.

The unfortunate lump groaned and stirred, not dead. "I say! Was that really necessary?"

It was Naoise's turn to groan.

"Father's mercy, no. Please, no." He closed his eyes, willing this not to be happening. "Dairinn? Is that you?"

The man on the ground rolled to his feet with alarming agility for someone of his size and launched himself at Naoise before the prince could react. "Naoise! The god, but it's good to see you! You've no idea how long I've been tripping at your heels with the damned misfortune of never catching up."

One moment, Naoise's ribs were being crushed. The next, he was listening to his brother squeal like an embarrassed chambermaid as Sovoqatsu pried Dairinn away one-handed and dangled him by his throat several inches from the ground. The elder prince was hardly a small man, and he was in armor; it was an extraordinary sight.

"Shall I kill him after all?"

Sovoqatsu spoke no Common, Naoise realized. He would have no idea what was happening here unless it was explained to him.

"No!" Naoise caught his breath with difficulty. Had Dairinn broken one of his ribs? "No. This man is my brother."

The annoyance in Sovoqatsu's eyes congealed into something more dangerous as he continued to suspend the Crown Prince of Grenlec within his grasp. "Your brother? Another Grenlecian? What is he *doing* here?"

"Maybe he could tell us if you would let him breathe," Sefaro suggested mildly.

Sovoqatsu opened his hand and allowed Dairinn to fall again. The prince was markedly disgruntled as he climbed back to his feet and brushed the dust from his dark blue breeches.

He jerked his head in Sovoqatsu's direction while swiping at dirt and dry leaves. "Who's the total ass-head?"

Since Naoise's wish for this not to be real didn't seem likely to come true, he sighed and tried to decide what he could possibly say to his brother that wouldn't involve swearing.

But Dairinn hadn't stopped talking. "What in the nameless Void is going on? Da tells me you're going to Mysia to find out who's been putting a knife in our back, and I find you – what? Fleeing into the wilderness? What are you up to? Who is that?" He nodded in Sefaro's direction, then seemed to actually see Sovoqatsu for the first time. "Is that fellow even human?"

Sefaro sighed. The sound conveyed Naoise's feelings exactly.

"Dairinn. Calm yourself, please."

"Calm, you say? I hunt you all the way across the worst parts of Telrisht and Mysia only to get jumped in the forest by this beast – what is he, really? – and you want me to be calm? *Calm*?" The elder prince seemed to have forgotten his joy at finding Naoise and was now warming himself up to a spectacular rant.

"Yes." Naoise could feel himself approaching an anger that was unfamiliar territory for him, and forced himself to speak evenly. "I want you to consider that I am here on business I discussed with Father first, that I just might be acting for the good of Grenlec, and that I am amply able to take care of myself."

Dairinn replied with a snort. The sound was a spark flying directly into the heart of the tinder, nearly setting Naoise's temper ablaze. Had nothing he'd accomplished since the start of the war even registered with Dairinn? Did his brother truly still think of him as the moody child who had fallen apart after watching their mother die?

"You, on the other hand, have left your post if I do not miss my guess." Dairinn's grimace was confirmation enough and encouraged him to go on. "Had you considered that what I was doing might require some finesse, and that you might be endangering my mission by blundering in?" *That Father and I have done all we could to keep you safe, and now you're endangering that too?*

"Honestly? No." Dairinn set his jaw. "I was considering the likelihood that you're diving into waters too deep for you and you're too wrapped up in your own clever ideas to see it. It seems I was right." He eyed Sovoqatsu speculatively. The elf was glowering with such murderous intent the look itself should have been fatal. "*That's* an *elf*, isn't it?" He jabbed a finger toward the imposing figure. "I don't know how it's possible, but it is. Isn't it?" He sounded borderline hysterical, which wasn't all that surprising. "Has he kidnapped you? Are you in danger?"

"Oh, Creator," Sefaro observed wearily. He made himself comfortable on a fallen log and tried not to look as concerned as he no doubt felt.

"You have no idea how fortunate it is that he doesn't speak Common," Naoise told Dairinn frostily. He drew a deep breath and forced himself to sound less furious. "Yes. You are right: that's an elf. Now I really do need you to calm down, turn around, and go back the way you came. The situation is in hand, but it's delicate. Please, Dairinn. Go back and tell Father I'm well and that Mysia is not the enemy we're looking for. Tell him I'm following a lead with Mysia's cooperation, that I will have answers shortly. Please, Brother. Trust in me."

Dairinn was finally quiet long enough for the roar of the waterfall to be noticeable again. Naoise focused on it and tried to let his anger at his brother go. The only thing that could have led Dairinn so far, so intently, was genuine concern. As patronizing as it was, Naoise told himself, he needed to appreciate that much.

"No," Dairinn said finally. At least he had finally lowered his voice. In fact, he sounded disturbingly clear-headed. "I'm not going anywhere until you tell me exactly what you're up to. And then I'm going with you. I don't know what this is, but it's too big for just you."

"Oh dear," Sefaro said quietly. Naoise looked to see him shaking his head. "I can name at least one person by this river who isn't going to like that."

Sovoqatsu was watching them with narrowed eyes. When Naoise turned to him, he tightened his jaw. "This unseemly display is your way of dealing with him?"

A sick feeling began in the pit of Naoise's stomach, a premonition of where this was going. Even knowing, he wasn't sure he could stop it from happening.

"Just give me a moment more," he said. "All will be well."

The elf shook his head once. "I can see well enough what is happening here. I was not sent to lead even one Grenlecian back to Evlédíen. I tell you now, human, I will *not* lead two of you."

"What's he saying?" Dairinn demanded, advancing a pace.

Sovoqatsu had his sword out and trained at Dairinn's heart faster than Naoise could draw breath to reply. The echo of the twig snapped by Dairinn's boot seemed to go on forever.

"Naoise." Dairinn drew a careful breath. "Would you mind telling this mad bastard to SHEATHE HIS FUCKING SWORD?" Naoise saw the muscles tightening in Sovoqatsu's corded forearms.

"Stay your hand!" he cried, diving between the two men. The elf glared at him but did not strike. "He only wants to know where I'm going," Naoise explained breathlessly. "He's my brother. He fears for me."

Just as quickly as it had appeared, the sword was once again sheathed at Sovoqatsu's back. Without a word the elf strode to his horse, untied the creature, and swung up into the saddle.

He stared down at the two princes.

"Tell your brother his fears are ill-founded," he said, his voice just as hard as his eyes. "You are going nowhere, Grenlecian. Not with me. This was not my mission. And if we do meet again, know that we are not friends and mind my blade accordingly."

On that ominous word, Sovoqatsu Farínaiqa put lash to his horse and disappeared into the forest.

Naoise waited until his heartbeat slowed before he turned to face Dairinn.

His brother regarded him with eyebrows raised, for once lacking a quick retort.

It was Sefaro who summed the situation up succinctly, the two words drifting out on a weary sigh: "Well, damn."

"I can hear the falls!"

Trying to make her stupid horse go faster was too frustrating; Lyn jumped out of the saddle and ran past Cole's mount, eager to get her first look at Scathan Falls.

She was surprised to find herself restrained, a moment later, by Cole's gloved hand reaching down from the back of his horse to seize her by the collar. She thought maybe he was being playful for once until she craned her neck around to peer up at him and saw that he looked just as grim as ever.

"Hey, y'mind letting go?" she demanded indignantly.

Even more surprising, Cole's response was to jump down beside her and lean close to say, quietly, "We're not alone here."

Momentarily distracted by Cole's sudden closeness and his unmistakably male scent, Lyn didn't realize at first what he was saying. "You mean the men in black? They caught up?" She lowered her voice carefully to match his.

But Cole shook his head, then cocked it in the direction of the cliff's edge as if inviting her to listen.

She'd been so enchanted by the roar of the water that she hadn't noticed it before, but he was right: not far distant, the sound of male voices. Three? Arguing, it sounded like. Not trying to be quiet, and clearly not trying to take anyone by surprise.

Not the men in black.

"Sounds like they're right where we need to be," Cole observed, frowning. "Wait here. I'll have a look."

Lyn snorted indelicately. "What's the big deal? Some guys are yelling at each other by the river. We'll just slide on by and be on our way." She went back for her horse and grabbed it by the bridle.

Cole moved to block her. "The *big deal*," he said, "is that you're an elf. You don't seem to understand what that means out here."

"Do I really stand out that much?" He had to be making a great deal of fuss over nothing. "None of the humans I've seen since leaving the forest seemed all that different from me or Bryant. And *you* don't care."

The look Cole gave her was by far the most interesting expression she had ever seen on his unremarkable face, and she had no idea what to make of it. She had certainly never before seen him open his mouth so many times without saying anything. "Yes," he finally said. "You really do."

"How so?" Lyn insisted, planting her hands on her hips. A look that interesting, there was no way she was going to let it go.

But Cole only shook his head. "I expect you'll learn all about it when we get where we're going."

"You know what, when you say things like that, it just makes me not *want* to get where we're going."

The former mercenary stared at her for a long time.

"What?" Lyn finally demanded.

"Are you going to let me have a look or not?"

The tired patience in his voice almost made her concede. Almost. "No," she answered, grinning. "We're going down together. And if I end up needing to be protected, well. Protect me."

Cole visibly weighed his options for a moment, then sighed. It might have been just Lyn's imagination, but she thought she saw him briefly eyeing the length of rope hanging from her saddle. Imagination or no, he stepped aside and gestured tersely for her to proceed.

Random words spiked up out of the forest as they walked. "… insane… fault… moron." Lyn stopped and laughed quietly for a moment. But then a particular word leaped out and put a hiccup in her amusement: "Evlédíen."

Cole put a hand out to touch her shoulder.

She nodded. "I heard it." She didn't know what to *make* of it, but she'd heard it. Wasn't Cole always going on – in his not-saying-much way – about how no one knew elves were still around in this place Bryant called Evlédíen?

As she came through the trees to the rocky ledge where the Shenzasa spilled into Heart Lake, the first thing Lyn noticed was the dramatic absence of ground in front of her. Just a lot of sky and delicious air. Then she looked past the white mist and saw the lake, blue and vast, meeting the sky at the distant horizon.

Sitting on the black rocks above the falls, arguing, were three men.

"Afternoon!" Lyn called. There didn't seem to be much else to say.

The three men stopped their discussion abruptly.

They were an attractive bunch, Lyn noted. The pale, black-haired man reminded her of Bryant in some way she couldn't pin down, and there was something reassuring about the smaller one with the warm brown face even though he seemed to be upset at the moment. The big, square-jawed armored man was the one with the loudest voice, and he had been using it just a moment ago to defend himself. He had extraordinarily blue eyes. All three were armed, but none of them looked interested in posing an immediate threat to her. Whatever they'd been discussing, it was the only thing that mattered to them.

The loudest one, who was quite handsome, had been leaning toward his companions to reinforce his arguments, but he straightened when he saw Lyn.

"You *must* be joking." His face went slack, all expression draining off of it like he was a bucket with a hole at the bottom. "You seeing this, Naoise? I'm just imagining things, right?" His accent was nothing like hers or Cole's, rounded and full instead of flat and clipped. It made her think of tall castles in big cities she'd never seen, soft beds, and extravagant things to eat.

The man with the rakish black hair unfolded himself slowly from his rock. She watched with great interest as his bright, clever eyes shifted through several shades from the lower half of the rainbow as he studied her and then Cole. Interesting – was he doing it on purpose, like Bryant playing with one of his toys when he was bored? He pushed a hand back through his hair and drew a deep breath as if to steady himself.

"Good afternoon," he said with admirable calm. "I can't say the company is expected, but it is welcome all the same." He had a pleasant voice, low and cultured, the accent the same as the other man's. But he did not, Lyn noticed, say anything about the fact that she was an elf.

Lyn swung her smile in Cole's direction. "Look, they're friendly! And really, *really* polite."

Cole didn't look at her. He was busy staring down the large man, with his hand on his sword hilt. Lyn jabbed him in the ribs.

"What are you doing?" she hissed.

The man who had yet to speak slid from his black rock before Cole could answer, and took several cautious steps in their direction. Now that he was not arguing with his friends, he had a kind face. Lyn decided she liked him. "Perhaps we'd all be more comfortable after some introductions," he suggested. His accent was subtly different to that of the other two, as though he was imperfectly performing an impression of theirs, but still pleasant on the ears. Lyn was delighted. How many ways was it possible to speak the same language? "I'm Sefaro Shinju, ambassador for the Crown of Mysia." He gestured at the other men. "My... esteemed companions are Princes Dairinn and Naoise of Grenlec."

Lyn blinked. Princes? In the middle of the forest? Then she remembered she was supposed to be a princess and had to choke back a laugh.

"Very helpful," the big, loud one said, rolling his eyes. "Thank you, Mysian. It's best to go about blurting our names to every ruffian on our trail. Good to let them know just how much of a ransom they can expect."

"Dairinn–" the elegant black-haired man began tiredly.

But Lyn wasn't waiting to hear it. "I am not a *ruffian*," she objected. Well, maybe Cole was a ruffian, but that was beside the point. "And I am not on your trail. My name's Lyn and I couldn't give the broken tail-end of a single mangy raccoon who you are or what you're doing here – well, I could have, until you ended up being *rude*."

It was the man named Dairinn's turn to blink.

The one called Naoise moved closer so he could lower his voice. "Forgive my brother, please. We've... just suffered a great disappointment."

Dairinn snorted loudly.

"I hope you will pardon my asking," the polite prince went on, "but you are an elf, are you not?"

At Lyn's side, Cole tensed and gripped his sword hilt harder. "We have a problem, friend?" There was not the least trace of cordiality in the word.

"Not at all," Naoise hastened to assure him. "I can see you are concerned for the lady's welfare. That is commendable. Be assured, we mean harm to neither of you." Lyn realized she hadn't seen anyone speak to Cole with such respect before. It was an odd thing, and she found herself annoyed that it had taken this long to happen.

Cole grunted. He had definitely assumed a stance Lyn was not comfortable with, muscles taut and ready for violence. "Two Grenlecians making friendly with an elf. I've been around a bit, but I've never seen *that* before."

"Cole." Lyn used her sweetest voice. Bryant would have known to be alarmed. "You want to back off? Please? Before I have to kill you myself?" She smiled sunnily at the prince named Naoise. "Well, you've got an oaf and so do I. Looks like we've already got something in common."

Naoise returned her smile, slowly. "That is something. This might be too forward of me, my lady, but I'm hoping we share something else as well."

The man who had identified himself as Mysian spun quickly to face his Grenlecian friend. "My lord. You don't think–?"

The prince was nodding. "As I said, Sefaro: I hope." He turned his sharp attention back to Lyn. "You wouldn't by any chance be going to Evlédíen, would you? We've an invitation from the princess that we should very much like to accept, but I'm afraid we've lost our guide."

"The princess, huh?" Lyn winked at Cole, who shook his head. "What a coincidence."

"Please don't," Cole murmured at her side. His tone said that he already knew the request was futile.

She reached into her jacket. "Would this map help?"

# Chapter Twelve

In the early days of Asrellion, when the first elves awoke in the forest, they had an entire world to learn. What to call everything, how the seasons worked, weather, food – magic. They had magic in their blood, many of them. None more powerfully than Voroméasa, who joined her life to that of Selatho and became the first queen.

She put her insatiable curiosity to work, discovering the Art and its uses, with Vaian as her teacher it was said. The Raia bloodline carried that power down through the years.

Her grandson Véloro was commonly regarded as the most powerful master of the Art the world had ever seen, and he had died seeing how far he could go. An accident in his laboratory. Those who discovered it described the scene as horrific, but there was no disputing that the man had been a genius.

Loralíenasa, last of the line, had all the power expected of a Raia. She had been apprenticed to the greatest known master of the Art and trained from a young age.

And she hated it.

The Míyahídéna stood in front of a familiar door in Níerí Tower within the palace, sick to her stomach. The last time she'd spoken to her master, when she had informed him she was ending her studies, he had told her she was a disappointment to her ancestors and would never have his respect. He had also said a number of even harsher things. She had good reason to believe he'd be happy if he never saw her again.

Honestly, the feeling was mutual. She was able to enjoy a stab of sour amusement at the thought that with all of the terrible things happening in the world, even with a powerful sorcerer trying to kill them all and destroy Evlédíen, the prospect of having a conversation with Ítaja Qíarna was nearly the worse fate.

She drew a deep breath, told herself to grow up, and knocked on the glossy ebony door.

As ever, it was a while before he bothered to respond. He believed his time was more valuable than anyone else's – when he acknowledged the existence of other people. A surly voice finally called out for her to enter. Loralíenasa braced herself and stepped into the enchanter's laboratory.

It was no surprise to find the place just as she had last seen it. Precariously overstocked shelves, strange aromas, busy workstations groaning beneath the weight of books and tools and various bubbling flasks. As usual, he had the curtains drawn. Natural light, he liked to say, was the enemy of synthesis. One required a controlled environment for the Art's manipulations.

Also as usual, the man himself was lost inside his projects. Today he was working a mortar and pestle with single-minded vigor, his long pale hair tied out of his way at the nape of his neck. The furrow between his thin brows would have seemed too severe for the situation if Lorien didn't know for a fact that he always wore exactly that same expression of vague disapproval.

She lifted her right hand to her brow in a gesture of respect even though he wasn't yet looking her way. "I apologize for the intrusion, Ítaja."

He looked up swiftly at the sound of her voice. When his lips turned down and thinned like he had smelled something sour, it was a deliberate remark on her presence in his laboratory. "Míyahídéna. I told you not to come back here. I had thought I was perfectly explicit."

Ítaja Qíarna, once her master. The memories were not good.

Loralíenasa squared her shoulders. "You were." It was as though he had only just ordered her out a moment earlier, not nearly a decade ago. Her gut was in knots. "I would not be disturbing you without cause, Ítaja."

The older elf grunted and returned to his work. "Whatever the cause, I have nothing further to say to you."

Oh, Vaian. Lorien asked herself why she had thought this was a good idea. She had told herself he'd listen to her if only she could apologize enough. He had always liked to see her humbled. It was a matter of balance, though; he would dismiss her if he felt she was giving way to her emotions.

She cleared her throat, trying not to sound diffident. "I seek your council, Ítaja Qíarna," she said, "in a matter beyond my knowledge."

"You?" He did not bother looking up from his desk. "You have never respected my knowledge in the past, nor have you ever troubled to take my advice, even when it was sought. Why now?"

She had anticipated that question, or one like it, and was ready with an answer. Appealing to his vanity certainly couldn't hurt. "Evlédíen is in peril, and you are perhaps the only one with information that can avail us."

That earned a short sigh. "You are referring to that business on the training field. I have already told Lord Maiantar everything I know about this *Kataki Kuromé*, and that is nothing. I have never heard of him, nor do I know how he managed to work his Art within our barrier, though my guess would be that it had to do with that letter."

Venturing closer to his workstation, Loralíenasa felt she was wading into a fog of tangible resistance. She stopped. He watched her with cold eyes.

"You may know him by another name," she suggested. He hadn't thrown her out yet, even if he was telling her to go away. "Our intelligence tells us he was once called Soríjuhí Volarín."

The icy scowl smoothed suddenly into surprised blankness. Qíarna allowed the pestle to drop into the mortar with a muffled clatter as he stood upright and went through an obvious struggle to contain his reaction. It was the most intensely expressive she had ever seen him before. "Where did you hear that name?"

She tried to keep the impatience from her voice. "You recognize it?"

"I do," he replied, turning his back to her. She could see the tension in his shoulders. "We studied under the same Ítaja in Eselvwey. Though not at the same time; he was several years my elder. From my Ítaja I heard many stories of the student prodigy I could never seem to surpass in any facet of the Art. He was a bright flame, full of passion and ambition. It was as a compliment to me that my Ítaja bestowed upon me the name of Qíarna, for he wished to show me that there was at least one – if only one – way in which I outstripped my predecessor."

Loralíenasa was silent for a long time, processing this new information. "He was not always bad?"

Her former master shook his head, still speaking to the wall. "What does *bad* mean, in any case? So imprecise. At one time Ríju was one of the most vivid souls in Eselvwey, though he did struggle with various... social anxieties; he could not abide crowds. Kept himself isolated by choice. My Ítaja could not speak highly enough of him. He always said Ríju was so inventive and put so much passion into the Art, he could do anything he decided to try."

She felt her heart sink. This was her enemy.

Qíarna's voice took on a note of admonition as he finally turned to face her once more. "He is far too powerful and too cunning to be checked by you. Do not engage him, Míyahídéna. Make peace if you can. That is the best – the only council I can give you."

"If only I could," she replied, wincing inwardly at the harsh truth of the matter. "He is the one threatening Evlédíen."

Qíarna shook his head. He had control of his expression now, but so carefully and completely that it was statement enough of how hard he was trying. "Then we must pray our barrier holds. It was made by every mage in the Valley working in concert, and will not likely fail under the assault of one man alone, not even the great Soríjuhí Volarín."

His words reminded her too much of Tomanasíl's helplessness, and she felt them prompting a mulish obstinacy within her. "He has already breached it once."

To her surprise, Qíarna came out from behind his desk then, the aroma of strange herbs following him. He stood before her looking down, tall and imposing and every bit as forbidding as he had ever been when ordering her to repeat a lesson.

"There was a time, perhaps, when your feet were on the path to greatness, but you strayed from it long ago. You are unfocused, lazy in the Art; you do not respect it." He spoke softly, but his voice carried volumes of accusation.

She swallowed and forced herself to endure.

He was not finished. "You have wasted your talents on your fascination with hollow adventure and the vain waving of weapons. *You are less than you should be.* You will never now be great, and Soríjuhí Volarín is likely the most powerful wielder of the Art in Asrellion, easily the rival of Véloro Chalaqar. You stand not a flower's chance in a deep freeze against him."

"Then help me!" She did not stop herself in time; there was too much passion in her voice. His lip twitched in disdain at the loss of control, but she went on. There was no use pretending now. "*You* face him! Or stand with me, and we will face him together. The Valley needs you, Ítaja. We cannot simply ignore this and hope the threat disappears. If he is as powerful as you say–" and she did not doubt it– "then our only hope lies in you. Please, Ítaja."

She lowered her head respectfully and forced herself to take a steadier tone.

"Not for me. I know I am a disappointment. For Evlédíen, for the memory of Eselvwey that was. For the man Katakí Kuromé used to be. Help me. Help me find a way to stop him before he goes too far."

But her former master simply shook his head and looked down at her with cold, hard eyes. "Once more, you are not listening to me. You *cannot* stop him, Míyahídéna, nor can I. I fail to see how my assured death facing him would benefit Evlédíen. Yours is the reasoning of an over-emotional child."

He raised a hand before she could respond to that, and she found herself suddenly unable to speak.

"I told you I had nothing to say to you," he said, "and that has not changed. Neither have you, I might add. A pity. Evlédíen deserves more." He pointed at the door. "Now go, and do not return."

At least he allowed her the dignity of walking to the door under her own power.

"You don't remember anything? At all?"

Lyn figured she was probably supposed to be annoyed that Dairinn was being nosy after showing no interest in her story for two weeks. But the truth was, it was just nice to have so many new people to talk to. People who laughed at her jokes. She aimed a mental headshake in Cole's direction.

"Only thing I think I might remember is... I don't know." She shrugged. "It's maybe a memory, maybe not, but I think I have a feeling like I'm supposed to be – it's hard to describe. Like I'm half of something?"

The handsome elder prince shook his head like she made no sense. Maybe she didn't. But he didn't say so.

Instead he asked, huffing as they climbed ever higher, "But about the place you came from. The place we're going. Nothing?"

Well that was new. He hadn't seemed that interested in informing himself until now. Maybe the fact that they were getting close to their destination had him realizing he had no idea what to expect. Or maybe he'd finally gotten tired of talking about himself.

She looked ahead to see which path Cole was taking up the rocky mountainside and readjusted accordingly. "I told you already. I've lived in the forest since before I was old enough to talk. As far as I'm concerned, pal, *that's* where I come from."

"So..." He stopped and gasped for air.

They were high up now and the temperature had dropped dramatically. It interested Lyn to note how badly the humans seemed to be handling the cold that wasn't bothering her in the slightest. The younger brother, Naoise, had long ago stopped trying to talk through the chattering of his teeth, which was a shame because the questions *he* asked were actually engaging.

"So you grew up in a forest? Have you never even been to a city?" Dairinn gamely tried again, wrapping his cloak tighter about his body. He was built entirely unlike Bryant, she couldn't help but notice beneath the lines of the cloak. Unlike Cole too, who was shorter and more compact than the broad-shouldered Grenlecian. He wasn't even like his brother. Naoise's build was more like Bryant's, but taller. And then Sefaro, of course, was like none of them.

She was delightedly realizing how different it turned out people could be from each other. Not just physically, either. The two brothers proved the point.

"Sure I have," she said in response to Dairinn's question, beaming up the mountain at Cole's back. "We went through Telrisht City on our way south. *Horrible* place."

"I will not argue," Dairinn agreed with fervor.

Lyn shook her head at the memory. Her first experience with civilization had not endeared it to her. Telrisht City under Grenlecian occupation was a dirty, angry, overcrowded place straining with barely-held tensions.

"You should come to Zarishan one day," Sefaro said from the path behind her. "I daresay you would find it more agreeable."

"If you grew up in a forest," the prince huffed, trying to sound amiable with an effort, "then who is it raised you? Wolves?"

"Oh, no," Lyn said cheerfully. She appreciated that he'd finally asked. "I was raised by–"

"Cave up ahead," Cole's voice cut in from the slope above. She looked up and found him stopped, scowling down at the rest of them as the sharp mountain wind whipped his cloak back crazily. "We should think about setting up for the night. Not a lot of light left."

Dairinn checked the sky and seemed genuinely surprised to find the sun already hidden behind snow-capped peaks. "Well, then. Let's have a look."

He gave his horse an encouraging pat on the shoulder and pulled the animal forward by its bridle, past Lyn up what they were generously calling a path. Cole stood still a moment longer, watching Lyn. She wasn't sure, but something about the wrinkling of his brow suggested he had interrupted the conversation on purpose. Would he tell the truth if she asked him, she wondered.

Sefaro passed her by with a shy smile as she stood pondering Cole's weirdness. Naoise came up the path after him, looking every bit as uneasy as

Cole ever did, his face taut and paler than usual.

What he needed was a hug, she decided. Naoise and Cole both. Not that she imagined she could get close enough to Cole for it without finding herself on the end of one of his many hidden knives. It would be good for him, though. He looked, actually, like a man who had never been hugged properly in his entire life. Lyn felt sorry for him if that was true.

"You coming?" Cole called, impatience flattening his tone.

Lyn shook herself out of her wild tangent and followed the others.

The cave didn't turn out to be much of a cave – just an indentation in the side of the mountain that offered a bit of shelter from the howling wind on a stone shelf, with enough space for all of them and their horses to settle in with only minor crowding. It was the best they were likely to do. Lyn didn't know if these mountains were less hospitable than any others, but she felt that whatever the case, it was like the rocks themselves didn't want them to be there.

After two weeks on the road together, they had begun to understand each other's routines. Cole wasted no time getting a fire going from kindling he'd collected lower down the mountain while Naoise saw to the horses and Sefaro started on dinner. Dairinn pretended to be useful by laying out the bedrolls, but it was all just an excuse to sit down sooner and monitor the progress of the food while complaining about the pain in his feet. None of them seemed to want to let Lyn do anything, which was stupid, but she was perfectly content to watch them go through their various motions. She hadn't had entertainment like this in a while.

Cole soon had a roaring fire built up; Naoise gratefully huddled close to it once he'd finished with the horses. Giving everyone a glance of careful appraisal and finding the others occupied in their various ways, Cole plucked at Lyn's sleeve and gestured with his head for her to follow him out of earshot.

"You might want to, well..." He stopped and frowned harder. "These fellows seem decent enough, for nobility," he whispered, "but it might not be the best idea to go around talking about fairies and magic and whatnot. At least not while you're in human lands."

She grinned back at him and cuffed him on the shoulder. "Well we're not. Right? We're in the wilderness."

The man flicked his eyes toward his abused shoulder. "It's not that simple. Just... be careful."

She looked at him, really looked, and was touched to see more than just his regular caution etching lines in his forehead. He was genuinely concerned for her. She smiled. "Aw, Cole."

He took a step back, clearing his throat gruffly. "I'm trying to do my job. Lyn. It's harder when you put yourself in danger on purpose."

Like when she'd offered to let these men follow her to Evlédíen, she knew he was thinking but not saying. He'd been grouchy enough about it over the past two weeks to make her wonder if it had been a good idea, but she always decided it was for the best. If nothing else, they would be three more swords against the men in black, when they turned up again, and they were good company besides. Better company than boring, grim old Cole. Even if it looked like maybe he didn't hate her.

"You worry too much."

"You don't worry enough," he said when she turned away to head back to the fire.

Dairinn made such a great show of waving her over that Lyn laughed and had to accept the place he'd made for her close to the fire's warmth. He moved in beside her and leaned his shoulder against hers, winking when she raised her eyebrows.

"What? It's cold!" he deflected with a charm that would have made Bryant jealous.

Cole walked by, grunting, on his way to fetch water from the saddlebags.

"Tell me about your home," the elder prince said to her, still smiling.

Lyn opened her mouth, glanced at Cole, and decided to be kind to the man who spent so much of his energy worrying about her. "Just a forest. I'd rather hear more about Grenlec. What's it like, living in a city?"

He waved a dismissive hand. "I've been doing nothing but talk about my-self and Grenlec since we met."

"He finally speaks truth," Naoise said with a dry chuckle. "Maybe it's someone else's turn to talk, for a change of pace."

Cole returned with the water in silence, but Lyn could see that the lines of his shoulders had tensed, as if he was readying himself for trouble.

"Let's hear it, Lyn," Dairinn said, nudging her playfully. "You're well-spoken for a wild forest nymph. Who raised you and taught you to be so… graceful? A spirit of the forest?"

He laughed at himself as if the suggestion was embarrassingly childish.

Lyn glanced at Cole across the fire and raised her eyebrows. What did he expect her to do when asked directly? Lie? She was no good at that, as he would learn if she had to try.

"Maybe we could all share something about ourselves," Cole said quietly, with great weariness, "now that the prince is willing to let someone else have a moment of attention."

"Actually, you know who I'd like to hear from?" Sefaro agreed unexpectedly, looking up from his cookpot.

Cole sighed as if he knew what was coming.

"You, sir," the Mysian said to him with a friendly smile. "You must admit, you hardly say much. If you're willing to share, we should be pleased to know more about you."

Then Lyn understood that Cole had invited this in order to deflect attention away from her, and her earlier urge to hug the frown off his face grew even stronger. She couldn't think of a more selfless thing that anyone had ever done for her. Even if she did think he was making something out of nothing.

Her protector started talking haltingly, his voice quiet, which only made the things he said hurt more.

"I was born in Rosemarch, in a small village you've never heard of in the north. My mother was a dairymaid. I don't know who my father was. She never talked about him. Hit me when I asked. Walked out when I was seven, and I never saw her again." He pushed on through his companions' sudden uncomfortable silence. "I took work at the local inn, did the bad jobs no one else wanted. My pay was dinner and a place to sleep. Anything else to eat I had to scrounge for myself. The innkeeper used to beat me with a leather stropping belt each night to make sure I remembered my place."

Lyn's chest went tight and hot as she listened.

"I ran away when I was ten," Cole went on matter-of-factly, "and took to petty crime to keep fed. Picking pockets, robbing farms. Slept wherever I could. I was in and out of jail for a while until the local magistrate decided to solve my need for food and shelter with a hanging." He appeared to be gaining momentum now, but he spoke looking into the fire and not at any of them. "I was fifteen then and I didn't want to die. I got free and left the area. Crossed Rosemarch on my own." He heaved a deep breath. "I finally found a tradesman willing to take me on, a blacksmith. That lasted about a year and a half, until the people found out I'm a bastard and a thief and ran me out of town. Didn't want 'my kind' around their women and children.

"I ran into a company of mercenaries. They let me join up even though I didn't have any experience fighting. Said I looked like I could pick it up in a hurry." He shrugged. "They were right. I stayed with them more than seven years.

"I found Bryant while I was with Rogue Company." He smiled grimly into the fire. "Spying on our encampment on my watch. I didn't know what he was. I wanted to haul him over to my superiors and dump the problem into their hands, but he talked me out of it with that silver tongue of his. I guess I was as strange to him as he was to me, because he followed us to winter quarters, kept pestering me. We got to be friends after a while. He was like a ghost, the way he made sure none of the others ever saw him. Mostly we only met when Rogue Company quartered for winter, but a few times he hunted me down on a job. Said he wanted to see what I did for a living. Said he didn't like it.

"He finally convinced me to quit the company and lead a more upstanding life," he said with a single mirthless chuckle. "So I tried again in a village close to where Bryant and Lyn lived in the forest – carpentry, this time. I'd learned a little wintering with the company.

"That's where I was when Bryant told me he remembered being a prince and Lyn was his sister. He made me promise to take care of her if anything ever happened to him, which of course it was going to after he made me agree to something like that. He always *was* determined to make a gentleman of me," he said with a shake of his head. "I don't know why he bothered.

"So there you go – that's my story," he concluded. "He was killed and I stayed to protect Lyn like I promised. Now here were all are."

After that, when the food was ready, they ate in silence. Lyn knew she couldn't think of anything to say.

The Qíarnos forbade displays of anger.

Tomanasíl often told Loralíenasa what a terrible student of the philosophy she was, but she did try. At the moment, she considered it an enormous triumph of control that she had not yet struck the Captain's insubordinate, ill-tempered guardsman right in the face.

"Explain to me," she said through a clenched jaw, "why you felt you had to disregard your orders?"

The man Lanoralas had told her she could trust – the one they had sent all the way to distant Mysia on the most important of missions – lifted his chin at the Míyahídéna.

"My orders said nothing about bringing enemies into Evlédíen," he replied tersely. "I might be willing to apologize for my lapse in judgment if you say I ought to have disposed of the Grenlecians and continued on with the Mysian.

I do not apologize for aborting a botched mission."

Behind her, Lanoralas sighed. It was a sound of frustration, not weariness.

"Guardsman, you were told to bring the Mysian ambassador to the Míya-hídéna. That you did not do."

Loríen had never heard him use this voice before, cold and hard and towering with authority. He was suddenly the Captain of the Guard and not her friend Lanas.

But the heavily-armed elf being dressed down by his superior officer looked not in the least repentant. Tired, irate, dusty and somewhat ragged in clothing that had seen a long road, but not apologetic. He stood at attention while Lanoralas went on to explain that this was not acceptable behavior for one of his men and would not go unpunished.

The Qíarnos forbade displays of anger.

Loralíenasa drew a deep breath and tried to summon a mental image of her favorite spot in the gardens, beside the pond. The placid water under a setting sun, a soft breeze in the leaves.

"Captain," she interrupted when she felt she could do so without raising her voice. The look on Lanas' face matched the unpleasant feeling in Loralíenasa's stomach.

"Where did you leave them?" she asked the guardsman slowly. He had made contact with Mysia after more than three thousand years of silence, assured them of her goodwill, and then left the Mysian ambassador all alone in the middle of the wilderness during wartime. She really felt she could kill.

Sovoqatsu Farínaiqa frowned, but could not pretend she hadn't asked. "At Scathan Falls. The Grenlecians were all but home."

"But the man you were sent for," Loralíenasa reminded him as calmly as she could manage. She kept an image of that tranquil pond before her and breathed slowly. "He is *not*. You will go back for him, before he comes to harm." *Before* you *come to harm, she added mentally.*

"Loríen–" Lanoralas shook his head.

Sovoqatsu interrupted. Loralíenasa could see the annoyance flashing across Lanas' face as he did so. "My lady, that was two weeks ago. Even if I agreed to go back–"

"You would disobey me?" she snapped. "*Again?*" The man seriously did want a thrashing.

The guardsman's severe eyebrows drew into a fierce line. "It *is* against the Regent's law to leave the Valley."

Lanas took a step back from the guardsman in order to speak closer to her ear. "Loríen. This man disregarded orders. I can't let that go. Even if I wanted to send him back for the Mysian – even if he could still be found. I must maintain discipline amongst my men."

She shook her head. "I understand. But what about giving him a chance to carry out the order? For a chance to lessen his punishment, perhaps?"

Sovoqatsu answered flatly though the suggestion was not made to him. "No."

"Hold your tongue, Farínaiqa," Lanoralas said. He was less stern when he turned to Loralíenasa. "I wouldn't send an unwilling man into the field, even if I felt it could do any good."

"But–"

He put a hand out to stop her. "I've no wish to fight with you, Loríen, but the Guard is my business and I have to handle it as I think best or I am not serving you or Evlédíen to the fullest of my ability. Disobedience in the ranks cannot be ignored."

No. Loralíenasa was *not* going to lose her temper. She breathed slowly. "Then what do we do next?"

The Captain turned a forbidding scowl on the waiting guardsman. "To start, we don't discuss our plans in front of someone who has already proven himself disloyal."

"With respect, Captain, I disagree with the accusation of disloyalty," Sovoqatsu argued, standing tall. "I did what I felt I had to in order to keep Evlédíen safe."

"Honestly, man, you showed yourself all the way through Mysia and back again," Loralíenasa replied with some exasperation. "You were bringing a Mysian ambassador here to talk about peace and a possible alliance. How long did you imagine we were going to keep ourselves a secret from Grenlec after that?"

He grunted and didn't answer.

Lanoralas didn't wait for one, anyway. "Guardsman Farínaiqa, you are stripped of your arms and confined to the tower until further punishment has been determined."

Loralíenasa closed her eyes and wondered how much worse things could possibly get.

Bryant's map showed their pass lying between the curving, jagged horns of the two peaks they hoped they were heading for. Other than the brief mention of a gate and a password, the map gave no indication of what they should expect when they got there.

Lyn spent most of their morning hike working up her courage while they were buffeted by increasingly sharp gusts. Finally, she just decided to do it. She made her way up beside Cole at the head of their struggling column. He glanced at her with his usual frown, but said nothing.

"So." She smiled, hoping it would help. "Those things you said last night."

He grunted.

"Were they true?"

"Yep."

Lyn thought about that as she hiked next to him. All true. Not that she'd expected him to confess a fondness for wild storytelling. She wished Bryant was here.

After she'd gone a while without responding, Cole looked over at her and raised his eyebrows. "That all you wanted?"

"No, I..." She shook her head. "I'm trying to think of what to say. I'm sure there's a normal response for these situations and I just don't know it because apparently I grew up feral. Or something."

Cole jerked his head at the path behind them, toward the three other men toiling their way up the mountainside. "You notice none of them have said anything either? It's because there *isn't* a normal response. I broke the unspoken code: men don't talk about things that hurt."

She thought about that for a minute too. "And you did it so Dairinn would stop asking about me."

He shrugged, leather doublet creaking.

"So I owe you."

"I was doing my job. You don't have to go on about it."

"But I want to." As soon as she said it, she realized what was bothering her. She didn't think less of Cole after what he'd shared last night, but it was easy enough to see that he was used to people thinking poorly of him and it was what he expected. And he had been nothing but honest and decent with her from that first moment in the forest. It wasn't fair. "People have always judged you on where you come from, not who you are, and you deserve more than that."

That prompted an unexpected anger like she'd never seen in him before. "I don't deserve anything, Lyn. All you get from life is what you can take from it. There is no *deserving*."

Lyn hurried to catch up to his suddenly longer strides. "You don't believe that." When he didn't answer, she added, "Bryant knew all of that about you, right? And he always believed in you anyway. Isn't it nicer to think it's because you deserved it?"

"I've never known why he trusted me," Cole countered. "You mattered to him more than anything. Why he would go to someone like me for–" He glanced at Lyn again and the set of his mouth shifted from anger to sadness. "I'll never understand. But we don't need to talk about this. Let's just get where we're going, all right?" He surged ahead of her with his powerful stride and didn't look back.

She followed him up through the rocks, toward those looming peaks. She was uncharacteristically deep in thought, some moments later, when she looked up to realize that he had stopped. He was staring.

Lyn stared with him.

She had never seen two such improbably massive gates before in all her life. Straddling the gap between the peaks with authority, they were as tall as the giant wych elm that had grown by the lake at home, but wrought more delicately in silver and twisting gold than anything so enormous had a right to be. The design was almost hypnotic; she found herself unable to follow one gleaming tendril all the way through the pattern. It shimmered in a way that had nothing to do with the sunlight shafting down onto its many curved surfaces. A way that seemed to say, *No. Turn back. This is not for you.*

"Well," Sefaro said behind her, subdued. "I suppose we've found it."

Dairinn shifted uneasily. "I say. What do we... *do*?"

"I believe the map said something about a password," Naoise said in a hushed tone. It was strange, Lyn thought, but somehow proper that they all seemed to feel there was something here they ought to avoid disturbing. Or perhaps awakening.

She swallowed and pulled the map out of her doublet. Bryant had scrawled three words of gibberish at the bottom.

"*Chanar thasa vaia,*" Naoise murmured, reading over her shoulder.

Lyn snorted. "I'm glad you can read it. I don't speak a word of this nonsense."

"That's going to be... interesting, when we get inside," Dairinn observed.

They all looked at the gates, hoping they were going to do something. No matter how they all stared, though, nothing moved. Cole drew a deep breath, squared his shoulders, and approached the gold-and-silver behemoths. After a moment, Naoise joined him.

"*Chachor?*" Naoise called, attempting to peer through the gates. "*Ídartaso qaio-qío lan?*"

"Handy in a pinch, your brother," Sefaro murmured to Dairinn.

Lyn shushed him.

She was still staring at those massive gates, expecting something to come through them, when she heard the granite shifting behind her and suddenly a sharp point was pressing against her lower back. Dairinn exclaimed without words in the same moment. Lyn smiled thinly at Cole and Naoise when they whirled at the sound, hands on sword hilts. She tilted her head back toward the handful of armed elves in blue uniforms that had materialized from the rocks behind her.

"Hey, Naoise. I don't suppose you know how to say, *'Please don't stab me, I'm your princess'?* "

## Chapter Thirteen

Lord Tomanasíl was not an elf given to excessive displays of emotion, so Loralíenasa had grown adept over the years at reading the lines of his body, the set of his face, the minute changes in his eyes and coloring. When he set his papers down and ordered them meticulously in a corner of his desk without looking at her as she came into his office, the formality of his movements told her he was furious enough to commit murder.

In truth, she had been waiting for this ever since she'd started working with Lanoralas in secret to protect Evlédíen.

She gestured respectfully. "You sent for me, my lord?"

His eyes were blue ice. "Loralíenasa. I'm so pleased you decided to answer my summons promptly, for a change."

She didn't blink at the rebuke. She was *usually* prompt, but to him she was the wayward ward and he saw what he wanted to see. "My lord, you said it was urgent," she replied. "Of course I would never neglect such a message."

His eyes narrowed a little. "Quite. Well then, Míyahídéna, to the matter at hand."

Loralíenasa found herself fascinated by a single throbbing vein at the side of his forehead. She could only remember seeing it once before, when he had first discovered she'd been traveling outside the Valley. She shuddered at the memory.

He continued quietly. "I was given some news today. Would you like me to share it?"

Under the circumstances, she felt it was best to keep her mouth shut. She merely raised an eyebrow and wondered what new headache was on its way.

Tomanasíl's tone remained level, but that vein was pounding and his color began to change, the rich dark hue blanching from his cheeks. "I've received word from the mountain gate."

If he expected her to give something away, she was determined to disappoint him. What could they have contacted Tomanasíl about that would have him this angry, anyway? Her scouts were all accounted for – but for poor Iríjo, whose fate was all too evident. If the gate sentries had intended to inform on her, surely they would have done it already.

Her guardian stood and walked slowly around the desk to stand directly before her. The muscles in his jaw were jumping. "I confess I am at somewhat of a loss. You see, what they tell me makes little sense. Something about a clutch of humans at the gate, with one of our passphrases, demanding to be brought safely to the Míyahídéna *who invited them to Evlédien.*"

Loralíenasa blinked. How, in the name of Everything, had they managed to find their way to the gate? With a passphrase?

"You feign surprise?" There was an alarming wrath in his eyes, made more so by the calm silk of his voice. "You dare to pretend this is not your doing?"

She swallowed and gathered her courage. "No. You are correct, my lord: I did invite Mysia to the Valley, so that I could warn them and discuss our mutual enemy. You weren't going to do the right thing; someone had to. I will not see them destroyed after they risked everything to protect us."

That vein in his forehead had practically taken on a life of its own, and his face was now close to the shade of bleached sand. He bared his teeth for a moment in an expression of rage that was so unlike him she felt the fabric of the world sliding out from under her feet.

He turned his back to her, which was more terrifying still. "I don't... know what to do with you, Loralíenasa."

Past him, outside his office window facing the royal gardens, a handful of snowflakes flurried down – the first of the season. She watched them settle and disappear against the glass and wondered what her guardian intended to do with the humans. What he intended to do with her. She sank into the nearest chair and waited with held breath for him to speak his mind.

"It is high time you took your position and your duties seriously, Loralíenasa."

What did he *think* she'd been doing?

"You are no longer a child and I will not suffer you to behave like one," he went on, cold judgment building in his words. "Acting against my express orders, betraying your own people, inciting our soldiers to commit treason, sneaking and conniving and exchanging secret messages...? This is no game.

You've exposed us all to the gravest of danger, and for what? Because you were bored? Feeling thwarted? *Grow up*, Loralíenasa. Our survival depends on staying hidden, and you have just negated that. Does it excite your little girl's heart to know the Valley will be destroyed because of you?"

It was almost impossible to keep her voice level in the face of his unfair accusations, his deliberate antagonism. She wanted to launch herself from her chair, to yell out that she had only done what was right. But she knew that Tomanasíl would never change, just as no elf would ever change, and that arguing with him about this now would only worsen her plight. He was Regent, and in his eyes she would always be a defiant child incapable of rational decisions – and he was now the one dooming them all because his fear had him blind to reason. The brutal unfairness of it–

"It's not a game, and I never thought it was," she murmured with effort. "I did what I had to."

"As I will now be forced to do," he replied quietly, turning to face her.

Loralíenasa had never been frightened of another person in all her life. She was afraid of her guardian now. She gripped the ebony arms of her chair until her fingers went bloodless. "What do you intend to do?"

His teeth flashed again without mirth. "Ah. Now we come to it, don't we?" His tone almost froze her blood in her veins. "I intend to see that you are made to feel sorry for what you have done."

That was as expected. She was afraid to breathe as she asked, "The humans: what will you do with them?"

"I might well be forced to kill them, thanks to your foolishness in bringing them here. They know the way into the Valley, a secret that must be protected at any cost. Know that their deaths will be on your head if that happens."

"Our *real* enemy already knows the way in," she argued with some heat.

He didn't respond to that. "I am having them brought to Efrondel, where they will be confined until I can decide what is to be done with them. They have… made a wild claim that I must verify before taking further action."

"You cannot kill foreign ambassadors," Loralíenasa pointed out. "We are not murderers."

"What we are," her guardian replied in a deadly whisper, "is nearly extinct. If you will take no care for that fact, then I must."

She shook her head, nearly tearing the arms from her chair with the sheer effort of not yelling her frustration. "This is wrong. My lord, you are in the wrong. And you wrong *me*."

Tomanasíl finally showed a crack in his veneer of calm, folding trembling hands behind his back. "*I* wrong *you?*" His voice shook with barely-restrained anger. "After all of the years I have devoted to you, all of the undeserved abuse from you I've weathered, all of the care I've taken to raise you to be something your family might not be ashamed of, the life of my own I've been made to set aside in order to be here for you – and you continue to disrespect me at every turn, to treat me like an enemy, a fool, worse. Even you, I would not expect to have the *gall* to say such a thing to me after this gross betrayal of what trust I have invested in you."

Loralíenasa knew she was too angry to speak reasonably, and clamped her mouth shut. Her face felt like it was in flames.

Her guardian was silent for a moment, visibly returning himself to a more appropriately calm state. He settled carefully behind his marble-topped desk once more and folded his hands on its smooth surface. When the frigid rage had left his eyes, he drew a deep breath and said, "In a moment the Guard will remove you from my office, Míyahídéna. You will be taken from my sight, and you will not enter it again until you are sent for."

The journey, once it began, passed quickly.

They all spent some time shivering in a guard tower at the pass while the elven guards – an even mix of men and women, Naoise noted with some be-musement, all of them armed and intimidating – conferred and sent a message to their superiors. It had started to snow. The elves didn't bind them, but they disarmed them and made it clear that they were prisoners. Even Lyn.

She mystified them, shrilling demands to be released and taken to her sis-ter in a language not their own, and completely unable to speak what should have been her native tongue. Naoise felt sorry for her, but her plight seemed the least of their troubles. He doubted *her* life was in danger for trespassing, after all.

Their status as prisoners became even more clear when they were forced into a march down the treacherous mountainside – into the hidden kingdom. That was a surprise, given their reception. Naoise wondered that they hadn't simply been turned away, or killed on sight. They traveled at the rate set by their captors, stopping only when one of the humans was unable to go farther without rest. Suddenly Naoise understood the relentless pace Lyn had tried to set south from the lake; it had seemed normal to her.

The guards didn't say much by way of explanation when Naoise asked where they were going, just that they were being taken to the Lord Regent. From there everything seemed to move at an unnatural speed to bring them to a moment in which he stood, awestruck, at the top of a ridge looking down upon Efrondel.

When he had read the name of the city on the map, he'd wondered if it was meant to be poetic or metaphorical. But when he looked down at the capital of Evlédíen, and saw the sunlight glinting off the many-faceted surfaces, he knew it was not. The city was literally constructed of crystal.

It was a painful kind of beauty, difficult to look at; it reminded him of a certain young elf woman he had met once.

Efrondel had been meticulously laid out from the first moment of its conception in the mind of the artisans who had built it, clearly. Not a single detail of the city seemed without serious premeditation. Even the overall shape was exact, outlined in the form of an eight-pointed star across the River Efron, oriented to the points of the compass. At the city center, the marketplace of Efrondel circled a massive star-shaped fountain, and from it radiated the eight main roads that extended down the rays of the star – four of them shorter than the other half. The streets themselves, improbably, seemed to be paved with silver cobblestones.

Naoise could hardly comprehend the volume of the precious metal that must have been required for that, or fathom the character of a people who were content to tread casually upon it without a second thought.

But their elven guards allowed them no pause to gather their wits, ushering them quickly down into Efrondel.

Within the careful layout of the city, each sector was immaculately organized. Residential, business, artisan, arts and recreation – each element had its own proper place. The river was crossed by three bridges. Each impossibly delicate span was covered in gold and ornamented with precious gems – ruby, diamond, and black onyx, respectively. Naoise couldn't imagine such a thing in a human city, nor how it was that the jewels had not all been pried from their settings by thieves long ago.

And there seemed to be no defense in place against military attack – another insanity. At the city limits, the larger rays were enclosed only by filigreed golden fences, the shorter rays by neat lines of trees of a kind Naoise had never before seen, with bark and leaves that looked to be made of silver though they were living things. The tall silver towers at each point were there for aesthetics only, as far as he could tell, not to guard the city.

They made their way due south down the main road, crossing the river on a bridge so exquisite it should have been unable to bear their weight. Naoise was too dumbfounded to be afraid, though a part of his mind was still able to tell him he should be.

The buildings were each a work of art unique and beautiful unto themselves, no two exactly alike and yet all crafted of the same materials: crystal, gold, silver, and white marble. Towers rose toward the sky in graceful spires, most of them capped with burnished silver. Golden domes also filled the skyline, contrasting artfully with their slim, lofty counterparts.

Silver fountains were everywhere in profusion: large and austere, small and ornate, tall and elegant, artistic and strange; on rooftops, in porticoes, in courtyards, in parks, on balconies, in the spaces between buildings, flowing down walls. The music of droplets of water rising and falling was everywhere upon the air. Wherever the eye chose to turn, there was some wonder large or small to delight the senses. The city was immaculately clean, bright, and precise.

But the architectural lines of many of the sprawling, airy buildings played to an aesthetic his human tastes could only term alien no matter how open-minded he tried to be. And however beautiful the city was, however complete in its perfection, it was the beauty of the symmetry of a snowflake. It was a beauty that offered no warmth, no comfort, no welcome. It was a beauty that froze the heart, rife with symbolism and ancient pain. Meant to remind the people who lived there each day that they inhabited a world of exile – not only from their homeland, but also from joy and innocence and laughter and the noontide glow of their history.

They continued south through the busy market circle, passing elves dressed in bright, loose fabrics. In fact many of them wore the same style Naoise had seen in Zarishan, but instead of wide leather belts, they had on complicated knotted sashes over their knee-length outer coats. The boots were slightly different, more like the Telrishti style: suede or tooled leather turned up at the toe into an exaggerated point.

Others had on fashions that were even more varied and exotic, asymmetric dresses that draped and flowed over lithe bodies, many of them sheer or showing more skin than Naoise had ever before seen in a public place, even despite the chill weather, and ladies were not the only ones wearing garments that he would classify as gowns. What made it even more strange was the utter lack of passion he would have expected such a display of flesh to provoke. The elves moved about their business with cool grace, unhurried and for the most part unsmiling.

The figures themselves were as odd as the clothing they wore. They were beautiful, to be sure, but they were decidedly not human. It was all in little differences, but as a collective those differences added to an unsettling feeling of otherness. Cheekbones too high or too wide, eyes too large and set at an angle to which he was unaccustomed, movements too fluid as if their bones and ligaments were assembled differently. Features too sharp, too perfectly balanced. Ears tapering into distinct points instead of rounding off and often adorned with elaborate jewelry designed to emphasize them. Skin tones that ran through a more varied spectrum from actual black to stark white than he would have thought possible, even after seeing the diversity in Zarishan.

As Naoise and his companions passed, surrounded by grim soldiers, the people of the city fell silent and gave them a wide berth.

When they approached the southern ray, it became clear that it was dominated entirely by the massive palace and its grounds. Its tall crystal towers soared into the clouds like an entire city made of giant icicles. They passed through another set of gold filigree gates into a garden-like courtyard filled with more of the beautiful silver-skinned trees with silver leaves. A stable-hand came forward silently to take their animals. Naoise and his companions stood there on silver paving stones feeling lost and so out of their depth they might as well have stepped into a different world after crossing those mountains.

How these people had been destroyed by the barbarians of ancient Grenlec and Telrisht, Naoise could not work out.

Thirteen steps led up to a pair of ebony and crystal doors etched with abstract patterns of stars inlaid with silver. Before they had moved toward the stairs, however, the doors opened and an imperious elf clad in flowing green and white garments came out onto the landing. He instructed the guards to bring them directly to the Lord Regent. Their presence had been *known*.

Naoise passed the message on to his companions before the guards had to push them forward.

"I…" Lyn swallowed. "I don't know if I can walk."

Cole put a hand briefly on her shoulder without saying anything, then started forward. Dairinn followed his lead in uncharacteristic silence. Naoise tilted his head back to look up at towers so tall they seemed to be part of the sky itself, and had nothing to say. He pushed a hand through his hair, squared his shoulders, and made himself go after his brother.

Their escort fell in behind them, shepherding them inside. The steward closed the doors after them.

Naoise looked around, feeling short of breath and unable momentarily to form a coherent thought as he stood in the entry hall of the most opulent palace in the most beautiful city he had ever seen.

The glossy black marble of the floor reflected the gleam of the ubiquitous crystal. The interior walls were like black glass etched and inlaid with delicate veins of silver in complex, fantastical patterns that mingled nature and geometric lines knotted together, and a carefully contained stream of the clearest water followed the perimeter of the hall to disappear through some sluice into another part of the palace. Along the walls glowed silver sconces holding a light that was not fire. An enormous staircase rose from the floor in crystal magnificence beneath a chandelier which cast prisms over the entire hall. At each corner of the room stood a silver sculpture of a tree rendered with perfect, lifelike accuracy – down to the veins on the individual leaves.

If this was just the entry hall... Naoise shook his head slowly. What wonders did the rest of the palace hold? Madness. Sheer madness. It was like... like these people weren't even living in the same flow of time as the rest of the world – like they existed hundreds of years further into a future so incredible it had not yet been imagined by humanity. Efrondel was like a dream of perfection, but worse than a nightmare because it was real.

"I'm afraid to breathe," Lyn whispered loudly to Cole. "What if I get something dirty? What do you think they'd do?"

Her taciturn bodyguard simply shook his head, and Naoise could not fault him. What was there to be said?

"You will wait here," the leader of their escort told Naoise, having established that he was the only one who could understand him. He gave the prince an extra glare as if to reinforce the point, then glided off into the palace's mirror-like black hallways.

"Look on the bright side, Lyn," Dairinn said with an unconvincing laugh. "They wouldn't kill us in here. Too messy."

"No one is going to be killed," Naoise murmured. He wished he knew for a fact that he was telling the truth.

It came to him suddenly that he knew exactly why everything about the city was so alien and inhospitable: they *wanted* it that way, for their home to offer nothing in the way of warmth to their human enemies, for the place to be a sanctuary that would deny a human any comfort. After the events that had driven them to flee their homeland and build their city here, he could hardly blame them.

Not that it helped him to feel particularly safe, now.

"This can't be where I'm from," he heard Lyn saying quietly to herself, more than once. She stared up at the ceiling that was so high Naoise wondered if the air was thinner there, and shook her head.

They were not made to wait long. Their escort returned in the presence of an imposingly tall elf clad all in shimmering silk. He had high cheekbones the color of the rich dark clay of the Shenzasa riverbed and a fiercely curved nose, straight wheat-brown hair worn loose nearly to his waist, and the coldest blue eyes Naoise had ever seen. This new figure radiated authority and disapproval so strongly there was no questioning whether or not he was the one they'd been brought here to see.

The Lord Regent swept Naoise and his fellow humans with that icy gaze and dismissed them just as quickly, focusing instead on Lyn.

The girl swallowed and stared back at him with her chin up. Naoise admired her courage.

"I am told," the cold elf said quietly, "that you cannot speak your own language."

"Can't understand a word you just said," Lyn returned in the flatly-accented Common of a Rosemarcher, voice cracking with nervousness. "I told your guards that already. Well, tried to."

The elf lord sighed pointedly.

"This one speaks Elven," the guard told his master, gesturing at Naoise.

The Lord Regent turned his attention to the younger Grenlecian. "I will not ask where or how you learned, human. Be brief, if you understand me: is it true that this young woman claims to be a daughter of King Andras?"

*You're the child of a king too*, Naoise reminded himself. "It is, my lord," he replied with all the dignity he could summon. "Her name is Lyn, and she has but lately been living in Rosemarch with her brother, until he was taken from her by assassins."

Against all reason, the Lord Regent reeled at that as if struck. His eyes darted back to the trembling blonde girl.

"What's going on?" she whispered to Naoise.

He watched the elf lord process the information, weigh it. Something about the particulars must have rung true, because the cool dismissal had left his demeanor. He actually appeared shaken. "I think he may believe you are who you say you are," Naoise told her softly.

"Why is it she cannot speak Elven?" the Lord Regent demanded.

Naoise relayed the question.

"Because no one ever taught me," Lyn answered with a shrug.

When the imposing elf lord did not seem satisfied with that answer, Naoise elaborated, "The prince had no memory of his true self until recently. Apparently he was wounded badly, when the two of them were separated from their party in Rosemarch, and he awoke with his mind empty."

The Lord Regent further surprised him by closing his eyes and walking several paces aside to face the wall, denying them access to the sudden raw emotion he was unable to conceal.

"What in damnation did you say to him?" Dairinn hissed at Naoise's ear.

But the younger prince gestured for him to wait, struggling to cling to his bearings here in this place where everything was so strange. Had that been grief in the frigid elf's eyes before he turned away? Was he at least that normal, that he had shared some bond of friendship with Lyn's brother and now mourned the news of his death?

"My lord?" Naoise prompted after a moment.

The Lord Regent drew his shoulders back and turned to face them once more. His face was again a mask of cool control as he examined Lyn.

"There are too many coincidences for your story to be untrue," he said to her, expecting Naoise to translate, "and at any rate, that you are a Raia is clear in your face. You look quite like your mother, and you have your father's eyes." He sighed, a reassuringly normal sound. "I must tell you that your death and that of Harunomíya Gallanas were mourned here more than a century ago and we did not look to see a return by either of you. That said, I am not displeased by your arrival. I simply question the company in which you travel."

Far from being cowed, Lyn picked up her own courage in response to that and stood taller before the Lord Regent to say with considerable heat, "Cole here was Bryant's – I mean Gallanas' – best friend and he got me all the way here safely even though he had better things to do and there were people trying to kill us. And these other guys, well, they're just here to talk about making peace. Because *you* invited them." She folded her arms across her chest. "Who are you anyway and how dare you treat them like prisoners after asking them to come here? Where's my sister? What's going on? I think we could all use a lot of explaining right about now."

Naoise braced himself and considered his translation carefully before relaying Lyn's words.

"I," the Lord Regent said with great, offended poise in the face of her tirade, "invited no one, child. It is unfortunate that the one whose fault this is will suffer the least of the consequences, but there it is." He drew a deep breath and did not order Naoise to be killed for his presumption. "However, I do apologize for the manner of your reception, Hídéna Lyllíen. You are correct that I've not introduced myself. It is my surprise at your return. I am Tomanasíl Eldoreth Maiantar, Lord Regent of Evlédíen. I was your brother's *jíai–*" Naoise paused to explain quickly, swallowing his own surprise, that the word had no direct translation but was a term indicating a bond of a romantic nature– "and for his sake I have raised your sister since that day in Rosemarch."

Lyn started forward at that. The guards made no move to stop her. "She's alive? I still have a sister?"

"For the time being," the Lord Regent replied with a mirthless smile. He gestured at the guards, who closed ranks around the humans again. "Allow me to take you to her."


It seemed at first they were going to be thrown into a dungeon. Flanked by palace guards who replaced their counterparts from the mountain pass, the humans and Lyn were escorted deeper into the extraordinary palace. Then, inexplicably, they found themselves heading outside again, into the back gardens. Like the rest of the city, the gardens were spectacular, even in winter. Not as formal as the royal gardens in Dewfern or Alanrad, but lush and vast.

"Where are we going?" Naoise asked their guards.

"To the Míyahídéna," came the implacable answer.

"Well this is nice," Lyn said, gesturing widely at the palace grounds. It was obvious she was getting tired of being left out. "Inside it's all black and dead. Out here it's white and dead."

"It's snowing," Cole countered. "It *is* nearly winter."

"Have you ever seen a tree like that before?" Dairinn asked the group at large, pointing.

The question was met by a chorus of denials.

"Well it never snowed in the forest," Lyn retorted. "You're saying it's normal for everything to die when it snows? That's terrible."

"It never snowed in the forest?"

"What did you ask?" Sefaro said quietly to Naoise while the others argued about the peculiarities of late autumn weather and Lyn's forest home.

"Just trying to get someone to tell us what's happening around here." Naoise glanced at their guards, who walked beside them in silence. "Nothing makes sense. There's fear, but I don't think it's us they're afraid of. And the business of Mysia's invitation lacking the Regent's approval... ? So that's dissent on top of the fear and whatever trouble they've got. I'll feel a lot better when I know how things stand."

Sefaro nodded his agreement. "I don't feel like we're in any immediate danger. But then, it's hard to get a read of any kind on these people. They're... not what I expected."

Naoise opened his mouth to respond, but suddenly found himself looking at something that froze him in place.

A pond, reed-fringed, marble bench at its margin. Tall willow bent to dip its boughs into the water, more trees receding into the distance on the far side. He realized he was expecting to see flowers there, and sunset, and a swan or two drifting by.

He had seen this place before.

The dreams... there had been many, over the years. It hadn't surprised him. In them the elf woman had taken on a quick mind and acerbic sense of humor to go along with the physical beauty he remembered, and had provided good company during the long war. It had made sense to him that he would cling to something fairer in his dreams than what the waking world provided.

But this place.

It was *real*. Whatever it was that had happened to them that day, though he didn't understand it, had joined them in some way and they had been sharing dreams ever since. Because as insane as that idea sounded in his own mind, it made the only sense that could explain how he was standing in a place where no human had ever stood before, knowing that if he walked over to the bench he would find a chip missing from the rose sculpted on the far corner.

His face burned. The things they had done in those dreams, believing none of it to be real...

"You there," the leader of the guards called to him, shaking him out of his reverie. "We have some way yet to go. Please come along quietly. We have no wish to subdue you."

Naoise swallowed several times and concentrated on the feel of his legs. They didn't want to move. The rest of the group was several paces ahead, looking back at him with intense curiosity.

"I say. You all right, little brother?" Dairinn called, frowning.

"I..." He swallowed again. His throat was dry. The entire substance of his universe had just shifted for the second time in one day. "I'm fine, Dair. Must have had a dizzy spell, but I'm fine now." He picked up one foot and put it in front of the other, made himself do it again.

The guards watched him for a moment, then continued on their way.

At his side, Sefaro peered up into his face with some suspicion. "Are you sure you're all right? What happened back there?"

Naoise shook his head. What *had* happened? He felt adrift, confused, but there was also a strange lightness rising within him. *It had all been real.* Everything they had shared. It had not been his imagination simply creating the companion he needed as a comfort in dark and lonely times. She was real and she was here, somewhere, and she would want to help him. He... was fairly certain she loved him.

If everything he had dreamed was real, he was fairly certain he loved her back.

"Nothing," he replied, forming the syllables with effort. "I just had one of those moments, you know? Thought I saw something familiar."

The Mysian studied him for a moment, then shrugged, sensing the evasion but evidently deciding he wasn't going to get a better answer than that. "Just be aware that if anything happens to you, I'll kill you myself for leaving me alone to deal with this."

Naoise forced a smile. "We can't have that."

They kept walking. The guard had told the truth: they walked for what seemed like hours, deeper into gardens that had even less of a cultivated feel the farther they went. At some point, Naoise realized they were simply walking through snow-dusted woods. The only thing that convinced him they weren't being marched off to a remote location to be executed out of sight was the definite trail they were following. At length, as the short near-winter day was losing its light, they stopped in front of a gleaming tower like the one they'd first passed upon entering the city. It rose out of the trees almost at random until Naoise realized they must have walked all the way to the southernmost tip of Efrondel, the lowest point of the star.

A guard wearing the same blue and silver uniform as their escort stood to either side of the tower door. They exchanged a few quiet words – Naoise wasn't able to overhear anything that helped – then one of them unlocked the door.

The foremost of their guards met Naoise's eyes and addressed him more bluntly than he expected. "Lord Maiantar commands that you and the rest of the humans be detained here until it can be determined what is to be done with you. You will not be mistreated while you are here: on that you have my word. But you are prisoners and you will be confined."

Naoise felt a surge of rare anger at having been misled. "You said you were taking us to the Míyahídéna."

"Naoise, what's happening?" Dairinn demanded, pushing his way closer. The guards blocked him.

"We *did* take you to the Míyahídena," the guard replied. "She, too, is a prisoner here. I did not lie."

"We're being locked up," Naoise told his brother with a scowl. If he could speak to Loríen in his dreams, perhaps he could find a way to do it consciously. If she knew he was here, captive, maybe she could do something about it. "I suggest we cooperate. Apparently the woman we're here to see is in there; it seems to be what happens when you cross the Regent."

Sefaro snorted. "At least we'll have plenty of time to talk things over."

"What about me?" Lyn asked, frowning prettily. "They're not going to lock me up too, are they? I didn't do a swilling thing!"

When Naoise relayed this concern to their elven captors, the leader of the guards said, "Lord Maiantar has ordered that the hídéna be allowed to meet her sister, and then we are to escort her back to the palace."

"You do know she doesn't speak a word of Elven," Naoise replied. "What does the Lord Regent imagine is going to happen when he tries to talk to her without a translator?"

"One will be found."

Naoise sighed.

"You're not a prisoner," he explained to Lyn. "You're just here to meet your sister."

"Oh. That's... All right." She made a strange face. "Let's do it."

The guards opened the door.

"She'd better be nicer than that Regent fellow," she added before stepping inside.

Naoise had to agree.

The humans followed Lyn into the tower; the guards remained outside and locked the door behind them. It was a terribly final sound.

"I say, isn't this cozy?" Dairinn snorted, eyeing the silver-etched walls and the tall, twisting staircase. "Can't say I've ever been in a prison like this one before."

"I don't think they have prisons," Cole observed quietly. "None of the ones I've been in were anything like this."

That wiped the smirk from Dairinn's face.

Naoise's eyes were drawn to movement on the staircase. Two figures were descending, a man and a woman.

The man was tall, handsome, slender by human standards but cut and corded with visible muscle definition. He had long ash-blond hair drawn back into a tail at the nape of his neck, a healthy pink complexion, and a strong jaw, and though he regarded the newcomers with friendly curiosity, Naoise could tell that this was not a man he wanted to cross.

The other was Loríen.

# Chapter Fourteen

Naoise stared.

In fact, he couldn't imagine a future, a few moments from now, in which he would be able to *stop* staring. The woman coming down the stairs in a sumptuous silver velvet gown – looking like a queen and an integral part of these strange, cold surroundings – was his forest elf from all those years ago, and she hadn't changed a bit. No, that wasn't true. She had to be even more beautiful now, because he didn't feel like it was possible that he could have let her walk away from him back then if she'd looked this way.

It was Loríen, and she was the Míyahídéna. And he had been sharing his dreams with this woman for the last seven years.

She didn't notice him at first, her sharp green eyes taking in the full collection of them before settling finally on Naoise. She stumbled on the stairs when she saw him. The elf beside her put out a sure hand and caught her elbow before she could fall, but her gaze never left Naoise's face. She had gone, if it was possible, even whiter.

"Look at that," her escort said with a dry smile. "For all of Farínaiqa's efforts, they made it anyway." He had the voice of a man who knew how to give orders.

She didn't answer, still focused on Naoise.

Her companion turned to her. "Loralíenasa?"

She made a visible effort to gather herself, murmuring something to the other elf. The two of them came the rest of the way down the steps. As they did, Naoise felt something jabbing him between the ribs.

"You're up," Lyn whispered nervously. "Introduce me to my sister, if you don't have something better to do."

Naoise couldn't look away. For a moment, he was afraid he'd forgotten how to make words.

"Welcome, friends, poor welcome though it is," the blond elf said, sur-veying the group standing before him. "I am Lanoralas Andreqí Galvan, Cap-tain of the Royal Guard. Which one of you is the genius Farínaiqa tells me can speak Elven?"

Naoise cleared his throat, hoping it would work. "That would be me." It came out as a whisper. He was pleased to find himself still capable of speech. "And this, I assume, is the Míyahídéna?"

"Míyahídéna Loralíenasa Níelor Raia," the man who called himself Cap-tain replied with a formal gesture at the woman who so far had remained si-lent. "Please allow me to apologize for Lord Maiantar. He's... not sure how to deal with what's been happening in Evlédíen of late."

"I have a feeling he's not the only one," Naoise murmured, eyeing Loríen. She blinked.

"This is much less fun when you don't tell us what's happening," Dairinn hissed.

Naoise struggled to clear his head. As if on cue to addle him further, the lights that ringed the walls came on suddenly without any motion from either elf. Magic? He drew a deep breath and let it out slowly.

"Also, *I'm* over here," Lyn said. "Why is it she won't stop staring at *you*?"

"Naturally, it's because my brother is so charming," Dairinn said with a snort.

Lanoralas was watching him with his eyebrows raised. "Your friends have a lot to say. Perhaps we should get down to it?"

"Before we do that." Naoise drew another deep breath and met Loríen's vivid green eyes. She stared back at him. "I am aware of how strange this is, but I find myself in the position of being responsible for introducing you to your sister." He gestured. "Please allow me to present Lyn."

Hearing herself named, Lyn stepped forward and offered her sister a shy wave. "Um. Hello? I wish I remembered you, but I guess we were pretty young the last time we saw each other."

"Lyn," Naoise said carefully, "this is Loralíenasa. Although I suspect she'll want you to call her Loríen."

"Sister?" Loríen's voice was just as Naoise remembered it, low and soft, with the sort of control that suggested training – a singer, perhaps – but it bore an edge of incredulity at the moment that matched the sudden hard glitter of anger in her eyes. "My sister died more than a hundred years ago. Who does this person think she is, to claim such a thing? Is this another of Katakí's games?"

Lanoralas put a hand on her arm as if to restrain her though she hadn't moved. "Loríen," he said quietly. "Look at her."

"What's she saying?" Lyn said, prodding Naoise in the ribs some more.

"She says you can't be her sister."

"Oho, so that's how it is." Lyn put her hands on her hips and scowled back at the Míyahídéna. "Maybe I don't *want* to be her sister."

Naoise managed to drag his eyes from Loríen's, turning toward Lyn. "Perhaps you could tell her your story. It certainly seemed to convince the Lord Regent."

"Well." Lyn huffed. "I guess."

As awkward as the situation was for so many reasons, Loralíenasa's primary complaint was that she just wished she could stop staring at Naoise. It didn't help that he was the one she had to talk to because her Common was so poor. She'd spent the last few years working on it, since coming back from Grenlec, but only on her own and not with any sense of urgency. It had been a subversive hobby, not a necessity. She could kick herself for that now. It also didn't help that his voice was so pleasant to listen to.

She made herself study the girl who did in fact bear a striking resemblance to the portrait of King Andras and Queen Melíara that had always hung in her bedroom. Lyn, she insisted, not Lyllíen. She was the strangest, most emotive elf Loralíenasa had ever met, constantly waving her arms in grand gestures and speaking with a gusto that seemed almost… inappropriate. After hearing the particulars, supported by the man Cole who claimed to have known her brother for many years, she had to admit that she agreed with Tomsíl: this Lyn's story was too specific to be false.

She had a living sister.

The trouble was, Loralíenasa didn't know what to *do* with the fact. Even though she knew on a rational level that this was one of the most important things that had ever happened to her, she simply couldn't get her mind around it. Not stewing in Tomsíl's makeshift prison with a powerful enemy out there plotting the destruction of everything she loved. Not with Naoise sitting there across from her in all his living warmth, instead of staying in her dreams where he belonged.

How was she supposed to handle this, on top of everything else?

Far too much of her attention was focused on feverishly calculating the odds of him being here, as if proving his presence impossible would make him – and her sudden headache – vanish.

Almost as much of her was trying to pretend that she wasn't noticing how attractive she still found him. He was older than she remembered him from that day in the forest – there were lines of care and time visible now at eyes and lips – but he was still the same solemn, courteous man with intense eyes that couldn't decide what color they wanted to be. It was also *not* him. He had changed. The wit and bright curiosity were still there, but they no longer burned. Now he appeared more wary. Guarded. Perhaps even a little resigned. Loralíenasa was sad to see it.

He looked, actually, the way she had last dreamt him. The thought brought an unwelcome heat to her cheeks. Vaian. If he knew half the indecent things she had imagined doing with him in the last seven years...

"The poor Harunomíya," Lanoralas murmured, dragging her out of her wildly improper thoughts. "Alive all this time, remembering nothing."

The poor Harunomíya indeed. Loríen couldn't help but think, perhaps bitterly, that it might have been nice of him to stick around so that none of this nonsense with Katakí would be her problem to worry about. She felt justified, having no actual memories of her brother to inspire her sympathy now.

She frowned at Lyn and searched her scant command of Common. "So. Sister."

Lyn's entire demeanor brightened. "You believe me?"

"I believe," Loralíenasa allowed grimly. "But you... come at not the best time."

"I'll be damned," Dairinn said, hitting his own knee with his gloved fist. "Naoise, your forest woman speaks Common after all."

She understood enough of that to hold up her hand in a gesture indicating a minuscule quantity.

"Dairinn," Naoise said with an urgency that was nearly amusing, "you do realize this *forest woman* is the Crown Princess of this kingdom? Don't you think we're in enough trouble already without–"

"Sure, whatever," the elder prince cut him off with a careless wave of his hand. "I just want to know why you lied to me. Mysian, my spectacular ass."

Lyn leaned over from her position sitting against the wall to smack Dairinn on the knee. He jumped in surprise. "No, we're still on me. My new sister may or may not be admitting that I exist. This is sort of a big moment."

Naoise saw that Loralíenasa was having difficulty following along and re-layed his companions' dialogue for her in Elven. She hated that she needed him to do it.

"Lyn," she said carefully, slowly. "Your words... feel? true to me. I am apology you come home to this. I cannot give to you welcome. But Tomanasíl is... good." Oh, but it felt so awkward to speak in the humans' language, and she knew she sounded like an idiot. "He will treat you with care."

"Sure," Lyn laughed. "There's just this little problem where I can't under-stand a jiggering thing he says, my sister's in prison, and so's the man I dragged here with me. Best homecoming ever."

Loralíenasa couldn't figure out why Lyn was laughing. In fact, little about her sister − strange even to think it − made sense. She shook her head and re-sisted another impulse to look at Naoise. "I mean not to be cruel, but there is no thing I can do for you more at this time, and there is matter I have waited long to discuss with the Mysian."

"That's it?" Lyn made a wordless sound of indignation. "This is what I came all the way here for? You're kicking me out?"

"I..." Vaian. It was hard enough to think of what to say without having to worry about doing it in Common. "You may be where you wish. I mean only that this is not a time for−" She stopped in frustration and tried to choose the right words.

"I think she's a bit overwhelmed," Naoise said quietly to Lyn. "Give her some time. She'll warm up to you."

"Do not overstep your bounds, Prince Naoise," Loralíenasa snapped in her language.

She regretted how cold she sounded as soon as she said it, but she didn't apologize. This wasn't going to work if he got too friendly. It was difficult to know which of the things she thought she remembered about him were facts and which were simply her incredibly vivid dreams. It was all too likely she'd overstep the bounds of propriety herself by accident, with or without his en-couragement.

He raised his expressive eyebrows at her. "Forgive me, Lorí − Lo-ralíenasa," he said in Elven. "If you prefer that I *not* continue assisting the two of you to understand one another, I will stop."

She glared at his charming smile.

Lanoralas looked back and forth between the two of them and frowned.

"Lover's spat?" Dairinn ribbed with a grin.

Loralíenasa wasn't exactly sure what the elder Grenlecian prince had said, but it was clear enough from the sudden high color in Naoise's white cheeks that she wouldn't like it.

"Dairinn," he murmured earnestly, "please don't–"

"Perhaps we could get on with our business," the Mysian interjected.

Welcoming the distraction, Loralíenasa gave him her attention. He had a disarming, unstudied, boyish look about him that she imagined might have played a role in his being chosen for this ambassadorship. "Please, yes," she agreed.

"Really?" Lyn sighed. "You're done with me already?"

The man Cole remained notably silent in his corner, wedged in against the foot of the winding staircase.

"We will talk more at another time," Loralíenasa said, trying to convey an apology with her tone if not her words. "My vow that I say truly."

There was a sudden knock at the tower door, a courtesy, then the lock clicked open and a handful of guardsmen stepped in. They were good men and women all, loyal to their Captain, and Loralíenasa knew how much they were suffering by being made to play jailor. She also knew not a single one of them would fight her if she decided to break out. The trouble was, without a plan, what good would it do?

"Our apologies Míyahídéna, Captain," the lieutenant said, saluting. "We have orders to take Hídéna Lyllíen back to the palace in time for dinner."

"She prefers to be called Lyn," Loralíenasa said wearily. "Has a translator been found?"

"Not yet, Míyahídéna."

"Then Lord Maiantar might consider allowing the Grenlecian into the palace to help as needed," she suggested without looking at the man in question. "She talks a great deal and has many questions."

The guardsman looked rightfully skeptical. "I'll pass the suggestion along, but we both know how likely Lord Maiantar is to take it."

She twisted her fingers into the gesture known as subtle abdication. "If he wishes to be foolish, that's his headache."

The guardsman saluted again and turned to Lyn.

"It's time for you to go up to the palace," Naoise told her gently. When it looked like she was going to protest, he added, "It's obvious they mean you no harm. Just be agreeable, let them welcome their lost princess, and come back to visit as soon as they let you. All will be well."

"He talks good sense," Cole agreed from his corner. "Don't worry. We'll still be here when you're done getting pampered."

"I… Well, dammit." Lyn scowled. "It's just this is going to be a problem, me not able to tell them when to stop fussing."

Cole snorted. "I think you'll get the idea across."

Lyn studied each of them for a moment, as if to memorize their faces in case she never saw them again. It was almost comically tragic, given that she was on her way to be bathed and fed and dressed in fine raiment, and generally treated like a minor deity for a while. "I *will* come back soon," she proclaimed. "If nothing else, I'm going to need someone to teach me a few Elven swear words after tonight, I'm sure."

The long-lost princess trudged out sullenly in the care of the Royal Guard, leaving Loralíenasa alone with the men.

She sighed and finally let herself look at Naoise once more, doing her best to ignore the stupid fluttering in her stomach. "Now I think I really need to hear how it is that my invitation to Mysia managed to net such a large Grenlecian contingent. From the beginning, please."

Lanas grinned suddenly at that. "Maybe we should fetch Sovoqatsu down here just to make him listen. I don't think he's been punished enough."

"Please tell me I just heard mention of our *delightful* guide," the Mysian put in.

"He's here too?" Naoise asked with apparent amusement.

The Captain of the Guard grinned even wider. "Oh yes. And he refused to come down from the upper platform when we saw the lot of you being brought here. I would say it's because he's shy if I thought he was listening and might be annoyed by it."

Loralíenasa found herself wanting to smile at her old friend, but managed not to. It was truly amusing, just how angry he still was at Sovoqatsu. Not that he blamed Sovoqatsu for their current incarceration, exactly, but he was certainly willing to extend some amount of fault in the prickly guardsman's direction and it seemed to help him feel better.

"Patience," she said wryly. "Business first, entertainment afterward."

Lanas laughed.

The best thing about humans, Loralíenasa decided, was that they were easily tired out and had to sleep. Leaving her in peace.

There was so much to think about now. The situation in Mysia, Grenlec,

Telrisht. Katakí. Tomanasíl's unexpectedly extreme threat to kill the human ambassadors. The sudden appearance of a sister who was supposed to be dead, and the knowledge that her brother had been alive until so recently the thought hurt.

Naoise. The Galvanos. That was too big, too important to come to terms with, so she pushed it aside.

She shook her head and stared out at her starlit city from the guard platform at the top of the tower. Sovoqatsu had eventually gone down to catch some sleep himself; she had the platform all to herself, and it had stopped snowing. The quiet was nice after such a tumultuous evening. In fact, though she would certainly never tell Tomsíl, being locked up had been nice too in its own way. No unreasonable expectations, running between lessons, unrelenting tutors, study sessions that never ended, tedious meetings with boring courtiers, pressure to adhere to the Qíarnos, or dinners with scabs like Qroíllenas Qaí. And of all the people she could have chosen to be trapped in a tower with, Lanoralas was the most tolerable of possibilities. It helped that Sovoqatsu rarely said much, and got right to the point when he did.

As relaxing as it was to have a vacation from her life, she could no longer afford the luxury. She had as many pieces of the puzzle as she was ever going to get, hiding behind her mountains here in Evlédíen, and Katakí wasn't going to wait for her to make up her mind about whether or not she had the courage to do something about him.

A familiar tread made its way up the stairs. Loralíenasa braced herself to deal with people and their demands again.

"Busy day," Lanoralas said, coming up beside her at the tower wall. He looked out at the sleeping city, then leaned on hip and elbow to face her. "How are you handling... everything?"

She gave a short, dry laugh at the prospect of answering that question.

"That's what I thought." He shook his head. "You know, the Houses are going to implode when they find out the Harunomíya was alive all this time. They haven't had something new to punish themselves over since your parents died. It'll be like Festival in reverse."

Loralíenasa smiled at that thought, and at his attempt to lighten the mood, but the smile soon faded. "I just don't know how I'm supposed to feel about..." Anything, really. Any of this. "...suddenly having a sister. How *can* I feel anything about it?" She'd spent her entire life knowing she was alone, letting that pain cultivate within her until it was a dull ache she wasn't herself without. "I don't know her. And you saw her, the way she is; she's a stranger here. She doesn't know anything about me, about her own people, about anything that makes us what we are. She can't even speak our language."

Lanoralas nodded. "We place a great deal of importance on knowing what to feel, don't we?" he sympathized.

"What does it matter, anyway?" she replied with an indelicate snort. "If Tomsíl has his way, we'll all be dead before the new year. Then I won't have to worry about the fact that I have absolutely no idea what I'm doing."

He pushed at her foot with his own booted toe. "That's hardly productive. Why did we bother getting ourselves thrown in jail if you're just going to sulk and give up?"

She pushed back, trying not to smile. "I never said I was giving up. You know things got pretty weird in a hurry down there, Lanas. You can't blame me for being thrown off balance."

"Speaking of weird."

Loralíenasa sighed, dreading what she knew he was about to say.

"*What* is going on between you and that Grenlecian?" he asked, punctuating the question with a low whistle.

"Which Grenlecian?"

He merely stared back in response to that feeble attempt.

"There is nothing *going on*," she finally answered. She didn't want to be talking about this. With anyone. Ever. Damn him for being so observant. Or more likely, damn herself for being so painfully obvious. "We've met before, that's all." She ignored the sudden alarmed widening of Lanoralas' eyes. "In Grenlec, the last time I left the Valley."

The Captain scowled hard enough to have terrified his troops. "That doesn't explain—" He cut off whatever that alarming thought was going to be and changed his attack, pushing off from the wall to stand up straight with his sudden realization. "Is it that man's fault I had to carry you back to Efrondel? Is he the villain who nearly killed you?"

Loralíenasa shook her head. "You have the wrong idea about what happened. He didn't... it's not his fault."

"Enlighten me." Lanoralas folded his arms across his chest and glared down at her. She had rarely seen him so serious. "What is the *right* idea?"

"This isn't productive," she objected. "And it's irrelevant. What we need to be talking about is what to do now. Mysia still needs to be warned, and we have to decide what our move is against Kataki."

Lanoralas smiled grimly. "Loríen, I've spent far too much time with a sword in my hand not to know a parry when I see one."

"I don't care." She could be every bit as mulish as the Captain if she needed to. "It's the truth. My private life isn't the most important thing happening
in the Valley right now. You heard what Prince Naoise said about the war. It
can't be much longer before Katakí means to make his final play, and we're
not ready."

The Captain allowed himself to be drawn from the subject with obvious reluctance, as she had known he would. "I've said before, if it comes down to a
frontal military assault, we'll *never* be ready for that. You know our survival
in Evlédíen has always relied on secrecy and strategy." He began to pace with
mounting agitation. "We simply haven't the manpower or the training for outright war. I could muster the whole of the Guard and it would scarcely give us
bodies enough to fill the pass. We're dead where we stand if he manages to
navigate the fjords to Chastedel. A march on his fortress in Mornnovin is out
of the question."

"Not a march, then," she returned, thinking. "Something more subtle."

"A tactical team?" He stopped pacing, brow furrowed in thought. "You
think, with his magic, we could get anyone close enough to him for an assassination?"

As soon as he said it, a chill slid down Loralíenasa's spine as though she
had been doused in glacier runoff. "Not just anyone," she murmured through
numb lips, voicing the thought in the moment it came to her. "Me."

"Loríen–"

"No, think about it." It was her turn to pace, restless energy propelling her
back and forth across the guard platform as the idea took shape within her. "I
could go to him as a diplomat, as Míyahídéna. I tell him his ideas are compelling but I have concerns about his plans for Evlédíen. Tell him I wish to talk it
over. Really sell the impression of a frightened princess. When his guard is
down, I strike."

"That's insane. I can't let you do it."

She was getting excited now as she thought about it. Excited and slightly
queasy, which told her she was serious. "You wouldn't be saying that if we
weren't friends," she pointed out coolly. "You know what I can do with a
blade. You know you'd send another agent with my skill if you had one."

Concern creased the corners of his mouth. "I might not be saying it if you
weren't Míyahídéna and I wasn't responsible for your safety."

"It's only because I *am* Míyahídéna that I have a chance of getting close to
him," she countered.

Lanoralas shook his head vehemently. "No. Loríen. This is a war veteran and a sorcerer. It's not that I doubt your skill. It's that I don't trust him not to have a response to it."

In his words, she heard again Ítaja Qíarna's searing judgment of her short-comings. *You do not stand a flower's chance in a deep freeze against him.* She tried not to let her disappointment show as she said, "I encourage you to suggest a better plan."

He took a deep breath and calmed himself. "We invite him here," he said, clearly thinking aloud. "Same premise: you wish to discuss a treaty. But we do the meet on *our* terms, lay a trap for him."

"And how do you know it isn't his plan to get us to do just that?" she retorted. "What if he's just waiting for us to deactivate the barrier and let him in so he can unleash everything he has behind our lines? It seems like what he wants. That was some rather transparent provocation, you must admit."

"How would it be worse than walking blind into *his* trap?" He shook his head. "Either way, we're facing a stronger opponent. We must use what tools we have."

"It would be worse because if *I* fail, in Mornnovin," she said, "you and Tomanasíl will still be here to defend Evlédíen, our barrier will still be intact, our soldiers and our mages at the ready, our people still alive to repel him. And Tomanasíl would no longer be able to deny the threat."

Lanoralas was silent, breathing quickly, unable to refute that.

In that silence, another thought came bolting down into her mind like a blinding strike of lightning and she could not believe she hadn't seen it sooner. *What tools we have. A flower's chance.* "Oh Vaian." She swallowed. "The Nírozahé."

The Captain stared at her, awaiting an explanation.

She struggled to marshal her suddenly chaotic thoughts.

"The Nírozahé. It… My great-uncle, Véloro Raia Chalaqar, he made it. The most powerful tool of the Art ever created, and only those of the blood of House Raia can use it."

She didn't mention that the Nírozahé was what had killed him. Everyone who studied the Art knew that Véloro Raia Chalaqar had been a genius but also too ambitious and more than slightly mad. What mattered was that the power to defeat Katakí was locked safely in the royal vault and only she could use it. The answer had been there all along.

"With the Nírozahé, I could easily overpower Katakí's defenses, whatever they are," she stated with mounting excitement. Between the power of the Nírozahé and the strength of her own sword-arm, she offered their best hope.

Lanoralas didn't seem to share her excitement. "If this talisman is so powerful, why wasn't it used to turn the tide of the War?"

"Véloro was dead and King Moraní was no mage. Nor was my father," she explained. "As I said, it has to be used by a Raia." She also didn't mention that King Moraní had declared the Nírozahé too powerful and had expressly outlawed its use. That seemed to be its strongest recommendation at the moment.

The Captain remained skeptical, observing the agitation of her pacing with a deepening furrow between his brows. "I… mean no disrespect – you know I love you, Loríen – but you aren't exactly a mage yourself."

They both knew what choice she'd made when Qíarna had issued his ultimatum, the sword or the Art. But that didn't change anything right now.

"It's in my blood," she said, meeting his gaze with all the steady conviction she could muster, "and that is enough. The Nírozahé will do the rest."

Her friend shook his head, unconvinced. "This is insane. I'm supposed to let you just climb right into the mouth of the beast? Because a magic flower is going to protect you? I'm Captain of your Royal Guard. It's my *duty* to see that you don't do these kinds of things."

She stepped close and took his hand, pressing it between hers, as if she could will him to understand through that contact. "No, Lanas. Your duty is to House Raia, and to Evlédíen. Those will both still be here without me, and you must protect them."

In the aftermath of her excitement, the silence rang loud as he thought about that.

Finally, he drew in a deep breath and let it out for what seemed like an eternity. "I can't tell you I approve of this plan," he said softly. "I also can't tell you I have a better one. I hate this, Loríen. I hate everything about this." He took his hand away and walked over to the table and chairs at the center of the platform.

"Two things," he said in an entirely different tone, now brisk and business-like. "One, Sovoqatsu is going with you, or you go nowhere. We will not debate on that point. Second, I'll be damned if I'm letting you do this without planning it down to the last jot." He shook his head as if he couldn't believe what he was saying and gestured at the other chair. "Sit down, Míyahídéna. We have a lot to cover before morning. Start by telling me how you're getting into the Royal Vault."

Naoise woke earlier than he wanted to because it was bitterly cold inside the tower. At that point, remembering where he was, there was no way he could fall back to sleep. He stumbled to his feet in the pre-dawn greyness and wrapped his cloak tighter about his body.

The others were still asleep on their cots, exhausted after the long week marching across Evlédíen at an elf's pace. He moved quietly, careful not to disturb them. As he passed his companions, he saw Sovoqatsu asleep by the door and had to smirk. The bad-tempered elf had waited for the rest of them to drop off before coming down to catch his own rest. The Captain of the Royal Guard, incarcerated for helping Loralíenasa defy the Regent, was asleep in a cot at the back of the tower.

Loralíenasa was nowhere to be seen.

He shuffled to the water closet in the frigid morning air and relieved himself. Tried not to be alarmed by the magic or advanced technology at work there when the pot drained itself. It was too early in the morning for such weirdness. He splashed some water in his face at the wash basin, gasping at the cold but also suddenly wide awake.

He took a deep breath, pushed a hand through his hair, and started up the long, winding staircase to the top of the tower with no idea what would happen when he got there.

It was so strange, seeing her like that – standing against the white marble rail in her silver gown with the glow of first light in the sky behind her – and knowing that for once this was not a dream. As if to underscore the timeless, unreal quality of the moment, the snow started drifting down again in unhurried clouds.

She turned her head at his approach and stiffened visibly when she saw that it was him.

Naoise came up to the rail beside her – close, but not touching. He wasn't sure what would happen if they made contact again, and he was more than half afraid to find out. She never took her eyes from him, and she never relaxed the alert wariness of her posture. He could almost *see* her thinking the same thing.

"Míyahídéna," he said, quickly lowering his voice to fit more comfortably within the muffled quiet of their pre-dawn solitude. "You might have told me that, when we first met."

"Why would I have?" she murmured, taking cue from his low tone.

He smiled in the grey half-light. "You knew who *I* was."

She did not return the smile or any of its warmth. "*Your* life was not in danger."

"No? I seem to recall something about this bear..." When that got no re-action of any kind, his smile faded. "I thought you knew you could trust me."

"Even if I did," she returned primly, "that would have been no reason to expose myself to unnecessary danger."

"More than you were already in, you mean."

If anything, her expression grew even more chill.

"Did I... offend you in some way?" Naoise moved as close to her as he dared.

She recoiled subtly. "You are about to."

Naoise studied her and found nothing in her of the dear friend from his dreams, only cold suspicion. Was it possible he was wrong? How then to ex-plain his moment of recognition by the pond?

He drew a deep breath. "A curious thing has happened, these past years."

A snowflake landed on her cheek but she made no move to brush it off. It rested there a moment, glittering like a jewel, before melting against her pale skin. She stared at him and said nothing.

"Later that day you left Grenwold," he said quietly, "I fell ill. The doctors could not tell me why. There was no cure, they said, no explanation for my sudden malady. I was as weak as a grandsire on his deathbed, delirious. Even though Telrisht had just declared war on Lang and my father was preparing the army to march to their defense, he spared the time to visit my bedside. Be-cause he believed those would be our last moments together in this world. I was that ill."

Loralíenasa had grown so still she might not have been breathing. He re-sisted an impulse to reach out and make sure her marble-white skin still held the warmth of life.

"One night in my illness," he went on, "after weeks close to death, I had a dream." He felt almost like he was in a dream now, or a spell, such an odd mood had descended onto the guard platform with his carefully-chosen words. "In this dream, I was again in the forest where we met, you and I. Beside that great tree. And you joined me there, and we walked among the trees, and when I awoke my fever had broken."

She still said nothing, but he did not expect her to.

"After that night, my condition improved," he said. "It was some time yet before I was well enough to join the war, but the worst of it had passed. And ever since that night, Míyahídéna, you have appeared often in my dreams." He breathed slowly, bracing himself. "I thought I was seeing you because I wanted to, because seeing you was better than what I had to face in my waking hours, because I wished we'd had more time to come to know one another and I wasn't ready to say goodbye.

"I didn't realize until coming here that you were seeing me too."

The Míyahídéna's cheeks flushed from white to red. "What are you talking about?"

"The dreams. Yesterday I saw things walking through your city that should have been strange to me, but I knew them because I'd seen them before, with you." He watched her involuntarily register the truth of his words. "They were never just dreams, were they? All this time."

She blinked quickly as if to stave off tears, but her eyes were quite dry. Her hands clenched and unclenched on the marble railing. "I... Even if it were true, it wouldn't matter."

It was Naoise's turn to blink. He could feel the aura fading. "Even if it were true? It *is* true. You know it is. Tell me I don't look different from the way I did that day, and then tell me I didn't look just the way you remember me anyway when you came down the stairs and saw me."

"It doesn't matter," she said again. Her cheeks burned with color.

He stared at her for an incredulous moment before spluttering, "Doesn't matter? How can you–? It matters almost more than anything that ever– Don't you understand? Whatever this thing is that happened to us, we're *connected*. I've been telling you all of my most intimate secrets for the last seven years! We've been – by the god, you and I have had more sex than my brother has with every strumpet in Yeatun!"

Loralíenasa bared her teeth as she visibly wrestled against a desire to strike him.

"Prince Naoise." Her voice shook. She drew her shoulders back, lifted her chin, and tried again. "You know why you came here. You know why I defied the Regent to contact Mysia. You know, now, the threat we all face. You know how little there is we can hope to do about it." She was gaining momentum, her voice taking on a cold note of accusation. "You are not a fool. You know how serious this is. And you will stand there making eyes at me and telling me it's supposed to change my life to learn that I've occasionally shared dreams with a man I once met?"

There. Finally. A little of the passion he knew she was capable of, a break in the icy veneer she seemed so desperate to maintain. She was his Loríen after all. And she had just admitted it.

"You trivialize it in order to escape its significance," he said. "Or perhaps you know more about what happened between us than you've been willing to share."

"Of course I do," she snapped. She looked again like she wanted to hit him, but she was in control now. "That doesn't change the fact that *everything else* is more important than this right now. You're in prison, or hadn't you noticed? The entire world is about to go up in flames, and we're trapped here *talking* about how mad it is that we've had a few dreams together."

He tried to keep his voice level. "It seems to me there's precious little else to talk about for the time being. Or hadn't you noticed that we're in prison?" What he really wanted to do, irrationally, was grab her by the face and kiss her hard until she stopped telling him he didn't matter.

"I thought we might get out of here and stop the world from ending," she said, eyes glinting in the growing half-light. "I thought you might like to escape before Tomanasíl decides he can't let you or your brother return to Grenlec alive."

Naoise thought about that for a moment while he fought the need to touch her. "You have a plan?"

She nodded slowly and seemed to relax a little as she understood that he was allowing himself to be led down this new conversational path. "I do, and I may need your help. When... my sister–" her lip twitched– "comes back to the tower, there is something I must ask her to get for me from the palace."

He wondered how good an idea that was. Even though Lyn was the only one of them still free to move about, it was unlikely the Lord Regent wasn't having her watched. He said so.

Loralíenasa shook her head. "He'll have her watched, but the Guard is mine. He won't learn anything the Captain doesn't want him to."

"I see."

"If she can get what I need, we have only to wait until Lanoralas' men let us know they've gathered our supplies. A day or two at most, and we'll slip out under cover of darkness. We'll be long out of the city before Tomanasíl knows we've gone. He will not dare give chase past the mountains. You'll have a clear run back to Dewfern."

"And you?"

She lifted her narrow chin. "I intend to speak to Katakí."

Neither of them spoke for a long time. All of the things that mattered most were still there, filling up the space between them, unresolved and unable now to be addressed after the shift in the discussion. The snow had started coming down faster and Naoise knew he couldn't stay up here much longer without freezing to death.

He sighed. "I'll help in whatever way you need me to."

The Míyahídéna sagged with relief.

"But Loríen–"

"Don't," she interrupted, tensing again so suddenly it was like watching a cat arch its back in alarm. "This is not something I'm willing to talk about, Prince Naoise. Not ever. If I can't trust you to respect my boundaries, I'm going to have to leave you here when I escape and hope Tomanasíl realizes he can't kill foreign ambassadors."

A dozen responses to that played out in his mind before he decided he could say none of them. In the end, he nodded and wished he'd had the courage to kiss her. But he suspected that touching her would mean being unable to part with her again without suffering another illness like the one that had laid him flat all those years ago. This was the wrong time and place to take that risk.

"About those supplies," he said instead. "Do you think you could ask for some warmer bedding? I'm not fond of waking up before the sun because I'm about to die of frostbite, as charming as the company has been."

She did a fine job of pretending not to read anything into the remark as she nodded and told him she'd do everything she could to keep him and his friends alive.

Below, inside the tower, they heard Dairinn shouting to be told where his brother had been taken, and Cole's lower tones requesting that he shut up so people could sleep.

Whatever the moment could have been was lost.

# CHAPTER FIFTEEN

Lyn ran back to the tower.

The poor guardsman tasked with keeping track of her was put to his limit just to keep up. She tore through the palace gardens like pain itself was clipping at her heels.

It wasn't that she'd had a *bad* day. Just that she wanted to punch all of these elves in the face and she would have preferred to be anywhere else and the only people in this horrible place who could even talk to her were locked up and her heartless sister who already hated her was in there with them.

At the tower door, the guards were surprisingly tolerant of her shouted requests to be let in. It didn't even seem like her friends had been mistreated.

A row of cots had been set up on the far wall to accommodate the tower's new inhabitants. Prince Dairinn was lounging indolently on his, saying something to Cole who was sitting with his back to the wall near the winding staircase. The Captain of the Guard and the elegant princess were playing a complicated game with many pieces set up on a board at a table near the door; Lyn couldn't tell who was winning and neither of them got up when she entered, but they did both stop playing and offered her their attention. A third elf, coppery and angry-looking, sat cross-legged on the floor engaged in some kind of meditation exercise and also didn't move. Sefaro and Naoise were nowhere to be seen. Cole stood slowly and studied her as if searching for injuries when she walked into the room.

"She returns!" Dairinn shouted with a smile, levering himself up from his cot. He seemed no worse for wear, as handsome as ever and in better spirits than she was after the night she'd just had. "And in a *dress*. What have they been doing with you up in that great pile of glass, my dear?"

"They stole my clothes!" She gestured angrily at the fancy blue gown draping what she felt was ridiculously from her shoulders. "Those rotting nut-jobs. They made me take a bath that wasn't even a *bath* because I had to stand up and the water was falling out of the ceiling, and then when I came out, *my clothes were gone*."

Cole snorted. She shot him a suspicious look and found him not smiling. *Not smiling* so hard that she was sure he really wanted to be smiling, and she didn't know if she should congratulate or hit him.

"Mock my pain, will you?" she said, attempting dignity. "*Look* at this aw-ful thing they're making me wear."

"I am," Dairinn replied, sweeping her with a head-to-toe gaze that was un-like any look she'd ever been given before. She was suddenly uncomfortable and felt her cheeks burning. "My word as a prince that you look as far from awful as is possible."

Lyn found she didn't have a response to that.

"They've been treating you well, then?" Cole interjected, surprising her.

"Haven't you been listening?" she huffed, turning her attention to him. "They made me wash, and stole my clothes, and then they kept *feeding* me. Like they were trying to make up for every meal I've missed since I was in Rosemarch."

"They probably were," came Naoise's amused voice floating down the staircase. He himself followed a moment later, Sefaro smiling behind him.

"*Weird* food, too," she elaborated. That made everyone accounted for, and she was glad to see them all safe.

"We know," Dairinn replied meaningfully. "You should have seen what they brought us last night. And fruit for breakfast. A man is like to starve in this place."

"That's not even the weirdest thing, either," Lyn said. She was still trying to make sense of the event she'd witnessed while fleeing through the gardens. It was *almost* like the elves she'd passed had been playing a game, some kind of recreational battle with packed handfuls of snow as their weapons, but eve-rything about the game had been so methodical – ritualized. "Is it possible they literally don't understand the meaning of *fun*?"

The prince snorted, pointedly not looking at the two elves sitting across from one another at the game table.

Which drew Lyn's attention to them. Loralíenasa was watching her with sharp eyes that were too much like Bryant's for her comfort. She was discon-certing to look at, actually – like seeing Bryant's and Lyn's own faces eerily blended together in a mirror and then stripped of all natural emotion. She was still wearing yesterday's ethereal silver gown, reminding Lyn that as palatial as the tower might seem by her standards, her sister was in fact incarcerated against her will. It was easy to be fooled by Loralíenasa's air of utter control into forgetting that she was not exactly where she wanted to be.

"Naoise," Lyn said, quelling her nervousness, "could you say good morning to my sister for me?"

"Good morning," the elegant elf woman carefully said before Naoise could open his mouth or even finish coming down the stairs. Her accent was thick, the words obviously unfamiliar. "I trust you are well?"

It was difficult and unsettling, not knowing how much or how little the other woman could understand of what was being said. Lyn swallowed and forced a smile. "I'd be better if your people would stop trying to make me comfortable."

"*Rajo*," Naoise supplied helpfully when Loralíenasa didn't seem to understand the word. He took up a position between the two ladies, anticipating being needed, while Sefaro walked over to sit on the edge of his cot.

Loralíenasa lifted one corner of her absurdly pretty lips once she understood what Lyn meant. "I can just imagine." Lyn was still trying to work out how she meant that to be taken when she added, surprisingly, "I offer regret for my... receiving of you last night. Many things happening all together. I do not mean to be unwelcome."

Lyn smiled, deciding not to correct her sister's Common. It was good to see there might be a real, flawed person in there somewhere, behind the perfect face, the grooming that was still impeccable though she was locked in a tower, and all the layers of so many years of careful upbringing that it sort of made Lyn's hair hurt to even think about what she might have been subjected to herself if she hadn't ended up in Rosemarch.

"Don't worry about it," Lyn replied with a careless wave. "You're right: there was a lot going on."

"I hope," Loralíenasa said slowly, choosing her words, "that Tomanasíl has been good to you?"

"Ha!" Lyn grinned. "I can just tell he's itching to start *fixing* me and it's annoying the spit right out of him that he can't get on with it because I don't understand a word of what he says. I have more than half a mind to keep pretending I can't speak the language even after I learn it, just to keep seeing that look on his face."

Loralíenasa appeared confused for a moment until Naoise supplied another quick translation. She smiled slightly and said to Lyn, "Slower, please."

"Sorry." Lyn grimaced. She was about to oblige by saying something one word at a time, but realized she couldn't think of anything else to say to her sister. What did you say to a person you'd shared a womb with and then hadn't seen for most of your life? They needed to learn literally everything about each other, but there was too much ground to cover to know where to begin.

"Well that's lovely," Dairinn declared before Lyn could fret over the lull. "But I don't see how your day could have been worse than ours. I mean, you weren't locked up with Sovoqatsu."

The third elf opened his eyes, unfolded himself from his meditation pose, and offered some kind of salute to Loralíenasa. He snapped something at her in Elven in a distinctly non-respectful manner and left with neat, abrupt steps, heading up the stairs.

"What's his problem?" Lyn asked, nodding her head at his retreating back.

Dairinn snorted. "Don't mind him. We're the best of friends."

Sefaro laughed out loud at that.

Lyn wandered over to the stairs and peered up. "What's up there anyway?"

"An amazing view," Naoise answered fervently. "I highly recommend it."

She shrugged and sat on the bottom step. "Maybe in a bit. Tell me what happened after I left last night."

The elder Grenlecian prince paced restlessly within the narrow confines of their prison, giving the impression of being far too large for the place. "A lot of talking."

Lanoralas stood suddenly and said something rapid to Loralíenasa in a voice pitched low for privacy, then walked past Lyn toward the tower door. He knocked in a curious way and proceeded to have a quiet conversation with the two guards on the outside when they opened the door.

Dairinn lifted his eyebrows. "And what's that all about, I wonder?"

Lyn's dark-haired sister made a complicated gesture with her fingers entwined. It was strange and mesmerizing. "He has… business with his men," she explained.

"But about last night—" Lyn pried.

Cole reclaimed his place against the wall, near where she was sitting. "We talked about the war between Grenlec and Telrisht," he explained wearily. "Turns out your sister knows a few things about the man behind it all. Also turns out he's another elf. Prince Naoise seems to think it was this fellow's men who came after Bryant."

"And it's not just Grenlec and Telrisht," Naoise added, frowning. "This is bigger than that. We're all in trouble if we don't do something to stop it."

"Lucky us," Dairinn growled, still pacing. "Special intelligence no one else in the world has, and we're locked up in prison unable to do a damn thing. We need to get out of here, Brother, and soon."

Naoise nodded. "We will."

He seemed about to say more, but Loralíenasa spoke over him. "I promise you will not be confined long, Prince Dairinn." She cast a cool glance in Naoise's direction before turning her attention back to Lyn. "Could we speak together, you and I?"

There were some weird tensions in this tower, Lyn found herself noticing suddenly. Between her sister and Naoise, between Dairinn and his brother, between Cole and everyone else. Between that other elf, Sovoqatsu, and the Grenlecians before he'd gone upstairs. What in the sweet damn had happened while she'd been away? She couldn't help but feel that things had been *much* more exciting here than at the palace, where she'd merely been pampered and fussed over all night and morning and nothing made enough sense to be interesting.

Lyn swallowed and nodded. Best not to let her scary sister see how little she liked the idea of a private conversation. "Sure. That sounds nice. I guess."

Loralíenasa beckoned with a slender white hand and started up the stairs. Lyn followed nervously.

"Won't that other guy be mad that we're bothering him?" she wondered aloud. "He came up here to be alone, right?"

Her sister did not turn. "I am Míyahídéna. He will endure it."

"Míy – what does that mean?"

The soft, strongly accented voice floated back reluctantly. "The humans have a phrase that is like it. 'Crown Princess,' I think. Gallanas was Harunomíya: next in the line to the crown, if it was known that he lived. I would be only hídéna."

"Like me," Lyn observed, remembering how the maddening elves up at the palace had refused to call her by her name. Always Hídéna Lyllíen, or hídéna, but never just Lyn.

Her sister nodded once and continued up the long staircase. "We were born not long from one another, you and I. This is how I am told. I come first, and then you not more than one hour after. Gallanas had many more years before us – I am not good with numbers in Common. More than one hundred and another half of that."

Fascinated against her will, Lyn realized that the people here probably knew a lot of things she didn't about Bryant. Especially if he was that old. He'd had an entire life here before getting lost with her in the forest and waking up without his memories. What had *he* thought of all the cold crystal, and the snow, and the black glass? Had he enjoyed any of the weird things they ate? Who had his friends been and what were they like? Because certainly none of them were anything like Cole. Where was his room? Were any of his things still there? Any of his drawings, maybe? What else had he found to do for fun in this place?

She thought about him having a girl here in Evlédíen, a lady-friend, and felt an uncomfortable, confusing surge of jealousy at the idea. Sometimes it was hard to remember that he had been her brother. Then she remembered what Naoise had said about Tomanasíl, what that man had called himself. That didn't seem possible. He was too cold for the Bryant she knew.

Had he been someone else entirely when he'd lived here?

"In fact," Loralíenasa went on, surprisingly talkative, "it is soon our birthday. Do you know this?"

"Birthday?" Lyn echoed.

That stopped her sister. Loralíenasa turned on the step above her and regarded her with both sharp eyebrows raised in surprise. "The day marking our being first alive. Do I misspeak the word?"

"Huh." Lyn frowned. "People keep track of that?"

The Míyahídéna stared at her for a long time, maybe trying to decide whether or not she was being mocked. Lyn smiled sheepishly. It was intensely uncomfortable to be looked at like that by eyes that were just like Bryant's without any of the mischievous fun she was used to seeing in them.

"They do," Loralíenasa finally said. "Do you mean to say you never… *sídaia-íta.*" She paused a moment and considered her words. "You never know your birthday?"

"Nope." When that elicited an even frostier look, Lyn tried putting more sunshine in her smile. "I mean, it's not like I was old enough to know it, and Bryant – Gallanas – couldn't remember anything, so…"

Loralíenasa studied her a moment longer, blinked, then continued up the stairs. "One week from today," she said, "we will be *thonalí na díalí-sílí.* I will ask for Prince Naoise to tell you how many years that is."

"Naoise." Lyn grinned at the other woman's retreating back. "Now if I didn't know better – and I don't – I'd say something about him bothers you."

Her sister said nothing.

"And if I had to try to guess what–" which Lyn absolutely intended to do because there were few things she liked better than wild speculation–

"Please do not," Loralíenasa interrupted curtly. She walked faster.

Lyn grinned and followed her sister up into the sunlight.

Sovoqatsu frowned while Loralíenasa said something to him in their language, but he didn't go back downstairs. He made that saluting gesture at the Míyahídéna again and withdrew to the far side of the platform, where he proceeded to ignore them both completely. Lyn wondered again what his problem was, and decided to say so.

"It is… not easy to explain," Loralíenasa answered. "And not why I would talk with you." She walked over to the railing but did not look out, instead facing her sister.

Following Naoise's advice, Lyn did have a look at the view. He was right; it was spectacular, the city laid out like a frost-covered jewel below. Still, the place was alien and cold and no matter what anyone said, Lyn knew it wasn't home. She didn't see how it ever could be.

"Tell me of Gallanas," the Míyahídéna said.

Lyn shivered. Didn't her sister's face have any other expression besides that one – cool, alert control? Didn't any of the people here *feel anything*? "What do you want to know?"

"I have no memories of him and Tomanasíl speaks of him never." Loralíenasa made another one of those slow, complicated gestures with her hands. Lyn decided it was supposed to be a kind of shrug. These elves were so bizarre they couldn't even *shrug* like normal people.

That thought made her feel strangely sorry for her sophisticated sister, and she decided to cooperate. "He was really good to me when I was little," she answered, thinking back. She tried to speak slowly so Loralíenasa could follow. "Had a great sense of humor – that was maybe the best thing about him. Sometimes his jokes went a little too far, but you always knew he was just trying to make you laugh. But when anything needed doing, he was right there. Steady as a rock. And he was so serious about honesty it was almost another funny thing about him."

Loralíenasa listened intently. Lyn didn't know how much of it she understood, but the sparks were clearly firing as she processed Lyn's words.

"He liked to hunt," Lyn added, stretching for more. "And he played with magic sometimes. Sun said it was 'in his blood.' And he liked to draw. He drew this." She reached for the sketch she kept in her doublet, the last drawing of his she had, before remembering that those damn creepy elves had stolen her clothes. "I swear by anything you like, if those silly minions of yours ruined Bryant's rose–"

"A rose?" Loralíenasa's thin eyebrows were arched once more. "That he drew for you?"

Lyn flushed angrily. They'd better not have burned her clothes or anything. They were out of their minds if they thought she was going to keep wearing these dresses. "Yes. He drew a lot of them for me."

" 'Lyllíen' is 'rose' in *Evlé'í*," her sister said quietly. "It is maybe that he still did remember some things, beneath."

Lyn didn't know what to say to that. If it was true... Well, that raised some interesting questions. She studied her pale, slightly-older sister and realized something. "You don't hate me."

That elicited the first thing like a smile Lyn had seen yet from Loralíenasa. "Why would you think that?"

"That you do or you don't?"

The sort-of smile turned into something more recognizable, and for the first time Lyn saw something almost Bryant-like in her eyes. "Will you do a thing for me, Lyn?" she asked unexpectedly.

The sun felt warmer as Lyn smiled back at Loralíenasa. "We're sisters, right? I guess it means we do things for each other. What do you need?"

The Míyahídéna leaned close as if to prevent anyone overhearing, even though they were nearly alone and Sovoqatsu didn't give a moldy grapeseed what they were talking about. "I need a thing in the Royal Vault, a flower. Will you get it for me? I will tell you how."

"A flower?" Lyn deflated somewhat. This wasn't exactly what she had expected her sister to request as her first gesture of trust.

But Loralíenasa nodded as if she was discussing the most serious thing in the world. "Not a live flower. It is... *jahar tíunos*? Glass. A glass flower. White, with also some colors on the edge, purple and red. This size." She held her thumb and forefinger apart, no more than the width of a small crabapple.

"Why do you need a glass flower in prison?"

When Loralíenasa visibly withdrew instead of answering, Lyn swore at herself. They'd been coming close to some kind of breakthrough. It didn't matter why her sister wanted a flower, glass or otherwise. The point was, she was acknowledging Lyn's existence. More than her existence – their relation to one another.

"Never mind. A flower it is. I like flowers." Lyn conjured up another smile.

She'd get the bleeding flower and whatever else her sister wanted, and maybe when Loralíenasa got out of prison she'd be grateful enough to tell Tomanasíl to let Lyn have her clothes back.

It was just possible, Dairinn acknowledged, that he had made a terrible mistake.

Of course he had no intention of admitting this to any of the people locked in the tower with him. There were the three elves with their horrible way of seeming to know everything and feel nothing and being far too pretty, and one of them was Sovoqatsu anyway. There was the Mysian. There was that common criminal, the Rosemarcher – definitely shady. And then there was his own little brother.

No. He wasn't about to tell any of them that he realized now he probably shouldn't have crashed Naoise's mission.

He also wasn't going to admit that Naoise was far more capable than he'd realized. In fact, without Naoise – the only one who hadn't panicked – they all would most likely have died in that mountain pass. Or on the Lord Regent's fancy doorstep. Or here in this tower, killing one another in a legendary brawl born of inactivity and frustration.

The elves seemed to be practicing for the inevitable moment of social decay: Loralíenasa and the Captain were having one of their sparring sessions and from what Dairinn could see, they were both exceptional. He was honest enough in private to admit that he wouldn't stand a chance against either of them if came to that. Sovoqatsu he still wasn't sure on, as he had as yet declined to join his princess or his superior officer at their practice.

Dairinn realized he was thinking of the people he was trapped with in terms of enemies and combat and forced himself to take a deep breath. Naoise didn't seem worried. Not about their safety, anyway. A few weeks ago, he would have put that down to naïveté, but now he wasn't so sure. His brother was keeping calm enough that he wasn't picking pointless fights with people he had no choice but to share space with, so Dairinn accepted that he should probably take something from Naoise's example. In this matter.

In other matters, Naoise was being a bit of a mopey child. Dairinn got up from his lounging spot in the sun on the guard platform and made his way over to Naoise, who was watching Loralíenasa spar with a droop in his shoulders and a wistful look on his face. His eyes, Dairinn noted, had gone their most serious color. He didn't even acknowledge his brother's approach.

Dairinn punched him in the arm.

"Oi!" He looked more surprised than angry, despite the glare he leveled at Dairinn while rubbing at the aggrieved spot.

"You've been idle long enough." Dairinn threw his arm around Naoise's neck and dragged him toward the stairs. "It's time we learned how to play elf chess."

Naoise stopped resisting him, for the obvious reason that he had nothing better to do, but sounded churlish as he said, "It's called *suji*. They keep telling you."

"Yes, well." Remembering all of that elf nonsense was Naoise's job and it wouldn't even matter once they got out of here. "We're playing. I'll be the garnets, or whatever they are. How hard can it be?"

"Er–"

They managed to reach the bottom of the stairs without tripping and falling to their deaths, which was a real accomplishment with one of them muscling the other along in a near-chokehold. The taciturn mercenary gave them a suspicious glance, but apparently didn't find them alarming enough to oust him from the spot he'd claimed beside the foot of the staircase. The others were still up enjoying some fresh air and what was left of the day's light.

"And how do you propose we play a game whose rules we don't know?" Naoise asked as Dairinn deposited him into one the chairs at the game table.

Pulling the closest thing he could manage to a serious expression, Dairinn said, "Now is that the attitude of a man who means to win this war?"

His brother made a sound of exaggerated disgust, just as Dairinn had hoped.

To their enormous good fortune, the princess and her Captain had re-set the board after their last game, so all of the pieces were already in their proper places. Only then did Dairinn realize he wouldn't have had any idea how to set the board himself if he'd had to. No one needed to know that.

"I'm sure we'll figure it out," Dairinn said. "You've been watching them play, yes? Time to put that memory you're so proud of to work." Of course it wasn't the *game* Naoise devoted so much of his attention to, any time a certain black-haired elf princess was in the room, but that was exactly the problem Dairinn wanted to distract him from. "Those shiny ones? I think they're first. Come on, put one of them somewhere and let's get on with it."

"I believe they're moonstones," Naoise informed him grudgingly. "But there are rules governing their movements. As well, I believe each side claims two sets. One primary, and one in support."

"You *have* been paying attention."

Naoise sighed.

"Then I'll have the black ones also," Dairinn decided. Black and red would make for an intimidating force in the field, he thought. It certainly worked for Telrisht.

"Thanks for giving me a say."

"Hey, you don't want to be playing in the first place. Why shouldn't I please myself?"

"Of course." Naoise's look now was wry rather than peevish, which was an improvement. "When *don't* you please yourself?"

From the other side of the room, Cole could be heard chuckling. For the sake of his brother's mood, Dairinn ignored him.

They had scarcely taken a pair of turns each when Sefaro came wandering back down from the guard platform. He grinned when he saw what they were attempting, declaring them ambitious, then dragged his cot over so he could perch on the edge within view of the game board.

"Do you know the rules?" the Mysian asked pleasantly enough.

"I assume my brother means to devise his own," Naoise drawled, "and then devise them over again as need arises."

Cole was not the only one who chuckled that time. Dairinn smiled across at his brother, blinking innocently. "Are you accusing me of cheating? Already? You wound me, sir." He moved a stone that looked like a hard sugar candy; he had no idea whether or not it was a legal play.

"I think that piece can only move the length of the board," Sefaro said before Naoise could come up with a retort. "Oh dear. And that's not where the rose goes at *all*."

This was even better. If the others got involved too, Naoise would be more engaged. More responsive. Less likely to sink into despondency.

"And I think you're trying to help my brother win," Dairinn said.

The Mysian smiled. "I think we all know that's going to happen anyway."

"Why do you think he's cheating?" Cole put in with a grunt.

"Let's make it interesting, if you think the conclusion is so foregone," Dairinn teased. "I get Aiqa back if I win."

A predictable, protective defiance flashed in his brother's eyes – a welcome sight. "Impossible for so many reasons."

The three of them bickered about the right way to move the pieces for at least a quarter of an hour with occasional input from Cole, until Sovoqatsu came down, drawn by their heated tones. He said something that sounded cutting, but to Dairinn's surprise, he did not go back to ignoring them afterward. In fact, he settled on the stairs within easy view of their game and folded his arms across his chest, staring down at them acidly.

"Pray, what was it our good friend had to say? I don't suppose he offered to help?"

Naoise snorted. "That's an arrow will never be fired. What he said was *'You and your brother are contemptible idiots. A pair of blind mole rats stand a better chance of teaching themselves suji.'* I get the impression he doesn't have a great deal of faith in us."

"When *will* the strife between our people end?"

Even though he used his most absurdly sarcastic tone, his brother didn't smile at that. Dairinn kicked himself, then decided to actually kick Naoise under the table.

"Oi!"

"Make your move already."

"Not until you correct your last one."

"Fine."

"Not there either," Cole said. Had he even looked?

Dairinn bristled. "How do you know?"

"You guessed. Obviously."

He was having marginally less fun now, but it often amused Naoise to see him ribbed, so he played up his aggravation. "I didn't realize they teach clairvoyance at Mercenary School. I see they've got insolence well represented, though."

For a moment, Cole looked like he might be about to show an emotion that wasn't related to aggravation or the various ways to go about violent crime. Dairinn snuck a glance at Naoise to see if he noticed and was entertained. In fact, his brother's attention seemed to have been caught by something on the stairs. A moment later, Loralíenasa and the Captain came into view, conversing in low tones. They both noticed they were being observed and stopped talking at the same time. Naoise drew a deep breath, put his shoulders back, and ran a hand through his hair. Bracing himself to take on more cares.

Dairinn sighed. So much for getting Naoise's mind off of what ailed him.

At first, Lyn thought she was going to have to do some sneaking and she was a little excited about it. Sneaking in a palace had to be different from sneaking in a forest, and she liked trying new things.

When it came time for it, though, she went right to the room in the palace Loralíenasa had told her to, and none of the creepily detached elves made any indication that they cared. They didn't stop her from going inside either. They simply glided about their business, whatever it was, and didn't interfere with hers. The guard following her said something to the guard at the door, who opened it and stepped aside.

"Thanks," she told them both. There was no sense in being rude just because they had no idea what she was saying.

The vault guard nodded once, clearly inferring her meaning.

Well, even if they were *letting* her do this, Lyn decided she might as well pretend she was having more fun than she was. She slipped nimbly into the Royal Vault, prepared to engage in a stealthy hunt through piles of riches for a single glass flower. Not, of course, that she had any real idea of what a pile of riches would look like if she saw one. Shiny, she imagined.

She stopped inside the doorway of the Royal Vault, and stared, and discovered what riches looked like.

Not *piles* of them, though. The room was surprisingly neat, given how much stuff was in there. Row upon row of the glittering trappings of luxury, trinkets and armor and jewels more beautiful than anything she could ever have imagined, basking in the light of a cut glass window in the high ceiling. So many crowns, delicate or ornate or imposing, all of them finely crafted in patterns evoking nature and flaunting a staggering wealth. Necklaces on velvet displays. Colorful bejeweled gowns on mannequins, like a silent crowd of court ladies admiring the spectacle of the vault. Silver bowls, crystal chalices, and giant gilt-frame mirrors. A suit of armor so brightly polished it was almost white. Weapons far too pretty to be functional. Boxes carved of strange woods. Baubles and ornaments whose purpose she could not even guess at and had no name for, resting importantly on marble plinths.

Loralíenasa had explained to her that everything in the vault was also hers, because it belonged to the family. Lyn stared, somewhat breathless, and tried unsuccessfully to get to grips with the idea of owning so many *things*.

And. Nuts. She was supposed to find a particular small glass flower in here.

She shuffled deeper into the vault with considerably less vigor than she had brought in. With no one watching to put on a front for, she admitted wholeheartedly that she was intimidated by the task before her. She closed her eyes, drew a deep breath, and forced herself to approach the matter rationally. The back half of the room, she could pass over entirely because it was dedicated to arms and armor. And because Loralíenasa had explained that she was looking for a large-ish display case, she could ignore everything that was lying loose.

That didn't stop her from pausing to admire a gold tiara resplendent with rubies and pearls, and the tiered necklace and ear baubles that went with it. She tried to imagine what kind of clothes she would have to wear in order to put on such ornate jewelry, and found herself smirking at the idea of herself in a gown as fancy as the ones on display here.

Mutinously, she moved toward the weapons in the back. The flower could wait a moment, and she had spotted some nice-looking bows. All of this was hers too, anyway. She picked her way through some of the less stupidly decorative weapons and found one she liked the feel and flex of. There was even a matching quiver, tooled white leather decorated with a twisting vine pattern, stocked with a fair quantity of white-fletched arrows. If anyone tried to take the bow from her, she decided, she'd clip them in the face with it.

Feeling better with the bow in hand, she went back on the hunt. It was impossible not to let herself get distracted by all of the stuff; she had a feeling she'd be coming back here a lot, just to look and try to figure out what some of it was.

The larger cases were in the middle of the room, and she eventually got there. For a moment, she was worried that she might have to break them in order to get in for the flower, but then she realized they weren't locked in any way she could see. She circled the cases, eyeing jewels and figurines and stranger items that she supposed might be the trappings of magic.

And finally, resting in a velvet-lined box in one of the more exotic displays, she spotted it just as her sister had described. A glass datura, smaller than its living counterpart, white in the center but darkening to a blood-like purple at the trumpet's delicate edge. The flower appeared to grow out of a milky translucent bulb that looked maybe to be stone, nestled within five glass leaves. On closer inspection, the flower itself seemed to be a funnel leading to the bulb, which Lyn could have sworn had been glowing a moment ago.

There was an inscribed plaque beside the box, but the swirling letters meant nothing to Lyn. She was more interested in the uneasy feeling she got when she looked at the flower anyway.

Shrugging mentally, Lyn put her hands on the glass door of the case and was relieved when it slid away. She picked up the small silver box, snapped it shut with the flower inside, and congratulated herself on having passed her sister's test. Also on her shiny new bow. With any luck, she was well on her way to securing Loralíenasa's… well, friendship didn't feel like a viable word when she imagined her twin's cold white face. But maybe one day they could be sisters.

Lyn whistled as she strode out of the vault victorious, sneaking forgotten.

# CHAPTER SIXTEEN

Ninety-nine elves and one human raised their glasses and drank to the Lord Regent's long-winded toast.

"Does he expect me to believe any of that?" Lyn whispered loudly in Naoise's ear once she'd set her glass down. "He's known me all of a week, and I'm pretty sure he's spent it discovering how much he hates me."

Naoise chuckled dryly and considered what *he* had learned over the last week.

That elves used magic every day for perfectly mundane tasks, whether they were the magic-wielding type or not. That they didn't sleep much, that their approach to food was distinctly at odds with his human palate, that they were unaffected by the elements – or less affected than humans, he hadn't yet come to a conclusion. That their ability to stave off boredom was what he could only term uncanny. That his brother was more of an ass than he had already suspected, when forced to inactivity, and that even when you liked a person it wasn't pleasant to be doing nothing at all with them in the same small tower for an entire week.

That it was intensely difficult to avoid touching someone you were imprisoned with, and harder to make yourself be serious about the effort when in fact you wanted nothing more than to hold her.

He shifted in his borrowed suit of silk and velvet – he also now knew that elven fashion was sinfully comfortable – and told himself, again, that he was an idiot.

The thing was, he knew she was right. She was right about all of it: there *were* more important things to worry about, and he *couldn't* afford to be so distracted by a beautiful woman while the fate of the world was at stake. He *was* worried about those important things, every bit as deeply as when he'd convinced his father to let him follow leads across Asrellion to figure out how to save his kingdom. It was killing him to sit idle, knowing that things were falling apart out in the world.

Unfortunately, he could do little else. Loralíenasa had told him she had a plan, and that he had to be patient. And with nothing productive to occupy him, forced to be constantly in her presence, how was he *not* to notice her?

Tonight, certainly, there was no pretending not to stare at her draped in that elegant white silk gown and all those diamonds – none of it covering her as much as he was accustomed to seeing women covered in public. She looked unreal, like a concept, a dream of glamor and grace. Seated between them, Lyn was more eye-catching in her bright red dress and matching rubies, but the ethereal image of Loralíenasa gleaming in white silk haunted him even when he looked away.

"You're staring again," Lyn added in an even louder whisper.

The blood flooded into Naoise's face and he fixed his gaze down at the black marble table top, hoping Loralíenasa had her attention directed else-where.

"If it makes you feel better," the blonde elf went on, this time mercifully lowering her voice to an actually confidential volume, "she's glanced your way a few times, too. Can't blame her. You look good."

Resisting an impulse to smooth his extravagant, colorful borrowed clothes yet again was difficult. Never as a prince of Grenlec had he worn anything so ostentatious; even the undergarments were silk, and embroidered too. He wasn't sure whether to be impressed or horrified by the cost of the garb he had on, but he nodded once and was able to say, politely, "You're too kind. You should know you look beautiful yourself, hídéna."

"Don't *you* start hídéna-ing me," Lyn snapped. "You're the only thing making this bearable, but if you're going to be like that, I'll have them drag you back to prison."

The summons had come without warning, though Loríen hadn't seemed surprised. She had explained on the long walk up from the tower that it was a matter of appeasing Lyn, providing her with a translator for the evening. The guards had been reporting that the newly-returned princess and the Regent were not getting on at all well.

Nor was Loríen's temporary release born of any desire to be lenient as a birthday reward. She had made it perfectly clear, when the guards extended the invitation, that she knew her guardian must have bowed to pressure from the Houses. They already thought he was outright draconian with her on his best days. Too much of an outrage, for the Míyahídéna to be barred from celebrating her first birthday reunited with her long-lost twin, and the Valley had been craving a glimpse of the sisters side by side ever since Lyn's return. It was edifying, good for public morale. The general mood needed lifting just now.

Naoise didn't want to think about the politics involved. He didn't even really want to be doing this, though there was no way he would have refused. The chance to have a better look at the elves and their palace was impossible to resist, and he wasn't fond of the idea of being locked in the tower while Loríen was somewhere else.

"But how will you tell them to do it?" he said to Lyn with a wink, keeping things light for her benefit.

She was nervous almost out of her mind, and he could see it no matter how she pretended not to be overwhelmed by the crowd and the luxury, or how many jokes she made at Lord Maiantar's expense. He looked up at the intricate chandelier, gold and silver and fine crystal giving off a light that did not come from fire, and couldn't blame her.

"I've gotten to be pretty good at letting them know what I want," she said, grinning. "Mostly I wave my arms around a lot and growl until they either give me things or stop doing things."

"Ah. So you get on by pantomiming an enraged bear."

Lyn smacked him wordlessly on the back of the head.

The entire table hushed suddenly and turned their way, staring at Naoise.

Lyn swallowed. "Uh." She forced a smile and lifted her hands palm out. "We're just playing? He didn't do anything to me. Ah, squirrel drops. It doesn't help for you to be the one to translate that, does it?"

Loralíenasa cleared her throat and said in Elven into the tense silence, "The hídéna has learned to show affection in strange ways."

Most of the elves at the table went back to their plates and their conversations, only a few giving Naoise an extra moment of study to be certain he wasn't on the verge of a bloody human rampage.

Lyn let out a long breath that terminated in an anxious laugh. "Sorry about that. These people."

The Míyahídéna leaned close so Naoise could better hear her. She was wearing a delicate perfume that drifted over him like starlight. "Please tell my sister we're not in the habit of hitting each other at the table," she said dryly. "She might want to trim that back, if she doesn't want to get both of you thrown out."

"If it's all the same to you, I'll not relay that message," Naoise replied. "A way out might be just what she wants." He was pleased that Loríen was speaking to him after a week of trying to pretend he didn't exist, but he made an effort not to show it.

The corner of her lip twitched. "In that case, just tell her that dinner is nearly over."

He smiled.

The elf on Naoise's left sighed too loudly and shook his head. The prince did his best to ignore it.

"Oh, before I forget," Lyn said suddenly, and with no further explanation reached into the gold sash tied at her slender waist.

When Naoise glanced over in curiosity, he briefly saw something shining in her hand, but she poked her sister in the shoulder and passed the item to her under the table. Loralíenasa didn't look down, but from her cool look of satisfaction as she closed her fingers over the object, she seemed to know exactly what it was. She thanked her sister and made the small, glittering thing disappear somewhere on her person.

True to her word, the dessert course was brought out a moment later – another alien extravagance, some airy, dark, bittersweet concoction that left Naoise feeling he'd just committed crimes against decency. They were released from the table not long after that to mingle in the Grand Ballroom, where mages spun ornamental magic for the entertainment of those gathered. Of course none of the other guests shared Naoise's deep unease in the presence of magic, and their nonchalance was itself even more unsettling.

He kept close to the young woman he was translating for and struggled to stay afloat amidst so much strangeness. Lyn kept close to Loralíenasa.

The nobility milled about the spectacular hall, brightly-colored and beautiful as butterflies, glancing their way and occasionally venturing over to meet their new princess in emboldened silken clusters. It was a flurry of names: Qroíllenas, Daríallas, Taréna, Víqarío, Víara, Qévalos. Dozens more, too many to keep track of. Naoise did begin to notice the same few surnames being repeated – the Eleven Noble Houses. He also noticed how few of these glittering, important personages Loralíenasa paid any real attention to.

Lyn was as overwhelmed as he. "By all that crawls on four, Naoise," she hissed at him before the hour was half gone, "*save me from this*. If another person asks me how I'm liking Efrondel–"

"*Me* save *you*?" He snorted and was about to say something witty when Loralíenasa interrupted him.

"On your guards, both of you," she murmured softly in Common. "Lord Maiantar."

Naoise turned quickly to see the intimidating Lord Regent parting the crowd, making for their position. He did not look happy, but Naoise couldn't imagine how the man could ever look happy.

Lyn slid closer to Naoise and grasped his arm for support. He patted her hand reassuringly.

The tall elf inclined his head to Lyn when he reached her, ignoring Loralíenasa. He glanced coldly at Naoise to be certain the translator was ready and listening. "Allow me to express again my fondest wishes for you in the coming year, hídéna. I hope everything tonight has been to your liking."

The princess frowned when the message had been translated for her. "Naoise, can you please tell him to stop calling me that? It's Lyn. I don't care who my parents were or how they do things here. If everyone's going to treat me like I'm made of glass, I swear I'm running away to live with the wolves."

Naoise couldn't tell whether Lord Maiantar was trying not to smile or shout when he rendered that, but his lips twitched. "I apologize if we've made you uncomfortable. That is not our intent."

"Well maybe if you'd let me have someone here to translate…" She made distinctly un-subtle gestures in Naoise's direction.

The Lord Regent blinked and ignored the insinuation. "We have been trying most diligently to find someone suitable. Common is not a language our people have been proud to speak in some years."

Naoise could detect the bitterness in Lord Maiantar's voice, the gall at the fact that their princess had been returned to them after all this time broken and out of place, tainted by humans and their ways. He was on the verge of feeling sorry for the man, but then he looked at those cold eyes and the sympathetic impulse froze dead.

Loralíenasa cleared her throat delicately. "With respect, my lord, you have a more than adequate translator standing before you."

Lord Maiantar lifted his chin and continued to ignore her. "I appreciate your willingness to help, sir," he said to Naoise, "despite the unfortunate circumstances."

Naoise opened his mouth to reply, but Loralíenasa again spoke before he could. "The circumstances are only unfortunate because you will it so."

"My fondest wishes to you on this day as well, Míyahídéna," Lord Maiantar said shortly, losing some of his composure. "Sometimes, when I think back over the last one hundred and seven years, I can scarcely believe you've survived so long in my care."

Naoise abruptly did not want to be standing between them.

Loralíenasa smiled frostily. "Nor can I. Between us, I do not have sole province over the making of *terrible* decisions."

Tomanasíl flicked his cold eyes in Naoise's direction. "This is a discussion I will not have in this setting, Loralíenasa."

"Well you'll have to forgive me," she replied, voice like silk, "but you haven't given me the opportunity to discuss it with you in any other setting. And I'm not expecting you to pay me a visit in my prison any time soon."

This time it was to the subtly attentive crowd surrounding them that the Regent glanced before replying, his body language all stiff discomfiture. "I have nothing more to say to you on this," he murmured. "And as you clearly have not yet arrived at the proper state of contrition, do not expect to be restored to your privileges any time soon." He offered Lyn another nod as if about to take his leave, but Loralíenasa's voice stopped him before he could turn away.

"But I have something to say to you." Naoise wasn't certain, but he thought he saw satisfaction in the tightened lines of her mouth. "You will release the man Cole."

One of the Lord Regent's severe eyebrows went up incredulously. "Oh will I?"

"What are they saying?" Lyn whispered fiercely in Naoise's ear. "They're talking about Cole now. What's going on?"

"She's trying to get him set free," Naoise whispered, gesturing for Lyn to be patient.

Loralíenasa nodded at Tomanasíl. She had unfortunately drawn an audience now. "Gallanas *made* him come here, made him swear to protect Lyn when she would otherwise have been lost and alone in a far-away place. It isn't right to punish him for his loyalty, or for your anger at me."

The eyebrows snapped together now. "I appreciate his loyalty; I am not punishing him for it. The timing of his presence here is simply unfortunate."

"Everything is so *unfortunate*," Loralíenasa drawled. "It's your new favorite word, isn't it, Tomsíl? Erases any responsibility you might have to do the right thing. It's all just *unfortunately* out of your control."

"You will address me with more respect," he snapped back at her.

She smiled, and Naoise could see that she was pleased to have forced an emotional response from him. The rules here, he suddenly understood, were vastly different from anything he was used to in polite society at home in

Grenlec. He saw his conversations with Loríen since coming to Evlédíen in a new light – as well as the fact that she had not seen the need to adhere to those rules with him in dreams.

"And if I do, *my lord*," she said in a lower voice, "will you release the human whose only crime is honoring an oath made in the name of friendship?"

Tomanasíl was silent for a long time. He was actually thinking about it. Naoise realized then that the man did in fact value reason and loyalty, and hadn't simply imprisoned them out of hatred for humans. As difficult as it was to impose such an emotion on a man who appeared so in control, he had been reacting to simple fear.

And Loralíenasa was calling him to account for it, in front of his subjects. Naoise finally did feel a pang of sympathy for the man.

"I will consider," Lord Maiantar said at last, "allowing the human the freedom of Efrondel, for Gallanas' sake as much as for Lyllíen's. But he can never again leave Evlédíen. Not so long as the threat remains."

Naoise realized he'd been holding his breath. He let it out slowly.

The Míyahídéna shook her head. "You're just telling him to be happy with a larger prison."

"Evlédíen is not a prison, Loralíenasa."

Not even Naoise was convinced when he said it like that.

But the Míyahídéna smiled. It was not an expression of joy or pleasure, and made Naoise's heart do uncomfortable, arrhythmic things inside his chest. "As you say, my lord."

Lord Maiantar bowed stiffly and made an angry escape before she could embarrass him further.

Lyn was looking up at Naoise expectantly, but he couldn't take his eyes away from the fierce satisfaction on Loralíenasa's face.

"And Lanas didn't think I could do it," she said, too quietly for anyone else to hear. "He owes me a silver."

"Naoise! If you don't tell me what's happening *right now*–" This time, when Lyn hit him, she made it hard enough to be clear that he was a dangerous miscreant.

As several armed elves converged on them, Naoise had to admit that she was right: she *was* good at letting them know what she wanted.

Cole was not as excited about the news of his possible release as Lyn wanted him to be.

"But I'll finally have someone to talk to!" she informed him. She was still bright and beautiful and looking entirely like a princess in her red party gown with its gold sash and matching jewels.

Maybe because of that, or perhaps for other reasons, Cole just didn't have much to say. "Thanks for trying to help," he muttered to Loralíenasa, "but one prison's as good as another."

Lyn was indignant when he refused to share her enthusiasm, and she was made to go back to the palace not long afterward.

Loríen was by now sitting cross-legged on her cot, waiting. She had taken the opportunity, up at the palace, to change into clothes better suited to the situation – a shirt, síarca, and soralos all in shades of black and grey linen, tied at the waist with a black sash, and her favorite black boots pressed with star patterns. Much more appropriate for the work that lay ahead.

"You have a plan," Cole said bluntly as soon as Lyn had gone. "You want me on the outside."

She rewarded his observation with a small smile. "Yes."

"It's high time, too!" Dairinn exclaimed far too loudly, springing up from his cot. "You've sat around doing nothing long enough."

Loríen didn't spare a glance for the impatient prince. "You can work the lock on the tower door?" she asked instead, meeting Cole's gaze steadily.

He nodded without taking time to examine the lock, and she understood that he already had. As she'd expected. Dairinn hadn't exactly been shy about bringing up Cole's history and asking the man all manner of uncomfortable questions over the past week. It was a wonder Cole hadn't laid him out yet, but Loralíenasa now knew a great deal about the Rosemarcher that she wouldn't have learned in more tactful company.

"With the right tools, no problem," Cole answered. "What about Lyn?"

He was sharper than he let on. "She must not know," she confirmed. "She would follow. But she must stay in Efrondel. For safety." In fact, it was an essential element of her plan that House Raia survive if she failed in Mornnovin. She needed to know that her sister was alive and being taken care of, no matter what happened.

"Are we really talking about this?" Sefaro put in from the other side of the room. "About escape? I mean, I'm not eager to die here, but I came here in an official capacity for my crown. Won't fleeing send the wrong message on Mysia's part?"

"It is your choice to be making, Lord Sefaro," Loralíenasa said carefully. "But know that I too plan to leave. I can do naught for your safety here when I am fled."

The Mysian's brow creased with concern.

Lanoralas looked at her and asked the question with his eyes, unable to follow the conversation in Common but guessing well enough what it was they discussed. She nodded confirmation. He seemed to brace himself.

"So that's it then," Dairinn said. He began to pace. "We're running."

"We have little choice," Prince Naoise observed. She looked at him with reluctance and found him meeting his brother's eyes as if to steady him. "Unless you want to rot in this tower until our enemies have destroyed Father and laid waste to Grenlec, and come looking for us here."

"Lord Maiantar will lie without sleep tonight, thinking," she said before anyone could raise more form objections. "In the morning, he will send his decision." She met Cole's mild blue eyes and hoped her brother had been right to trust him. "Tomorrow night, we leave this place."

In the darkest hour of the night, Naoise awoke to the sound of voices.

Once he had sat up and blinked the sleep from his eyes and tried to catch the words that had woken him, he couldn't believe he'd heard the voices at all. He must have been in the lightest sleep indeed to have caught the whispers up on the platform. Or perhaps his senses were all starting to pitch toward her, so he would have been aware of her faintest sigh from the deepest of sleeps. He could believe that.

His first instinct was to roll over and try for more sleep. She was entitled to her privacy and he'd be getting no rest tomorrow night. But because of what they had planned, and because there was so much she wasn't telling them, he hesitated a moment then climbed out of bed and up the stairs as close to silently as he could.

Owing to the unique acoustic properties of the stairwell, he only had to go about three quarters of the way up before he could hear them both with perfect clarity as though he was standing beside them. He stopped and held preternaturally still.

"… tried yet to do anything with it?"

"Tried, yes. There's some trick to it that I haven't figured out."

"That doesn't worry you at all? Your entire plan pivots on this thing being stronger than Kataki."

Naoise listened with more care.

"To be blunt, no it doesn't worry me. I can sense the power in it. It's like a presence I can feel in the room. The way I would still know you're standing there even if I closed my eyes. Everything I need is here, waiting to be tapped."

Naoise felt the stirrings of the deep unease he'd been taught to feel in the presence of magic. He had never realized Lorien was a mage, but then he knew so little about her people, and they treated magic with a casual acceptance that he found alarming.

"I daresay, but that doesn't do us much good if you can't get to it."

"I will. The journey to Mornnovin is a long one. I have time to learn."

"I'm not liking the sound of this," the Captain of the Guard responded.

Naoise agreed.

"You have my word: I won't approach Kataki until I've mastered the Nirozahé."

"And what if you can't?"

"I will."

The Captain responded to that with a charged silence.

"What do you want me to say, Lanas? It's a risk, we both know that, but it's a risk we have to take, and the odds are in my favor. I promise I won't be stupid."

"I'm holding you to that promise, Lorien." There was a pause. He sounded even less happy when he spoke again. "I know we agreed to this, but now it comes to it, it's so hard to let you go. Without me. I'd feel much better if..."

"I know."

"You know I love you, right?"

Naoise swallowed.

"Of course."

"And not... Vaian, this is hard. Not only as your friend. I genuinely do... *love you.* If anything happens to you, and I'm here just standing idle while Tomanasíl decides what to do... Please come home, Lorien."

Naoise wished he wasn't hearing this, but couldn't make himself walk away.

It was a long time before Lorien said anything.

"Lanas. I didn't realize."

"Well now I've told you. Do with it what you will, but for friendship's sake at least, do me the favor of not dying."

There was another long silence. Naoise started to feel twitchy, imagining her in the tall Captain's arms for a farewell kiss. The feeling surprised him – he'd never thought of himself as a jealous man.

"I wouldn't do that to you," she finally said with another small laugh. "You will take care of Lyn, won't you?"

"I imagine your sister will take care of herself. She's not as unlike you as you seem to think."

"You've been locked up too long."

"Ha! One day you'll see what I mean. Until then, yes, I'll keep an eye on her. It's Tomanasíl you should worry about."

"I do."

Another silence. Naoise considered going back downstairs. Then:

"One more thing, before I let you do this."

"*Let* me?"

"That human prince."

Naoise felt the gooseflesh rising on his arms.

"Which one?"

"No, no. Not this game again. You know perfectly well how you've been acting. I'm about to turn you loose into the world with him. You will tell me what's going on."

Naoise realized he was holding his breath. He let it out as quietly as he could.

It was so long before Loríen said anything that it seemed unlikely she would answer. Finally, she whispered, "I could explain, Lanas, but I give you my word on Nuvalin's First Text that it wouldn't make you feel any better."

"And that only makes me feel worse."

A sigh. "I've never told anyone. Not even Prince Naoise himself…"

"But?"

"And I don't know how it's possible! No, I'm mad to even suggest it…"

"Loríen."

A sigh. "It's the Galvanos. I don't know how, or why, and I hope by Vaian I'm wrong, but all those years ago in Grenlec when we met, I think we were Joined. And then when I left him behind…"

"Oh, Vaian." The Captain sounded ill.

"I know. It doesn't make any sense. He's Grenlecian. I just… need to be wrong about this."

Even though Naoise had no idea what she was talking about, he knew she was giving him the answers he'd always wanted and that this was of vital importance. He concentrated so hard his head started to ache, hoping she would give him anything that would help him understand.

"Oh, Vaian," the Captain repeated. "The Galvanos? Loríen, what... Do you love him?"

"What would that have to do with anything?"

She sounded so defensive that Naoise felt like he'd been kicked by a horse.

"If he's your galvaí–"

"That's not how it works. It's a bond, one I had no say in, not a love spell. He's human; that's the end of that. It sort of simplifies everything for the rest of my life. I don't have to worry anymore that I might make the wrong choice. No matter who I choose now, I know it is."

"I don't think you would have said that just now, if you'd considered how much it would hurt."

"... I'm sorry."

"I know."

"I told you it wouldn't make you feel better."

"Qotsu, Loríen. What if you–"

"Could we please leave it? I don't enjoy discussing it, and there's nothing I can do about it."

"Just tell me, is it like it was before? When you part ways, will you be in danger?"

"No, I don't think so. The bond seems to be dormant."

The Captain sighed.

"Needless to say, I expect this to remain between us."

"You know I would never betray your trust."

"I do know. Lanas, I love you too."

He didn't respond to that.

Acting on instinct, Naoise began making his way down the stairs as quietly as he had come up. He had more questions than ever, but he wouldn't be getting the answers tonight. He rolled himself back up in the blankets on his cot, only then discovering how chilled he was.

A moment after he had stopped shifting and settling, he heard footsteps coming down the stairs – not Loríen's.

The Captain sighed as he sank onto his cot, a sound of deep anxiety. "Please, take care of her," Naoise heard him whisper. It wasn't clear who he meant it for.

In that moment, Naoise realized she had never said *no*.

When the time came, Loralíenasa tried again to make the Nírozahé respond to her, but it remained cold and silent in her hand. She concentrated instead on her own power, long neglected, centering herself as Qíarna had taught in order to focus her will into a single simple command. She was limited by her own understanding of the natural laws and her ability to direct the energy that surrounded her, she reminded herself, not by her strength. She had more than enough of that.

Breathing carefully, she concentrated on the feeling of the two guards standing just outside the door, on their breathing, their heartbeats, their sudden need to sleep *now*. She felt the old dizzy, rushing sensation, as if all the blood was leaving her head, and struggled to keep her focus. A moment later, she heard two bodies hit the ground.

She drew a shaky breath. It had been a long time.

"Any moment now," she said to Lanas.

He surprised her considerably by reaching out and taking her hand. When she looked at him for an explanation, he just stared back with worry drawing his lips flat. She wasn't used to seeing him so serious. But then, he had been acting strangely ever since their talk last night.

She didn't blame him.

"Shouldn't he be here already?" Dairinn wondered, practically vibrating with anticipation.

"Patience, Brother," Naoise soothed predictably. Loríen closed her eyes and let herself be calmed by his low voice – the smooth, warm accent.

"Forgive me if I'm just entirely done being in this tower," Dairinn snapped.

"I second that, actually," Sefaro said.

A moment later, they could all hear the sound of tools in the lock. Then the door opened and Cole was standing there, as placid and unassuming as ever.

"Probably could have just lifted the key," he pointed out. "Guards are fast asleep. Your doing?"

Loralíenasa nodded as the man stepped over the threshold and determined with a glance that they were all ready and waiting.

"Sovoqatsu too?" he asked, eyes widening in mild surprise.

The elf grunted, hearing himself named.

"Come on, come on!" Dairinn urged, pushing forward. "Let's get out of here before something goes wrong!"

The human captives made a surge for the door, Cole stepping aside to let them pass.

Loríen turned to Lanas. He was still gripping her hand.

"Don't take any unnecessary risks," he said in the voice he used on his men. "Whether you succeed or fail, you are needed back here."

She swallowed, nodded. "I know."

"I'd rather you succeed," he added, trying for a wry smile but too anxious to pull it off. "Come back alive, Loríen."

She nodded again. Her throat was suddenly tight and the mad hammering of her heart told her that this was real. She was about to flee into the night to confront the most powerful sorcerer in Asrellion, and she might never see Lanas again.

Lanoralas gave her hand one last squeeze, then released it. "Now go, and luck speed your way."

"Thank you, Lanas," she whispered. Just as she had with the two door guards, she felt for his need to close his eyes and sleep, and brought it forward. She caught him before he hit the ground and eased him down carefully. The idea was to give him deniability, not a concussion to go with it.

"Stop wasting time!" Dairinn hissed as she grabbed her things and followed him out the door. His eyes were alight with excitement and he didn't seem to be complaining. If she had been more comfortable with the language, she would have rebuked him.

As it was, she simply gestured for them to follow her.

The city wall here was lost amid the trees, but she knew where the gate would be and led them to it. Cole helpfully picked that lock too, and they were free.

Efrondel seemed so much larger as they skirted it in stealth than it ever had when she'd simply passed through it in daylight, but the winter night was still deep and dark when they arrived at Nevethas Tower at the northern point. There was no door guard here – no prisoners inside to mind – but the tower's sole night guard was waiting for them. She let them inside and showed them the stockpile of provisions that Lanas' people had spent the week gathering.

Dairinn's eyes danced as he took up his sword. "By the god, how I've missed you!" The weapon was straight-bladed, wide and heavy, with an ornate crossguarded hilt, completely unlike an elven sword. From the grin on his face, he might have been greeting a childhood friend.

Loríen shook her head and tried not to be as ridiculous while strapping her own sword, Líensu, to her back.

"And the Father bless your man for rescuing our things," the prince added, all expansive good humor. "I'm ready to take on anything now. Let's get out of this pit!"

"Efrondel is hardly what I would call a *pit*," Sefaro objected before Loríen could tell the Grenlecian to quiet himself.

"Your humans are *loud*, my lady," the guardswoman observed with a frown.

Loríen sighed. "Just that one, really. Are you ready and still willing?"

The guardswoman stepped to attention and saluted. "I am, Míyahídéna. My name is Víelle Sívéo and it is an honor to accompany you."

"Do you speak Common, Víelle-*so*?"

"Not a word, Míyahídéna."

Loríen resisted the urge to sigh again. "That should make Prince Dairinn marginally more tolerable." She glanced at her human companions and saw that they were nearly geared up. A careful mental probe told her the pursuit had not yet been raised.

"Where are the horses?" Sovoqatsu asked Víelle. It was the first thing he'd said in hours and his voice was rough.

"In the hills, out of sight of the city," the guardswoman replied. She was pretty in an un-fussy way and had a brisk manner; she seemed competent enough, but Loríen hoped Lanoralas had known what he was doing when he chose her. The plan required this woman to pass as a lady-in-waiting when they got to Mornnovin.

Sovoqatsu nodded once and put his head outside the door to check for signs of trouble.

"Let's go," Dairinn said impatiently when he'd finished collecting his gear.

Naoise calmly helped Sefaro shrug into his loaded knapsack, then found Loríen's eyes and nodded. Cole, too, was already waiting.

"Well, then," she murmured. "Nothing left but to do this."

She took a deep breath and stepped out into the diamond-clear night.


Víelle had spoken truly – their animals were waiting just beyond the city, stomping and champing in the snow to keep themselves warm. Even though it was a short march, the humans were huffing from exertion in the frigid air by the time they reached the spot. Loríen frowned. If they were this fragile, she didn't like to think how they would fare on the journey.

As they mounted up and turned their faces north toward the mountains, Loríen reached out with her mind one more time to assess the pursuit. It was a farther reach this time, more difficult, all the way south to the castle and the tower beyond. But Efrondel still lay wrapped in winter sleep, cold and quiet. She finally allowed herself to smile.

It was then, at a full gallop, that the exhaustion hit her.

Her vision went black for just a moment and she struggled to catch her breath. She felt herself slipping from the saddle. Her well-trained horse, sensing the lapse, slowed and eased his gait to help her keep her seat. Loríen blinked and struggled to regain her hold.

"You all right?" Cole called, directly behind her and first to notice the change in pace.

She shook her head to clear it. The sick dizziness had passed, but she still felt as weak as if she'd just come off of an eight-hour training session with the Captain.

"I am," she replied. She urged her horse back to his former tempo.

It really had been a long time since she'd tried to access her own power. Too long. She knew the dangers. In the same way her swordwork required the development of certain muscles, the Art needed mental exercise if she didn't want to hurt herself. But that was fine. It was a long way to Mornnovin, and she would bend the Nírozahé to her will before then.

Loríen put her head down and kept riding.

## CHAPTER SEVENTEEN

Once the excitement wore off, it became obvious that the humans would have to stop to rest sooner rather than later. Loríen would have been more worried about it if she wasn't still trying to shake off a certain amount of fatigue herself, for different reasons.

They rode until her companions were nodding, then stopped at a discreet grove she knew of, some way distant from the path they would be expected to take to the mountains. Víelle stood guard while Sovoqatsu went back to obscure their tracks through the snow. Everyone else slept.

Loríen was disoriented when she woke. It wasn't completely dark, but the light was not the grey of predawn. It felt unspeakably strange to be waking up as the day was ending. At first she couldn't figure out what had woken her; the others were still asleep, and neither Sovoqatsu nor the guardswoman had made a sound.

Then she heard it again: the distant crunch of shod hooves in snow. She climbed to her feet.

"It's just one rider," Víelle whispered. She sounded confused, and rightfully. The entire Guard would be after them, if Tomanasíl could get anyone to go at all.

But just as soon as Loríen asked herself the question, she realized she knew the answer. She sighed. "That will be my sister."

Sovoqatsu scowled as if she'd insulted him personally. "There is no trail she could have followed to us. How did she get here?"

Loríen considered a number of explanations, but ultimately it didn't matter. Lyn had found them — or would, in another moment. Impressive, Loríen had to admit. "I suppose we can take this as confirmation that we've been missed."

The ill-tempered guardsman snorted and folded his arms across his chest. "Excellent. Now get rid of her."

"Is anything the matter?" Naoise said behind her in sleepy Elven. She turned to find him sitting up in his bedroll, yawning and pushing a hand through his perpetually disordered black hair. It irritated her to an irrational degree how polite and concerned he was able to sound just after waking.

"It's Lyn," she said briskly. "Get ready to move."

Even as she spoke, she strode back toward the circle of bedrolls and bent to touch Sefaro on the shoulder. They were all up and getting their things together in a matter of moments, Dairinn grumbling about the cold.

"Do all Grenlecians whine like children who've just been told no for the first time," Cole snapped unexpectedly, "or is it just you?"

Loríen looked up from saddling her horse to see the two men staring at each other over the small firepit. There wasn't enough light to tell whether or not Dairinn was going to kill Cole over that. Well, try to. She doubted the prince's chances against the former mercenary, if it came to it.

"It's just Prince Dairinn," Sefaro said after a moment, tone light, defusing the mounting tension. "Don't worry: he grows on you. Rather like a rash."

Cole didn't seem amused. He glared a moment longer, then grunted and turned to go about his business without another word.

"Someone's prickly when he doesn't get enough sleep," Dairinn snorted.

"Dair, I wouldn't–" Naoise started to caution, but his brother waved him off.

Loríen didn't know the word she heard the elder prince mutter with a dismissive glance in Cole's direction, but she didn't have to.

"Sirs, please," she said. "We have not the time for such things." *And I don't have the patience for it,* she added internally. *Oversized children.*

Dairinn sketched an exaggerated salute as he knelt to tie up his bedroll.

"As you wish, Princess. My most abject apologies. Perhaps when next we stop, you can teach me how it is you always remain so calm. Or I could teach you how not to, if you like."

Something must have been missing in her understanding of what he'd said, because she could explain neither the lascivious wink he followed that with nor the sudden sharpness in Naoise's tone as he snapped his brother's name. Trusting Naoise's response, she sniffed and ignored Dairinn.

Instead, she focused her mind and searched for her sister's presence. Lyn was making straight for their grove, would reach them in another moment. She could probably hear their bickering already.

Loralíenasa had to do something about it.

If Lyn had found them because she could sense the Nírozahé in some way – plausible, she'd had it on her person for several days and was, after all, a Raia – then there was little to be done. But maybe she had found them another way. Maybe she had better tracking skills than Sovoqatsu was giving her credit for; she *had* been raised in a forest. Or perhaps it was even more intuitive. Perhaps she was tracking Loríen herself, trusting her instincts to lead her to her twin. The idea didn't seem nearly as insane to Loríen as it would have two weeks ago, before she had met her sister.

In any case, there was no more time to think about it. Loríen extended her mind to Lyn's. It was easier to form the connection than she would have imagined it could be with an almost-total stranger, but it was less easy to sow confusion there. Her sister was angrily single-minded about finding them. But Loríen concentrated on feeling the energy that surrounded her, channeling it, turning her thoughts into a mental blade cutting through Lyn's focus. Presently, Lyn was convinced that north was south and was no longer heading right for them.

Loríen let out an unsteady breath. Her hands were shaking. The misdirection wouldn't last long, but hopefully it would be long enough. She wasn't going to be able to keep doing this. It wasn't a thought that gave her great hope in thinking about the job she had to do in Mornnovin. She needed the Nírozahé, and she needed it now.

"She's heading the other way," Víelle announced. Naoise quickly translated that for the others.

"Then let's get out of here," Dairinn said. He was by now tightening the straps on his saddle and preparing to mount up.

"A moment," Loríen said. The strain showed in her voice more than she liked. "Give her a moment," she elaborated when several faces turned her way with varying degrees of concern, "to make more distance between us."

She didn't need to tell them the truth: that she was waiting until her hands stopped shaking enough for her to climb up into the saddle.


It was Loralíenasa's turn to stand watch while the others slept.

They had reached the base of the mountains after five days of riding flatout as often as their horses could endure it. In the morning they would begin the difficult ascent. And then... they would deal with whatever situation they found at the gates. She could see two scenarios: gate wardens who were loyal to the Lord Regent, or to the Captain. It was certain they'd received orders from both parties by now. The days of them letting her pass with a wink and a head turned the other way were long gone, lost when she had returned from Grenlec on the verge of death and the Lord Regent had come down on everyone involved with the hand of righteous fury.

This was larger than that, of course. Loralíenasa just hoped she was lucky enough to find guards at the pass who agreed.

Back aching after a long day in the saddle, she slid down from the flat-topped boulder where she was keeping watch and had a long stretch. She'd walk the perimeter of the camp, stretch her legs, before settling in again for the long vigil until dawn.

When she got back to her boulder, it was already occupied.

"I ought to pop you in your pretty mouth right now," Lyn said matter-of-factly.

Loríen was not entirely convinced she wasn't seeing things. It had been a tiring few days. "Lyn? How... how is it that I heared not your steps?"

"It's 'didn't hear,' " Lyn corrected, thin-lipped and annoyed. "I have skills, you know. Had to, living with Bryant. His sense of humor was hard to dodge." She wasn't bothering to keep her voice down; the others would soon be wakened. "But that's not what we're talking about. We're *talking* about what a lying, sneaking, *sneak* you are, and how I can't think of anything bad enough to call you. What the slithering crap, Loríen? How could you leave me in that horrible place and take *everyone I know* with you?"

She jumped down and stood eye-to-eye with her sister, none of the light-hearted geniality Loríen already knew her by to be found anywhere.

Once more Lyn had on the red doublet and white breeches she'd worn on her arrival in Efrondel, her honey-blonde hair hanging down her back in a single thick braid beside a beautiful white bow and quiver that Loríen recognized from the Royal Vault. It had belonged to their twice-great-aunt, Éhaia the famed huntress, who had died helping to lead the retreat from Eselvwey, and as such it was a nearly priceless heirloom of their house. Not that Lyn would know any of that – or care, Loralíenasa thought sourly.

"I did what is needful," Loralíenasa replied, chin out, prepared to be as stubborn as she had to. "One of us must be safe."

Lyn's chin jutted to match. "Let me see if I've got this, because I think I can just guess: you're planning to run off against Tomanasíl's orders and fight this Katakí person all by yourself, with only a handful of humans to watch your back? And he's like the most powerful person in the world and you're going to defeat him with, what, that little magic flower you had me steal for you? And it's my job to sit on some throne back in Ice Town where I don't understand a hopping thing that's going on or what anyone wants from me, and wear pretty dresses while you take all the risks and have all the fun? Sister, if that mountain of squirrel droppings was any taller, you'd need special equipment to scale it."

Lyn was talking so fast by the end that Loríen wasn't sure she was catching all of it, but she got the idea and it wasn't good. "That is it near enough," she replied, folding her arms across her chest. "I am not taking the men. They go their way after the mountains. You can have anger about it, but nothing changes. I go and you stay."

"And who the galloping frot do you think you are to decide that?" The heated words fell oddly from Lyn's tongue, as though she had no comfort and little practice with rage. "You think I care if we grew inside the same person or that you came out a whole hour before I did? Two weeks ago I didn't even know who you were. I *still* don't know who you are. You might as well be a total stranger for all that I mean to go or do or be what you expect me to. Especially if you're not even going to bother to talk to me about what your plans are."

"Talk to you? I know it will be this," Loríen countered, her own anger flaring to match Lyn's. She had never been spoken to like this by anyone. "I know you will not stay in Efrondel if I ask it."

"Of course I damn-well wouldn't, but that's not the point!" Lyn yelled. Her face flushed red. "You don't have the right to *manage* me. And do you know what happened the last time I let a sibling go off alone without telling me anything?"

The others had woken; Loríen could hear them stirring in the camp, muttering in confusion and some alarm. She flushed as red as Lyn at the thought of them hearing what should be a private conversation, but there would be no asking Lyn to lower her voice.

"Do you want to know?" Lyn pressed, still far too loud, fists clenched at her sides. "He got himself *murdered*. Heart cut right out while he was still alive. I know because I had to watch the whole thing happen – he was looking at me when he died. Maybe you remember me saying something about it? Maybe you can understand if I don't think your idea is the best idea ever? Maybe I don't want to lose everyone I've ever had and be left all alone in a terrible place that'll never be my home?" She stopped abruptly, breathing hard.

Loríen swallowed. "Lyn…"

"What?" Lyn looked like she was either going to cry or hit her and couldn't decide which would be better. "I *dare* you to say something right now. Do it."

Loríen swallowed again. Her own breathing seemed to have picked up somewhere along the way; her chest felt tight. She was also unpleasantly aware that they now had an audience, standing silently just beyond swinging range, watching with round eyes and tensed muscles.

The truth was, she hadn't considered how Lyn would feel. About being left to shoulder the burdens of their house in Evlédíen if anything should happen to her, about being alone in such a strange place, about losing everyone she knew and the last family she had in the world all in one night. About how hard it would hit her in the wake of their brother's death. Loríen hadn't even been thinking about her *own* feelings – everything else had seemed so much more important. So much more pressing. The world was ending, after all.

She met Lyn's infuriated blue eyes and realized she didn't know how to respond.

Lyn snorted without mirth after a moment when she didn't answer. "I think I might hate you a little." Her voice was tight. "You couldn't be any less like what I was expecting. You're high-handed and controlling and smug and I'm not even sure you have feelings, and I'll be jiggered if I'm going to let you order me around just because you're a princess and you're used to people doing what you want. And no matter who you think you are, you're not walking into an obvious trap by yourself."

Loríen blinked and struggled to breathe normally. "If you hate me, wh–"

"Because I'm your *sister*, you donkey!"

Someone's foot crunched loudly in the snow and Lyn swung to face their audience. "What?" she snapped. "Go back to bed!"

"Be happy to," Dairinn said, "as soon as you stop screeching like a lost soul in a lichyard. I say. Some of us were snoring quite happily before you got here."

Naoise cleared his throat and met Loríen's eyes across the distance. "Maybe we could all talk about this in the morning? Decide what to do after we've had our rest?"

"No one's *deciding* anything for me," Lyn pronounced. "I'll go where I want to go. You bet your fine princely buttpads that doesn't mean playing board games in Efrondel all winter and practicing how to wear dresses while the rest of you get to face the guy who murdered Bryant." She turned toward

Loríen again and jabbed a finger in her sister's face. "And I'm sure as sunrise not sticking around to be Queen if you snuff it out there."

Cole took a step forward, separating himself from the cluster. "Lyn, Bryant made me promise–"

"*You.*" The blonde elf drew herself up, eyes blazing with purpose. She took several resolute steps across the camp, closing the distance to him.

And put her fist square in his face hard enough to knock him down into the snow.

Lyn stood looking down at him as he sat there in a daze, both hands clenched at her sides, and shook her head once. "I trusted you."

She spun on her heel before he could say anything and started walking back down the slope. "Getting my stupid horse," she called over her shoulder. "Don't even think about running while I'm gone. You'd *regret* it."

Loríen watched her go, at a loss for words, then turned to see Cole, still on the ground where Lyn had left him, wiping a trickle of blood from his lip. The look on his face pretty well expressed the way Lyn had just made her feel too.

"I'd like to start by saying I'm sorry about last night."

Half a dozen faces looked up from the fire-side with varying degrees of surprise and attentiveness. Dairinn crammed half a day's bread rations into his mouth and chewed while waiting for her to go on. No one told her an apology wouldn't be necessary.

Lyn kicked her boot into a snow drift that turned out to be a rock.

"Ouch." She made a face. "I was in a bad mood – *someone* made me get lost out there in the snow – and I probably shouldn't have yelled at all of you."

Loralíenasa listened to the apology with the same cool detachment she turned toward every situation, except last night when she had seemed upset for the first time that Lyn had seen. Either she wasn't buying her sister's contrition or she just didn't care. It made Lyn want to yell again to get a reaction.

"Also I'm sorry I punched you, Cole." Lyn did feel bad about that, even if the rest of the apology was just to make them feel better.

The Rosemarcher grunted. His split lip looked like it would be fine even if the rest of him was more unhappy than usual.

Lyn drew a deep breath, lifting her chin. "But I want to *finish* by saying there isn't going to be a discussion." She met Naoise's eyes defiantly; he was the one who had suggested talking about it. "None of you get to tell me where to go."

Naoise cleared his throat in that polite way of his and set his breakfast aside, giving Lyn his full attention.

"Well. You are certainly right that your actions are your decision. What then do you intend to do?" He frowned. "For that matter, the rest of us have yet to solidify our plans beyond getting free of the Valley. To what end and purpose would you accompany any particular one of us? This is what I proposed discussing."

"What do you mean?" Had they really just *run*? "You're not going to go do something about this Kataki person?"

Prince Dairinn looked first at Lorien, then at his own brother, and swallowed his food. "I don't know about anyone else, but I'm just keen to not die in some bizarre fairyland. The rest of you can do whatever you like. I'm going to Dewfern. My father needs to hear about all of this."

Lorien nodded primly. "It is best that we part after the mountains. We have tasks each to be enacting." She looked at Sefaro, beside her at the fire. "You will be making to Mysia with word for your prince?"

"That's right," Sefaro confirmed.

"What about you?" Lyn asked of Cole.

The man shrugged, still looking deeply unhappy. "I did my job. Saw you safe back to your people. Figured I'd go home."

"And what about you?" Naoise asked Lorien unexpectedly, solemn and intense. "You *are* going to Mornnovin, I trust?"

All eyes turned to the black-haired elf. She made one of her complex gestures. "Yes." She did not elaborate.

"What do you hope to accomplish there?" the prince pressed.

"I will talk with Kataki," she answered. Evasively, Lyn thought. "I am Miyahídéna. He will see me."

Dairinn snorted. "Somehow I doubt he'll stop murdering everything in sight just because you ask him to. Even if you put on your best dress and ask *really* nicely."

She made that complicated gesture again. "I must try. Tomanasíl does nothing."

"Uh-huh," Lyn said dryly. She'd spent enough time with Bryant to know a wild fabrication when she heard it, even if Lorien was a cool liar. "You're going to *talk* to him. Then what's with the magic thingummy you made me steal for you?"

The others shifted uncomfortably.

Loríen blinked. "I said nothing of magic."

"Please." Lyn scowled at her sister and tried to decide just how stupid Loríen thought she was. "You mean to tell me you just wanted a little something sparkly out of the Vault to spruce up your prison cell? I don't think I'm as thick as you think I am."

For a moment, Loríen struggled to work out what Lyn had just said. Then she shook her head. "Yes, it is magic. Protection, should our talks go ill."

"That still isn't the truth," Naoise interjected quietly. Lyn and Loríen both turned to him in surprise, but he was staring into the fire. "You mean to confront Katakí and defeat him, or die trying. And you have been training yourself to use that device of yours since Lyn gave it to you at dinner, but it isn't going well."

Loríen glared harder at him.

"So." Lyn folded her arms across her chest and stared at Loríen until her sister paid attention. "Like I thought. You're going to try to kill the man who murdered our brother. You're off your head if you think you can stop me from going with you."

The fire crackled and a wind howled between the stones of their encampment, but no one said anything for a while. Loríen visibly weighed her response. Finally, she drew a deep breath and said something long and complex to Naoise in her strange language. She looked almost like she was having a feeling as she said it.

Naoise listened carefully, then sighed and raised his face to Lyn's. "She says she's having a hard time explaining herself in your language. She wants you to understand that she's not trying to tell you what you can do. She says she's used to people listening to her – respecting or fearing her because of who she is, only Tomanasíl excepted – and that she has never had an equal. I gather she has no idea how to talk to you, Lyn."

Lyn felt herself growing warm with irritation, but Naoise went on.

"She says she needs you to know that she has a plan but you don't fit into it. She will seek a diplomatic audience, with Sovoqatsu and Víelle posing as her attendants, and strike when she has Katakí unaware. There's no place for a second princess, one with no knowledge of your people or the Valley, in this ruse."

Naoise stopped and said something to Loríen in Elven. She answered curtly in the same language. Lyn made use of the pause to breathe deeply and not punch her sister in the face.

"No place for any of us, apparently, even if we wanted to help," he added with a rueful half-smile.

The Míyahídéna spoke again, and again Naoise waited until she had finished to translate.

"I'm going to render her exact words: 'I cannot *make* you stay in Efrondel, but I can beg. Please believe that I mean only good for you. Please, for the sake of our people and our house, do not expose yourself to needless danger. Bad enough that I am doing this against common sense and Tomanasíl's wishes, with no official sanction. And if you don't care about our people, do it for our brother. His last wish was for you to be safe. Or do it for this man Cole, who risked his life and freedom honoring that wish.' "

Hearing himself named, Cole looked up. He wiped his hands on the sides of his brown leather trousers, then climbed to his feet in order to stand eye-to-eye with Lyn. "You should listen to your sister," he said carefully. "I think she's just looking out for you, not trying to be overbearing. And... if you do go back to Efrondel–" he braced himself– "I'll go back with you. So you're not alone."

Lyn's eyes widened so far she feared they might fall out of her head. "You'd really–?" He looked like he meant it. Then again, when didn't he look like he meant what he was saying?

But that was beside the point.

"No," she said to Loríen. "You don't get to ask me for things yet, and I already got you that flower." The elder twin deflated visibly. "But you know what? If you do this right, we might just know each other well enough by the time we get to Mornnovin that I *could* be willing to talk about my part in your plan instead of barreling in with an arrow nocked."

"You make threats," Loríen said coldly.

Lyn shook her head. "Just saying the way it is."

Loríen thought about that for a moment, but was interrupted before she could respond.

The bad-tempered elf, Sovoqatsu, appeared from the edge of camp where he'd been watching for signs of pursuit while they ate. He said something terse and grim in Elven, and Loríen nodded.

"He tells us we have not this time to spend in talk," Loríen explained to the group at large. "He has it right. If Lyn was so near behind us..."

Without further prompting, Sefaro stood and began to clear away the remains of their quick breakfast, and Naoise set about covering their fire with fistfuls of snow. Dairinn stretched, gave the two princesses a long, curious stare, then moved to pack up the camp. Sovoqatsu and Víelle were already saddling the horses.

Only Lyn, her dark-haired sister, and Cole remained still – waiting. Lyn didn't want to repeat her declaration, but she did want her sister to acknowledge it. Cole, she assumed, wanted to know whether or not he'd just condemned himself to spend the rest of his life in captivity.

In any case, Lyn was right in at least one thing: Loríen couldn't *force* her to go back. She even seemed to know it.

At length, Loríen sighed. "I cannot argue this more. Perhaps later." Another one of those weird gestures. "Come if you wish, but know I will not allow my plan to be... unmade." It obviously wasn't the word she wanted and Naoise had already moved away, but she put her shoulders back and stood by it. "Just take care, Lyn."

Well, that was as much of a triumph as Lyn could have hoped for. She grinned, the grin becoming a laugh when she saw the dour expression on Cole's face.

"Relax. I mean, the alternative is life in prison, right? How is this worse, even if we all get killed?"

He grunted but didn't say anything, instead moving off to help hide their camp.

Soon they were on their way up the treacherous mountainside, toward freedom and Katakí and maybe their deaths, and away from the icy sanctuary that lay behind in Efrondel. The sun was shining, the air was clear, and Lyn wasn't doing what anyone else wanted her to.

It was a beautiful day.

By the time they neared the pass beneath the two great horned peaks, their tracks were sunk more than a hand deep in new snow. And it was as the shining gates came into view, indistinct and surreal in the low, snow-laden clouds, that Efrondel caught up with them.

Loríen had known for some time that the Guard was not far behind, but it would have been a waste of time to hide their trail; they could have only one destination, up here, and it was impossible to run under the conditions.

The humans were already moving as fast as they could, plagued by snow and mists on a difficult path while under assault by the dangerous, unpredictable mountain gusts her people called the *jíjíro*. Even with the cold-resistant gear Lanas' men had gathered for them, Naoise in particular was suffering in the extreme temperatures and the higher altitude. He'd begun the hike in good spirits, teasing Lyn over her temper-driven use last night of the word frot, which she blamed on Dairinn. But he hadn't spoken in several hours. Hadn't been able to. Loríen was more worried than she wanted to be.

All they could do was press on.

They approached the gates as the first of the Guard came into view on the path behind. Loríen called out to the gate wardens, willing them to appear before it was too late.

Two uniformed guards stepped out of the mists at her call; it was clear they'd been following her progress up the mountain for some time.

"Please, let us pass," she said above the howling winds, making her way toward the gate as quickly as she was able through the snow. " *'Chanar thasa vaia'*. "

They didn't answer until she was closer, the older of the wardens shaking his head. "Míyahídéna, you must surely realize the Lord Regent changed the password the moment humans came to this pass with knowledge of it."

She pressed on despite the chill that gripped her at his words. "Nevertheless, I ask that you let me pass. As your Míyahídéna I ask it, but also as a woman of the Valley ill-content to see it fall without a fight. Please, allow me to go about my business for the good of us all."

The others were catching up to her now, coming to stand before the gate as she tried to negotiate their passage. She could hear the Guard on the path behind them, tack jingling, boots crunching in the snow.

Lyn turned her head at the sound, peering into the swirling mist. "Um. Loríen."

The younger of the two wardens was about to say something when his superior preempted him. "I understand your need to act, Míyahídéna," he said sternly, "but we have our orders from the Lord Regent. Not all of us have your facility for insubordination, or your immunity from the consequences."

Loríen heard a mirthless laugh and realized it was coming from her. "Immunity? Do you truly not know that I've been in prison since these humans entered the Valley?"

"That is no inducement for me to come in on the side of your rebellion."

The younger warden, black-haired and serious, cleared his throat and stepped forward. He looked at Loríen, not at his superior, as he said quietly, "I must ask that you help me now, Míyahídéna. I fear I cannot take the lieutenant myself without hurting him gravely, and I would spare him if I can."

The senior warden darted a surprised glance at his companion. Loríen, just as surprised and suddenly surging with nervous adrenaline, whipped her sword from its sheath before the soldier could react. Her young ally reached back to draw his weapon but was prevented by the lieutenant, who struck him hard and fast in the gut. The icy mountain air rang with the sound of several swords leaving their sheaths in response to that.

"Stand down!" a voice commanded from the path behind.

Dairinn was the first to swing in the direction of that sound. He swore vividly when he saw that the Guard had caught them up, seemed to be noticing it only now.

Apparently deeming further violence unnecessary, the senior gate warden stood waiting with his sword bared as a dozen uniformed soldiers streamed into the pass. Loríen drew a deep breath, tried to find a calm, focused place inside herself despite the pounding of her heart, and reached out to the energy around her. She had no idea what she might be able to manage if she had to, but she didn't want to have to use her sword against her own men.

"We *will* be leaving the Valley today," she said to the guardsman who had called out, once he stood before her. "I would prefer not to do so at the expense of elven lives."

The guardsman met her gaze frankly with his own dark-eyed stare before saluting. "Lieutenant Asagaos, Míyahídéna. We're here to see you safely off."

It took a moment for the words to assemble themselves into anything that resembled sense within Loríen's mind, poised as she was for conflict. She blinked once, then blinked again and struggled to slow her breathing. "I beg your pardon?"

"Stand down. All is well," she heard Naoise desperately insisting to Dairinn and probably Cole in Common.

The guardsman inclined his head once. "We were sent to bring you in, of course. A pity we arrived at the gate too late to prevent you going through."

"Guardsman!" the warden snapped. "We have our orders."

"As do we," Asagaos replied coolly, meeting the warden's eyes. "From the Captain. Unless you want to die in this pass some weeks from now, failing to prevent an invasion that will destroy the entire Valley, you may want to rethink what it is you're being loyal to by keeping the Míyahídéna here."

There were a lot of drawn weapons and even more strained nerves as the warden weighed that idea in a silence broken only by the wind and tense breathing.

At length he shook his head. "I cannot." But he sheathed his sword with a defeated motion.

The younger gate warden had by now recovered his feet. He stepped forward and reached into the lieutenant's síarca, pulling out a black crystal rod. The lieutenant made no move to stop him.

"Both rods have to be activated at once," the young warden explained quietly, extending it to Asagaos before producing his own.

"Is what I think is happening actually happening?" Lyn asked breathlessly.

Loríen sheathed her sword and let out a shaky breath.

"I believe we're getting out after all," Naoise answered, incredulity fringing his tone. He also returned his sword to its place at his belt.

Dairinn sighed loudly.

Loríen watched as the two guards deactivated the barrier. The senior warden also watched, with considerably less relief. Once the barrier was down, the young guard applied a more conventional key to the lock and swung the massive gold-and-silver gate open on eerily silent hinges.

A dozen guardsmen from Efrondel and one timorous gate warden saluted as Loríen guided her companions through to the other side.

"For Evlédíen," Asagaos called as the gate was closed behind them. "Vaian guide you and protect you, Míyahídéna."

It wasn't until the adrenaline had worn off, some way down the other side of the mountain, that Loríen realized she had never thanked those men.

*For Evlédíen,* she thought back at them, gratefully. *For all of us. I won't let you down.*

# CHAPTER EIGHTEEN

With the sun now on the far side of the mountains, behind them, they lost their light even earlier in the day. They were not long out of the pass when they were obliged to find a place to stop for the night, where they could take shelter from the gusts and the still-falling snow. Loríen led them to a cave she'd used before on occasion, humans and horses all crowding in close to one another for warmth.

Víelle announced that she would stand first watch and took position just outside the cave mouth. Lyn wedged in cheerfully between the two princes despite Naoise looking distinctly unwell, while Sovoqatsu surveyed his options with distaste. He evidently decided that he had a duty to Loríen to help keep her companions alive, because finally he grunted and settled in with the others, building a small fire and contributing his body heat.

Loríen was only amused for a moment before having to face the very real challenge of figuring out where she could sit without danger of making contact with Naoise. It grew more awkward when Lyn waved her over. She had to pretend not to notice while planting herself safely between Cole and the way out.

Cole glanced at her but said nothing.

Very quickly it became close and hot within the cave, full of steaming breath and all the smells of men and beasts that had spent a hard day laboring up the mountain. But outside was falling night and howling winds and a cold that would be lethal to her human friends, driven by a storm that gave every indication of worsening before morning. Loríen steeled herself to ignore her own discomfort and made herself relax against the sparkling granite at her back.

"I say," Dairinn sighed after he had stopped shivering. "I did *not* think we were getting through those gates without a fight. Was I the only one planning my last words back there?"

"To fight would not avail, at the gates," Loríen replied while Dairinn's question met with chuckles. "The barrier. They have to... permit? us through."

"You had no way of knowing they would," Naoise said.

It was not a question, and he did not sound amused. Loríen wasn't used to seeing him angry, but he seemed like he might get there in a moment. He also looked like he was possibly about to be sick. She blinked, surprised; he stared back at her intently.

"Oh, it all turned out," Dairinn said, expansive in his relief, leaning past Lyn to slap his brother on the shoulder. The younger prince's color took on a definite greenish cast. "Don't be so high-strung."

"High–?" Sefaro laughed. "The wrong brother is speaking, I think."

Loríen was sitting close enough to Cole to catch his one quiet chuckle at that.

But Naoise wasn't joining in. "What was your plan, then?"

She wasn't sure exactly what he was upset about this time, but she could sense the coiled danger in his voice. She was hit by a feeling of being back out in the howling winds, clinging to the mountainside and doubtful of her footing. "Happily, I need not to tell it," she answered carefully. "It turned out, as Dairinn says."

The lines around Naoise's mouth tightened. "You honestly expect that answer to be good enough?" Something in his tone made everyone else stop what they were doing and give him their full attention.

Loríen sat up straighter, considering her response. She was interrupted before she could give one.

"What's this all about, little brother?" Dairinn asked, leaning forward again to look across Lyn at Naoise. "What's eating into you?"

Naoise turned a surprisingly severe gaze on his brother. His eyes were a lighter blue than their normal shade, icy and unsettling. "What's eating into me? I'm cold and I'm tired and I've had too many days now that I was sure would be my last. The experience has lost its charm." He shifted his too-perceptive stare in Loríen's direction. "And I'm afraid for the ones I love."

She swallowed and refused to let herself acknowledge what he meant.

"There are things I know you're not telling us," he said. His tone matched the frost in his eyes. "I want to hear more about your plans in Mornnovin. We do all have an interest in seeing this Katakí Kuromé defeated, after all, and you are undertaking to face him by yourself. I'd like to know how much of a chance you have against him, and I hope to be comforted by the answer as you insist on refusing help from those who would give it."

For a moment, no one else in the world existed for Loríen besides the man meeting her eyes from across the cave. She had never seen him like this. Intense was an inadequate description. Not angry, exactly, but holding tightly to something that lived close to his temper.

Loríen switched to Elven. "What is it you want to hear?" she asked quietly. "You seem to have your own ideas already as to what I intend. I don't know that I see the use in arguing against them."

He drew a careful breath as if to keep himself from shouting, though his voice was as low and smooth as ever. "What I want," he said in Common, giving no quarter, "is for you to succeed. Survive, even – if such a thought is permitted, Míyahídéna."

She felt the heat of anger rising in her cheeks.

"I want my kingdom safe and for this war to end with those I love still alive," Naoise went on. "I want to do my part to make that happen. I want to do what I can, even if it's not enough in the end. I want you to have a plan that's more certain than what we saw back at the gates, because failure is the *last* thing I want. And I want you to admit that people have a right to want to help you, that our stake in victory is as vital as yours."

As quickly as the anger rose in her, it was replaced by something else, more complicated and more difficult to name.

"Couldn't have said it better myself," Lyn murmured at Naoise's side, reminding Loríen that the world did in fact contain other people.

It was because of the profound silence inside the cave as everyone held their breath, awaiting Loríen's response, that they all knew something was wrong even before Víelle's warning cry came.


Sovoqatsu was the first one on his feet, but Loríen made it outside before him because she was closer. Just in time to hear Víelle cry out again. Visibility was poor, but Loríen saw the darkness of a black-clad figure dropping down onto the guardswoman from above, saw them struggle, saw the unknown figure twisting Víelle's neck too far to the side.

Saw him toss the soldier's suddenly limp body over the cliff face.

Loríen knew she needed to draw her weapon, but she couldn't stop staring at the empty space where a living woman had been standing only a moment ago. Sovoqatsu was already rushing past her, a snarl in his throat. He leaped upon Víelle's killer with his weapon drawn; the two went down in a violent spray of snow.

"Get down!" Naoise called behind her.

Freed from her paralysis by the urgency in his voice, she didn't even pause to question the warning or to look for the source of the danger. Dropping flat against the mountainside, she felt the whistle of some sharp object slicing through the air where her head had been. She looked up to see several throwing knives embedded in the rocks behind her.

Ahead, she saw Naoise spinning away from a scything sword-blow, then allowing the momentum to bring him around behind his attacker. The stranger in black tried to turn, but Naoise had already taken him by the throat with one hand and buried his sword at the base of his spine, twisting the blade with brutal proficiency.

A spray of blood joined the swirling snow.

Loríen heard footsteps speeding her way and rolled to her feet, pulling her sword from its sheath at her back. She only just turned to face her attacker in time to block the knife that was trying to find her kidney. The enemy now gauging her for another attack was armed with a pair of long knives, swathed from head to foot in black like the others, fully concealed but for a slit at the eyes. He moved like an animal, a predator. Like someone who had killed before and no longer had to give killing a moment's thought. He pressed in, filling all of her senses until she felt an overpowering need to escape. She parried his second attack, feeling clumsy and sluggish. This was supposed to be what she was good at, she thought.

As his steel ground against hers and the impact shuddered all the way up her arm to her shoulder, her brain finally churned to life. She had the reach with her longer blade; there was no reason to let him control their distance. She sprang back before he could thrust again. When he tried to follow, she let him have the deadly point of her curved sword on his advancing thigh with all the force of his own forward motion.

He dropped to one knee with a grunt, the snow darkening beneath him. One of his hands came up almost too quickly for her eyes to follow. She knew more than she saw that he was throwing his long knife. Her instincts, honed by years of hard practice, brought her blade up at the right angle to deflect the weapon flying toward her heart. And because Lanoralas had taught her to waste no motion once the energy was committed to it, Loríen dropped the point to come down above his other knife, sliding her blade in between his neck and his collarbone.

It didn't occur to her until a moment later that she had just killed a man.

His body was still falling as she turned to assess the rest of the battle. She could see four black shapes lying motionless in the snow; another fell at Cole's feet with a sickening crunch of bone before she could see just what the man had done.

And then it was still and quiet on the mountainside.

Loríen looked for her friends. The wind had died down for the moment and the night was almost peaceful now. Lyn was standing just inside the cave mouth, bow in hand and arrow nocked, looking wildly terrified. Sovoqatsu was down on one knee, already cleaning his reddened blade in the snow. The others were standing where they had fought, struggling to catch their breath, all of them also looking from one to the other to be certain everyone else was all right.

Except for Víelle. The guardswoman was no longer among them.

When Sovoqatsu was done seeing to his weapon, he knelt beside one of the black-clad bodies and yanked the hood off with brisk precision. He glanced down into the face for a moment, then looked up at Loríen and nodded once, angrily.

An elf. One of their own.

Only then did Loríen realize what had been so unnerving about these enemies: no visible heat outlines. They'd been dressed to mask their glow. Which meant they had *planned* to attack their own kind.

Naoise spotted Loríen and took two steps in her direction before stopping himself. She didn't know what to do with this image of him with a bloody sword in his hand, his muscles tensed for more danger as the breath sawed in and out of him, his eyes alight with focus. Or with the memory of his lethal grace with that sword, his efficiency at taking life. It was such a far cry from her impression of the quiet, shy young man she'd met in the forest, the scholar – the one she had not feared, whose life she had needed to save. She was disoriented enough without this too.

"Are you all right?" he asked, doing a visual sweep of her condition and relaxing a little when he saw no obvious wounds.

Loríen swallowed. She had just killed a man. One of her own. "I... yes." She looked down at her sword and found it covered in someone else's blood.

Very carefully, she crouched down and cleaned it in the snow as Sovoqatsu had. Later, she would have to oil it and check it for nicks. Lanoralas had been adamant about proper blade care. He would be furious with her if she didn't respect the weapon that had just saved her life. She didn't want to disappoint him. As she dried the blade with her sash, she was hit by a wave of dizzy nausea. She kept her head down until it passed. Her throat was still tight when she climbed back to her feet.

Naoise had sheathed his sword and was standing less than an arm's length from her, watching her intently.

"I'm going with you." His tone was difficult to read.

Dairinn stopped excitedly recounting his version of the fight to Sefaro and stepped closer to his brother. Lyn drifted out into the night in their direction as well. Some of the wildness had left her eyes, but she was shaking now.

Loríen lowered her hands to her sides and drew a careful breath. "No."

"No?" Naoise shook his head and gestured curtly toward the cliff face where Víelle had disappeared. "Half of your guard just died and you're telling me the entire world has to hold its breath to find out if we all live or die while you and that angry hate machine stroll into the enemy's lair by yourselves? That's lunacy. I have as much right to fight for my people as you."

The others were all listening now. A strange tension was building on the mountainside as the wind thought about picking up again, surreal after the heat of the battle just passed.

"I do not question your right to act on your own," she replied in Elven, "but your coming with me would only endanger my plan. I explained this already. I can gain access to Katakí as a diplomat, but not with humans in my company."

"We'll think of something," he said stubbornly. "Even if all we do is go with you to Mornnovin and make ourselves secure while you have your audience. Why should you refuse the extra protection on the road?"

It was Loríen's turn to shake her head. "No. I am not discussing this." She couldn't, not right now. She felt as rational as Lyn looked.

Even though Dairinn could only follow one half of the conversation, he evidently had enough of an idea to have an opinion about it. "It goes without saying that where Naoise goes, I'm following," he decreed. "I can't allow my little brother to march right into the dragon's lair without me. Especially if there's going to be opposition like this all the way there."

"The road isn't exactly safe," Cole said slowly. It sounded like it might have been an agreement.

"And it looks like your plan needs a new lady-in-waiting," Lyn observed, the bravado in her tone doing much to conceal the fact that she still had the battle shakes.

Loríen looked from face to face and saw only resolve and some defiance.

Naoise folded his arms across his chest. "You seem to have a problem."

"No." Now Loríen was just angry. Not that she wasn't used to being thwarted, especially by Tomanasíl, but she certainly didn't like it. And in particular she didn't like the idea of putting any of these people in danger. "I am sorry," she said in Common for all of them to understand. "Sovoqatsu and I go on alone."

"If we follow, you can hardly stop us."

Loríen's pulse was still racing from the battle and the strangeness of Naoise's mood, and she felt queasy when she thought about the limp rag-doll quality of Víelle's body before the man – the elf – in black had thrown her down into the night. It was possible she wasn't thinking clearly. She reached into her sash for the Nírozahé, had it in her hand before she'd decided what she was going to do with it.

"In fact," she said, "I could."

Naoise lunged forward and grabbed her hand, his gloved fist closing her fingers painfully tight over the glass flower. And before she was able to sort past her anger, or her relief that he was wearing gloves, Naoise braced himself with a quick breath and bent the only exposed part of his body – his face – down to touch her brow.

A riot of sound seemed to explode around her, but Loríen couldn't make sense of any of it because of the electric jolt suddenly wracking her body. For what could have been a moment or a year, she seemed to be outside herself, outside time. The only thing there with her was Naoise, and they were joined in a way that left her confused as to her own identity. Which one of them had spent the past seven years at war with Telrisht? Then she seemed to be behind his eyes looking across at herself, feeling the desperation that had driven him to reawaken this terrible bond.

When the lightning-struck feeling passed, Loríen found herself on her knees in the snow facing Naoise, a number of voices shouting all about her. She dragged her gaze upward with difficulty. Sovoqatsu had his sword out and was being forcibly restrained by Cole and Dairinn while Sefaro pleaded with him in Mysian. His teeth were bared in a fierce grimace.

"If you don't take your hands from me this instant," Sovoqatsu growled at Dairinn in barely-accented Common, "I swear by Vaian your precious little brother isn't the only Grenlecian who will die on this mountain."

Dairinn was so stunned he lost his grip on Sovoqatsu's sword arm. The elf wrenched free but was immediately tackled to the snow by Cole.

"Stop!" Loríen called shakily. She climbed to her feet, as disoriented and unsteady as a newborn colt. Sovoqatsu twisted his head up from the snow to look at her and registered that she was again lucid. He stopped struggling against Cole, but his dark eyes continued to spit fire.

There was just too much. Loríen went to the most obvious and least vital thing: "You speak Common?"

Sovoqatsu grunted. "I *can*. I've had nothing to say to any of these animals before now."

Cole carefully levered himself up off of the downed elf and stepped back to allow Sovoqatsu room to climb to his feet. The elf brushed snow from his síarca angrily, his breath steaming.

"You speak Common?" This time it was Dairinn who asked, in an entirely different tone.

Sovoqatsu glared back at him.

"You've spoken it *all this time*?" The Grenlecian was going red in the face, whether from cold or apoplexy or some other reason entirely, Loríen wasn't sure. "You lying *bastard*!"

"I never said I didn't," Sovoqatsu snapped. He still had his sword in his hand. He lifted it and pointed it at Naoise across the distance between them. "More importantly, just what in the black Abyss do you think *you're* doing?"

Naoise blinked as if he was having trouble following things in the wake of his foolish action – Loríen hoped he was – and stood slowly.

"I was…" His words sounded strangely labored, as if they were coming from a place in his mind not usually tasked with creating language. "I did what I had to. I must go where Loríen goes now."

Loríen wanted nothing more than to smash her fist into his face the way Lyn had done to Cole, because he was right. He was right, and in that moment she hated him for it. There could be no more argument, and she had been robbed of choice. They were stuck with each other now, all the way to Mornnovin and whatever came afterward.

And she could no longer try to pretend that this bond had been her imagination, or that it wasn't obvious what it meant.

"Damn you," she said quietly to his face.

If he had responded by looking smugly pleased with himself, Loríen might have punched him after all. He didn't.

"Explain yourself," Sovoqatsu demanded.

Naoise swallowed and pushed a hand through his hair. He opened his mouth, looked at Loríen, could easily now sense the murderous rage pouring off of her. Closed it again.

Loríen turned and stalked back into the cave.

"*Qotsu!*" she hissed at the restive horses. Everything was terrible.

After they dealt with the bodies, it was decided that someone should say a few words about Víelle. The wind had started to pick up again. Lyn convinced her sister to rejoin them, and Sovoqatsu surprised them all by volunteering to speak for his fallen colleague, which he did generously and in Common so they could all hear what he had to say about the guardswoman.

Once that was done, they all went back to their small cave for warmth and a subdued evening meal, and Sovoqatsu took up the watch.

On her way inside, Loríen noticed that Lyn was looking pinched and anxious and far more vulnerable than usual. She recognized on her sister's face many of the emotions she herself was struggling to contain.

During the fight, she had been just on the edge of a panic that had lent a feverish surge of energy to the encounter – but there had also been a kind of clarity, a simplicity that was strangely *relaxing*. No decisions to be made, just the need to trust her training and survive. And once it was over, with her heart still pounding and someone else's lifeblood on her blade, everything had felt too real. Too immediate. She had killed one of her own people and that fact was both impossible and the most genuine truth of her life. She'd been overly conscious of everything, down to the feel of her own skin and the fragility of her body, experiencing a string of impulses that made no sense and couldn't even be expressed.

Lyn hadn't taken part in the battle, unable to get a shot off in the crazy wind and the bad light, but she had to have been every bit as frightened as her sister. And then Loríen realized something else: those men had been Gallanas' killers, if not the actual men themselves then at least part of the same team of assassins. Lyn would be dealing with that, with the memories.

She paused by Lyn and squeezed her sister's arm wordlessly. Lyn blinked at her, then forced a smile. Loríen held the other girl's gaze for a moment, hoping she was managing to convey some kind of solidarity. Lyn's smile relaxed a little, and they went in together.

"It's odd. I can *feel* that you're awake." The words being whispered in Elven, it was inescapably clear who Naoise intended them for. As if it wasn't in any case.

Loríen stared up at the cave ceiling, watching the weird shadows thrown by their small fire. Sovoqatsu was outside, guarding them against a second attack that they all knew wouldn't come tonight, but everyone else was asleep. There was no escaping this, no hiding from it.

"I'd forgotten how strange it feels," Naoise went on. "What else can this thing between us do, I wonder?"

Loríen sighed and rolled away from the sound of his voice.

He chuckled quietly. "No, I didn't suppose you would answer that."

For a long time he was silent. The fire cracked and shifted, and she began to hope he would leave the subject for the night.

"Loríen," he said. "I... need to apologize." All trace of amusement had left his voice.

She hated how much she enjoyed hearing him speak like this, so solemn and giving her so much of his attention, of himself. Annoyed at herself, and at him – and not sure what she wanted to say in any case – Loríen waited and said nothing yet. *You're damn right you do,* she thought at him into the silence.

It was his turn to sigh. "I'm sorry. It was terribly autocratic of me, and I have wronged you. I hope you can understand my reasons for doing it, even if you can't forgive me."

"As it happens, I do understand," she answered coldly, keeping her voice low so as not to wake their companions. "Your thoughts were coming through quite strongly at the time. That doesn't make me willing to excuse what you've done. We're bound together through this for good or ill, and we both know which it will be."

"It doesn't have to be so bad." There was a lightness in his tone that stirred her anger, as though he was trivializing their awful plight. "We have common goals, so it's not as though we'll be hindering one another. And while we're working to save the world, the company will be good." He paused. "Loríen, you must know how I feel about you."

The entire world seemed to darken for a moment as she found herself suddenly facing exactly what she most needed to avoid. "Don't," she whispered.

"Why must I not?" He waited, allowing her time to answer, but she didn't. "The dreams, all those years... I've never been closer to anyone."

Oh, Vaian. Why did he have to mention the dreams? Just thinking about them was distracting, and the sound of his voice was making this difficult enough already.

But he went on. "I confess after that first dream I started going to sleep hoping I'd see you, actively wishing it, because I had things to tell you and there was no one else I'd rather share them with. I... still feel that way. I still hope that Loríen will be with me, my friend and lover, so that I can share with her all of the enormous things that have been happening." There was such longing in his voice that far too much of her wanted to reach out and hold him. "It's like I'm trapped in the wrong dream now, because in this one, Loríen looks at me with so much coldness, so closed off, and I don't know what she's thinking. She won't laugh with me, love me..."

"Naoise, I said *don't*." It hurt. Literally, physically *hurt* to hear him talk this way when what he wanted was impossible and listening to him made her want it too.

"Maybe your people place a great deal of importance on silence, and denying one's feelings." Even though it was a kind of accusation, he managed to make it without sounding like he meant to pass judgment. Which was unfortunate, because Loríen desperately needed a reason to be angry with him. "Mine value honesty. I'm only speaking my mind, not trying to bewitch you."

But he was. His voice, his words, they were like a spell and far too much of her wanted to be enchanted. In fact, if she was honest with herself, a part of her was *relieved* that Naoise had reawakened the Galvanos. There was inexorability in play now, an excuse not to fight against what she wanted to feel for him, what she wanted to do with him... But she hated that part of herself, and hated not being in control of what was happening to her, especially when it was so important. She was angry, and she disliked the fact that she was apparently so easily manipulated.

And, frankly, she was afraid.

She braced herself and forced a chill into her tone. "That Loríen you're talking about: she is a dream. In the real world, I will be Queen of Evlédíen, and you're a Prince of Grenlec. Your people *destroyed* mine."

Even at their distance from one another across the cave, even in the darkness, Loríen could feel how Naoise winced at that. "If you truly feel that way, why not let Katakí carry out his plan?"

Too much of a chill, apparently. Loríen wished it didn't make her stomach feel like it was full of hot lead to hear him sounding so hurt. She drew a slow breath and tried again. "What I mean is that there's no place in this world where we could ever be allowed to *be* a 'we'. Our goals may coincide for the moment, as you said, but what do you suppose will happen when I must return home to rule? You just escaped from prison and possible death there. And do you not even realize that I am at least a century older than you and I'm *young* for an elf? When you die of old age, I'll still be little more than a child."

"...and that's why I can't be with my dearest friend now, for as long as the world allows?"

She closed her eyes, grateful that he couldn't see how that hit her. "You would choose to pretend, to ignore what's before us? I wouldn't."

He shifted in the darkness; she could tell from the sound of his voice that he had turned toward her within his bedroll. "It wouldn't be a pretense. It's called living. We humans don't *have* forever. We have *now*, and we must do with it what we can."

"Well I'm not human," she snapped. "And I'm not *your* Loríen. But this is all terribly beside the real point. Even if I can respect your need to fight for your people, I can't forgive you for reawakening the – our bond." Vaian, she had almost said it. Naoise did not do good things to her ability to think clearly. "I am not some tool you can use to fight your battles."

"Dammit, Loríen, you know that's not why I did it." Somehow, hearing that she had made him angry was not as satisfying as she'd hoped it would be. At least his voice had lost its hypnotic quality. "You're just trying to–"

In fact, he had spoken loud enough that Cole stirred and sat up with a hand on his sword, looking around sleepily for the source of the disturbance. A moment later, he settled back down again. Loríen could feel Naoise's frustration from where she lay.

She breathed a quiet sigh of relief.

## CHAPTER NINETEEN

"Your mountains are stunning, Loralíenasa," Dairinn said, collapsing into a dramatic heap. He looked behind him at the steep, snow-covered slopes they had just quit. "But it's good to be on flat ground again, it is."

"Hear, hear!" Lyn seconded, flopping down beside her discarded gear as if mortally wounded.

Naoise too looked back at the mountains with a clear wish never to meet them again, but he said nothing as he sank to the ground beside his brother. In fact, he hadn't spoken much since nearly falling from a cliff face taking Dairinn and both of their horses with him.

Although they still had possibly another hour of light, they were all so thoroughly spent from the arduous descent that they couldn't contemplate going any farther.

They had left the snowline behind them some way up the slopes, which was a mercy, and they no longer had the dangerous jíjíro to contend with, but it was still terribly cold. Cole built a fire before moving some way apart to dress the mountain goat he had taken down earlier in the heights. Loríen and Sovoqatsu took care of the horses while the others got a head start on their rest, then they came over and collapsed as well. They all lay around for a while, immobile, enjoying the solid footing and the warmth of the fire.

"I don't remember the last time I was this tired," Lyn announced, lazily watching Cole prepare their dinner.

After shucking his armor, Dairinn edged over to Lyn's place by the fire and nonchalantly draped an arm about her shoulders. She giggled self-consciously but didn't pull away. "I can think of a few enjoyable ways to make you more tired yet."

Lyn blinked back at him, obviously not sure what he meant.

He leaned closer, his face now less than a hand's breadth from Lyn's, smiling in a manner that was entirely too charming. Loríen suddenly understood why Naoise was wary of his brother with women. "You really don't know what I'm talking about, do you? Not to worry. I can teach you everything you need to know."

Although it was manifestly clear that Lyn lacked the experience to know what Dairinn was implying, the man emanated too much sexual energy for even her to miss. It showed in the sudden reddening of her cheeks.

"Prince Dairinn," Loríen said in her coldest tone. "Take your hands off from my sister and stop looking upon her as prey."

The smile faded from Dairinn's face. He even managed to look hurt. "I don't like your implication, Princess. I am a gentleman."

Naoise snorted.

Dairinn ignored him. "You are both lovely women," he said, more serious than usual, "and I will not pretend that I don't harbor certain intentions, but I would never do anything unwelcome to you or your sister." He turned to look intently into Lyn's eyes. "You do know that?"

She stared back at him, brow wrinkled, clearly struggling to find something to say. Loríen was on the verge of again commanding Dairinn to leave her alone when Lyn burst out laughing.

"I'm sorry," she hooted at Dairinn, shaking with laughter. "It's just... you're so..." She gestured vaguely at the entirety of his being. "Look at you!"

They all stared at her as though she had cracked. All except Dairinn, who shifted uncomfortably and finally took his arm from her shoulders, mumbling under his breath. After a moment, as Lyn's laughter showed no signs of stopping, Naoise joined in. The tension left his shoulders and his face changed completely when he laughed, his eyes sparkling and the worry lines around his mouth relaxed so that he looked like a different man. Loríen realized it was the first time she had seen him like this, in person. She found herself smiling as she watched.

"All right, that'll do," Dairinn grumbled at his brother. "I think you've wounded my ego enough for the moment."

Naoise raised both hands in a gesture of surrender, but it took him a moment to put a stop to his laughter, and Lyn took even longer. Sefaro made a sound that bore a suspicious resemblance to a chuckle beside Naoise at the fire, earning a glare from the elder prince. Cole, some way apart from the group as he finished dressing his kill, was conspicuously unamused.

By the time they finished dinner – Cole's cooking was surprisingly good – Dairinn was in much better spirits and had shifted his attention to a new target.

"So tell me, Princess." He lounged back onto his bedroll with a contented smile. The firelight danced over his impressive cheekbones. "We've been together for a couple of weeks now, and we still know so little about you. Oh, we know you like taking crazy risks and telling other people what to do, and that you're handy with a blade. But I'm sure there's more to you than that."

"What would you ask?" Loríen said, wary of his sudden mood. He was a little like the winds that came to Efrondel at the end of winter: unpredictable, shifting from playful to destructive without the least warning. It was exciting to be around him, but dangerous too.

"What do you do for entertainment in that glass city of yours?" the prince asked.

The word was unfamiliar. She shook her head to show her incomprehension. He sighed exaggeratedly and waved a hand in the air as he considered how he might rephrase himself.

"How do you like to have fun?"

Naoise provided a quick translation when she still didn't understand.

She nearly laughed at the absurdity of the question, and settled more comfortably beside the fire. To her left, Sovoqatsu was sitting with his legs crossed, eyes closed, hands resting lightly on his knees as though he intended to meditate. Cole had taken the place at her other side and was watching her now with something like curiosity.

What *would* she do for her own enjoyment, if she had the ability to choose and the time to do it? There were her lessons with Lanoralas, of course, but she'd had to fight so hard to keep them that they were not recreation but a careful guarding of her essence against the world's endless incursions. There were her subversive explorations outside of the Valley, when she was younger, but that had been about more than entertainment. Other than that, when she was able to snatch the time for it, she most enjoyed just being allowed to have a quiet moment alone.

"You met Lord Maiantar," she answered. "Think you that he allows me the time for this *fun*, Prince Dairinn?"

His eyes gleamed with mischief. "I think you don't always do what you're supposed to. Good girls don't end up in prison for treason. But perhaps you don't want to tell us what kinds of things pass for your idea of entertainment."

She sniffed, not dignifying the implication. "You do not understand my people."

"Efrondel intrigues me," he pressed. "And your people. There's so much I want to know. I should think you're not *able* to feel anything if Lyn didn't prove otherwise. So why is it you choose not to?"

Loríen blinked. She wasn't surprised that he was asking her about her people or Evlédíen – in fact, he hadn't asked much while imprisoned there, and she'd been waiting for him to start. What surprised her was the unexpectedly astute observation that lay behind the question. She was impressed enough that she decided not to take offense.

"It is our way," she answered simply.

"Yes, but *why*?" Dairinn pressed.

She made the sign of the open basket. "We *do* feel. It… we call it the Qíarnos, the way we learn to be controlled. We do it because…" She paused to consider her words.

"Why make the effort, Míyahídéna?" Sovoqatsu said, not bothering to open his eyes. He had stopped speaking anything but Common now, as belligerently as he had pretended not to speak it in the first place. "Even if you had enough of the language to explain, which you know you do not, these animals would never understand."

"*You* don't seem to be too good at this Qíarnos business," Dairinn shot at the prickly elf. "You're angry all the time and I can tell perfectly well what you're feeling."

Sovoqatsu opened his eyes and blinked slowly. "Can you?"

Dairinn's smug smile faded a little.

"You see what I want you to see, human," the guardsman said dismissively. "That is the purpose of the Qíarnos."

"No," Loríen corrected. She met Sovoqatsu's surprised look with a cool one of her own. "That is the purpose we give it now, *i barolan*. We forget it was not always."

Sovoqatsu's eyes spat fire at her.

"Explain that," Lyn said unexpectedly. She sat up and leaned forward. "I'd like to know. Why *do* you all pretend not to feel anything? Why would anyone want to live that way?"

Loríen stared into the dancing flames for a moment, trying to put together the right words.

But Sefaro surprised her.

"I know this, actually. I think. If you don't mind me trying to explain, my lady," he said. He offered a shy smile. "We still teach the Seven Principles in Mysia, too. We rarely do as well with them as your people do, but we try."

Loríen felt a surge of affection for the Mysian. "Oh?"

Sefaro directed his boyish, almost-apologetic smile at Lyn. "It all goes back to the legend of the Creation. I won't bore you with the long version, but the story is that the first elves were so curious and so innocent that they got themselves into a lot of trouble with the Farín – fairies. Many died, not having the wisdom to know when they were being led into danger. It was the first king who taught his people how to be more cautious, not to give action to any emotion until it had been examined and understood. The point was to keep them from doing rash things that would get them hurt."

Loríen nodded. "Yes. Selatho Raia. He made the Qíarnos, to keep us safe."

"But now it's a superiority game," Naoise observed. "Who-is-better-at-staying-in-control. You consider you've scored points off one another when you make each other slip and show your feelings."

He had been to exactly one court function. He was even sharper than Loríen had given him credit for, if he had picked that up already. She tried not to show how impressed she was, aware of the irony even as she made the effort.

"Yes, that is true," she admitted.

"That's twisted," Dairinn said.

"It's stupid," Lyn added flatly. "I mean, I've embarrassed myself before, and sometimes I've wished later that I hadn't said something, but I haven't literally *died* of feelings. And I don't think you deserve some kind of prize if you can manage to fool me into thinking you don't care about things. Mainly I just want to punch you."

Loríen tried to decide whether or not to explain to Lyn just how offensive that was, striking at everything she had been raised to be.

But Dairinn was nodding. "I think I understand your Valley much better now." He smiled his too-charming smile at her. "And it's a relief to know you're just as much of a burning, chaotic mess under there as the rest of us. Makes you somewhat less terrifying."

She lifted an eyebrow at him. "Terrifying?"

"I warn you not to become overly familiar, Grenlecian," Sovoqatsu said ominously.

Dairinn casually made what might have been a rude gesture in the guardsman's direction. "Don't worry. I'll stay terrified of you if you want."

Lyn laughed as the guardsman stared him down.

"I say, Loríen," the elder prince added with alarming suddenness. He sat up, his eyes gleaming mischievously. "You allow us to call you by a short-ened name rather than Loralíenasa, and I heard you calling that Captain friend of yours by a more familiar name as well. What do our dear Sovoqatsu's friends call him? Assuming he has any."

"I think that's enough, Prince Dairinn," Cole said quietly at Loríen's side. The mildness of his tone was belied by the sudden tension in his sword arm.

"Just trying to get to know our elven friend," Dairinn replied with a brittle smile. "No harm in that. Come now, Loríen. Do share."

There was an unpleasant spirit developing around the fire, and Loríen had no desire to encourage it. In fact, she had begun to wonder how to put a stop to it. She looked up at Naoise, instinctively wondering if he shared the feel-ing. He was staring back at her. When he saw her looking at him, he frowned and shook his head inconspicuously.

Loríen was unsettled by how well he could read her.

"They call me Sotsu," the man on her other side snapped before she had decided what to say. He held Dairinn's gaze steadily, the firelight turning his eyes into flickering chips of black onyx. "And as we are not friends, if you call me that, you have my solemn word that I *will* put my fist in your face."

Dairinn met the elf's intense stare over the fire. "Why tell me, then?"

Sovoqatsu smiled fiercely. "I'd very much like to have a reason to do it."

Loríen looked back and forth between them and hoped she wasn't going to have to hurt either one of them before the night was over.

The prince laughed suddenly. "Excellent. I knew I liked you."

Sovoqatsu did not join in the laughter.

"I'll take first watch," Cole mumbled, pushing himself to his feet as he spoke.

Loríen breathed a guarded sigh of relief. Lyn was shaking her head.

"Idiots," the girl said. "All of you. Just a bunch of idiots." She grinned. "It's almost like home."

The mood broken, Dairinn and Naoise both stood and went about various mundane items of business, and Sovoqatsu cleared away the remains of din-ner. Lyn moved to help. Loríen suddenly found herself alone at the fire with Sefaro, who was staring into the flames with an unwontedly pensive look. She realized it was the first time she had ever had the opportunity for a conversa-tion just between the two of them.

She also realized what had to be weighing on his mind.

Loríen got up and moved to his side of the fire, sitting beside him on Naoise's bedroll. "It is rare that we hear of you, Lord Sefaro," she said gently. He looked up at her in surprise. "How is it you came to be here – chosen for this?"

He made that strange hunching gesture the humans had, accompanying it with a small smile for her benefit. "I'm afraid I'm not terribly interesting, Míyahídéna."

Loríen returned the smile carefully. "You interest me, Lord Sefaro. *Jaín.*"

Sefaro shook his head, but he was still smiling. "You know how I got here, my lady. When your message came to Zarishan, my prince was unable to accept the invitation himself due to the circumstances there. He seemed to think I would discharge the duty adequately, and here I am."

"And why you?"

Again that strange gesture. "The prince trusts me. Mine is but a minor noble family, distantly connected with the royal house. I've had the fortune of being a lifelong companion to Enyokoto, as we are so close in age. We were playmates as children; now we are friends." His lips twitched into a lopsided smile. "That is well for me, having no other prospects as a younger son."

She smiled back. "Well indeed."

He seemed to be warming up a little now. "I've an older brother, Asahi, and a younger sister, Anara. She was married not too long ago, into a good house thanks to my royal connections. So apparently I'm good for *something*," he added with a self-deprecating chuckle. "And that's nearly everything there is to know about me. I enjoy racing, dicing, and hunting, I've a better than passable knowledge of what elven history there is to study in Mysia, and I have extraordinary luck – now you may call yourself an expert on Sefaro Shinju," he added with something like a grimace.

"So you are here to…" Loríen paused, truly frustrated this time that she couldn't think of the word. "*Tsuriqaia téas.* Make your name." It wasn't exactly what she meant. "Be Sefaro out of the prince's shadow."

That seemed to unsettle him. "No, not really."

"What then? What now will you do?" Loríen asked. "I see there are no words of parting ways tomorrow for Mysia."

That took him by surprise, but he didn't deny it. "I'm here because it's what Enyo asked of me," he said slowly. "But now, I… Well, I'm not sure which way my duty lies most true."

She nodded. "There is a choice you must make."

"I confess I am of two minds." Sefaro sighed. "My charge is to return to my prince with the tidings you shared in Efrondel, but…"

"Worried we'll snatch all the glory for ourselves?" Dairinn asserted as he returned to the fire's side.

The Mysian bristled at that, the first time Loríen had seen him show any kind of temper. "Worried that were my lord here, he would do other than I am doing," he contradicted. "Would he run cowering back to Mysia while mighty Grenlec rushes in to save the day? I think not." As quickly as it had appeared, the anger seeped out of him. "On the other hand," he murmured, "it is my duty to tell him what I've learned."

Naoise moved back into the circle of light almost silently and looked down at Loríen in his spot. She blinked up at him, pretending not to notice the slight flush in his cheeks, then returned her attention to Sefaro. He drew a deep breath, pushed a hand through his hair, and claimed her place across the fire. She could still feel him even from there.

"Frankly, Lord Sefaro," Naoise said as he sat down, "I think the worst thing you could do is strike out on your own. You would be an easy mark for Katakí's assassins, and what good then your embassage?"

"I say, he's got a point," Dairinn agreed, slapping a hand to his thigh. "Come with us as far as Dewfern at least. You can be sent on with an armed escort from there. It would be foolish to try for Mysia by yourself."

"We do not go to Dewfern," Loríen objected coolly.

Both princes turned to her.

It was to Dairinn that she directed her explanation. "For *my* safety. I am an elf, if you will please recall."

"That might have been a necessary precaution when you were planning on making the journey alone," Dairinn responded, "but it no longer makes sense, under the protection of two princes of the realm. No harm will come to you in Dewfern, I swear it."

Loríen sniffed. "Your *protection* is not a thing I would depend on."

"It's a long way to Mornnovin," Naoise said gravely. "It's simply a fact that we will need to re-provision. And we too have a duty to deliver our news where it can be useful. Our father needs to know what we've learned of the enemy."

"But will he let you leave again?" Lyn put in, wandering back to the discussion. "Maybe the one thing I've learned about family already is that they like to tell you what you can and can't do when they think it might be dangerous." She jutted her tongue out at Loríen most indelicately as she sat down.

Loríen could see from the tight lines around Naoise's mouth that it was a genuine concern, but he shook his head. "We shall have to address that when it presents itself. I'm afraid there's no help for it." He nodded at Sefaro. "And I hope you'll join us."

Her plan was looking precious little like her plan anymore, and she'd had no say as it had spun out of her control. Loríen had to stop herself from grinding her teeth.

The Mysian cast Loríen an apologetic glance, but he seemed relieved. "You speak reason, Prince Naoise. As always."

Dairinn scowled. "Hey, now. This one was *my* idea."

Sallendale was a dark spot against the massive snow-covered backdrop of the Royal Forest, smoke rising from its many chimneys into the chill winter sky. Unease filled Loríen, just looking at it.

Dairinn rode up beside her and reached across the distance between their horses to pat her firmly on the thigh. "Relax, Princess. I said we would make sure you are safe, and you've my word you will remain so."

She glanced down at his hand on her thigh and back up at him. He showed a lot of his teeth in an especially wicked smile.

"You know, we needn't do this," Sefaro said, turning in the saddle to look back at both of them. "I can go into town for dinner and supplies while the rest of you wait here."

"No," Dairinn retorted quickly. "Have you any idea, my friend, just how long it's been since I've had a bath and a solid meal and a decent sleep in a real bed?"

Cole grunted. "It's not even close to dark yet."

"Are we truly going to waste an entire day because Lord Pampered Ponce wants a bath?" Sovoqatsu added from the back of the column, loud enough to be certain Dairinn could hear.

Loríen turned to let Sovoqatsu see her smile at that. He didn't smile back.

He was the real problem, of course. Lyn could let her long hair down and hide her ears as well as Loríen could, but Sovoqatsu's many braids kept his blond hair swept back and would take hours to undo. He declined to do so. Worse, the inhuman shape of his ears was accentuated by the elaborate silver jewelry he wore through his earlobe and wrapping upward to cap the sharp point at the top. He'd had to borrow Dairinn's second cloak and hope the hood stayed up while they were in town.

Not that hiding their most conspicuously elven feature would make any of them look human. Loríen had a bad feeling.

"Pretty ripe yourself, Marigold!" Dairinn shot back. "I'm not the only one who could use a good scrub."

The elf sneered at Dairinn.

Despite Sefaro's gallant offer and Loríen's misgivings, they rode into Sallendale anyway.

Loríen had actually been here before, once. The experience was firmly in the *not for Tomanasíl to know* category of things she had done in the past – one of her many youthful indiscretions. The glamor she had cast to make herself appear less alien had not prevented people from staring.

Sallendale was not among Grenlec's great cities, but it was an important one, guarding the trade route to the sea on the Nanayaska River. A massive, ugly castle loomed over the river where it flowed into the western edge of the city. Sallendale itself was no more beautiful, constructed largely of shale and black river clay and dark timber from the forest, many of the buildings so old and precarious they seemed in danger of collapse at the next strong wind. The river rock paving the tortuous streets had been worn to loose scree. The bridges too were crumbling, and Loríen wasn't sure she wanted to cross them.

"Mighty Grenlec," Sovoqatsu grunted as they passed under the stone archway marking the city limits.

The few remaining citizens of Sallendale did not improve the ambiance, and there were not enough of them to give the city a truly inhabited feel. They were frightened, tired, dispirited, thin and hungry and feeling the end was near but not knowing which way to look for it. They watched the newcomers with suspicion and too much curiosity for Loríen's comfort as they scurried about their business through the sad marketplace.

Loríen considered what Naoise and Dairinn had told her that first night in the tower, about the war and the state of Grenlec. If she had been inclined to think they were exaggerating when they said their kingdom was on the brink of collapse, she was convinced by what she saw here. It was grim.

She braced herself and stayed close to the two princes. Naoise took the lead once it became clear that Dairinn was making for the seedy tavern district.

"We talked about this," he said to his older brother.

Their story was supposed to be that the princes were escorting an official Mysian embassy to Dewfern, which at least had the grain of truth in it. It made no sense in that scenario for Dairinn to bring them to some noisome watering hole in the worst part of town. Naoise led them instead to the high houses on the west side to find a respectable inn for the night.

Dairinn grumbled, arguing that they'd have more fun where he was leading them, but they all wisely followed Naoise instead. Loríen wasn't especially interested in finding out what kind of fun Dairinn preferred.

Decent neighborhood or no, when Naoise finally declared himself satisfied, the courtyard they rode into was bleak and silent and distinctly unwelcoming. Dirty snow was pushed to the perimeter into mounds of black slush, and Loríen couldn't tell if the high clay walls were naturally black or grime-darkened. A stablehand appeared only after Naoise shouted their presence, and he seemed as startled as if they had marched a parade of clothed badgers into the courtyard. Loríen doubted Sallendale saw many travelers at this time of year. Or perhaps at all, lately.

"This is kind of exciting," Lyn whispered to her sister as they handed their horses off to the surprised lad. "I've never been Mysian before."

Loríen wasn't sure whether to smile at her sister's enthusiasm or scold her for not taking the danger seriously. It was still against Grenlec's laws to be an elf on their sovereign soil.

Dairinn took Loríen's hand and looped it over his arm, grinning. He began to walk with her toward the front door. She made an instinctive effort to draw back, but he placed his other hand over hers and held it in place.

"Come along, my lady," he said cheerfully. "Now you get to see what Grenlecian hospitality is like."

"Prince Dairinn, if you will not take your hands from me now–"

He pulled her closer against his distressingly firm body. "If you don't mind, could we save the sexually-charged banter until after we've both bathed and eaten? We'll be able to enjoy it better then."

A moment later, once Loríen had managed to close her mouth, she walked into the inn behind her sister and Sefaro, shaking her head in disbelief at Dairinn's audacity.

Prince Dairinn didn't follow because he was sitting in the black slush of the courtyard, looking dazed and holding a hand to his suddenly bruised jaw.


"I don't mean to make anyone jealous," Sefaro informed the group in a stage whisper, leaning across their large oak dinner table, "but I think they're all admiring me."

Naoise enjoyed seeing Loríen allow herself to smile at that. She'd been markedly anxious ever since Sallendale had appeared on the horizon, and that hadn't changed despite her amusing rebuff of Dairinn's attempts at flirtation.

Their nervous, reed-thin innkeeper had done little to put any of them at their ease. The fact that most of the group was foreign and the rest were the sons of his king had him in a state of near-panic. They were literally the only guests staying at the inn, but that didn't mean they were alone; the locals were keeping the place in business by patronizing the common room for its better-than-passable ale and its selection of Arden reds. Every single person gathered there had spent the evening staring at their table, at the three elves trying to take a quiet meal – but especially at the two ladies, both of whom were uncommonly beautiful by any standard as well as distinctly *other*, even if no one had yet figured out what they were.

Encouraged by Loríen's wolfish smile, Sefaro passed a hand through his nut-brown hair and winked back at her. "It's because I'm so very pretty. A constant burden, I assure you. I hope I'm not making it too difficult for you to concentrate on your meal."

That was met by more than one laugh, and Naoise was pleased to hear Loríen's among them. Something about Sefaro always put her at ease, and Naoise was grateful to the man for it.

"I struggle, Lord Sefaro, but I must manage," she said in a perfect deadpan once she had stilled her laughter.

Lyn put her mug of ale down a little too solidly. "By all the stars and the sun too," she said brightly. "You *can* laugh. I was beginning to wonder if the muscles for it were broken from lack of use or something."

The tension returned to Loríen's posture as though it had never left.

Naoise sighed. "How many of those have you had?" he asked Lyn, nodding at the nearly-empty mug.

She shrugged. "Not enough. Dairinn says it's an acquired taste, and it still tastes awful." She sounded entirely too sober for a young woman who had drunk as much as she had.

Dairinn was less sober; he had been trying to keep pace with her, drink for drink.

"Waste of a fine brew," the elder prince slurred. "Leave it for someone who can 'preciate its... its subtle herbal notes." At least he was in better spirits about his bruised jaw. Naoise just didn't like to think of the headache complaints they'd all be hearing tomorrow.

"I think it's safe to say you've 'appreciated' more than your share for the evening, my lord," Sefaro observed with a chuckle.

Dairinn swore indelicately and drained his mug. "Ah, that's the stuff. Now tell me this wasn't the best idea."

"It *is* good to be clean again," Lyn agreed.

Loríen looked especially nice after her bath, Naoise couldn't help but notice – her dove-white skin and black hair glowing in the light of the common room's fireplace and many lamps. She had washed her clothes and changed into her spare set while they dried, and her second síarca was the same vivid green as her eyes. Naoise was freshly-bathed and fed, warm for the first time in weeks, and he couldn't pretend that the thing he wanted most at the moment was not to retire upstairs with the woman he loved and fall asleep in her arms.

"I think I am for bed," Loríen murmured, pushing her plate back.

Naoise stared down at the table until he felt the heat receding from his cheeks, only looking back up at her when he thought he could speak without revealing his inappropriate thoughts. "It's early yet. Do you perhaps intend to spend some time studying that jewel of yours?"

"It is no jewel," she corrected, but she did not refute his suggestion, instead meeting his eyes for the first time in hours and offering a minute nod. The attention from her – always complete, always intense – made him feel like he'd had far more than two glasses of wine with his dinner. "It was my thought, yes."

"Be careful," he said before he could stop himself, knowing she would hate both the unwarranted advice and the show of concern from him.

But she surprised him by simply nodding again. She stood and gave the table at large a final farewell glance, then headed toward the stairs.

Lyn stood up suddenly, smiling all around. "I'm going too. This stuff isn't getting any better. Just makes me need to visit the necessary, if you know what I mean. And I think it might be starting to make me feel kind of funny. G'night!"

Naoise watched Loríen and her sister as they left. He realized he wasn't the only one, as four of the probably-drunk locals drifted in the direction of the stairs for no legitimate reason.

Cole and Sovoqatsu exchanged a wordless look, then both of them pushed to their feet. A moment later the local men in question found themselves deposited perfunctorily in the snowy courtyard and the innkeeper was calling shrilly for order to be restored in his common room. The two returned to the table still without a word. Cole reached across the wide oak surface to claim

Lyn's unfinished mug of ale for himself.

"Wha'a le'down," Dairinn growled. "Wanted t'see a brawl."

"I don't think they would have found quite the reception up there they had in mind, anyway," Sefaro said with a wry smile.

Dairinn snorted loudly and mumbled something lewd and impractical about Loríen's sword.

When the brief moment of levity passed, so did the cheer from the table. It was as though Lyn had taken it with her, and now the rest of them could not help but face the reality of the situation they were in. On their way to a place they only knew from ominous legend, caught in the middle of magic and myths and unstoppable forces, to face an enemy they had no real hope of defeating in order to put an end to a war that was far larger than any of them. And if he was honest with himself, Naoise knew he was afraid of the situation he would find when they reached Dewfern. Of what his absence from the war these past months might have affected in Grenlec's standing, or his father's well-being.

Dairinn put his head down on his arms and was snoring a moment later. The rest of them stared sullenly into their cups.

Their nervous innkeeper approached the table himself, clearly not trusting his staff to deal with such important guests. "Anything more I can bring for Your Graces this evening?" He flicked his eyes in Dairinn's direction, then Naoise's, before lowering his gaze to the table-top.

Naoise smiled, thinking it fortunate his brother had passed out or he would have called for another round. "No, we thank you. We are well-supplied. All we require is that your people please see to it we are not disturbed in our rooms." He nodded in the direction of the staircase.

Though he said it mildly, the man colored a deep red to the tip of his sharp nose. "I do apologize for that, my lord. You've my word there will be no more such lapses."

The prince nodded. "Then that will be all."

They were alone again, their host having departed with several awkward bows, when Naoise was hit by the sudden feeling of alarm. Pulse-pounding, instant fear that he knew was not his own.

Naoise surged to his feet with a single word on his lips: "*Loríen.*" He was halfway up the stairs before he realized his friends were right behind him.

When he burst through the door into the room the two women were sharing, Naoise did not know what he would find, only that Loríen was afraid and something was wrong. He spotted her quickly – back to the wall, eyes wide, the long, curved knife she always kept in her sash now out in her hand and held before her in defense. Lyn, sitting on the edge of her bed, just seemed surprised to see him.

The white-haired woman standing in the middle of the room turned slowly and swept him with a coolly amused glance. "Prince Naoise Raynesley. How gallant. But if you don't mind, I was about to have a quiet word with my daughter."

## CHAPTER TWENTY

Although Loríen had been telling herself that the journey was a long one, that she had plenty of time, the fact was that the Nírozahé remained a mystery to her and they would all be in serious trouble if she couldn't figure it out.

Lyn flopped down on the edge of the large bed they'd be sharing for the night. It was a nice room, if not what Loríen was accustomed to at home. All finished woods and fine carpeting, upholstered in rich tones of brown and ivory, much more comfortable than the inn's lacklustre exterior had promised. Naoise had done well.

"So what's your game?" Lyn asked without preamble.

The question made no sense, but Loríen was getting used to that with her confusing sister. She settled on the rug before the fireplace, where she intended to meditate as she tried to unravel the Nírozahé's mysteries.

"Game? Which game?"

"With Naoise." Lyn pulled her boots off and tossed them in a corner, then stretched her feet out before her on the carpeted floor with a sigh of relief. "I mean, the way you look at him, the way he looks at you; it's obvious you two want to smash your faces together and probably some other parts too."

Loríen was too astonished to do anything but breathe her sister's name in horror.

"What? I'm not *that* uneducated," Lyn went on, rolling her eyes at Loríen's tone. "Well. Not that Bryant and I ever... That would've been gross, since he ended up being my brother and all. But you know. I'm guessing you guys are acting out some traditional courtship ritual I just don't know about? A stupid game where you pretend you hate him and he pretends he doesn't mind? Seems like a waste of good kissing time. I was just wondering how much longer it goes on, because it's kind of exhausting to watch."

Loríen realized she was gaping for the second time in one day and snapped her jaw closed. "There is no *game*, Lyn. I do not– How can you–" She drew a careful breath. "I came here to *focus*."

"Because you can't when he's around? I get that. He *is* nice to look at. They all are." Lyn nodded sagely. "I admit I get a little distracted sometimes when he talks. What a voice. Dairinn's probably jealous."

Forcing herself to breathe deeply instead of snapping a furious response, Loríen gathered herself before saying quietly, "Hear me on this, Lyn. Naoise and I, there is nothing–"

Before she could finish putting that lie together, a painful white light flashed in the middle of the room. Loríen threw a hand before her eyes to protect them against the sudden brightness, but it passed quickly. When she lowered her hand again, a woman stood before her.

A woman like no other Loríen had ever seen.

In a way, she was even more painful to look at than the light. Gleaming pale-gold tresses, skin nearly as blindingly white as Loríen's, eyes a grey-shadowed sky blue – by all appearances an elf woman of surpassing beauty, clad in a gauzy gown that was like the shifting of sunlight through the clouds. Her aura was so intense, so powerful, that it hurt Loríen's mind to try to make sense of it, to accept it as real. Then she realized why.

This was no woman. This *was* power, pure energy.

This was one of the Farín.

Loríen was on her feet with her knife out before she had even finished thinking to herself that she was about to die. There was no standing against a power like this, no resistance to be made, but she had no intention of dying on her knees.

Then the door burst open.

Naoise came rushing in, pale with worry, Cole and Sefaro and Sovoqatsu so close behind they nearly knocked him down when he stopped abruptly just inside the door.

The Farín turned to face him. It was like vortices were shifting within the room. "Prince Naoise Raynesley," she said. There was unexpected amusement in her bell-like voice. "How gallant. But if you don't mind, I was just about to have a quiet word with my daughter."

*Daughter.*

Lyn strode forward insolently. "Sun. Where the prancing bellwether have you been?"

Daughter. This was Lyn's Farín, Sun. Loríen would have breathed a sigh of relief if she had been able to breathe.

The not-woman called Sun laughed and returned her attention to Lyn. "Where leaves go in autumn." She smiled. "If you are going to come in," she said without looking back at the men, "then you had better come in, and close the door behind you."

Naoise seemed to force himself to step forward, terror radiating from him as he moved.

"Please, gentlemen," Sun said in her musical voice. "Do be seated."

The four of them accepted her invitation with varying degrees of wariness, each of them finding a seat within the spacious room. Naoise and Sovoqatsu both settled on the sofa before the fireplace, closest to Loríen and the Farín.

Loríen swallowed, and sheathed her knife. The sound drew Sun's full, frightening attention.

"You are Loralíenasa." She nodded as if at an old friend. "How like Bryant you look. I'm glad Lyn found you."

"No you're not," Lyn said before Loríen could respond. Loríen hadn't heard her this flat and deadly serious since that night in the foothills. It didn't seem like the best way to talk to an all-powerful being of pure energy from the dawn of Time. "You didn't want Bryant to remember who he was, and you didn't want us going back where we came from. Or else you would have taught me to speak Elven."

The Farín merely smiled at that. "You always were sharper than you let on. Then let me say instead: I'm glad you're not alone, Lyn."

Loríen dragged her attention away from the gleaming creature of light long enough to meet Naoise's eyes, which were unusually dark at the moment. He was making a visible effort to hold to his courage. Seeing that helped Loríen to find hers.

"You are the Farín who rescued my sister and brother," she said with all of the cordiality her training was able to provide. "I thank you for that. We are to call you Sun?"

The creature waved a delicate white hand. "We don't have names, as such. But Sun is what Lyn has called me, and it will do for this reunion."

"Where were you when Bryant died?" Lyn demanded bluntly. She had her arms clasped about her body as though to hold something in – her temper or her grief, perhaps. Her self-control. Loríen didn't know her sister well enough to do more than speculate.

Sun shook her head, but it was a difficult gesture to interpret. "I'm sorry things turned out that way." She didn't appear sad in any traditional sense.

Lyn was no more impressed than Loríen. "Sorry? You don't seem like it."

This time the Farín seemed to make an effort to approximate an expression of remorse. It didn't look right on her. "I am, in my way," she assured her one-time daughter, reaching out as if to pat Lyn though she was too far away to reach. "But you must understand, Lyn, that your ways are not mine. You never were willing to accept that."

Loríen looked at her sister and swallowed again. She couldn't help but feel she was intruding on a private conversation, even though the Farín showed no awkwardness. This time when she spoke, Lyn's voice was small and young and bare of bravado. It made Loríen's heart hurt.

"Then why did you just let him die?"

Sun sighed. She turned away and studied them all one at a time, as if bored already by the conversation. "That was not by my choice. When he chose to reenter the world, he rejected my protection."

"You could have done something." Lyn had reclaimed some of her spirit, perhaps angered by the Farín's show of inattention.

As nervous as she was, Loríen admired her sister's bravery.

"There is much you don't understand about my kind, Lyn," Sun said lightly, giving Sovoqatsu a careful examination before moving on to Cole. "What we *can* do, we may not always do."

"That doesn't make any sense."

Sun finally looked at Lyn again. She no longer seemed amused. It was like watching a heavy sea-sky change into a squall – terrifying and sudden. "I am bound by certain laws. There is little to make sense of. I should not be speaking to you now."

Lyn shrank back, but managed to find her voice anyway. "Why did you even take us in?"

It was a long time before the Farín answered. "He intrigued me." It had the sound of a guilty confession. "I wanted to know what made him nearly give his life to save yours, and you such a small, helpless thing. He always just wanted to protect you."

Lyn drew herself up, scowling as hard as Loríen had ever seen her scowl. "I think I'm tired of people feeling like they have to protect me."

"Then maybe you should stop needing it."

"I…" All expression drained from Lyn's face, and the color with it. If Loríen knew her sister better, she might have said the girl was struggling against a sudden, powerful rage. Lyn unfolded her arms to let her hands hang down at her sides, where she clenched them into white-knuckled fists. "Why are you here, now?"

The creature's mood changed again and the weather metaphor seemed more appropriate than ever. This was, after all, a natural force. "I come to warn you, Lyn, my daughter." Even her voice was deeper as she delivered the ominous words. "You're walking into something that is greater than all of you, and death will come of it."

The room was utterly silent. Loríen reminded herself to breathe.

"Walking into what?" Lyn finally managed to whisper. "Could you be a little more helpful?"

But Sun shook her head. "No. My being here at all, telling you that, is already a violation of the laws that bind us."

Loríen surprised herself, finding her voice when Lyn looked more perplexed than ever. "When Vaian made our kind, Lyn, the Farín he forbade to involve in our... our *etharían'í.*"

"Affairs," Naoise murmured automatically, swallowing hard when he realized he had drawn attention to himself.

Lyn was shaking her head. "Now I really don't understand. Wasn't it some pretty serious involvement to rescue Bryant and me from that ambush and keep us safe all those years?"

"It was... well, it's complicated." Sun made a dismissive fluttering gesture with one hand. "Some called it meddling, but what I did was remove the two of you from the world for the time that you were with me. *That* is the protection your brother rejected when he resolved to return home, having remembered his true identity. I was censured by the others for what I did – they feared I would bring the Maker's wrath down on us all. I had to release him when he chose to break free of the glamor I had spun, for the safety of all my kind."

For the first time since the Farín's sudden appearance in their room, Loríen started to feel like something made sense. She nodded her comprehension, but Lyn wasn't looking at her.

"I still don't follow," her sister said stubbornly. "It just sounds to me like you make up your own rules."

"No." Whatever levity might have been present in the Farín earlier was entirely absent now. "Believe me when I tell you that there *have* been consequences in the past."

Loríen was well aware. She wondered if her sister would listen if she tried to explain what the Farín were and how their history had affected that of the elves. Probably not. It was terrifying but also somewhat impressive to watch

Lyn speak to this creature made of power as though she were no more than a mildly frustrating old aunt.

Lyn stared back at Sun. "But if you can push some of the rules, why can't you work a little give out of this one and at least tell me what you're warning me *about*?" She blinked, then grinned suddenly. "Please? You know you never say no when I beg."

Whatever response Lyn had expected, they were all surprised when the Farín sighed again and turned toward Loríen. "You're distracted, and you're not thinking clearly."

Loríen swallowed. "I beg your pardon?"

"Nírozahé," Sun said, carefully enunciating each syllable. "You know what it needs. Or you would, if you weren't trying so hard not to be frightened of the power you hold. Stop thinking about it and you'll know what to do."

Loríen stared back at the Farín, hoping for more. For something less cryptic. Willing her brain to function even though her entire being was blinded by this creature's presence. But she realized that not a single thing Sun had said so far had been a wasted word. And if she was pushing the rules, as Lyn had suggested, to say this much, then it had to—

"Blood," she found herself murmuring through numb lips. "The blood of House Raia."

The Farín did not nod, but her eyes like snow-shadows gleamed with approval.

Lyn shifted uneasily. "Is this helping?"

Loríen felt a surge of excitement. Sun was right: she should have seen it sooner. Of *course* the Bloodflower needed her blood before it would respond to her will; she simply had to forge the bond. She'd been a fool.

"Yes," she told her sister. "This is help." She inclined her head in gratitude at Sun, all of the tension of the moment dissipating in her relief. "*Chanaqai.*"

But Sun turned to look at Lyn, and at each of the men in the room. "This is the Míyahídéna's task," she pronounced sternly. "There is no room for the rest of you in the work that is required of her. It would be better for you to return to your homes." She offered Lyn an almost gentle smile. "Especially you, my child. It isn't safe for you."

"But I want to help," Lyn said indignantly. "We all do. This man killed Bryant. I want to stop him."

"Stop him," Sun echoed flatly. She met Lyn's eyes for a long time, the silence between them growing into a strange thing that Loríen started to fill with her imagination, and not in a pleasant way. What made it worse was that the Farín had no need to blink. After a while, finally, she crossed the distance to put both of her hands on Lyn's shoulders. "Stopping him is not for you to do," she said quietly. "Please, Lyn. Believe me and be safe."

Before anyone could say anything in response to that, the Farín was gone. No one saw her go; she simply wasn't standing there any longer and her presence was no longer filling the room.

A terrible stillness took her place.

They all jumped nearly out of their skins when the door crashed open a second time and an impressively drunk Dairinn came staggering through. "*There* you all are. Whad'ya mean leaving me down there all alone? And why is there a party in here? And who died?"

Against all reason, Cole was the one to break the oppressive silence.

"Are you all right?" he asked Lyn. He studied her with more intensity than he usually allowed himself to show.

Sefaro and Naoise were escorting Dairinn back to his room to sleep off the many tankards of ale he'd unwisely consumed. It was just the elves and Cole now, along with a great many unspoken questions and a lingering air of unease.

Lyn smiled. "Sure. Why wouldn't I be?"

Loríen stared at her sister. Could it truly be possible that she found nothing odd or upsetting about what had just happened?

"I'm guessing that didn't go exactly like you wanted it to," Cole explained after a moment. Loríen had a sense that he had wanted to say something else instead.

"Oh, that." Lyn perched on the edge of the bed, arms out straight to rest her hands on her knees. "Most things don't go like I want them to. I'm just glad I got to see her one more time."

Loríen shook her head.

"So, that..." Cole seemed to lose his nerve for a moment, which was as alarming as anything else that had happened tonight. He cleared his throat and started again in a firmer tone. "That's the woman – the fairy – who raised you? That's what you and Bryant lived with?"

Lyn cocked her head at him. "Yes. Well, that was Sun. But she was in a strange mood. She isn't usually so..."

"Ominous?" Sefaro filled in, returning from the princes' room with Naoise at his side. "Mercurial? Cold? Unnerving?" He closed the door then stood near it, but Naoise reclaimed his place on the sofa before the fire.

Lyn shrugged. Loríen hated seeing her make that graceless human gesture. "Like I said, she was strange tonight. But I *told* you she was a fairy. Bet you all feel pretty silly now, not believing me."

"Why was she here?" Naoise asked after an awkward moment. "I mean, why come to you now, tonight?"

Loríen's elation at finally knowing what to do with the Nírozahé faded a bit at the suspicion in his tone. He had a point.

"Why not tonight?" Lyn returned. "She does things when she feels like it."

"Are we going to keep stepping around the real issue?" Sovoqatsu growled suddenly, pushing himself to his feet. Loríen looked at him with some surprise. "Who cares why it was here, or about the timing, or whether anyone's feelings were bruised? That Farín had some rather specific things to say about the little party we've assembled here. Perhaps the rest of you don't understand what it is, but *you don't cross the Farín*. Will you all pretend it didn't tell you to go home and stay out of the Míyahídéna's affairs?"

Sefaro swallowed. Cole stood looking at Lyn, his hands twitching at his sides.

Naoise shook his head. "It doesn't matter." His voice was barely audible, but Loríen heard every softly-spoken word. "I must go where Loralíenasa goes, for good or ill. It is out of my hands."

Loríen's temper flared. How *dare* he behave as though their predicament was beyond his control, when he was the one who had reawakened the Galvanos – deliberately? "That was *your* choosing," she snapped back at him before she could stop herself.

Every eye turned to her.

She composed herself quickly but declined to explain.

"Well, look," Lyn said. She sounded weary. "I don't see how anything has changed from the last time we argued about this. Yeah, it's dangerous. We all knew that already. And this insane plan of yours–" she waved a hand at Loríen– "still depends on that magic gizmo and what you can do with it, same as it ever did. So what if Sun told us to go home? Not like I always did what she told me to anyway."

"Not *she*," Sovoqatsu ground out. "You don't comprehend what that thing really is, girl. You have no idea what it's capable of."

"You may not believe it," Lyn said, "but she cares about me. She just wants me safe. She said so. It's not in her nature to lie. Please, trust me. Sun is the only mother I've ever known."

"That thing is no one's mother," Sovoqatsu said flatly.

"Well, I'm not staying behind." Lyn folded her arms across her chest. "If Naoise gets to go, so do I."

Cole sighed.

Sovoqatsu opened his mouth to argue, but Loríen forestalled him with a raised hand. "Please. This is not expected, I know, but I came up to sleep. You remember?" The angry elf subsided with a scowl. "If there is arguing to be done, maybe the morning can wait for it? Though I think all is settled already."

In spite of black looks and some grumbling, the men were persuaded to shuffle out of the room. Except Naoise. He hung back and stopped at the door after the others had gone. The prince dragged his fingers back through his forelocks and breathed in slowly, exhaling with just as much care. He raised his now-violet eyes to Loríen's face.

"Don't do it," he said in Elven.

She stared back impassively.

"What the fairy told you, about the blood," he clarified. "I know I have no right to tell you what to do, but I can beg. Don't, please." She understood then that he meant his words to be private, despite Lyn's presence.

"You don't understand," Loríen answered in the same language. "It won't work otherwise, and I *need* it to work."

Naoise shook his head. A worry line had appeared between his eyebrows.

"No one said I have to bleed my veins dry," Loríen said irritably. "Just a drop or two, to awaken it to me. You don't know anything about magic, you Grenlecians."

"No, I don't," he said. "What I do know about is blood. I've seen enough of it, spilled enough, lost enough of my own. Blood is life, which means blood is power. You're talking about pouring your life, your essence, into that device. It's not giving you power, it's *taking* yours. Don't you see?"

Well that was... unexpected. Loríen blinked.

"It's a bargain – a bargain struck in blood – and you don't know the terms." He reached out and took her hand in earnest. His skin was warm against hers, the magic of the Galvanos crackling between them like tiny invisible forks of lightning. "Please, Loríen. Don't."

She pulled her hand back with a frown. "Prince Naoise–"

"I know, sorry." He grimaced. "Don't touch you. You needn't put your fist into my face too. Just, please, consider what I've said. Sleep on it at least."

There was so much grave good intention in him that Loríen couldn't bring herself to dismiss him entirely, despite her irritation. "Very well. I will sleep on it." She flexed her hand behind her back, the skin still tingling, and ignored the corner of her mind that was wondering what prolonged contact would feel like. "Good night, Prince Naoise."

He offered a low, formal bow. "Good night, Míyahídéna."

Loríen stared at the door long after he had gone. Her thoughts were interrupted by an exaggerated sigh from her sister. She turned to see Lyn shaking her head.

"There's no game, huh?"

"Everything all right, then?" Blinking blearily at them in the pre-dawn firelight within the common room, their innkeeper did not appear to have passed anything like a restful night. He simply had not been shaped by his creator to handle the strain of housing such important guests as both Princes of Grenlec. "Seemed like might your lordships saw a bit of trouble last night, the way you tore out on your supper." He flicked his watery eyes in Loríen and Lyn's direction, but added nothing further.

Dairinn groaned a wordless complaint at the volume of the man's voice.

"No, not at all," Naoise replied. It was the best Loríen had ever heard him manage to lie, but what else could he have said to their host?

*Oh, we were having a quiet evening until one of the guardians of the Maker's Creation, a being of pure energy and unlimited power, decided to pay us a good-night visit to discuss the fate of the world. I assume your accommodations weren't up to her standard, as she didn't stay long.*

"We thank you for your hospitality," the younger prince said. "We should like to settle our account and be on our way directly, if that is convenient to you, sir."

As he reviewed the particulars of their bill with the innkeeper, Loríen tried to ignore him and the fact that it impressed her how unfailingly courteous he was to those of lesser rank. She could not help but think of cold, self-important Qroíllenas, and the many lords like him back in Efrondel who believed themselves above the world and the other people in it. The two men could hardly be more different. And her elders had always taken such pains to convince her of the barbarism of humans.

Naoise was not even the only example of human decency she could point to, not the aberration her teachers would claim him to be. There was Sefaro, gentle and kind and unpretentious. Cole, who, despite a dark past and obvious personal struggles to be a better man than nature inclined him, had displayed nothing but admirable loyalty and selflessness where Lyn was concerned. Even Dairinn was impressive in his own way: devoted to his family, and un-questionably courageous.

None of them had ever made her feel unsafe as an elf in their presence, in spite of what she'd been led to expect. She was not so naïve as to think that every human in Asrellion would be so open-minded, but the fact remained that her people were wrong. There *were* good humans, and they were worth saving.

Loríen toyed with the handle of the long knife she wore in her sash. Just a small cut, a few drops of blood. She had promised Naoise she would sleep on it, and she had. She'd expected to wake with her mind clear on the subject and ready to move forward, but she found herself troubled – not so much by the things Naoise had said, but by the grave sincerity that had driven him to say them. She needed the Nírozahé – that was not in question. But whether she was angry at Naoise or not, she could hardly deny the grace of his mind. If he had concerns, they were worth considering.

Loríen remained lost in her ruminations until she heard Naoise concluding their affairs with the innkeeper. She followed the others outside in silence. Dairinn groaned again when the cold morning air hit his face in the courtyard.

"And I was just starting to remember again what it is to be warm. By the great horns of Ardash, *why* are we traveling at this time of year?"

Loríen found herself smirking at his flamboyant Telrishti curse. "One charge more I will lay to Katakí's name, when we meet," she said dryly.

"And the state of my head," he added miserably. "Might as well bill that to his tab too." He eyed his waiting horse with trepidation. Loríen understood why when swinging up into the saddle shaded his face green.

Sovoqatsu mounted up and brought his horse alongside Dairinn's in order to slap the prince heartily on the back. His smile was as friendly as a case of daggers when Dairinn moaned and nearly pitched back onto the snow-covered flagstones. "Oh, no. You've only yourself to blame for that one, *friend*."

"It's too early in the morning for truth of that character," Sefaro said mild-ly from the back of his placid brown gelding. "Give a poor fellow some time to come properly awake before you remind him of his failings."

"They'll keep," Dairinn agreed sepulchrally. "I promise."

The heavily-armed elf blew out his breath sharply in amusement. "At last. For the first time in his life, the Grenlecian speaks sense."

The party met with no trouble leaving Sallendale, but that was unsurprising given the early hour. It wasn't until midday that they rode straight into a trap.

They were following the road now, nearly due north toward Dewfern through the snow and mist of the Royal Forest. Naoise and Cole led the column in companionable silence, followed by Sefaro and Lyn cheerfully exchanging childhood stories. Behind them rode Loríen and Sovoqatsu, with Dairinn trailing miserably at the rear. In some ways it was a relief not to be picking their way through difficult wilderness anymore, but having entered inhabited lands carried its own share of worries. The only mercy was that traffic on the road in winter was blessedly sparse.

That ceased to be a good thing when, all alone between settlements, they were greeted suddenly by a hail of sharp steel. Several things happened at once, then.

Naoise's horse went down with an ear-shredding scream before anyone knew what was going on. Stunned, Loríen watched the prince leap clear, landing badly after a delayed start. She heard a rasp of metal beside her and knew that Sovoqatsu was arming himself. At the same time, Cole shouted what might have been an expletive. He kept his seat, but the pain in his voice was unmistakable. Loríen drew her sword and braced herself for battle.

Lyn fumbled for her white bow, but there were no enemies in sight to fire upon; they were well-concealed amongst the trees and underbrush. Sefaro drew his sword grimly and moved closer to her, perhaps intending to shield her with his body.

At the back of the line, seeing his brother go down, Dairinn gave a great cry and powered his horse past Loríen, up to where Naoise lay dazed in the snow. More knives flashed by him. One struck Dairinn's back plate with a clang and fell harmlessly away. Another sliced through his green cloak. He ignored them and dismounted to haul Naoise upright by the doublet. The younger prince was unsteady on his feet, but he managed to get his sword into his hands and stumble for cover without his usual grace.

The rest of them followed suit as quickly as they could move. As Cole dodged behind a tree, Loríen saw the knife embedded in his thigh.

A snarl fixed across his fierce features, Sovoqatsu visually tracked the knives still hurtling through the trees back to their source.

"Farínaiqa, wait!" Loríen called when she saw his muscles tensing, but it was no use. He launched himself forward, disappearing into the forest mist with unnerving silence.

"Crazy bastard!" Dairinn called after him.

"We can't do anything while we're pinned down like this," Cole grunted, ignoring the blade in his leg.

Lyn squinted into the trees, then loosed an arrow. A gratifying cry followed. "I can't do much unless they show themselves. Pretty sure it's our guys in black, though."

"This is distraction theatre," Naoise said. He seemed to have regained his composure. "They will be flanking us."

Loríen turned to suggest that she and Dairinn press forward to put their enemies on the defensive and draw them out, but then she saw the blood – so much of it, covering Naoise's left shoulder and quickly blooming down the arm of his doublet – and her words died in her throat. She swallowed. "You are hurt."

He did not glance down. "I've had worse, I'm afraid. Cole, are you able to move?"

"Not quickly," the other man replied with terse battlefield candor. "I'll stay here with Lyn and guard her back."

"What are you–" Lyn began to object predictably.

Naoise cut her off. "Lyn. You can sight at this distance, yes? Assuming we flush them out of hiding?"

She nodded.

"Then this is where we need you. It does no one any good to put the archer in the thick of the fight where there's no vantage."

She grumbled but didn't argue.

"You're planning to charge out into that?" Dairinn asked incredulously. "This might not be the best time to ask why the bloody shit you're not wearing so much as a maille shirt, but do let's be clear on the insanity of walking out into a rain of sharps as you are."

Naoise patted Dairinn on the shoulder. "Have some faith in me, Brother. This isn't my first combat situation. Loríen, I need you to–" He stopped because he saw that she wasn't listening.

Doubts or no doubts, it was fairly clear to Loríen what she had to do now.

Her friends were wounded already, about to commit suicide against an enemy with a superior position. Who could say whether Sovoqatsu still lived or if he had sold his life already? Loríen firmed her grip on her sword and pressed the tip of her left index finger against its lethally sharp edge.

"Loríen, *no*," Naoise said, fear sharpening his tone. He lunged toward her, but Dairinn and Lyn were both in his way.

She took out the Nírozahé. Turned it so that the trumpet of the flower's petals pointed upward. Squeezed her cut finger against her thumb and held it over the waiting funnel. Several drops of her blood fell onto the delicate glass petals and disappeared into the translucent bulb in a flash of purple light. Instantly Loríen could feel the thing, its presence, its power, in a way that made it clear how little she had felt it before. It was a weight in her mind, a flame in her hand, an immense living presence consuming all of the air she needed.

Dizzy, breathless, she reached into the center of the Nírozahé's energy and felt herself vanishing there.

With all of the clarity of mind she could summon, she thought of how her enemies needed to be visible. Visible, vulnerable, open to attack. She felt herself projecting this need through the nexus of the Nírozahé's power, felt it become real.

She realized her eyes were closed when it took a great effort to open them. Once she could see again, she saw that Naoise was crouched in front of her, holding her by the shoulders. He was watching her with an expression of worry and such regret that in the raw state the Nírozahé had left her in, she was unable to control the tears that sprang into the corners of her eyes.

He shook his head slowly. "For a moment, I could no longer feel you."

Her lips refused to move, to form a response to that.

"What in the name of–" Evidently, not even Dairinn could extemporize an oath strong enough, because he stopped and stared off into the trees. "Wait. Is that… are they *glowing*?"

Loríen drew a careful breath and dragged her gaze away from Naoise's to look with Dairinn through the mist. Three, no four. And another six behind them. Beacons of purple light stretching up into the sky past the forest rooftop. As she watched, one of them flickered and went out.

Lyn cocked her head. "Well that's handy."

Naoise let go of Loríen and issued a new set of orders in a subdued tone. He came to Loríen last. "Are you able to wield a sword?"

"Of course I am," she managed to say with a hint of asperity. It was even the truth.

"Then let us not waste another moment."

Robbed of their concealment and facing experienced warriors, the assassins had lost the advantage. They had also lost some of their nerve, understandably. The fight didn't take long under Naoise's careful direction, even with Sovoqatsu off on his own, one light after another going dark amid the trees.

## Chapter Twenty-one

One of their enemies still lived.

When Dairinn and Loralíenasa moved among the fallen to be certain they'd all been dispatched, they found one of the black-clad assassins drawing labored breaths beneath a robinia shrub.

"Best to put him out of his misery," Dairinn said with a grunt, looking down at the long, terrible wound in the elf's side.

Kneeling in the snow, Loríen carefully peeled back the black hood obscuring the assassin's face. Suddenly she was staring at a surprisingly handsome man: ivory-skinned and dark-haired, with a strong, hawkish nose and austere jawline. He looked a great deal like Naoise, in fact. Her heart was a knot of pain in her chest as she met silver-blue eyes that were wide with the agony of his injury. There was blood on his thin lips. He looked up at her and shook his head, but she wasn't sure what he meant by it.

"Why?" she asked quietly in Elven.

Icy blue eyes met hers, but he didn't seem to be lucid because what he whispered back was, "I promised to come home, my love. I'm so sorry, Effí." He was slipping fast.

"Why?" Loríen repeated, holding him by the shoulders as if she could will the life back into him, will him to explain why her own people had taken arms against her and forced her to respond in kind. "I am not your enemy. Why did this have to happen?"

The wounded elf shook his head one more time. "We all... have our part in the song. Mine is finished at last."

He reached down to his sash, his movements slow and difficult, and pulled out one more knife. Loríen tensed instinctively to block an attack, but he raised the blade to his own throat even as Dairinn cried a warning and lurched forward. There was suddenly a great deal of blood on her hands.

Loríen didn't know how long she spent staring down at the dead elf, at the pale blue eyes that no longer held the spark of life, before she finally heard Dairinn saying her name. He had a hand on her shoulder, gripping gently.

She let go of the elf and pushed herself to her feet. She had no idea what she was supposed to feel. Worse, when she tried to imagine what Tomanasíl or Lanoralas or any of her teachers might tell her, she didn't think they would know either. That was the most terribly disorienting thought of all.

They returned to the others to find Sefaro and Sovoqatsu comforting the surviving horses and redistributing the load now that they were down a mount, while Naoise, moving awkwardly, stitched the wound in Cole's thigh. Lyn watched with an evident mixture of revulsion and curiosity, repeatedly asking Cole whether or not it hurt. Cole remained stolid as Naoise worked quite competently over his injury.

Loríen didn't want to imagine how much violence either of them had seen, that they were able to be so casual with so much of Cole's blood everywhere. The Naoise she'd met in the forest before the war had been young and innocent, a scholar; this man had watched friends and fellow soldiers die in the field. Had tried to put them back together, held them while they breathed their last when he couldn't. He had done this before. They both had. Either one of them would have known better than she what to say to the dying elf with the bright eyes.

"You need to get looked at yourself," Dairinn told his brother after draining an entire skin of water. He still looked fairly ill even though he'd pulled himself together for the fight.

"In due course," the younger prince replied, carefully attending to his work. "His wound is bleeding out faster than mine. But I'd rather first address the issue of traveling with a man who leaves his companions to fend for themselves during a battle." None of his usual solemn courtesy was visible in him as he looked over his shoulder at Sovoqatsu. "Perhaps you have no care if the rest of us survive, but you left your Míyahídéna in danger. You are a Royal Guardsman, are you not? It's your duty to protect her."

The blond elf lowered his forbidding eyebrows at Naoise. "Do not presume to instruct me, boy. You have no idea why I'm here or where my duty lies."

"Tell me, then," Loríen said. She pushed away the intimidation she always felt when speaking to Sovoqatsu and strode so close to him she had to tilt her head back to meet his eyes. They were as hard as black glass as they returned her stare. "Why *are* you here?"

Sovoqatsu shook his head with a sneer. "Not for you. You are nothing, a child, the last echo of a family that long since fell from greatness." If he had spat the words at her, she would have been able to summon anger as a defense against them, but he hissed them at her in a terrible, damning whisper. "It is your grandfather's fault we lost the war. *His* fault that the appropriate measures were not taken to save Eselvwey before it was too late. And you do not yet even wear his crown. My duty is to our people, not to you."

Loríen forced herself not to fall back a step. Never before had she heard anyone speak of her grandfather the king in this way. She lifted her chin. "Our people have little hope against Katakí, if I die before I reach him." A chill slid down her spine. "Or is it that you mean to make your own peace with him?"

For a moment, Loríen thought Sovoqatsu might be trying not to strike her. His eyes narrowed to dark slits and he bared his teeth in something like a snarl. "If you dare again accuse me of disloyalty—"

There. She could allow herself to feel anger at that. "I will address you in what manner you earn from me," she said coldly. "*You* will remember your place, Farínaiqa."

The snarl twisted into a ferocious smile. "Impressive words from a spoiled child who has never had to prove herself."

Loralíenasa swallowed a quick response. Only then did she realize that the others had fallen silent, stunned by their confrontation and Sovoqatsu's vicious candor. Naoise had even stopped treating Cole's wound and was watching them intently. Dairinn seemed torn between fascination and a readiness to fight Sovoqatsu if it came to that. A calm descended over her as she realized what needed to happen. A part of her had known it was inevitable.

She drew her sword slowly. A strange gulping gasp escaped Lyn.

"Let us to it, then," Loríen invited, choosing to continue addressing him in her broken Common so the challenge would be heard and understood by all of them. "If you require that I prove myself, come and have your defeat, and then let us go on with the work before us."

Somewhere behind her, Dairinn sucked in a sharp breath.

The Mysian took a step toward them both. "Don't you suppose we should all just—"

Sovoqatsu drew an axe for each hand from their holsters at his narrow hips, flourishing both in perfect synchronicity.

"—keep calm," Sefaro finished, voice rising.

"Well you have backbone, I will concede," Sovoqatsu sneered. "That is more than could be said for your grandfather."

She kept her chin up. "You knew him?"

"Who, I?" He snorted and took a deliberate step back, withdrawing from her reach while keeping her well within his long-limbed range of motion. "Who am I to have been on terms of any kind with the great Moraní Raia? Just a guardsman then as now, with no skill to my name but the one I was not allowed to employ for our kingdom's salvation."

Loríen had a sudden moment of clarity about the angry guardsman and the source of his resentment, but she had a point to prove before she could explore it.

Sovoqatsu would want to make the first move, would want to make her work to keep him at bay before putting her in her place. He was letting his temper hold too much sway, and while that maybe served him in facing the long-standing frustration he lived with every day, it would do him no service here, against this opponent.

As a precaution, Loríen focused on the old familiar command to give her sword a practice edge. She needed to educate the guardsman, not kill him. Unexpectedly, she could feel the Nírozahé seizing on the open avenue to her power, drawing it in. It took all of her attention and will to pull back from the dizzying well of energy. For just a moment, she was blind and disoriented.

"Loríen, look out!" Lyn shrilled.

Loríen ducked and rolled away from the axe blade as it came whistling toward her shoulder. She had to allow her well-trained instincts to take over in guiding her away from the guardsman's reach until she could see again.

"This is madness," Sefaro said on a note of incredulity. "We are all friends here. I know you don't want to hurt each other."

The two combatants ignored him.

Sovoqatsu pressed in with a swift, angled chop that would have taken off half her face if it had connected, but she was already regaining her bearings and was able to drive the attack down and away with her sword. From the feel of the contact, she could tell that he had not given his weapons a practice edge.

Apparently he shared none of her concern over wounding his opponent. She was glad; if he gave this everything he had, the outcome would have more of an impact.

Undeterred, he transferred the deflected motion through his body into a swipe at her midsection with the other axe. Loríen recognized the pattern; she met his hand with a high kick and sent the weapon spinning off into the snow.

He brought his remaining axe down, catching her sword on the haft just below the head as she swung low for his knees. She knew he would try to trap her blade between the haft and the beard of the axe and yank it from her hands; she was already rotating smoothly around him to keep the angle flush as he began to twist his grip. She stepped in at the same time, sliding her sword farther along the haft until her point was ripping into the linen of his soralos.

Sovoqatsu reversed his grip with impressive speed, freeing his axe and her sword from their entanglement and spinning away from the near contact. He reached into his sash for the long knife he kept there, but he no longer looked like he was enjoying himself.

Armed with an axe in his right hand and the knife in his left, he bore down relentlessly in a crossed slash meant to scissor her head from her shoulders. Loríen had to catch both weapons on her sword's edge. He was anticipating the deflection and kicked her square in the diaphragm below their locked weapons. The blow drove all the air from her body.

She could feel his metal rasping against hers as he withdrew for another attack. Acting on pure instinct, she dropped to the left and rolled past him. She came back up onto her feet and whirled to see him recovering from a failed strike at her sword arm.

They paused a moment to reassess each other. It was time to end this. Loríen could see that Sovoqatsu thought so too.

She waited for him to come in for a two-handed attack, dagger out to block her sword as his axe raced downward to the base of her neck. It was predictable. Instead of trying to stop him, she made straight for the hand that held the dagger, slicing upward hard into his wrist. He dropped the weapon with a grunt of pain, her practice edge having effectively simulated severed tendons. Bringing her sword up and across in one beautiful, continuous motion, she cut what would have been deep into his other forearm. The axe fell out of that hand too. She ducked aside to let the weapon pass her harmlessly by.

Then, straightening without any great hurry, she lifted the point of her sword and held it steadily trained at Sovoqatsu's throat.

He stared back at her with eyes that spat fury, ignoring what had to be searing agony in his wrist and forearm.

She returned his gaze without blinking.

"Does that prove what you need it to, guardsman?" she asked coldly. "Do I earn any more of your respect than you accord the memory of my grandfather?"

Sovoqatsu straightened out of his ready stance and raised both hands in surrender. It had to hurt. "Whatever else you are," he growled in response, "you are not him."

She lowered her point and spoke the word to annul the practice edge, which also ended the simulated effects of Sovoqatsu's wounds. Not as much tension went out of him as she expected.

"Tell me, then," she said more gently, "the answer to my question: why are you here, Sovoqatsu?"

It was as silent as if they were the only two living beings in the forest. He still didn't want to give an answer, but she had earned the right now to demand one. He took a deep breath, clenching both hands into fists. "I kill, Míyahídéna," he ground out. "I am quite good at it, and I always have been." He was as angry as ever, but she could see now that the anger was not meant for her. "It is the *only* thing I'm good at."

Loralíenasa found herself nodding. "But you could do nothing to stop the Exile."

Sovoqatsu's teeth flashed angrily. "How could I have? I never saw the front line. My superiors felt I was better suited to *protection duty*."

Just like now.

"We *will* save Evlédíen," she told the guardsman, breathing carefully. "You and I, Farínaiqa. If I fail, you will be there to see it through."

"I know," he growled, but there was no force behind it this time.

She nodded and, after a moment of gathering her courage, stepped forward to grip his shoulder. He looked down at her hand but said nothing. His upper lip twitched in what might have been a repressed snarl before he turned away from her and went to collect his scattered weapons.


The others started moving again, almost hastily, as though none of them wanted to be the one caught staring at the angry elf after his moment of almost-vulnerability. Dairinn started cleaning his blade, and Lyn was suddenly studiously interested in counting her arrows. Sefaro was somewhere out of sight among the horses. Naoise went back to taking care of Cole's wound.

Loríen sat down and tried to look like she wasn't feeling unsteady.

But Dairinn had been right; Naoise was hurt too. His movements showed it, even had the left side of his green doublet not been stained dark. By the time he finished sewing up Cole's thigh, binding the wound with the shredded remnants of his second shirt, he had to collapse with his back to the nearest tree stump to catch his breath. Sweat beaded on his forehead despite the chill winter air, and he'd gone even whiter than usual.

"You want me to see to that?" Dairinn asked with a gesture at his shoulder.

Naoise smiled faintly. "I'd prefer to live, if you please."

He shrugged carefully out of his doublet to expose a lot of blood-soaked linen that had once been white. Loríen's heart shot up into her throat. It took him longer to get his shirt off, his teeth bared against the pain as he wrestled his way free of the clinging material. The realization that he was now wearing nothing on the upper half of his body was far more distracting than she liked. In conjunction with all of the death around them, and the blood, and the hollow feeling as the adrenaline from her fight with Sovoqatsu rushed away, Loríen grew disagreeably lightheaded.

Then she noticed the trinket he wore about his throat, ordinarily hidden beneath his clothing – a single dark claw, enormous and fiercely curved, suspended on a silver chain. A bear claw? Was there any possible way he could have–? She was intensely relieved that she was already sitting down.

"What in the frosty Void did you do to yourself, anyway?" Dairinn wondered when the wound was finally visible. He bent to study his brother's mangled shoulder despite Naoise's quiet pleas to be left alone.

"I landed on something when my horse went down," Naoise said, craning his neck to get a look at the wound. "A branch in a snow bank, I think."

Loríen looked at the jagged gouge in Naoise's shoulder, at the dark clots and uneven edges of raw meat, red and black where it should have been whole and white, and had to choke down her own dizzy nausea at the sight of his blood. His mortality.

Dairinn clicked his tongue against his teeth. "I say, that's messy. The kind of wound will take infection."

Lyn had shifted her attention to the new spectacle, staring at Naoise's shoulder with wide blue eyes. "That's disgusting," she declared, entranced.

"I'll have a look if you want," Cole said.

But Loríen – surprised at herself and refusing to wonder what was driving her – was already kneeling at Naoise's side. She could feel his eyes on her but she didn't look up to meet them. Her hands mercifully did not shake as she lifted them to probe the dimensions of his wound. He flinched when the contact sent energy surging between them, but tension froze him in place beneath her hands.

"You will not use that flower on me," he said with quiet insistence.

If she had ever been able to claim any sort of excellence in the Art during her time as a student, it had been in the field of healing. A fact that would not inspire any of her companions with confidence in terms of her ability to face down Katakí, but that was another matter. She shook her head.

"I have not the need of it, for this."

Moving with great care, she cleaned as much of the blood from Naoise's shoulder as she could before bending her attention to the task of repairing the damage. She felt it every time he hissed at the pain.

"Yes, let's talk about that flower of yours," Dairinn said. "Suddenly it works?"

"That was *outstanding*," Lyn interrupted before Loríen could try to answer. She sprang to her feet and began miming combat moves with terrible form. "You made them glow! Poor luckless gobs didn't even know what was happening."

Loríen could not share Lyn's enthusiasm. She recalled the handsome face of the dying elf, the look in his eyes as the light left them, and swallowed with difficulty. How many did that make, now? How many of her people were dead simply because she had left Evlédíen? How many of them by her own hand?

How many more deaths would she be responsible for before this business was done?

This was not exactly the way Naoise had imagined coming home for the first time in more than a year. Dewfern didn't seem to know what to do with him, either.

There was a tension in the air, a sense of looming disaster, that reminded him of Zarishan. But it was worse, because he knew what Dewfern *should* be like. Gone were the brash, energetic crowds, empty the many public parks. The market was sparsely populated by starving farmers and struggling craftsmen and a citizenry that scurried from doorway to doorway as if afraid to be caught out when the inevitable axe fell. The once-beautiful russet cobblestone streets, lined with majestic oak and pine and maple, were in a shabby state of neglect, filth piled high and half-buried in un-shoveled snow. It broke the heart.

Dairinn made much of their arrival at the gates, unable to contain his joy at being home again; it had been even longer for him. The guards were less pleased to see their princes home again than Naoise had anticipated, instead seeming to view their arrival as a harbinger of more bad news. Dairinn was undeterred by this, calling an enthusiastic greeting to anyone who looked their way as they rode through the city. By the time they reached the castle, at the lake's edge, word of their return had gone before them so that the courtyard was thronged with nervous courtiers and servitors hoping their salvation had come.

The crowd eyed what rumor had told them was a Mysian envoy with enough suspicion to send Naoise's heart even lower, into his boots. The press was so close that the travelers had no room to dismount. They backed away only when a well-dressed knot of ladies swept onto the scene, filling the courtyard with their round skirts and their air of purpose.

The tallest of these ladies, auburn-haired and firm-jawed, regal in a blue brocade gown, stood scowling at the two princes with her hands on her hips. "And exactly *where* have you been?"

Naoise smiled and climbed down from the saddle with great care. Scarce more than a week old, the wound in his shoulder still pained him despite Lo-ríen's surprisingly gentle and skilled interventions. He let caution set his pace as he approached the redheaded woman. "That's all the welcome you have for two weary soldiers back from the front lines?" Before she could answer, he wrapped her in a one-armed embrace and pressed his cheek against her glossy red hair, assuring himself of her reality. It had been far too long.

"It's all the welcome I have for two shiftless older brothers who can't bother to write letting me know they're still alive more than twice a year, while they're off trying to get themselves killed in some terribly impressive manner," she said, voice muffled against his shoulder. But her arms were tight around his middle as she spoke.

"Alyra!" Grinning near wide enough to split his face, Dairinn jumped down and caught both of them in an embrace that forced a cry of pain from Naoise. "Ah yes. The shoulder. Sorry."

Their sister drew back and studied Naoise, eyes the same bright blue as Dairinn's narrowed with concern. "You're hurt?"

He made himself smile, aware that it possibly had more the look of a gri-mace. "It's nothing serious, less so now that I'm home. By the Father, it is good to see you. You look well, and more like Mother every day. Have you grown taller?"

"Don't you try to charm me, Naoise Raynesley," she said, still scowling. "We've been so worried about you two; you can't just ride in here all faint with heroic battle wounds and wave my concern aside as though you don't deserve to be kicked in the knee for making me fret so."

"Kick *me* in the knee instead." Dairinn threw an arm over her shoulder, grinning. She tried and failed not to look intensely pleased to see him. "I'm less likely to fall over."

"You'll fall over when Da gets to you," Alyra replied with vigor. She had an arm around each of her brothers now and could not have been emanating a greater sense of relief. "Let us be tactful and say only that he was *not pleased* when you abandoned Alanrad."

Dairinn made an indelicate noise and waved carelessly with his free hand. "Oh, that. He'll be *far* more upset later, after he's had the news we carry."

Naoise shot his brother a quick warning glance. Alyra intercepted the look and finally smiled, sharing a moment of wry amusement with her more sensible sibling.

"My lord Dairinn," Sefaro called through the crowd as he dismounted behind them, "I do hope you plan to introduce us to this lovely young woman before you drag her off to regale her with tales of your grand adventures." Naoise felt he knew the man well enough to guess that he was doing his best to tactfully prevent Dairinn from blurting things that ought not to be shared in public. He felt a warm surge of liking for Sefaro.

Dairinn turned and showed Sefaro a lot of teeth. He hadn't been so demonstrably happy in a long time. "Get over here, Mysian, and I shall." Whether Dewfern was happy to see them or not was less certain, but at least the visit was doing the elder prince some good.

Naoise craned his neck to catch sight of the rest of his companions. They had all managed to dismount now, and although he could hear Lyn calling brashly for Cole to be given some space so he could limp in peace, all he could manage to see through the mob was a glimpse of tall Sovoqatsu's hooded head. He could feel Loríen, though. She was close, and apprehensive. Every bit of the fear and uncertainty he'd experienced riding through Efrondel came back to him in a wave, and her people hadn't tried to exterminate his. This had to be even more terrifying for her.

The castle guards finally managed to impose some order within the chaos of the courtyard and the crowd parted to let the new arrivals through. Naoise saw Loríen then, the carefully composed mask of cool dismissal allowing no hint of the fact that her heart was pounding so hard Naoise could practically feel it inside his own chest. He was sorry he had talked her into coming here.

She looked his way and squared her shoulders as if bracing for a blow.

Alyra freed herself from her brothers' fond embrace and stepped forward once the group had gathered. Her smile showed none of the unease the rest of the crowd was brimming with. "I am Alyra, daughter of King Lorn. Enter, friends, and be welcome to Dewfern. And on behalf of all Grenlec, I apologize for these two fools."

Lyn and Sefaro laughed while Dairinn made predictably loud complaints.

Following Alyra's gracious lead, the princes and their guests made their way into Dewfern Castle. It was the first time an elf had set foot there in more than three thousand years.

Naoise was suddenly having the worst feeling about this.

## Chapter Twenty-Two

As it happened, the king was not in. Naoise chafed at the delay, anxious to brief his father before gossip spread through the city, but there was nothing to be done. Thus it was that Loríen found herself having a well-catered soak in an ornate brass bathtub, attended by Alyra's many ladies-in-waiting.

Despite the pleasures of being clean and fed and allowing her tired muscles a moment to relax, the experience made Loríen deeply grateful for her life in Efrondel. No matter what other indignities Tomanasíl subjected her to, at least he didn't make her try to function while constantly surrounded by an army of fawning servants. She had no idea how Naoise's sister tolerated it.

Several of the women were having an animated discussion that Loríen wished she was not overhearing, about which of them would get to welcome Prince Dairinn home properly later. She felt she was missing out on most of the subtleties, as the conversation was largely idiomatic, and she was glad of that.

Interestingly, none of them had anything to say about Naoise. It irritated her that she even noticed the omission.

In an identical tub on the other side of the room, Lyn was making a considerable row as the ladies tried to wait on her. According to her tart declaration, she'd never before been in one place with so many women all together and it was exhausting, and she just needed all of them to take at least ten steps back and let her wash her own tossing hair.

Finally, Loríen agreed with her sister on something. She leaned back into the hot water with a glass of tolerable wine in her hand, and tried to drown it all out.

When she finally dressed and emerged from the bath chamber some time later, she was surprised to find her companions gathered in Princess Alyra's charming green-carpeted parlor. The princes were regaling their sister with the full tale of their adventures; they had each so far made it to Mysia. Dairinn sat perched on the edge of a low bench, leaning forward in his excitement as he spoke, looking energized and ecstatic to be wearing fresh clothes. Sefaro and Cole were listening with differing levels of interest – Cole propping his injured leg up on a stool with evident relief – while Sovoqatsu sat aside trying to be inconspicuous.

Loríen noticed with some annoyance that Naoise was clean-shaven for the first time since Efrondel and looked quite princely indeed, dressed for his audience with the king in dark green velvet breeches and a tooled black leather doublet.

He looked, actually, a great deal like he had on that first day in the forest.

She cleared her throat, but Naoise had already started turning in her direction as soon as she entered the room. He quieted at once to let her speak. Loríen ignored him, addressing Dairinn instead.

"Do you think, maybe, this is a story not meant for... all ears?" She looked pointedly at the many sumptuously-dressed ladies hanging on Dairinn's every word.

"Rubbish," Dairinn declared. "You're safe here. People are going to find out soon or late, so it may as well be now."

Sovoqatsu shifted uncomfortably.

Alyra frowned at her oldest brother. Loríen could see her wanting to ask, but afraid that he would answer if she did. She clearly had experience with her brother's indiscretions and didn't want to encourage him to do another foolish thing he shouldn't.

"Find what out?" Lyn asked brightly as she came into the room, still shaking out her wet hair. She too had managed to escape without letting the ladies dress her in one of their absurd hoop-skirted gowns.

Dairinn pushed himself to his feet and paced the distance to the door and back again. By the time he came back to his bench, he had clearly made up his mind.

"She's right, Dair," Naoise cautioned, shaking his head. "Think about–"

"That woman there," Dairinn said over his brother's warning, pointing at Lyn, "and that one, and the fellow in the corner? Elves."

There was a flurry of gasping motion as all of the ladies quickly turned to look. Loríen suddenly wished she could disappear into the wall behind her. Two things were obvious right away: Alyra and her ladies were frightened, and no one had any idea what to say. Cole leaned forward wearily, easing his leg down off its stool back to the floor, and let a casual hand fall to the knife at his right hip.

"But how is that possible?" Alyra finally managed to say, looking at her brother and not at the mythical beings she had just been asked to believe in. She was so stunned the words were bare of inflection.

"Is it really that strange?" Lyn asked. For answer she received several incredulous stares.

Naoise reached across the distance between his chair and Alyra's, laying a hand on her arm so that her gaze swung over to him. "Please trust me that they mean us no harm, Sister. There is no cause for fear. Not from them."

In his corner, Sovoqatsu laughed. The sound did not convey amusement.

"Íyaqo, Farínaiqa," Loríen snapped. "You are not a help."

Alyra breathed slowly, trying to hold in her panic. "Ladies," she said carefully, "what you have heard and will hear in this room today is to go no further. Is that clear?" When the question met only with silence, she repeated herself in a firmer tone. This time her attendants murmured hasty acknowledgments. She nodded and took another deep breath, and finally lifted her eyes to look at Lyn and then Loríen, and then Sovoqatsu, as if seeing them for the first time.

Loríen tried not to appear terribly threatening as she met the princess's gaze.

"I believe you were going to explain how you come to be traveling with… elves," Alyra said to her brothers, folding her hands in her lap. Her voice shook only a little. "But first, now that the bell has been forever rung, perhaps we can finally have the introductions you've been holding out on."

Dairinn laughed, and Loríen knew then that he had simply forgotten. Naoise sighed and did as she requested. Surprisingly, it was Cole she seemed most interested in despite the presence of elves.

"I've never met a Rosemarcher before," she said, eyes wide with fascination. "Is it true you have never had a king?"

Cole leaned back again and let his hand fall from his knife, but whatever he was about to say to the princess was cut off. The door opened suddenly and two fully-armored guards swept in to take up positions on either side, carrying pikes and uniformed in Grenlecian green.

Behind them entered two more guards, and a tired-looking older gentleman whose pallor stood out against the fine black velvet and silk brocade of his raiment. He was neatly-bearded, with thoughtful grey eyes and black hair running to silver. And he looked enough like his sons that Loríen had no need to ask who he was though he wore no crown. She was proven right when every Grenlecian in the room rose and either bowed or curtseyed.

Naoise started forward after offering his bow, but his father was not looking at him. Lorn, King of Grenlec, crossed the room to Dairinn in three purposeful strides and backhanded his eldest son square across the jaw.

A surprised cry escaped the prince's lips. Naoise froze in place.

"How *dare* you show your face so casually in Dewfern after deserting Alanrad?" the king said to his son, voice tight with control. "Have you no shame? No sense of honor? Do you honestly not know what your actions have done to the spirit of this kingdom, to the army? I know you've no mind for the worry you have subjected me to since your disappearance, but *dammit* man, you might just show a little pride in your duties as heir!"

"I– Da–" Dairinn half-raised a hand toward his reddening jaw before dropping it again, clenched to a fist.

"*Do not* embarrass me further in company, boy," Lorn boomed. "I should have you whipped for insubordination. If another soldier deserted as you had, he would get far worse."

Naoise braced himself and moved to his father's side, head bowed.

"My lord, temper your anger I beg. He acted rashly when he left his post, but he has comported himself valorously since and we have come to Dewfern through mortal danger with much to tell."

Lorn rounded on his younger son, jaw clenched, but the anger light slowly went out of his eyes. He reached out a moment later and gripped Dairinn firmly by the shoulder.

"I thought you both dead."

Loríen swallowed and wished again that she was somewhere else.

"You will return to Alanrad immediately," the king said to Dairinn. "Your troops need to see that you are alive and well and ready to lead. Telrisht is readying for a final push at the start of spring. We cannot afford to be ill-prepared."

Dairinn, so relieved when his father had seemed to be on the verge of forgiving him, bristled and shrugged off the king's hand. "No."

"No?" Lorn's jaw hardened again.

"No." Dairinn was a kind of angry Loríen had never seen in him before, lacking any of the blustery drama that ordinarily characterized his temper. He met his father's eyes steadily. "I know what everyone thinks of me. You all think I'm useless. I know I'm not as smart as Naoise. I know he's the one who has really been fighting this war for you all along. I'm nothing but a pretty figurehead. Father, please. Don't... send me back to that. Not now that I'm finally *contributing* something. Maybe we're doomed to fail, but I'd rather die trying than live and be *irrelevant*."

Naoise looked back and forth between his brother and his father, searching for words, for the proper response to the moment and the fact that Dairinn had just said these things. He was breathing heavily, as if he had just run a footrace. Loríen watched him struggle and felt his distress as if it was her own.

Lorn sighed. "I have never thought you useless, son. But perhaps we had all best calm down and you can tell me what it is you're talking about." He looked around the room at their rapt audience and raised an eyebrow. "Will you walk with me?"

As the king and his sons left the room, guards trailing behind, Loríen realized she was holding her breath and had to make herself start breathing again.

Naoise glanced at Dairinn behind their father's back as they walked down the familiar hallways of Dewfern Castle. The elder prince was still tense following his outburst and wasn't meeting anyone's eyes. Naoise wasn't sure how *he* felt. He had never once suspected that his boisterous, handsome, overly-confident brother harbored the kind of resentments and insecurities he had just revealed. Or that Dairinn thought of him that way.

Dairinn was eldest and had always treated Naoise like...

Naoise thought back to their argument by Scathan Falls, when Dairinn had asserted that he was coming along because he believed his younger brother couldn't handle the mission alone. In his memory, the incident played itself out in a much different light now.

His brother envied him?

"So tell me, Naoise," Lorn said, walking at a slower pace now that they were alone. "How is it that your mission to Mysia ended in your disappearance from Zarishan under mysterious circumstances? Your message was unsatisfactory, to say the least."

The disapproval in the king's voice did not nearly match the anger he had shown toward Dairinn, but it was still a note Naoise was not used to hearing from his father and it filled him with unease.

It didn't help that he felt he deserved it after the vague missive he'd sent home with Lonan and Nicol upon setting off for Evlédíen. He had *wanted* to tell his father everything, but feared to put so much into a letter. Or to reveal the existence of elves in such a manner.

He cleared his throat. "I apologize for that, Father. With respect, may I first ask after the situation here in Dewfern? Things seem…"

"The situation is not good," Lorn said shortly. He cast a narrow-eyed glance at Naoise over his shoulder. "You already know that which presses most: that Telrisht is massing at Nastrond for a spring strike. If we cannot meet it, we are finished. To that end, we are mustering what troops are not holding down the line in Alanrad. But I asked you a question, son. Anything you can tell me to help us prepare might just save our lives. Speak."

Naoise had never seen his father this way. This close to desperate, robbed of grace and warmth. It shook him worse than staring into the face of combat, because it did not fit into the shape of the world as he understood it.

"My lord father," Dairinn said, uncharacteristically quiet, "please don't be upset with Naoise too. He tried to talk sense into me. It's not his fault I'm too much of a fool to listen."

Lorn stopped walking and turned to Dairinn. The guards and his sons halted around him. He didn't say anything, just looked at Dairinn for a long time before starting forward again.

Dairinn swallowed and hastened to catch up.

"I am not angry with you, Naoise," Lorn said a moment later. "But I have been worried."

Naoise sighed. "You know the reason I went to Zarishan," he said, following his father's agitated stride. "I believed an unseen hand to be guiding this war, and I feared that hand might be Mysian."

"Yes, I well recall."

"I learned there that I was wrong only in one thing: Mysia is not our enemy. That much came clear with little enough digging, upon my arrival. In fact, they too are sore beleaguered. They believed their enemy to be Telrisht, foraging for provisions to continue the war. Tense as our relations have been in the past, they were willing enough to welcome the possibility of finding a friend in Grenlec. They've been driven near to desperation."

In profile, the muscles in the king's jaw could be seen leaping. "As have we. Go on."

Naoise braced himself. What he was about to say, he could not bring himself to just blurt with Dairinn's utter lack of tact. "As distressing and as mysterious as I found the situation there, I was not left long to wonder at it. While I was in conference with Mysia's prince, he received another foreign emissary. An elf."

The king did not react at first, but then his steps slowed and finally halted altogether as the meaning of Naoise's words sank in. He turned to face his son, brow pinched into anxious lines, searching for any sign that Naoise was having him on. Naoise returned his gaze steadily. The guards shifted, struggling to maintain their professional demeanor.

"An elf." Lorn blinked several times. "This is no laughing matter. Had your brother said that to me at a time like this, I should have administered that whipping after all."

Dairinn grunted but said nothing.

"I assure you I am in earnest, my lord," Naoise said. "This messenger was sent to warn Mysia, because I was right. Someone *is* manipulating us, all of us. I could not say more in my message when I left Mysia, because I went with the elf to the valley where they yet live in secret."

"You... went with the elf." Lorn blinked again. His voice was disturbingly flat. "As prisoner?"

It was Dairinn who spoke quickly to refute that suggestion. "No!"

Naoise glanced at his brother, willing him to remain silent while he explained the complicated situation. It did not help that they actually had been taken prisoner upon their arrival, and he didn't need Dairinn letting that slip. "No," he said, more calmly than his brother had. "To hear this warning, and learn more of our common enemy. His name is Katakí Kuromé, and he commands a force based in Mornnovin. His plan all along has been that we destroy one another while he watches us burn, as vengeance for the Purification."

The king shook his head slowly, eyes on the floor. "All the world is consumed by the unrelenting maw of war, and you ply me with fairy tales."

Dairinn laughed shortly at that. *Fairy tales.* Lorn raised his head and frowned.

"We've seen much that strains belief," Naoise replied, "but what I say is true, I assure you." He met his father's eyes in earnest.

"Elves are not real, son," Lorn said unhappily. "I know you harbored a strange fascination in your youth, and your mother encouraged it, but you're too old now for such nonsense."

"Truly, Father?" Naoise felt his temper flaring, which would not lead to anything good. He fought down a shouted response with some difficulty. "You will pretend to be ignorant of what Mother was? What people say about the House of Devon?"

Lorn's expression twisted alarmingly in mingled pain and rage, a combination Naoise had never seen before in his mild-mannered father. "You will not insult your mother by repeating those hateful lies!"

Clenching his fists, Naoise stood his ground with difficulty in the face of that. "We both know they are not lies. This is real, and so is the threat I speak of. It is imperative that we stand together now, that we *not* fight Telrisht. It's what Kataki wants. He is our true enemy, and we must stop him before all is lost. This is the mission Dairinn and I have undertaken, with the help of the elves themselves."

"With the help of…" Lorn stopped himself and shook his head again. "This is madness, Naoise." He took his son by the shoulders in a steely grip and stared closely into his face. "But your eyes… You believe what you are saying." That seemed to shake him worse than anything yet. "What has happened to you, son? I know I've asked much of you in this war, but it was because I thought you capable. Has the strain broken your mind?"

Naoise struggled to slow his breathing. "If you will believe what you can see with your own eyes, then believe our companions. We travel in the company of three elves."

That got a reaction as nothing else had.

"And you left your sister alone with them?" the king roared, red-faced with horror. Not even sparing another glare for either of his sons, he turned and raced back the way they had come at a respectable jog for a man of his years.

Naoise and Dairinn exchanged worried looks, and followed him down the hall surrounded by alarmed guards.

It was a relief, when explaining everything to Alyra, to discover that although she looked so like Dairinn, her mind was more like Naoise's. She grasped it readily, though she'd been struck bloodless by the seriousness of the situation.

"So all this time we've been killing each other, he's been laughing at us?"

"It does gall, does it not?" Sefaro agreed amiably.

Cole grunted from deep within his armchair, injured leg outstretched once more. "Our reasons for killing are never as good as we think they are. It's always better to admit that before you start."

Lorien stared, surprised by the philosophical observation from the former mercenary. He kept his eyes fixed on his hands.

Alyra cocked her head at him. "I can't imagine… What you're doing, heading into the heart of the enemy's domain with little more than confidence and the weapons at your sides – it's terribly brave. To be honest, I love them, but I had no idea my brothers were so heroic."

"In Dairinn's case," Lyn laughed, "I think he just doesn't have the good sense to be scared when he should be."

The princess joined her laughter. "I see you have my brother figured out." But the laugh quickly subsided into an earnest smile. "Is there anything I can do to help? You're all doing so much, and here I am forced to sit idle, wringing my hands while I wait to find out what becomes of my kingdom. Grenlec has little use for princesses, I'm afraid."

Loríen was considering what to say to Alyra when the door opened again.

This time when the king entered with his guards, it was with a palpable sense of menace that impelled Loríen to her feet. His eyes raked the room in harsh judgment, quickly singling out the three elves he had ignored before. Dairinn and then Naoise stumbled in behind him looking far too worried for Loríen's liking. In his corner, Sovoqatsu stirred and then stood in a way that was more alarming still.

"Alyra," King Lorn rasped, "you and your women are unharmed, I trust?"

The princess hurried to her feet to offer a hasty curtsey. "Of course, my lord. Is something the matter?"

King Lorn gestured with one gloved hand, the command obviously meant for his guards. "Take them."

Naoise surged forward. "Father, no!"

Ignoring Naoise's exclamation, the king's armed escort gripped their pikes and strode past him. One of them was heading right for Loríen. Too stunned to speak, she drew her sword and moved to Lyn's side. Cole was already there, also armed and grim-faced. Sovoqatsu came to stand behind her, a long dagger in each hand. The princess's ladies-in-waiting launched into a high-pitched cacophony of panic.

Loríen suddenly found herself looking at Naoise's leather-clad back as he interposed himself between her and his father's guards, arms outstretched.

"No," Naoise repeated firmly.

The soldiers halted, unwilling to harm their prince.

"Stand aside, boy," Lorn ordered. "You bring this threat into my house and then presume to tell me how to handle it?"

"*Threat*?" Lyn echoed shrilly. "Would someone mind explaining just what the damn is going on?" She took a step forward, scowling, but Sefaro caught her arm and pulled her back before she could advance any further into the volatile layout of the room.

"Lyn darling," he said with a tight smile, "you really need to learn how to swear properly."

Princess Alyra moved toward her father slowly, as if approaching a feral dog. She put a cautious hand on his arm, ignoring his grimace of impatience. "Yes, Father. I'm afraid I'm a bit lost here. What *is* going on?"

"By law," Lorn said, holding himself under tight control, "no elf has been permitted in these lands on pain of death since the days of Ronan the First. I will not be the king to disregard that law to Grenlec's utter ruin. Not in these times."

All three of Lorn's children replied to that in raised voices, drowning one another out. Loríen only caught enough to make her wince that they would address their father so. Dairinn cut himself off and sent a sober stare in Naoise's direction, nodding an invitation.

"These elves are not our enemy," Naoise said, lowering his voice to more diplomatic tones. "And I cannot imagine that you would choose to make war upon foreign royalty." Loríen couldn't see his face, but she could feel the desperation pouring off of him as he paused to meet his father's eyes. "These ladies are princesses both, and their cause is Grenlec's. Please, Father. You granted me your trust that day in the Ghadeer Mountains. Do not revoke that trust now."

"We're going to Mornnovin, together," Dairinn added staunchly, "to destroy Kataki Kuromé. These are our allies, Father. Battle-tested and true."

Past Naoise's ear, Loríen saw the king shaking his head. "Can neither one of you see this for the trap it is? At best a distraction meant to draw our attention away from the real threat? While you go off chasing shadows and lies in the far corners of the continent, led by these demon spirits, we are dying here at home. We *will* die, when spring comes, and you would have me ignore the enemy massing on our doorstep in order to let you be carried off by a couple of eldritch sorceresses!"

"Now see here–" Lyn began with some heat. This time it was Cole who quickly begged her to be silent.

"My lord," Loríen said, stepping around Naoise to stand beside him, "I am Loralíenasa Níelor Raia, heir to the throne of Evlédíen. Whatever the history that lies between our people, know that I am your ally in this. Upon my word as queen-to-be, I am not a threat to you."

The king blinked at her, jaw twitching, terrified and struggling with emotions Loríen couldn't even begin to understand. He saw something more than Loríen when he looked at her, that much was obvious.

"Father, please," Naoise said when the king's brow only darkened further.

"Stay your hand, I beg. This woman has saved my life. She risks hers now for all of Grenlec. This is not how honor repays such service."

Lorn stared at his son with heart-sore eyes. "The law is clear, and so is my way," he said. "And much as it pains me to say it, my sons, you are not of sound mind. I grieve for what this war has taken from us all. Now you *will* stand aside, or I will call in more guards and you will be subdued along with those you harbor."

The entire room seemed to hold its breath.

Loríen knew what Naoise was going to say before he said it, because she could feel him thinking it as clearly as if the thought was her own. Her own frantic heartbeat slowed to a calm murmur as she realized it was up to her to end this without bloodshed.

"I'm sorry, Da," Naoise said quietly. "I can't let you do this." Moving as if against a strong current, he slowly drew the sword at his hip.

The king's grey eyes creased with pain. "Then I'm sorry too, Naoise. This is for your own good." He gestured to the guard standing nearest to him. "Fetch reinforcements, an entire company. This threat stops here."

The guard saluted, then started for the door. With a cry, Dairinn threw himself into the man's path and laid him flat with a single blow to the face.

The room exploded into chaos.

Loríen dove into the Nírozahé, thinking desperately of sleep. Of a sudden weariness, quiet, a need to lie down and rest. She poured herself into the thought, into the need for it to become real. The chaos around her faded and grew calm. Everything went away into a blur of purple light that enfolded her, drawing her inward, ever further in, toward the power at the heart of the flower. She emerged only when someone smacked the Nírozahé out of her hand and sent it flying. Opening her eyes, she saw that it was Lyn.

She also saw that the king and his men were on the ground.

"—get you out of here," Alyra was saying to her brothers over the sound of several frantic female voices. "We can keep anyone from entering this room until they wake, but I suspect you haven't long."

"Damn it," Sefaro murmured at the floor. "Damn. I *need* to get back to Mysia, and you louses promised me an escort."

"You also promised we'd be safe," Sovoqatsu hissed with less affection.

Naoise had sheathed his sword and was staring down at his father.

"I had no idea... I could not have known he'd react this way." He shook his head. "Lyr, what has been *happening* here?"

Loríen drew several deep breaths and tried to get her head back into the moment. She felt disoriented, disconnected, as though she was the one asleep. She put out a hand and felt for the nearest object to steady herself against, which turned out to be Sefaro's shoulder. He gripped her arm helpfully. Lyn was watching her with a scowl.

"You all right? I don't think I like what that thing does to you."

"I…" Loríen shook her head. "I am well. It just takes… effort."

Lyn stared at her a moment longer, distinctly unhappy, before moving off to find where the flower had landed. "Yeah, well. Maybe too much."

Alyra was saying something about the king, but Loríen wasn't ready to focus on that yet. She watched Lyn scrounge under a bookshelf, emerging with the Nírozahé. Lyn deposited it dismissively in Loríen's hand.

"I can only say I'm sorry," Dairinn offered in response to whatever Alyra had just said. "But we all know I'd do it again. Though maybe this time I'd let Da know what I was about so he wouldn't lose all hope. This was… I've never seen him like this."

One of the ladies-in-waiting, a willowy girl with big eyes, was crying distractingly in one corner. Alyra went to her and held her by both shoulders.

"You've got to brace up, Rian," she said sternly. "If you must cry, do it after we've saved the princes and their companions. Right now I need you. Run down to the kitchens and have provisions for seven sent to the stables. Tell them it's an emergency, whatever you must to see it done right away." She turned to a second lady. "Caron, I need you to get to the stables and see that their mounts are made ready. Let no one stop you with questions; tell them you are under royal order. Go, both of you."

Naoise looked up at his sister, grim-faced and weary. "Alyra–"

"There's no time. You've got a world to save, haven't you?" Alyra smiled, and there was an unsettling amount of Dairinn's charm in it. "Just make sure you do save it, and come back alive, or I shall be terribly cross with you." She went to each of her brothers and held them close for a moment.

"Thanks, Lyr," Dairinn said gruffly into her hair before letting her go. "You are the best of sisters."

"I know."

Loríen drew a deep breath and ventured to let go of Sefaro's arm. The Mysian gave her a searching look. She nodded back at him. Everything kept happening.

Dairinn swept the room with his gaze. "Not exactly how I pictured setting out from home again, but let's go. While we still can."

Sovoqatsu and Cole made for the door immediately, Lyn following. Sefaro approached Alyra with a small, shy frown.

"My lady, I hate to impose as you have already been so kind, but–"

The princess was already nodding. "You need word sent home if you cannot make it there yourself."

Sefaro smiled and offered a gallant bow. "You are a credit to your kingdom, my lady. Please, let my prince know everything we've told you. Tell him where I go and what it is I do. Tell him not to step to the tune Kataki Kuromé plays for Mysia. He *must not* march against Telrisht, no matter what his Council says. Do this for me, my lady, and I shall be forever grateful."

She returned the smile. "You have my word. And it was a pleasure meeting all of you. May your luck be better elsewhere."

"Come *on*," Dairinn urged, glancing nervously at his father and the downed guards.

For once, Dairinn was right. Pausing only to thank Alyra for her kindness and clear-headed courage, Loríen followed the others out into the hall.

And they ran.

# Chapter Twenty-Three

The weather took a bad turn, matching their mood, as the group fled Dewfern knowing a pursuit would not be far behind. It was colder than it had been in weeks, the wind driving ice into their faces hard enough to burn. They left the road at Naoise's insistence that he knew the area well enough to guide them. For a while, Sovoqatsu rode behind to conceal their trail, but he caught up to them again when it became clear that nature was going to take care of destroying any sign of their passage.

It was well into the night by the time they stopped and they were all of them exhausted, more than physically. Naoise brought them to a hunting lodge deep in the forest, boarded up and abandoned for the winter, but tidy and well-appointed once they pulled the sheets off the furniture. Huddling close for warmth while the chill seeped out of their bones, they sat in sullen silence for a long while instead of discussing their plight as they should have.

Everything was different now.

Gone was the hope, the almost foolish optimism, that had driven them in their escape from Efrondel and onward. They were no longer going to save the world – they were just trying to keep the world from tearing itself apart.

A large part of the changed mood lay with Dairinn. Both brothers were despondent, but it was surprising to find how much of their energy they had been drawing from him alone. Now that he was shaken and uncertain about their course, they all could not help but be infected by his apprehension. Loríen wanted to feel more sympathy for the princes, but she was still too rattled and frankly angry that they had so blithely put her in that situation.

"What happened back there?" she finally asked when no one else seemed willing to speak.

Naoise sighed and stared into the dead hearth.

Dairinn ground his teeth. "My brother's famous powers of diplomacy failed him at precisely the wrong moment."

His brother's head snapped up. "You blame me for this?" Naoise's voice rose on an incredulous note lacking any of his usual polish.

"You wanted me silent, so I remained silent," the elder prince said bitterly. "And a *fine* job you did handling the situation, wouldn't you agree?"

The temperature in the lodge rose by several degrees.

"Look me in the eyes and tell me you knew Father would react that way to the news that elves yet live in the world," Naoise challenged, jaw clenched. He was more upset than Loríen had ever seen him before, lost inside his bewilderment and almost child-like with it. "Who knew he would turn out to be a Purist? In this age, with that war so far behind us?"

"Of course he's a Purist," Dairinn spat. "It's because of Mum."

The words struck Naoise visibly with the force of a blow.

"Oh, the two of you were thick as thieves and no one else mattered half as much," Dairinn went on. "Must be the only way you could have missed seeing how it boiled Father when people said those things about her. All the elf talk. And the two of you with that gibberish language. Father *hated* it."

Naoise sat gaping in horror at his older brother.

Sefaro cleared his throat softly, staring down at his own hands. "I can't help but feel the rest of us are intruding on what should be a private matter."

But Loríen leaned toward Dairinn. Her heart was suddenly hammering. "What do you mean by 'elf talk'?"

"Rumors," Dairinn answered, scowling. "Vicious rumors, circulated by enemies of the House of Devon, our mother's family. There was some objection when she married a Raynesley, claims that she was an elf in disguise, or part elf. There was talk of forcing her to renounce her future rights to the throne in order to appease the dissidents, but nothing came of it. No evidence was ever produced to support the lies. It was a major scandal. And then she died." He spat the word.

Loríen was having trouble keeping her breathing under control.

"They were not lies," Naoise said quietly to his brother, "and we all knew it. I never understood why you and Father were so intent on pretending otherwise. Do you feel the same way he does?"

"This doesn't matter right now." That wasn't an answer, Loríen noted. Dairinn pushed himself to his feet and put several agitated steps between him and the hearth where Naoise huddled with the rest. "What's done is done. And I can't help but think we've *royally* dropped the biscuits into the kettle this time, little brother."

"He was going to kill her," Naoise replied. He seemed to realize what he'd said too late and amended, "Them. What choice did we have?"

Dairinn raked both of his hands down his face. "This is a nightmare! What are we *doing*, Naoise? We attacked Father and ran away like criminals from our own home! We have to go back and set it right. Surely you can see how much he needs us there. He's falling apart. Alyra said he's been ill. What if he—" He stopped as if unable to make himself say what he feared.

"That's not the best idea you've ever had," Cole said. He frowned self-consciously when all eyes turned on him. "I thought our mission was what mattered, not earning your father's approval."

The elder prince took an angry step in Cole's direction, hands clenched into fists.

"You don't have any idea what—" He stopped himself with obvious great effort. "For once, I *am* trying to think of what matters most, and this is all wrong. We have to go back."

"That's not going to happen," Sovoqatsu said, folding his arms across his chest.

"I'm sorry we had to do that to your dad," Lyn offered apologetically, glancing at Dairinn and then turning to Cole, "but we're just sort of in this now. Nowhere to go but forward and all that."

Dairinn went back to pacing. "For the rest of you, perhaps. I can't make you go back." He swung to face his brother. "But Naoise, we must."

Loríen watched several thoughts crawl miserably across Naoise's face and was sure she could identify every one of them, down to the desperate regret that settled there as he gazed back at Dairinn.

"I can't."

"Naoise." Dairinn dragged in a slow, frustrated breath. "I love you, Brother. And I've learned to respect you enough in these last months to show me I never really did before. But I've had it as far as I can stand with this mulish insistence on playing the hero. And *I'm* saying this." He smiled tightly, the expression too tense to stay on his face for long. "Loríen is well-guarded; she'll carry on just fine to Mornnovin without us, and you'll come home with me even if I have to lay you out and drag you back draped over my saddle-bow."

Naoise closed his eyes. "No, Dairinn. You don't understand. I *can't*." He opened them and looked woefully at Loríen.

She shook her head back at him, at what she knew the look meant. *Naoise, by all the lost souls in the Abyss, don't you dare.*

He sighed. "I have to."

A chill gripped her when she realized he was responding to a threat she had not made out loud. The Galvanos was getting stronger.

"Have to *what*?" Dairinn demanded. "What in the name of damnation are you talking about?"

Naoise drew himself up slowly, passing his hand through his hair. They were all watching him. Loríen stood quickly before she was forced to hear him say it, and stalked with as much dignity as she could muster to the room at the back of the lodge. As she was closing the door behind her, Naoise started speaking.

"I don't have any choice but to go where Loríen does. I don't know what to call it, but we–"

She shut the door decisively.

It was a bedchamber, unsurprisingly. Loríen didn't bother to light any of the candles and it was far too intemperate outside to open a window; in the near-blackness, she slid to the floor with her back against the wooden footboard and buried her head in her arms.


A chorus of shouts rose from the other room. Loríen tried to block out the individual voices, but she was sure she heard Sovoqatsu being lethally angry. Maybe he'd kill all of them in a fury and save them the trouble of sorting out their loyalties.

The silly thing was that Loríen knew there was no reason to be feeling this despondent. Nothing had changed – nothing that *mattered*. She was on her way to face Katakí just as she had always planned, and Dewfern had never been her idea. Why should she care that they'd had to leave sooner than intended? Why did it feel like the ground had shifted beneath her feet just because she'd discovered that the old hatred was still alive and well? She was stopping Katakí because it was the right thing to do, not to make friends in Grenlec.

Unfortunately, while that argument had been easy enough to make in abstract, back in Efrondel, it rang a little hollow after having to run for her life from Naoise's father just for being an elf.

In the end, she was thinking about Naoise again. It was inevitable, no matter how much else there was to worry about. She hated that. But willingly or no, she came back to Dairinn's words. *An elf, or part elf.* Certainly strange enough things had been happening lately that she couldn't dismiss the prospect, as unlikely as it seemed. It finally offered a reasonable explanation for the Galvanos being possible between them.

But it didn't *mean* anything, she told herself impatiently.

The door opened and a single figure slipped in, his heat glow faintly visible in the darkness. Loríen wondered which of them was presumptuous enough to have decided this was a good idea. She was surprised to recognize the particular creak of Cole's leather doublet as he slid to the ground against the footboard, a respectful distance from her.

"You all right?" he asked quietly, not wasting her time.

Because she appreciated that, and the concern, she didn't lie to him. "No."

He drew one knee up and looped his arm over it. "Didn't think you'd admit it."

"What do you want, Cole?"

He hesitated for the first time. "Lyn's worried about you," he finally said.

"And you worry about Lyn."

In the darkness, she could hear his doublet shifting as he shrugged. "I made a promise."

There were also men like this, Loríen reminded herself. Some of the tension went out of her. "You are very decent," she said out loud.

Cole snorted his disbelief. "I know what I am."

If only that were true, Loríen thought, and true of all people. She doubted they would find it so easy to live with hate if they looked it honestly in the eye. But that wasn't a helpful meditation.

He sighed after a moment. It was a resigned sound. "Look, I don't know what to say about any of that stuff between you and Naoise–"

"Good," she interrupted.

"–because it's none of my business," he went on staunchly. "Whatever's going on there, or isn't, it won't be an issue to me. That's all I wanted to say. We have a job to do. Let's do it."

Some part of her wanted to reach out and hug him for that, even if it didn't actually help anything. His decency, and his solidity, just somehow lifted the black mist a little. And he was right: none of what she was feeling changed the nature of the task at hand. Knowing that he would be there at her back made it seem more possible to see it through.

"Thank you, Cole."

The words were inadequate to convey everything she felt for him in that moment, but they would have to do.

Eventually, the shouting and the heated talk died down and they all fell into exhausted slumber. Naoise volunteered to keep watch; he knew he was too agitated to sleep. Frankly, he had no idea how Dairinn was snoring so peacefully. He wrapped himself in his cloak and his bedding and settled by one of the front windows where he could look out through the cracks in the shutters, though he expected no one to approach in this weather. Outside, the storm howled around the lodge with almost supernatural fury.

It seemed appropriate.

The others were all asleep before the hearth, Dairinn monopolizing the one sofa. Loríen had never emerged from the other room, but Cole had come out some time ago reporting that she was well and only wanted solitude. Naoise wasn't going be the one to take it from her, as much as he wanted to talk about their situation. As much as he wanted other things as well.

He sighed, leaning his forehead against the cold window. What a mess. He couldn't remember feeling so drained in spirit since the early days of the war, when his unit had lost the Battle of Najal after five days of brutal attrition. He'd had to flee with only a demoralized handful of survivors nearly twenty leagues across enemy land, back to the main body. He had known he was lucky to be alive, but all he could feel was the shame of defeat, in every joint and sinew of his body. He felt that way now.

How could his own father turn out to be so fearful and so small-minded that he would give in to the senseless old hate? And Dairinn – his brother envied him, blamed him, resented the closeness he'd had with their mother, repented of what they'd had to do to protect their elven companions. Their way had seemed so clear only that morning; now Naoise felt like nothing he'd ever known was true.

Behind him, by the low-burning fire, he heard someone stir and then rise to cross the room to the window. He knew that light tread and forced his tense muscles to ease.

Sefaro settled with his back to the wall, wrapped in his own bedding, where he could look up at Naoise in the window-seat. He didn't say anything for a while, just sat there looking sleepy and more than a little bemused. Naoise couldn't tell if he'd come over because he had something on his mind, or because he wondered what was on Naoise's.

"Strange day, my lord," Sefaro said after a while, the dry understatement detectable despite his low-pitched tone.

That earned him a single, sad chuckle.

"I'm sorry about your father," Sefaro added after a moment.

"As am I." It came out more revealingly lost than Naoise had intended, but he did not regret it. Appearing emotionless was Loríen's game, not his.

Sefaro peered up at him. "I'm sorry too about that escort you made promise of, you rogue." He managed just the right combination of petulance and lofty outrage to provoke the smile he'd been aiming for.

"And the provisions we expected," Naoise agreed.

They shared a moment of grim amusement, and Naoise was again grateful that the man was traveling with them. Although, he *had* meant to go his own way from Dewfern. Another plan gone wrong.

Naoise suddenly thought of something he should have long ago. "You know, my holdings at Grenwold lie not far off from where we are now, and we were quick in the saddle today. If we make an early enough start, weather permitting, we could reach it ahead of any word from Dewfern. We can supply ourselves from my household, and I can send you on from there in the company of my own men."

Sefaro's smile was a flash of white in the darkness. "I should be most grateful for it, my lord."

Naoise reached down to press a hand against Sefaro's shoulder. He was sorry he hadn't been thinking clearly enough to make this suggestion while they were fleeing his father. He who was supposed to be the smart one, the strategist. He shook his head at himself. "I ought to have brought this suggestion before my brother, but…" They had been on better terms before, that was certain.

The Mysian seemed to follow his train of thought. "His temper does run hot, it's true," he said with a fond chuckle. "But you must know he loves you no less for that. And he's fortunate to have you beside him to keep his heels to earth."

"I wonder if he sees it so," Naoise said grimly, knowing the answer.

"Pish, my lord, that's nothing but grief talking and should not be heeded."

Naoise looked down at Sefaro in some surprise. The other man met his eyes steadily, as if *challenging* him to cling to his melancholy. "Perhaps it is at that," he allowed. "Strange day."

Another flash of teeth as Sefaro acknowledged the return of his own words, but the smile soon faded. "Naoise. If we are indeed to part ways soon, there's something I feel I must tell you before I go." He paused, all levity lost. "There is much the Míyahídéna is keeping from you."

Naoise laughed quietly without mirth, hating how much it hurt just to think about her. "I know that already, good Sefaro. The woman is inscrutable."

"But this touches you as well, my lord," Sefaro said decisively, "and so I do not think she has the right to keep it from you."

"Go on."

"The spell that binds you—"

"What know you of it?" Naoise could hardly pretend he didn't want the answers she'd been withholding. He was even desperate enough to berate himself for not putting the matter to his resident elf scholar sooner.

Sefaro nodded, evidently pleased to have engaged his interest. "That it is no spell at all, if I know my elven lore." He frowned. "From what you described tonight, I believe it is something they call the Galvanos."

Naoise recognized the word: Loríen had said it to the Captain, the night he'd overheard them speaking on the tower platform. He remembered well the things she had said about him that night, and what the Captain had seemed to think it meant. His heart started to race.

"And what can you tell me of that, my friend?"

"It's one of their oldest stories," the Mysian explained. "It is said the Creator so admired the partnership between Selatho and Voroméasa, the first king and queen – the way they were so evenly matched, complemented one another so perfectly that together they formed a single greater whole – He swore forever to ensure that any two so well-suited would always know they'd found one another. And so that they would be in no doubt, He would bind their souls together as a sign, and a gift." He stopped and stared up at Naoise, eyebrows raised meaningfully.

For Naoise's part, he found himself not knowing what to think. From the evidence he had suspected something like this, almost exactly this, but hearing it confirmed was disconcerting and his thoughts were already in some disarray. The only thing he could draw from these tidings with any clarity was that he understood why Loríen would keep this from him. Because if it was true, it meant they had been touched with purpose by the god and that a choice lay before them both – and Loríen would not like the side she'd feel compelled to come down upon. She would prefer to pretend no choice existed, the better to remain numb to the disappointment.

Sefaro watched him struggle for a moment. "Desperate as she may be to keep this from you," he advised after a time, "it is not her right. This impacts your life too."

Naoise shook his head and sank back against the window. "But this matters little, for she will not have me."

He was surprised when Sefaro's response was to laugh at that, hastily quieting himself before waking the others. "Pardon me, Naoise, but I am an observer and I know what I've seen. Have you not found it odd how hard she struggles to ignore you and yet can never manage it?"

The wind howled in response to that, for Naoise had none.

Sefaro patted him smartly on the knee. "Now I know there is much to be done and more to worry over, but–"

"I'll never have another chance." The reality of it hit Naoise like a slap in the face. They would confront Kataki, they would die there or complete their purpose, and if they lived, Lorien's duty to her people would call her home again beyond a border he could not cross. And he would never see her again.

"Don't waste it," Sefaro advised.

Naoise looked down at the other man, at the well-meaning kindness in his boyish face. The events of the day and night had unmoored the prince such that he felt a suspicious stinging in his eyes and had to blink instead of offering thanks. But he *was* grateful. Sefaro was a true companion and Naoise would miss him.

The Mysian climbed to his feet suddenly and stretched his back with an audible crack. "Why don't you get some sleep, my lord, and I'll take the watch." He smiled ruefully. "I'm up anyway, and you must lead us in the morning."

Naoise clasped the other man by the shoulder before moving to claim his abandoned place beside the fire. But he knew, no matter how much he needed it, he'd not be getting any sleep tonight. He had far too much to think about.

The sky was still dark, a heavy grey threatening more snow, when the towers of Grenwold reared up against it from the surrounding forest. The travelers had risen well before dawn to get underway and, as Naoise promised, arrived in advance of the king's men.

At first Lorien wasn't sure, but the guards and the household staff received their master with such surprised joy that her nerves were calmed. A familiar black and white dog with golden-brown markings came trotting out of the castle and made a good attempt to devour Naoise with kisses.

"Aiqa!" Naoise cried in a tone she'd never heard from him before, and threw himself to his knees with an enormous grin on his face to greet the dog. Loríen was even more pleased than she had expected to be to discover that the old fellow was still around, her heart doing obnoxious melty things as she watched master and hound shower each other with love.

Dairinn came up beside Naoise in the courtyard as stablehands tripped over themselves to lead their mounts away to shelter. "This was well thought of," he said discreetly. There was an unexpected kind of searching in his voice, almost like an apology, that made Loríen stop and watch for Naoise's reaction.

Naoise heard it too. He stood up slowly from hugging Aiqa and looked at Dairinn with wrinkled brow. The two brothers studied one another in silence, speaking without words in the language of long familiarity. At last Dairinn reached out and gripped Naoise's uninjured shoulder, nodding once, and the tension went out of the younger prince. A small smile stripped his face of years and worldliness so that for a moment he was but a boy relieved to have his big brother's approval, and Loríen knew this wasn't about coming to Grenwold.

"If a bit late," Naoise replied with that small, child's smile that said something his words didn't.

Dairinn smiled back, a bright flash of goodwill, and he clapped Naoise hard with the hand on his shoulder. "Well, we can't *all* be perfect."

Naoise laughed.

Just like that, all was right in the world again for the sons of Lorn.

Leading the way into the castle, Naoise stopped beside the iron-banded door to have necessary words with his steward and gestured for them to proceed without him. Aiqa remained by his side, nuzzling for more attention; Naoise kept one hand resting fondly on the dog's massive head in a pose that seemed familiar to them both.

Dairinn hung back while the others passed and plucked Loríen by the sleeve when they were alone in the courtyard.

She looked up at him expectantly. Honestly, she was surprised no one accosted her sooner about last night's revelation, but she still wondered just what he would have to say. It depended a great deal on how Naoise had framed it. She chided herself for allowing emotion to drive her from the room. As little as she wanted to face the reality of being Joined with a human, she couldn't change it by pretending and it was time she accepted that.

The prince chewed at his lower lip for a moment as he considered his words with a care that was unusual for him, and she knew he'd been giving the matter some thought. "It isn't in your nature to trifle with my brother," he said after a moment, "and for that I give you praise. But... is there no way for you to undo this hold you have upon him?"

Sadness gave weight to her response. "If that hold was of my doing, I would have long ago. I offer my word on that."

"Well then." He nodded slowly, clearly having expected that answer. "You know Naoise would die to protect you." He speared her with a stare that was nearly accusatory, but she could see enough love for Naoise in it to make it bearable. "Don't let it come to that."

Loríen swallowed. She wished she could answer that with the promise he wanted from her, but she knew she had no control over Naoise, and that what Dairinn said was true.

But he didn't stay to await an answer. He simply nodded again, as if satisfied that all had been said, and followed the others into the castle.


They did not waste time foolishly on luxury, as they had at Dewfern. Knowing the king's men could not be far behind, Naoise gave concise instructions to his staff and then sent the group with Dairinn to raid the storehouse while going himself to oversee the assembly of an escort for Sefaro.

Naoise rejoined them there with Aiqa at his heels just as they were choosing the last of their gear, and seemed content that all was in order. Something must have changed for him in the night, because all his doubt and disquiet of the previous day had congealed into a quiet sort of determination. He stroked his dog's ears contentedly as they loaded up.

One corner of his mouth rose slightly when he saw Loríen studying him. "It brings back memories, does it not, being here again?"

"You've been here before?" Lyn shrilled, nudging her in the ribs.

Loríen raised a wry eyebrow at Naoise. *You see what you've done?*

Naoise seemed to be fighting back a smile. *Sorry,* she distinctly heard him thinking at her with more amusement than contrition.

Oh, wonderful. Their connection wasn't enough of a distraction already, but now he had figured out they could share their thoughts directly.

She shook her head at him but addressed Lyn, "Yes. This is where Naoise and I met."

"In point of fact, we met in the forest," Naoise said, in markedly better spirits by the moment. "This is only where I brought you to recover after you decided to try your strength against an enraged mother bear."

"You–" Lyn shook her head in wonder. "This is a story I need to hear."

Naoise smiled at her, eyes bright. "On the road," he said, patting Lyn's arm in passing. "We've not the time to tarry here, as pleasant as that would be. It's been so long since last I was at home it surprises me they still acknowledge me master here."

As if on cue, Aiqa casually licked his hand.

"It would seem you have been missed," Sefaro observed as he tied up his pack. "It is unsurprising to learn you are a good liege-lord to your people."

Loríen wondered idly if the willful girl Issa still served here, and how the many fine musical instruments in Naoise's collection fared after the years of neglect the war had enforced. Perhaps she would have played some of them, or convinced Naoise to, if she had been able to stay longer that last time. Perhaps other things would have been different too. Perhaps there would have been no need for the dreams.

Dammit, being here *did* stir memories. She glared at Naoise for setting her upon this thought trail, and found him smiling at her. It was nothing but an annoyance that his smile did such amazing things to his eyes.

"Shall we away, then?" Dairinn said, hoisting a pack now bulging with extra weapons and warmer clothes. He threw a second pack to his brother, who caught it adroitly.

Loríen tore her attention away from Naoise and his too-charming smile. "I do think we are all in readiness." She glanced at Sefaro and found the Mysian frowning down at the floor. Crossing the distance between them, she reached out to grip his hand. He looked up at her in some surprise. "Sad it is to say farewell, friend Sefaro, but we know your prince needs you."

A fond smile creased his eyes. "It has been an honor to travel with you, Míyahídéna." He returned pressure on her hand. "With all of you. You have my word that Mysia will not be drawn into Katakí's machinations. We will stand with Grenlec and with Evlédíen against this chaos."

Dairinn stepped forward and clapped Sefaro on the shoulder. "I say. I wasn't sure about you when we met, Mysian, but I'm sorry to lose you now. I would have a dozen more like you at my back any day."

"A dozen more like me and you would never win a single copper chit at dice ever again," Sefaro said with a wink.

The elder prince laughed as Naoise drew Sefaro into a fond embrace. "You will be missed, my friend. May the Father watch over you on your long road."

"And you on yours," the other man replied, all levity gone from him.

Lyn next pulled him close, informing him that she'd have some stern things to say to him if he got himself killed. Cole chuckled at that before clasping the Mysian's forearm and bidding him safe travel.

Even Sovoqatsu gave him a solemn nod. "May your return do Mysia a good turn, for it surely needs one. Be safe, Lord Sefaro."

The Mysian regarded them all with wide-eyed innocence. "Now shall we away? I don't think I could ever forgive myself if I should wring tears from our good Sotsu."

When Sovoqatsu's blow only rocked him back and did not knock him from his feet, Loríen couldn't help but smile. Dairinn laughed so hard he was the one crying.

The warm mood of fellowship remained with them as they gathered once more in the courtyard, six of them bound for Mornnovin, the seventh surrounded by an escort clad in the green and black livery of Grenlec. The steward had to hold Aiqa back by his collar to prevent him trying to follow Naoise into the forest. The small sad sounds coming from such a large dog were truly pitiable.

"The Creator smile upon your enterprise," Sefaro said with a nod for each of his companions in turn. "And if He is kind, we'll meet again in better days. Farewell."

They rode out into the winter-white forest together, parting ways at the guard house. And as Sefaro and his entourage disappeared from sight amongst the trees, Loríen hoped with every breath and every drop of blood in her body that the Creator was kind.

# Chapter Twenty-Four

The most merciful aspect of riding so far north was that they shed the worst of winter's chill in favor of more temperate weather. Less pleasant was the discovery of why it was that none but outlaws and the truly desperate ever came to Mornnovin: as they approached the border, they found themselves crossing a foul marshland that went on for days.

Engulfing them now was a tangled, fetid mass of creeping vines and stinkweed overshadowed by twisted willow and stunted, black-barked pine. Rancid, nearly unbreathable air, a fog which did not obscure enough of the hideous scenery, the random cries of strange beasts and the sucking sound of their own feet fighting for escape from black clay – Loríen felt she would soon go mad from the horror of their surroundings.

She did not like to imagine what the place would be like in summer heat, when the humidity would be as robust a force as the smell to contend with. But she reminded herself that she would have to be much stronger than this before her errand was done, and could not allow herself such fragility now.

Even Lyn was markedly unhappy as they picked their way single-file between islands of sure footing. As much as she liked to say she hated her horse, she seemed terribly concerned for its safety now. Every hour of their trek that they were still surrounded by the noisome bog, she grew more irritable.

"How will we know, do you think?" Lyn wondered aloud while toiling under a fog-choked sky. "When we've crossed over into Mornnovin, I mean. Do you think we'll be able to tell?"

Dairinn muttered something vaguely combining an assurance that they'd get where they were going eventually with a surly claim that it didn't matter where the border lay. Lyn made it clear that she didn't like that answer or his attitude. When the expected remark gracefully defusing the tension never came, Loríen missed Sefaro. She had missed him now too many times to count, since their parting at Grenwold.

Loríen watched them bicker for a moment, wishing the Mysian were back with them, before interrupting. "You cannot already feel it?"

Lyn and Naoise both turned their heads briefly in her direction, eyebrows raised. Dairinn kept on miserably at the head of their disheartened column.

She'd felt it for some time, since before the swamp – a deep, festering anger, and a sense that they were advancing against the will of an enormous power that wanted them gone. She was certain the only reason they were able to carry on was that this power was not aware of their presence specifically. It was an unwelcome reminder of Katakí's strength. "We are not wanted here."

None of them seemed to appreciate that observation.

"I say," Dairinn grumbled, "this fen is shattering work. A man could do with a moment's rest."

Loríen glanced to either side, taking note of their treacherous path and the general lack of hard ground. "Say but where," she invited somewhat irritably, "and the man shall have it."

The prince responded idiomatically.

"How much farther on is our destination? A castle, you say?" Naoise said, drowning out his brother's complaints. Despite the horrific conditions and the sweat standing out on his brow, he managed to ask graciously.

Loríen carefully picked out her next step before answering. "Some way – *sílíví* leagues, or so." Numbers in Common were still difficult.

"Thirty," Naoise translated for their companions' benefit.

Loríen went on. "I am told Katakí commands a castle looking over the Red River."

"How do you know that?" Dairinn asked over his shoulder.

"We lost good men to learn it," Sovoqatsu said flatly from the back of the column.

The prince had nothing to say to that. Loríen sent out a thought for brave Iríjo, who had died to get her what intelligence she had within the enemy's borders.

"Thirty leagues," Cole repeated thoughtfully, behind her. "We won't make that tomorrow through terrain like this."

Naoise shook his head, agreeing. "But probably the day–"

"Hush!" Loríen hissed. She raised her head to listen, hoping she was imagining the sound of footsteps that were not theirs. After a moment it was clear her hope was in vain. "A patrol, I think," she whispered when the others looked to her for an explanation. "Hide if you are able."

There wasn't much they could do, cramped as they were onto the limited area of solid footing, but they did huddle against the foul greenery as close as they could. Soon the footsteps came near enough for her companions to hear too. Two sets, moving with purpose and direction – an established patrol.

The companions kept themselves painfully still and quiet while waiting for the danger to pass.

Lyn let out an exaggerated sigh of relief some moments after the last trace of the squelching footsteps had receded into the distance. Dairinn stretched his cramped legs with a groan.

"Could we not have dealt with two sentries?" he complained.

"And raise an alarm when they don't check in," Cole replied, frowning.

Loríen breathed carefully to slow her heartbeat. At least one of her companions was sensible. "Cole is right."

"Look, I just *really* hate this swamp," Dairinn said. "Deeply."

Lyn snorted. "I think it hates us too."

"But this makes a point," Loríen said. "We must talk about where I leave you and go on with Sovoqatsu." No time better for it, and she had been looking for the moment to raise the issue.

"And me," Lyn put in.

Loríen glanced at her sister but didn't argue. "We run more the chance of discovery, the farther we go in. If I am taken traveling with humans–"

"Yes, yes," Dairinn growled. "We mustn't spoil your elf-in-exile reunion before it starts. We know."

"It cannot be too far from the castle," Naoise said quietly, as if he meant only for her to hear. When she looked at him, he nodded once but did not elaborate. She appreciated that.

"Where we stop tonight," she decreed, "I think will be the parting of ways."

Cole frowned at Lyn but said nothing.

Naoise sighed and pushed a hand through his hair. "We shall see."

Instead of arguing further, he urged his horse forward by the bridle and guided it out again onto their treacherous archipelago of a trail.

Loríen followed.


During their meager evening meal, all huddled around a pathetic, guttering fire, they listened while Loralíenasa outlined the specifics of the plan at Lyn's insistence.

Naoise could not argue that there was sense in what the Míyahídéna proposed, or that there was no place for him in her strategy, but still. It was difficult to listen to her talk so calmly about diplomatic immunity, magical artifacts and the sealing of power, and subduing the sorcerer who had the world on the edge of total chaos. Difficult to believe that this was it, that the time had finally come after all their long weeks on the road together preparing for just this moment.

Difficult to accept that this might be the last time he ever saw her face.

After explaining what would happen when she came before Katakí, after answering all of their questions, she excused herself. To see to her horse, she said, though Naoise knew she just needed a moment alone. She was far more nervous than she was letting anyone see.

He allowed her some time to herself, then followed her to the tussock where their horses were tied. She was stroking her stallion's white neck, head bowed, her mind clearly elsewhere. She looked up at his approach, wariness instantly tensing every line of her body. It made Naoise sad that his proximity always elicited that response.

Both hands raised in submission, he advanced only until he was close enough to speak in a voice the others would not overhear at the campfire. She watched his every step with narrow-eyed suspicion.

"I won't try to convince you that I should come along tomorrow," he assured her. "I know why I can't."

Some of the tension went out of her, but none of the suspicion. She lowered her hand from the horse's neck and turned to face him fully, though she didn't say anything. He knew she was waiting for him to explain what he *did* want with her.

What could he say? "Just know that I'll be thinking about you." He smiled away the pain of his own ineffectiveness. "I'm always thinking about you."

Predictably, that bit of truth made Loríen uncomfortable enough to flick her eyes away from his evasively. More surprisingly, she did not simply snap at him to leave the matter. She seemed, in fact, to be struggling for the correct response. "You have been a loyal companion," she finally said with great dignified care, in that flat tone of hers that her guardian would surely have been proud of, giving away no hint of her feelings. That she even *had* feelings. "Thank you."

With a small nod, she stepped around him and started back toward the fire.

Gently, but without hesitation, he reached out and caught her wrist before she could disappear from his life. Her thin eyebrows came down in disapproval.

Naoise shook his head. "It's to be like this between us? Even now?"

It was exhaustion, not anger she was trying so hard to keep him from seeing. She swallowed and drew a deep breath that was shakier than she wanted it to be. "What is it you expect from me?"

If he pushed too hard, she would melt away from him. But this was his last chance to push at all. "We may never meet again."

Loríen didn't say anything for a long time. She looked down at the ground beyond his boots. "I do not... have anything to give you, Naoise."

"What about the truth, just once?"

It was her turn to shake her head. Her eyes caught a strange flash of moonlight. "The truth between us is too large, too real." That was far more vulnerable, far more honest than he had expected. And that, more than anything else, told him just how worried she was. "It is... not possible."

He stepped closer, near enough that he could feel the warmth of her body reaching for his – an effect of the Galvanos that he quite enjoyed. "Never?"

Her lips thinned against one another and she made no answer.

"I'll speak the truth, then, if you can't." Naoise watched her begin to withdraw and spoke quickly to her retreat. "I love you, Loríen." As much as he wanted her to, she would not look at him. She just stared at the ground, breathing a little too hard. "You needn't know what to say, or what we ought to do. I don't expect you to have all the answers. Just love me back."

During the long silence while Naoise waited for Loríen to respond, he imagined several extreme possibilities. The jumping muscles of her jaw suggested she might lose control and murder him, but there was something else going on in the energy she was putting forth. Something sadder and more complicated than the anger his presence usually provoked. There was a hesitation in her posture that he wasn't used to, and seemed to be an unwelcome surprise to her.

When Loríen lifted her gaze finally to meet his, Naoise was convinced he was about to hear, in great detail, all the ways he would be made to suffer if he ever presumed to touch or speak to her in such a way again.

Instead, she kissed him.

She closed the distance between them with two careful, almost ritual steps, lifted both hands to either side of his face, and pressed her lips against his with a familiarity that confirmed the reality of their shared dreams as nothing else had before.

It took Naoise only a moment to realize she wasn't murdering him in some exotic fashion and to return the kiss. The feel of her in his arms was even better than he remembered, because it was more real than it ever had been. Those were actually her hands cool and strong against his cheek. It was really her body arching into his, seeking more of him. The Galvanos was a warm glow between them, feeding their energies into one another in a way he had no words to describe. He pressed her to him by the small of her back, his other hand buried in the soft black hair at the nape of her neck as he earnestly made love to her mouth.

Just as unexpectedly as she had given herself into his arms, Loríen pulled away again. The distance that suddenly existed between them was tangible.

She braced herself with a deep breath and shook her head once. He silently willed her not to say what he knew she was about to.

"Goodbye, Naoise. Take care."

Even if Naoise knew how to respond, how to make her stay, he couldn't have. He couldn't anything. He could hardly breathe.

*Immortal Father,* he thought as he watched her walk away, *let this not be the end.*

He stood still while his heart slowed its frantic racing.

"We're going after them, yes?" Dairinn said behind him, startling him almost out of his skin. Naoise whirled to see that his brother had evidently been watching for some time, leaning against the tree his horse was tied to. His smile was too pleased. "If things should go wrong, don't you suppose we would be of more use within shouting distance rather than a day's ride off?"

Naoise managed to nod, amazed to find himself capable of it.

Dairinn winked. "I know our laconic friend from Rosemarch will agree."

No matter how hard Naoise tried to order his thoughts into some reasonable response to his brother's take on what had just happened, he simply could not. He could only nod dumbly, reliving the last few minutes in his mind in an attempt to force more sense from them.

The elder prince strode forward and cuffed him on the shoulder. It didn't even hurt; Naoise realized he'd gone numb. "I've never seen you like this before, little brother. I'd mock you for it, but…" He shrugged, and smiled mischievously. "Be ready, tomorrow."

Naoise watched a second person walk away from him, but this time he managed to find his voice.

"Thank you, Dairinn."

Lyn was the one, after a moment of stunned silence, who expressed it the best:

"Did we all eat the same bad mushrooms?"

Loríen blinked, and blinked again. What she was seeing still didn't make sense. No matter how she tried to reconcile the fact, it still didn't seem possible that they had just been ejected from such a horrible, grim, terrifying swamp – so like a scene dragged straight out of nightmare – into this.

This spring-like paradise of gently rolling turf dotted with wildflowers beneath an azure sky.

It was like they'd crossed a portal into another reality, because there was no logical way that this idyllic pastoral tableau could be what lay at the heart of Mornnovin. The land notoriously peopled by criminals, now held within the iron grasp of a tyrant bent on vengeance and the destruction of all mankind. Loríen had been expecting, perhaps unreasonably, that the countryside itself would have absorbed his hate. It didn't seem possible for someone so powerful, driven so entirely by his own festering malevolence, not to leave his mark upon the very earth that surrounded him.

The truth was, Loríen felt like she'd come back home to Evlédíen. And after spending close to two months crossing the face of Asrellion to reach this place, bracing herself to look into the eyes of a man so angry he wanted all the world dead for the wrong it had done to him, only to be greeted by this–

Sovoqatsu seemed even unhappier about the disarming beauty of this strange new scene than he had been at the horror of the bog, which she would not have thought possible. It was worse that there had been no transition.

"It's a trap," he growled, darting a suspicious stare from tree to perfect tree as if he expected Kataki himself, attired in flames and wielding a hammer forged from condensed hate and the bones of his enemies, to leap out from behind one of them.

Loríen wished she didn't agree. It would have been nice to simply enjoy the early return of spring, to admire the picturesque landscape for what it was.

"Be watchful," she advised both of her companions.

The soldier grunted, but Lyn made a face. "I'm always 'watchful.' "

Loríen found herself smirking at that claim, but she didn't argue. They rode into the deceptive peace of Mornnovin in wary silence.

"This guy likes playing with our heads," Lyn announced after they'd gone some distance without incident. "Doesn't it sort of feel like maybe he's just lonely?"

Sovoqatsu twisted his body in the saddle to look back at her with sheerest haughty disdain. "Yes, I'm sure he'll stand down and make reparations for all the destruction he's caused once you offer to be his friend. Maybe you can even take tea together."

"You don't have to be an ass."

They kept riding.

With such easy terrain before them, they were able to pick up a much more effective pace. It didn't exactly make up for all the time lost crawling through the swamp, but it was a balm to Loríen's nervous impatience. They even let their horses run off the bridle for a while, which was exhilarating in itself despite Lyn's complaints that she was going to fall off and die.

In due course they began to see signs of civilization. Loríen's informant had told her there were several farmholds and a sizable city directly adjacent to the castle; she felt foolish for not realizing that would mean a habitable landscape.

She lifted her head high and rode as though she belonged as the people watched their passage. It was a shock to see so many elves outside the Valley.

Sovoqatsu's earlier assessment that they would not reach their destination by day's end notwithstanding, the black bulk of a castle loomed against the sky well before the light began to fade. It was an ugly structure, built for defensive purposes and not aesthetics – standing out like a malevolent growth against the fair green pastures and the mild blue sky.

When they drew closer, it could be seen that the castle was surrounded all about by a dense grove that from a distance was invisible against the fortress because of its blackness.

"I don't like it," Lyn said bluntly. "Doesn't feel right. *Nothing* here feels right."

"No, it does not," Loríen agreed. "But that is not what surprises." She urged her horse into a brisk canter before Lyn could say more, not slowing until the grove itself rose before her.

She turned to her sister and waited until Lyn was paying full attention. "Give mind to your role," Loríen said, trying to keep the uncertainty from her voice. She had little faith in Lyn's capacity to pretend even mild servility, but this was the plan they all had to live with now. "You are my maidservant. In that guise, there is no need for you to speak." *Please, do not speak.*

"I know," Lyn replied, waving one hand airily. "I don't even understand your swirly old elf gibberish anyway. Let's just do what we came here to do, yeah?"

Loríen sighed. One day, if they lived through this, she might just snap and the two of them would come to blows over Lyn's disrespect for her own culture. But there was no room for that particular frustration today. "Yes. And may Vaian grant us the luck we need."

Sovoqatsu leading the way in the obvious role of bodyguard, Loríen and her sister side-by-side behind him, they rode into the dark wood before Katakí's castle.

From a distance, the grove had seemed another barrier, like the swamp. Like the power Loríen could still feel pushing at her. But now, she could see that she had been wrong. Projecting her own bias. Because in fact it was almost immediately clear from the deliberate, ordered layout of the varied flora that this was someone's functioning garden. Despite having given up her study of the Art well before getting into the more complex areas of herbal alchemy, she could easily recognize this assortment of barks, leaves, and blossoms as the staples of a mage's kit.

This impression was made more strongly when Loríen spotted a gardener just off the path, carefully pruning a young hawthorn tree. He looked up in some surprise at the sound of their approach, straightening from his task. Frowning, he slowly wiped the gardening shears clean on his russet linen síarca before tucking them into his sash. For better or worse, they had his attention.

Loríen rode up to him as though she believed herself expected. The unknown elf watched her warily. He was small and pasty pale, with the tousled hair of someone whose appearance was never his primary concern. The closer she got to him, the steeper grew the anxious slant of his dark eyebrows.

"We do not often see strangers in this place," he said when she was near enough to address quietly. It was as much of a question as a statement, his Elven crisp and markedly formal. His hazel eyes flicked to take in Lyn, and Sovoqatsu's more imposing presence.

Loríen nodded politely. "I don't imagine you do. I am Míyahídéna Loralíenasa Níelor Raia, come from Evlédíen to speak with Lord Kuromé."

"That is a long way for a Míyahídéna to travel," he murmured, still studying all of them as guardedly as though he expected them to erupt into violence at any moment. In Sovoqatsu's case at least, it wasn't an unreasonable fear. "And as you may surmise, diplomatic envoys are even more of a rarity here than strange faces."

Conjuring up a polite smile, at least in part to ease some of the poor man's anxiety, Loríen said, "But not unwelcome, I hope."

His frown only deepened as he drew a deep, bracing breath. "Come. I shall bring you to Lord Kuromé."

Loríen waited as the gardener bent to collect the pile of deadwood he had accumulated. She was aware of Lyn's eyes on the side of her head, but she could hardly risk explaining the situation in Common for her. All she could do was offer a reassuring smile and hope for–

Well, just hope.

Inside, the castle was another world again and nothing like home. Loríen had to remind herself that to the people who had fled here from Eselvwey, Evlédíen might feel even stranger than this did to her.

Their mousy guide took them past a pair of guards at the door, where they were not divested of their weapons. Loríen wanted to take that as a sign of good faith, but she had accepted that she couldn't trust any of her assumptions here.

Though ostensibly quite large, Katakí's castle had an enclosed feel from within. Minimal lighting and small spaces joined by twisting passages contributed to this warren-like sense. Where Efrondel was all crystal and marble and precious metals defined by wide-open spaces and light, there was a more naturalistic ambiance in Katakí's home – wood and stone, woven fabrics in warm tones, lighting that mimicked the glow of firelight. Everywhere Loríen's eye fell, she beheld some beautiful item of elven workmanship that seemed to belong to another era.

It was... she didn't want to give it *cozy*, though it was obviously homey to someone. Actually she found it stifling, but that was because she could not shake an impression of being deliberately manipulated by the unsophisticated intimacy of the atmosphere. Or maybe she was imposing her own bias again.

From fen to paradise to sorcerer's wood and now this, she had passed through so many layers of cheated expectation to reach her final goal that she was no longer trying to pretend she knew what was happening. Now she was just trying to take it all in fast enough to stay alive.

Loríen had no idea what was real.

The gardener led them deeper into the castle, past many curious faces. Loríen tried not to view all of them as potential threats, but she had to be realistic. She knew what she was here to do. They came finally to the most spacious room they had yet seen – a high-ceilinged dining hall dominated by a polished walnut table large enough to seat probably thirty. At the moment it was laid out with four place settings at one end, including rose-scented wash basins and hand towels.

Four places.

Katakí had been expecting her, and that meant a whole host of things that were not best discovered only now. Her fear rose up within her like a wave of black bile and threatened to choke the reason out of her. She put a hand to her sash, over the Nírozahé, for reassurance.

Their guide gestured at the red-cushioned chairs carved into the shapes of twisting branches. "Please do be seated."

But instead of disappearing through the far door to fetch the master of the castle, he seated himself with a sigh at the head of the table. Lyn gasped. As Loríen stared at him in astonishment, he allowed the shield he'd been maintaining to fall away. Now that she could see the gloriously complex aura of power that surrounded him, she could hardly doubt he was the man whose magic had bypassed Evlédíen's protective barriers. But he didn't *look* like... well, anything special.

Small and slight, pallid, dark-haired, eyes somewhere unremarkable between green and brown, he was not at all what she had anticipated. In his face she saw none of the insanity or rage she'd thought to find there, nor the arrogance of a man who would order an entire kingdom to bow to his will. All she could see was lingering grief of the kind she saw at home every day, and an apprehension that nearly mirrored her own.

"Katakí Kuromé, I trust?" she managed to say with some semblance of control.

He inclined his head in acknowledgment. His attention was all focused on her, overwhelming in its intensity, and he did not seem to think much of what he saw. She had never been looked at that way before, as though he expected her to try to earn his respect and doubted she was up to it.

"You arrived somewhat sooner than I looked for," he observed, "but dinner will be served anon. I hope you will join me at table while we discuss the reason for your visit."

This man had murdered her brother, her sentries, Víelle; had threatened her kingdom. And he had been expecting her. Her scripted dialogue for this moment was suddenly meaningless.

She was now improvising.

"Do not permit fear to hinder you," he said with a frown of mild vexation when she made no move to join him. "That will hardly be productive."

She drew a deep breath and deliberately took the seat at his right hand. Sovoqatsu immediately moved to fill the seat at Kataki's other side, and Lyn took the remaining place beside her sister.

"I am pleased to be meeting you under such cordial conditions," she made herself say, relieved to note that her voice was quite steady despite her sudden overwhelming terror, "given the flavor of your last communication with Evlédíen."

That drew something like a dark smile from the Lord of Mornnovin, though it spoke of pain rather than predation and was quickly gone. "I suppose I am to feel sorry for having sent to you in such strong terms."

Lorien blinked back at him, uncertain whether she was meant to believe he could be so cavalier about the deaths he'd ordered. But he ignored her astonishment, bending his attention to cleaning his face and hands. She decided that the best course for the moment was to gather her thoughts while doing the same. Her companions followed her lead.

Just as she was drying her hands, servants entered to carry the basins away, and several more followed behind to lay out a sumptuous feast. Not standing on protocol, Kataki served himself at once and began to eat. It was almost like he had forgotten the presence of his guests. Almost, for there was nervous tension in every line of his body. Improbably, it seemed *she* was making *him* uncomfortable.

Feeling Sovoqatsu's eyes on her, Lorien looked across the table at the guardsman. He flicked his gaze down to the food and back up at her, and shook his head. But Kataki had served himself from the same platters they would all be dining from, and whatever else she could expect from him, it seemed at least that he was not about to leap upon her with unsheathed claws in the next few moments. He had also demonstrated clearly that he expected her to behave with the decorum appropriate to her station.

In any case, Lyn had already tucked in with enthusiasm.

Lorien nodded once for Sovoqatsu's benefit and reached out to pour herself a glass of the pale white wine Kataki was already sipping. Sovoqatsu's scowl deepened but he said nothing, filling his plate reluctantly once she had served herself.

"You appear prepared to fly away, Míyahídéna," Kataki said after a moment of tense silence, not looking up from his food. "A strange reaction, given that you traveled all this way of your own accord and against my express word. I'd expect it should take more backbone than that to make your way across a continent at war."

She nearly choked on a mouthful of sweet bread and had to wash it down with a healthy gulp of wine before she could answer. "You will forgive me if I seem suspicious of hospitality I have done nothing to merit."

An aggrieved frown pulled at Kataki's thin lips, though he still did not look up at her. "A visit from my kin in the Valley is cause enough for hospitality, whatever your intentions," he said quietly. "It has been too long since I've had tidings of our people there."

Incredulous, she made a concerted effort not to shake her head, listening to the sorrow in his voice. "Is that why you slaughtered a company of my soldiers? For tidings?"

Sovoqatsu made a low sound in his throat that may have been a warning.

Kataki's brow twitched. "It begins already, and we've not even had our soup."

"I believe you know why I'm here," Lorien replied, spreading her hands. "Why play games and dissemble with one another?"

"I do not invite deception," her enemy said flatly, "but we are not savages, you and I. There is no reason we cannot treat with one another in a civil manner. And perhaps you would like to hear my point of view before you decide you simply must have my head, Míyahídéna."

# Chapter Twenty-Five

As hungry as she was, Loríen had little appetite. Her stomach was too fiercely knotted from fear. Katakí, however, displayed no such compunctions. He worked through his dinner as though the act itself was a ritual and its performance relaxed him. Lyn seemed to have arrived at the conclusion that whatever happened, at least she was going to die with a full stomach. Sovoqatsu remained vigilant. His presence was somewhat reassuring.

Watching Katakí Kuromé, Loríen could not discard the notion that he was as nervous as she – though not due to any fear on his part. In fact, he could hardly have appeared less frightened of her if she had been a tiny mouse in a trap. It was just that he avoided looking at any of them directly if he could, but was still so obviously aware of their presence that their every move drew a twitch. She wondered if Lyn's naïve assessment had been close to the truth – that he was isolated whether by choice or circumstance, and was so unused to company as to be unsettled by it.

Loríen summoned all of her courage. "In your message," she said to the sorcerer who had threatened the Valley, "you spoke of a 'remedy' to our ancient defeat that includes 'destroying our enemies.' "

He nodded curtly.

"From what I have seen," she went on carefully, adapting the script she had prepared with Lanas back in Efrondel, "you seem to mean this in a sense more literal and absolute than I can condone. You would exterminate the humans as if they were a virus to be cured. Though this may have been their intention with us in the days of their ancient antiquity, yet this makes you as wrong as the worst of them then. That is why we must be at odds, why I must stop you. If you intend to explain yourself, Lord Kuromé, now is the time for it. Evlédíen will not countenance a slaughter in her name, by you or even by

Moraní himself returned from his eternal rest."

"I don't believe I expressed an intention to *explain myself*," Kataкí replied with some contempt without raising his eyes from his dinner. "As though I am a froward child who stands in need of correction from his betters, and you the wise elder sent to deliver it. I also did not invite your judgment. What I offered, Míyahídéna, was an insight into my motives, if such a thing is of interest to you. But it makes no matter to me if you will not hear it. There is no price you might name that I've not already paid to see this through. I'll not be chid by the likes of you for my determination."

"Enlighten me, then," she allowed.

He looked up at her with a reproving frown, setting his knife and fork down in a deliberate motion that was terrifying because it meant he was focusing more of his attention on her. "Enlightenment is entirely your responsibility; I hope you know better than to look to anyone else for it. But perhaps that is a foolish hope on my part. The craven skulkers who infest your Valley have never given me any cause for it, and I can see that despite the early loss of your parents, you have been raised with the same rank sense of entitlement that has marked House Raia since the beginning of time."

Whether from fear or anger, Loríen's heart was suddenly pounding so hard she had to catch her breath before trying to respond to that. "You reveal your true nature, sir, in speaking so vilely of the kin you claimed a moment earlier to have so much concern for."

For a moment, she honestly wondered if those would be the last words she ever spoke.

Then Kataкí Kuromé favored her with a genuinely quizzical smile. "My true nature?" He shook his head and took up his utensils once more, digging into his food. "I should ask when you imagine I have ever sought to conceal it, but you understand as little about me as you do your own reasons for being here."

In her mind, she formulated a polite yet intrepid request for him to explain those last words to her, but her voice refused to cooperate in a timely manner.

He ignored her inability to speak and went on in a tone that was no longer amused. "Do not mistake me, Míyahídéna. Our people are my *only* concern, I assure you. They sink always deeper into their torpor, dying a little more every day, as those who lead in Evlédíen seek only to keep them complacent in their slow surrender. That concerns me gravely."

His words struck near the heart of everything that hurt Loríen most about Evlédíen and her role in it, and she was left almost gasping as from a blow. "I am not as you describe me," she countered with a tight hold on her passion that left her voice nearly flat.

"No?" Katakí studied her doubtfully. "But it matters little. You ask why I favor so stringent a solution to the human problem in Asrellion. I propose that you do not fully grasp the situation if you can ask such a thing, but you are not entirely at fault for that. You were not alive in the days of the War. You have not seen the depths of the savagery these monsters are capable of. I was and I have. One does not share the village with the wolves that ravage it, Míyahídéna, and merely driving them out is an invitation to reprisal. A beast cannot be reasoned with."

"Humans are not beasts."

"We must disagree on that point."

Loríen swallowed. "Can *you* be reasoned with, Lord Kuromé?"

Sovoqatsu seemed to be trying to murder her with his eyes. She could hardly blame him, having trouble herself believing she had just been so bold.

"No," Kataki answered bluntly. "Inasmuch as I exist solely to exact vengeance, and nothing you could say has the power to alter my nature."

Loríen swallowed again, with difficulty. It was hard to decide how to respond to that. She couldn't help but feel like she was passing through a narrow gorge, surrounded on all sides by archers waiting for the fatal signal. Sovoqatsu shifted in his seat, drawing Kataki's sharp attention for a moment.

It was not a relief when Kataki broke the silence. "In the name of transparent communication," he said too loudly, "I feel I must mention that I find this pretense distracting. Do you suppose I am *not* perfectly aware that is no serving woman but in fact your sister, the Hídéna Lyllíen?" He blinked owlishly at the girl in question, who sat upright upon hearing herself named. "Shall I speak in Common for her benefit – will you be able to follow along, Míyahídéna?"

There was no point in trying to lie to him. "What else do you know?" Loríen asked in Common.

He seemed, of all things, relieved when she didn't try to press the deception. "Everything you don't want me to, I suspect," he replied in the same language.

They all stared at each other.

This man had ordered her brother's assassination. The Nírozahé almost seemed to be a thing alive at Loríen's side, demanding to be used, impossible to ignore. If Kataki was going to attack, she had to be faster. But he still had offered no threat. And he seemed willing to talk.

It finally occurred to Loríen to wonder why.

"So who wants to tell me what's going on?" Lyn asked into the uncomfortable web of tension. Though Loríen had her back to her sister, she could hear the brittle smile in Lyn's voice.

Kataki Kuromé ignored Lyn, frowning instead at Loríen. "Tell me: in Evlédíen, what do they teach regarding the cause of the War?"

The subject change was so sudden that Loríen would have thought he was trying to hide something had he not been so disturbingly frank all along. It was difficult to imagine the topic he would shy away from. She felt that she could ask him which method of murder he liked best and he would provide an unashamed and detailed answer. That sort of candor was harder for her to handle than all the veiled threats he could have thrown her way.

Loríen had to make herself relax her fists, clenched beneath the table in her lap. She placed her hands carefully flat on the walnut table top as she sought the words in Common. "Tensions between humans and our people grew for a long time," she said. "When Murasaju Raia went to Telrisht as envoy, only his head was returned to Eselvwey. It was the final weight that broke the scale."

As she spoke, Kataki started shaking his head. When she finished, he punctuated her explanation with an annoyed sigh. "And what do they have to say about your aunt?" His eyebrows angled down fiercely.

Loríen blinked. She knew little about her father's sister, and nothing that was relevant now. "Tsuru? She died in the War."

For the first time, Loríen could feel anger pouring off of the man at the head of the table, tapping into something hot and dangerous that she rightfully feared. "Thaníravaia," he corrected curtly. "Is *that* what they say?"

She would have asked what he meant, but it was clear that he intended to go on.

"Your father, the great and golden Andras, was ever the beloved one," he bit off, his anger building with every word. "Thaníravaia was lesser in their parents' eyes. Quiet, shy, her ambitions so mean they could never bring her or the family glory. Of all the Raia line, from the first days down through to these, the only one not marked by an uncommon beauty." He gestured brusquely in Loríen and Lyn's general direction. "When they called her Tsuru, it was not fondly, though they claimed otherwise. It does not surprise me she would be overlooked even now."

Lyn shifted in her seat; Loríen could feel her sister almost bursting with the need to ask what this had to do with anything, but she managed nothing short of miraculously to hold her tongue.

"She was rarely thought on by the king," Kataki went on, rage driving his voice ever quieter, "until she shamed the name of Raia by loving an unsuitable man. The youngest son of an irrelevant family, a recluse, who was also an embarrassment to *his* father. He had shunned society to live apart. Deepest of all ironies, they only met because their families forced them both to attend the same Autumn Festival against their will. One is not meant to fall in love at Festival."

Suddenly Lorien knew exactly where this was leading, and she wanted him to stop, but she was strangely fascinated too. A combination of the hurt anger in his voice, a need to understand why she was sitting here having to call this man her enemy, and a morbid curiosity about this piece of her family's history that she had never been taught.

"A time came when she finally convinced her father the king to let her pay a visit to the man she loved," Kataki said. The doom in his voice now made it clear that the story was nearing its end, and that Lorien's premonition was correct. "But she was taken on the road by Telrishti soldiers. The man, knowing she was on her way to him, had been watching her progress on the road by means of the Art. So he saw it all, had to watch, too far away to do anything. Certainly you have heard the stories. What the Telrishti liked to do with elven captives." A grief that had not diminished through the years twisted his unremarkable face into something dark and ugly. "Shall I tell you anyway? Shall I *show* you?"

Sovoqatsu tensed and tried not to look like he was reaching for his nearest weapon, but Kataki ignored him. Leaning forward quickly in his seat, he covered Lorien's hand with his own upon the table.

And he showed her.

They weren't even like memories, as when she had been joined with Naoise. The vivid reds, the laughter and the screaming, the heat of the campfire were all as real as if Lorien herself were standing there three thousand years ago, watching as a Telrishti patrol amused themselves with the daughter of their enemy and her captured escort. Having heard the stories had in no way prepared her for the savage brutality. It could not have.

In the space of a heartbeat she lived that entire night, the most horrific torture she could never even have imagined. And then it was over, and she found herself engulfed in a cold sweat, struggling for breath, being watched by three pairs of eyes each looking for something different in her face.

She bent double in her chair and was sick onto the flagstones beneath her.

"Loríen?" Lyn asked tentatively. Sovoqatsu had not even had the time to draw his sword.

Kataкí Kuromé stared at her until she was able to raise her eyes to his face once more. "*That* is what they are, why there can be no peace," he whispered, as pale and shaken as if he had seen the memory with her. Perhaps he had, putting himself through it again to remind himself why he was doing this, or because he thought he deserved it. "Why they must all be destroyed."

Loríen wiped her lips. The air was roaring in her ears, and for several minutes she had to concentrate on staying upright. She realized there were tears in her eyes and wiped at those too. "The man," she finally managed thickly. "What happened to *him*?"

Kataкí blinked. With that one small act, he seemed to distance himself from the raw emotion that had been struggling to break free, and he was once more merely intent. "Her death destroyed him," he said calmly. "He lives now only for revenge."

It felt like she had been struck by a mailed fist directly in the heart. She tried to remind herself that Kataкí Kuromé was not the proper subject for her pity, but she couldn't entirely convince herself of it. "There is none to be had, anymore," she made herself say. "The humans who killed her are long dead. No human living today could prove a link back to them. And they have changed. Humans reach for more than they have, strive to be more than what they are. That is their gift, and their curse too."

"As long as a single one of them lives," Kataкí hissed, "that war will always be doomed to repeat itself, with all its atrocities."

Loríen shook her head, struggling to find the words.

Sovoqatsu surprised them both instead. "But it is over," he informed Kataкí bluntly, drawing the enemy's attention. "Your plan has already failed. The humans know you are the one who began this war and turned them upon one another to your own ends. They know that to prolong the conflict would only serve your will. They will unite against you now, and there is not power enough in Mornnovin *or* Evlédíen to repel them. Our people will suffer a second and final fall, and it will be your doing."

Kataкí listened to the soldier impassively, only sighing when Sovoqatsu was done. "*You* haven't the power. I have." He threw his napkin down onto his plate and stood suddenly. "Come," he said, encompassing Lyn and Loríen both in his gesture of invitation. "Let me show you."

Everything within Loríen screamed at her that this was it: the moment. That following him would be a mistake. And yet... she was curious. And dismantling his power would be easier if she understood just what resources he had in play. It wasn't even just her fear and uncertainty talking. There was a narrative at work here that she had to see through to the end.

Against her better judgment and Sovoqatsu's whispered warning, she followed Katakí from the dining hall. Her companions came up protectively on either side of her.

"This is crazy," Lyn whispered as they walked. "You know this is crazy, right?"

"Most likely," she answered quietly. "Be ready."

This time Katakí led them skyward through his castle, up several flights of stairs to the top of the tallest tower. The room they entered there took Loríen again by surprise: starkly empty but for the complex runes carved into the floor, entirely encompassed by windows from the floor to the apex of the domed ceiling. The moment they stepped through the silver-banded door, Loríen knew she was in a place of tremendous power.

And the moment she saw the chair, the throne-like carved stone apparatus standing by itself exactly in the center of the room beneath that glass dome, she knew she had made a mistake.

Kataki Kuromé crossed the floor to stand beside the chair.

"Do be seated," he said quietly. Even though he was looking at the chair, Loríen knew the invitation was for her.

She took a deliberate step back. "I think not."

"I must insist."

To her horror, Loríen found herself compelled forward by a will not her own, her steps as fluid as if she was directing them herself. All the way to the chair. She settled into it without pausing.

"What is this?" she demanded, cold to her core with fear. "This is what passes for civil in your house?"

Kataki frowned down at her. "You shall have to forgive me, if you can."

Across the room, sensing the wrongness of what was happening, Lyn and Sovoqatsu both moved to help her. Kataki gestured with one hand and they both stopped in place.

"For your own sakes," he said on a sigh, "I would advise you not to bother struggling. The herbs you all consumed in your food will render you entirely vulnerable to my manipulations for several hours at least, I do assure you. You will only do yourselves harm, trying to fight me."

They were making for the dark castle with all the stealth and speed they could muster when Naoise felt it. Cole noticed the sudden change in his horse's gait and slowed his mount to match.

"What is it?"

Naoise cast about for the words to describe what he was experiencing. "It's Loríen," he explained. "Something is wrong. She's..." Not just afraid. She had been afraid ever since Dewfern. This was more. "Something has... changed. She believes she's lost what control she had of the situation. They are in danger."

"Right," Dairinn said over his shoulder. "That's our cue, I should think. Shall we put spurs to it, gentlemen?"

Stealth be damned. Their time was up.

The castle was close, but still such a terrible distance if Loríen was in danger now. Another ten minutes might see them arriving too late to help her. Cole urged his mount forward past Naoise, catching up to and then passing Dairinn. Naoise would have called a warning if they were not so near the enemy's stronghold.

Following Cole's lead, they galloped through the eerily dark woods at the castle's base. Through some kind of luck, they encountered no one until bursting from the trees into the cobbled courtyard. There they found two guards waiting at the door, standing at attention and armed with a halberd each. Interestingly, Naoise thought, they were human.

The men did not pause to exchange words or formulate a plan. Dairinn simply hopped down from the saddle and made for the door with enormous, purpose-driven strides.

"Halt and state your purpose," ordered one of the two guards.

Dairinn walked up to them, seized each of them by a fistful of leather jerkin, and heaved them together hard so that their heads collided.

He opened his fists and they both slid to the ground against the stone wall.

"That's *one* way to go about it," Cole muttered. He climbed down from the saddle and crouched over the downed guards, searching them for keys or anything else that might be of use.

Naoise hunted in his saddlebags and produced a length of rope. There would be little sense in leaving the guards to wake and bar the door against them, when clearly they would be needing to make a hasty escape.

"Good thinking," Dairinn said, nodding at the rope.

"I do try," Naoise replied.

Then the courtyard filled with soldiers.

It was like a nightmare, only far worse, because it was really happening.

Loríen had no choice but to sit motionless in the stone chair as Katakí Kuromé knelt before her with genuine regret in his hazel eyes. She felt certain she was about to die. Her fear only mounted when he took hold of her sash with one hand, tugged it forward, and reached past it with the other.

When he stood, he was holding the Nírozahé.

Loríen swallowed. Could he possibly know what it was? What it could do?

Raising it high to catch the light artificially glowing out from the windows though night had fallen, Katakí studied the glass flower with intense curiosity. After a moment he shook his head and made a scolding sound in his throat. "You brought it."

She stared back at him, not wanting to give anything away he didn't already know, but aware of the danger in lying to one so powerful.

He lowered the flower to hold it more comfortably within her line of sight. "Do you know what this is?"

"You cannot think I would have brought it if I did not," she temporized.

Kataki's smile was distinctly unhappy. "I cannot think you would touch it if you did. You haven't the stomach. This is your uncle's finest work in a lifetime of marvels – a masterpiece of audacity."

The words stirred the deepest unease in the pit of Loríen's stomach.

Kataki stroked the glass petals almost reverently with careful fingers. The bulb began to glow softly in his hand. "A thousand – a hundred thousand souls and all their power are bound within this small flower, to be used by the man with a will strong enough to bend them to it. The mind almost cannot encompass such an idea," he added wistfully, "and yet your uncle wrought it into reality."

For the second time within the hour, Loríen could feel her gorge rising. *A hundred thousand... souls? Trapped? And I've been...*

"Your parents' essence and your brother's have I held in trust for this day, to be added to the Nírozahé's stores," Kataki explained gravely, eyebrows slanted down again with anxiety. As though he needed her to understand how seriously he took the responsibility he had shouldered. *A hundred thousand souls.* "They will help save the world, Míyahídéna. And you will join them, the gift I allow you for your part in this."

"My parents...?" *No.* He couldn't be saying that he–

"That's why you took Bryant's heart!" Lyn cried, straining forward ineffectually. "You sick son of a crazy person!"

Loríen's heart was pounding. "But that would mean..." He claimed credit for her parents' murder, more than a hundred years ago. Gallanas' death too had taken place even before Kataki's message had arrived in Efrondel. As if he had known, had planned...

Her mind recoiled from the acknowledgment of just how completely she had been used.

"No. You could *not* have known I would bring the Nírozahé. Of all the weapons and all the treasures and all the artifacts in the Royal Vault. You could not have known." She licked her dry lips as another thought struck her. "You could not even have known I would come. Your message threatened harm to the Valley if I did not stay away."

The sorcerer cocked his head at her, a complex mixture of pity and incredulity drawing the sad lines of his face down even further. "Oh, my dear. Is it more comforting to you to think so? To think that any of this was your choice, and not my plan exactly? I am no monster; hold to that if it helps you now."

"Not a monster?" Loríen argued, breathing now so fast the words came out as a gasp. The room and its air supply seemed to be shrinking as everything she had thought she knew fell down around her. "You murdered my family! You are so bent on your revenge that there is nothing sacred to you anymore. Not just sacrificing our people's lives, but *taking* them for your cause...?"

Kataki's look of pity cooled and hardened. "I would ask you to explain how we are so different, you and I, but I need no such assurances from an untried child." He raised the Nírozahé again before her eyes. "Did you not set out to kill me against your people's will, armed with a power those wiser than you knew well enough to fear, because you were convinced you knew what was best for them? Am I not engaged in the same task – saving them without their consent by means they would deplore?"

"It doesn't matter," Lyn blurted courageously. "You can't use it."

He half-turned to her with a puzzled frown. "No?"

Loríen lifted her chin in defiance. "It responds only to the blood of House Raia. And I will die before I will wield it at your command."

"Ah." Kataki drew the sound out long and regretfully. Loríen held her breath. "You are *partly* correct, I fear. It must be awakened by the blood and will of a Raia, yes. And if I am not mistaken, my ally saw to it that you did just that."

"Your... No."

Lorién had not known how to awaken the Nírozahé until the Farín had come to them in Sallendale. And Naoise had asked her not to. Begged. His warning had been too entirely, eerily accurate.

She had never been so terrified in her life.

"What are you saying?" Lyn demanded shrilly. "Sun would never. She raised me. She came to warn me, to tell me to stay away from you."

"It is somewhat endearing," Katakí observed, "that you believe your cause so righteous that every living being *must* be on your side against me. But I ask you, when have the Farín ever been known by their fondness for mankind?"

Lorién could no longer help it; a sob rose in her throat as she began to understand just how terribly she had failed. Because he was right, and she should have seen it. There was no reason she should even have believed the Farín who visited them that night was Lyn's Sun – incorporeal beings, they could show themselves in whatever form they chose. Now Katakí would kill her and use the Nírozahé to murder every living thing on the planet, and he would only be able to do so because she had so kindly brought it to him, primed and ready.

"How will you do it?" she asked quietly, ignoring the tears pooling in the corner of her eye because she couldn't move and had no choice.

Katakí eyed her speculatively for a moment before producing a long knife from some mysterious location on his person. "I could explain, but... as much as I had hoped you would aid me willingly if you understood, our dialogue has nothing left to yield. You are even more intractable than I expected to find you." He cut the tip of his finger as Lorién had her own, allowing a single thick drop of his blood to fall onto the Nírozahé's petals.

There was a flash of purple light, just as she remembered, but he didn't seem as disoriented by the Nírozahé as she had been. He drew a breath and knelt again beside the chair.

"Just know that your death will not be in vain." As he spoke, he set the flower carefully into a depression in the left arm of the chair that seemed to have been made for it. "Your power will add to the Nírozahé's reserves, and with it I will protect our legacy, refashioning Asrellion into a paradise for our people. And there is no need for both of you to die. Your sister's power is negligible and not worth harnessing; she will be of more use alive."

"What?" Lyn cried, voice skirling upward incredulously. "You're insane if you think you can get me to do *anything* for you."

Loríen noticed that there was a channel cut into the arm of the chair, leading to the depression where the Nírozahé sat.

Katakí half-turned his head in Lyn's direction. "Would you truly choose to mar your sister's last moments with needless strife? Surely you can find it in yourself to let her die believing that you will live." He looked up at Loríen and shook his head apologetically. "I shall do my best to see there's no pain. You've earned that much at least for acting out my plan so flawlessly."

"You need not do this," Loríen whispered ineffectually, because there was nothing else she *could* do. She was, as he had promised, entirely under his control – unable even to twitch her hand if he willed otherwise.

He smiled sadly at her. "You know that's not true."

"If you touch her," Sovoqatsu boomed, to as little avail as her plea, "I *will* kill you. Spell or no."

Katakí Kuromé ignored the threat. He took Loríen's hand in his, positioning her arm over the channel cut into the chair, unbuttoning and then carefully drawing back her sleeve up to the elbow. Without another word, he laid open her forearm with a single fluid stroke. True to his word, there was no pain, only an awful tightening and pulling sensation. Her blood flowed the course cut for it in stone, down to the Nírozahé's waiting petals, where it disappeared into the translucent bulb with an ever brightening glow.

Loríen would not beg. But as she sat there, bleeding, helpless to stop herself from bringing on the end of the world, she clung to a futile relief that at least Naoise was safe. Faint though it was, there was still hope that he might be able to thwart Katakí's plan.

It was all she had.


Bound by his own rope with his hands behind his back, in the custody of half a dozen paid soldiers, Naoise was marched with his two companions to the top of the highest tower of the castle. And there they were brought into a scene that may as well have been pulled directly from Naoise's worst nightmares.

In a stone throne in the center of the room, limp and waxy-pale, her lips a lifeless blue, Loríen slouched with her eyes closed. Naoise had seen that complexion on the battlefield too many times not to know what it meant. Her left arm was slick with blood, which was flowing inexorably into a tiny glowing object set in the throne. Lyn and Sovoqatsu stood by as witnesses to whatever drama was unfolding here, armed but unnaturally still. Seemingly frozen in poses of arrested alarm beneath an eerily illuminated glass dome.

And beside the throne, one hand resting lightly on its edge, a man watched guardedly as the three humans were brought before him.

Small, dark, unremarkable in all ways save for the overwhelming air of grief that surrounded him – Katakí Kuromé. He let his hand fall from the chair and stepped forward to receive his prisoners with the grave formality he might have offered more welcome visitors.

"Ah," Katakí Kuromé said, studying them each in turn. "The Grenlecian princes." He flicked his gaze over Cole dismissively. "You have been expected."

"How lovely," Dairinn replied. "No cup of welcome for visiting royalty?"

At the sound of Dairinn's voice, Loríen stirred and pried her eyes open. They were dull and glassy. She slid them about the room until they found Naoise. "No," she breathed, defeat shaping the tired syllable. "Naoise, no…"

As hopeless as the moment should have been, relief left Naoise momentarily breathless. She was alive. For a while longer, at least.

But she was fading fast.

"Bravado," Katakí said to Dairinn, ignoring the Míyahídéna. "You want me to be dazzled by it, but I have never cared for dogs that perform tricks."

"Dogs?" Dairinn strained against his bonds, the cords standing out in his neck. "Mind your tongue, villain! You are addressing the Crown Prince of Grenlec."

Katakí blinked slowly. "Well I *am* pleased to hear it. I would rather not have wasted my antagonism on the wrong target."

"You reprehensible b–"

"Lyn," Cole interrupted. "You're not moving. Are you hurt?" He was carefully taking everything in with what Naoise had to think of as a professional attention to detail.

"This… this… *lumpfish juggler* has us under a spell," Lyn replied furiously, still entirely immobile. Despite her frozen state, her eyes were red with rage-fueled tears. "We can't move. And he killed my parents, and now he's trying to say Sun tricked us and he wanted us to come here all along and it was a trap, and he's a real *ass*. And he cut Loríen open and she's dying into the magic flower thing. We need to get her out of here."

"Of course, Princess," Dairinn snapped. "Please pardon the delay."

Naoise didn't know if Lyn could hear the taut worry in Dairinn's voice, but it was like a punch to the gut to him. Dairinn was the impetuous one who rushed in with foolish courage where a wiser man would know to fear. If he was afraid now...

Kataki Kuromé in no way acknowledged their exchange, but crossed the rune-carved floor to stand unsmiling before Dairinn. Height difference not-withstanding, he managed to convey a certain quiet menace. "Now that you've arrived, I have something to show you." He raised a hand to the glass ceiling.

Behind him, the Nírozahé brightened noticeably, the purple light somehow caught up by each of the massive windows all at once. There it brightened still further, resolving into patterns that seemed random at first until Naoise was certain he could make out the shape of a maple tree. After that it quickly be-came more obvious, and a moment later he was staring up – with a sick sense of vertigo – at the city of Dewfern laid out as though he was viewing it from a great height.

Even though it was night there, he could see it all clearly, the little houses all aglow with hearth-light. The moon glittering on the lake. The straight, ma-jestic line of tree-lined Redwood Road leading down to the familiar old castle. The torches blazing on the battlements. The ships bobbing at harbor.

The view itself was disorienting. The fact that he was being shown his home by his enemy was enough to make his innards quake.

"Dewfern?" Dairinn said dismissively. From the long pause, Naoise knew he was unsettled too. "I've seen it, you know."

Kataki frowned at the prince. "Not like this, I imagine. Observe." He closed his outstretched hand into a fist.

The most horrible thing was the total lack of sound. Naoise watched, breathless, unable to form anything like a coherent thought, while Dewfern died in silence.

They would be terrified, the people there, as the earth began to tremble. As their homes swayed too violently and were reduced to rubble. As streets split open, swallowing buildings whole, twisting the fair shape of his city. Then the lake rose. It all happened quickly, but not fast enough. It took more than enough time for his people to fear, for them to suffer. Naoise could imagine the deep growl of stone being rent, the explosion of glass, the roar of the floodwater. He could imagine the screams. But he couldn't hear any of it. He could only watch while his heart broke into pieces inside his chest.

*Da. Alyra...*

"That's not real," Dairinn shouted, straining against his captors as the de-struction unfolded. It took four of them to hold him back. "*This isn't real.*"

Dairinn was not the only one shouting, but Naoise was in too numb a state of shock to make out who was saying what.

Katakí Kuromé watched the annihilation of Dewfern with them in silence. Another man might have gloated, but Kataki's merciless calm was worse than any taunt. It was impossible to mistake the hatred he had for Naoise and his brother, for all of the humans dying in Grenlec right now at his will. There was nothing in him but that hatred, no room for anything else, not even the satisfaction of victory. Naoise understood that kind of single-mindedness, because he would have felt pity for Kataki if he was not himself so overmastered by heartache.

*"Naoise."*

It took him a moment to draw his thoughts down from the view in the windows, to recognize that he was being spoken to quietly in the midst of the furor. Cole was staring at him, waiting for him to notice. When he finally had Naoise's attention, he flicked his eyes toward his shoulder, in the direction of the distracted guard standing there. He raised his eyebrows at Naoise before repeating the gesture, then hunching his shoulders slightly as if to indicate pulling at the ropes that bound his hands.

The man had slipped his bonds. Of course. He had been in custody many times before.

Naoise nodded back. He had no plan, but there wasn't time for one.

With astonishing quickness, Cole snapped his left elbow up and back into the nearest guard's face, turning his body in toward a second blow with his right fist. At the same time, Naoise slammed the back of his skull into the nose of the man standing behind him and heard him go down. Cole took a knife off of his felled guard and brought it to Naoise's bonds in one swift motion. The ropes parted just as the other four guards began to realize what was going on.

Seizing hold of the nearest weapon, Naoise made a mad dash for the throne where Loríen sat. He had to get her away from there, and he had to destroy the Nírozahé, or all was lost. But the moment his boot struck the runes carved into the floor surrounding the chair, the air split with a deafening crack and there was a flash like lightning, and Naoise was thrown to the ground.

By the time his head stopped spinning, total chaos had broken loose. He looked up to see Dairinn still bound but keeping Kataki's guards at bay as Cole tried to fight through them to free the prince. And Sovoqatsu had joined the fray.

Under Kataki's control.

Naoise stumbled to his feet, sword in hand. "Sovoqatsu! Fight it! You don't want to do this!"

The elf turned to meet his blow with the edge of his sword, rage in his eyes. "You're damn right I don't! Do you think I can help it?" He turned Naoise's blade aside with all the ferocity that the prince had seen in him before, always with gratitude that he would never have to face it in battle.

"There must be some way you can break free," Naoise said, ducking a powerful swipe meant to remove his head. He tucked into a roll to get a bit of distance on the tall elf's superior reach and came back up to his feet having drawn Sovoqatsu farther away from Cole. It also saved his life as an arrow whistled through the place where his heart had been.

"Crap. Naoise, I'm so sorry!" Lyn called, nocking another arrow to her bow. "Keep moving around!"

"If there was," Sovoqatsu answered him, "don't you think I would have done it *before* everything went to shit?" He drove in mercilessly, pressing Naoise back toward the runes that would knock him flat again if he touched them.

"I concede the point," Naoise panted. "So what do we do?" He watched his footwork carefully as Sovoqatsu pressed the attack, dodging when he heard the twang of Lyn's bowstring again. This one nearly caught him in the shoulder, scraping over the leather sleeve of his doublet.

The elf grimaced. "I'd say we have to go for the source." He caught Naoise by surprise with a kick to the kneecap, which sent the prince stumbling back awkwardly on one leg to avoid a quick death.

"Little busy at the moment," Naoise gasped. He tried putting his weight down on the injured leg and had to ease off right away. If it was broken, there was no way he was getting out of here alive. Not that his chances of that seemed good in any case.

"Naoise!" Dairinn called. Naoise spared a glance for his brother and found him still bound; Cole had not been able to break through to him, with all four of Kataki's remaining guards focusing their attack on the armed former mercenary. "Naoise, they need you more than they need me. Save her and get out of here. I'm sorry, Brother."

Before Naoise could ask what Dairinn was talking about, the elder prince charged forward with his head down. Straight at Kataki.

The sorcerer's attention was drawn to the prince only after he had burst free of the melee. His eyes flickered with something like annoyance as he pulled a dagger from a hidden sheath in his boot.

Naoise watched in horror. "Dairinn, *no!*"

Teeth bared in a fierce grimace, Dairinn barreled onward, right onto the waiting blade. He cried out in wordless pain.

Katakí opened his mouth as if to speak. But Dairinn had not stopped. Joined now to Katakí by his grip on the dagger buried in his abdomen, Dairinn powered both of them forward with a determined roar.

*"Dairinn!"*

Even though he knew what was coming, Naoise could do nothing to stop it. He had to block another attack from Sovoqatsu and struggle to stay upright on his hurt knee just to keep himself alive.

Dairinn and Katakí both crashed through the glass wall and seemed to hang there a moment, suspended in the night. Then they were gone.

Dairinn was gone.

The glow from the shattered dome vanished, and suddenly the only light in the tower was coming from the moon and the stars outside. In the same moment, Sovoqatsu was no longer trying to kill Naoise. Without a word, he turned to address the guards who had Cole pinned to the now-dark wall. Lyn's bow sang twice.

Then all was silence.

# CHAPTER TWENTY-SIX

"Loríen? Loríen!"

When she registered that they were calling her, she also realized with a shock that she had been out and unaware for some time. She tried to open her eyes. It seemed an impossible act, her eyelids were so heavy. Angry that such a simple command should be met with such resistance, she redoubled her efforts and finally pried her eyes open.

It was dark, and for a disorienting moment she thought she hadn't managed to open her eyes after all. Then she saw the shapes of her friends in the darkness, standing all around her at a distance she could make no sense of. Why were they so far away? She was slouched at a painful angle in an uncomfortable chair, but when she tried to sit up, her body did not respond.

"Oh thank everything fuzzy and good, she's awake." Lyn leaned forward, but came no closer. "Loríen? You all right?"

Loríen swallowed thickly. Her throat was painfully dry. "No, I – Lyn, I think I'm–" She stopped when she realized she was speaking in Elven and her sister wouldn't understand, but when she tried to call up the words in Common, she came up empty. Her brain was plodding at an agonizingly sluggish rate.

"Loríen, can you stand?" Naoise said. There was a terrible, bleak urgency in his voice that made her stomach churn. "We can't get any closer to help you. I know you're hurt, but we need you to come past the runes."

Memory started to crystallize, images of the last few horrible moments before she'd blacked out. Loríen looked down at her arm and fought off a surge of nausea. So much blood, the parted skin, visible tendons. It hurt now as it had not before, but the pain was distant, almost as though she was hearing it described by someone else. Her body had become a foreign thing, lethargic, beyond her control.

Because it was dying.

"I... I can't," she told Naoise with difficulty. Keeping her eyes open was proving to be the hardest thing she had ever done. "Just leave me. Save Lyn."

He leaned forward. "Please. Loríen. Please try. We have precious little time, and I'm not going to lose you too."

"Too?" Finally realizing that something was wrong with the tableau before her, she looked again, and again only saw four faces peering back at her anxiously. "Where's Dairinn?"

Naoise shifted his focus to something behind the chair. His expression was heartbreaking.

Loríen's entire being congealed into a single silent cry of negation. She refused to accept anything that had happened since she'd walked into this tower. Katakí's manipulations, the truth about the Nírozahé, and now this. Dairinn. Even her own helplessness, she denied with every drop of life still within her.

This could not be allowed.

Slowly, agonizingly, Loríen pushed herself upright. She looked down at the arm of the chair. The flower – the horrible, cursed soul-prison she'd been carrying all this way for her enemy – was no longer there. That made her even angrier, for reasons she was not lucid enough to articulate.

Getting to her feet was never going to happen. She slid instead out of the chair, down onto her knees. And there, driven by all of her rage and grief, she crawled. Slowly. Agonizingly. Every second seemed like it would be her last, and each one dragged on for an eternity. It was only two meters, but in that short distance she lived an entire lifetime of effort.

She collapsed finally at Naoise's feet and drifted at least halfway out of consciousness again. There were voices saying earnest things about getting out of the castle and seeing if he had survived, and how there was no time, and someone was binding her arm so tight she stopped feeling it at all, but she couldn't focus on any of it. Then Naoise's voice was inside her mind.

*I need you to live. Do you understand, Lorien? This isn't over. If there is some way for you to draw my... life, my energy, across the bridge of this bond between us, do it now. Take what you need. Live.*

Forcing her eyes open again, she found herself cradled in Naoise's lap, looking up into his solemn face. He nodded once and took her hand into his. Her own energy sparked only weakly against the contact. That fact provoked a visible twitch of distress in the lines around his eyes.

She had no idea if this was even possible, but there seemed little purpose to her agonized struggle a moment earlier if she was only going to give up now. Concentrating on the solid feel of him, the warmth of his hand, she reached out with her will and pulled his vitality close as if she was drawing his arms around her. She felt him resist for the briefest moment, reflexively, then he was wholeheartedly pouring his energy into her weakened body.

The rush of it was dizzying, and for a confused moment she wasn't sure who she was or where she ended. And she realized for the first time, with a twinge of fear, that Naoise was *strong*. His power, the essence of him, just went on and on like a taproot reaching for an aquifer miles beneath the ground.

It was hard to focus in the face of the inrush of energy, but Loríen struggled to harness that energy. To direct it. She had no idea how long she spent fighting to make her body begin to heal, but Naoise was there throughout. Solid, generous, willing her to live.

When she opened her eyes again, it wasn't an ordeal to do so. She was weak, and she ached everywhere, and she didn't think it would be a good idea to try standing under her own power, but she was alive. And she would stay that way, for now.

Naoise looked down at her, startled and a little winded. He nodded again when he saw that some color had come back into her lips.

"If you're done holding hands," Sovoqatsu growled overhead, "we need to get out of here. I don't trust that weasel to be dead and I don't want to be standing here like an ox waiting for the slaughter when he comes back up to finish us."

Loríen sat up with Naoise's help. The rush of blood to her head was loud and horrible. "What happened?" she asked when she could.

"No time for that," Cole answered. He was already waiting by the stairs that led down to the silver-banded door, watchful and unhappy.

"He's right," Naoise said. He stood up slowly, then offered her a hand, but Sovoqatsu preempted him by bending to scoop Loríen up into his arms.

"Sorry about that knee," the elf grunted at Naoise over her head.

Naoise acknowledged the apology with a grim nod. When he moved to join Cole, she saw that he was limping with painful effort. Now that she could think a little more clearly, her curiosity was almost unbearable. What in the name of the Abyss had she missed?

Sovoqatsu led them when it became clear that no one else could find their way back through the maze of staircases and narrow hallways. They met with only two regular patrols, and Cole dealt with them both handily. At the door, they had to fight their way out, but they were driven by such desperation that they made quick work of the guards there.

Loríen was confused when, having retrieved their horses, they rode not back the way they had come, but north to the far side of the castle.

"It's too dark," Sovoqatsu said to Naoise, inexplicably. Sitting before him in the saddle, Loríen looked back over her shoulder but found him inscrutable. "We'll never find him in this wood."

"I'll not leave him here," the prince replied, short and clipped.

Suddenly Loríen understood, and she sagged against Sovoqatsu weakly.

They were all tilting their heads back to look up at the tower, gauging. The moonlight glinted off of countless tiny shards of glass scattered through the trees. Lyn sat upright and told Naoise with unwonted hesitation that she could smell blood. Naoise squared his shoulders and nodded his acknowledgment, following her lead.

When they found what they were looking for, Naoise jumped down from the saddle without waiting for his horse to stop moving. He cried out in ignored pain as he landed on his injured knee, dashing forward to the silent form that lay broken on the ground.

The rest of them remained mounted, as though they feared to intrude.

Loríen's throat was tight as she looked down at the two brothers. She surprised herself by wanting to put her arms around Naoise and hold him. "Will someone tell me how it happened?"

"He saved all our lives," Sovoqatsu answered behind her. "He went for Katakí when no one else could. The brave fool." He dismounted then and knelt beside Naoise. "Let me help you."

Weeping unashamedly, the prince reached out and clasped the elf's shoulder. Sovoqatsu returned the gesture without words. Together, the two of them cut Dairinn free of his bonds, wrapped him in his cloak, and draped him over the back of his horse. Loríen was too raw to stop herself from crying as she watched.

"Where *is* Katakí?" Lyn said as they were securing Dairinn to the saddle.

Cole glanced up sharply, studying the ground. A moment later they were all hunting – except Loríen, who knew she would only fall down if she tried to move. But she closed her eyes and searched for the Nírozahé's familiar presence. It was not there.

"He's gone," Cole declared flatly after a fair search.

They were all silent for a moment as they absorbed what that meant.

Dairinn's funeral was a bleak affair, as brief as they could respectfully make it. There was no time to dig a grave. They had to assume the whole of Mornnovin was behind them, but Dairinn deserved whatever they could give him. So they rode through the night and morning, pushing the horses hard, until they reached the reeking fen.

There, in quiet solemnity, they prepared the prince for his final rest. Naoise knelt beside his brother one last time and offered his words of farewell before Sovoqatsu helped him lower the body carefully into the murk. Looking down at Dairinn's face, the only part of him not wrapped tightly in his green cloak, Loríen was struck by how small he looked. Small, and not at all like himself; he had never worn that slack, vacant expression in life. Without the fire that had animated him, he was just clay. No longer human. It was deeply upsetting.

Lyn turned her face to Cole's doublet and wept like a lost child when Dairinn disappeared beneath the surface of the opaque water. He was gone. Truly, irretrievably gone. They drifted apart afterward, each to their own thoughts.

As Naoise saw to Loríen's wounded arm, she had trouble knowing where to look. Watching him meticulously sew the long gash back together made her stomach do unpleasant things, but looking up at his face was worse. Evlédíen had not prepared her for this. She had never seen a grief so vivid, so fresh, no attempt made to cloak its intensity.

And it was her fault. Dairinn was dead because she had misjudged so terribly. She owed him her life, but she owed Asrellion even more than that.

On their mad dash from the castle across hostile terrain, Sovoqatsu had filled in the gaps for Loríen. The destruction of Dewfern. The chaotic battle. Dairinn's heroic sacrifice. Now Katakí was armed with the Nírozahé and ready to reshape the world into a sanctuary free of humans, and it was all because she had blindly done exactly what he wanted.

What was she supposed to say to Naoise? What could she say to any of them?

Naoise worked in silence, eyes achingly red. The twitch of every muscle in his face, the flex of his throat every time he swallowed, struck her as hard as if he was shouting his loss at her as an accusation. Every moment that passed seemed like it would be the one when he could no longer hold back.

The waiting was unbearable. Loríen gathered her tattered courage and said what she knew she needed to. "Naoise, I am… *so sorry*, about your brother. It was my doing, my folly. I was arrogant. I've failed you all, and I am sorry."

His hand faltered for a moment with the needle. He reset his grip before answering, his voice quiet and sorrow-roughened. "Thank you. But you haven't failed until you stop trying."

She blinked. How could he say that, when his brother was dead because of her mistake?

Sensing her surprise, he raised his eyes to hers. "You think I blame you."

"Don't you? I blame myself."

Naoise stopped working on her arm entirely. "Loríen, listen to me. My brother… was a brave man, and he made his own choices." He fumbled achingly over the past tense, but pressed on. "He was here because he believed in what we were doing, but more than that, he trusted me. So if anyone is to blame, it isn't you."

The self-recrimination in his eyes nearly made her interrupt with an objection. She bit her lip and let him speak.

"But he chose his death," Naoise continued, "and he chose to die fighting because even to the end he still believed we had a chance. So the only way you could fail him is if you give up." He looked back at her intently; he had started crying again. "But know that you can never fail me."

Loríen tried for several minutes but could think of nothing to say to that. Nothing she wanted to say aloud.

Naoise went back to stitching the cut in her forearm.

They were sitting there awkwardly without words when Lyn came and sat beside her sister.

"Disgusting," she observed, peering over at the wound. The declaration lacked her usual enthusiasm. "So what's our plan now?"

The prince frowned down at his work. "I don't know how much of Dewfern may remain, how many survived, but I must return. Dairinn was right: they need me."

Lyn's lips tightened. "Well. But we're not done fighting, right? That man has now messed with everything I care about, and I'm not just going to sit around while he's still out there hurting people. So we go back to Dewfern, but what's the *plan*?"

Naoise sighed. Loríen could tell from the tugging she felt on her forearm that he had begun to tie off the stitches. Lyn leaned across and helped him secure the knot. "We regroup. See what resources we have at our disposal. Then we come at him with everything we have."

"And what of Telrisht?" Loríen asked, switching to Common with careful concentration. "What of this spring assault?"

The poor prince had never looked so weary. "We will deal with that as we must," he answered, "but our priority must obviously be Katakí. We don't know if he needed that magic observatory to work his destruction, how long it will take him to rebuild it if he can, or if the Nírozahé alone is enough. His is the advantage; we cannot afford to wait on his next move."

He reached for the pile of clean rags ready at Loríen's knee and gently bound her arm. Loríen was unable to deny that she enjoyed being cared for, as weary and soul-sick as she was.

Lyn was nodding. "Good. Good. Because I owe him something special." She struck her open palm with her fist. "Bryant, my parents, now Dairinn and Dewfern – and he tried to kill my sister too."

Loríen put her free hand on Lyn's arm and was surprised to find her sister shaking. "Lyn. Remember that revenge is *his* purpose. This has to be more than that, or we are him."

Naoise glanced up at her thoughtfully, but said nothing.

The blonde elf sighed. "Oh, I know. It is. We have a world to save, right? But I can't help it if I'm going to enjoy seeing that weedy moldwarp get his."

"I think that should suffice," Naoise said to Loríen, tying off the last of the bandages. He did not, she noted, seem to be in any hurry to let go of her arm. Even more of a surprise to her, she was not particularly anxious to pull it away. "I believe I know just how you feel, Lyn. Don't worry. We're not done fighting." He met Loríen's eyes steadily; his were quite dark. "Are we?"

Loríen looked back and forth between the two of them. At the determination in Lyn's eyes and the quiet trust in Naoise's, visible even through the grief. It made no sense that they could still believe in her when they knew she had failed so entirely, but their faith would have to be enough to carry on with. For now.

"Of course not. Lyn is right: we have a world to save."

The five companions stared up at the sky through the trees. Not a single tower rose above the treeline to disrupt the view.

After their momentary pause, they spurred their horses on toward a scene none of them truly wished to see. When they emerged from the forest to what should have been their first view of Dewfern, a silence descended.

What had once been a great and fair city was now a flattened, barren patch of ground dotted eerily with the odd standing wall or pillar. Much of it was fire-blackened, and even all these weeks after the event it still bore the squalid signs of flooding – jetsam littering the site almost disrespectfully. Not a living soul stirred among the rubble but the unnerving caw of the carrion crows could be heard echoing over the otherwise silent field, the sound itself calling attention to the pervasive stench of rot.

Loralíenasa put a hand to her mouth. "Merciful Vaian." This was the destruction her failure had wrought. Staring it in the face, breathing in the realness of it, was almost like being dealt another physical injury and hurt even more.

Naoise gripped his reins so tightly his gloves screeched.

Lyn reached across the distance between their horses and patted his knee. There was nothing to be said.

"Surely there must be *some* survivors," he posited in a not-quite-convincing tone. His brow was glistening, his hand flicking the reins back and forth across the saddlebow as if of its own volition.

"Better search, anyway," Cole said, and urged his horse forward.

Lyn watched him ride into the lonely wasteland for a moment, then drew a deep breath and followed him in.

Naoise rode behind her, his lips pressed tight together. His eyes had a glassy look, as if he were not really seeing what was before him.

But there was no escaping the smell.


Cresting the high point of the city, and looking down unimpeded toward the lake from there, brought a different view. Naoise sighed and braced himself as if preparing to take up a great weight.

Campfires. Movement. Little of either.

Their arrival at the edge of the dispirited camp was met with suspicion. The people here were bedraggled and afraid – not that Loríen blamed them. Their entire world had literally fallen away in a single night of chaos. It was painful to watch Naoise shoulder that suspicion, that fear and downtrodden weariness. As if he felt it was his responsibility to bear it with them.

She knew that particular burden, as princess of a conquered people, and she ached to see it come to someone else.

The further in they rode amongst the frightened refugees, the more beaten

Naoise appeared.

"My lord! Oh, my lord Naoise! By the Father, is that you?"

They reined in at the call, and Naoise swiveled in the saddle to search out the speaker: a tall, thin grey-haired man whose court finery had seen far better days. He was hurrying toward them so quickly he nearly stumbled through a family's cookfire. He paused to apologize in haste before continuing on to meet the newcomers.

"Lord Mostyn." Naoise climbed out of the saddle and passed a hand through his hair, straightened his doublet. Nervous gestures, Loríen had come to recognize, not vanity. " 'Tis good to see you alive and well, old friend." He clasped the old lord's forearm when the man had come near enough. "I had feared to find only the worst here."

The older man grimaced. "Alive, my lord, but well may be overstating. As you can see, Dewfern has seen better times. It has been all we could do to keep what little order you find here."

Naoise was nodding. "And who is we, may I ask? Is the king–?"

Mostyn's face fell. "Dead, my lord. Lost, like so many others, when the castle came down. I am so sorry. The princess has been leading in his absence."

Naoise turned and stared down at the lake for a moment. Loríen couldn't see his face, but she could read the loss in him well enough. Although he'd spent the journey here expecting this news, and worse, at least some part of him must have been holding out the hope that the whole thing had been no more than an illusion. Finally he drew a deep breath and gave his attention back to the tattered courtier. "Will you take me to her?"

"Immediately, my lord. Her Highness will be transported with joy to see you. Your return is the only good news we've had since..." He trailed off, evidently realizing that Naoise might not know *what* had happened and coming to the conclusion that he'd rather not shoulder the responsibility of telling him. "Please pardon the question, but your companions. They are...?"

"Elves, yes," Naoise answered shortly. "And they are Grenlec's allies."

Mostyn blanched, but did not argue. "As you say, my lord." He gestured, and they followed.

"Well, I mean. It could be *worse*, right?" Lyn whispered un-secretively to Cole. His scowl of concentration deepened but he did not answer.

The Grenlecian lord led them down to the waterfront, following the curve of the lake south before descending sharply into an unexpected series of caverns. Naoise balked at the entrance.

"Do not fear, my lord," Mostyn assured him. "Your horses will be safe if you leave them here. I shall see to it they are as comfortable as we can make them."

Loríen must have been the only one to see the momentary flash of animal terror in Naoise's eyes, because no one gave him a second glance when he said, with careful enunciation that denied the presence of fear with every cool syllable, "Forgive me, Lord Chamberlain. I am not terribly fond of caves."

"Ah, well, it's a roof overhead, isn't it?" the lord sighed, proceeding without the least bit of doubt that they would be following. "We're lucky to have found these at all, when... when the shoreline changed."

Naoise swallowed hard. Loríen touched his arm briefly and nodded once when he looked her way, to show her understanding. He closed his eyes, squared his shoulders, and drew a deep breath as if preparing to dive underwater. She knew that he was accepting this – his own fear – as just another burden he could not escape, and her heart hurt for him.

They navigated the red-walled caves with Mostyn guiding them until they came to an especially wide grotto that was mercifully open to the lake all on one side – with a sheer drop to the water below. There they found a patchwork reconstruction of life in the castle with what wreckage had been salvageable. Everyone was busy at some task, moving with purpose. At the center of it all, overlooking an improvised map, was Princess Alyra. Weary, haggard, her clothes just as worn as those of any of the refugees they'd passed on their way through the camp. She had discarded the hoop structure beneath her elaborate skirts. As they approached, she registered her awareness of another imminent demand with a bracing of her posture – not unlike her brother – but the expression that settled on her face when she looked up and saw them spoke of something else entirely.

"Naoise! By the– You're alive!" She all but vaulted over the map table to launch herself into her brother's arms.

Naoise caught her hastily, wearing a dazed smile.

Alyra pushed back after a moment to study his face. Her joy was dimmed by what she saw there but she kept her smile. "By the Father's love, it's good to see you. I only wish we could offer a proper welcome. But you don't have good news either, do you?" Then she took in the rest of the group. She seemed to know already the answer to the question she was about to ask. "Dairinn?"

The prince's entire body sagged, his smile vanishing, but he drew a deep breath and made himself say it.

"Dairinn is dead. We failed to defeat our enemy in Mornnovin; he died bravely so we could escape."

A hush descended upon those in hearing distance, spreading like a black fog until the entire vast cavern was heavy with the silence. Alyra found her way back to the edge of the table without looking and allowed it to support her. She was speechless for a long time.

"Another blow, when Grenlec has already suffered so many," she finally said. "That we still have you is a mercy we should give thanks for." She tried to force a smile, but her eyes were too wet to sell it. "We have little else to rejoice at. But I suspect you already have some idea as to what has passed here, as you have not yet asked."

Lyn leaned in conspiratorially. "We were… sort of… *there*, when he made it happen."

When Alyra met that revelation with a puzzled frown, Naoise offered the quick explanation. "The tremors that swallowed Dewfern were caused by Kataki Kuromé's magic."

"I will want the longer version of that," Alyra replied, "but it can wait. You all look like you desperately need to sit and catch your breath. I'll have something found for you to eat and drink and we shall speak when you've rested."

Lord Mostyn took a hesitant step forward, drawing everyone's attention. "Forgive me, Your Highnesses both. The last thing I wish is to add to anyone's burdens in these times, but… I must point out that things have changed with the news of Prince Dairinn's death." He frowned at Naoise. "My lord, with your father gone, the crown passes to you. Yours is the rightful rule of Grenlec now."

Even though he must have known, must have been preparing himself for this possibility ever since that day in Mornnovin, Naoise blinked rapidly as if to stave off tears of exhaustion.

"Yes, Lord Chamberlain." His voice was a mere husk of a whisper. "I am aware."

Naoise was King of Grenlec. That fact filled Lorien with an inexplicable gloom that she didn't think was only a response to the deep misery radiating from him.

But he shouldered this burden too, visibly adjusting his posture to accommodate the new weight. "Well," he said gruffly, "if I can just get a place to sit and something to wet my throat while I listen, I'd like to hear about the numbers and disposition of the camp, including the army. We have more than mere survival to contend with and we need to be ready."

Alyra bit her lip. "Oh dear. Naoise. There is no army."

Her brother turned to her slowly.

"Father had called a muster to meet the Telrishti attack he feared. The army was assembled at the harbor barracks, preparing to sail." Alyra shook her head – half apology, half disbelief that their luck could be so bad. "Not a man of them made it."

By nightfall, news of Dairinn's death had spread throughout the camp. And the survivors of Dewfern mourned.

Grenlec's living king did not have the luxury of joining them. He sat with Alyra and what officials he had left by the open cave wall, where he could look out over the lake and pretend he wasn't buried under the earth, hearing what each of them had to say. A steady rain was coming down, the fresh promise of spring a hint on the air. But of course, winter's end was no mercy. It meant Telrisht could have been on their doorstep yesterday.

Naoise listened to his advisors with a heavy heart. All he had ever wanted was to protect his family, and not only had he now lost nearly everyone he cared about, but he was being given so much more responsibility than he could possibly bear. What was he to do with no army and his capital in ruin? How was he to stop the inevitable now? What kind of king ruled from a hole in the ground while his people cowered in rags above? He resisted the urge to bury his face in his hands.

"We've sent to the governors of Yeatun and Arden both for aid," Alyra was telling him, "but they've returned only blankets and some meager food-stuffs, and their regrets that they have no more resources to spare." She smiled somewhat bitterly. "Though I suppose a king might be better able than a princess to compel cooperation."

Sitting beside Naoise at their improvised council table, mostly gazing out at the rain rather than following the discussion, Lyn snorted at that. "Now that's just rude. I bet they'd sing a different song if they came down and saw the state of things here."

Naoise shook his head dolefully. Both of them were correct, not that it did anything to help them just now. He looked up and saw that Loríen was quirking her lips at him in a small, sympathetic smile.

He could not help but be reminded of the night he had felt those lips on his in Mornnovin. A strange, sudden moment before everything had fallen apart. They had not shared another kiss since that night or even talked about it, but something indefinable in their dynamic had shifted and he could see it every time he looked at her. He just wished he knew what to do about it. Or had the focus to spare.

Naoise pushed a hand through his hair and drew a deep breath, returning to the demands of the moment.

"We cannot afford to wait upon anyone's mercy, and neither can we stay here in this graveyard. We are entirely indefensible," he told his tattered council. They sat up to listen, hearing a decision in his voice. "Spread word through the camp that the host will be split in two and we will march severally to Arden and to Yeatun as soon as may be. If we halve the burden on each, both will be better able to bear the imposition." He turned to his sister and met her eyes. She looked back expectantly.

"Alyra, you will lead the way to Arden, and I to Yeatun. Make fast the city against the possibility of siege, though it is more likely Telrisht will strike at Yeatun if they mean to break us."

Her left eyebrow puckered, her habit when thinking. "I thought you were trying to convince us all that Telrisht is not the enemy," she objected.

Naoise smiled dryly back at her. "They're not, but *they* don't know that yet." Some of the men chuckled. "Our task is to stay alive until they do."

"But this means nothing with the true threat remaining," Loríen pointed out coolly.

Lord Mostyn hemmed nervously before speaking up. All of the Grenlecians were having trouble handling the presence of elves at their council table, no matter that their king had ordered them to accept it. "But what can we do against a sorcerer? A man who can apparently flick his hand and exterminate us with no more effort than he would use to swat a fly?"

"I don't think he can," Cole put in quietly, speaking for the first time all night. He scowled his discomfort when all eyes turned on him, but went on to explain anyway. "I think he needed his observatory to work his magic from such a distance, or he'd have had the rest of Grenlec and Telrisht flat by now. If I had to guess, I'd say he's grudgingly leading his forces out of Mornnovin right now. Probably making for Yeatun."

Sovoqatsu grunted his agreement, drawing the table's fascinated and understandably nervous attention. "The man speaks sense. We'd all be dead already if Katakí had the range for it."

"Wonderful," Alyra sighed. "Not just one army but a second we must meet with our utter lack of one."

Loríen sat up and cleared her throat. "I believe my people will answer the call now, should I sound it. This has come far enough that even Lord Maiantar cannot deny what is happening."

Though he had his doubts on that, Naoise supposed she knew the mettle of her own people better than he did. But that was hardly the only concern. "Even so," he objected, "by the time a message could get through to Efrondel and back again, we would be beyond all help."

Loríen returned his gaze steadily. "I have the means of speaking with Captain Galvan tonight – now, if you wish it. He has not been idly waiting. He could reach us with his men within a fortnight."

He accepted the news and the unsettling hint at magic in stride, forcing himself to smile back at her. "Unless he's still in jail."

Lyn laughed at that outright as Naoise's gathered advisors stirred uneasily.

Loríen didn't blink. "He is not, but even were he."

A fortnight? Naoise wanted to believe in this unexpected aid, but that seemed a bit too optimistic. Still, he was in no position to turn down even the possibility of an ally. His smile faded as he started to run scenarios. "Can you give me numbers?"

She gestured vaguely with fingers entwined, glancing with an almost unnoticeable caginess at the Grenlecian lord sitting beside her. "No? I truly cannot say how many would be willing to march. But no matter the size of the force he might lead, the Captain will be enough to engage Kataki's attention. Of that, be assured."

Sovoqatsu nodded his agreement.

As Naoise considered that, he had another thought. "What of Dairinn's wing in Alanrad?" he asked his sister. "Have they been recalled or do they still occupy the city?"

"I sent the order to recall them after the tragedy. Alanrad will avail us little if we die here at home." The princess answered quickly, defensive, and Naoise realized this must have been an unpopular and contested decision. "But I did leave the main force at Nastrond."

Naoise found himself nodding his agreement. It was what he would have done in her position. "That's – what? Five thousand?"

"Five thousand sounds better than none," Lyn pointed out.

"Not exactly a scale-tipper against the entire Telrishti army," Alyra said with a frown.

"But serviceable to man the walls at Yeatun," Naoise countered. "We don't actually want to fight Telrisht. All we need is time to treat with the Ayiz."

The pronouncement was met with murmurs and a general shudder from the Grenlecians. "That is not a task I envy you, Sire," Mostyn declared.

Nor was it a task Naoise looked forward to.

He glanced around the makeshift table, seeking confirmation in every pair of eyes. They all had so much faith in him, as though they believed his return would bring the nightmare to an end. Just the sight of that much expectation drained the energy from him. But he nodded at each of them in turn, collecting their belief, taking up the burden. There was no one else left to do it. He desperately wished for his father back.

"Well, then." Naoise flattened both his palms on the table top. "I believe we have enough to be getting on with. Prepare the camp to pick up with all possible haste." He met Loríen's eyes. "And contact your people by whatever means you have." Then he sought Sovoqatsu's attention, and could see that the elf was surprised to be singled out.

"I know I have no authority to ask this of you, but I can think of no man better for the task: would you be willing to do some reconnaissance? If what Cole says is true – and I do not doubt it – we would all feel better, I think, if we knew how close Kataki is and what manner of force he has with him."

The martial elf frowned, but not with displeasure. "You are right: there is no one better. Yes, I'll go."

"Thank you, my friend."

Sovoqatsu glowered at him but made no verbal protest to the appellation. Naoise had to consider that progress of some kind.

# CHAPTER TWENTY-SEVEN

Lyn hated feeling useless.

She wondered what she was supposed to be doing with herself as she watched the meeting break up. For the first time since setting out for Evlédíen, she had no idea. Even worse, it didn't seem like there was anything she really *could* do.

Naoise and his sister stepped apart to talk about things Lyn had no urge to intrude upon. She couldn't even imagine what she would say to Bryant right now if they could talk one more time. The six Grenlecian gentlemen who were all the leadership left in Dewfern disappeared quickly the moment they were dismissed. Either they shared Lyn's feelings about intruding or they just feared for their lives in the presence of elves, but whatever the case she had no time to introduce herself to any of them or even ask where she was supposed to settle down for the night.

Cole stayed with her, predictably, even though she was sure he had no such doubts as to his role here. He would probably be wanting to claim a proper dinner, check on their horses' accommodations, and get as much sleep as possible before being called upon next. She envied his pragmatism.

While Lyn sat at the makeshift table feeling unnecessary, Loríen excused herself with a murmured word and a grim look. The angry elf followed her; the two of them disappeared down some dark side-tunnel. Lyn felt herself seeming to shrink as she eyed their retreat. Agitation sent her to her feet and after Loríen before she'd given any thought to what she was doing.

Clearly surprised, Cole hurried to join her. "You know she's just contacting the Captain, like she said she would? I don't think she needs your help for that."

Lyn rounded on him with an entirely involuntary snarl on her lips. "And *I* don't need *your* help to be a nuisance to my own sister. Why don't you go find someone else to play nursemaid to for a while?"

The former mercenary withdrew in hurt surprise. The look on his face made her feel like she'd eaten something that had already gone off, but she was feeling too sorry for herself to apologize.

He was not following when she turned off into the tunnels to look for her sister.

It was actually no challenge to find Loríen and Sovoqatsu. Evidently they had a light with them, and all Lyn had to do was trace the glow to its source. But when she emerged to see Loríen carefully wiping clean the surface of a small mirror, Sovoqatsu holding one of the elves' weird flameless light spheres behind her, neither one of them seemed terribly pleased to see her.

And now that Lyn was being looked at like that, with so much impatient expectation, she admitted she wasn't sure what she'd thought would happen.

"What's that you've got there?" she asked fatuously, wishing she could disappear into the red rock walls.

"A mirror," Sovoqatsu said with carefully slow and offensive enunciation.

Loríen lowered her eyebrows at him before offering Lyn a slightly less forbidding expression. "It is a... *rovanan*." She searched her memory for the words she wanted. "A... talking glass?"

Lyn came closer and peered at the unassuming piece of reflective glass held within a ring of carved ash wood. "It can talk?"

The impatience returned, sharpening Loríen's movements as she pulled the mirror away from Lyn's scrutiny and settled on the tunnel floor. "No. We use them to talk with each other over great distance. Lanas has one like it with him. But I must–"

"Concentrate," Sovoqatsu filled in curtly when Loríen paused to think of the word. He stared at Lyn meaningfully.

Lyn sighed gustily. "Fine." When Sovoqatsu kept glaring her way, she backed up with reluctance and retraced her steps toward the main cavern. After a moment she heard Loríen's soft voice floating on the tunnel's strange air eddies, gliding quickly over strange words Lyn was certain she'd never learn herself.

Lyn sighed again, less dramatically.

Instead of going back to the giant cavern where she would have to find Cole and tell him she was sorry, Lyn followed a branching of the tunnel that smelled of rain. As she hoped, it led to another window to the outside, this one much smaller – just the right size for her to climb through. She put her head out and examined the rocky cliff face until she spotted a serviceable ledge at a reasonable climb down. The rain made the rocks more slippery than was strictly safe, but Lyn was careful and she'd done this sort of thing enough times not to give it a second thought.

She settled on the ledge in the rain, looking down at the lake with her knees drawn up to her chest, and gave in to her feelings of uselessness.

No one needed her. And for all her insistence on tagging along to Mornnovin, to help protect her sister and defeat their enemy, she had accomplished exactly nothing there. Katakí had hardly even noticed her presence.

And now Dairinn was dead. A second time she'd been forced to watch, powerless to save someone she cared about.

She recalled that awful feeling, when Katakí had taken control of her body. She had been worse than useless then, she had been a weapon against her own friends. A liability. In fact, since leaving the forest she had done nothing but cause Cole undue stress and occasionally annoy a scowl out of her sister.

"Brooding isn't your style, Lyn."

Lyn's head snapped up at the sound of the unexpected voice. She stared, trying to decide whether to bother getting up. "I should punch you right in your face," she finally said instead.

Sun smiled back. "I don't think it would do you much good, but you're welcome to if you want. I suppose." She sat down on the ledge beside Lyn. Strangely, even though it was still raining, the drops were no longer hitting the ledge or the two women on it.

Lyn studied the fairy who had raised her – the smiling, beautiful face that hid a nature Lyn could never understand. "Eh. Not worth it." She shook her head. "You lied to us. To me. You sent us into a trap." It occurred to her belatedly that she should maybe be afraid right now, but she couldn't conjure up the proper sense of self-preservation for it.

But Sun offered no threat, and Lyn's accusation seemed to make her light go dim. "No, I didn't. I really didn't."

"Ha."

The fairy sighed. "Lyn, you do know what I am, right? We can look like anything we want. We can look like nothing. That wasn't me."

Lyn hugged her legs tighter against her body. She wasn't sure what to believe, but it would have been nice if the only mother she'd ever known had not in fact sent her into an ambush to die. And it was certainly possible that she was telling the truth. Sun *had* behaved oddly that night. Not like herself.

This Sun was much more like the one Lyn had known all her life.

"Listen," Sun explained earnestly. "There are those of my order who don't entirely disagree with this elf, this Katakí Kuromé, and who also want to see the humans gone. We're not allowed to act directly upon you flesh creatures, but some of the others have tried to work around that. But that was before they understood what he meant to do. Now he's twisting the bones of Creation itself – precisely the thing we're charged to prevent. That's going to have repercussions for the ones who helped him, I promise you."

Hearing the unstudied candor in the fairy's voice, Lyn let go of her knees and sat up. "So you'll fight him with us now that he's crossed the line?"

Sun shook her head. "We *can't*. I'm sorry. I really am sorry, Lyn." She reached out and touched the girl's arm gently. "About Bryant too. More than I can say."

Lyn swallowed past a sudden lump in her throat. "Then what good are you? Why are you here?"

"To apologize."

"Yeah, well." Lyn swallowed again. She wished she didn't feel like she was about to cry. "You can save it. Your apology is about as useful as I am. I should've just stayed home, not that it was home anymore."

Sun put an arm around the elf she had raised from infancy and pulled her close. And as though she had drawn them forth with magic, Lyn's tears started to come after all. "You're wrong. Can you know yourself so little? You're strong, Lyn. You've always been strong. When you've decided you want to do something, nothing can stop you from doing it. You help others find that strength in themselves, too."

Wiping at her face with both hands, Lyn snorted at the reassurance, but she didn't push Sun away. "Sure. I'm a sidekick. That makes me feel so much better. So, what, I'm here to convince Loríen to decide that she actually wants to beat Katakí, and suddenly she'll be able to?"

The fairy smirked. "Not exactly. Your sister has all the tools she needs to defeat her enemy already, if she just stops fighting herself. And you will help her. Never doubt that you matter, Lyn." She squeezed Lyn's shoulder. "You changed *my* life. I want you to think a while about what that means."

Lyn opened her mouth to ask Sun what she was talking about. Before she could get even the first word out, she was alone again on the ledge, in the rain.

By the time Loríen came looking for Naoise, he was standing by himself before the open view of the lake and the night sky – alone in a cavern teeming with life. The slim line of his body looked vulnerable against that great black void in a way that made Loríen's chest tighten. It reminded her of something she couldn't put her finger on, something that frightened her. She approached him with care.

Naoise cast her one quick, enigmatic glance when she came to stand beside him, but his body language was more telling, subtly oriented toward her though he hardly moved. She tried to ignore that, with limited success.

"I've spoken with Lanoralas," she said briskly in Elven. "He'll contact me in the morning after he has broached the subject with Lord Maiantar, but he believes he will be able to field four hundred fighters within two days." She was stupidly aware of Naoise's hand, just a short reach from hers, and how much she wanted to hold it. He looked so sad.

"Four hundred?" he echoed. "That's… not a lot."

Because his day had already been difficult enough, she answered as gently as she could instead of hurling in his face the bitter fact that if four hundred elves were to die in this, her people would nearly be extinct in Asrellion. "That is more than we can spare," she said instead, "and yet we will."

Perhaps her tone told him enough, because he gave her a longer glance and something like a smile ghosted across his face. "Well. If they fight anything like their Míyahídéna, then every one of them is worth at least five men. And we need every body we can get." All traces of his short-lived good humor melted away. "Did you know this city was once home to more than eighty thousand souls?"

She swallowed. What could she say to that?

He smiled unhappily out at the night. "Although perhaps it's asking too much to beg your sympathy for the deaths of so many Grenlecians."

Loríen felt as though she'd been kicked in the lungs. "Naoise." She reached out and held him by the sleeve of his doublet until he turned to face her. "If that is what you think of me, then I don't know why you imagine I'm here at all."

The drizzle of rain and the susurrus of the crowd behind them were the only sounds for a moment. Naoise's gaze drifted despondently away from hers.

She watched the rain on the lake, the steady stream of it. Each drop that fell exploded outward into a circle touching and overlapping, subsuming and being subsumed by those they touched. There was no predicting how the rain would fall; it was chaos. And yet the fact that it did, that it kept on falling – that it would fall again and always until the end of time – was the most regular, the most predictable of truths. As brief the life of each of those exploding circles, there were always more after it and each was part of that eternally shifting mural.

She watched the rain, and she thought of human life and felt at once indescribably sad, and unbearably joyful. There would always be life, and the rain did not mourn its own fall. How could she tell one drop to envy those that came after?

Naoise's voice had lost its brittle edge when he spoke again. Now he just sounded tired. "Why *are* you here? Why do you care what happens to us?"

She answered carefully, meeting his eyes. "Because one cannot claim to revere our maker and be so eager to destroy any part of creation. Because life itself has inestimable value, no matter how different it is to mine – perhaps even more when it *is* different, because that difference enriches us all. And because," she braced herself, "I've seen how good humans can be."

From his sudden stillness and the intensity with which he stared back at her, it was clear that Naoise had read far more in that than she meant him to. The distance between them seemed to shrink; Loríen was well aware of every inch of him, so close to her, just a single invitation away. Of what it had felt like to kiss him that night. No matter how hard she tried not to dwell on it, the memory was never far from her thoughts.

Naoise leaned toward her just slightly before checking himself with a pained grimace. Loríen knew exactly how far the memory of that night was from his mind too.

He was King of Grenlec.

"I'll keep you informed as soon as I hear from the Captain," she said, brandishing the words as a shield. She took a deliberate step back. The powerful sadness in his eyes made a full return. "Good night, Naoise."

She could feel him watching her as she walked away.

Although four thousand was a pitiful remnant of eighty thousand, it took several days to organize and supply such a large host to march. On the morning they were ready to get underway, Naoise moved among his people and strove to impart some sense of hope. He was not so certain of the things he told them, but he said them convincingly enough to lift their spirits. What else did he have to give them?

At length, he stood at the verge of the lake and finally had a quiet moment as his poor beleaguered people prepared themselves for another hardship at his behest. He just had to believe things would be better for them where they were going. They would rebuild Dewfern in time – this he swore to himself – but first they had to survive.

Alyra found him there keeping his silent vigil. She came up beside him and put her hand in his.

He found a smile for his sister. "Are you ready to do this?"

She smiled back innocently, batting her lashes over blue eyes that were so like Dairinn's. "I've been fancying an Arden holiday for some time now. I'll be sure to give your love to the cousins."

That drew a chuckle.

Alyra squeezed his hand. "I would tell you not to worry about us, but I know you. So just don't worry *too* much, all right there big brother? And that reminds me." She rose up on her toes to plant a kiss on his cheek. "I wish you joy of the day."

He stared back at her blankly.

"Don't tell me you've got your head so turned around you've forgotten your own birthday?"

Naoise blinked. He had lost track of the days somewhere in Mornnovin, but he didn't doubt she was right. The season had already turned, after all. "I... Thank you." This was not exactly how he had imagined himself spending his next birthday. He resisted a surge of despair.

The princess stepped back and he saw that she was carrying a small wooden chest under her other arm. She held it up for him to see. "Perhaps this will cheer you. It was found washed up on shore."

"Is that–?" Naoise reached out and opened the chest, immediately heartened to see that it was in fact his mother's collection of family treasures. Amazingly, the box seemed to have done a fine job of keeping the water out. "I'll be damned. Who could have imagined we'd ever see this again?"

"I wish we could have saved more," Alyra said, "but I think this is a start."

He pushed a finger through the familiar old pieces – a delicate diamond necklace of strange antiquated design, a bright silver and red-gold brooch depicting the sun half-hidden behind steep mountain peaks, an ornate ring set with a purple stone. Others their mother had worn more often. He had seen them all so many times it was like reuniting with old friends, and it was a comfort after everything else they had lost.

Naoise closed the lid on the chest and sealed the catch. "Take this with you to Arden and keep it safe," he said. "I'll fight better knowing a piece of home yet endures." He put an arm around his sister and pulled her close.

They parted ways, each to their separate duties. Naoise offered a silent plea to the Father that he would see Alyra again.

He found his friends with the horses at the head of the column, waiting to march – except for Sovoqatsu, who had been gone for days, scouting the enemy as promised. He would find them on the road when he had news. Lyn grinned brightly when Naoise came near.

"Well let's get moving," she declared. "For seeing the world, I really picked the right people to tag along with."

Loríen shook her head at that, but Naoise was mostly certain he saw the hint of a smile on her lips. He briefly contemplated telling them that it was his birthday. Remembering the princesses' birthday back in Efrondel and Lyn's utter confusion over the fact that anyone cared what day she'd been born on, he decided not to. If that ritual torture Lord Maiantar had called a court dinner was anything like the typical elven birthday celebration, Naoise doubted that Loríen would greet the news with any particular warmth either. And Cole...

Not that Naoise generally let himself indulge in what would have been a condescending pity for the man, but he wondered for a moment if Cole had ever been given a gift of any kind in his life.

He swallowed his own feelings of injustice and mounted his waiting steed without comment. He nodded to Lord Mostyn, who passed the signal all the way down the line. Slowly, at the walking pace of the weakest of his people carrying what was left of their households, they left ruined Dewfern behind.

They had traveled scarcely a mile beyond the former city limits when Loríen sat up straighter in the saddle beside him, lifting her head like a wolf that had caught a scent. Naoise watched her, but she offered no immediate explanation.

"Loríen? What is it?"

Eyes narrowed in concentration, she did not look his way. He could see the tension in her profile. "Someone approaches. There is the thunder of many horses. Not as many as half one hundred, I would say."

Naoise peered through the trees, but whatever it was Loríen heard, it was still too far off to be seen. Behind him he heard Cole loosening his sword in its sheath.

A party of fifty horse. Naoise considered carefully in the moment allowed him. Surely that was too few a number for Kataki to have sent to finish them, even knowing that Dewfern lay in ruins. And if the Ayiz were to send an envoy offering to accept Grenlec's surrender, fifty would be too many. Obviously it was too soon to be Loríen's people, and he could not think why Mysia would–

He felt himself relax to the point of smiling. Loríen blinked at him, clearly demanding an explanation for his sudden insanity.

"Well," he said lightly, "we can hardly hide. There's nothing to do but ride on and be vigilant." For good measure, he asked the Lord Chamberlain to pass a warning for readiness back through the host, but he had a sudden strong feeling it would not be needed. In fact, he felt more hopeful than he had in weeks.

Loríen continued to watch him doubtfully. He smiled back at her.

When Naoise could finally hear the drum of horse hooves for himself, it became clear that the riders were moving at speed. Not long after that, the first of them came into view down the Greater Forest Road, and Naoise didn't even bother to keep his relief from bursting out of him in a wholehearted laugh.

"Oh, hedge-pigs," Lyn sighed. "Naoise's lost his mind. Which one of us is going to hide all the sharp things before he hurts himself?"

That only made Naoise laugh harder.

"Naoise?" Loríen asked him quietly. To her credit there was no longer any trace of doubt, only a request for clarity.

"It's all right," he assured her. She did not argue.

The double column of riders – forty, in fact – slowed as they approached. Naoise raised a hand, calling a halt to the march behind him. The trees echoed with a seemingly endless ripple of muttering and the creaking of cargo. When the foremost of the uniformed riders had reached Naoise and his companions, he dismounted and offered a crisp military salute.

Naoise grinned down at the man in the road. "Lieutenant Reid. It's a long way from Telrisht. To what do we owe the pleasure?"

His former second-in-command dropped his hand when acknowledged. He did not look nearly as pleased as Naoise at the reunion. "We heard the news about Dewfern. Came as soon as we could." He stopped to frown at Loríen and Lyn. "Mysians?"

"Elves," Naoise replied. There was little point in trying to hide it now.

Reid continued to glower at the ladies. He evidently had no trouble resuming his old habit of questioning Naoise's judgment. "Naoise, what in the black Void has been happening here?"

"Sire," Naoise corrected gently.

The soldier stared back at him with incomprehension that visibly shifted through all the expected stages to the same grim acceptance Naoise himself had to bear. "I see." He drew a slow breath before lowering himself to one knee in the dust of the road. Behind him, the rest of his soldiers dismounted and did the same.

Naoise was suddenly lost for words.

"The Father bless your reign, Sire," Reid said only somewhat mechanically. "What has happened, and how can we help?"

"On your feet, soldier," Naoise managed to say. It was a relief when the man rose again so quickly and without further ado. "Instruct your men to escort these people, then come and ride beside me. I shall explain everything as we go. We make for Yeatun."

As Reid moved to do as ordered, Naoise felt almost on the verge of more laughter. Forty men would hardly defeat Katakí or protect them from Telrisht, but the unexpected appearance of Naoise's old unit was the first good thing to have happened in so long that he had to take it as a fair omen. And he knew these men, had trained them, knew what they could do. He would happily take these forty over any other thousand.

Even though a part of him felt foolish for this new optimism, he held fast to it. They needed every possible advantage they could get.

Suddenly he no longer minded so much that it was his birthday.

"You hear it too?"

Naoise held perfectly still and Loríen could see that he was trying to un-wish from reality the faint rumble they could all feel in their bones, but with no success. "I hear it." He sniffed the intermittently acrid air and grew more solemn. "And that smell. I know it well, I'm afraid."

Cole urged his mount forward without comment, breaking away from the trudging mass of refugees. Loríen followed, knowing that Naoise and Lyn would be with her. More surprisingly, Reid appeared at Naoise's side, grim and determined. Despite what was apparently a long history of personal differences, Reid seemed to have appointed himself and his unit as Naoise's royal security escort.

The five of them together rode out in advance of the throng to investigate, although Loríen was already certain of what they would find. They left the road, which cut through the middle of a butte, and dismounted to climb up among the giant standing stones at the apex of the hill. When they peered down through the maze of boulders, they could see it all laid out before them, through the smoke.

Yeatun was besieged.

Without taking his eyes from the Telrishti lines, Naoise reached out and gripped Reid by the shoulder. "Ride back and tell Mostyn to halt the march. *Now.*"

The soldier saluted his king and turned back without arguing.

Naoise's lips moved soundlessly as he scanned the scene below, counting. He swore in what Loríen assumed were strong terms. "We *have* to get our people into the city. They're completely vulnerable out here."

"I'm guessing these guys won't just stop and take lunch while we march by?" Lyn quipped. "Maybe if you ask politely. You're good at polite."

No one laughed.

Loríen looked down at the sprawling city of Yeatun by the lake. Not Grenlec's capital, but its largest city by far and desperately proud of its urbane sophistication. The many white towers were an homage to Eselvwey that was lost, though there was not the human alive who would know that fact anymore or admit to it if he did. Those soaring white spires were threatened now by an army that disappeared against the horizon – more bodies than Loríen had ever before seen in one place, more than she could comprehend. They had a line of enormous black cannon levied against the walls of Yeatun, not yet close enough to bring the defenses down, but that would not be true much longer.

"How long can the city hold, do you think?" she asked Naoise.

It was Cole who answered in precise, professional tones. "That depends on a few things. Yeatun's guns are bigger and their walls give them range, but it doesn't look like they have the manpower to run them all. Telrisht will keep them sweating and blowing through shot while their engineers work on advancing that line. They have the numbers to keep up the bombardment and switch bodies out all night while they dig." He drew a deep breath before continuing. "How long Yeatun can hold out depends on how many men they can put on the walls at a time and how many they can cycle in for relief, how much ammunition they've got stockpiled, whether or not they had time to lay in adequate provisions for a siege, how fast Telrisht can mine, and how much heat the city can bring against them when those guns do come into play."

Loríen blinked back at Cole in surprise, but Naoise was nodding with the grim assurance of an experience she was glad she did not share.

"That's about the size of it," Naoise said quietly. "And we're only going to tax their ability to withstand a long siege by bringing more hungry mouths into the city, but there's nothing for it. In any event, we have no hope of defeating that army."

Lyn leaned back from the edge and folded her arms across her chest. "So you're giving up."

"No," Loríen answered. "We must convince them to stop the attack."

"So we're back to Naoise asking politely." Lyn snorted. "That's going to go well."

Loríen looked at Naoise, saw him thinking furiously, frustration drawing furrows between his brows. "Worth a try, is it not?" When they all looked at her like she was insane, she smiled back. "I have a thought. Can you get a message into the city?"


Naoise had been party to many diplomatic dealings of one character or another in his life. He had to remind himself of that, and order his nerves to fall in line, as he rode toward the Telrishti army under banners of truce. The fact was, he had never done anything exactly like *this* before.

The sun had set over the lake behind Yeatun, painting the sky with fire in a more beautiful echo of the incendiary action below. Soon it would be full night. The timing mattered.

Their flags were shabby, scavenged from the wreckage of Dewfern and restored to the best of their ability with limited resources. He was escorted only by a handful of guards. Naoise tried to make up for these shortcomings with the majesty of his bearing, but he was well aware that his time on the road had left him looking more a bandit than a king.

"Steady," Cole said behind him with the unaffected stability of an old oak tree. "This is your game and you have it in you."

Naoise turned in the saddle to give the man a grateful nod. Whether it was blind luck or some other force that had brought them into one another's paths that day by Scathan Falls, it remained true that Cole was the best companion and comrade-in-arms Naoise could have asked for on the road these past months. More than that, he was a friend and Naoise was grateful to have him by his side for this.

They were met by armed and hostile Telrishti soldiers some distance out from the camp. Cole spurred his horse forward in advance of Naoise's guards.

"Stay your swords," he said in passable Telrishti. "The King of Grenlec comes in peace to hold conference with your general. Upon your honor, you are bound to observe the laws of the field."

The Telrishti met this declaration with suspicious, disdainful stares, examining the supposed king by the light of their torches. Naoise drew himself up and tried to look as regal as possible.

After a brief discussion between themselves, one of the soldiers gestured curtly.

"You will dismount and give us your weapons," he said in heavily accented Common.

Naoise swung down from the saddle with all the grace at his command and raised his arms to show his sides clearly. Those with him followed suit. "We bear no weapons. We hereby place ourselves under your protection."

The Telrishti laughed. It was not a friendly sound. "Then you will come with us quietly, men of Grenlec," their spokesman said. They moved to surround Naoise and his retinue, but made no threat of violence. Escorted now by a score of men who wanted him dead more than they wanted their next meal, Naoise advanced into the Telrishti camp.

He drew a deep breath, steadying himself, and thought deliberately, *We're in. Stand by.*

*Be careful,* a familiar voice said back to him within his mind. Stupidly, it helped just knowing she cared enough to actually say it.

They were led in amongst the larger tents behind the active line, where the Rahd and commanding officers were waiting to be needed. For all that this was an army presently engaged in battle, there was little tumult here. If not for the constant percussion of cannon fire and the occasional armored clatter of units jogging to their appointed posts, there would be no indication that this was anything more than a field exercise. Naoise didn't know whether to admire the Telrishti's aloof and disciplined approach to combat, or to be horrified by their decadence in the face of violence.

The general's pavilion was unmistakable amid the rest, massive and brightly-colored as it was. The soldiers bade him wait outside while their leader went in to inform the general of the unforeseen visit. Naoise imagined them all having a nice laugh at his expense before the man came back out with word that the general would see him.

Inside, the tent was appointed with every luxury one might have expected to find in a fine villa in Alanrad. Naoise was not surprised but he was, after the squalor he'd lived in lately, just the slightest bit jealous. The general himself was lounging back on a rug strewn with pillows when they entered, incongruously dressed in full formal armor. He looked up at Naoise with a hard smile, studying the Grenlecian for a moment before he bothered to stand.

The Telrishti general was an imposing man, as tall as Sovoqatsu and much broader through the shoulders, skin the deep brown of walnut wood, with a thick mane of black hair bound carefully into a tail at the nape of his neck. His immaculate black beard was peppered with grey, but he in no way appeared diminished by years. And his dark eyes, as he studied his guests, were even more fierce than the angry elf's ever had been. He walked right up to Naoise and stood no further than a hand's distance from his face.

"I am Shafiq dal Nayil, Lord High Rahd and General of all the armies of the great and glorious Ayiz Tarek the Fifth, and I am no fool," he decreed in elegantly accented Common. His deep voice filled the pavilion. "*You* are liars and brigands, for I have met the King of Grenlec and not one among you is he. What is the meaning of this shabby pantomime?"

Naoise did not flinch from that relentless stare. "Things have changed in Grenlec. My father the king has joined our ancestors," he returned. "Likewise Prince Dairinn, his heir. I am Naoise, younger son of Lorn, and the crown has fallen to me in these dark times. I call upon your hospitality now, Abir Shafiq, one lord to another, as honor demands. We have much to discuss of import to both our kingdoms before this night is done."

Shafiq hissed between his teeth at the sound of Naoise's name, nor was he the only one to stir ominously.

"*You* are Naoise?" The word was a curse in his mouth. "The Ghost of Ghadeer, you are called in Telrisht. The Scourge of the Zahra. You have caused the deaths of many of my people, Naoise son of Lorn. You must know I would sooner put this dagger through your coward's heart than welcome you into my tent." Despite the polished beauty of his ornate scale armor, the dagger in his sash that he gripped now was no mere ornament and Naoise did not for one moment doubt his sincerity.

"It is true that in the course of my duty to Grenlec, I have not had the liberty to be a friend to Telrisht," Naoise replied evenly. He had heard the titles, knew the hatred they had for him. It had served him on occasion; this was not one such. "I would hope that, as a soldier, you would understand that what I have done has been for the protection of my own people."

"You speak of duty with the mouth of a sneakthief," the general growled. But he took a deliberate step back and offered a begrudging gesture of respect with both hands together over his heart. "Yet as you are a *king* and you have claimed my hospitality, you must have it. Take your ease and be welcome, Your Majesty."

It was too soon to relax, but Naoise did feel a flickering of hope. So far, this was going nearly exactly as planned. "Thank you for your generous welcome, Abir."

Shafiq bared his teeth. "It looks to be some time since last you had a meal fit for better than a beggar, Lord. I should be honored if you would join me at my table."

Naoise inclined his head. "You are kind to offer it." In fact, this was all still standard and Naoise was trying his best not to show his triumph. He had never been much of an actor, but he tried to tell himself he was simply mirroring his host's manners. "I assume you will honor the terms of diplomacy while I am a guest in your camp. A hold on all combat whilst we conduct our business."

The general seemed amused by that. "You do know your city will fall whether I cease the assault for one hour or one hundred."

Naoise acknowledged that with a single curt nod.

Shafiq turned to his soldiers and barked a series of commands in Telrishti. Ordering an increased guard and the laying of a sumptuous feast to remind the Grenlecian upstart of the difference between men and dogs. And commanding that the troops stand down while diplomatic talks were in progress.

"You have some audacity to come here like this," the general said to Naoise. It was unclear whether he meant the remark in scorn or with grudging respect. "You of all men, Grenlecian."

Loríen had been right: the only thing more reliable than Telrishti hatred for elves was their pride. No amount of time passed had changed that, and Naoise doubted it ever would.

*It is done,* he thought carefully as he followed Shafiq to the low table where their feast would be set. *I've bought you the time. Do not waste it.*

When night fell, not a single light burned in the city of Yeatun.

Loríen stared out at the Telrishti camp in view of those dark walls and waited. As confidently as she had presented her plan, she could not pretend that she wasn't worried about Naoise. If the Telrishti hated him even half as much as he'd said they did, it was just possible they might decide the laws of honor could be put aside for this one exception. She doubted it, though. They would not kill a king – not without the express decree of the Ayiz, which would give her time if she needed it.

It was all a calculated risk, and Naoise had agreed to do his part.

"Don't worry about it," Lyn said. "They're going to be fine. If there's one thing Naoise's good at, it's talking." She sounded more nervous than Loríen felt.

Loríen glanced at Lyn and was surprised by what she saw. Was that concern for Cole? Was that something Loríen had to worry about now, to crown everything else wrong in the world – her sister and a human? Not that Lyn cared at all about her people or their ways.

No. That was unfair. Lyn had never been given the chance to care. Her heritage was just another thing Katakí had stolen from her, along with their parents and Gallanas. Along with everything else. The life they could have had. Loríen had to breathe carefully for a moment, wrestling a surge of anger. She *would* stop Katakí, and it was likely she'd have to kill him when she did, but it couldn't be for that. Not for the sake of revenge.

But she couldn't deny that she did want him dead.

Loríen was jolted back to the moment by the sudden reception of a message. The one she had been waiting for. She stood quickly, drawing several eyes.

"He did it. We must move."

Naoise's elite soldier Reid had been vocally distrustful of this plan ever since it had been described to him, primarily because he couldn't get his head around the magic. He clearly wanted to argue now, or at least make her explain exactly how she knew what Naoise was doing in the hope that the answer might somehow be more to his liking. She could feel the force of his scowl even if the darkness obscured some of its intensity.

"I told you it would be fine," Lyn said. She climbed to her feet and slapped her sister on the shoulder.

It wasn't worth telling Lyn not to do that again, Loríen reflected tiredly.

Instead she found Lord Mostyn. The man looked up at her with surprise tempered by fear. Some of it was probably even the result of what they were doing now.

"The way is yours to lead, Lord Chamberlain," she told him before he could grow truly agitated by her presence.

The aging lord licked his lips and nodded. "I am ready. Although I had thought this sort of lunacy long behind me in my youth."

Loríen found a smile for him. "We all surprise ourselves in war, I think."

He blinked at that, obviously torn between wanting to be polite in the presence of a lady and fear that she was a demon and no lady at all. None of them knew what to do with her, when Naoise was not around. She spared him the indecision by turning to Reid, who had followed her, and exchanging a few last words regarding what they were about to do. Lord Mostyn did not wait to be told twice; he rode ahead escorted by two of Reid's men to open the city gates.

In the dark of night, in the brief moment of peace bought for them by their king's courage, Dewfern's refugees broke from cover and made for Yeatun in a concentrated sprint. Those who could not run were borne on the backs of what horses they had, or were carried by those more fit than they. It was, as Mostyn had described it, lunacy.

Reid led the desperate charge, his squad helping the people along as they could. Loríen lingered in the rear to shepherd them on. They were as quiet as they could manage to be, but every sound excited Loríen's nerves. Even with everyone ready, everyone helping each other, it took what felt like an alarmingly long time for two thousand bodies to sneak into the city before their enemies spotted them.

By the time Loríen passed through the gates with the last of the refugees, she was certain Naoise's truce must have ended ages ago.

And chaos had taken the city.

# Chapter Twenty-Eight

They dined in silence, for which Naoise was grateful. The longer the Telrishti general allowed him to wait before opening their dialogue, the more time his people would have to do what they needed to. And it allowed Naoise to enjoy the extravagant spread. He hadn't seen so much food in one place since the feast in the Crystal Palace. It took a deliberate act of will not to let himself succumb to the accumulated exhaustion of his many labors.

The general himself ate little, clearly observing no more than the form of breaking bread with him. Naoise could imagine the man entertaining bitter thoughts about the impossibility of having an appetite in his presence.

General Shafiq wasted no time or words, however, as servants cleared away the remnants of the meal.

"I cannot be guilty of sharing in your lies. I am a soldier and not one for games. Therefore I must inform you that I am well aware of that rabble you hope to hide from me on the other side of those hills."

Cole remained blessedly still and silent.

Naoise cleared his throat, considering his response carefully. The moment the other man felt Naoise was trying to manipulate him, this would all be over. On the other side of the scale, his people needed as much time as he could buy them. "Is it a lie to hope to protect innocent lives?"

The general grunted. "I simply wish to spare myself the torture of watching you labor to convince me that you are here for any purpose other than to negotiate their safe passage into the city."

Alarmed at first, Naoise felt his surprise shifting to a dry amusement. He kept himself from smiling for fear that General Shafiq should think he was being mocked. "As it happens, that is not what I've come to discuss."

The Telrishti narrowed his eyes in suspicion. "Oh?"

Naoise tried to make himself comfortable on the ornate rug. This might take a while. Or he might be thrown out in the next moment. Either outcome seemed equally likely. "No. I've come to propose an immediate truce between our two armies."

Shafiq stared for a long time without answering.

"The motley ill-becomes a man of blood. It is not meet that a king should act the part of his own fool." He raised a hand to smooth his black beard; despite his words, he did not appear in the least amused. "Or perhaps I should do you the greater kindness of believing you mad."

"I am entirely serious, and I would not disrespect you with mockery," Naoise said. "But you can hardly judge my sanity until you've heard me out."

"Speak then. And I shall judge."

The King of Grenlec drew a slow breath. "We share an enemy in common, Grenlec and Telrisht. One who is on his way even now to destroy us both. And Mysia too, and Lang, and Rosemarch. Seland has already fallen. This conflict between us is his plan and serves only his purposes, which is why we must put a stop to it at once." He pushed on despite the sudden lowering of the general's brow. "Will you tell me you've not felt it – the tug of the puppet strings as we've acted out this farce for so long? Have you not found it strange you never could achieve a final victory despite having the advantage of us on so many occasions?"

"I am not prepared to discuss my professional assessments with you," Shafiq said stiffly, "and you are doing little to convince me that your judgment is sound. A mysterious enemy to Grenlec, Telrisht, Mysia, and everywhere else too? Who is left but the Great Horned One herself? You forgot to weave fairies and the little men of the mountains into your tale for good measure."

*Fairies.* Once again Naoise had to keep the smile from his face, though it would have been a dark one.

"You have no idea how near the mark you strike," he said instead, as much to measure the general's mood as to gain time.

Shafiq narrowed his eyes, studying him. "I am a man of sword and strategy and I have no time or patience for the stories told to children. I must say it comes as a surprise of unwelcome flavor to find the dreaded Scourge of the Zahra to be no more than an idle dreamer. I had expected the architect of Telrisht's greatest losses to be more ruthless, better worthy of those victories."

Cole shifted at Naoise's side, obviously itching to speak, but he only frowned and managed to hold his peace. Naoise cast his comrade a glance, considering what Cole might have wanted to say. It was a welcome distraction from his own unhappiness at hearing that he was thought ruthless.

"You do not, then, believe in the old tales?" Naoise asked.

General Shafiq's scowl of contemplation became something more severe at the question. "You are a source of frustration, Lord. I do begin to feel manipulated – by you. Clearly you waste my time for a purpose. You, I suspect, are more devious than you appear."

It was nothing but sheerest bad fortune that a messenger came into the tent at that precise moment driven by urgent steps, before Naoise could respond. He crossed the lush rug to deliver his news directly into the general's ear in an impassioned whisper. All pretense of idleness was shocked from Shafiq's posture by what he heard, and he turned a flinty stare on Naoise as he listened. After a moment, the general waved his messenger back but did not yet dismiss him.

"I suspected duplicity from the moment of your arrival," Shafiq said to Naoise, "but it is no less a disappointment to have it confirmed, Grenlecian."

Naoise drew a careful breath. He could feel Cole tensing beside him, readying to fight their way out of the camp; he half-turned in Cole's direction and shook his head once, inconspicuously. "Of what am I accused now?"

"Your lies are inexcusable," the general snapped. "Fear drives the coward to desperation, but it is a truth beyond escaping that your city will fall. It needs not for you to come here with false talk of peace, demanding terms of honor, while your forces sail in from behind and lay waste to my ships." Naoise sucked in a startled breath, but Shafiq ignored his surprise. "All you have succeeded in achieving tonight is my ill-will."

The Primary Wing. They must have sailed across the lake and, seeing Yeatun besieged, they had come to her rescue. At the worst possible moment. Naoise didn't know whether to weep or laugh.

"You have no reason to trust me, I know," he replied, choosing his words with redoubled care, "but I swear to you upon the memory of my mother that I have been out of contact with the army these many months and have given no such order. When I ride from this camp I will see that they stand down."

"When you ride from this camp," the general echoed bitterly. "Such gall you have, to imagine I will allow you to do any such thing after this brazen double-play."

Naoise tried not to react while he furiously calculated their odds of escape.

"You *will* allow him to leave," Cole said, quietly forceful. Naoise and the general both turned to regard him with equal surprise, "because you agreed to honor the terms of diplomacy, and your honor is not contingent upon his."

The music of armor in motion sounded behind them as the guards at the tent flap surged forward. Shafiq raised his hand and they halted.

"I need not to be reminded of my duty by a low-bred mercenary dog," the general said coldly. "You would do well to mind your tongue in the presence of your masters or I shall allow my men to teach you how." He stood, a swift, uncoiling motion, and looked down at Naoise from his great height, ignoring Cole.

Naoise climbed to his feet somewhat less nimbly, stiff and sore as he was. Beside him, Cole also stood. They both watched the Telrishti general carefully.

"You will take your men and go in peace, Grenlecian," General Shafiq said, hand casually resting on his sword hilt. He took a step closer, asserting his commanding stature. "Know that you have forever doomed yourself into the lowest dungeon of my regard with your deceitful practices, and never again try to work me like one of your cheap tavern harlots."

Naoise drew himself up. "I meant every word I said about peace between our armies," he asserted as calmly as he could while he still had the chance. "Our true enemy is an elf driven out of Eselvwey in that long ago war, and he approaches even now to finish us off while we spend our strength at one another's throats."

A snarl of frustration curled the Telrishti's moustached lip.

"If you cannot trust me," Naoise added before the general could respond, "at least look into it yourself. Send your own scouts; they come on from Mornnovin." He smiled wanly. "As you said, Yeatun will fall soon or late. What harm in a small delay?"

Shafiq drew a deep, slow breath.

"You will take your men and go in peace," he repeated in a low rumble. "I regret, Lord Naoise, that I am no longer able to entertain you as my affairs take me elsewhere at present. Fare you well." He brought both hands together over his heart, the respect of the gesture utterly belied by the murder in his dark eyes.

Naoise returned the gesture. "Fare you well, Abir. Thank you for the meal, and for your time. If the Father favors us both, we will meet again soon under more cordial circumstances."

Cole plucked at his sleeve and Naoise followed the man out of the pavilion. It seemed best to leave before the look in Shafiq's eyes became something more palpable.

"You are killing your own king."

Loralíenasa had the Governor of Yeatun by two fistfuls of his red velvet doublet – an unfortunate color choice for him, given the natural ruddiness of his plump cheeks – because it was the only way she could get him to look at her. She had already been turned away by the captain of the City Guard, the commander of the local barracks, and the harbormaster. Naoise's man Reid was the only one who seemed to understand what she was saying, but he lacked the rank to get results. He could only travel with her from office to office and watch as she met with repeated dismissal.

The redness rose in the governor's shiny face as he sputtered back at her. "Unhand me this instant!" He looked back and forth at his guards, but they pointedly failed to meet his gaze. It seemed no one was willing to touch her.

Convinced now that she finally had his attention, Loríen let go of his doublet but refused to back out of his personal space. The governor looked around for a way out, but he was hemmed in by his enormous marble-topped desk and his armed guards. He had to settle for taking a single step back that did not put nearly enough distance between him and the angry elf woman, then made a great show of smoothing out his expensive garment where she had clutched it.

"I don't know who you think you are, young woman, but you will show some respect for my office."

With a great effort, she did not sigh at him. Spending time with Qroíllenas had helped prepare her to manage it. "I have told you already: I am Loralíenasa Níelor Raia, heir to the throne of Evlédíen, and you are therefore nothing to me. But that is of no matter. What matters is that you listen to what I tell you. Your king is even now in the Telrishti camp. You doom him if they learn of this battle while he is at their mercy."

The man glared. "I did not order the attack."

"But it is you who must put a stop to it," she replied diplomatically.

"And anyway," he added, going redder and more indignant still, "I have my hands full already dealing with this mess the king dropped on me."

"Mess? These are your *people*. They have survived a terrible tragedy. You should be *grateful* so many came out alive."

The human's fleshy red face was shaking now. "I am, of course, and I do not welcome your implications. I don't even have the authority to issue orders to the army."

Behind her, Reid snorted.

"You will kill the man who does," she said.

"I didn't make him go into that camp," the governor snapped, sweating his discomfort. "Now, if you please, I will need you to leave me to do my job in peace. I've just had word that Mysia is on the march, and I have two thousand refugees camped on my doorstep who are waiting to be told where to lie their heads and whether they get to eat tonight. And understand, *my lady*," he added with narrowed eyes, "that under other conditions I would be enforcing the law against you right now." He flicked his attention briefly over to Lyn. "Against *both* of you."

Lyn took an annoyed step forward, gesticulating wildly. "Me? I haven't done anything to you, old man. *Yet*."

It came as no surprise when Loríen found herself ejected from the governor's office along with her sister. Reid followed in some agitation.

"*Íyaqo los qotsuín qíjano*," Loríen spat at the closed door.

"That sounded unpleasant," Lyn observed. "I'm guessing those are the first words I'll want you to teach me if I ever go back to the Valley."

Loríen couldn't let herself even begin to think about what her sister meant by that *if*. "The fool," she fumed instead. "*Useless*."

"If the entire world is full of people this stupid," Lyn said, "then I don't understand how someone hasn't managed to, I don't know, torch the entire place to the ground already."

"They do try," Loríen murmured dryly.

"But Mysia," Lyn observed. "How about that? Good old Sefaro."

Loríen tried not to snarl. "We may all be dead before he arrives."

Reid watched her pace out her frustration, torn between mistrust and the horrible knowledge that Lyn and Loríen seemed to be the only people of reason around him at the moment. The only ones who understood why it was not a good thing that the army was attacking the Telrishti blockade. "I don't know whose orders they think they're under," he growled, "and they probably don't either. The lack of discipline here is appalling."

She stopped pacing. "Who is there left to address? Where can we go?"

He gritted his teeth and adjusted his sword belt on his hip. "Nothing for it but to get out on the water if I have to row myself out in a leaky yoal, and *make* them halt the attack."

Loríen raised her eyebrows, but lacked both the authority and the will to stop him. Someone had to do something. "Let us to it."

Reid scowled, but it was not at all the same kind of scowl she'd been meeting with all night from the men of power in Yeatun. "If you truly mean to help the king, you'll leave this to me."

As much as she wanted to argue, as much as she wanted to be doing something, anything, she had to admit he was right. Her presence and her voice hadn't exactly produced results yet in Yeatun. Not the good sort. She nodded briskly. "I will come with you as far as the harbor," she announced, her tone brooking no argument.

The scowl remained, but he simply grunted what might have been assent before making off down the hallways of the governor's palace.

The streets of Yeatun were even more crowded than Efrondel at Festival, bodies milling together in the darkness waiting to be told what to do with themselves. Instead of music and laughter, the night was filled with fear and the crack of cannon fire over the lake to the west. No one knew what was happening, not even those in charge. It was panic-choked chaos.

The city guard were scuttling about like ants whose hill had been kicked. Loríen didn't bother asking to be let through the gates into the harbor district; she simply pushed past and continued on her way.

"Halt and turn back, ladies," a guard called. "The city is under attack. This is no place for a stroll tonight."

Loríen ignored the warning, but her sister was not so collected.

"Then you'd better be getting home to bed yourself, before you see something that upsets you!" Lyn taunted, preempting whatever Reid had been about to say.

"Oi!" the guard shouted. They could hear his booted footsteps pounding up behind them.

"Vaian's love, Lyn," Loríen said. "*Must* you make everything harder?"

The guardsman caught up to them quickly and made to reach for Loríen's arm. She turned to face him with her chilliest glare.

"You do not want to touch me, Grenlecian."

The guardsman – young, nervous, dark eyes wide in his pale face – fell back with a strangled sound in his throat.

The elves and their Grenlecian companion kept walking.

"Which one of us does things the hard way?" Lyn muttered.

Loríen kept walking until Yeatun harbor lay before them.

On the coast of Evlédíen, nestled safely within a complicated network of fjords cut over many years by the collective effort of the mages of the Valley, the port city of Chastedel looked out at the dawn and the route to Vaian's side. Loríen had visited several times. She loved the fresh sea breeze whipping her hair and the salt spray into her face, the keening cry of the gulls, the sun sparkling on the water, the shifting moody hues of the sea, the soothing rhythm of the surf.

She loved the white marble and the glossy blue tile of the city – the clean, simple lines of the architecture there. She loved the tall ships waiting at harbor; the slow, graceful glide of them when they cut through the water like enormous swans. She loved the way the men of the sea had their own language, their own code, their own relationship with the waters they sailed – a relationship so intimate and yet so casual that she could almost believe the sea itself was a living being.

The harbor at Yeatun was almost entirely unlike Chastedel. Perhaps on another day she might have seen something more familiar, but tonight it was all fire and fear.

Loríen, Lyn, and Reid stood at the harbor wall looking down, where the darkness was periodically pierced by the glow of orange water and coiling smoke when the ships' cannon spoke. Every now and then, the wind shifted just right and a single roaring wave of the shouts of the fighting men drifted across the surface of the lake. The smell of burning was not far behind.

"Well then." The lieutenant squared his shoulders. "Let's see what we can do about clearing up this disaster."

An amused and weary voice came floating out of the night behind them.

"Going for a night swim then, soldier?"

Loríen felt him before she heard his voice and was already turning to face him by the time he spoke. "Naoise!" Her heart suddenly seemed to be trying to jump out of her chest. She didn't even care, for a moment, that she was grinning ridiculously or that she was so happy she wanted to put her arms around him to make sure he was real. Naoise was here and he was visibly unharmed, Cole at his side. She started toward him.

The smile was startled off her face an instant later.

Lyn dashed past her crying a single word. "Cole!" Before the man could reply, Lyn threw herself into his arms and crushed her lips against his.

Loríen stared.

No one was more startled than Cole, who flailed for a moment to regain his balance. Once he was finally able to set her down on the ground in front of him and take a step back, the blank surprise on his face was almost comical.

Loríen turned her gaping stare to Naoise and found him smiling at Cole with one eyebrow quirked. Sensing her eyes on him, he looked at her. She snapped her jaw shut. His smile closed and became something more private, just for her, that left her every bit as confused as she was sure Cole felt.

She cleared her throat carefully and drew herself up into a more dignified posture. "We worried for you both. It is good to see you safe."

"We were never in any real danger," Cole said, not meeting Lyn's eyes.

Naoise laughed. "I'm glad at least one of us thought so." But despite his words, he did seem to be fine. He was still smiling at Loríen.

Reid stepped forward deliberately and cleared his throat. "Sire, shall we do something about this battle I assume you don't want happening?"

The smile disappeared quickly as he offered his lieutenant a brisk nod. "Yes, quite." He turned to his friend. "Cole?"

"I'll stay here, if that's all right," the blond man replied.

Nodding as though he had expected to hear just that, Naoise flicked one last, small smile in Loríen's direction before disappearing down into the madness of the harbor. "Wish us luck."

"I saw the way you looked at him, by the way."

Loríen strained to keep her eyes on Naoise's boat through the darkness and the smoke. "What look is this?"

Lyn clouted her on the arm, not hard enough to bruise but with enough force to show she wouldn't be playing anymore if her sister kept being so obtuse. "You know what look I mean." The wink and nod Lyn followed with were not terribly subtle.

"I do not," Loríen returned stubbornly. She glanced over her shoulder at Cole. Now that Lyn had finally stopped grilling him about his adventure in the Telrishti camp, the man was resting on a freight box and seemed to be putting considerable effort into not paying them any attention. Lyn had seriously rattled him.

Lyn eyed her sister for a moment, gauging whether or not it was worth forcing a fight. She changed tactics. "Don't pretend you weren't happy to see Naoise back safe. I saw your face."

"Of course I was. The Telrishti could have killed him, and it was my plan put him into danger. I have no idea what it is else you suggest."

"Please."

They were both silent for a moment that resounded with distant shouting over the water. Lyn fidgeted with a loose thread on her sleeve.

"I just…" Lyn paused for a moment to choose her words, which was odd enough to demand Loríen's attention. "I want to understand you, but I can't. Refusing to be happy… is this really what our people had in mind with the whole Key-yarns thing? Why is it so important to pretend to be miserable all the time? Can't you just… not?"

Loríen stopped herself short of blurting that she didn't do that and correcting her sister on her carelessly mangled Elven, and considered her answer instead. Was Lyn serious about wanting to understand their people's ways? Or was she just being judgmental again? "There is no pretense, Lyn," she said cautiously, still thinking. "It is different for you. It will be always, I suspect. You may do what things bring you joy, but I…" She made the sign of white surrender with her fingers entwined. She wasn't sure she knew how to explain what she meant in Common without Lyn accusing her of condescension.

"I have duties. When this is over, if we survive, Naoise will be needed in Grenlec and I in Evlédíen."

Her sister scowled. "So? What does that have to do with a minute ago when you wanted to kiss him because you were glad to see him alive? Your guardian isn't here to wag his finger at you. No one cares if you follow all those stupid rules. Why can't you let yourself have even one happy moment?"

Although it seemed like she should be able to, Loríen couldn't think of a response to that.

"I think it's stopped," Cole said behind them.

Loríen realized then that she hadn't heard cannon fire for the past few minutes. She let out a sigh of relief and tried not to think about what Lyn had said as they waited for Naoise to return.

"Dammit, man," Naoise snapped. The Governor of Yeatun bore the rebuke frozen in a half-bow with a brittle smile on his face. "Had you any reason to doubt him when he said I was expecting him?" It was the first time Loríen had ever heard him be sharp with a subordinate, but he wasn't exactly pleased to have returned to the news that Sovoqatsu had arrived at the city gate in his absence only to be imprisoned by the guards there.

Naoise went on instead of allowing the governor to answer him in the way he obviously would have. Loríen was grateful; she'd already heard enough aspersions cast on her kind for one night. "He brings intelligence I am sorely in need of."

"Your Majesty," the governor said, "I would like to extend my apologies over any misunderstanding that may have occurred in regard to your... your allies." He was gripping his marble-topped desk hard with both hands, his plump face going redder by the moment. "It is only my diligence in protecting Yeatun that... If someone had told me to expect... I mean, *elves*, Sire? In this century? How was I to know?"

"You could have trusted my chosen representatives while I was out risking my life for our people's safety," Naoise replied coldly. Loríen had never heard that tone either. "Now tell me of this news from Mysia."

The governor gulped a deep breath. "The courier arrived only last night, Your Majesty. Meant for you, though I'd no idea where to send it. According to the message, the Mysian army is on its way, led by one Lord... Shinju."

Lyn let out a cheer. Naoise glanced at her but quickly returned his grave attention to the other man, who was still sweating under his king's scrutiny.

"How far out and how many?"

The governor had not formulated a response to that when Sovoqatsu entered the office escorted by Reid, and flanked by a humorously large guard detail carrying all of his weapons. Lyn laughed outright, much to the governor's discomfort, but the angry elf looked no worse – or angrier – for the wear of his temporary imprisonment.

"Ah," Sovoqatsu said with a curt nod in Naoise's direction. "You're still alive, then. I trust this farce is concluded and we can be getting on with the business of fighting our actual enemies." He cast a venomous glare at the governor, but seemed to decide addressing that terrified old gentleman was a waste of his time.

"Let me make this plain, Sorley," Naoise said to the governor while Sovoqatsu took his weapons back from the uneasy guards, "since apparently it needs to be said." He inclined his head at Loríen. "This lady and her sister are foreign royalty, and are to be accorded every honor befitting their station. This man–" he clapped Sovoqatsu on the shoulder– "is the princess's escort and trusted agent. And what is more than this, all three are our allies and my proven companions."

The governor dropped his eyes. "Yes, Sire." It was a barely intelligible mutter.

"If I hear a single objection to any of this involving the word elf, you will be divested of your title," Naoise said. "That holds true for every last soul in your employ, down to the lowest rat-catcher. We've been given a second chance with our elven cousins. We'll not begin by being just as viciously wrong-headed as when we left off. Consider Ronan's Law abolished across Grenlec as of this moment. Am I understood, Sorley?"

"Yes, Sire," the governor repeated with a little more life. "I understand." He drew his bulk up into an almost dignified posture and offered Loríen and Lyn both a bow. "I do apologize if you have found my reception previously lacking."

Lyn snorted loudly. "Lacking? What was it *supposed* to be made of?"

Loríen blinked, gathering her thoughts. A part of her wanted to keep the man discomfited for a while; he deserved no less. But she was more mindful of her duties than that. Unfortunately. "Your apology is acceptable."

Sovoqatsu grunted but didn't say anything aloud.

Naoise spared a brisk nod before sinking into a chair across from the governor's desk. He gestured for his friends to find chairs as well. Lyn and Cole were quick to claim the only two plush chairs in the room, on either side of the door, while Reid seated himself closer to his king. Loríen chose to remain standing, taking position beside the desk. She was itching with too much restless energy to relax. Sovoqatsu dragged a chair over from the far side of the room and settled beside her.

"Very good. Now." Naoise frowned at the governor. "Tell me how it goes. We have reached a watchful armistice for the night, out on the water. Are our people in the city quartered and cared for?"

The Governor of Yeatun checked a sigh and offered another half-bow before reclaiming his own seat behind the desk. "We are seeing to it, Sire. Your Majesty has my word, all that can be done is being done. You need not trouble yourself on that front any further."

"That's good, because you have other things to worry about," Sovoqatsu put in bluntly, cutting off Naoise's response. "Kataki is coming on. At the rate they're moving, I estimate no more than seven days before he'll be at Telrisht's back. I can show you on a map where I left them."

Loríen swallowed hard. "How many come with him?"

"Ten thousand," Sovoqatsu reported succinctly. "Thirty-five hundred elves, the rest human mercenaries."

The governor let out something like a whimper.

That was so many more of her people alive than Loríen would ever have guessed possible.

"Could be worse," Reid grunted.

"It's true," Naoise said, "but that doesn't solve our most pressing problem:

how do we stop him using that magic flower to destroy Yeatun as he did Dewfern?"

"Keep him from getting here," Cole suggested.

Naoise nodded. "How?"

"Lanas must be near them," Loríen said. "I will instruct him to harry their progress."

Naoise met her eyes. "Yes, good. And the army: we've got to get them into the city. The walls are nearly bare."

"Shafiq won't like that," Cole pointed out.

"We *have* to convince him we're on the same side," Naoise murmured. "We haven't the time to be eyeing one another like this."

"There's still that flower, though," Lyn said.

Several faces turned to regard Loríen. She resisted the urge to retreat.

"Any chance you can use it – turn it against him?" Lyn asked her.

Loríen's gut churned at the thought. She shook her head. "Even was Katakí not so much stronger than I, he spoke truth when he said I would have not the will if I knew what it is."

Naoise watched her carefully, but said nothing.

"Well then we're jiggered," Lyn declared. "If you can't do anything–"

"We keep him busy," Naoise said quietly, "and we keep him away from Yeatun. And the sooner we can make Telrisht see reason, the more likely we all are to come out of this alive."

Lyn fell back in her chair with a chuckle. "Oh, yeah. We're jiggered."

It was still dark out when Naoise woke almost as exhausted as when he had closed his eyes. He had too much on his mind to allow him any real sleep. He threw on the fresh clothes he'd been furnished with and went for a stroll to shake the sleep dust from his mind. With no clear destination in mind, he allowed his feet to carry him where they would.

Dawn was darkly reddening the clouds on the horizon as he found himself stepping out onto the mansion's rooftop garden. They were common enough in Yeatun, where the urban crowding meant little space for anything green and growing at street level. Even the poorest tenements had functional kitchen gardens on the roof where the sun could reach them. This garden, however, was a wealthy man's well-groomed paradise – useless in practical terms but aesthetically pleasing, even so early in spring, softened by a fine morning mist.

Naoise wandered the main path at a contemplative pace. Even though he couldn't yet see her, he already knew he was not alone in the garden. He didn't know what would happen when he found her. He never did.

The path wound a sinuous line to the eastern parapet, to a clear view of the whole city and the Telrishti camp beyond and the brightening dawn. Loríen was there, relaxing against the wall, gazing down. She turned when his boots made a noise on the gravel path behind her, but after a passing glance she went back to her study of the view. He thought of the entirely different way she had looked at him last night, down by the harbor. All her studied composure stripped away, leaving only the fierce blazing of her joy to see him alive.

His memory was suddenly reaching back through the horror of the past weeks, toward another quiet moment like this one. The tower in Efrondel, a deep winter morning feathered with snow. A stillness that was like a spell, in a time between times. Not so long ago, but everything had been different.

He couldn't find anything to say that felt right, with both moments happening at once within him. Careful of the stillness, and the silence, he came up beside Loríen at the parapet and looked out with her, and said nothing.

She didn't say anything either.

The mist dissipated as the blue of the sky lightened from midnight to pale turquoise. The dawn that unfolded slowly before them then was like iridescent dragonscale from one side of the sky to the other, so beautiful that Naoise knew he would never be able to describe it if he tried. He was simply glad to be seeing it, to be alive, to be sharing it with the one person who mattered most, and to be standing beside her.

Loríen reached out and took his hand in hers.

They watched the chimneys of Yeatun awaken one by one, sounds of life slowly rising to join the smoke of morning cookfires. They watched the vast camp beyond the walls begin to stir with martial order.

Even though no words had been exchanged, Naoise knew that Loríen was watching time happen, watching the night become another day that might be the one to take away everything they had left. He knew she was struggling to deal with the thought of time as fleeting, that every instinct of her nature and her upbringing wanted her to let go of the moment and concern herself with the longer view. That something in her had changed and she was trying to catch up to it.

He could also tell that she was glad to have him there, so close. Another thing that was different.

Naoise turned away from the world below and faced the woman at his side. She returned his steady attention. This moment would never come again, but that was not important. It had become something perfect that would soon come to an end, and they would both carry it with them into these last days. Naoise lifted a hand to her cheek and just held it there, feeling the warmth of her skin. She leaned into his palm.

"I'm sorry." Her voice was so soft that Naoise wasn't sure she had actually spoken aloud.

He gave up on trying to decide which of many things she might mean. "For what?"

She sighed quietly. "That this is all we have."

There was so much Naoise wanted to say to that. Too much. He struggled to put even any of it into words and ended up saying, "I love you."

A small smile pulled at one corner of her mouth. "I'm sorry for that too."

Before Naoise could regret that she still wouldn't say it, or couldn't, she had raised herself onto her toes to kiss him on the mouth. Gently at first, but soon she was giving all of herself to it, and Naoise realized that whether she could say the words or not, she was telling him right now.

He held her close and kissed her as he had wanted to ever since that first day in the forest – long and deep. Unlike their one sad kiss in Mornnovin, this was no farewell. This was simply the present unfolding, and she was right: this was what they had. It wasn't enough, but it was theirs. She pressed herself against him as if she hoped to melt into him; he buried his hands in the dark softness of her hair and breathlessly devoured her lips with his.

Because time had not stopped for them, no matter that it felt otherwise, the spell was broken by the boom of cannon fire. Their faces froze no more than a breath apart as they accepted the reality of this.

Naoise looked at Loríen, at the gentle curve of her cheek, the line of her nose, her arched brow, the parted lips, memorizing it all. Collecting the moment forever. She blinked back at him with a smile so shy and full of regret he wasn't sure he was looking at the Loríen he knew. Slowly, slowly, she drew back, out of his embrace. She held his hand between hers a moment longer before letting that go too.

He sighed unsteadily. Together they went down to the world again, to deal with the latest horrors.

# CHAPTER TWENTY-NINE

As the morning progressed, two things became clear: that Yeatun had been on the verge of collapse before Naoise's arrival, and that General Shafiq did not believe in the threat of an elven sorcerer he had never seen. When he renewed the battery at dawn, his navy also fired on the harbor. The Grenlecian army's vessels had been chosen for speed and were not fitted to give serious battle. Yeatun's guns were well-placed to keep the attacking ships at bay, but that would only be true for as long as their supplies lasted.

Loríen was up on the walls with her sister, Sovoqatsu, and Cole all day amongst the bowmen, spelling out the tired soldiers who had been on duty since the siege began. Naoise was kept running between those who needed him. The few times she caught a glimpse of him, he looked so harried she nearly felt it in her own bones. She had her own troubles, though.

If anyone had ever tried to tell Loríen before today that there was a particular sound to air literally splitting in half, she would have scoffed. She had now stood beside far too many active cannon to call it hyperbole. The only mercy was that her ears were beaten into submission after the first few hours so she stopped really hearing it, but it was difficult to be appreciative with the grit of black smoke choking her lungs.

Sometime after noon, the intermittent mist turned into a steady drizzle of rain, slicking the stones beneath her feet. And the Telrishti kept coming.

Any time Loríen allowed herself to look down at the thousands of tents sprawled across the plain, she was struck by a sense of vertigo. She found herself imagining, against her will, what the sight of that army must have felt like to her people long ago. Imagining the bleak, inescapable realization that there could be no victory. That they were all going to die. She wondered what it must have felt like to the units tasked with keeping that army engaged so that some pitiful remnant of their civilization could escape – the assignment Sovoqatsu had wanted. They would have been acutely aware that their own deaths were assured, but they had fought anyway.

She thought of Naoise, of the look on his face when he agreed to ride into the Telrishti camp in order to distract them while his people fled into the city.

Cole approached the battle with the same stoicism he brought to every task, and after a while Loríen realized why he had to. When she feathered her first few Telrishti miners, knowing she had to do it even though these were potential allies and she needed them on her side, and felt the guilt of those deaths subsumed by the remembrance of everything she knew the Telrishti had done to her people– She had to stop trying to think about what she was doing. It didn't make sense, and the more she tried to figure out how she felt about it, how she *should* feel, the less sense it made.

Though they seemed to be holding the walls for the moment, whatever good they hoped to accomplish, their time for it was almost at an end. No matter how bravely the Grenlecians resisted the assault, the Telrishti were simply too numerous. Sefaro's reinforcements were too far off. The defense of Yeatun might hold out for another day, three at most. If Shafiq could not be convinced to stop the attack by then...

As the sun made its way toward the western horizon and the end of the most exhausting day of her life, Loralíenasa saw Sovoqatsu sinking an arrow into a red-uniformed soldier who unwisely broke cover for the briefest moment. She wove her way through the chaos of bodies and roaring cannon on the walls to reach his side.

"I think we have a job to do, you and I," she shouted into his ear in Elven. "This has to be stopped."

Sovoqatsu returned the arrow he had in his hand to its quiver and turned toward her. He seemed content with whatever he saw in her face because he nodded once. "What about the hídéna?"

She only thought about it for a moment. "We'll need Cole's help to find the general, so there's no getting around her knowing."

Sovoqatsu nodded again. "If you say so. What do we tell Naoise?"

"Nothing." He raised his eyebrow at her. "He's somewhat occupied. It would be wrong to oblige him to abandon his duties to stop us."

"In that case," Sovoqatsu replied briskly, "two questions: how do we get out of the city, and how do we avoid getting killed in the Telrishti camp?"

"Those are excellent questions." Loríen was only marginally deflated. Details. She'd figure it out because she had to. Something had to be done.

The guardsman stared at her, awaiting a more reassuring response.

Getting out of the city would be the easier part, if they waited for cover of darkness. Trickier would be ensuring their safety among the Telrishti long enough to come before General Shafiq. Assuming they were successful. If they weren't, they also had to consider how to get out again alive. In the same way that Telrishti pride had kept Naoise safe after he'd claimed their hospitality, it was as much a surety that when they saw elves they would want them dead. Loríen could even understand. Once you've tried to murder an entire race, self-preservation would make you terrified of the survivors.

If only Loríen still had the Nírozahé. She could use it to make a shield, to protect herself and her friends, so the Telrishti couldn't– But no. Not now that she knew what it was. However, there were other powers in the world.

Yes. It was a remote chance and a mad one, but probably their best.

Sovoqatsu frowned. "You've just had an idea, and I already don't like it."

Loríen smiled back and propelled him by the shoulder, leading him down off the wall. "I daresay you will if it works."

"I can't believe this was your idea," Lyn said to her sister. "I knew you were crazy, but this is out there even for you."

"Wish you'd thought of it yourself?" Sovoqatsu asked with a snort.

Lyn made a face at him in the darkness. "Maybe."

The three of them walked toward the Telrishti camp at an assured pace. The last thing they wanted was to look desperate.

Lyn glanced down at her dress uncomfortably and tried to tug the bodice upward. "But I think this was maybe going a step too far."

Loríen and Sovoqatsu exchanged dry smiles.

"You know that is no fault of mine," Loríen objected.

Her sister mumbled something disgruntled under her breath.

They didn't try to hide as they drew near, and soon they had attracted the notice of the forward sentries. Both men were armed with wicked pikes, and both subjected Lyn and Loríen to a long moment of confused scrutiny.

"Gifts from the Grenlecian king?" the younger one scoffed doubtfully.

The sound Sovoqatsu made in response to that was sufficiently threatening to make both sentries firm up their grip on their pikes.

"We have instruction," the other man said. "The General will entertain no Grenlecian message that is not surrender."

Loríen produced a light globe and held it so that her face was illuminated.

"We are not Grenlecian."

The Telrishti soldiers both took a step back at almost the same time. Their shock lasted only a moment. One of them raised a horn to his lips and sounded a distinct call of warning, then joined his companion in leveling his weapon against the three elves.

"Demons! Turn thee back and leave us in peace," cried the guard who had sounded the warning. "We seek no quarrel with your kind." His eyes, like those of the other guard, were so wide with terror it was a wonder they were still in his head.

"Neither are we demons," Loríen said calmly. "We are elves." She thought it was important to say it out loud at least once so they couldn't pretend. The announcement caused another round of stunned silence.

"Halt and disarm," commanded the more senior guard.

Loríen took a step forward. "We will not."

"Then you will die."

"You will not touch us," Loríen declared. "We would speak with your general. Our purpose is peaceful, but we will defend ourselves if we are forced."

More Telrishti soldiers were hastening to the scene now, weapons at the ready, drawn by the warning call. They stopped in their tracks when they saw that they had been summoned to deal with a party of three – two of them women in fine array. But it was interesting to watch the cascade of delayed reactions when they realized what they were looking at.

"By Ardash, whatever you be, we will not allow you into our camp appointed so," the senior-ranking guard told her, "and you are mad to think it."

"We know too well what Telrisht did to the last elven envoy to willingly disarm," Sovoqatsu rumbled ominously at Loríen's side.

"And I say you shall not pass."

Loralíenasa looked at Lyn. Her sister seemed to be handling the tension well enough. Lyn raised her eyebrows – a question, and Loríen nodded. She gave Sovoqatsu a quick nod as well, and together the three of them walked past the guards into the Telrishti camp. They ignored the many furious cries of "*Halt!*" A pike passed through the air where Sovoqatsu's neck should have been, and he kept walking as though he had not been touched.

Because he hadn't been.

The terrified and enraged Telrishti swarmed about the elves, but they simply kept walking. Lyn laughed.

Loríen did not join in, but she understood the sentiment.

By the time another night fell over Yeatun, Naoise could not recollect when he had last been off his feet. The city's defenses were holding only just barely, morale in sore danger too, his bones and his brains had been rattled by explosions all day, and he knew he desperately needed to eat something before he fell down.

The most terrible thing was that this had nowhere approached being the worst day of combat he had ever seen.

He left Reid in charge and ducked out for a moment of breath and sustenance. As he inhaled some dried venison and the contents of a waterskin in a guardhouse below the wall, he realized that he hadn't glimpsed Loríen in some time. Any of his friends, actually. A swift panic gripped him, which he forced down through an act of will. If Loríen had come to harm, he would have felt it. As for the others, surely he would have been informed.

This wasn't the right place for it, if there was such a thing, but Naoise closed his eyes and tried to find a stillness inside himself. Loríen was there, as she had been since the night he deliberately reawakened their bond. She was alive. He felt a rush of relief.

That relief quickly became something else as he realized that his sense of her felt off in a way he couldn't explain. Not that she seemed to be hurt, just... He sent a questioning thought in her direction and got nothing in return – nothing clear.

Something was wrong.

Naoise was back on his aching feet without hesitation, letting his senses guide him almost blindly through the city, past all the chaos and the crowds. He was only dimly aware that he seemed to be headed back to the governor's mansion. It hardly seemed worth questioning when he realized he was being guided down into the cellar. Then he saw a light.

He was led around the next bend, where he found Cole sitting on the ground with his knees drawn up, his back to a storage room door.

Cole stood quickly when he saw Naoise. The look on his face was decidedly odd.

Naoise made unerringly for the door.

"Wait," Cole said, reaching out to grasp him by the arm. "Just, *wait*."

Naoise looked down at the hand that gripped him. "Cole, you want to tell me just what in the black Void is going on here?"

Cole grimaced. "Don't interrupt them. You can't. Please."

No, too strange. Especially coming from Cole. Naoise shook off his hand and pushed past into the storeroom.

And stared, uncertain what he was looking at.

Sovoqatsu, Lyn, and Loríen were kneeling in the center of the room around one of Loríen's illuminated globes, their eyes closed, all as motionless as if they were deep in sleep with the even breathing to match. And although Naoise could see Loríen right there before him, she felt far away.

He didn't know what prompted him to keep his voice low, but it came out as little more than a whisper. "Cole, what... ?"

His friend's voice was just as cautious. "They're in the Telrishti camp."

Naoise spun to look Cole in the eyes, as if he might find the other man poorly concealing some jest. "*How?*"

Cole met his gaze steadily. "Sun."

It took a moment for that to process through Naoise's battle-weary mind, but when it did, the thought exploded behind his eyes like a blow to the head. "What? The thing that tricked us and sent us into a trap to die?" For the moment it didn't matter that Lyn claimed they'd been visited by an impostor. Whether that was true or not, this was still a being of pure energy and no friend to humans. He surged forward with no clear thought but to carry Loríen away from danger.

Cole grabbed him by the shoulders and pushed him back toward the door. "I don't know what happens to them if you, if you break the spell or whatever it is, but I don't want to find out. Just *wait*."

If it came down to it, Naoise *thought* he could take the former mercenary, but he wasn't sure enough to try it and he had no wish to hurt his friend.

"Cole, this is madness."

"It was Loríen's idea."

Naoise stopped and pushed both hands through his hair. "That doesn't make it a good one. Trusting that fairy is like trusting lightning not to strike."

"*You know I can hear you,*" laughed a voice right beside his ear.

Naoise suddenly found himself staring into complex eyes like snow shadows. He drew a careful breath and forced himself not to back away from the luminous figure now standing before him. "What have you done to them?"

Sun sounded amused. "Done? Nothing. Why would I want to do anything to them?"

"Apparently they asked you to." He tried not to sound impertinent.

The fairy looked down at the three elves and waved a hand vaguely. "They're perfectly safe. All I've done is help them to project their consciousness and likeness remotely to the same location."

Naoise studied all three of them as he tried to make sense of that. They did seem to be fine, physically. It was just too eerie, their utter stillness and the distance he could feel between himself and Loríen despite the fact that she was right in front of him. It was even an interesting idea, but the fairy's involvement made it too unsettling. He chose his words carefully.

"Isn't this rather like interfering?"

"No, no." The fairy shook her head with an almost shark-like smile. "They're the ones taking action. I'm not actually *doing* anything." She shrugged in one sinuous motion. "The rules are flexible, and anyway I can't say the others were too pleased when this renegade elf decided to rework the bones of the world. Some might say we failed our charge. Some might say helping you flesh creatures to stop him from doing it again falls within our appointed function," she added airily in a way that reminded Naoise of Lyn.

He thought about what she was saying. "Some? You mean Loralíenasa called you out?"

Sun smiled again. As suddenly as she had appeared, she was gone.

Cole let out a ragged breath.

"I told you," the Rosemarcher said. "All we can do is wait."

Naoise sighed. "Why didn't you stop them? Or warn me?"

"Didn't have the option," Cole grunted. "It was guard the door or leave them to it. Have *you* ever tried to stop a force of nature?"

*I'm sure the fairy was formidable as well,* Naoise thought sourly as he settled outside the storeroom to keep watch with Cole.

At least he was finally getting a moment of rest.

When they found Shafiq, he was fully armed and armored and on his way to meet the commotion spreading through his camp. Needless to say, he was not in the softest of moods. That was fine. Loríen wasn't trying to make a friend of him.

She was aware, as she stood facing General Shafiq dal Nayil for the first time, that she had never seen a Telrishti before tonight. She didn't know what she had expected, but it was a surprise to look at him and see so much that was like Naoise. And Dairinn, Cole, Sefaro, Mostyn, Reid, Alyra – every decent human she had met since leaving Evlédíen. In the days of the War, she'd been told, Grenlecians had been ruthless in exterminating her kind, but the Telrishti had *enjoyed* it. So the stories said. They were the monsters she had always been taught to fear.

Shafiq was just a man. One who had been fighting for his country for so long that desperation had congealed into a ruthless kind of practicality in him. She had seen the same thing happening to Naoise. This was not a monster, and he was not her enemy. She had been taught wrong, as she had been in so many other things.

It was a disorienting adjustment to have to make.

He drew his sword slowly as he eyed each of them in turn, but he made no immediate advance and gestured for his men to hold their ground. With obvious resistance, he made Loríen as the leader of the group due to her bearing and the richness of the silvery white gown Sun had envisioned for her.

"Word flies through my camp," he said to her, voice as hard as the steel in his hand, "that we are attacked by elves. Some say demons. I confess some relief that I need not to have so many of my men whipped for spreading superstitious falsehoods." He narrowed his eyes at Loríen. "Whom – or what – do I address?"

She held herself proudly, with all the poise of her careful training, ignoring the many soldiers clustered around them. "I am Míyahídéna Loralíenasa Níelor Raia, heir to the kingdom of Evlédíen. This is Hídéna Lyllíen Raia, my sister."

General Shafiq continued to study the three of them. "Evlédíen," he said carefully. "I am not familiar with it."

"That is by design."

His smile was quick and fierce. "So the stories are true: your people survived, despite our concerted efforts to have it otherwise."

Loríen nodded once in acknowledgment.

"Then that Grenlecian cur did not speak entirely in lies," Shafiq went on without a trace of apprehension. She admired his forthright bravery. "And you come now to – demand our surrender? Gloat before drawing closed the trap? You shall have no satisfaction here in either case, by Ardash."

Loríen could feel Sovoqatsu tensing at her side, provoked by the Telrishti's hard-edged bluntness. She put out a hand and gestured for him to ease off. It was better this way.

"We come because you are fools," she said with equal bluntness. Shafiq's lips tightened into a thin and angry line, exposing the gleam of teeth, but she went on. "With the same warning the King of Grenlec tried to offer: your true enemy comes on from the east, and you doom yourselves by spending lives on this siege."

Her words were met by a roar of outrage from those surrounding her who could understand Common.

The General took a step in her direction, sword still in hand, but he made no threat with it. "I told you, lady, gloating will bring you no satisfaction from me. Either kill us or begone."

"If I wanted you dead," Loríen said, "you would be already." She lifted her hand and imagined tongues of blinding white lightning forking across the sky. The illusion that resulted was entirely convincing, if the startled cries of the men were any indication. She'd have to thank Sun if she got the chance.

Shafiq blinked but did not flinch. "What then do you want?"

"To warn you," Lyn said with an exasperated sigh. "She already told you that. Crumbs. You're just as thick as the men back in Yeatun."

If they had actually been standing in the middle of the Telrishti camp, surrounded by tens of thousands of men who wanted them dead, Loríen might have killed Lyn herself for that. As it was, she restrained herself with a great effort and managed not to snap her sister's name.

"Your enemy is an elf named Katakí Kuromé," Sovoqatsu said flatly while Loríen was taking a deep breath, "a veteran of the War of Exile, and a sorcerer. I can assure you he remembers the war vividly, no matter that it was so long ago for you humans. You could keep up the siege and have Yeatun down by the time he gets here, but I suspect you might regret the loss of allies as he's finishing you off. Although I suppose a man has to grasp at what little satisfaction he can get when his death is bearing down on him."

The general looked for a moment as though he wanted to kill Lyn and Sovoqatsu with his bare hands, but after some consideration he drew his head up and narrowed his eyes as he asked, "And why should you wish to warn me of this threat? Why should you not instead join with him and have your vengeance?"

Loríen glared at her companions, silencing them before either tried to answer. "There is no victory in destruction," she said carefully. "I would rather have peace."

Shafiq thought about that, watching her. Weighing her. After a moment, he returned his sword to its sheath as slowly as he had drawn it.

"Grenlecians proposing alliance with Telrisht, elves urging it, while a monster from ancient antiquity comes on to destroy us all with black magic." He shook his head. "It must be sure, these are the strangest times that have ever been lived. What is a soldier to believe but what stands before him?"

Loríen did her best not to show her relief, to look back at him with only the steady confidence that she had known he would come to see reason.

The general brought his hands together over his heart and nodded once, brusquely. "On behalf of my master the great Ayiz, Princess, I declare peace between us and ours until our common enemy is vanquished."

She returned the nod. "And beyond, I hope." If there *was* a beyond. If Vaian was kind.

They all came back to their small closet in the same moment, blinking at one another in the silvery glow of Loralíenasa's light sphere.

"I didn't think that was going to work," Sovoqatsu announced. He climbed to his feet and began to stretch pragmatically.

Lyn rolled backward and sprawled on the flagstones in her relief. "I knew Sun wouldn't let me down. Just don't ever make me wear a dress again," she added with some heat in Loríen's direction. "That was ridiculous."

"And not my doing," Loríen retorted. She allowed herself to smile. Their mission had met with even better success than she had hoped for, and no one had been hurt. It almost made her believe they might not all die horribly by Katakí's hand.

The storeroom door burst open and Cole came pushing in with Naoise at his side – Naoise, whom they had left out of this particular enterprise. He hauled Loríen to her feet by her shoulders in a Dairinn-like manner and pulled her into a quick, trembling embrace. After a moment he held her out at arm's length and studied her with concern tightening all the planes of his pale face.

She stood awkwardly stiff until he let her go again, then put a generous step between them. She couldn't say she was used to people feeling like they could just handle her if they wanted to, or that she liked it. Their moment together on the roof of the mansion was beside the point.

"Loríen, thank the Father you're safe, but I could just kill you," he bit off sharply. "I can't *believe* you would do something like this without at least discussing it with me first. Don't you think I might have liked to have a say?"

She narrowed her eyes at his imperative tone. "I am no subject of yours, Your Majesty," she said. "I am not answerable to you." Instantly regretting the way that made his mouth twist unhappily, she added, "You were engaged elsewhere. How are you here, even?"

Naoise's frown deepened. "You *know* I could tell something was wrong."

Sovoqatsu finished his stretches and spoke before Loríen could respond to that. "The Telrishti general would speak with you," he said to Naoise. "Not that he is pleased about the necessity. He really doesn't like you."

"My favorite thing about you," Lyn said sunnily, sitting up, "is your special way with words."

The guardsman made a gesture that Loríen was glad her sister was not familiar with. "Do keep talking. Your contributions are always so profound."

Cole cleared his throat. "So it worked? The general believed you?"

Loríen looked at him, and at Naoise. She didn't like the way either of them were looking back at her. "He did. He had little choice."

Lyn chuckled at that.

"*Va geléias*," Loríen said softly when Naoise continued to frown. His left eye twitched. She wanted to put her hand on his arm to reassure him, but she didn't.

He let out a careful breath. "Would the rest of you mind terribly if I asked for a moment alone with Loríen? Please?" He gave Lyn the courtesy of a small, apologetic smile, but returned his too-intense and deeply unamused attention to Loríen almost immediately.

Cole went for the door right away, wrapping one hand firmly around Lyn's arm and dragging her with him. The girl exclaimed indignantly but did not struggle. Sovoqatsu studied the Míyahídéna and the King of Grenlec for a moment with narrowed eyes before following, closing the door audibly behind him.

"Whatever there is to talk about right now," Loríen said to him in Elven, "you should be discussing with Shafiq. He is open to strategizing with Grenlec to bring Katakí down, and awaits your thoughts. We're wasting time."

Naoise stared at the racks of stored domestic goods behind her head, his lips pressed into a tight line as he composed his thoughts. When he did look at her, his expression was too complex a mixture for her to read. Worry. Anger. Disappointment. Stony resolve. Something warmer underneath, that just left her confused. His eyes were that subdued shade of purple they darkened to when he was at his most solemn.

"I know why you did it," he said in her language. "I know why you felt you had to, risky though it was. What I cannot understand is why you did it without me."

The simple, wounded accusation in his voice sent her heart down into her boots. She swallowed, and swallowed again.

He closed the distance between them slowly, giving her time to accept his nearness. She was all too aware of what had passed between them the last time they had been so close. "For good or ill," he said, voice still pitched low, "we *are* in one another's lives. Whatever may come of it. This morning I thought you had accepted that. I did a long time ago. You don't have to do this alone, Loríen. You're *not* alone."

"I'm sorry," she said again, and meant it. Naoise hadn't used the word *betrayal*, but she could feel it hovering in the charged space between them. The look on his face was almost more than she could stand. She took a deep breath and tried to find words that would make it all clear to him.

"When my parents died, when Tomanasíl took me in…" No, too much self-pity in that approach.

The fact was, Loralíenasa had been raised to be solitary. To know that she would always be surrounded by people who would want something from her because of who she was, and that she could trust none of them. That it would always be her responsibility to know best and she could rely on no one's judgment but her own. But if the past months had taught her anything, it was how wrong, how frail she really was. How much she needed other people, how much they all needed each other.

She tried again. "I *have* been alone. Do you understand? All my life, it has been only me. It's hard to remember anything else."

Naoise blinked, the disappointed grief in his eyes mingling with something else she was hesitant to name because she'd never seen it before. "You're not alone," he repeated. "Please don't treat me like you are. I exist."

It was like a slap, even though he had said it softly.

"Listen to me carefully, Loríen," Naoise said when she didn't answer him. "Remember *this*." He took her hand in his and held it flat against his chest, where his heart was pounding beneath his doublet. He didn't explain what he meant, but he didn't have to.

*I am alive,* his heartbeat told her. *I am here. I am yours.*

Loríen didn't tell him again that she was sorry, not out loud, but she made a decision in that moment. She took his other hand and held it, forcing herself to accept the contact, the warm rough feel of his skin and the strength in his lean musician's fingers. The heat of his energy flowing into her, hers rushing out to meet it. His physical reality. He had a scar across his second knuckle, a raised white line that stood out in sharp relief when his fingers curled around hers. She drew a deep breath and let it out slowly.

She wasn't alone.

# Chapter Thirty

Not for the first time nor the last since winter, Lanoralas Galvan wished he had Loralíenasa by his side. Midnight operations against a superior foe would have been a marginally less daunting prospect with his best and most determined fighter there beside him. He simply had to make do. He'd been carrying the Valley onward through the sheer force of his will since she'd left anyway; Lord Maiantar had been in no state to do it.

It was a grim sort of darkness that night, the moon and stars all veiled in cloud. A storm had rolled in at the end of the day, making for a dramatic, apocalyptic sunset. Now the sky was charged and heavy, promising rain that had yet to fall and probably lightning too. The Captain was too level-headed to be swayed by signs and superstition, but it seemed like the kind of night on which fates could be decided.

Well, if that were so, he'd grit his teeth and get on with making it happen. He gave the signal, and his men advanced.

Their target was located at the center of the encampment, so they had a bit of doing to get to it without being seen, but Lanas' soldiers were well-trained. Kataki had made no effort to hide the giant stone chair's presence or its importance. It was so massive that the wagon carrying it had to be pulled by eight workhorses, and in fact was solely responsible for the tortoise-like pace at which the entire army had been forced to travel.

They dealt swiftly with the black-clad sentries. Lanas took one of them out himself – a quick cut across the throat from behind while ignoring all possible feelings about what he was doing – because he didn't think he could fairly ask his soldiers to kill their own kind otherwise.

There was a unit protecting the wagon, even in the dead of night. Far more of them than Lanas had expected, but not enough to be a problem. He crouched in the darkness as his soldiers silently encircled the guards, waiting until he felt the slight prickling in the back of his mind that told him his second-in-command had just spoken his name into his tracking glass.

"*Íyéda*," he whispered back into hers.

Fifty arrows left fifty bows in the same moment; as many guards fell into the dust around the stone chair.

Lanas was the first one up and running toward the wagon, his soldiers right behind. He bent to the nearest fallen guard, checking for a heartbeat. Nothing. He saw the man to his right finishing off one of the downed Mornnovini elves with quick efficiency. Up close, the chair was even more alarming than it had been from afar. It was dark and massive and blunt, radiating an awful sense of power even the Captain was not senseless to, looming over the entire encampment from its position at the heart of it. He was happy to do his part in keeping this terrible instrument out of the battle.

They worked quickly. The wagon was up in a tower of flames and Lanas' soldiers already sprinting for the horse enclosure before their presence in the camp had been noticed. Which was all to the good, since he had no desire to find out what Katakí could do to them with his magic if they lingered.

The camp erupted into a riot of shouting soldiers running in all directions – to put out the flames, to catch the intruders – as Lanas' troops reached the horses. The time for stealth was over and it was now all about speed.

First to hit the line of guards at the enclosure, Lanoralas tore through the defense and came at them from behind, pinning the enemy between two relentless assaults. The twenty men tasked that night to guard the army's mounts never saw another dawn. Lanoralas and his soldiers drove the horses of Mornnovin out of the enclosure, scattering them to the wilderness and following close behind.

They left behind a camp in disarray, thousands of angry voices, and the glow of firelight filling the night.

The day had bled relentlessly into a night that seemed just as unwilling to quit. Although he would never have complained of the turn in their fortune, Naoise nevertheless did wish it could have fallen to anyone's lot but his to ride back to the Telrishti position to speak with General Shafiq. Or, failing that, that the meeting could have waited until morning.

But of course the sooner they agreed upon a plan, the more likely it was that some of them might survive.

Naoise did his duty and then came back into Yeatun ready to have his first sleep in some time.

But before that.

He stood in front of a certain door, hesitating to knock. It was quite a nice door, he observed instead of unpacking the reasons for his hesitation. Ironwood, decorative silver banding, an actual locking mechanism and not merely a latch. Either every door in the palace was this expensive, or Sorley had given the princesses a properly well-appointed room.

He squared his shoulders and knocked.

"Yeah?" Lyn's voice was muffled by the weight of the wood.

Walking away was still an option, and probably better than shouting his business out in the hallway for any passerby to hear. He would simply wait until morning. The results of his talk with Shafiq would not change if he delivered the news a few hours later.

The door opened suddenly in his face.

Naoise blinked in surprise at Sovoqatsu, who peered down at him for only a moment before opening the door wider without a word. He saw then that Cole was also in the room, sitting on the floor close to the fireplace with his back against the side of an armchair; Lyn was above him, curled up in the chair. Loríen was nowhere to be seen.

He was about to ask what was going on, but Sovoqatsu surprised him again by answering the unspoken question as he closed the door.

"The Captain was to stage his incursion tonight, but there has been no word yet. We're still waiting."

Lyn must have seen him looking, because she grinned a little mischievously as she said, "Loríen'll be back in a minute. She was getting – you know the way she gets when she's trying to hide how nervous she is. So she went to have a bath."

That was exactly the kind of distracting information Naoise did not need. "Thank you," he murmured. He found a place to sit where neither of the two beds were in his line of sight. This left him close to the fireplace, across from Lyn and Cole. Sovoqatsu remained lurking somewhere near the door.

"I've been trying to get Cole to tell me what happened when you two went into the Telrishti camp," Lyn said, "but his version is boring."

"That's because I'm boring," the blond man below her said flatly. Naoise couldn't tell whether or not he meant it in jest.

Lyn sighed. "I mean, you didn't have to fight your way to the general's tent or anything?"

"If we'd had to do that," Naoise said, "we'd both be dead now. You cannot imagine how many men *twelve thousand* is until you're surrounded by all of them and each one is armed."

Somewhere in the shadows, Sovoqatsu made a sound that might have been agreement or amusement.

The princess leaned toward Naoise restlessly. She was wearing pajamas that consisted of an overlarge red linen tunic and drawstring trousers that she must have demanded of the governor's people. "See, that's already more exciting than the way he tells it."

A look of something that wasn't annoyance flitted briefly across Cole's face, but it was gone before Naoise could decide what he'd just seen. The only thing he could tell for certain was that Cole wished he dared do more than sit at Lyn's feet – but that had been developing for such a long time and seemed so unlikely to go anywhere that it was hardly notable. Naoise could just imagine the objection Cole would raise if Naoise ever tried to talk to him about it. Something about not dishonoring the only promise he had ever made.

The door opened suddenly and Loríen stepped through. If she was at all surprised to see so many people invading her room, she gave no sign. Her hair was wet and she wore pajamas similar to Lyn's, in black.

"Feel better?" Lyn asked.

Loríen's movements were slow and methodical as she set her boots and clothing down out of the way. "I did," she replied evenly, "until I found a party taking place in the room where I am meant to sleep."

A plump pillow went sailing across the room in Loríen's direction. "You're as boring as Cole," Lyn declared.

The Míyahídéna easily evaded the clumsy projectile.

"You know why we're here," Sovoqatsu said unexpectedly.

Loríen turned toward Sovoqatsu. Whatever was in her face, Naoise had no view of it.

"And that didn't sound at all ominous," Lyn said with a snort.

"I have had no word," Loríen said to the imposing soldier. "But I–"

They all leaned forward at exactly the same moment when she cut herself off, tension straightening every line of her body as though she'd been dealt a blow. Her hand darted into her pocket and emerged again holding something small that caught the light as she turned it over.

Naoise stood abruptly, taking an uncertain step in her direction. "Loríen?"

She did not look up. "It is Lanas," she confirmed. "Yes, I'm here," she added in Elven at the shining thing in her hand. "No, I'm with the others."

The King of Grenlec stood frozen in place as he came to understand that he was again in the presence of magic and the unexplainable. He had a moment of cornered panic when she looked up at him and, beckoning, said, "Lanas says you may want to hear this too."

Sovoqatsu grunted.

Naoise hesitated, but she kept her eyes steadily on him until he forced himself to move. She indicated that he should stand beside her, which he did in full if distracted appreciation of the fact that she had invited him to do so. She was warm and her hair smelled of lavender soap. A moment later he felt himself being crowded in by the others as they tried to stand close enough to also see what she held in her hand.

Looking down, Naoise saw that the item she held was – or appeared to be – a mirror small enough to fit in her palm. The frame was ash wood, carved into a spare but beautiful knot pattern. Only, instead of their reflections, looking back at him from the glass surface was the visage of Loríen's friend the Captain of the Guard.

The elf's handsome face was smudged with what might have been soot, and the remembered good humor had been replaced by sober, professional intensity. It was impossible to make out his surroundings, but they were dark, and there was a sense of many other presences close about him.

"I understand I am to call you Your Majesty now," the image of Lanoralas Galvan said out of the mirror.

Naoise was uncertain where he could hear the elf's voice – inside his mind, or projected from the glass, it was impossible to tell. Whatever the case, when the face in the mirror spoke, Naoise could hear and understand him as clearly as if they had been standing face-to-face in the same room. Some part of him was deeply concerned, but a corner of his mind was busily calculating all of the many possibilities that could be opened up by being able to communicate instantaneously over vast distances.

He mastered his discomfiture and made himself speak into the mirror, ignoring the oddity of the fact that he was doing so. "You need not call me anything, Captain. I don't feel much of a king, and we've more than enough to be getting on with."

The image of Lanas smiled, a quick quirk of the lips, but the sober concentration never left his eyes. "Well. To it, then."

Loríen cleared her throat. "You made the attack on the encampment?"

A single, brisk nod. "And the news could be worse, but it's not good."

"Yes?" Naoise and Loríen both said it at the same time, and both resisted the impulse to look at one another when they did.

Lanas frowned. "We destroyed the wagon used for transport of the throne, and we scattered the horses."

"But that's excellent news!" Naoise said, wishing he dared to be excited about such a positive turn in their fortunes. Without the wagon or horses, Mornnovin's progress would come to nothing for several days at least. Possibly time enough for Mysia to reach Yeatun with reinforcements.

"And yet," Loríen said, "you are not pleased, so all did not go to plan."

The Captain nodded again while Naoise looked to Loríen, mutely asking for clarification.

"We planned for Lanas and some quantity of his men to get themselves captured," she explained, "in order to have someone inside when we make our move."

Annoyance surged through him that Loríen would dispose of one of their few assets without discussing the scheme with her allies first, but this was hardly the moment to revisit the subject of her bullheaded way of making unilateral decisions. And, he realized, she was Míyahídéna and he hadn't the right to tell her what to do with the lives of her own men. Instead he addressed the face in the mirror. "But?"

"They never gave chase."

Naoise thought about that for a moment.

"They just let you come in, burn their wagons, and walk out again?" Loríen asked incredulously.

"They resisted us," Lanas answered, "but when we fled, they let us go. We came in on foot so they would be able to follow, even without their mounts, but they just... didn't."

"They let you go?" There was something in Loríen's voice like the threat of distant storm clouds.

The Captain nodded briskly, a military confirmation. "It certainly felt that way. And they seemed driven by no urgency to recover the horses, either."

Naoise did not like the sound of that at all. Loríen, too, was silent in contemplation.

"I know I don't need to tell you how dire this news is," Lanas added.

Loríen was close enough to Naoise that he could feel it when she started shaking. "If Katakí doesn't care that he has lost his transportation," she vocalized, "he must already be near enough to destroy us all if he chooses."

No one said anything for a moment.

It was Lanoralas who broke the silence, stating a thought he'd obviously been weighing since the raid, "We must ask ourselves, then, why he hasn't. What is he waiting for?"

"Íyaqo," Loríen said, suddenly sounding exhausted.

Naoise looked at her and saw it in her face. He closed his eyes. "We are very foolish."

"Mysia," Lanoralas said. Naoise couldn't tell if he was just figuring it out along with them, or if he was tactfully hiding the fact that he had come to this painfully obvious conclusion already. "He wants all of us in one place."

"Íyaqo," Loríen said again, more quietly.

Suddenly Naoise felt her free hand squeezing his, offering reassurance, seeking it back. He returned the pressure.

It was what Katakí had always wanted, Naoise realized. Why he had driven them all toward a moment where the gathered might of three human kingdoms would be all together in the field. One catastrophic event, and all major resistance would be broken forever. All that would remain for him to do would be cleanup.

"Would one of you mind explaining what's going on and why you look like you're going to toss your baked goods?" Lyn said with less bluster than she'd probably intended.

Naoise gave a succinct summary. Cole swore just as efficiently.

"I don't suppose any of you have a backup plan," Lanoralas said, moving the world onward from the moment. "Our time is no longer even measured in hours."

Naoise smiled wryly. "This would be the ideal time for one, wouldn't it?"

"There is nothing else to be done," Loríen said in Common, her voice so soft now that Naoise wondered if she meant for any of them to hear her. "I will go to Katakí's camp and surrender. Let him take me into the Nírozahé. I will destroy it from within."

Several voices stated an emphatic *no* at the same time.

Naoise added, urgently, "If such a thing were possible, don't you suppose any one of the countless other souls trapped in there would have done it already?"

"Yes, exactly," Sovoqatsu said.

"No," Loríen replied simply. "They would have had to know what had happened, what was *happening* to them. They would have needed the will to do it, to fight back." She turned to Naoise and blinked slowly. "I know what it is I fight for and why."

Naoise shook his head, swallowed. Struggled to speak despite the sudden pounding of his heart. "Captain, would you give us a moment, please?"

Even through the device, Naoise could feel Lanoralas' skepticism, but then the elf's image faded and the glass showed Naoise's own face – his features all tight and stress-hardened. He hardly recognized himself anymore.

He swallowed again. "You're talking about dying."

"It is all right." Her voice was so calm he wanted to scream. "I was always willing to die for this."

"It's not all right!" Lyn screeched in the same tone Naoise himself was struggling not to use. "Are you *insane?*"

Cole was shaking his head.

"No," Naoise said. "I'm *done* losing the things and the people I care about. The line is *here*." He ignored the sudden threat in Sovoqatsu's eyes, focusing only on the woman before him. Despite her sudden trembling, she was as difficult as ever to read. "I love you. Loríen, *I love you*. I am not willing to lose you too."

She sighed, a sound of utter exhaustion. "You never had me."

"You're wrong," he replied as steadily as he could. "You are in me." He laid his hand over his heart. "And you have me as well."

Even as Loríen parted her lips to respond to that with what he could see would be another denial, an indescribable sound came out of Lyn, drawing everyone's attention. Her cheeks were aflame with color and her eyes blazed with triumph to match. Her entire body was nearly vibrating.

"Great god of goatswains," Lyn breathed. She grabbed Naoise by the front of his doublet and pulled him down to plant an excited kiss on his brow. "Naoise, you're a genius. *I've just realized what we have to do.*"

He took a long bath, for once glad to be king because it meant no one dared hurry him. As Naoise soaked in the blessedly scalding hot water, allowing the heat to work at the ache of his weary body, he forced his mind to seek a state of absolute emptiness. If he did not, he knew, he would inevitably be thinking of Lyn's insane plan. He didn't have the strength for that right now. He just needed to sleep, and forget everything until morning forced him to confront it again.

They would do it. Of course they would. They had no other choices. But what she proposed…

No. Not until morning.

When he climbed out of the bath eventually and wrapped himself in a plush robe, he felt blissfully loose-limbed and drowsy. Maybe he didn't have much sleep ahead of him tonight, but what he did have would be deep and dreamless. He dismissed his valet with relish.

*Bed.*

Then he registered that he was not alone in his room after all.

He felt strangely lightheaded as his body tried to decide whether it was suddenly energized by the sight of Loralíenasa sitting on the edge of his bed in her pajamas, or whether that was simply one thing more than he had the strength to handle at the end of this intolerably long day. He swayed on his feet.

She stood up once he had noticed her. Her hair and skin glowed in the fire-light and she was watching him with intense focus, as if she wasn't sure whether he might vanish if she blinked.

Naoise swallowed. He stood rooted in place by the door, tongue cleaving to his palate, simply absorbing the fact of her presence. He wanted to tell her everything in his heart, but he also didn't want to speak. She seemed more likely to vanish than he was. Still watching him with that careful attention, Loríen crossed the room to stand well within reach. He saw the muscles flex in her throat as she swallowed, and knew she was not as calm as she appeared.

"You're tired," she said in Elven after a long silence. There was disappointment in her voice though she spoke quietly, and the sound of it – of what that meant – nearly caused Naoise to forget to breathe.

"To the marrow," he replied carefully.

He bent his head to press his lips to hers.

She made a small sound against his mouth that might have been surprise, but he quickly felt one of her hands clenching in his hair tight enough to set his scalp tingling. Her tongue was delicate but insistent against his lips until he parted them, and then it was soft as it caressed his. Naoise groaned when it became clear what she was saying, what she wanted. He held her body against his, almost drunk with the feel of her and the realization that they were alone, together, within reach of his bed, that she wanted him, and that there was nothing to stop them from having one another here and now.

Almost nothing.

He broke the kiss slowly, with such reluctance he could hardly make himself do it. Touching his brow to hers, trembling, he sighed and made himself say, "I would pretend otherwise if I could, but I simply haven't the energy for what I'd most like to do right now." There was no way he would permit their first time making love to be the tired, desultory affair it would be if he attempted anything tonight. "It's just never the right time for us, is it?"

Loríen didn't say so aloud, but he could clearly see in her face that she believed this was their last chance. She drew a careful breath. "Then I'll leave you to your rest. We have much to do tomorrow."

Naoise wanted to tell her not to go. The moment wasn't right, but it wouldn't be their last. There was no way in the Father's creation he would permit that, not after how far they had come to get here together. He cupped her cheek in the palm of his hand. "This is not the end."

Her answering smile did not touch her eyes. She put her hand up to brush against his, briefly, but then she withdrew and turned away. Naoise watched her go, calling her back to him in his mind.

"Wait. Loríen." He only realized he'd said it aloud when she stopped and turned slowly back to him. He crossed the distance to her. "Wait." He caught her hand gently. It trembled in his.

She looked up at him, her expression carefully revealing nothing, but the bond between them had grown so strong that she could not hide her mingled excitement and apprehension. He also knew, as surely as he knew he loved her, that this might actually be their last moment alone together. In the morning they would set Lyn's utterly mad and bold plan in motion, and it would quite possibly kill Loríen and maybe the rest of them too, but would save the world if it worked.

"If I don't have another chance to say this, I want you to hear it now." He swallowed and searched for words that would be good enough; she watched him expectantly. "I have never known anyone more brave than you. Your courage shames me, and inspires me, and I count it an honor to have fought at your side. If you do not think me too presumptuous, and choose to accept, I believe you have earned another name: *Nuvalinas*."

She blinked at him for a moment, and he knew she was struggling to conceal great emotion. He wished she didn't feel like she had to, but he understood why she did. Her voice was so soft it was almost like a prayer as she murmured the ritual response to the naming, accepting what he had given. "*Loralíenasa Nuvalinas Níelor Raia*." She kept blinking, and now he could see she was genuinely struggling against a shining dampness at the corner of her eyes.

He smiled and pretended not to notice. "By the Father, what a mouthful," he teased.

"I've learned something valuable from Lyn," Loríen replied, also ignoring her almost-tears.

His smile invited her continue.

"The proper response to that," she explained, and cuffed him playfully on the shoulder.

Despite the gravity of their situation and the genuine fear Naoise had over Lyn's mad plan, he felt his heart lightening as Loríen smiled and walked out of his room wearing her new name with a pride that showed in her step.

There was no approaching the camp undetected by the watchful ring of sentries, and Sovoqatsu did not try it. He rode up directly to what looked like the main ingress, second horse and cargo in tow, and addressed the suspicious sentries in steely tones.

"My name is Sovoqatsu Zimají Farínaiqa. I bring a gift for Lord Kuromé."

In his right hand he carried an exquisite elven sword, crafted by a master for a master, and the most famous bow in their people's history.

That was not the gift.

"You treacherous toad! You slime from the underside of a rotten compost heap!" Lyn spat at him from the second horse. Her hands were bound and tied to the horn. Behind her, senseless and draped across the saddlebow, Loralíenasa said nothing at all. "When I get loose you're going to wish your parents never oozed in each other's direction across the sucking swamp that spawned you."

Sovoqatsu spoke curtly without bothering to look in her direction. "Be silent or be silenced." The deadly glint of his black eyes never wavered.

One of the two sentries vanished into the camp and returned a few moments later with a third elf, who gestured Sovoqatsu forward without speaking. This was no mere sentry, the quality of his kit and the authority with which he moved making clear that this was an experienced warrior who commanded respect within the encampment. More than an assassin. This was Katakí Kuromé's general, his second-in-command.

He was nearly as starkly white as Loríen, with the focused and dangerous look of a man who knew that he existed for no other reason than to end lives and wanted nothing else. He wore the same black uniform of the assassins that had followed them out of Evlédíen, but he had on black leather armor as well, intricately tooled with sharp, aggressive patterns. The sword at his back was an antique but it was not for show.

A crowd of elves followed their progress in near silence – but only elves, he noticed. The human mercenaries were absent, deployed into battle, only the elven warriors remaining behind to protect their lord. Sovoqatsu had passed the army on his way here; they would surely be at Yeatun soon if they were not already.

Despite the departure of the human contingent, the dimensions of the camp made for a long, tense journey to the far side of center. Sovoqatsu could see the pavilion that was their destination from a long way off. It was enormous, round, with red walls and a black top like a great scorched hole in the sky, the avenging eagle flag of Mornnovin flying at its pinnacle.

He dismounted while his guide disappeared through the tent flap. The trailing crowd of elves lingered, watching with more curiosity than suspicion but a fair dose of both. Katakí's dangerous-looking second remained in the pavilion for some time before coming out again.

"Lord Kuromé will see you." The warrior flicked his eyes in the direction of Sovoqatsu's second horse. "And he will receive your gift."

Without a word, Sovoqatsu loosed the hídéna from the saddlebow and pulled her down ungracefully onto her feet. She spat on his boots and tried to kick him in the shin, but she did not have her proper balance and was easily evaded. Katakí's man took hold of the rope binding her hands and waited while Sovoqatsu slid Loralíenasa's limp body from the saddle onto his shoulder like a sack of barley.

They went into the pavilion together.

As with the castle in Mornnovin, Sovoqatsu did not find what he expected inside. They stood in a vestibule cut off from the rest of the interior by thick walls of some beautiful material in autumn tones, shot through with leaf patterns in a muted gold. The fabric was so heavy that it blocked all light from the adjoining rooms completely, and the camp sounds without were nearly inaudible. Colored glass sconces – decorative glass, in the field – worked into the shape of artificial flames cast a muted glow over the chamber. The floor of the tent was covered in a plush dark rug. Once his eyes had adjusted to the sudden low light, Sovoqatsu saw that the intricate stylized pattern was meant to replicate the detritus of a forest floor. The decadent affectation set him instantly on edge.

"This way," Katakí's general said, and led him through a pair of curtains into the next room. This turned out to be a hallway of sorts, formed of the heavy fabric hangings, which wound and twisted its way toward the pavilion's heart. With every step he took, through more partitions, Sovoqatsu felt himself more removed from the reality of the encampment outside and the battle beyond – engulfed more fully by Kataki's will or his imagination or perhaps actually his magic. He breathed carefully and did not grind his teeth.

They passed through another pair of curtains. Kataki Kuromé was on the other side.

They only found the camp, Naoise realized, because Captain Galvan allowed them to. The force from Evlédíen was small enough, and the elves skilled enough, that their presence in the near vicinity of Kataki's army was all but undetectable.

Three elves in mottled green and brown leather armor appeared from what seemed to be nowhere, rising up suddenly from the brush almost within striking distance as Naoise and Cole searched out the coordinates they'd been given. Two of them had arrows nocked and drawn.

Naoise's horse gave a surprised whinny and took a hopping step back. A startled oath slid from Naoise's lips as well. Cole kept his mount under control with a stern hand.

"Peace," Naoise said quickly in Elven. "We are looking for Captain Galvan. He should be expecting our arrival."

"Yes," answered the elf who did not have an arrow trained on them. "That is why you still live and why you see us standing before you." She did not sound particularly friendly, but being fair she didn't sound hostile either. Naoise reminded himself that it was simply their way and she likely meant nothing by it – they *wanted* to be difficult to read.

"In that case," he said mildly, "perhaps the arrows are unnecessary?"

The elf gestured and her companions lowered their bows. "You will understand the need for caution. The enemy is near, and our presence is still punishable by death in these lands." She turned without another word and started to lead the way onward.

Naoise glanced over at Cole, who shrugged and dismounted, and followed the three elves on foot.

"You might like to know," Naoise said when he had caught up to the elf sentry, "that edict has recently been revoked."

She gave him an inscrutable look and kept walking. Her eyes were aggressively, opaquely copper and told him nothing.

"But yes, of course, the need for caution is clear," he added, still striving for a casual tone. He already didn't like this plan. Every moment they came closer to it only intensified his concerns.

Their guide said nothing to that either.

The camp they would never have found on their own was nestled in amidst a stand of dark basalt outcroppings and low-clinging shrubs. It was clear the force was on the verge of action, armored and busy with final preparations. They found the Captain inspecting another soldier's armor as they approached; he finished the task and sent the other elf on her way before turning to greet them.

"Your Majesty," the tall Captain said with a brisk nod that was frankly more honorific than Naoise expected. "You found us. Good." He also offered Cole a nod, looking a good deal more serious – and more dangerous – than he had during their time imprisoned together. He seemed to have put on, or perhaps revealed, a calm and lethal competence that he wore as naturally as the sword at his back.

Suddenly Naoise understood Lorien's unquestioning confidence in him.

He returned the nod. "It's good to see you again, Captain, on the right side of a prison door."

Lanoralas flashed a quick and sober smile.

"The moment is near, I think," Naoise said. "Tell me where I may set up. Cole will stay by me; you need not spare any of your men on my protection."

The Captain nodded and gestured with his head for Naoise to follow him. His strides were long and purposeful, the tail of ash blond hair at his nape flowing behind him as he moved. "These rocks have been good cover," he said. "They should serve you well when we move out." He showed Naoise to a hollow on the north face of one of the basalt crags, out of the direct sunlight and well-hidden.

"Perfect," Naoise murmured. He realized that his lips felt stiff and his heart was pounding. He had started to shake, unmistakably. He was terrified and there was no way to pretend otherwise.

*I can do this*, he told himself carefully. *It's going to work. I trust her. I trust them all.*

Lanoralas must have noticed his trembling but he said nothing of it, simply offered one last nod. "I must return to my preparations." He hesitated. "May Vaian guide and protect you on your way."

"And you on yours," Naoise replied.

The Captain saluted smartly, then disappeared behind the outcropping.

Naoise drew a deep breath.

Cole gripped him by the shoulder. "You can do this," he said, echoing Naoise's own reassurance. "I'm convinced you could do anything."

That took Naoise by surprise. The other man stared back at him steadily, refusing to allow any doubt that he had meant it.

The King of Grenlec drew another unsteady breath and settled into the spot Lanoralas had shown him, sitting with his legs crossed, protected from view by the dark basalt mass. Cole took up a watchful position nearby.

"Well then," Naoise said, closing his eyes. "Shall we make a miracle?"

# Chapter Thirty-One

It was dark and close inside the pavilion, mere feet away from the most powerful sorcerer in the world. Sovoqatsu had an uneasy sense that he was standing inside the innermost chamber of an enormous beating heart; he shook off the fanciful notion with an actual angry shake of his head. This was no time for nonsense.

Without ceremony, he threw Loralíenasa Nuvalinas Níelor Raia, heir to the throne of Evlédíen and the Raia legacy, onto the dark rug at Katakí Kuromé's feet. One of her eyes was swelling shut and dark blood trickled from her nose and mouth. She groaned and lay still. Beside her he deposited her magnificent sword, Líensu, and the great white bow of Éhaia Raia before taking Lyn's rope from the hands of Katakí's man and pushing her to her knees at her sister's side. The Mornnovini general stepped back until he almost disappeared against the heavy fabric wall and stood there looking as menacing as Sovoqatsu ever did.

Katakí Kuromé watched these proceedings with what seemed like mild curiosity, half hidden behind a table that was piled high with maps and various trappings of magic that meant nothing to Sovoqatsu, and a great silver basin filled with clear water.

Despite the fact that he was ostensibly the general of an army in the field, Katakí had not shed the look of the apprehensive hermit. He was just as small and unprepossessing as he had been when they'd found him tending his sorcerous garden. He wasn't even armored, still dressed simply in linen that was the color of old blood, and he bore no weapon but for the glass flower that he had attached to a silver chain about his neck.

Katakí listened to Lyn's ongoing stream of invective for a moment with his head cocked before saying to Sovoqatsu, "Why are you here, soldier?

What means this?" Although he seemed to be ignoring Lyn now, he spoke Common for what could only have been her benefit.

Lyn stopped speaking so quickly there was an audible snap to her jaw.

Sovoqatsu threw his shoulders back and clasped his hands behind him, to indicate that he had no need to be ready with his weapons.

"I am here because I can no longer stand by while this willful child betrays her people," he said succinctly with a nod at Loralíenasa. "She would make peace with the humans and sacrifice our own to do it. She is a fool, arrogant, defiant, disrespectful." He sneered down at the ground, where the Míyahídéna still had not moved. "The Raia have always believed they could do no wrong. I weary of following their orders to utter ruin. You, however, have proven you have the means to do what you promise. I believe you can end this."

The Lord of Mornnovin listened to him with both eyebrows slanted in concentration. "I see," he said quietly. "Why bring them to me?"

"As a gift, my lord," Sovoqatsu replied, "and assurance of my intentions. I would serve you on the field, if you would have me. But first, the satisfaction of seeing the Raia family humbled."

"I see," Katakí repeated in exactly the same tone. He finally looked down at Loralíenasa again, addressing himself to Sovoqatsu while studying the Míyahídéna. "You betray her after accompanying her so far to oppose me." It was not a question; Sovoqatsu waited. "Where are you from, soldier?"

"I was born in the hills above Eselvwey. I became a guardsman in the Royal Ward as soon as I was old enough to take the oath of service."

Katakí nodded again. He had not moved from his place behind his camp table, almost hiding, since their arrival. "Where did you serve in the War?"

The snarl that escaped Sovoqatsu may as well have been building for three thousand years. "I was assigned protection duty in the Pearl Palace, and afterward with the van of the retreat."

This time when Katakí said, "I see," it conveyed something else entirely. "You never saw combat?"

"No."

Katakí Kuromé nodded one more time. "I have taken in more elves disenchanted with Evlédíen than this girl or Lord Maiantar would care to know of, but none so late in the day." He met Sovoqatsu's eyes frankly for the first time. "I can see you are a skillful killer, but there may be little enough call for that left."

Sovoqatsu asked the question silently.

The sorcerer gestured at the silver basin on the table. "My mercenary army will be arriving at Yeatun shortly, as will Mysia, and then I shall square this mess for good and all." He blinked slowly. "You bested the Míyahídéna in combat, did you?"

For the first time, Sovoqatsu shifted uneasily. "No. I took her unawares."

Kataki nodded as if he had already known the answer to his question and was pleased that he had not been fed a lie. "I am told she is without peer with a sword, excepting only one man who is not you."

Sovoqatsu scowled fiercely. "That is true."

"You're damn right it's true," Lyn taunted with vicious glee. "She beat your boots off that one time you challenged her and we all saw it. Should have known you'd carry a grudge, you vicious viper."

"This viper does bite," Sovoqatsu snarled at her with teeth bared.

Lyn snarled right back.

"You will please conduct yourself with some dignity," Kataki said to the hídéna. "You and your sister are all that remain of the oldest family in all of Asrellion – the *first* family. Though I am aware you were raised in ignorance of that, surely even you must grasp something of the weight of what you are."

It seemed that Lyn might surge to her feet; Sovoqatsu pressed heavily down on her shoulder and forced her to remain on her knees.

"You are *aware*," she spat, eyes blazing. "Of course you're bleeding *aware* – you're the one who did it! You killed my family and saw to it I was left alone in the world, and now you want to take my sister from me too!"

He did not blink. "Yes."

She sputtered for a moment.

Very slowly, Kataki came around the table until he was standing before Lyn, nearly close enough to touch, but he made no threat to do so. A deep rage had begun to kindle beneath the surface, just visible in the tension of his slight body, the glint of his hazel eyes. Upon his chest, the Nírozahé began to emit an ominous purple glow. "Yes," he repeated even more quietly. Sovoqatsu strained to hear him. "I killed your family. It is only because I was judged an inadequate match for a Raia that she was ever in danger, and the worse offense lies in the hypocrisy of their own indifference toward her." His voice dropped still lower, his words seemingly for Lyn alone. "I swore on Níra's blood that I would have theirs, that before I was done in this world I would take everything from House Raia and make myself master of what once was theirs."

"So there it is," Lyn sneered. "All this noble talk about saving our people and doing what has to be done – it was all yakshit the whole time. You only ever wanted revenge on the guy who didn't like you for his daughter."

"It is possible," Katakí said with great and terrible clarity, "to hit more than one target with a single arrow, particularly when one is three millennia in taking aim."

Lyn snorted. "You're not even an archer, you pretentious mammet."

Katakí seemed confused as he looked down at Lyn, a furrow deepening between the slant of his brows. "I'm not..." He trailed off as if he had forgotten how to make words.

Sovoqatsu took a step forward. "My lord?" The almost forgotten soldier stirred against the wall.

The Lord of Mornnovin put a hand out behind him, feeling for the table to steady himself. "What... are you doing to me?" His confusion turned into a snarl in Lyn's direction. "*What are you doing?*"

Lyn drew herself up with a smug grin. "Me? I'm not doing anything. I'm just the distraction, obviously. You *are* dumb."

Sovoqatsu moved with all the speed he was capable of, placing himself between Katakí and the two sisters, when he saw the sorcerer's hand begin to raise. A diffuse glow of white light bloomed around Katakí's body, engulfing him. A protective field.

"This will avail you nothing," Katakí ground out with such difficulty it was no longer clear whom he was addressing. "I will repel you and you will have surrendered yourself for nothing."

Loralíenasa, until now motionless on the ground, reached out blindly in Lyn's direction. Sovoqatsu saw the hídéna shrug off the trick knot on her ropes and reach for her sister's questing hand, but he did not see what followed.

He was distracted by the warrior who came at him from the shadows with weapon drawn.

Lyn's plan had layers, even though it was relatively simple. She was proud of that, proud that she had seen it when no one else could. They had all listened with varying degrees of skepticism as she explained it, back in the twins' room in the Governor's palace.

"Look, you two." She had gathered Loríen and then Naoise with her gaze. "We all know you're in love like idiots–"

"We are n–"

Lyn did not allow her sister's aggravated interruption to stand. "–but more than that, even, you have this bond thing. That it's totally pointless to argue about," she tacked on loudly when it looked like Loríen was going to interrupt again.

Naoise said nothing. He listened, his eyes wide with either curiosity or an intense effort to stay awake.

"There was literally no way you could have predicted it would happen to you guys, right?" Lyn asked her sister.

Something about the way she asked let Loríen know that this was going somewhere, because she swallowed her arguments and shook her head. "None."

"And everything we *could* have predicted, Katakí is ready for, right?"

This time it was Naoise who nodded, slowly, concentrating.

Cole got up from his place on the floor and came to stand closer.

Lyn could no longer contain her grin. "So we use what we have."

"Vaian," Loríen breathed. From the mingled fear and wonder in her voice, it was clear she had begun to grasp what Lyn proposed.

"There's no reason to jump in and drown," Lyn said to her sister. "Not when you have someone to hold the rope."

Lyn had all of them hooked now. Even grim Sovoqatsu moved in to listen to her plan.


Whatever Loríen had expected to find when she went inside the Nírozahé, this was something else entirely.

There was a sky, a heavy and unsettling purple like the darkest overripe berry on the point of decay. The intense red of the ground – the color of thick heart's blood, churning sickeningly beneath her feet – did nothing to put her at ease. She was crowded on all sides by bodies, faces indistinct like smudged chalk drawings, and she could see no end to the throng. Otherwise there were no features to the landscape; there *was* no landscape, just an endless sea of faceless figures, impossible amongst them to distinguish young or old, man or woman, elf or human.

Then there was the noise.

Thousands – tens of thousands – of voices all at once, weeping, wailing, whispering. An unrelenting, crushing wave of fear and despair. It was altogether too much to bear.

Loríen tried to cover her ears, and found that one of her hands was held firm in the hand of another. She turned to the figure beside her. When she saw her sister's familiar face, determined and distinct, she nearly sobbed with relief.

They clung to each other until their shaking stopped.

"I wasn't sure I'd be able to do it, to bring you here with me," Loríen admitted. She had to shout to be heard over the cacophony. "I'm glad it worked."

Lyn laughed nervously. "Of course it worked. We're twins – two buds on the same branch, right?" She did not sound at all convinced. "But what about our escape route?"

Loríen took a deep breath that she knew wasn't really a breath – not here, not in this place – and reached for the corner of her mind where she had grown accustomed to feeling Naoise's presence. They had established contact before she tried diving into the Nírozahé, but–

*Yes.*

"He's there," she confirmed, reaching out to him as decisively as she was holding her sister's hand. She could feel him holding her in turn, a steady presence, an anchor. She sent what she thought of as a reassuring nudge across whatever physical or theoretical distance bridged them, and felt him nudge her back in reply. "He's ready. Let's..." She trailed off as she realized she had no idea what they were going to do, how they were going to accomplish what she had promised to. "Let's do this."

They both looked around and seemed to be having the same thought: *how?*

"Are you..." Lyn broke from her study of their surroundings long enough to give her sister a curious look. "Are you speaking Common, or do I suddenly understand Elven? Because you sound–"

Loríen shook her head. "I'm not sure. I suspect things like language are irrelevant, here." One of the smudged-chalk figures jostled her and she recoiled in near horror. For a moment the wave of voices seemed to reach a crescendo. Lyn gripped her hand tighter. "But that raises a valuable line of questioning," she added, carefully ignoring the cold heart of her terror. "What *does* matter here? What sort of things can we do?"

Lyn opened her mouth and seemed about to answer, but instead she closed it and scrunched her brow in concentration. Loríen let her try whatever it was she was trying.

"There," Lyn said finally. "What am I wearing?"

It seemed to occur to Loríen suddenly that until now she had only been registering her sister as a presence with a face, because now she stood beside her in her habitual red doublet, white breeches, and brown doeskin boots – all of which were a good deal cleaner and brighter than Loríen had seen them in months.

"Your usual clothes," Loríen reported with due curiosity.

Her sister nodded and made the concentration face again. "And now?"

Now she was dressed in gorgeous scale armor, polished so bright it was nearly white, gleaming like a beacon in the dullness of their hell-world. Lush blue and white plumes jutted from the helmet tucked under her arm, matching the velvet sash tied about her middle.

Loríen had seen it before.

"You're wearing Father's armor," she answered, wrestling several emotions she could not name or control.

Her sister grinned. "I saw it in the Vault, back in Efrondel. Didn't know it was his."

Loríen closed her eyes.

"Okay," Lyn said after a moment. "I can change myself, but I can't seem to change you."

Loríen got hold of herself and opened her eyes. Lyn was still wearing the armor. Carefully imagining her once more in her doublet and breeches, extending her will to give form to her vision, Loríen tried with all of her power to make it so. And, suddenly, Lyn was dressed in white and red once more.

"So that's not fair," Lyn said with a frown.

"We don't know what the rules are in this place. It could be because I've already bled into the Nírozahé," Loríen theorized. "Or it could simply be a matter of aptitude," she added with an apologetic grimace. "I've had training in the Art; you have not."

She imagined her sister once more into their father's armor. It seemed appropriate to this task and the sight of it gave Loríen a probably unwarranted feeling of confidence.

"And my 'power is negligible,' " Lyn added, glumly quoting Katakí's assessment of her. "Well. Looks like I'm going to be as useless here as I am anywhere else."

"No." Loríen gripped Lyn's hand tightly in hers, determined to hold onto it no matter what came at them. "You are many things, sister mine," she said with a grim smile, "and there are many ways in which you drive me mad, but useless you are not. Neither here nor anywhere else. You're already helping. Believe that. I'm glad you're here."

The hídéna continued to scowl for a moment, then looked up at the rotten-berry sky. "Well *I'm* not glad I'm here. Let's figure out how in the sweet, fluffy name of cheese curds we're supposed to bust this place open."

Loríen nodded. "Be on your guard. We are not alone; our enemy will be here somewhere."

In the end, the hardest part of negotiating the plan ended up being Cole.

Lyn had never seen him so obviously miserable, not even when listening to Dairinn's interminable tales of erotic conquest over the campfire. "No," he said, the syllable dragging out of him. "I'm sorry. I can't just sit by and watch while you go into the heart of the danger without me. I swore an oath, Lyn. The only oath I've ever sworn, to the only man who ever trusted me. I prom-ised him I would protect you with my life. I'm not going to break it now, I *can't*. Not now that– No."

Lyn was still deciding how to tell Cole he was being unreasonable when Naoise had spoken quietly:

"Not the *only* man who ever trusted you."

Cole blinked rapidly and seemed momentarily lost for words.

Into the silence, Lyn offered an appeal to reason. "Come on, Cole. Think about it. There's no way to get you into the camp with us. It just doesn't work. And Naoise will need you once he's vulnerable."

The blond man furrowed his brow doubtfully. "Anyone can stand guard over Naoise. He's got an entire kingdom to do that job. You're the only one I'm sworn to protect."

"But he's my – our – way out of this," Lyn had argued. "If something hap-pens to him, I'm done for. So, really, you're protecting me by keeping him safe."

Loríen made a sound of agreement and Lyn looked over to see her making one of her curious elven gestures with her hands. She was standing close to Naoise. Intriguingly close.

Still Cole seemed unconvinced. "If anything happens to you…"

Sovoqatsu had stepped forward, drawing all eyes. Something about him seemed decidedly odd. Then Lyn realized with a jolt: he didn't look angry. "I will protect her in your place," he announced flatly. He'd met Cole's eyes with his unsettling black gaze. "If it helps you to do your part in this, I will watch over her as devotedly as if you yourself were there. While you are ab-sent, I swear on the memory of lost Eselvwey, no harm will come to her so long as I live to prevent it."

They had all stared at him in astonishment.

"Will that do?" he said to Cole with something more like his usual level of irritation.

Cole approached Sovoqatsu and extended his hand. The two clasped forearms without a word more spoken.

"Well that's fantastic," Lyn said tartly, trying to pretend she wasn't moved by what she'd just seen, "but I'm actually free to follow my own plan whether I have anyone's permission or not. So if we're done being all paternalistic–"

The former mercenary turned to Lyn. His mild blue eyes, usually so calm, were like a sea in turmoil. She swallowed the rest of her words. He hesitated visibly, and that awkwardness from the man who was always so effortlessly competent was just as alarming as the look in his eyes. But after that brief pause, he abruptly moved close to her and landed a feather-light kiss on her cheek.

No one looked more stunned than Cole himself.

"Take care of yourself, Lyn," he mumbled. "Just take care."


It quickly became clear to Sovoqatsu that Kataki's man was a more skilled fighter than he. The important thing after that was to keep him from realizing it for as long as possible. And to keep him away from the two sisters, who lay completely helpless on the rug at Kataki's feet. His other responsibility – giving the signal that Kataki was out of play and vulnerable – was going to have to take the back tier.

Sovoqatsu met his enemy's attack with his twin axes, keeping his sword in reserve. With luck, he would be able to prevent the other man from nailing down the range of his technique for as long as Loralíenasa needed.

Kataki's man was almost as tall as Sovoqatsu with nearly the reach as well. His sword was old and beautiful, the weapon of a warrior aristocrat, and he wielded it with the skill of long familiarity.

"I remember you," he said, frowning with concentration, as he swept his blade in a graceful arc where Sovoqatsu's neck had been mere seconds ago. "Farínaiqa, yes? We served a rotation together in the Pearl."

Recognition settled in: he had been Sovoqatsu's commanding officer for a season. "I wouldn't say we served *together*." Sovoqatsu aimed a decisive chop at the other man's wrist while his guard was low, but of course it didn't land. "So you lead Kataki's army now, Tenchíechanaros?"

Kataki's general nodded curtly. "You know no one calls me that." He was briefly kept occupied by a flurry of cuts from Sovoqatsu's two axes, but he pressed back almost calmly.

Sovoqatsu had to watch his footing; they were dangerously close to Loralíenasa and her sister. "Well we're not exactly going to be friends, are we," he grunted, taking care not to tread on the Míyahídéna's foot. The sorcerer himself stood motionless within the protective shell of white light he had conjured, eyes closed, one hand clutching the Nírozahé. A purple glow could be seen escaping his grasp. Whatever he was doing, he was untouchable and far away, and Sovoqatsu could not afford to worry about it.

He took the colossal risk of closing with his opponent in order to swing past him and draw the fight in the other direction. Tencharo betrayed surprise in the widening of his eyes as they grappled. He also revealed, when he was the one to break the engagement without allowing it to play out, that Sovoqatsu at least had him overmatched in raw physical strength and he knew it. Sovoqatsu bared his teeth in a ferocious smile, allowing the other man to see that he had made the observation.

They stood apart for a moment, calculating. "We could be," Tencharo said unexpectedly. "Friends, or allies at least. We are much alike, Farínaiqa, and I know you to be a man of honor. I can't understand why you choose to oppose my lord instead of joining him in victory."

"Truly?" Sovoqatsu shook his head. "You are truly going to play this feint? I'd say it's a bit late now for me to earn your master's trust."

"It is not too late to earn mine." Tencharo put up his blade just enough to show his willingness to talk. "You could still do the right thing. Help me retake control of this mistake."

Hefting both axes, Sovoqatsu assumed a defensive stance. "The mistake here is not mine."

"Does the girl truly hold you so much in thrall?"

The guardsman all but growled his response. "In truth, she has little to do with it, apart from the fact that of the two choices – the Míyahídéna or your Lord Kuromé – she is not the homicidal maniac suffering from severe dementia."

Tencharo reeled as if struck, and responded by renewing his assault in one long stride. His sword carved an elegant line on a course for Sovoqatsu's midsection. The guardsman stopped the blade at hip height with one axe. Tencharo moved to the side only one step and twisted his wrist in a way Sovoqatsu could not follow, and the axe was torn from his grip to fly across the small room. The technique struck him as similar to young Lanoralas Galvan's way of moving.

Sovoqatsu had to bring his second axe around awkwardly to block the continued attack while reaching into his belt for his long dagger. He was able to spin away before Tencharo could press the advantage, and took a breath while firming his grip on both of his weapons.

"You studied at the Voromé School," he said as the other man assessed the new threat.

"And you," Tencharo said with an unmistakable sneer, "are self-taught, if I do not miss my guess."

Sovoqatsu swore internally. This wasn't going to play out much longer.

"I don't know if I can do this," Lyn shouted.

"Stop saying that and just keep trying," Loríen replied.

She wanted to be patient with her sister, but circumstances had drastically limited her supply of serenity. Something about being inside a hellish soul-prison, possibly trapped, maybe about to die, surrounded by the dwindling essences of several thousand unfortunate victims already suffering the fate she hoped to avoid, and not being sure she knew how to do what she'd come here to do.

"It's just I don't know what she looks like," Lyn added anyway. She had already made this point before, more than once.

Loríen took a deep breath. "Let *me* focus on that. Try to think of something else, any memory, even an impression or a feeling. But above all let me concentrate."

Concentration was hard enough already, with the faceless throng and its deafening roar of despair pressing in. With the awful rotten-berry sky above, and the bloody red of the ground below. The thickness, the closeness of the air. The lack of any distinguishing landmarks; the feeling like she was at the bottom of a paint cup and any moment the brush would dip down to swirl her and everything else into murky sameness and she would be forever lost.

This time, though Lyn continued to grumble under her breath, she obeyed and did not utter another word of argument.

Loríen focused harder than she ever had in her life, on the image of a single face. It was one she had seen every day of her life, always the same, as the artist had captured her. Wide, high cheekbones, small chin, smiling green eyes, the healthy glow of a woman in love. Loríen thought of her in the dress that was the color of new spring grass, imagined the ring on her hand with its great rose-cut garnet. Decided that she was more than a painting, that she was real, that she was *here*.

The shape of a woman solidified from out of the shifting and nebulous throng – took on color, a distinct face.

Lyn stopped mid-grumble and stared. Her grip on Loríen's hand tightened.

Now that she'd done it, Loríen wasn't sure what to say. At her side, she could feel Lyn echoing her apprehension.

"Melíara?" Loríen said uncertainly.

The woman turned her bright green eyes upon Loríen fully, but they were not smiling as they were in the painting. A small line appeared between her golden brows.

"My name." She seemed stunned by her words, by the fact that she had made them. "Yes. Melíara. I am that name. I… *am*." Despite her hesitance, her voice was as lovely as Loríen had ever heard it described by those who had known her – a rich contralto. Her hair was the same honey gold as Lyn's, her skin the same sun-kissed bronze. She studied Loríen more carefully, and then Lyn, a sleeper coming awake and only gradually noticing her surroundings. "You. The two of you. You look like… But you can't be."

"Mother." Loríen was surprised to hear herself say it. Then she realized that Lyn had said it at the same time. She squeezed her sister's hand and felt pressure back.

The woman they had conjured fought against unseen resistance to shake her head slowly. "My daughters? Grown?"

Lyn was now holding onto Loríen's hand so tightly that it would have been a problem if these were their corporeal bodies. She started forward, but stopped herself and bit off whatever she had been about to say.

Melíara continued to study them both. "How is it you are in this… place? Am I dreaming this?" Even as she said it, it was clear in her face that she knew there was something wrong in the idea, that dreams should not be possible – had not been possible for her – under the circumstances.

"You know where you are?" Loríen asked, uncertain how else to address this woman when there was a lifetime between them and only this moment to say any of it. Uncertain even what she felt right now. She was confused in a hundred ways.

The woman who had been their mother in life looked at Loríen, and more awareness came into her eyes. "I know I am not living, but that this is not where I should be. Not where any of us should be." She stepped closer, removing herself from the unformed multitude. Loríen found herself breathing faster. "You cannot be here. Loralíenasa. Lyllíen. You must be alive."

"We *are* alive," Lorién replied, "and we need your help, desperately." She swallowed. "Haojí."

Melíara closed the distance between them and reached out to touch them searchingly, gripping Lyn and Loríen both by the shoulder. "This is real," she whispered. "My little girls…"

A sound rather like a sob escaped Lyn, who threw her free arm around their mother and drew her close. Loríen found herself cheek-to-cheek with the woman who had not been allowed to raise her, locked in a three-way embrace with the twin who had been stolen from her side in infancy. It was difficult not to cry.

But there wasn't time for that.

"This place," Loríen explained, pulling back just far enough to look into her mother's vividly green eyes, "is the Nírozahé. We are inside the heart of its power."

Horror blossomed slowly across Melíara's face as she came to understand what that had to mean.

"We need your help," Loríen repeated urgently. "Yours, and Father's."

"And Gallanas', " Lyn added, not bothering to hide her tears.

Melíara looked back and forth between them, the horror fading, replaced by a distinctly stubborn determination. The roar of the crowd seemed to recede. She took a deep, steadying breath and let it out slowly, as Loríen herself often did before accepting yet another responsibility. "I don't know how you're here — I don't know how *I'm* here — but tell me what you need of me and you shall have it."

"We're going to destroy the Nírozahé, but first we need to find our father and brother," Loríen said. "Can you help us? Lyn knew Gallanas, but I did not. And Father…"

Their mother flashed a quick smile that seemed familiar. "Yes, of course."

Lyn crowed in triumph. "Ha! Katakí wants to take on our family? He'll get his Raia fight!"

Loríen winced. "Lyn. I may not be an expert on how this place works, but I wouldn't say his name. He's here somewhere; I suspect attracting his attention before we're ready would be a bad idea."

Just as Lyn opened her mouth to respond to that, Kataki Kuromé suddenly stood before them. Distinct and fully defined, Kataki all but loomed from the drab and murmuring throng that surrounded them. He was close enough to touch, and he did not look happy.

Loríen sighed. "Honestly, I would have preferred not to be right."

If there was a stranger thing than observing events transpire in a mystical energy-world held inside a small magical glass flower through the linked consciousness of an elf woman, Naoise could not imagine what that might be.

The wildest part was being also aware of the perfectly normal world around him while experiencing the other place. The cold black basalt at his back, the pebble starting to annoy beneath him, the sharpening breeze that carried the scent of more spring rain. The murmur of elven voices and the all-too-familiar clatter of arms, mounts, and equipment as they prepared for a battle that would be quite real. Cole kneeling an arm's length away, doing his best to hide his concern, giving it away in the regulated pace of his breathing.

While Loríen and Lyn stood beneath a looming sky the color of a bruise and fought to summon whatever remained of their family.

Naoise could feel Loríen's thoughts as clearly as his own, joined as they were. She was frightened, but that was no surprise. He was frightened too, for most of the same reasons. When she succeeded in summoning her mother the queen, Loríen's confused feelings stirred and mingled with impressions of his own mother lost, overwhelmingly.

The idea of being able to see her one last time, as Loríen was now doing, but under such conditions... Would it be blessing or curse? Was it better or worse that Loríen had never known her mother, had no relationship with her to mourn having lost? Would he be able to focus on the task at hand if it was him in Loríen's place? Would he be able to say goodbye again?

It was a mistake, he knew, to let any of that bleed over into her awareness while she was trying so hard to concentrate on what had to be done, but it was vital that they stay connected and he didn't know how to partition off his own thoughts while keeping an open channel between them. He tried as hard as he could to be aware only of what was before her, what she was thinking. The sounds of man and beast faded; the purple of the sky darkened.

Then he felt steely hands digging into his biceps, shaking him stoutly.

He blinked and was looking into Cole's eyes.

"Focus, Naoise," the other man was saying to him urgently. "Stay here. You're only their way out if you stay *here*."

Naoise put his head back and took a deep breath. Cole watched him carefully. "Thank you. It's... I didn't know what to expect, but this is– I don't know how to be in two places at once." Or how to process two sets of thoughts at once.

"Yeah," Cole said. It wasn't entirely clear what he meant. "I have your back."

That was clear enough. Naoise took another breath and re-settled himself, keeping in his mind the world of the Nírozahé while reminding himself of his physical place in the real world. Cole retreated an arm's length and sat back on his heels.

Just as Naoise was finding his equilibrium again, Katakí appeared before Loríen.

"Dammit," Naoise said aloud. "The nameless, bleeding Void."

"What?" Cole did not bother to hide his sudden alarm.

"Katakí. He's there. Sovoqatsu never gave the signal."

Which meant that the guardsman was either dead or in trouble.

"Shit," Cole said quietly.

"Go," Naoise ordered with as much authority as he could muster while concentrating. "You have to tell the Captain."

Cole tensed as if about to stand, but looked at Naoise doubtfully.

"I'll be fine," Naoise assured him. "I'll stay grounded until you get back. You have my word."

The former mercenary studied him a moment longer, concern obviously battling the knowledge that someone did have to tell the elves they were missing their assault window. For Sovoqatsu's sake, at the very least. This would be their only chance to make an armed approach without the risk of instant annihilation.

"I'm holding you to that," Cole finally said as he pushed himself to his feet and took off at a flat sprint to find the Captain of the Guard.

Naoise breathed carefully. He was not in the habit of breaking his promises, but he also wasn't in the habit of getting himself involved with sorcerers and magical half-worlds. Anything might happen now.

# CHAPTER THIRTY-TWO

Even though there wasn't much point to imposing the illusion of physical distance in an incorporeal world, Loríen pulled her mother and sister back, out of the appearance of Katakí's reach. It felt important.

"I observed long ago," Katakí hissed at her, "that you are possessed of more courage than wisdom. I thought then that it made of you a charming antagonist. Now I see you are long overdue for a correction which it will be my pleasure to deliver."

"You talk pretty tough for someone who had to build himself a tent cave so he could hide from his own men," Lyn retorted.

Katakí's lips pulled back against his teeth – a grimace or a snarl, Loríen could not tell, but it was the first time Lyn had gotten a reaction from him.

If she was guessing correctly, it was his anxiety around people that had led him to meet Thaníravaia Raia in the first place and also had been the primary source of the king's disapproval of him. For all that Katakí was a tremendously powerful sorcerer capable of immense destruction, Loríen thought she was beginning to understand the fierce protectiveness of his followers.

"Perhaps I chose the wrong Raia to allow to live," he ground out. "Although you both are fairly odious, I must confess. Know that the only pleasure I will derive from our marital union will lie in my triumph over your insufferable family."

The sisters shared a horrified look, then Lyn shook her head slowly. "That may be the most disgusting thing you've ever said. And there's a list."

While Lyn tried to upset Katakí, Loríen studied him. Beyond appearing frustrated by Lyn, tension had him pulled taut. He was concentrating hard on something that was not either of them, and he was radiating a faint glow that had grown slowly since he'd first appeared before them. So he had some idea of what he ought to be doing in order to evict them from this place – or perhaps trap them here forever – but so far she had yet to feel any change in her own being. Whatever he was doing, it was indirect.

It would be wonderful, she thought with more frustration than self-pity, if only there were someone who could help her understand the Nírozahé as well as Katakí seemed to. But ultimately, as Tomanasíl had always taught her, there was nothing for her to rely on but her own wits and judgment.

*No,* a voice she recognized told her across the distance between them. *You know that's not true.*

He was right, of course. It wasn't true. It had never been true, although the isolation she'd always felt had made it true enough in practice. She had Lyn, Naoise, Lanas – *all* of her friends and companions, more than one army, the trust of all of them. And, here, she also had what Katakí had been so confident as to boast of.

Melíara, who had been Queen of Evlédíen until she was murdered by Katakí's men for revenge and power, raised her golden head and stepped forward so that she stood between Katakí and her children.

"Who are you, and by what supposed right do you address my daughters with such insolence?"

The Lord of Mornnovin shifted his intense focus to the queen. "I owe no answers to a phantom summoned to assuage the fears of frightened children."

"You just answered her anyway," Lyn taunted. "I mean it was a terrible answer, but still."

Katakí's scowl deepened, the noise of the multitude rising as if voicing his displeasure for him. Loríen suddenly realized that the sound had been building since he'd arrived, and that the glow was now radiating not just from him but from the grey masses around them.

She touched her mother's arm urgently. "That thing we talked about?" she whispered when the queen looked back at her. "There's no time to figure it out. We need to do it *now*."

Melíara nodded and took a deep breath. "Andras, jíai, I need you."

As soon as Melíara had spoken those words, two things happened. The first, which Loríen noticed immediately, was that Lyn cried out and doubled over in apparent pain. Her hand wrenched free of Loríen's, and she suddenly felt much more distant than an arm's length away. She too, had begun to glow, an unsettling purple like the color of the awful sky. Loríen doubted that Lyn was doing that herself.

The second was that a golden-haired man coalesced beside their mother.

Loríen wished she had time to spare more than a glance, but that was enough to recognize in the tall, regal figure the second subject of the portrait she was so familiar with. It would take him a moment to acclimate, as it had Melíara, and longer to figure out what was going on, but they could not wait for that. Loríen just had to hope he was as quick-witted as people had always said her father had been. She needed to focus on Lyn, on trying to stop whatever it was Katakí was doing to her.

"One more," she said to Melíara.

"This is your grand plan?" Katakí sneered. "You believe that you can imagine your dead haojí and yají protecting you from the wicked man, and it will be so?"

Loríen did not answer. She was busy concentrating on her sister, on feeling her presence, holding onto her concept of who and what Lyn was. Remembering all of the ludicrous things Lyn had said and done over the past months, the outrage she had often made Loríen feel. The reality and immediacy of that.

"Lyn." She knelt beside her sister and reached for her hand, but couldn't seem to find it. "Lyn, look at me."

Her sister raised her head with obvious effort and searched for a moment before finding Loríen's eyes. Her own features had started to become difficult to make out. "This is awful," Lyn gasped. "It's like I'm... like I..." She shook her head. "Can't words."

"Since when," said a new voice sparkling with amusement, "have *you* ever had trouble *talking?*"

Loríen whirled to see the newcomer and was surprised to find herself looking into a face almost entirely like her own.

"Gallanas," she murmured, unable to produce a less fatuous observation under the circumstances.

Her brother was looking down at Lyn, who was emitting much less of the alarming glow now as she returned his attention.

"Nice of you to finally show up," Lyn managed to grumble at him, which Loríen took as a good sign.

The sound of Katakí's laughter was less encouraging. Loríen stood slowly, keeping the sorcerer in view. Gallanas bent to Lyn's side.

"Come on. I made sure you'd be safe so you'd *live*, not die ridiculously in a weird nightmarescape while some lunatic laughs at us." He sounded effortlessly amused in a way that Loríen envied. Taking Lyn's hand, he pulled her to her feet beside their sister.

The purple light around Katakí now was almost blinding, like looking directly into a patch of absolute blackness. She could feel Lyn trembling, but she didn't think it was from fear; she put her arm around her sister and held her close anyway.

"This begins to be absurd," Katakí chuckled. "Big brother, now? Am I meant to fear this parade of family members I've already killed, already taken from you?"

It was Lyn's turn to laugh scornfully, but in a display of surprisingly good judgment she added nothing further. She simply held tight to Loríen and stepped back until they were surrounded by their family. It was a strange feeling, to be standing between her parents and the brother she could not even remember and to know they were *hers*, that she belonged to this collection of people, that they were here for her.

"I dislike this fellow," Melíara said, lip curled in distaste. "He thinks he can hurt our children and laugh about it?"

King Andras lifted his proud, golden head. "You do not fear to face us, villain? Then face *all of us*."

Melíara nodded.

Suddenly it was not merely the five of them against Katakí Kuromé amid a sea of faceless, murmuring grey shapes. Now they were standing at the center of an army abruptly awake.

Power surged through Loríen – not just a feeling of strength, but a burst of actual energy she knew she could use.

"Lyn," she started to say, but her sister answered with an audible grin.

"Yep. Let's roast this creep."

More than anything else, the problem was that Tencharo was faster than Sovoqatsu. Form, education, reflex, confidence – the guardsman could overcome those and often had, because victory came down to patience and will more often than not. When he wanted to win, he simply didn't allow anything to stop him. It was why he respected the Míyahídéna for besting him. She was the same and had backed her skill with the determination to see it through.

But his former commanding officer had more than skill on his side: he had speed that Sovoqatsu could not match.

He'd watched fights like this one before. He'd been on the other side of fights like this one. Soon it would become a game of attrition, where Tencharo picked him apart piece by piece until he could fight no more. He was already nursing a bleeding gash to his bicep and feeling grateful the wound was not two inches closer to his armpit.

At the moment Tencharo was trying to addle him with a blindingly fast series of attacks. Another reminder of Lanoralas Galvan's style, but lacking the young Captain's preternatural grace. Sovoqatsu knew he had to break the other man's rhythm or he would find himself drawn into a fatal trap. He blocked and blocked again with his dagger and axe, watching for an opening, feeling the first signs of fatigue.

"It's not too late to surrender," Tencharo said. He batted the axe aside and nearly got his sword edge across Sovoqatsu's chest before the dagger rose to push him back. "We could still use you."

"I've had my fill of being used," Sovoqatsu grunted. He dropped his guard low to chop at the other man's thigh with the axe, but his blow was met and repelled so quickly it was almost like Tencharo could read his mind.

"That's not what I meant."

They were getting close to a rather precarious stack of crates against the tent wall, but Sovoqatsu dared not glance behind him to see how close. He glowered at Katakí's man while evading a near-hit. "Yes it was. The problem is, none of you people are willing to admit it."

"Us people?"

Tencharo re-set himself with his weight on his back foot and raised his sword at a downward angle across his own body, and suddenly Sovoqatsu knew exactly what he was about to do because he had seen Captain Galvan do it before. He tried his utmost not to broadcast his familiarity with the form.

"Those in power," he answered while Tencharo swept his point upward, nearly catching him on the chin. "Our illustrious leaders. Users, all of you." He watched as the general brought his blade around through the rest of the attack, toward his left flank, right where he knew it would be.

And was there to drive the point of his sword into the ground.

Surprise flashed in the general's eyes just before Sovoqatsu smashed the crown of his skull into his nose. Tencharo staggered back, momentarily blinded, flailing his sword up in sightless defense. Sovoqatsu danced out of its range.

"That's how it is to be, then," Tencharo gasped. His face was smeared with blood.

"If you ever imagined this was a friendly duel between gentlemen,"

Sovoqatsu sneered, "you're as delusional as your master."

An unhappy smile deepened the lines of the general's brow. "Very well. You seek a death in battle? I can give that to you."

Whether he had been holding back before or was enraged that Sovoqatsu had drawn blood, he redoubled his assault with a terrible ferocity. He struck so hard that Sovoqatsu felt the force of it vibrate all the way up into his shoulder and down through his ribs when he blocked the blow. The guardsman had to withdraw while he absorbed the shock, but Tencharo was there, crowding him with flashing steel and bared teeth.

Suddenly Sovoqatsu felt his back hit the stack of crates, and he detected the acrid taste of desperation in his own mouth. He half-turned and reached behind him to the top of the stack, heaving the uppermost crate down toward Tencharo's head. The general lunged aside in the only direction he could; Sovoqatsu launched his axe to meet him as the crate crashed into pieces.

The axe hit squarely in the center of Tencharo's chest, met armor, and fell to the ground.

The general smiled. He picked up the fallen axe and threw it back, but as the guardsman gathered himself to dive out of the way, he saw that it was not aimed at him.

It landed with a deep *thunk* in one of the wood posts supporting the internal wall. Sovoqatsu followed the sound just in time to see heavy, dark fabric descending over his head.

His thoughts a solid stream of desperate profanity, he cut his way out of the cloth wall with his dagger. He expected to see Tencharo's bared teeth bearing down on him the moment he caught a strip of light, and was alarmed when he didn't.

*Lyn. Loralienasa.*

He fought his way free of the fabric pulling him down, abandoning his dagger in its weighty folds. Tencharo was kicking his way through the wreckage of the crate, sword in hand, on a course for the vulnerable sisters. Sovoqatsu roared for his attention, but the general did not stop.

There was nothing for it. Sovoqatsu launched himself across the almost impossible distance, catching Tencharo in the midsection just as the general started turning to face the renewed threat. The two of them went tearing through the wall into another room, landing hard together. Pain blossomed in a hundred places on Sovoqatsu's body. When he tried to move, he found himself full of as many pieces of broken glass.

And Tencharo was angry.

As fine a thing as it was to be surrounded by family in this horrible place, it was also distracting. The need to turn, to look at all of them, to study them until she knew all of their faces from memory, was so strong. It had not occurred to Loríen earlier that this might happen.

Lyn was obviously having the same difficulty, or one similar, but she wasn't fighting it. Maybe she had so much faith in Loríen's ability to get the job done that she could afford to lose focus. Or maybe she needed the reminder of who she was, after Katakí's assault on her being. Whatever the case, she stared at the throng of elves that continued to emerge behind them, at the king and queen who had summoned them, at the brother she had lost not so long ago. She was visibly overwhelmed.

"What do you need us to do?" Gallanas asked either or both of them, standing between his two sisters.

Loríen opened her mouth to answer, but her first syllable was drowned out by a sudden clap of thunder that seemed to reverberate all the way inside her mind. It was accompanied by a fork of violently red lightning cracking open the terrible sky. Thick rain the color and consistency of congealed blood came pounding down all at once. It clung to her skin where it struck, burning on contact with an intensity that left her doubled over and gasping. The sudden smell of sulfur was like another assault in itself.

It wasn't long before she was surrounded by screaming.

Katakí stood scarcely more than an arm's reach away, watching the effect of this gambit with an eerily flat expression on his unassuming face. The blood rain had not touched him.

"Loríen!" Lyn cried out, a plea.

*It's not real. Our bodies are elsewhere,* Loríen reminded herself forcefully. This was about will. The sense of physical pain was meant to scatter their focus.

Concentrating as hard as she ever had on anything, she ignored the real and immediate feeling that her flesh was being boiled from her bones. *It's not real.* She imagined a dome made of pure white light, imagined that no pain could penetrate its serenity, imagined this white light enveloping her and all of her family. Holding them in safety. She envisioned Katakí being cast out and away, unwelcome within its protective glow.

*It's not real,* she told herself again, blocking the pain. *Real is what I decide it to be. This place is what I decide. I am in control.* She clung to a mental image of that dome, of safety.

There was a flash of white light in the sky overhead, but it was soothing rather than hurtful to the eye. Like a giant flower, the illumination blossomed outward and down until it met the deep red of the ground. The sulfur rain struck the dome in viscous gobbets and slid off harmlessly. Loríen refined her imagining; the awful sounds became bell chimes every time a glob of the blood-like rain hit the dome, so that they were now surrounded by a veil of sublime music and light, and Katakí had been banished to the other side.

He stared at her implacably.

Loríen let out a long breath. Lyn stood beside her and did the same.

"It's not real," Loríen murmured, reminding herself.

"Feels real enough," Lyn countered.

Loríen stared back at Katakí. "He's just trying to keep us occupied. Distracted."

One corner of the sorcerer's mouth twitched in the hint of a smile.

"While he does what?" Lyn asked uneasily.

"Does it matter?" Gallanas cut in.

Loríen finally allowed herself to look at Gallanas properly. It was disconcerting how much he looked like her. How much she looked like him, she supposed. This was her older brother. And he looked so familiar though she had never seen him before. The determined glitter in his green eyes was something she'd seen often enough.

She was surprised by the sudden feeling of a hand on her shoulder. Her father's. At his side, Melíara reached for Lyn's hand. They all shared a look that warmed Loríen down to the blood coursing through her veins.

"Did you really suppose it would be so easy?" a voice hissed in her ear.

In the same moment, she found herself standing upon a high, flat-topped rock spire with a sheer drop on every side, battered by punishing winds that threatened to send her over the edge.

Katakí was there with her.

"You still think this is a game," Katakí Kuromé ground out, his teeth nearly touching Loríen's face. "You still think to *win*."

She brought her fist up to crash it into his jaw, but it passed through the place where his head should have been as though through air. Snarling, he reached out and grabbed her by the throat. The contact was substantial, and she could not breathe. She could feel her windpipe buckling beneath his hand, her lungs panicking and screaming for air.

*No,* she reminded herself. *I decide what is real.*

But she couldn't *breathe.* She clawed desperately at his hand. It was like an iron vise she could not pry open. He watched her struggles with terrifying dispassion, then he faded before her eyes as her vision alternated between airless bursts of white and black. Her heartbeat was pounding in her head so hard that it became almost the only thing she could think of.

*No,* another voice said in her mind. *You are stronger. This is an illusion, his illusion. Reject it.*

Though she was no longer entirely convinced that anything here was an illusion, Naoise's voice took the edge off of her panic.

She tried to decide that her lungs had plenty of air, but she wasn't able to convince herself of that reality with the feeling of Kataki's hand crushing down so persuasively on her throat. Instead, head swimming, she decided that if his hand was solid, so was the rest of him. With that thought in mind as firmly as she could make it, she brought her knee up sharply into his groin.

He staggered back with a strangled cry.

Lorien sucked air gratefully while Kataki was doubled over. She thought that if she had her sword, he would not dare touch her again. An imagined version of Liensu manifested in her hand, its bright edge reflecting the purple of the sky, but she was still too close to the brink of asphyxiation to use it. She leaned on the sword and took several more gulping breaths.

"Do you not understand," Kataki gasped, "that it makes no matter what you do to me? I control the Nírozahé. Our true battle is not being fought here, by means of such crude violence. You can imagine a thousand wounds upon me, and the power of this relic will yet be mine to wield."

Because Lorien had just summoned her sword with thoughts of defense, she was able to see that Kataki was doing the same thing. He was afraid. Or at least concerned.

She did her best to sound calm. "I suppose you could end me with a single thought."

The Lord of Mornnovin straightened, the fierceness of his glare not hiding his indignation. "You cannot taunt your way out of your death. But you can still save your sister."

"My sister and I will be just fine," Lorien replied, "but your concern is touching." Of course, if she couldn't find Lyn and escape with her, they would both be far from fine. And she had a horrible feeling that if she let Katakí explain what he meant, things would suddenly get much worse than they already were.

As if he didn't even consider her worth the effort of an explanation, Katakí gestured at the great red plain stretching far beneath them. Loríen did not fear heights, exactly, but their rocky platform was so tall, the drop so precipitous and the winds so strong, that her mind and her stomach fought with each other while trying to process how far down the ground was. She edged carefully close enough to the overlook to see whatever it was he wanted her to.

A battle, fierce and desperate. Two clear sides, even from this remote height – Kataki was certainly not trying for subtlety. One full of color and vitality and even the unmistakable flash of a figure in blinding white armor, beaming with the glow of power; the other a terrible, unstoppable grey mass, like a spreading fungus. The island of color looked so small, so inadequate against the crushing sea of sameness. As she watched, she saw individual beams of light overtaken and swallowed by the grey tide, to become part of its inexorable advance.

"There is no need for both of you to die here," Kataki said. "You have the power to end this." He came to stand beside her, looking down at the battle below. There wasn't anywhere for Loríen to escape to on their rock, so she didn't bother. And suddenly the Lord of Mornnovin sounded... not tired, but something like it. Not remorseful – he hadn't earned that grace from her.

Loríen remembered seeing his memories, back in Mornnovin. Being connected to the bottomless well of his grief and pain, a dizzying abyss that sustained him but had also driven him mad.

He was desperate.

"You could end this yourself," she said. "It's not too late."

Kataki turned to her, incredulity and some amusement crinkling the corners of his eyes. "It's to be an appeal to my better nature, is it? After everything I've already done?" He gestured down toward the battle. "Ask your dead parents if they think I have a better nature to appeal to. Ask your brother what it felt like when his still-beating heart was carved from his body."

That struck as hard as any blow from a mailled fist. Loríen reeled, but stared back at him. "Why?" she said before her question had formed fully in her mind.

He cocked his head.

Loríen took a deep breath and reset herself. The feel of her sword in her hand, real or not, was an absolute. It was simple, direct, a manifestation of her strength and a tangible extension of her will. It helped her thoughts to cut through in a straight line. "Why do you want me to hate you?"

It was Kataki's turn to take a step back as if struck. The strong winds abated for a moment, and in the sudden silence Loríen could hear the cries of the distant battle.

"This is simpler for us both," Kataki said quietly. "I exist for one purpose only. We must play out our roles."

"No." She shook her head slowly, then with greater vehemence as she utterly rejected the reality he wanted to believe in.

"No. You do not *exist*, you are *alive*. You are not the avatar of our people's vengeance. Yours is the grief of one sad man. I will not help you convince yourself that none of this has been your choice." She manifested a sheath at her back and made a show of returning her sword to it. "This role you have cast me in, I refuse to play it. My grandfather may have done you wrong and maybe he did not, but I am not him. There is no ancestral grudge; you are not my nemesis. I will stop you, but I will not hate you. You will not fuel yourself on my rage."

Kataki listened to her with disgust blooming across his face in a red flush. "Fear not, child," he whispered, "for I've more than enough to destroy us both."

*Loríen!* Naoise cried in warning.

The sky and everything else went black.

It was darker in this part of the tent; Sovoqatsu could not make out what it was they had broken with their fall, he could only feel the dozens of glass shards cutting into him all down his left side and smell the coppery tang of his own blood. At least one of the wounds was going to be a serious problem in another handful of minutes.

Tencharo recovered faster, levering himself over and then behind Sovoqatsu in an attempt to wrestle him into a chokehold. Sovoqatsu scrambled for purchase amid the strewn glass but could find none. The general's arm found his throat and clamped down hard. There was no give for Sovoqatsu to slam his skull back into his enemy's face, and he couldn't reach his sword.

Wielding the only weapon he had access to, Sovoqatsu swung his left arm up behind his head until he felt contact, then dragged the glass shards in his forearm across the general's face.

Tencharo screamed horribly. The pressure on Sovoqatsu's windpipe let up enough for him to struggle free.

He drew his sword while climbing to his feet. The tight, sharp ache in his side made it impossible to ignore the large piece of glass buried several inches deep in his vitals. There was blood everywhere, obscuring the extent of the damage.

Kataki's general looked little better as he found his weapon and struggled to his feet after Sovoqatsu. Though it seemed he had not taken the brunt of the fall, he was still cut in several places, including a fresh and terrible gash in his left cheek that gushed blood with every beat of his heart.

Tencharo bared his teeth in a pained grimace. "You've no idea what you have done."

"I may have ruined the view in your looking glass," Sovoqatsu replied, gesturing rudely at Tencharo's face, "but you won't mind when you're dead."

The general let out a growl. "You have destroyed something precious to Lord Kuromé. Were it not my duty already to end your life, it would now become so, and you should beg of Vaian that you will be dead before my lord returns."

Fear was not an emotion Sovoqatsu permitted himself, but a prickle of some cold premonition entered his heart at the recognition that those words were not a threat but a statement of truth. The general stepped over the carpet of shattered glass with a care that spoke almost of reverence despite the murder in his eyes. Sovoqatsu firmed his grip on his sword. The blood sliding down his wrists made that more difficult than it should have been.

Tencharo's attack this time was relentless, driven. When Sovoqatsu took the first swing on the edge of his sword and felt his arms wanting to go slack, he knew he didn't have much left. He just hoped it would be enough.

Then he heard the voices.

For a moment, he thought maybe the blood loss was already too much and he'd started hearing things, but Tencharo took a step back and cocked his head to listen. In the respite, it was impossible to mistake the sounds and shouts of sudden combat outside the tent. Captain Galvan. Even though Sovoqatsu had not been able to give the signal, the Captain had come anyway.

Good. That meant Sovoqatsu had only one thing to worry about, one job to do until he couldn't do it anymore.

He lunged toward Tencharo with everything he had.

Loríen was alone in the dark.

No, it wasn't just darkness. It was *nothing*. No light, no sound, nothing to touch, not even the feeling of air to breathe or of open, empty space around her. Not even a *her* for space to surround. Katakí was gone. The battle was gone. It was like nothing existed in all the world but her consciousness.

Or maybe it was the other way around. Maybe she was dead and the world was carrying on without her. Maybe this was the Dark One's Abyss.

Dissent. Naoise's voice in her mind assuring her she was still alive. But she could just as well be reassuring herself in his voice, she supposed. She had never felt so entirely, oppressively alone.

*As much as I like knowing you would choose to imagine my voice as a comfort, I'd rather you believe me when I say that you are still alive, and you are not alone.*

The warmth in his perceived tone provided a baseline that allowed her to identify the feeling around her as cold. It was something.

She tried to fill the silence with her own voice, but nothing happened. Not even the sound of air passing wordlessly through her lips.

*But then where am I?* she asked inside her own mind. *What has Katakí done?*

*Shall I bring you out?* A sense of bracing, of readiness from the man at the other end of her thoughts.

*No! I've lost Lyn. If you bring me out now, she might be trapped in here forever.*

Not that Loríen had any idea how to un-trap herself.

If she was to believe that she was still alive and still inside the Nírozahé, she should be able to control this too. Whatever Katakí had done to her, he couldn't have changed that. Unless he'd won and was now in command of the Nírozahé.

That wasn't useful. Loríen took a deep breath and concentrated on feeling herself do it. Yes, good. Concentrated on feeling her lungs expand within her chest and then deflate as she let the breath out again. She was still here. And wherever *here* was, she needed to be somewhere else. Forming an image of that battlefield in her mind, she willed herself there with every ounce of her being.

Nothing happened.

She tried again, focusing on every detail she could think of. She thought of Lyn in their father's gleaming armor, of their mother's green eyes. The flower of white light she had summoned to protect them from the blood rain, and the chiming of the bell-tones. The encroaching wave of grey shapes. No matter how hard or how clearly she concentrated on any of these images, she could not make her surroundings change. She could not even summon a single spark of light to banish the darkness that engulfed her. It felt unquestionably as though she had been put into a lightless, lidless box and there was no way out.

Which was unacceptable. She was prepared to die if she had to, but not like this.

*Naoise! I need you.*

He let her feel that he was ready to do whatever she asked.

*If I was able to bring Lyn into the Nírozahé with me, that has to mean I was able to form a connection to her. And if I'm connected to her, you must be too.*

His thoughts registered doubt.

*Find her,* she insisted. *Find the connection. It has to be there.*

Despite his doubt, she could feel Naoise inspecting the corner of his awareness where his bond with Loríen resided. She knew, because they were sharing thoughts, that this was something he had done before. She wasn't sure how to help him, but she held onto every memory, thought, and image of her sister that she could conjure. They were connected; they were twins. It had to be possible, somehow, for him to find his way to Lyn through her.

It had to be.

*I have her!*

Loríen's heart leaped up into her throat. *Help me.* But he was already showing her the way, steady and patient and strong.

Suddenly the darkness was gone and Loríen was standing in the midst of a deafening battle at Lyn's side. The white dome was starting to fail, disintegrating in places where the burning blood rain now fell through. Katakí's red lightning veined the dark sky overhead. Her sister shouted something while kicking a clinging grey shape off her leg, but it was too loud for Loríen to hear. And there was no time. She could not afford to suffer any more of Katakí's tricks.

In the distance, she could see the impossibly tall rock column in what had previously been a featureless landscape. At the top, a lone dark figure with arms raised to the looming sky.

Loríen looked around and saw her family fighting to hold back the tide of Katakí's power. She allowed the sight of them to settle within her. She allowed herself to feel the connection with Lyn that had brought her here until she could see it as a ribbon of white light stretching between them. It extended out from her sister in turn, joining her to Gallanas, and Melíara, and Andras, and from there to every soul awake and fighting.

She gathered the feeling of so much kinship, of their support, and let the power of it blaze through her like fire in her veins. Raising her arms high, she sent that power streaming up into the dome of white light. It brightened and bloomed outward, and still further and higher, fuller and brighter until it was pushing against the sky.

Katakí pushed back.

It was like the feeling of sorrow striving against joy, but Loríen was replete with the radiance of her family's determination and strength. She forced the dome higher, straining against the confines of reality until she could feel them melting away like ice in the summer sun, unmade. There was no more sky, no battle, no wailing throng, no Katakí, because there was nothing left to contain them. There was nothing. Not even fear.

*It's over,* she thought, at peace. *They are free.*

All of Naoise's being was bursting with bright white light, and it was the most sublimely beautiful thing he had ever felt.

So beautiful that it was a moment before he realized. *Loríen.* He searched desperately for the feeling of her in his mind and found an impression only, not her distinct awareness. The terror that sent shooting through him was cold enough to banish the feeling of pure beauty. He reached from Loríen to the link he had established with Lyn and found the same thing.

He held them both and pulled them back quickly, sparing no time to ask himself if he was doing it right.

"Naoise?" Cole could see the sudden alarm in him and leaned forward so far it was a wonder he didn't topple over.

Naoise waited only long enough to see the mundane view of a tent interior through Loríen's eyes before surging to his feet. "Come on," he said to the man already following almost at his heels. "I think it may be over."

Together they both sprinted for all they were worth.

Sound was the first thing to happen in the whole of time. Loralíenasa lay on her side listening for an eternity, picking out a hundred sounds before remembering that there were words to describe each of them. Loud, muffled, sharp, *close*. Then she rediscovered that she had a body for her to be lying on the side of.

She climbed to her knees, slowly.

Lyn was lying on her back beside her, eyes open wide, blinking up at the ceiling. It looked like she was unharmed.

Katakí stood no more than an arm's reach away, both hands on the table for support, shaking a daze from his head. The shattered remnants of the Nírozahé lay on the table before him. He looked up when he saw her moving, and hate flooded his visage.

"*You!*" The sound tore from him, the essence of pain distilled into a single syllable. He lurched toward her, dagger suddenly in hand. The thought came to Loríen with strange certainty that it was the same dagger that had killed Dairinn.

Líensu lay on the rug where Sovoqatsu had thrown it down beside her. Loríen took it up with the speed of desperation and swung the blade in a defensive arc as Katakí bore down on her. A thin line appeared across his throat, followed by a terrible red spray. It all happened so quickly that he was upon her before he knew he was dead. They tumbled back together, Loríen wrestling the dagger away from her face as they fell. Lyn screamed her name.

Katakí lay still.

Then Loríen heard another cry, another voice, that reminded her the world had not stopped. She pushed the sorcerer's body off of her and rolled to her feet in time to see Katakí's general coming at her with weapon drawn. Behind him Sovoqatsu had collapsed to his knees, so pale and covered in so much blood she wondered how he'd had the strength to call a warning.

But just as she brought her sword up to deal with the new threat charging at her, the general stopped short. Confusion bloomed across his face. Loríen watched, breath held, as he turned slowly to look back at Sovoqatsu.

She saw the long, horrible glass shard protruding from the back of the general's neck when he turned.

Sovoqatsu's outstretched hand hovered a moment longer as he watched his opponent fall; then he toppled as well. Loríen dropped her sword and rushed to catch him.

He was virtually covered in cuts, many still embedded with broken glass, and he had the ashen pallor to attest to their seriousness. It was obvious he'd seen quite a fight, but the real problem was the jagged hole in his side that was pumping blood vigorously. She could guess where the shard he'd thrown had just come from. He had to have known that pulling it out would kill him.

Fingers fumbling over each other in her haste, she tore at her sash until she had it off, and pressed it hard against the wound until he hissed in pain.

"Loríen," Lyn said again, in a completely different tone. She was on her feet now, looking down at Sovoqatsu with her jaw clenched.

From outside the tent came the muffled sounds of battle. Loríen finally realized they'd been going on all this time.

The guardsman bared his teeth in a fierce smile. "He thought he had me. Elitist *qíjano*."

"*Íyaqo*, Sovoqatsu," she swore. "You fool. Why did you do that?"

His grin widened, terrible and bloody, before his eyes rolled up in his head and he lost consciousness.

"*Íyaqo*." She looked around her for anything she could use to help him. This entire section of the tent was in ruins. She was going to need to hear the story of his fight with Katakí's general. "You are not dying, do you hear me?" she informed the guardsman's senseless face. "Lyn, I need you to find things." She threw a look over her shoulder and saw her sister standing ready. "Water, more cloth, bandaging, something for–" She realized she didn't have the words for "needle and thread" and mimed the objects' use instead. It looked like Katakí had brought nearly his entire castle with him. He *had* to have a medical kit around somewhere.

"I have a smarter idea," Lyn said. "Why don't *I* hold that, and *you* go looking, since you know better than I do what will suit."

Loríen made a face and gestured with her head for Lyn to take her place. She kept pressure on the wound until she was certain Lyn had it.

"You are *not* dying," Loríen repeated more quietly before standing up. She'd already lost enough today. She couldn't even identify which emotions were making her eyes swim with tears, not yet. She suspected it had something to do with the parents and brother she'd just met for the first and last time and had not gotten the chance to bid farewell to; the life she had just taken; the wrongness of everything if Sovoqatsu of all people died protecting the royal family.

She looked around again, carefully sliding her eyes past the two bodies without letting herself focus too closely. She had killed one of those men. In spite of everything, she would have preferred not to.

Well. Everything in this room was smashed to useless kindling. Stepping through a long rent in the tent wall, she found herself wading through broken glass into a dim room lit by two of Kataki's flame-shaped sconces. She told the lights to brighten.

All of the breath left her body in a sudden rush, as though stolen from her by the vacuum of the Abyss, when she saw where all the broken glass had come from.

Enough of the object remained intact for her to discern that it had been a long glass box, joined at the seams by bands of rune-inlaid gold. Twisted on the rug amidst the wreckage lay its terrible contents.

Thaníravaia Tsuru Raia, preserved in death for more than three thousand years by an Art that was now unraveling rapidly.

# Chapter Thirty-Three

When Cole and Naoise reached the Mornnovini camp at a mad gallop, they found it eerily quiet for what should have been the site of an ongoing battle. Enough bodies lay in their path to attest that a fight *had* taken place. They slowed their steeds to a walk and made for the only thing that seemed to be happening: a towering inferno near the center of the camp. As they drew near they finally heard the sound of voices as well as the roaring of the flames.

What had once been an enormous pavilion – Kataki's, Naoise could guess – was all but destroyed now, the fire groaning at its contents. In a clearing nearby, Loralíenasa stood atop the seat of the massive stone chair on its high platform. Surrounding her were the elven armies of Mornnovin and Evlédíen, both of which had apparently been listening to her speak. Weapons were still out, but no more fighting seemed to be taking place. The mood was... not *calm*, but an odd kind of still, like the uneasy quiet at the eye of a storm.

As they approached, Naoise saw Captain Galvan help Loríen down from the throne then turn to address one of his soldiers. Loríen seemed dazed. She was also covered in blood.

She looked up at the sound of their horses. Her absent look receded when she caught sight of him.

"Where's Lyn?" Cole asked predictably while leaping from the saddle.

"Right here," the princess replied before Loríen could say anything. She was crouched beside something at the base of the throne platform that Naoise only realized after a second glance was Sovoqatsu. The guardsman was so pale and blood-soaked, and somehow small and fragile-looking, that he was nearly unrecognizable as himself. Lyn, however, seemed none the worse for wear.

Cole hauled Lyn to her feet and drew her into a crushing embrace. "You're okay," he murmured into her hair. "That was crazy, Lyn. That was so crazy."

She laughed breathlessly. "You don't even know."

Naoise approached Loríen more cautiously. He couldn't find the words to talk about what they'd just experienced together, but the connection they had forged for her journey into the Nírozahé was still so strong that he didn't have to say anything at all. He could also feel that something else had happened since then, something that had shaken her badly.

Around them, Lanoralas' men began disarming the Mornnovini elves.

Loríen looked at Naoise and said a thousand things silently that she couldn't find the words for either, aloud.

Needing to make contact – wanting to do more but knowing this was not the place for either of them to reveal how desperately worried they had been – Naoise reached out and touched her cheek briefly. She leaned into his hand before he pulled it away. He would almost have sworn he could *see* the Galvanos flaring between them now. His eyes went to her reddened síarca, the blood covering her hands up to the elbow. "Are you all right? What happened?"

She slashed one hand toward Sovoqatsu in a gesture of condemnation. "That fool tried to end himself." A small smile twitched over her lips. "He is fortunate that healing is the only branch of the Art I ever had any skill at."

After what she had just accomplished inside the Nírozahé, Naoise wasn't sure what to say to that.

"Ingrate," the guardsman choked out. He hardly looked alive enough to have made the sound, but then Naoise didn't suppose Sovoqatsu would let a thing like a mortal wound get in the way of winning a fight. Or insulting his Míyahídéna.

"They surrender," Loríen added softly, as though she could hardly believe it. "It was like they woke up. I think… I think he…" She stopped and shook her head, still working out what had happened and what it all meant.

Naoise wanted to smile, but the moment was too large for that. He couldn't make his face decide what to do. "We did it," he managed to say quietly. "It's over."

"Yes." Loríen's eyes slid past him to take in the remnants of the battle. So many elves dead. "It is over." It was not a declaration of victory. She seemed to be having some difficulty breathing; Naoise realized she was forcing back heavy sobs.

Lanoralas Galvan asserted himself at her side, bloodied sword in hand, dotted with black and red from boot to crown. "No. No self-recrimination," he said to her in Elven. "We did what we had to do, and it was enough. If we hadn't, or hadn't found the nerve, things would be a vastly different kind of *over* right now."

Naoise wondered briefly if the Captain realized he had just revealed that his comprehension of Common was better than none.

Lorien offered Lanoralas a look that was almost a smile and allowed herself to lean against him wearily. Naoise tried not to envy him the contact. "I know. Thank you for that." She almost-smiled at Naoise. "And you. What you did, what you helped me do today... You know there are no words. *Chanaqai*."

All around them, Kataki's elves were surrendering their weapons to the Captain's soldiers as the pavilion burned to cinders. It really was over. His father, Dairinn, Dewfern – so much lost to one man's rage, so much more nearly lost. And it was *over*, because Loralienasa Nuvalinas Nielor Raia had decided she would not let hate define the world they lived in.

Naoise drew a deep breath. "Well," he said. "Back to Yeatun, I think. Let us see what Shafiq managed to make of the *other* half of Kataki's army."

*And hope he doesn't decide to finish off Yeatun afterward,* he thought, but did not say.

The moment was bittersweet enough already without voicing that doubt.


Somehow none of it felt real because it all felt *too* real.

It came at Lorien in bits and pieces – fighting a battle she didn't want to be fighting, against her own people; elves of both sides working together to put out the fire before it took the entire camp; Sovoqatsu covered in blood, alive only because she had been on hand to save him; standing atop the stone chair with two armies looking on, crying out words that must surely have been given to her by Vaian until the fighting stopped; an elf who had been her enemy half an hour ago surrendering to Lanoralas; Lyn and Cole in one another's arms. Naoise, looking at her that way. The memory of those last seconds with Kataki; taking his life; discovering what he had been carrying with him all this time. The war, over.

She felt like she wasn't entirely inside her own body.

Naoise watched her expectantly, waiting for a response to his suggestion. She drew a deep breath and tried with all her will to be inside just one moment out of all the ones that seemed to be happening at once.

"I just need to speak with Lanoralas," she told him. It seemed odd to have to tell him anything. Not so long ago, they had been in one another's minds and now the distance between them that made words necessary no longer felt right.

On any other day, she realized, she would be angry about that. The thought felt foreign and far away, like it was someone else's.

Naoise nodded. Loríen drew the Captain aside.

"What do you want me to do with them?" Lanoralas asked quietly, anticipating her thought.

It was a good question, and Loríen wasn't sure if there was a right answer. She knew what she *wanted*, but she also knew that what she wanted might not be best for everyone. She glanced over the ongoing surrender, tried not to count the dead.

Out of the corner of her eye, she caught sight of Lyn and Cole. Their embrace had turned into something rather more, oblivious to their current surroundings. Loríen's words were momentarily stunned out of her mouth and she had to collect herself before speaking her mind.

"Mysia is on its way to the ruins of Dewfern, to begin rebuilding."

Lanoralas nodded attentively.

"I'd like you to take whoever will go and meet them there, to help."

"That's..." Lanoralas thought it over. A sober frown drew the lines of his face taut. "They may not follow me there, Loríen."

"If they will not follow you there, then perhaps it would be for the best if we didn't try to bring them to Evlédíen."

She could see Lanoralas process that thought, its meaning. Finally he nodded again. "As you wish, Míyahídéna." He cleared his throat almost tentatively. "And... you will join us at Dewfern?"

Loríen deliberately did not look in Naoise's direction, but she didn't have to. She could feel his presence even more powerfully than the heat of the nearby flames. "In due course. First I would return to Yeatun to see the outcome of the battle there for myself. I need to know this is over."

Understanding showed in Lanoralas' expression. He was a soldier. "Of course." His eyes flicked toward Naoise even though she hadn't looked that way. "Then take care of yourself until we meet again."

They clasped forearms and Loríen dismissed him to carry out the task she'd charged him with.

It was her hope that most if not all of Katakí's lost elves would follow her back to Evlédíen, though she knew better than to expect it. But if even one of them did, it would help her to feel she'd taken something back from all of the death and destruction. They had all paid such a heavy cost; she needed it to have purchased more than mere survival.

For the sake of her own future, she needed to believe in possibility.


Sovoqatsu stayed behind with Lanoralas and the army medics, while Lorien convinced Lyn and Cole to emerge from each other's eyes long enough to ride back to Yeatun accompanied by two of Lorien's Royal Guard. When they passed through the remains of a bloody battle, hoping for the best but fearing the probable, they found the Telrishti army still encamped outside the city walls.

Victorious.

Lorien couldn't tell whether it was exhaustion, relief, or renewed dismay that caused Naoise to sag within his saddle. Possibly all three.

A sentry was waiting at the gate expressly to deliver a message to the king: General Shafiq would not quit the field until they had shared words.

"Perhaps it would be best if you were to await me in the city," Naoise said doubtfully to his companions.

Lorien spoke up even before Cole could voice the predictable objection to Naoise going anywhere alone. "No. If we are to go forward into this new world Kataki has made, Telrisht must do it knowing that Evlédien is part of the discussion."

Cole subsided, content with the strength of that argument. The doubt did not leave Naoise's eyes, but he allowed that she had a point.

Five hours later, something like peace had been agreed upon between Telrisht, Grenlec, and the now-known Evlédien. Naoise had sworn to the immediate and unconditional withdrawal of the Grenlecian army from all positions in Telrisht, and had admitted in front of witnesses that Shafiq was a good and honorable man who kept his word. For his part, Shafiq was willing to concede that Naoise was an improvement over his predecessor and that he had the potential to be tolerable; and that enough damage had probably been done already as a result of the Purification. Naoise and Loralíenasa, respectively, were willing to take that as a fair start.

After nearly eight years of continuous war, Grenlec and Telrisht were officially at peace.

By the time Naoise was able to lead a host of builders and re-settlers back to Dewfern with supplies, the wreckage had already been cleared and work on the first structures was well in hand. Mysians may not have been known for their skill at warfare, but they did know how to build a fair city; and elves had experience with starting over. It seemed to please them both to be working together again.

When Naoise asked for the man in charge, they were pointed toward the Chief Architect's command center. They found it easily by the lakeside, one of the few standing structures not currently under construction. It was essentially no more than a white canvas tent stretched over a timber frame, making clear that other work was the priority. Despite that, when they entered the office they found it tight and secure and filled with every tool the architect could need to draft his plans for the new Dewfern.

And there was a long-absent friend waiting to greet them.

"Sefaro!" several voices cried at once when they saw who it was bent over the drafting table.

The familiar Mysian looked up from his work, brightening considerably at the sight of his friends. He looked none the worse for his time on the road or with the Mysian army; in fact, he seemed delighted with the task he'd been assigned. More than he ever had as ambassador to Efrondel, or in the even more perilous role of accompanying a handful of mad royals halfway across the world to face down a genocidal sorcerer.

Lyn rushed to embrace him as the others filed in at a more relaxed pace.

His smile dimmed somewhat when the hídéna finally let go of him and he was able to look the rest of them over. "I heard about Dairinn. Naoise, I am so sorry."

The King of Grenlec answered with a solemn nod. "Thank you. He died as bravely as he'd ever wanted, but I would much rather he were still with us."

"So you didn't have to be King," Lyn added too observantly.

Naoise grimaced.

Loríen said nothing.

"But our good friend Sovoqatsu is yet alive and as angry as ever," the Mysian said after an awkward silence. His smile reappeared. "Angrier, perhaps, because the physicians won't let him perform any labor."

They chuckled at that and began sharing their news of all that had passed since they'd parted ways at Grenwold. Sefaro's tale was straightforward enough: he had raced across a beleaguered Asrellion to deliver his news, and had found Mysia readying to march against Telrisht, pushed into action by the Royal Council despite Prince Enyokoto's insistence that it would be a mistake.

Then King Eselakoto had finally died.

As sad as it was to lose the beloved old king, his father, his passing was a boon to Enyokoto who was finally able to take rightful command. Heeding Sefaro's warning, he'd sent the army on to Yeatun to join forces against Mornnovin. The rest they knew. Once they had figured out that this was precisely what Katakí wanted and that he was awaiting Mysia's arrival on the field, they had advised Sefaro to divert to Dewfern. The only insane part of that plan had been Lyn's idea: asking Sun to baffle Katakí's scrying tools so that as far as he knew, the Mysian army was still on its way to Yeatun.

If it hadn't worked, if Sun hadn't agreed to help, Katakí might have made his move with the Nírozahé early and they would all be dead now. Loríen was glad her sister had convinced the fairy that she owed them the help after her kind had allowed Katakí to remake the bones of the earth at Dewfern.

They were still catching Sefaro up to their story, Lyn and Naoise carrying most of the narration while Cole and Loríen listened, when a commotion outside the office let them know that another large group had just arrived. Naoise didn't seem surprised, which told Loríen something about who it might be. He drew himself up and pushed a hand through his perennially unruly black hair as though to make himself more presentable, though the gesture only ever made his hair more unruly. Loríen smirked.

A moment later, the door opened and a pair of guards entered; behind them came Princess Alyra. Naoise was across the room and had his arms around his sister before the second pair of guards had come in after her. Loríen looked away when she noticed tears in the brother and sister's eyes.

Lyn was leaning back against Cole and grinning as she watched the reunion. That was another sight Loríen found difficult, but she knew she had no choice but to accept it however she could.

"I see everything is under control here and I need not have come," Alyra said, wiping her eyes surreptitiously, once she and Naoise had released each other. "But I brought a thousand carpenters, masons, ironworkers, glaziers, and their tools, if that will be of use to anyone," she added with a distinctly Dairinn-like wink.

"My lady," Sefaro said with a low and gracious bow, "as before, your help is a gift from the Creator Himself."

Naoise cleared his throat. "Lord Sefaro, are you flirting with my sister right in front of me?"

The Mysian sputtered something as a red flush crawled up his face.

Alyra shook her head at her brother. "I brought something for you too, Your Majesty." She gestured behind her, and one of her men went outside, returning with what looked like a jewelry chest. "The crown jewels may have been destroyed," she said, passing the chest to Naoise, "but these are yours now, and may they serve better than none."

Naoise took the box from Alyra with suddenly shaky hands. The next breath he drew was slow, careful. Loríen knew, even before he started speaking, that Something was about to happen. She could feel the waves of nervous energy pouring off of him. He loosed the catch and opened the box.

Because she knew, could feel it coming, she looked into the box with him. It was full of jewelry, as she had surmised. A breathtaking diamond necklace, several smaller pendants and rings, a beautiful gold circlet set with garnets. She recognized the style unmistakably.

There was also a bright silver and red-gold brooch showing the sun setting behind steep mountain peaks, and an ornate knotted ring set with a purple stone – the emblem and ring of House Faríel.

"How did you come by these?" she breathed without meaning to speak.

Naoise glanced at her sharply, but it was difficult to tell whether or not he knew the significance of the question.

"These were our mother's," Alyra answered with reverence. "Heirlooms of her house. They washed up on the lakeshore after the city was destroyed. I thought she'd given the ring to Dairinn. What is it doing in here, I wonder?"

"It had been too small for him for some years," Naoise murmured. "He'd returned it to the chest for safekeeping while he was away in Telrisht." He reached out and drew a finger carefully over the brooch, tracing the line of the mountains. "This she gave to me."

Loríen was having some difficulty breathing. "Heirlooms of her house?"

*Faríel,* she thought dazedly. *The Exiles. Of course.* She thought back to the night they had hidden from pursuit after fleeing the King of Grenlec. When Dairinn had explained that their father was so venomous toward all things elven because of what he'd considered scurrilous rumors that his wife had been an elf, or part elf.

It wasn't just a rumor, or her imagination. Naoise really did have elven blood in him. He was a Faríel.

He nodded, but he was looking at Alyra now. "But I cannot keep them," he said quietly.

His sister quirked an eyebrow at him, inviting explanation.

Naoise closed the box. "I cannot stay in Grenlec." He spoke slowly, as if weighing each word carefully before letting it go. "I cannot be King. I... can't say I know what my future holds–" he did not look at Lorien– "but I know it is not here."

Lorien stopped trying to breathe altogether. She held herself perfectly still, waiting.

"Naoise." Alyra stopped herself and visibly re-thought whatever it was she'd been about to say, set her shoulders, and raised her head. "I would tell you this is madness, but honestly I've expected it since you came back from Mornnovin." She met Lorien's eyes for a moment. Lorien finally had to take a breath. They shared a long look that seemed to satisfy Alyra, for she nodded almost imperceptibly. "I love you, Naoise. I would have you follow the path you must follow, though it will pain me to lose you. Go where your heart leads you, and the Father speed your way."

Lyn let out a loud and unattractive sob. When they all looked at her, they found her watching the scene play out with her eyes shining, both hands fisted at her mouth as if to hold her smile in. Sefaro laughed at her; with that, the tension was broken.

"Damn you, Naoise," Alyra said on an unsteady chuckle. "You're lucky I like you, that I have a soft spot for impossible love stories, and that I actually *want* to be Queen."

Naoise laughed and looped an arm around her shoulders, kissing her auburn hair. He looked suddenly years younger, almost like the boy Lorien had met in the forest so many years ago. "Just please do a kindness for me?"

"Another, you mean?" Alyra did not sound displeased.

Her brother grinned. "Take care of Aiqa. The poor boy's too old to be adventuring anymore."

Alyra laughed and agreed to give the dog all the love he could want.

For her part, Lorien was still having trouble with air. Something had just happened, something enormous, something that meant her life was going to change. Just like that, and it was done. She hadn't even asked – had never thought to suggest it. She would never have imagined he would leave his kingdom, his family, his entire world behind. For her.

She did not know what was going to happen now. She only knew, as he did, that whatever happened, it had to be at one another's side.

They stayed on through the spring and summer to help rebuild Dewfern and to watch Naoise pass the crown to his sister Alyra – the first Queen of Grenlec in her own right – but finally Lanoralas convinced Loríen that it was time to be getting back to Evlédíen. They had an accounting to make before Lord Maiantar, consequences to face for their potentially treasonous actions.

One thousand and eighty-six elves from Mornnovin who had once been their enemies agreed to go with them.

It was more than Loríen had looked for by almost all. The rest were allowed to leave with a standing invitation to join their people in Evlédíen. Perhaps one day, Loríen hoped. The group made the journey with ease through a recovering countryside now at peace, and arrived in Efrondel as the first leaves of autumn were starting to turn.

Tomanasíl Maiantar was waiting for Loralíenasa amid the cold silver and glass of the palace foyer, dressed in grey silk that nearly disappeared into his surroundings. She didn't know what to expect, but was fully prepared for him to throw her back in the tower. She was surprised to see that he looked different, but even more surprised when she realized a moment later that actually, he looked *exactly the same*. She was the one who had changed, and she was seeing him now as she never had before.

He was young. He had been afraid. And he had absolutely no idea what to do with her now.

The Lord Regent watched with a near-perfect mask of calm as Loríen, Lanoralas, Lyn, Sovoqatsu, Cole, Naoise, and a handful of representatives sent by the Mornnovini refugees waiting outside the city gathered in the glittering foyer before him.

Ever the gallant hero, Lanoralas stepped forward to take the brunt of his anger. "Lord Maiantar, we–"

Tomanasíl put out a hand and the Captain fell silent.

Moving with great care, the Lord Regent of Evlédíen crossed the glittering obsidian floor to his ward and took her hands in his with awkward gentleness. She tried, but couldn't remember another time he had ever shown physical affection. In her entire life. That nearly brought her to tears.

"Loralíenasa," he whispered, "we have been so worried."

She put her arms around the man who had raised her and held him close. He felt frail and not at all terrifying. "I'm sorry, Tomsíl. I'm home now."

Between having to repeatedly explain the events of the last several months and deal with the various consequences, trying to make places for all the refugees and planning the formal embassy to the non-combatants who had remained behind in Mornnovin, the struggle and demands of resuming her interrupted life, and handling her concerned people as they made much of her return, Loralíenasa found that being home again was not as restful as she had hoped it would be. Not nearly. And did not involve as much Naoise as she needed it to.

Part of the problem was that she had no idea how to explain his presence to her guardian, which meant that the terms of his stay were somewhat vague and did not often bring him within the circle of her company.

It was more than a week before Loríen was finally able to sneak a moment alone, and that only by stealing away from an interminable state dinner well before Tomanasíl was prepared to let her leave.

Slinking through the hallways of the palace, hoping not to be noticed, she was surprised to come upon her sister standing at the top of the grand staircase looking down wistfully.

"Have you ever tried sliding down the rail?" Lyn asked before Loríen could say anything.

Perhaps it was merely her relief at having escaped, but Loríen could not stop herself from laughing at the question. And as a matter of fact– "I thought Tomsíl was going to kill me."

Lyn's eyes sparkled with amusement. "I knew it! Not as stuffy and repressed as you always wanted me to think you are."

"Repressed?" She understood the implication if not the word.

"That's what I said." The mischievous smile playing about her sister's lips faded after a moment. Loríen didn't have to be connected to her mind to know that she was thinking about all of the things they still hadn't talked about. Their experience together inside the Nírozahé. Meeting their family, seeing Gallanas. What they'd discovered hidden in Katakí's pavilion. Evlédíen, and Lyn's plans – her life – now that the war was over. Cole. Each other.

Every time they had tried, the world had found ways to pull them in other directions. Now, it seemed, there was finally nothing to distract them.

"Loríen I can't stay here," Lyn said in a single breathless stream, as if to be certain she got all of the words out before something stopped her.

Even though Loríen had known her sister felt that way, it still hurt to hear her say it. But she knew too well the Valley was a prison. She would not cage Lyn here to waste away with the rest of them, not when she was full of so much life. Loríen breathed carefully. "I know."

Lyn lowered her jaw from its distinctly defensive angle. "You do?"

"I hope that will change one day," Loríen replied quietly. "I also hope we will have at least one real talk before you go. There is... much we have not said to one another, I think."

Lyn leaned against the stair railing, looking unusually thoughtful. "There's a lot of that around here, isn't there? A lot of not talking, especially when it's important. Maybe work on that before I come back for a visit." For once, she didn't sound judgmental in talking about her people's alien ways. And she looked, fleetingly, so much like their mother, whom neither of them had ever known.

Loríen offered a small smile to the sister she still hoped to know a great deal better, if time and the world allowed. More than the smile, she tried to offer a piece of herself. Some of the vulnerability Lyn was always asking her to admit to. "You know, I used to have dreams about it. Getting to meet... her, one last time. There were so many things I planned to say." So many things she still wanted to say to her sister, too. "Nothing goes as we expect."

"Maybe not." Lyn gave it a moment of thought. "Sometimes it's better."

Loríen raised a doubtful eyebrow.

"The first time I met you," Lyn explained seriously, "you looked so much like Bryant that I kind of hated you for not being him." Her eye contact was steady, assuring her that she wasn't joking about this. "But you turned out to be something else I didn't know I needed. A sister. I didn't know what that would be like. I'm glad you were the one who showed me."

That was, without question, the most wonderful thing anyone had ever said to her. Loríen caught her breath and struggled to respond without embarrassing herself.

"You're supposed to say something nice about me now," Lyn prompted indignantly.

The absurdity of Lyn's tone allowed Loríen to say, "You must know you are not at all what I expected. But I think you are just what I needed." The smile she offered was genuine.

The light of mischief sparked in Lyn's eyes once more. "You're damn right I am. Now, if you don't want to get blamed for this, you should probably clear off fast-like." Lyn set her jaw and took hold of the staircase railing.

Laughing outright, Loríen did as she was advised. At least Lyn would be taking the focus off of Loríen's disappearance from dinner. After more than a hundred years it was probably her turn to absorb a little of Tomanasíl's ire anyway. Loríen's mood improved with every step closer to Naoise's room.

It was late, and she hoped he would still be awake. She had only seen two brief glimpses of him since their arrival in Efrondel, and the need to touch him and hear his voice was eating away at her in a way that would have inspired her rage, less than a year ago. They had been through too much for her to deny it now though, no matter how much more convenient it would be if she could.

She stopped in front of Naoise's room and composed herself before raising a hand to knock, but the door opened before she could make contact with the polished ebony surface. Naoise stood haloed by the glow of light from his fireplace, his eyes bright and blue and alive at the sight of her.

"I felt you coming up the stairs," he explained quietly. Without another word, he opened his door wider in invitation. She stepped past him. The sound of the door closing – a sound that meant they were finally, finally to be granted a moment alone – sent a tremor through her.

Naoise's arms came around her from behind, pulling her close against his body; she could feel him trembling too. He lowered his head to rest upon her hair. "I've missed you." His voice was doing odd but warm and agreeable things to her blood.

"Naoise, we need to have a talk," she made herself say while she still had the power to say anything at all. "About us."

He nodded against her hair. "Unquestionably." He turned her within his arms and bent his head to capture her lips with his own. Loríen melted against him, allowing herself to drown in the sudden wash of euphoria as he kissed her with so much force and passion she could hardly think.

Talking could wait.


Safe within the warm circle of Naoise's arms on the sofa before his fireplace, it was difficult for Loríen to make herself say what she knew she needed to. It would bring an ending, and she wanted desperately not to do that. There was only one thing she wanted more than to stay here in this moment forever. That was what ultimately made her speak up.

"Naoise."

He nuzzled his face against the back of her neck. "Mmm?"

She had to draw a deep breath. "I love you."

No response came for such a long time that finally Loríen craned her neck to look back at him. He had his head back against the sofa, lips parted with shock.

And he was crying.

When she saw that and made a noise of dismay, he offered a smile with some pain in it. "You've... never said that before."

"I know." She closed her eyes. "I am a fool." He didn't argue. "But I do. I love you, and I don't want to lose you. I can't."

His arms tightened about her. "You never will. I am yours, Loríen."

"But you can't promise that." Loríen had started shaking. There was no going back from this now. "You are human. Mortal. You will age and die, and I might as well die with you when that day comes. I can't. I can't, Naoise."

Naoise pushed her away gently in order to turn her by the shoulders so he could look into her eyes. His had darkened to a sober purple, still sparkling with the tears he'd shed a moment earlier. "No. We will find a way. I don't believe Vaian would have made us galvaí if he did not mean for there to *be* a way. I'll ask him myself if I must, but I swear to you that I *will* find a way for us to be together."

"Do you..." she gulped. "Do you truly mean that?"

"You know I do."

Now that the moment had come, Loríen almost could not make herself say it. Perhaps it would be better to keep him here for what time they were allowed, as little as that would be. She had no right to ask him this.

"You know a way," he said calmly. It was not a question.

She folded her hands in her lap, looking down at her own interlaced fingers. "It is true, yes, that you are descended of an elf?"

She watched as his larger hands came up and over hers, enfolding them. "It is no secret within the House of Devon, though my father denied knowing," he said softly. "My mother's grandfather was an elf named Síthas."

*Síthas Faríel. Son of the Exile.* Loríen closed her eyes again. There was a tragedy somewhere in that story.

"I see." She breathed carefully. "Then you should know that would make you Lord Faríel. The family is... much reduced in the Valley in these times."

"I don't... Does that help us somehow?"

Loríen made herself meet Naoise's eyes and almost couldn't bear to look at the hope she saw in them. It was a terrible thing she was doing to him, and he was taking it as a blessing. "In the early days, Vaian used to walk among us wearing the likeness of one of my people. But after humans came into the world– No, that's not how I will tell this." She sighed and started again.

"When he left these shores, he wanted to leave us with the means to speak with him as we once did. In the eastern sea, beyond Trajelon, there lies a series of small islands we call the Islands of Vaian. It is said that one may call upon him at the temple there, and he will come."

Naoise inhaled sharply. He already knew what she was about to say.

"You could go there," she said, "and face Vaian, and request the right of your Elven blood." She paused. Her hands were shaking. She gripped them harder. "But you should know that this is a journey no one has ever come back from."

"I'll do it," he said without hesitation. "You knew I would do it."

She nodded. Now that she had said it, speech was failing her.

"But what about the Galvanos?" There was still no doubt in his voice, only the need to work through a problem. "The last time we parted– There must be a way we can avoid endangering one another like that again."

"There is. We've already done it." Loríen chose her words carefully. "I knew it was the Galvanos all along, or suspected. After what happened when we separated that first time, once I was well enough I did some research. Apparently, the bond becomes passive once it is consummated."

Naoise mouthed the Elven word, evidently uncertain he understood its meaning, but knowing came into his eyes after a moment. "You mean...?"

"No, not that." She shook her head. "The Galvanos is a bond between souls, not bodies. We consummated it when we opened our minds to one another completely and became one."

Confusion bloomed across his face. "You knew this all along? You knew it in the mountains, when I reawakened the Galvanos to force my way on your quest. You could easily have negated my gambit."

"No," she said again. "For two reasons. One, we both had to be willing to open ourselves. I could not have forced you to do that. And two." She drew a difficult breath. "I knew that once we did it, once I *saw you*, I would never want to let you go. That's the point of it, I imagine."

Her galvaí offered a smile so beautiful it landed with a sensation of actual pain somewhere in her chest. "In that case," he said, "it is settled. This is just the chance I've been praying for. I'll do it, and I *will* come back to you." With carefully formal movements, he climbed down from the sofa and onto his knees on the green and silver rug before her, still holding her hands between his. "And when I do, Loralíenasa, will you consent to take me in marriage?"

Loríen had known he would say that – almost exactly that – but still she felt her heart clutch with love for this man. It was possible that he would fail, that she was sending him away to die and that she would never see him again. It was also possible he would succeed at something no mortal man had ever attempted and would return to be with her forever. That thought was almost equally terrifying. She nodded.

"With all my heart. But I must add one caveat."

The smile in his eyes did not falter. "Yes?"

"I cannot wait for you indefinitely," she whispered, hating that she had the need to say this. Hating, for this moment, that she was Loralíenasa Raia. "I will be Queen of Evlédíen. Galvaí though we may be, if you do not return I must one day choose a consort."

"Then I swear this to you as well." He paused and raised her hands to his lips as though he could no longer contain the need; he kissed one, and then the other before continuing. "I will face Vaian and return a worthy match for the Queen of Evlédíen by the day you take the crown, or I will not return at all and you will know that I am dead."

That would do. It was a terrible vow, and it would do. Loríen nodded once. "So be it." She held his face, wishing she never had to let him go and that she had told him how she felt about him every day she'd had the chance. "My love."

Though she had saved the world, Loríen felt like she was losing everything else. She waited on the steps of the Crystal Palace in the weak dawn light with a coldness creeping into her heart that had nothing to do with autumn's wane.

Lyn's announcement had come as a surprise, in spite of everything. Loríen mused that the past year may have changed her, but not enough, apparently, to make her understand her sister. Or entirely approve of her choices, though she knew that was not her place – as if she had the right to tell anyone else to be sensible in matters of love. She would not withhold her blessing on those grounds.

"Cole asked me to marry him and I said yes," the hídéna had blurted without preamble when they finally sat down for their long talk. Later, after they'd both calmed down, she had gone on to say, "You know we can't stay here.

Maybe one day I'll be ready to give the Valley a chance at becoming Home, but not with Cole."

That much, Loríen could understand.

So it was that at the tag-end of the season, Loríen found herself bidding farewell to three people she had come to love dearly as they set out to catch the last ship from Chastedel before winter. Lyn and Cole would go to Trajelon, they said, and travel on from there as the mood took them. Naoise, of course, had a much longer sea voyage before him. Loríen could almost feel herself becoming a thing of ice, the frozen embodiment of bereavement. Finally the Míyahídéna that Evlédíen had always wanted her to be.

Wrapped in the warmest cloak she could find for him in Efrondel, Naoise finished seeing to his gear before mounting the stairs to bid her farewell. When he caught sight of the look on her face, the coldness, he brought both hands to her cheeks as though to force some of his warmth into her.

"I *will* return to you," he said. "Never doubt it."

Loríen nodded. "I trust you."

He nodded his satisfaction before kissing her thoroughly. She held him close, memorizing the way it felt to do so. When he let her go, his eyes were a sharp, wintry blue. "Remember that," he murmured.

Though she had spent so much time lately trying to stop herself from crying, Loríen wished she could conjure a tear now. She wished she did not feel so cold, so bleak. It was difficult to imagine feeling this way for the next nine years and surviving.

Below in the courtyard, Lyn and Cole tactfully did not rush them. But the horses shifted restively.

Loríen reached up to her throat and removed the brooch at the high collar of her silver gown – a stunning diamond cut into the shape of a many-rayed star. She clasped it onto Naoise's cloak and stepped back. "Go now, or I will never have the heart to let you leave."

He glanced down at the brooch, then back up to her eyes. Letting her hands go slowly, he reached up to his own high collar and unclasped something at his neck which he pressed into her palm and closed her fingers over. He said nothing, not aloud, but they had come beyond words. He turned and joined the others at their waiting steeds.

She gripped the single bear claw he'd just given her so hard that she could feel it pierce her skin.

"Take care of one another," she said to Lyn and Cole.

They both smiled back, tearfully in Lyn's case. Their goodbyes to Loríen had already been spoken. This was simply the moment of departure, and Loríen could not find it in herself to prolong it. What she needed now, finally, after so many months, was to be alone with her pain.

Loralíenasa stood on the steps of the palace long after they were gone from sight, wishing she could cry.

Tomorrow, she already knew. Tomorrow she would be able to do little else but cry.

For now, it was time to go back to work.

## Appendix A: Elven Glossary

**aiqa:** dog

**andras:** just; fair

**andreqí:** idiomatic word with no direct translation, approximating something like "as invincible as a dragon," "dragon-like," or "dragon-hearted"

**asagaos:** "a gentle man"

**callas:** strong

**"Chachor? Ídartaso qaio-qío lan?":** "Hello? Is anyone there?"

**chalaqar:** singer

**"Chanar thasa vaia.":** "Sorrow without end."

**chanaqai:** thanks; "thank you"

**Chastedel:** "Sea City"

**daríallas:** "one who is kind"

**díaros:** ray of sunlight

**efron:** crystal

**Efrondel:** "Crystal City"

**efronía:** "like crystal"

**éhaia:** delicate

**eldoreth:** steadfast

**Eselvwey:** "Land of Hope"

**etharían'í:** affairs

**Evlédíen:** "Elf Valley"; the name is literally meant to convey that the place is for elves only

**evlé'í:** elven; this is also the plural form of "elf"

**Falaríyu:** "day of leaving"; the fifth day of the elven week

**faríel:** dusk

**farín:** guardian

**farínaiqa:** "guard dog"

**gallanas:** one who is brave (or stout)

**galvaí:** a person who is joined to another through the Galvanos

**galvan:** strong; steadfast

**Galvanos:** "The Joining"; the little-understood and rare phenomenon in which two souls are literally bound together by Vaian

**haojí:** mom; mommy

**Harunomíya:** "Crown Prince"

**hídéna:** princess

**í barolan:** "in error"

**ílím:** perfect

**íríjo:** an amalgamation of the words **íríj** (joy) or possibly **íríhí** (sunset) and **jo** (brother)

**ítaja:** master; the title of respect given to someone who is a master at their craft or in their field of expertise

**íyaqo:** damn

**"Íyaqo los qotsuín qíjano":** "Damn that fucking piece of shit."

**íyéda:** "one with the eyes of an owl"

**jahar tíunos:** colloquial phrase meaning "how does one say"

**jaín:** please

**jíai:** a term of affection used to indicate romantic involvement

**jíjíro:** colloquial name for the sudden dangerous gusts in the high mountains surrounding Evlédíen

**jouai:** term of (familial) affection

**katakí (qataqí in Modern Elven):** loyal

**kuromé (quromé in Modern Elven):** avenger

**lanoralas:** "one who is honorable"

**loralíenasa:** "falling star"; a poetic amalgamation of the components **lorailo** (to fall) and **líena** (star)

**líensu:** starfire

**"Losí? Valo daiquro'í íta-qaior-qo sovora? Téo orían hana val jía? Aia, sur'lí jéha téo qaian chubíra.":** "What? My parents were not enough? You must have me too? Well, at least you're consistent."

**lyllíen:** rose; rose-like

**maiantar:** "most noble"

**melíara:** nightingale

**Míyahídéna:** "Crown Princess"

**moraní:** kingly

**nevethas:** to reach

**níelor:** defiant

**níerí:** dawn; sunrise

**nírozahé:** bloodflower

**nuvalin:** courage

**nuvalinas:** courageous

**ovasuo:** to hide

**qévalos:** "quiet one"

**qaí:** to be; as a proper noun, it is understood to mean "at one with being"

**qíarna:** "one who has mastered the Qíarnos"

**Qíarnos:** the Qíarnos, or "The Seven Principles of Wisdom," is the philosophical theory upon which elven culture is founded, espousing the strict regulation of all emotion

**qíjano:** "piece of shit"

**qíjí:** shit

**qotsu:** fuck

**qroíllenas:** "of aristocratic bearing"

**Raia:** Royal; this is a proper noun that has only ever been used to mean the surname of the royal family

**rajo:** comfortable

**rovanan:** "talking glass" (from **rovano** – to talk)

**selatho:** shining

**séochoría:** poetic amalgamation of the words **choríala** (misty) and **séo** (morning)

**síarca:** in elven fashion, a long sleeveless coat worn over a shirt, typically left open or held closed only with a sash worn about the waist

**sídaia-íta:** celebrated

**sílíví:** thirty

**síthas:** one born in the month of Sítha (the eighth month of the year)

**síthí:** hunter

**sívéo:** bell

**so:** he/she/singular they; when hyphenated at the end a proper name, it indicates formal respect offered from one of higher rank or status to one of less-er

**sònoreth:** literally "strike the string"; the name of a musical instrument which closely resembles the modern Earth piano

**soralos:** pants, specifically the type of pants worn in elven fashion that are full and baggy through the thighs and form-fitting over the calf

**soríjuhí:** amalgamation of the words **soríj** (cold) and **juhí** (tree), possibly an allusion to an evergreen

**sovoqatsu:** amalgamation of the words **sovílo** (flame) or **sovai** (to burn) or possibly **sovos** (endless), and **oqatsu** (hatred)

**sují:** beyond; the name of a popular elven strategy game

**taréna:** "one who is imperious"

**tenchíéchanaros:** "gates of sorrow"

**thaníravaia:** poetic amalgamation of the words **thanrai** (fair; beautiful), **nírava** (emblem) and **vaia** (eternity)

**thonalí na díalí-sílí:** one hundred and twenty-three

**tomanasíl:** "one who is beloved"

**tsuriqaia téas:** "distinguish yourself"

**tsuru:** difference

**"Va geléías":** "I'm sorry"

**vaian:** endless; eternal

**véloro:** green

**víara:** beauty

**víelle:** "one with a heart-shaped face"

**víqarío:** amalgamation of the words **víqar** (instead) and **qarío** (to be silent); a tongue-in-cheek way of saying "talkative"

**vísairajenré:** amalgamation of the words **vísaira** (alive) and **jenré** (soul)

**volarín:** crescent

**voromé:** "crescent moon"

**voroméasa:** "she of the crescent moon"

**yají:** dad; daddy

**zimají:** amalgamation of the words **zím** (fierce) and **ají** (fang)

## Appendix B: The People of Mornnovin

**Elves**

**Andras Raia:** King of Evlédíen until his assassination, father of Gallanas and the twins Loralíenasa and Lyllíen

**Asagaos:** a Lieutenant of the Royal Guard

**Avorí Faríel:** formerly patriarch of the Noble House of Faríel, banished from Evlédíen in Loralíenasa's childhood for attempting to foment war

**Callas:** a sergeant of the Border Guard

**Daríallas Díaros:** Lord of the City of Chastedel and formal suitor to Loralíenasa

**Efronía Faríel:** oldest daughter of Avorí Faríel; banished from Evlédíen with her parents and her siblings Mitallí and Síthas in Loralíenasa's childhood for attempting to foment war

**Éhaia Raia:** famed hunter and daughter of the first King and Queen

**Gallanas Vísairajenré Raia (Bryant):** son of King Andras and Queen Melíara; heir to the throne of Evlédíen until his death

**Iríjo:** an illusionist serving as a scout in Mornnovin for Lanoralas and Loralíenasa

**Íyéda:** a Lieutenant of the Royal Guard, second-in-command to Captain Galvan

**Katakí Kuromé:** formerly the hermit Sorijuhí Volarín of Eselvwey, who lost his love during the War of Exile and suffered a mental breakdown as a result; now Lord of Mornnovin and a powerful sorcerer

**Lanoralas Andreqí Galvan (Lanas):** Captain of the Royal Guard of Evlédíen and widely held to be the finest swordsman the world has ever seen; friend and formal suitor of Loralíenasa

**Loralíenasa Nuvalinas Níelor Raia (Loríen):** daughter and middle child of King Andras and Queen Melíara, twin to Lyllíen Raia; heir to the throne of Evlédíen after Gallanas' death

**Qévalos Síthí:** patriarch of the Noble House of Síthí

**Lyllíen Raia (Lyn):** daughter and youngest child of King Andras and Queen Melíara, twin to Loralíenasa Raia

**Melíara Raia:** Queen of Evlédíen until her assassination, mother of Gallanas and the twins Loralíenasa and Lyllíen

**Mitallí Faríel:** oldest son of Avorí Faríel; banished from Evlédíen with his parents and his siblings Efronía and Síthas in Loralíenasa's childhood for attempting to foment war

**Moraní Raia:** the last King of Eselvwey and founder of Evlédíen; father of Andras and Thaníravaia

**Murasaju Raia:** King of Eselvwey before ceding to his son Moraní; attempted to broker peace with Telrisht before the War of Exile but was killed during his ambassadorship

**Nuvalin Galvan:** twin brother of Selatho, the first King; founder of the Noble House of Galvan and the first sword master in Asrellion; his text on sword work is still studied by students of combat

**Qíarna:** the preeminent Master of the Art in Evlédíen and formerly Loralíenasa Raia's teacher; after earning the name Qíarna from his master, he discarded his birth name and is known ever after only as Qíarna

**Qroíllenas Qaí (Qroíllen):** formal suitor to Loralíenasa Raia

**Selatho Raia:** twin brother of Nuvalin Galvan; the first King, and creator of the Qíarnos; with Voroméasa Raia the first galvaí

**Séochoría Ílím:** a well-known poet

**Síthas Faríel:** son of Avorí Faríel; banished from Evlédíen with his parents and his siblings Mitallí and Efronía in Loralíenasa's childhood for attempting to foment war

**Soríjuhí Volarín (Ríju):** a hermit and powerful mage of Eselvwey who fell in love with Thaníravaia Raia before the War of Exile; after her death fled to Mornnovin and took the name Katakí Kuromé

**Sovoqatsu Zimají Farínaiqa:** formerly a palace guardsman in Eselvwey, now a member of Lanoralas Galvan's Royal Guard

**Taréna Díaros:** matriarch of the Noble House of Díaros; mother of Daríallas

**Tenchíéchanaros:** formerly an officer of the palace guard in Eselvwey, now General of the army of Mornnovin

**Thaníravaia Tsuru Raia (Níra):** daughter of Moraní Raia and sister of Andras; taken and killed by Telrishti soldiers while traveling to see her lover Soríjuhí Volarín

**Tomanasíl Eldoreth Maiantar (Tomsíl):** Lord Regent of Evlédíen and guardian to Loralíenasa Raia after the deaths of King Andras and Queen Melíara

**Véloro Chalaqar:** grandson of the first King and Queen and commonly held to be the most powerful wielder of the Art the world has ever seen; creator of the Nírozahé

**Víara Galvan:** niece of Lanoralas Galvan and friend of Loralíenasa Raia, known for mischief and an ability to see hints of the future in her dreams

**Víelle Sívéo:** a member of the Royal Guard, accompanies Loralíenasa on her escape from Efrondel

**Víqarío Voromé:** formal suitor to Loralíenasa Raia

**Voroméasa Raia:** the first queen and first master of the Art, having learned from Vaian Himself; with Selatho Raia the first galvaí

## Humans

**Adan:** Lord of the Rosemarcher city-state of Ravenwood during the reign of King Andras; organized an ultimately fruitless international council with the aim of cementing a lasting peace between the human nations of Asrellion

**Captain Adar:** a Telrishti mercenary, leader of Rammad Company

**Alyra Raynesley, Duchess of Crestwood:** daughter and youngest child of King Lorn

**Caron:** lady-in-waiting to Alyra Raynesley

**Cole (possible pseudonym):** former mercenary; friend of Gallanas Raia during his time living in Rosemarch as "Bryant"

**Dairinn Raynesley, Duke of Northdown:** eldest son of King Lorn, heir to the throne of Grenlec

**Doran:** a scout in Naoise Raynesley's strike team

**Edelmar:** a captain in the Grenlecian army serving under Prince Dairinn in Alanrad

**Enyokoto:** Prince of Mysia, eldest son of King Eselakoto

**Eselakoto:** King of Mysia, father of Prince Enyokoto

**Farid:** a Telrishti swordmaker

**Husam:** a Telrishti swordmaker

**Issa:** a maidservant at Grenwold Castle

**Lonan:** a Grenlecian valet, Naoise's escort to Mysia

**Lorn Raynesley, King Lorn I of Grenlec:** King of Grenlec during the war with Telrisht, father of Dairinn, Naoise, and Alyra

**Mostyn:** Lord Chamberlain of Dewfern

**Naoise Raynesley, Duke of Lakeside:** younger son of King Lorn

**Nicol:** a Grenlecian soldier, Naoise's escort to Mysia

**Raza:** a Telrishti swordmaker

**Reid:** a lieutenant in the Grenlecian army, second-in-command to Prince

Naoise over a strike team of forty men

**Rian:** lady-in-waiting to Alyra Raynesley

**Ronan:** the King of Grenlec who began the ancient War of Exile; instituted a law prohibiting the presence of elves within the borders of Grenlec, punishable by death on sight

**Sefaro Shinju:** Mysian nobleman sent as Ambassador to Evlédíen by Prince Enyokoto

**Seyam:** a messenger in the royal palace of Zarishan

**Shafiq dal Nayil:** Lord High Rahd and general of the Telrishti army

**Sorley:** Lord Governor of Yeatun

**Tarek the Fifth, Ayiz:** the ruler of Telrisht

**Zahir:** a Telrishti swordmaker

**Other**

**Aiqa:** Naoise Raynesley's dog, an enormous shaggy-coated black-and-white creature with distinctive golden brown markings

**Ardash:** also called "the Horned One"; the Telrishti name for the fairy who tried to destroy men and elves in the early days of Asrellion; to the elves, simply "the Dark One"

**Sun:** a fairy, or farín; rescued Lyn and Gallanas in Rosemarch after the ambush that killed King Andras and Queen Melíara

**Vaian:** the elven name for the deity who created Asrellion; known in Grenlec as "the Father", or "the Father god"; known in Mysia as "the Creator"; in Rosemarch simply "the god"; and in Telrisht as "the One"

I would like to offer a heartfelt and eternal thank you to my very special Kickstarter backers, without whom this book would have remained no more than a file on my hard drive for all time:

A. Kennerley, Abi Godsell, Adam Watts, Alek and Becky Balobeck, Alexander Makk, Amber Edmunds, Andrew Alexander Miller, Andy Neville, Annelise Jensen, Arwen aka Woody, Beth Raney-Yancey, Brian "Big Daddy" Nielson, Bryony "R2-Bree2" Mackey, Callisto Almasy, Carolyn Chrisman, Cherilyn diMond, Cheryl R, Charlie D, Christina Nordin, Clarice Rose, Clinton R Moore, Damon, Daniel Crowley, Daniel Hunt, Danika Lagorio, David Coan, David K. Wheeler, David Mulhern, Dexter Morgenstern, Dr. J, Elina and Callum Cotterill, EP Eriksson, Erin Kate Mead, Fermin Serena Hortas, Heike Irion, Heather Asay, Helen Wright, Ivan Tamayo, James Gunn, Jamie Carey, Jamie Wyman, Jason Anderson, Jennifer Shumway, Jesse James, Jessie Warr, Janet Lunde, Joe Ashcroft, Joeleen Kennedy, John Athitakis, John Moore, Jon Skocik, Julia Hoefer, Julianne Poston, Julie Gatti, Kaj-Nrig Thao, Kate Kockler, Kate Schaich, Katelynn Cuciak, Katie Agren Andersen, Kayla Adams, Keith Spears, Kerri Stover, Kerstin Bodenstedt, Kim Wincen, Laurelin, Linda Johnston, Lore Cox, Mary Campbell, Matt Matt, Matt R. Lohr, Megan "FG" James, Mel Dadoly, Mel Reams, Melinda Dixon, Michelle Moreno, Michelle Yeargin, MichiMusic, Natalie Robinson, Nick Ridout, Oulin Yao, Paula N, R. Corley, Raven Meier, Rebekah Delling, Roger Siggs and Sasha Davis, Rolfe Westwood, Ron Lunde, Ruthan Freese, Sarah Wells, Siavahda, Sithrenity, Slightly Avocado, Sonja Purser, Stephan Nagel, SueBC, Summer Brighton, Susan K. Fountain, Tamra Mathias, Tasha Gonzales, Todd Watson, Tom "Nuvelle" Abbott, Tyler Patton, Vijay Myneni, Wendy Grube, Wil Bastion

# About the Author

Alyssa is a lifelong fantasy fan and all around Nerd of Many Colors who has been writing her own stories since the first grade. She's into trees, water, books, cool science facts, photography, dogs, music, and making things. After spending 36 years burning to death in the Arizona desert, she ran away to the frozen moonscape of southwestern Pennsylvania, where she now lives with the most adorable husband and husky. She shares her nerdy scribblings with Pittsburgh writer's group Rust and Ink and has grand plans for many fantasy novels yet to come.

Look for *Trajelon*, the Way of the Falling Star Book 2, coming soon!

www.alyssabethancourt.com

CPSIA information can be obtained
at www.ICGtesting.com
Printed in the USA
LVHW032042290419
616026LV00006B/638

9 781733 648004